The
MX Book
of
New
Sherlock
Holmes
Stories
Part XXVII – 2021 Annual
(1898-1928)

CONTENTS

Forewords

Adventures

(Continued on the next page . . . .)

(Continued on the next page . . . .)

These additional adventures are contained in
Part XXV: 2021 Annual
(1881-1888)

These additional adventures are contained in
Part XXVI: 2021 Annual
(1889-1897)

(Continued on the next page . . . .)

These additional Sherlock Holmes adventures
can be found in the previous volumes of
The MX Book of New Sherlock Holmes Stories

(Continued on the next page . . . .)

PART III: 1896-1929

PART IV – 2016 Annual

(Continued on the next page . . . .)

PART V – Christmas Adventures

(Continued on the next page . . . .)

PART VI – 2017 Annual

(Continued on the next page . . . .)

PART VII – Eliminate the Impossible: 1880-1891

PART VIII – Eliminate the Impossible: 1892-1905

(Continued on the next page . . . .)

Part IX – 2018 Annual (1879-1895)

(Continued on the next page . . . .)

The Lambeth Poisoner Case – Stephen Gaspar
The Confession of Anna Jarrow – S. F. Bennett
The Adventure of the Disappearing Dictionary – Sonia Fetherston
The Fairy Hills Horror – Geri Schear
A Loathsome and Remarkable Adventure – Marcia Wilson
The Adventure of the Multiple Moriartys – David Friend
The Influence Machine – Mark Mower

Part X – 2018 Annual (1896-1916)
Foreword – Nicholas Meyer
Foreword – Roger Johnson
Foreword – Melissa Farnham
Foreword – Steve Emecz
Foreword – David Marcum
A Man of Twice Exceptions (A Poem) – Derrick Belanger
The Horned God – Kelvin Jones
The Coughing Man – Jim French
The Adventure of Canal Reach – Arthur Hall
A Simple Case of Abduction – Mike Hogan
A Case of Embezzlement – Steven Ehrman
The Adventure of the Vanishing Diplomat – Greg Hatcher
The Adventure of the Perfidious Partner – Jayantika Ganguly
A Brush With Death – Dick Gillman
A Revenge Served Cold – Maurice Barkley
The Case of the Anonymous Client – Paul A. Freeman
Capitol Murder – Daniel D. Victor
The Case of the Dead Detective – Martin Rosenstock
The Musician Who Spoke From the Grave – Peter Coe Verbica
The Adventure of the Future Funeral – Hugh Ashton
The Problem of the Bruised Tongues – Will Murray
The Mystery of the Change of Art – Robert Perret
The Parsimonious Peacekeeper – Thaddeus Tuffentsamer
The Case of the Dirty Hand – G.L. Schulze
The Mystery of the Missing Artefacts – Tim Symonds

Part XI: Some Untold Cases (1880-1891)
Foreword – Lyndsay Faye
Foreword – Roger Johnson
Foreword – Melissa Grigsby
Foreword – Steve Emecz
Foreword – David Marcum
Unrecorded Holmes Cases (*A Sonnet*) – Arlene Mantin Levy and Mark Levy
The Most Repellant Man – Jayantika Ganguly
The Singular Adventure of the Extinguished Wicks – Will Murray
Mrs. Forrester's Complication – Roger Riccard
The Adventure of Vittoria, the Circus Belle – Tracy Revels

(Continued on the next page . . . .)

(Continued on the next page . . . .)

PART XIV: 2019 Annual (1891 -1897)

(Continued on the next page . . . .)

(Continued on the next page . . . .)

(Continued on the next page . . . .)

Part XIX: 2020 Annual (1892-1890)

(Continued on the next page . . . .)

The Adventure of the Matched Set – Peter Coe Verbica
When the Prince First Dined at the Diogenes Club – Sean M. Wright
The Sweetenbury Safe Affair – Tim Gambrell

Part XX: 2020 Annual (1891-1897)
Foreword – John Lescroart
Foreword – Roger Johnson
Foreword – Lizzy Butler
Foreword – Steve Emecz
Foreword – David Marcum
The Sibling (A Poem) – Jacquelynn Morris
Blood and Gunpowder – Thomas A. Burns, Jr.
The Atelier of Death – Harry DeMaio
The Adventure of the Beauty Trap – Tracy Revels
A Case of Unfinished Business – Steven Philip Jones
The Case of the S.S. Bokhara – Mark Mower
The Adventure of the American Opera Singer – Deanna Baran
The Keadby Cross – David Marcum
The Adventure at Dead Man's Hole – Stephen Herczeg
The Elusive Mr. Chester – Arthur Hall
The Adventure of Old Black Duffel – Will Murray
The Blood-Spattered Bridge – Gayle Lange Puhl
The Tomorrow Man – S.F. Bennett
The Sweet Science of Bruising – Kevin P. Thornton
The Mystery of Sherlock Holmes – Christopher Todd
The Elusive Mr. Phillimore – Matthew J. Elliott
The Murders in the Maharajah's Railway Carriage – Charles Veley and Anna Elliott
The Ransomed Miracle – I.A. Watson
The Adventure of the Unkind Turn – Robert Perret
The Perplexing X'ing – Sonia Fetherston
The Case of the Short-Sighted Clown – Susan Knight

Part XXI: 2020 Annual (1898-1923)
Foreword – John Lescroart
Foreword – Roger Johnson
Foreword – Lizzy Butler
Foreword – Steve Emecz
Foreword – David Marcum
The Case of the Missing Rhyme (A Poem) – Joseph W. Svec III
The Problem of the St. Francis Parish Robbery – R.K. Radek
The Adventure of the Grand Vizier – Arthur Hall
The Mummy's Curse – DJ Tyrer
The Fractured Freemason of Fitzrovia – David L. Leal
The Bleeding Heart – Paula Hammond
The Secret Admirer – Jayantika Ganguly

(Continued on the next page . . . .)

Part XXII: Some More Untold Cases (1877-1887)

(Continued on the next page . . . .)

(Continued on the next page . . . .)

The following contributions appear in this volume:
The MX Book of New Sherlock Holmes Stories
Part XXVII – 2021 Annual (1898-1928)

The following contributions appear in the companion volumes:
The MX Book of New Sherlock Holmes Stories
Part XXV – 2021 Annual (1881-1887)
Part XXVI – 2021 Annual (1888-1897)

Editor's Foreword
A Series of Tales
by David Marcum

A few weeks ago, I was exchanging messages with a Sherlockian friend, and the topic of editing came up. We were discussing a new Holmes anthology which neither of us has yet read, containing stories by several authors that my friend likes and several other authors that I like (and also that I know by way of their previous participation in various anthologies that I've edited). I mentioned how it might be a little while before I would actually have time to dive into this new book, as a great deal of my free reading time nowadays is now spent editing submitted stories, which I print on 8½ x 11-inch paper and read with red pen in hand. Over the last few years, I have less time for purely recreational reading than I used to, as I currently receive around 200 traditional pastiche submissions per year for various collections that I edit, and each of those gets multiple read-throughs.

"I can't imagine," my friend, who is a noted editor himself, replied, *"wading through 200 traditional Sherlock Holmes pastiche submissions in a year. You've got my respect and sympathy for that."*

That response has stuck with me for several weeks. *Sympathy?* Why *sympathy*? Right now I'm having my Sherlockian wish come true – people send me new Sherlock Holmes adventures nearly every day. Decades ago, when I first found my way to 221b Baker Street, new stories beyond the original Canon were very few and far between. I'd be lucky to find a new pastiche *once or twice a year*. Now, in terms of new Holmes tales, we're living in the most golden part yet of the Golden Age that started when Nicholas Meyer published *The Seven-Per-Cent Solution* in 1974.

There are a lot of newer Sherlockians who don't know what it was like back then –before the internet, when one couldn't instantly research anything as soon as the idea crossed one's mind, or reach out to an author directly with praise, or to ask a question or offer a comment. One couldn't simply download something or buy a physical copy within minutes of seeing it. Back in those days, one generally didn't know about a new book or its release until it was there in front of you at the bookstore, serendipitously discovered on the shelf. And in those long-ago days, the idea that the majority of writers could write and then get their work in front of the public with any kind of ease was almost laughably impossible – akin to getting a rich man into heaven or a camel through the eye of a needle.

Publishing then was an elitist club with a closed door – even more than so than today, if that can be conceived. (Back then, it took so long for a new story or book to grind through the process then set in place that very few made it, and if something was picked for publication, it might be *years* before it actually physically appeared.) There were certainly a lot of potential Sherlockian authors in that era who would have brought forth Watsonian manuscripts if there had been any hope at all of them reaching the hands of the true fans. Thankfully for both writers and readers, this is a different and better time.

When I was ten years old in 1975, and obtained and read my first Holmes book, there was relatively very little out there beyond The Canon for those who wanted additional adventures. There was some scholarship, but it was generally very esoteric, and extremely difficult to locate, as most of it was published in very limited runs, which quickly vanished into private collections.

But some could be located if one was lucky. I remember when I was in high school in the early 1980's and had reason to go to the nearby University of Tennessee Library for the first time. It was then housed in a vast building that was more akin to a castle than a university building – that is to say, it was perfect. On my first trip, I happened to check the card catalog – if you don't know what that is, kids, Google it – and found that there was a whole section of Sherlockian scholarship upstairs. I was stunned and amazed.

When I navigated the Library of Congress method of cataloging and shelving – which makes no sense if you've been trained on the sensible Dewey Decimal System – I found that they had a complete run of *The Baker Street Journal*, all the way back to the first issue. There were other legendary titles that I'd only seen in mentioned in footnotes – Bell's *Baker Street Byways*, Blakeney's *Sherlock Holmes: Fact or Fiction?* and Holroyd's *Baker Street Byways*, among many others. Over the course of the next few years, I spent a goodly number of hours up there, working my way through the *Journals* and the other volumes (which I could not check out), standing at a Xerox machine and plowing through mounds of dimes to copy items from them, one page at a time. And what was I copying? *Pastiches*, of course. For those books sometimes – although quite rarely – contained a very few of them, buried amongst the scholarship, and it was worth my time and money, because *I wanted more Holmes adventures!*

It was tough then for people like me who had read through The Canon at a dead run and burst out the other end still wanting more. One option was to start in and re-read the pitifully few 60 stories again, and then again, and again, in whatever way seemed best: Straight through in the order that they were collected in book form, or jumping around randomly, as influenced by whatever tale seemed most interesting that day. (My parents gave me Baring-Gould's biography, *Sherlock Holmes of Baker Street*, early on, with its very influential chronology, but it hadn't yet occurred to me the wisdom of actually reading the stories in chronological order.)

My initial exposure to extra-Canonical adventures was first by way of the previously mentioned *The Seven-Per-Cent Solution*, followed soon after by Nicholas Meyers' much better sequel, *The West End Horror* – still one of my favorite Holmes adventures to this day. (I'll never forget the surprise ending.) I found a few others through the mid- and late 1970's – Sean Wright and Michael Hodel's *Enter the Lion*, for instance, and Michael Kurland's *The Infernal Device*, along with those reissued treasures, the Solar Pons volumes by August Derleth – and these encounters with new Holmes adventures in those days came primarily from what showed up on the drug store paperback rack. One can easily imagine how rarely something Sherlockian appeared there.

As I grew older, other methods of obtaining Sherlockian volumes became available. One could write letters to certain specialty bookstores (advertised in the back of a few mystery magazines) requesting their "catalogs" – usually nothing more than a set of poorly Xeroxed and stapled sheets. (How many Sherlockians – like me – still have those precious documents saved someplace?) There were a few dealers that put out nicer brochures and catalogs a couple of times per year – the place in California called *Sherlock's Home* and Carolyn and Joel Senter's wonderful *Classic Specialties*. And of course there was Otto Penzler's amazing *The Mysterious Bookshop* – still going strong today. My family knew that when my birthday or Christmas rolled around, I would provide them with these various catalogs, with pages suitably marked and Sherlockian items specifically requested. I imagine that Sherlockians all over the country did the same thing, and they probably learned the same lesson that I did: If you come across a Sherlockian item that you want, you'd better go ahead and get it now, because it will soon be gone, and trying to find it again later is either going to be nearly impossible or very expensive!

And so it went for several more years – Every once in a while, a traditional pastiche could survive the publishing gauntlet and appear for the hungry public in a real bookstore. Carole Nelson Douglas's definitive Irene Adler novels came along during this time, as did some anthologies by editors like Martin Greenberg and Marvin Kaye. And several small publishers offered Sherlockian titles for a while – Magico and Ian Henry, for instance. Some canny authors like Master Pasticheur Denis O. Smith self-published his initial efforts in chapbook form – and thankfully I have all of those in my collection, proving again my point to grab these things when you have the chance.

And then: *The Internet.*

The Internet changed everything in terms of Sherlockian Pastiche. (It changed everything, period, but this essay is more tightly focused on Sherlockian pastiches and publishing.) I found The Internet in the mid-1990's, when I went back to school for a second degree, this time to be a civil engineer. As an adult student, I worked full-time at night in addition to going to classes during the day, and I had lots of time to kill in between some of those. It was spent hanging out in the school's computer lab, where I received my first real exposure to The Internet. (A dial-up modem at home on a small computer that wasn't much more than a solitaire-playing machine/drink coaster combo was no help at all.)

Naturally, I spent a lot of time going down various Sherlockian rabbit holes. (My wife, a gifted reference librarian, taught me some great search tricks, and I figured out a few more on my own.) By way of the original and very useful *Sherlockian.net* (before it changed), I found links to many on-line pastiches. As an adult student, I was forced to pay certain fees to the university for things that I would never use, such as intramural sports, so I felt no guilt at taking advantage of the free printing that I was allowed in the computer lab. Thus, I was able to print hundreds – nay, *thousands!* – of traditional online pastiches that I winkled out over several years through searches into ever-more obscure places. Often one led to another, or to five more. Thankfully I did print and save them all. I still have them archived in my collection, and many of them have long-since vanished – lost Sherlockian treasures, some of which are as good or better than the Canonical stories.

At one point, I probably had a six-foot-high stack of printed Holmes stories on my desk at home, and I slowly worked my way through them, along with reading all the other Holmes volumes in my collection. (It was during these years that I was initially constructing my Holmes Chronology of both Canon and pastiche, now well over 1,000 dense pages, breaking down novels, short stories, radio and television episodes, movies and scripts, comics and unpublished manuscripts, and fan-fiction by book, chapter, page, or paragraph into year, month, day, and even hour.)

Besides printing online pastiches, I was also requesting many many obscure volumes by way of the university's interlibrary loan program, and Xeroxing them for my collection, until some future date when I could obtain the real thing – once again standing at copy machines and feeding in dime after dime. It was time and money well spent. Additionally, I was able to find many more pastiche titles for sale through The Internet than I'd ever been able to locate before using those irregular catalogs, and I started acquiring those too. My endeavors to track down as many traditional Canonical pastiches as I could was vastly aided by the late Phil Jones's online pastiche list, which allowed me to identify even more that I wanted. Thus, I built a formidable traditional pastiche collection.

And even as I was obtaining these new adventures by way of The Internet, The Internet was allowing previously suppressed and stymied Sherlockian authors, without hope, to connect with readers in ways that had never before been possible.

Who could have known that there were so many people out there who had access to some really excellent material from Watson's Tin Dispatch Box? The call to pull forth these stories might have been so strong that they would have done so no matter what, but The Internet allowed a connection between author and reader in such a new way, and with such instantaneous feedback and gratification, that it became almost addictive to keep producing stories.

The old publishing paradigm, as alluded to above, was Darwinian, with only a few survivors able to see actual publication. Often it wasn't – and isn't – fair, with material being published "professionally" that is nowhere near as good as "amateur" writings. Granted, some like Denis Smith had the gumption to produce their own pamphlet-like publications, but very few knew about them, and only a tiny number of them in the great scheme of things were ever physically produced. The Internet allowed authors – not just Sherlockians, but of any fandom – to write and publish with nearly instantaneous turnaround. And here the publishing paradigm began to shift. The old established behemoth publishing companies continued to follow the model of printing thousands of copies of the few authors' works that survived their gauntlet, with carefully calculated mathematical models to determine just how many copies had to be sold to make the thinnest margin of profit. In the meantime, copies sat on bookstore shelves, more unsold than sold, and then they rotated into remainder bins or were destroyed, like food that has gone past the expiration date.

But others had vision – like Steve Emecz of MX Publishing – who recognized the incredible value of *print-on-demand* technology, wherein an order is placed for a book, which generates that book being printed at a specialized factory where the file is already loaded. As soon as it's produced, it's then shipped, and thus into the hands of the happy reader just days later – while the author accumulates a royalty. With that simple brilliant realization, Steve Emecz managed to make the connection between the Sherlockian authors who had tales to tell and no effective way of sharing them to their benefit, and the Sherlockian readers (like me) who want more new Holmes adventures, every day.

5

I was aware of the MX books before I ever became involved with them. As a Holmes collector, I was thrilled when this new company showed up, and of course I started buying the books as the appeared. A few at first, then more and more as Steve perfected his system. My own first book, *The Papers of Sherlock Holmes*, was originally published in 2011 by a small Canadian press, and according to that publisher, it has yet to sell a single copy. (Curiously, I know that copies were in fact sold, because I know people that bought them. Yet I've certainly never received a single dime in royalties for that edition, although it's still available on that publisher's website.) When I saw that an excellent Sherlockian pasticheur, Gerard Kelly – who had also been with that Canadian press – had jumped to MX for a new edition of his book, I reached out to Steve Emecz (on December 13th, 2012), asking for him to forward a message to Gerard. Steve did, and Gerard and I discussed our mutual experiences with the Canadian publisher. He then advised enthusiastically that I also switch to MX. So finally, on January 11th, 2013 I formerly introduced myself by way of an email to Steve, pitching my book. That turned out to be an amazing life-changing email for me, and once again proof that if you don't ask, you'll never know. A few months later, my first book was reissued as a two-volume set (and later as a hardcover and an Audible audio book too). And there was no looking back.

I believe that MX initially began as a typical for-profit company, but Steve and his wife Sharon quickly pivoted it to become a non-profit organization, supporting several charities, including the Happy Life Children's Home in Kenya. Initially, MX was involved in saving Undershaw, one of Sir Arthur Conan Doyle's former homes, from developers who would drastically alter or destroy it. When Undershaw was saved, MX shifted to supporting the Stepping Stones School for special needs children, which is now located at Sir Arthur's former home. In addition to these charitable works, Steve has another unofficial mission: He gives Sherlockian authors who would otherwise be unable to do so the chance to have their books published. Some MX authors are quite prolific, and some of their titles are tent-poles for the broader business, while other authors just have the one story in them. Still, they are also a part of the MX family, and they've had an opportunity that wouldn't be offered by most publishers.

In 2013, the year MX re-published my first book, I made my initial Holmes Pilgrimage to London and other British locations, and I was able to meet Steve in person for the first time. It was a rainy afternoon in the bar of the Sherlock Holmes Hotel in Baker Street, where I was staying. For those who don't know, Steve is just as nice in real life as he seems when you read about him or hear him interviewed. And he's very supportive – for instance, on the occasions when I wrote and published my next two books of original material, and also when, in early 2015, I had the idea for *The MX Book of New Sherlock Holmes Stories.*

For early that year, I woke up from a dream where I'd edited a book. In spite of all the new pastiches I'd found over the past years, I wanted more – particularly to reinforce the traditional Canonical heroic Holmes, as there was too much insidious infiltration of late into pastiches of elements from a certain television show that had the word *Sherlock* in the title, but nothing else to do with Our Hero. As this show started to creep into the public consciousness, I was starting to read pastiches by people who should have known better giving Holmes a "mind palace", or indicating that he was a "high-functioning sociopath", or implying that Watson's wound was psychosomatic, or that Irene Adler was a dominatrix – all ridiculous ideas. A strong push-back was necessary.

I asked Steve about my idea for a new book of traditional Canonical adventures, and he was very supportive, so I began reaching out to some authors that I admired to see if they would be interested. I had pictured – if I was lucky – a trade paperback of maybe one- or two-dozen new stories, pleasing me but gathering little attention otherwise. Fearing failure, I overcompensated and sent invitations to every Sherlockian author that I could think of, particularly authors of books in my Holmes collection – and there were a lot of them. I also wrote to some Sherlockian friends who had never actually written a pastiche before to see if they were interested, and they we were. (I'm especially proud of recruiting first-time writers, many of whom have gone on to successfully write quite a few more pastiches since then.) Amazingly, people were interested and willing to join the party. Word spread, and more people wanted in, including many that I hadn't heard of before. This was really going to happen.

Part of what attracted these participants – besides the desire to contribute to The Great Holmes Tapestry – was the fact that early on, Steve and I had decided to direct the royalties from the project to the Stepping Stones School, and people were thrilled to be able to help in that way. Through 2015, the stories rolled in and the editing continued. Then, it was publication time. I had my second in-person meeting with Steve in October 2015, on my second Holmes Pilgrimage when I was able to return to the Holmesland for the launch of the three-volume initial set of *The MX Book of New Sherlock Holmes Stories* – for by then it had grown to over 60 new adventures, the largest collection of its kind in the world. Steve had an amazing launch party on top of one of London's skyscrapers – which just happened to hold the office where he was employed at the time. It was an amazing night, and I was able to meet a number of wonderful Sherlockian contributors in person – and my biggest regret is that I didn't get to spend more time with each of them and think to make photographs there that night.

While on that second Pilgrimage, I was able to spend some time with Sherlockian Nick Utechin, who gave me an in-depth tour of Oxford – Sherlockian points of interest and otherwise. While we ate lunch, he expressed that he wished he'd been part of the three volumes, but he'd be interested in being in the next set. *Next set . . . ?* Back home a few weeks later, I started to hear from previous contributors and the newly interested, also indicating they'd like to be in the next volumes. *Next volumes . . . ?* I'd never thought of it as anything but a one-time thing. But suddenly the future got a little brighter than it already was. *Why not another set?* Steve and I had already done the heavy lifting in setting up the previous volumes, making decisions about formats and style. We had an existing pool of contributors – Sherlockians with more stories to tell and anxious to do so. And it was for a great double cause – the Stepping Stones School, and the continued support of the true traditional Canonical Sherlock Holmes. So a week or so after I returned from Holmes Pilgrimage No. 2, the call went out for more stories, and Part IV was published in Spring 2016. There was such interest that another volume was scheduled for Fall 2016, and since then, we've published spring and fall collections every year, sometimes single volumes, but more often then not having so many stories that they run to double- or triple-volume sets. (And I'm mightily thankful that Steve is the kind of publisher who indicated that with more stories, we simply grow to more volumes, without slamming the door at a certain page count and cutting off willing authors and hungry readers from more excellent adventures.)

Since the series started, we've now produced almost 600 new Holmes adventures in 27 volumes from nearly 200 contributors around the world. And as of this writing, the donated royalties to the Stepping Stones School are somewhere over $75,000 – with no end in sight. Many of the contributors have provided enough stories that they now have enough of them accumulated to publish their own books, and there have also been a number of other Sherlockian anthologies – particularly from Belanger Books – that have started to promote the same kinds of Canonical Sherlockian tales. (I've also edited a number of those, and I think of them as MX Anthology annexes – they're set up with the same story requirements, and the same typeface and layout as the MX books, and usually submitted by the same authors. I highly recommend them.)

So when I think of my friend's comment about *Sympathy*, I'm frankly dumbfounded. Personally, I'm having the time of my life, and I expect that I'd be somewhere far outside the Sherlockian sandbox looking in if not for my initial emails to Steve Emecz in late 2012 and early 2013 and his subsequent positive response. (Thanks Steve!) And beyond what these books have done for me personally, I think they provide an amazing service for others – not just the royalties for the school, or as an outlet for the authors who have tales to tell, or for the readers hungry for more of them. No, in these crazy times in which we live, there's a true *need* for Sherlock Holmes – maybe more than ever.

It's unnecessary to delve in great depth upon the calamitous events of the past few years – the COVID-19 pandemic, and the rise of fascism coupled with the need of many to race toward the cliff of stupidity. Holmes's adventures provide a much-needed escape from the idiocy of today: They show order being brought to chaos, and justice being administered to injustice. But Holmes also serves as a reminder and example of how we should be as people. For Holmes would not be a science-denier. He would not support those oppressors who would steal basic human rights from those whom they can exploit. And he would not support fascist wanna-be dictators. He would speak truth to the liars and the corrupt, and that's why he's a hero for any age.

Of course, it must be noted that Holmes the scientific supporter would have had little use for these additional Watsonian narratives of his adventures. In *The Sign of the Four*, he explains his position to Watson, when discussing the published version of *A Study in Scarlet*:

> *"I glanced over it," said he. "Honestly, I cannot congratulate you upon it. Detection is, or ought to be, an exact science and should be treated in the same cold and unemotional manner. You have attempted to tinge it with romanticism, which produces much the same effect as if you worked a love-story or an elopement into the fifth proposition of Euclid."*
>
> *"But the romance was there," I remonstrated. "I could not tamper with the facts."*
>
> *"Some facts should be suppressed, or, at least, a just sense of proportion should be observed in treating them. The only point in the case which deserved mention was the curious analytical reasoning from effects to causes, by which I succeeded in unravelling it."*

More pointedly, in "The Copper Beeches", Holmes says:

> *"You have degraded what should have been a course of lectures into a series of tales."*

9

So Holmes was a hero, but he was also capable of being wrong, as shown with this simple statement. For Watson is a hero too, taking the time and effort to bring us these heroic adventures – not just those few in the original Canon, but all the others that have been pulled from his Tin Dispatch Box in the years since, by way of those later pasticheurs who open their minds to receive them and then transcribe them for the rest of us. Now, with this latest set of *The MX Book of New Sherlock Holmes Stories*, we have 59 more of them, and they'll help brighten the current (but thankfully brightening) darkness and push back on the seemingly endless evil and willful ignorance until the next set of MX Sherlockian tales arrives. Thank heavens the paradigm shifted so that so many talented and willing people could get these *"series of tales"* to so many of us who want and need them.

* * * * *

"Of course, I could only stammer out my thanks."
– *The unhappy John Hector McFarlane,* "The Norwood Builder"

As always when one of these sets is finished, I want to first thank with all my heart my incredible wonderful wife of nearly thirty-three years, Rebecca, and our amazing son and my friend, Dan. I love you both, and you are everything to me!

During the editing of these particular volumes, I obtained employment at my dream job. When the agency where I was a federal investigator closed in the 1990's, and I was figuring out what I wanted to do with my life, we lived near a beautiful park, and as I would walk there with my son, seeing the trails and springs and streams and culverts big enough that kids were exploring them, and I realized that I was interested in infrastructure – and particularly working for that city. That led to my return to school to be a civil engineer. After a number of years working at various engineering companies, and getting my license along the way, and still wanting to work at the city, I was finally able to. That has kept me extremely busy for the last few months, which kept me from replying to emails as fast as I would have wished, so I'm very grateful to everyone who patiently waited to hear back from me about their stories.

I can never express enough gratitude for all of the contributors who have donated their time and royalties to this ongoing project. I'm constantly amazed at the incredible stories that you send, and I'm so glad to have gotten to know so many of you through this process. It's an undeniable fact that Sherlock Holmes authors are the *best* people!

The contributors of these stories have donated their royalties for this project to support the Stepping Stones School for special needs children, located at Undershaw, one of Sir Arthur Conan Doyle's former homes. As of this writing, and as mentioned above, these MX anthologies have raised over $75,000 for the school, with no end in sight, and of even more importance, they have helped raise awareness about the school all over the world. These books are making a real difference to the school, and the participation of both contributors and purchasers is most appreciated.

Next is that group that exchanges emails with me when we have the time – and time is a valuable commodity for all of us these days! As mentioned, I don't get to write back and forth with these fine people as often as I'd like, but I really enjoy catching up when we do get the chance: Derrick Belanger, Brian Belanger, Mark Mower, Denis Smith, Tom Turley, Dan Victor, and Marcia Wilson.

There is a group of special people who have stepped up and supported this and a number of other projects over and over again with a lot of contributions. They are the best and I can't express how valued they are: Hugh Ashton, Derrick Belanger, Deanna Baran, Craig Stephen Copland, Matthew Elliott, Tim Gambrell, Jayantika Ganguly, Paul Gilbert, Dick Gillman, Arthur Hall, Steve Herczeg, Paul Hiscock, Craig Janacek, Mark Mower, Will Murray, Robert Perret, Tracy Revels, Roger Riccard, Geri Schear, Brenda Seabrooke, Shane Simmons, Robert Stapleton, Kevin Thornton, I.A. Watson, and Marcy Wilson.

I also want to particularly thank the following:

- *Peter Lovesey* – I first became aware of Mr. Lovesey by way of Sergeant Cribb, hero of eight novels (and later a short story), and a set of original television episodes. I saw *Cribb* when it first appeared on PBS in 1979 – consisting of two series of filmed versions of all eight novels, as well as six original cases, as written by Lovesey and Jacqueline Lovesey. This led me to read the one Cribb volume in our house, *Invitation to a Dynamite Party* (1974), inexplicably in my dad's massive book collection – "inexplicably" because that wasn't the type of book that he read at all. (And after that he didn't own it anymore, as I took possession – and I still have it.) That one book led me to quickly acquire all the rest of them, which I read in a white heat over the next few weeks, and have re-read countless times in the years since.

11

These fifteen tales (novels, original TV episodes, and short story) make up the entire Cribb Canon, and I've desperately wished for decades for more of them. When, through the aforementioned *Internet*, I was finally able to communicate with Mr. Lovesey, I expressed as much to him, but sadly I haven't (yet) convinced him to write more adventures of that heroic Sergeant. I've also floated the idea several times of having a Holmes and Cribb share a co-adventure, as they most certainly knew one another, and Holmes would have liked and respected Cribb. Additionally, Mr. Lovesey has written several especially fine Holmes pastiches. So far no luck – but I did have an off-screen Cribb Easter-egg appearance in one of my own short stories, "The Tangled Skein at Birling Gap" in *Sherlock Holmes: Tangled Skeins*.

After Sergeant Cribb, Mr. Lovesey went on to an incredibly honored writing career, including other series featuring Peter Diamond and Bertie, the Prince of Wales. While I've tried for years to recruit him to write a Holmes story for these volumes, I'm thrilled that he's a part of them by way of his brilliant foreword – wherein I learned that he has a knowledge of Undershaw that I didn't know about.

Thank you, Peter!

- *Roger Johnson* – I'm more grateful than I can say that I know Roger. His Sherlockian knowledge is exceptional, as is the work that he does to further the cause of The Master. But even more than that, both Roger and his wonderful wife, Jean Upton, are simply the finest and best kind of people, and I'm very lucky to know both of them – even though I don't get to see them nearly as often as I'd like, and especially in these crazy days! In so many ways, Roger, I can't thank you enough, and I can't imagine these books without you.
- *Steve Emecz* – As mentioned, when I first emailed Steve from out of the blue back in late 2012 and early 2013, I was interested in MX re-publishing my previously published first book. Even then, as a guy who works to accumulate *all* traditional Sherlockian pastiches, I could see that MX (under Steve's leadership) was *the* fast-rising superstar of the Sherlockian publishing world.

The publication of that first book with MX was an amazing life-changing event for me, leading to writing and then editing more books, unexpected Holmes Pilgrimages to England, and these incredible anthologies. When I had the idea for these books in early 2015, I thought that it might, with any luck, be one small volume of perhaps a dozen stories. Since then they've grown and grown, and by way of them I've been able to make some incredible Sherlockian friends and play in the Holmesian Sandbox in ways that I'd never before dreamed possible.

All through it, Steve has been one of the most positive and supportive people I've ever known, letting me explore various Sherlockian projects and opening up my own personal possibilities in ways that otherwise would have never been possible. Thank you Steve for every opportunity!

- *Brian Belanger* – Brian is one of the nicest and most talented of people, and I'm very glad that I was able to meet him in person during the 2020 Sherlock Holmes Birthday Celebration in New York. (Hopefully I'll see him there again when travel resumes.) His gifts are amazing, and his skills improve and grow from project to project. He's amazingly great to work with, and once again I thank him for another incredible contribution.
- *Scott Monty and Bert Wolder, Lenny Picker, and Adrian Braddy* – I very much appreciate being interviewed by these men – respectively at *I Hear of Sherlock Everywhere (IHOSE)*, *Publishers Weekly*, and *Sherlock Holmes Magazine* – and having the opportunity to spread the word about these anthologies.

And last but certainly *not* least, **Sir Arthur Conan Doyle**: Author, doctor, adventurer, and the Founder of the Sherlockian Feast. Present in spirit, and honored by all of us here.

It was particularly unusual editing this collection through the latter half of 2020 and into 2021, as the world continued through a deadly globe-spanning pandemic. Many people ended up being stuck at home, and my first thought was that a number of them would take advantage of that newly carved-out time – although for terrible reasons – to write. However, it soon became apparent that everyone's lives were turned upside down to greater or lesser degrees, and even if they had the *time* to write something, they didn't necessarily have the *heart* to do so. I was concerned that Parts XXII, XXIII, and XXIV (published Fall 2020) might not have enough stories – at least not to the level which many have come to expect and look forward to.

But as people found their footing and their spirits, the stories began to arrive, more and more of them – both for those books, and also for other Sherlockian anthologies that I've edited at the same time. And the same was true for this current set. It's been amazing, and it showed that in these dark times, people have found great comfort in writing about Holmes and Watson and those bygone days, and also that they want to share those tales with others who will find comfort as well.

For everyone who dug deep and found a way forward and is a part of this collection, and for all of you who will be reading it, thank you so much.

As always, this collection has been a labor of love by both the participants and myself. As I've explained before, once again everyone did their sincerest best to produce an anthology that truly represents why Holmes and Watson have been so popular for so long. These are just more tiny threads woven into the ongoing Great Holmes Tapestry, continuing to grow and grow, for there can *never* be enough stories about the man whom Watson described as *"the best and wisest . . . whom I have ever known."*

David Marcum
March 4th, 2021
The 140th Anniversary of Watson
first beginning to understand why
Holmes is a hero, during the events of
A Study in Scarlet

Questions, comments, or story submissions
may be addressed to David Marcum at

thepapersofsherlockholmes@gmail.com

Foreword
by Peter Lovesey

I'm delighted to be providing a foreword for this latest collection of stories inspired by Sir Arthur Conan Doyle's great detective. By the time I was fourteen, I had devoured the entire Canon. I know this because in 1951, armed with notes I had made in the complete short stories, I went to London to visit Abbey House in Baker Street. A national effort was being made to escape the post-war gloom with a Festival of Britain, and part of the fun was a Sherlock Holmes exhibition. Between May and September, over fifty-thousand people flocked to see it.

I remember being enraptured by original manuscripts, Sidney Paget's illustrations for *The Strand*, and a selection of the many letters addressed to Holmes that were delivered to Abbey House because it was deemed by the Post Office to be the site of number 221b. The main attraction was a re-creation by Michael Weight of the great consulting detective's living room as it had looked on a given day in 1898. As I entered, I heard sound effects provided by the BBC of a barrel organ playing and the clop-clop-clop of cab horses from the street below. A cluttered interior had numerous reminders of the room's occupant: *The Daily News* open at a page reporting the death of the long-serving prime minister, William Gladstone; shelves of books and case files; a Persian slipper containing tobacco; unanswered letters jack-knifed into the fireplace; cigars in the coal-scuttle; bullet-holes in the wall; chemical apparatus; a table set for afternoon tea; and, if you looked for it, a hypodermic syringe. Holmes himself wasn't present, but his likeness was, against one of the windows, the wax bust from *The Empty House*. I believe purists protested in the press that there should not have been a deerstalker cap hanging on the back of the door with the Inverness cape, and that Holmes could never have smoked a curved pipe because the first ones in Britain were brought back after the Boer War ended in 1902, but none of this bothered me as a schoolboy. I was enchanted.

The magic stayed with me. My first attempts at crime writing nearly twenty years later were set in Victorian London. Sensibly I made my sleuth, Sergeant Cribb, an ordinary working policeman, more shrewd and dogged than brilliant. Much later, I tried a couple of short stories meant to celebrate The Master, but I'm not proud of them. The stories in this fine collection get much closer to the spirit of the originals.

By then I was living in Sussex, the county where the Great Detective lives on in endless retirement, but I never had the privilege of meeting him. My reason for mentioning this is that my route into London took me regularly through a notorious bottleneck in the village of Hindhead. This was before the tunnel was built that now allows traffic to by-pass the place. I would look out of my slow-moving car at a sad sight: A large, derelict building that had once been the home of Conan Doyle. He had the house built and lived there from 1897 to 1907 while writing *The Hound of the Baskervilles* and the stories in *The Strand* later collected as *The Return of Sherlock Holmes*. Undershaw had been declared a World Heritage site in 1977, but its crumbling exterior suggested nothing so grand.

What heartening news it was in 2016 that Undershaw had been completely refurbished and was opening as an alternative special needs school called Stepping Stones for children with a variety of handicaps including hemiplegia, autism, and cerebral palsy. And how fitting that the profits from all the stories in this and other volumes in the series are donated to this worthy cause.

Seventy years after I visited that exhibition, I am treated to these new adventures of Sherlock Holmes. The spell is cast again.

> *"Come, Watson, come!" he cried. "The game is afoot! Not a word! Into your clothes and come!"*
> *Ten minutes later we were both in a cab and rattling through the silent streets . . . .*

Peter Lovesey
November 2020

16

"Veritable Tales"
by Roger Johnson

Nearly seventy years ago, in the October 1953 issue of *The Baker Street Journal*, Edgar W Smith wrote: *"There is no Sherlockian worthy of his salt who has not, at least once in his life, taken Dr. Watson's pen in hand and given himself to the production of a veritable tale."* After briefly mentioning his own two contributions to the apocrypha, he continued: *"The point is that the writing of a pastiche is compulsive and inevitable, and nothing to be ashamed of. It is a wholesome and welcome manifestation of the urge to be intimately a part of the Baker Street scene; a sublimation of the desire that is in us all to revel in the glory of the Saga, not only receptively, but creatively as well."*

Some will disagree – I've known people who regard Holmesian pastiche with a rabid hatred that sometimes suggests actual mental disorder – but most of us, surely, realise that the Blessed Edgar expressed, far better than we could, something which we had always instinctively known even though we may not have given it much thought.

He had more to say on the subject, however, and this too may stir a thought or two that were hitherto unrecognised. *"And yet I like to think,"* he said, *"that pastiches are made to be written but not to be read. They are the stuff of dreams, the projection of our fancies, the release of our repressed desires, in which we, but not others, should be expected to take delight."*

To sum up, then, we should all feel free to create new exploits for Holmes and Watson, but we shouldn't inflict them upon others.

Now, what sort of statement is that to make in a foreword for the latest in David Marcum's admirable series of *New Sherlock Holmes Stories* for MX Publishing? Well, Edgar Smith went on to say: *"Once in a while, when there is one superbly done, it may with some trepidation be, shared with those who understand and sympathize."*

His standards were possibly higher and less flexible than mine. Where he required the superb (and remember that many of the sixty canonical tales don't qualify for that description) I can be satisfied with ingenuity, atmosphere, historical authenticity, wit, style . . . In short, I like a story that's neatly planned, written in good English, and written with real knowledge and love of Holmes, Watson, and Conan Doyle.

Which is to say, the sort of story that you'll find in this remarkable collection, and it makes this – and its companion volumes – the sort of book that you can confidently hand to almost any Sherlockian, with the recommendation, "This is good. I think you'll like it!"

Roger Johnson, BSI, ASH
Editor: The Sherlock Holmes Journal
February 2021

An Ongoing Legacy
for Sherlock Holmes
by Steve Emecz

Undershaw
Circa 1900

*T*he *MX Book of New Sherlock Holmes Stories* has now raised over $75,000 for Stepping Stones School for children with learning disabilities, and is by far the largest Sherlock Holmes collection in the world.

Stepping Stones is located in Undershaw, the former home of Sir Arthur Conan Doyle, where he wrote many of the Sherlock Holmes stories. The fundraising has supported many projects continuing the legacy of Conan Doyle and Sherlock Holmes in the amazing building, including The Doyle Room, the school's Zoom broadcasting capability (including Sherlock themed events), The Literacy Program, and more.

In addition to Stepping Stones School, our main program that we support is the Happy Life Children's Home in Kenya. My wife Sharon and I have spent seven Christmas's with the children in Nairobi. Due to the global pandemic we didn't visit Africa this year.

It's a wonderful project that has saved the lives of over 600 babies. You can read all about the project in the second edition of the book *The Happy Life Story*.

In 2020, our *#bookstotrees* program where every book bought on our *www.mxpublishing.com* website resulted in a tree being funded at Happy Life. We reached our target of 1,000 trees in August.

In 2021, we are working on *#bookstobooks* which sees us donating 10% of the revenues from *mxpublishing.com* to fund schoolbooks and library books at Happy Life.

We've launched the Sherlock Holmes Book Club where fans can get a hardcover edition of *The MX Book of New Sherlock Holmes Stories* every month plus exclusive free books, events and competitions:

> *https://mxpublishing.com/products/sherlock-holmes-book-club-hardcover-subscription*

Our support of both of these projects is possible through the publishing of Sherlock Holmes books, which we have now been doing for thirteen years.

You can find out more information about the Stepping Stones School at:

> *www.steppingstones.org.uk*

and Happy Life at:

> *www.happylifechildrenshomes.com*

You can find out more about MX Publishing and reach out to us through our website at:

> *www.mxpublishing.com*

Steve Emecz
February 2021
Twitter: @mxpublishing

The Doyle Room at Stepping Stones, Undershaw
Partially funded through royalties from
The MX Book of New Sherlock Holmes Stories

A Word From
Stepping Stones
by Jacqueline Silver

Undershaw
September 9, 2016
Grand Opening of the Stepping Stones School
(Photograph courtesy of Roger Johnson)

Undershaw provided much inspiration for Sir Arthur Conan Doyle. It was the backdrop to many of his works which gained him such literary reverence. Those large south-facing windows which, in days gone by helped ease the symptoms of his wife's tuberculosis, now provide an inspirational setting for the next generation of scholars. Undershaw is seminal to the future of Stepping Stones School.

We have missed much of its magic over the past twelve months with the restrictions around the Covid-19 pandemic and the heart-breaking but necessary loss of our social interactions. However, for the most vulnerable members of our school, it has remained a safe place and we have kept our doors open for these students.

We long to return. To hear the building teeming once again with life, noise and bustle; to hear the creak of the green front door as it opens and shuts with each passing student, parent, and teacher. Undershaw has provided our school community with a sense of calm amidst the unpredictability of the outside world, this year more than ever. It did the same for Conan Doyle as he supported Louisa: An oasis amidst the tumult.

In the autumn of last year, we enjoyed a brief respite in restrictions which meant we were able to return fully. Shortly after this, we were honoured to receive a Royal Visit from Her Royal Highness the Countess of Wessex. The Countess was delighted to see such a happy and vibrant school looking ahead to the future with fresh leadership and a team of staff passionate about delivering the very best Special Educational Needs education. The students spoke proudly of their school and what it meant for them to call Undershaw home.

As we turn the year, our educational offer continues to evolve. We are wholeheartedly committed to our pursuit of raising standards for those with additional learning needs and to foster a fearless and aspirational mind-set regarding their capabilities, potential, and their futures. In our work going forward, the school is resolute in unearthing ways to *"Eliminate the Impossible"* for these fantastic young people.

On behalf of the students, staff, and families we support with our work here, I remain so grateful for your interest in the school. I consider us very fortunate to have such a strong and committed network of benefactors.

Jacqueline Silver
Headteacher
February 2021

"When you have eliminated the impossible,
whatever remains, however improbable,
must be the truth."

Sir Arthur Conan Doyle

"Undershaw," Hindhead, Conan Doyle's House.

Sherlock Holmes (1854-1957) was born in Yorkshire, England, on 6 January, 1854. In the mid-1870's, he moved to 24 Montague Street, London, where he established himself as the world's first Consulting Detective. After meeting Dr. John H. Watson in early 1881, he and Watson moved to rooms at 221b Baker Street, where his reputation as the world's greatest detective grew for several decades. He was presumed to have died battling noted criminal Professor James Moriarty on 4 May, 1891, but he returned to London on 5 April, 1894, resuming his consulting practice in Baker Street. Retiring to the Sussex coast near Beachy Head in October 1903, he continued to be associated in various private and government investigations while giving the impression of being a reclusive apiarist. He was very involved in the events encompassing World War I, and to a lesser degree those of World War II. He passed away peacefully upon the cliffs above his Sussex home on his 103rd birthday, 6 January, 1957.

Dr. John Hamish Watson (1852-1929) was born in Stranraer, Scotland on 7 August, 1852. In 1878, he took his Doctor of Medicine Degree from the University of London, and later joined the army as a surgeon. Wounded at the Battle of Maiwand in Afghanistan (27 July, 1880), he returned to London late that same year. On New Year's Day, 1881, he was introduced to Sherlock Holmes in the chemical laboratory at Barts. Agreeing to share rooms with Holmes in Baker Street, Watson became invaluable to Holmes's consulting detective practice. Watson was married and widowed three times, and from the late 1880's onward, in addition to his participation in Holmes's investigations and his medical practice, he chronicled Holmes's adventures, with the assistance of his literary agent, Sir Arthur Conan Doyle, in a series of popular narratives, most of which were first published in *The Strand* magazine. Watson's later years were spent preparing a vast number of his notes of Holmes's cases for future publication. Following a final important investigation with Holmes, Watson contracted pneumonia and passed away on 24 July, 1929.

Photos of Sherlock Holmes and Dr. John H. Watson courtesy of Roger Johnson

The MX Book
of
New Sherlock Holmes Stories

Part XXVII – 2021 Annual
(1898-1928)

Sherlock Holmes Returns:
The Missing Rhyme
by Joseph W. Svec, III

Once more I sat with pen in hand,
Before my typewriter so grand.
Engaged deep in the poets craft.
Why? Don't ask, I must be daft.

Again a rhyme was being vexing.
Finding it was most perplexing.
When suddenly upon my door,
There came a rap, and then one more.

"Now who could that be?" I declared.
And opened it, just somewhat scared.
Well, I'll be, and rattle my bones,
If it isn't the famous Sherlock Holmes.

"What are you doing here?" I said.
He answered, "This is the place that I was led.
You're looking for a rhyme, I know.
All the clues do tell me so.

"At first it was a foggy haze,
But then, it came like a Silver Blaze.
Delivered in a Cardboard Box
Disguised as clever as a fox.

"To miss it sure would be disgrace
Almost like a Yellow Face.
I knew that you could make it work,
As clear as any Stockbroker's Clerk.

"Or smooth as any sailing yacht,
Just like the famous Gloria Scott
I analyzed. (It is habitual.)
'Twas easy as the Musgrave Ritual.

"I was quite quick, I was on fire.
As slick as any Reigate Squire.
In color, and hue, it looked tan,

33

More so than a Crooked Man.

"With clues I am the Precedent facient
More often than the Resident Patient"
First I saw a meek conservator,
And then did find a Greek Interpreter.

"Twas obvious as a claval, meaty,
Clearer than a Naval Treaty.
The steps to you, why, I did Gobble 'em
Quicker than The Final Problem.

"So here at last, is your lost rhyme,
The best detective, surly I am,
Known by all, why even gnomes,
I am the famous Sherlock Holmes."

The Adventure of the Hero's Heir
by Tracy J. Revels

During the years that I shared a domicile with Sherlock Holmes, I never knew who I might find ensconced on our sofa when I returned from an errand. It was rare for me to step out to visit the tobacconist or the chemist's shop, or take a brief stroll about Regent's Park, without discovering some unique visitor had arrived at Baker Street in my absence. Holmes's services were offered to all. I might find a humble charwoman or a chimney sweep laying their troubles at my friend's feet. It was equally likely that a duchess or a baronet would be putting a case before him.

Therefore, it was with some great pride but no astonishment that I learned, one pleasant morning in May, that Holmes's newest client was none other than Colonel Edward Jasper, accompanied by a regally attired Indian servant who melted into the shadows as we talked. In the days of the Great Mutiny, Colonel Jasper had won fame for riding through mountain passes crawling with cultists, bandits, and mutineers, in order to save a fortress packed with women and children. Though his hair was grey and his brow wrinkled, there was still something of the gallant and determined officer in his great drooping mustache and his steely gaze. He curtly dismissed my praise and worshipful commentary on his record.

"Those days are far behind me," he grumbled, resuming his place, his back ramrod straight. "I have not come to talk about my past, but about my son's current problem. I would have Mr. Holmes get to the bottom of it."

He spoke these words with the air of a man accustomed to giving martial orders long into his retirement. I knew that Holmes was quite capable to reminding even the most highly placed officer that he was no private in the regiment. Much to my surprise, my friend merely nodded and asked the old soldier to tell his story from the beginning.

"The beginning? Very well, though I rather think it a waste of breath. Edward – Neddy, we always called him – was born just as I shipped out for the colonies. As you know, I had something of a career in India, but I saw far too many vile and wicked things there to ever summon my family to join me. Eliza, my wife, raised the boy on her own – I never laid eyes on him until his eighth birthday, and by then it was far too late."

"Too late?" I asked. Jasper gave me a look to freeze blood, and I immediately resolved not to inject any more questions into the conversation.

"Too late to make a man of him! He'd been babied by his mother. By the time I returned, he'd grown soft and weak. I did my best to take him in hand, test his mettle, but it was useless. He would never make a soldier of any rank, especially after his mother passed away that winter. I sent him off to a military school in Scotland, thinking that would help, but he sickened and almost died. There was nothing for it but private tutors, then Oxford. I told myself that he could study law and use the family name and wealth to stand for Parliament. Instead – " Here the man shook his head and puffed out his mustache in disgust. " – he was sent down in his second term."

"The nature of the trouble?" Holmes asked.

"Some scandal over a foolish girl he was said to have ruined – she killed herself afterward. I took a horsewhip to Neddy, then cut him from my will. We were estranged for a time after that."

I looked up from notes I had begun writing. How quickly my image of Colonel Jasper as a chivalrous knight-errant had been turned on its head. I saw him now as cold and callous, almost devoid of any feelings. Then I reminded myself that he had come about his son's problem, and perhaps was determined, in his own rough way, to extract his child from trouble.

"Neddy became a writer of novels. Of course, at my insistence, he published under a pseudonym – Charles Crusoe."

I must have made a sound, for the old man's head snapped in my direction. "I – I have read your son's work," I offered.

"And your review of it?" Holmes asked.

I stumbled, attempting to dredge up words that were truthful but would also not offend the war hero. "His novels are – engaging. Filled with adventure."

Jasper snorted. "What you mean is that they are childish claptrap! A schoolboy could write better potboilers than my son does. He gets everything wrong, especially when he tries to write about foreign lands and customs. I know, because my criticism sent him off to India, where he has been for the last five years."

"I had wondered," I said, "why he had not published recently."

"Yes – I suppose it was my fault. There were times when I regretted telling him that if he wished to write believably about thuggee cults and the practice of sati, he should go to India to learn. Years passed without me hearing from him. Then, last summer, I received a most remarkable letter. My son begged my forgiveness and promised to reform, if I would restore him to his inheritance. I agreed, but with certain conditions in place."

"What were they?" Holmes asked. The Colonel counted off on his fingers.

"First, he must return home from India. Second, he must find some more stable line of work. And third, he must woo and wed a decent girl and start a family. If he would do these things, I would settle one of his mother's properties on him. She was the heiress of Sir Lionel Balton, and as such had inherited several properties, most of which I sold following her demise. I retained a few, however, including a house in the city, which I was willing to place at my son's disposal, should he prove worthy of my trust. Much to my surprise, I received a telegram acknowledging my terms.

"My son returned to London last November. His experiences in India had significantly changed him – he was thin and browned by the sun, he had lost almost all his hair and acquired a squint, which he did his best to conceal beneath dark spectacles. His voice, once lipid and oily, was now a rasp. He had clearly suffered the ravages of tropical diseases, but I would not allow myself to feel pity for him. Much to my surprise, he immediately found gainful employment as a translator for the Museum of Indian Curiosities, and soon afterward presented a young woman for my approval as his bride. I gave them my blessing and offered Neddy his choice of dwellings. He selected Squire Hall, which is a crumbling manor house, set back in some woods an hour from London."

"One would have thought a fine city home would have been more to his liking – or at least to his bride's," Holmes mused.

"It did seem a rather poor choice, what with the roof leaking, the wallpaper peeling, and the drains broken – not to mention the family legend that the house is haunted! But Neddy said that he did not wish to live amid the rush of the metropolis, and that he could do his work just as well from the countryside, coming into London twice a week. He also claimed that a country home with an antique legend would be more romantic." Jasper snorted. "Such piffle. I settled an allowance on him, three-hundred a year, to be doubled when he gave me a grandchild – tripled if it was a male so that our family name would not die with him. In return, he gave me the services of his man, Namir." Jasper acknowledged the silent figure behind him. "I plan to send him back to India soon. I have people of my own to take care of me."

"So what has occurred," Holmes asked, with some sharpness, "that brings you to plea for my assistance?"

Jasper bristled. Clearly, he wasn't accustomed to being addressed in such a pointed manner.

"Celeste – Neddy's wife – has disappeared. Today is Tuesday. Late last evening, Neddy arrived at my door in a sorry state. He said that he and Celeste had quarreled and in consequence of this tiff, she had spent some days with a female friend in London, but returned on Saturday evening. The couple reconciled – it was nothing but a silly pique over some trinket he had denied her – and all seemed well. He came into the city on Sunday morning and returned in the afternoon, only to find the house empty. He searched all night, and the next morning made inquiries, but there was no sign of her." Jasper shook his head. "I would not have our good name dragged in the mud over some marital misunderstanding."

"The police have not been alerted?"

"No."

"That was unwise."

"I preferred to hire you, rather than those bumblers. Are you refusing me?"

"No, Colonel Jasper. But clearly you perceive how badly this will reflect upon your son if something unfortunate has happened to his wife."

"He would never hurt her! He is incapable of such! He doesn't have the manly spirit to whip a disobedient dog, much less – "

The Colonel's face had turned scarlet. He abruptly jumped to his feet, snatching up his hat.

"Will you take the case or not? There are other private inquiry agents in this town."

"None as successful," Holmes said. "I would prefer to speak with Edward Jasper the Younger before making my decision."

"You cannot. The boy was nearly raving when he came to me, and I mixed a strong sleeping draught, which I forced upon him. He was not awake when I departed, and he will be stupid until dinner. No – you must give him time. I will keep him at my house until he is calm enough to speak to you in a proper manner."

Holmes tilted his head. "I will ask one more question before I give you my decision: Whom do imagine is your daughter-in-law's lover?"

The Colonel's jaw dropped. He stammered, banged his cane against the rug, then pulled a key from his pocket, throwing it onto the table beside Holmes. "That is a key to Squire Hall." He mentioned the address. "You must go there, immediately. You'll not be disturbed, Neddy sent his housekeeper away."

"Not until you answer my question, sir. Whom do you suspect?"

"No one!" the Colonel shouted, waving a knotted first. "Celeste has all the appeal of a Jersey cow! I never understood what Neddy saw in her, much less what a real man might find attractive. She was a ticket-taker at

38

the Museum, a fat little wench in a striped uniform that made her look like a circus tent. God only knows who or what she would have attracted!"

With that dramatic proclamation, the great hero stormed out of our door with his servant drifting silently behind him.

"Charming fellow," Holmes said. "Did he live up to your expectations?"

"I am beginning to understand why it is said that one should never meet one's heroes."

"Yet you are willing to reside with me."

"I have never called you a hero."

Holmes barked a laugh. "You wound me, Doctor – though no more than I deserve. Still, I think I will take the case, if for no other reason than I am fascinated by the dynamic presented. Colonel Jasper clearly loathes his own son – yet he is strangely protective of him. And why does a man who married a 'Jersey cow' merely to gain an inheritance show such great passion when she disappears? What was the true nature of their quarrel – not even a child would believe the 'trinket' story. There are deeper and darker waters here, not to mention a haunted house in the bargain. Come, Watson – we shall begin at the Museum of Indian Curiosities."

A short time later we found ourselves at the establishment. A few discreet inquiries revealed that Edward Jasper's work for the Museum was irregular, with long periods where his expertise was not required. Holmes filed this information away with a nod, then asked about Mrs. Jasper. We were pointed toward a lady in a gay costume, who was said to have been a special friend of the former Miss Celeste Brown. As we approached, this pert, honey-haired little wren of a woman looked up with a start.

"Mr. Sherlock Holmes! Oh, sir – please – tell me Neddy has not killed her!"

We adjourned to a small, secluded restaurant. The lady's dress was covered by a grey cloak and she had exchanged her silly little hat for a modest bonnet, but none of the sartorial changes dimmed the brightness of Miss Anna Moore's eyes as she spoke.

"You are very much like your pictures, sir. And you as well, Doctor Watson. Now, please – you could only have come about Celeste. What has happened to her?"

"No evil, we hope," Holmes said. He had a most reassuring manner with women, and his gentle voice quickly calmed our excited witness. "But she has gone missing, and I have been engaged to find her and bring her safely home."

"Sir, you must. Apply all your powers to her aid. A better, dearer friend has never lived. If Neddy has harmed her – Oh, I wish I were a man, to handle a gun or a blade. I would surely cut his throat if he lifted a hand to her!"

"There will be no call for violence," Holmes said. "Tell me how you know the lady."

"Celeste and I grew up together. We were both orphaned as girls and taken in by families who lived across the lane from each other in our village. We decided when we were children that we would not settle on being servants in the country, and so we came to London together to find work. We had quite a time of it, as we were both nearly penniless, but we found employment at the Museum and were able to rent a suite of rooms from a kind widow. We had been in town only a few months when Celeste met Neddy Jasper, and before she had known him for a week, he proposed to her!"

The lady's face had taken on a bright flush, which could carry only one meaning.

"You did not approve of the match," Holmes said.

"It was hardly my place to approve or disapprove," Miss Moore answered tartly. "Celeste was of age and no one could have faulted Neddy's manners or his prospects. Celeste was quite taken with marrying the son of a great hero, and Neddy told her – in rather lurid detail – of all the properties he stood to inherit if he could just worm his way back into his father's good graces. But it was not so much Neddy's fortune as – Oh, how can I explain these things to a man? Celeste feared that she would be a spinster – she had a horror of it, she who was only twenty. She used to lie awake at night and cry, because she was so afraid that no one would love her, that she would have no family of her own. She believed she was too unattractive to ever find a husband."

"I have not seen an image of Mrs. Jasper, but her father-in-law shared her opinion. He described her as lacking in beauty."

"That cad! I don't care how many bloodthirsty mutineers he killed. See here!"

The lady pulled a locket from her blouse, opening it to reveal a tiny portrait of another young woman with dark brown hair, soulful blue eyes, and the merest hint of a smile. The face was too fleshy and simple for real loveliness, but far from hideous. It was hardly a visage for which a lady should have been ashamed.

"Celeste is the sister of my heart. She is good and kind and easily swept off her feet." Miss Moore snapped the locket shut. "I had misgivings, but what could I do? If I objected, she would think I was jealous of her success. I have briefly caught the attention of several bachelors, but none of Neddy's rank in society. She seemed to be succeeding where I had failed."

40

"Was there a wedding ceremony?"

"A very small one, with only myself and Neddy's Indian servant present. On that day, Neddy seemed impatient to get away, to go to the country home he had been bequeathed by his father. Celeste was not allowed to go with him – when I tell you that the bride spent what should have been her honeymoon in our old suite, playing with our landlady's spaniel, you may have some idea of what manner of man she married."

"But they did commence their lives together?" I asked.

"A few days later, she received a summons to join him."

"And what of the marriage?" Holmes asked. "Was it a happy one?"

"Celeste wrote me every other week. At first, the letters were light enough – he had given her money for a bit of decorating. She was trying to bring some cheer to the old pile. But soon her messages were plainer. The Indian man had been sent to serve Colonel Jasper. Neddy refused to return social calls in town and Celeste was isolated. Her only help was an elderly housekeeper who was nearly deaf and blind. And . . . I fear you will think her insane . . . but she was convinced Squire Hall was haunted. She heard footsteps in the dead of night, strange moans as if from an invisible invalid, and things were moved about. Once, she told me, she picked up her brush and found a mat of black hair tangled around it. She was absolutely terrified."

"And a week ago, she came to you?"

"Yes, the Monday before last. She suddenly appeared late at night, weeping so bitterly I thought she would die. She said there had been a terrible row with Neddy, that she had begged him take her from the cursed house. He refused, with rough language toward her, and she told him she was leaving him forever. But in a few days, she resolved herself to return."

"And you have heard nothing since?"

The lady nodded. "I am worried, for Celeste promised to send me a note and tell me how Neddy took the unexpected news she had."

"And what news was that?" I asked. Miss Moore's eyes stayed locked to her teacup. Her lips pressed together into a thin line.

"No," she finally whispered. "I have spoken too much."

"So," Holmes said, "Mrs. Jasper was expecting,"

The lady flinched. It was clear that his deduction was correct.

"Celeste swore me to the secrecy of the confessional. It is truly a woman's most private matter, but it might have some bearing upon her disappearance. Though, if I am wrong – "

"I would urge you to speak," Holmes said, "and assure you that if the matter has no significance to the lady's disappearance, the good doctor and I shall carry it to the grave."

Miss Moore looked up at us. Her eyes were moist and soulful. My heart went out to her.

"When Celeste arrived at my door, she was in a terrible state of anxiety – this I have already made clear. She feared that she had lost her husband's love, and that her life was blighted. But, as she stayed with me, I noticed that she was often indisposed in the morning. That, along with a few other things that only a woman and a dearest friend would note, made it clear to me that she was in a delicate condition.

"'CeCe, you are going to be a mother!' I said. 'You should be so happy!' Indeed, my friend was very maternal type. She could not even walk in the park without spending an hour cooing over every baby in its pram. But she only wept harder.

"'He will not love the baby if he hates the mother! Sometimes I think he loves the ghost in the house more than me!'"

"I spent most of the week working to convince her that Neddy would of course adore his baby, and that fatherhood would change him. I realize that I'm not a married woman, but I have noticed that fatherhood generally transforms even the coldest gentleman into a proud, babbling fool."

Holmes inclined his head. "And Mrs. Jasper responded to your advice?"

"Yes. I saw her to the train station, and when I kissed her goodbye, she promised me that if she returned with a daughter in her arms, the little one would be named for me."

Holmes frowned. I, who knew him so well, sensed that he – like the lady before him – was debating whether certain words should be spoken.

"Miss Moore – I fear I must put a very uncomfortable question to you. I would not ask it if there were any other witnesses to Mrs. Jasper's state of mind and her anxiety."

The girl proudly tilted her head. "I know what you are about to inquire, sir, and the answer is no. There was no other man. Celeste was the soul of propriety, a good Christian. She had never had a sweetheart before Neddy Jasper came along. She would not betray her principles by finding solace with another, no matter how coldly or cruelly her husband treated her."

Holmes lifted a finger. "Did she say he was cruel?"

Miss Moore frowned. "Not in those words. And sharing a chamber as we did, I would have seen wounds upon her body. But when a husband takes a wife and then treats her as if she is nothing more than a piece of furniture which he has added to his home . . . surely that is a cruelty equal to any beating." Miss Moore consulted the delicate watch that hung from her belt. "I must go. The Museum is very precise about my time."

"A remarkably perceptive woman," Holmes said, after the lady departed.

"And a very different story from what Colonel Jasper told."

"As one might expect it to be. It casts our mystery in a new light."

I applied myself to the remains of my meal, but a sudden thought turned the sandwich tasteless in my mouth. "Holmes, surely – "

"A man would not kill his pregnant wife? It is a wicked world indeed, if we must even consider a thing." Holmes leaned back in his chair and lit a cigarette. "If Jasper had tired of his wife, he might indeed get rid of her. But one must consider how much his allowance stood to rise with the birth of a child. If he even suspected his lady was *enceinte*, he would have been foolish to do her harm. Though at the moment, I find the house as intriguing as the husband. It is said to be haunted. Perhaps it is best visited in the light of day."

"You do not want to wait until you speak with Neddy Jasper?"

"Some instinct tells me we have no time to lose. Let us hurry, Watson, and we may yet catch the train."

Some two hours later, we had reached our destination, where Holmes quickly located the cottage of the Jaspers' housekeeper, a widow named Eliza Martin. Unfortunately, there was little we could learn from her, for she clearly was beyond the point of being useful, to either her employer or to us. Her cluttered home, which she navigated largely by touch, spoke to her near blindness, and Holmes was forced to bellow out the few questions he had for her, as she was clearly but one degree removed from being completely deaf. The only light she could shed was a confirmation that Mrs. Jasper had returned on Saturday – Mrs. Martin had seen a carriage being driven to the house as she departed from it. She had no idea whether the couple had been happy or quarreling. Her only complaint was that Mr. Jasper would not allow her to bring over some of her feline friends to patrol the attic, which she was certain was riddled with rats.

"That was rather a waste of time," I said, when we had freed ourselves of the two dozen cats that lurked in her dingy domicile. I snorted, hoping the fresh air would dispel their unpleasant scent from my nose.

"On the contrary, Watson, she gave me everything I needed to know. My theories begin to take definite shape."

"And they are?"

"What lovely roses they have in the countryside, this time of year. It is only a mile or so to the house. Let us enjoy the stroll."

It was pointless to press for details. Instead, taking my cue from Holmes, I let my gaze wander across the pleasant fields and hedgerows, amazed as always that such splendid natural scenery was but a short train

43

journey from the coal-grimed heart of London. After passing through a rather dense wood, the rutted road took us into a clearing and a small hill. Atop it, squatting like a malignant toad, was Squire Hall. It had seen much better days and showed every sign of neglect and decay. The paint was peeling, several shutters hung awry, and the roof was in desperate need of repair. The grass was high and the fountain just before the façade was green with algae.

"What kind of a man brings his bride to this place?" I muttered.

"A woman of spirit would have stomped back out once she'd been carried across the threshold," Holmes mused. "I doubt, however, that our lady had any sense of the injustice done to her." He pulled out the key and, with some difficulty, forced the door open. As it gave way, I heard a sound that froze my blood. It was a low moan, like a wounded man would give, and it seemed to rise out of the very air itself, swirling and curling around our heads. I looked about for a source of the cry but could find nothing.

"Steady, Watson," Holmes said. "We perhaps should have expected a greeting from the ghost. Let us see what else the house has to offer."

Nodding tightly, I followed my friend inside. The home had a close, nasty smell, the rancid odor of too many pipes smoked amid its festering, fetid walls. The furnishings were mostly new, but of the cheapest material. The faded and threadbare rugs clearly predated the sofas and chairs and showed every sign of having been chewed upon by generations of hounds. There was little of interest in the parlor, the sitting rooms, and the downstairs library, which was stocked largely with Indian curios and cheap editions of classic adventure tales. Holmes took out his handkerchief and wiped dust from the brass plates of a few old family portraits.

"There are no modern pictures here," he said. "One would think at least a photograph of the lady of the house might be displayed."

I opened a scrapbook that had been carelessly tossed upon a chair. It was filled with clippings from Indian newspapers, some of them in Hindi. One included an etching of an Englishman in tropical attire, standing atop the body of a tiger. The face bore a slight resemblance to the heroic Colonel Jasper, enough for me to deduce that I was looking at his son.

"Holmes, do you think some event in India – Holmes?"

I heard my friend walking up the stairs. I dropped the scrapbook and followed him. A single, gloomy hall led me to an open doorway. I stepped inside what was clearly a lady's boudoir, complete with a canopy bed and a vanity table littered with perfume bottles and little jars of cosmetics. Pictures of famous beauties were placed around the mirror, and combs and brushes were scattered about. I had a sudden vision of Mrs. Jasper, a plain and matronly woman, laboring to work some magic to make her husband fall in love with her. I was struck through the heart, remembering my beautiful wife, how naturally lovely she had been, without any need of paints or powders to make her attractive.

"Watson?"

"Yes."

"Consider this."

I turned. Holmes had removed a nightgown from the bed. He held it out at arm's length. It was a small, delicate, flimsy thing, all in white silk with a bit of lace at the throat and sleeves.

"Holmes, I doubt Mrs. Jasper would approve of your cavalier treatment of her – "

"Look at it, Watson. *Look!*"

I blinked and then, suddenly, I understood.

"Who wears it?"

"Certainly not the stately Mrs. Jasper – nor the rather substantial housekeeper. I believe it belongs to the ghost."

At just that moment, another low moan swirled through the air. Holmes dropped the nightgown and shot through the doorway. I ran after him and found him pulling down a ladder that led to a trap door in the ceiling. I was certain he would find it fastened tight, but to my surprise it easily gave way. I heard his cry of horror. As quickly as I could, I followed him up the steps.

The attic was low and dark, noxious with the odors of a prison. A single candle illuminated the grotesque figure crouched before my friend, huddled in a ragged blanket. It was a dark-skinned woman, kneeling in supplication, her long, matted hair falling to the floorboards. Holmes gently consoled her, assuring her that she was safe. I took in the room's furnishing: A single chair, a slop pot, a low iron bed, and a long, heavy chain that was fastened to a ring in the floor at one end and around the Indian woman's neck at the other.

"My name is Aarna Khatri," the woman said, after Holmes had coaxed her to take some food, and I had attended to her medical needs. She was badly bruised and fearfully emaciated. "I have been a slave to that wicked man who defiled me."

Her English was strong, and only slightly accented. In short, precise sentences, she told us how Jasper had come to her village while on a tiger hunt. He befriended her brothers, who served as his guides, and then made odious love to her.

"I was betrothed to another – my brothers made it clear to him that I was an honorable woman and told him to stay away. But on the last night, he and Namir, his servant, kidnapped me from my home. He dishonored me so that I could never return to my village and my family. He promised me he would marry me when we came to England. But until then, he treated me as his possession, lower than even a woman of the streets. He kept me hidden away in secret places, always guarded by the fierce Namir. At last they brought me to this house and locked me in the attic. A short time later, his wife arrived, and I knew that I would be a captive until I died.

"I tried to find a way to be seen or heard. I cried out, but each time I did, he hurt me more. Once, I escaped and fled to his wife's bedroom. I was nearly naked, and I pulled out one of her dresses, thinking I would put in on and flee. But he caught me, and grabbed the lady's hairbrush, and beat me with it until I was unconscious. For so long I could do nothing but moan. What . . . what day is it? Tuesday? Then . . . it was more than a week ago that I heard them quarreling. His wife left the house, screaming that she would never return. A few days later, he brought me down to her room. He had a gift for me – a pretty nightgown – and he said he did not care that his wife was gone. His father would be dead soon, he laughed, and he would inherit everything. His wife would not matter.

"But on that very evening, his wife returned. We were here, in this bedchamber, when she arrived. He did not have time to lock me away. I heard them on the landing, they were quarreling. I dared wait no longer – I fled from the room, ran out so that she would see me. She screamed – she seemed to think I was a ghost or demon. And then – it was horrible – she stepped backward, and lost her footing, and went flying, tumbling down the stairs. I heard a loud thud as she hit the floor at the bottom. She lay there, not moving. He said, 'She has broken her neck – you have killed her!' His eyes were wild, and I thought he would murder me! I must have fainted. When I awoke, I was back in my attic prison, wearing nothing but the dirty shift you found me in. Please, sirs, you must believe me. I never intended to make the lady take fright – I only wanted her to see me."

Holmes's frown deepened. "You are as much a victim as Mrs. Jasper – but do you know what he did with her? Where her body might be?"

Miss Khatri looked up with sad eyes. "Perhaps. There is a family tomb, at the edge of the woods. He locked me there once, like a dog in a kennel."

Holmes assured her we would examine the tomb, and then he would go for the authorities, while I would return to the house and stay with her. Darkness was falling, and we took two lanterns with us. The lawn behind the house was vast, and the ancient mausoleum rested just at the edge of the dense forest.

"This is one case I hope to see concluded on the gallows," Holmes muttered. "If ever a man deserved to hang, it is Neddy Jasper."

"I wonder if his wife told him that she was with child."

46

Holmes frowned. "Here we can only surmise, but if he was annoyed to see her back at Squire Hall, and initiated an instant quarrel, then it is unlikely he knew the truth. But let me have your professional opinion, Doctor. Did Colonel Jasper strike you as a man shortly destined for the undertaker's parlor?"

"Indeed not," I said. "He seemed remarkably fit for a man of his age."

"Therefore, his son's assertion could only mean – "

A terrified shriek, followed by a long, ghastly wail, silenced Holmes's speech. We halted, staring at each other.

"That is not the Indian lady," I said.

"Nor is it a ghost," Holmes replied, "even though it came from the tomb."

Once again, we were running, not for our lives, but to save another. Inside the crypt we found Mrs. Jasper on her knees, her hair falling loose, her face covered in blood, her hands bruised and battered from where she had broken free of a wooden box that had been shoved to the back of the marble chamber. She was weak and dazed, unable to speak. Together, we bore her back to the house.

"Watson, I must leave you," Holmes said, as we gently settled the lady onto a bed. "I think Miss Kharti will be an effective nurse, though it might be best to explain her presence before she is seen by Mrs. Jasper. It is imperative that I send a telegram and alert Inspector Lestrade immediately."

"Holmes, what is it?" I asked. He turned at the door.

"The only reason young Jasper could have been certain his father was about to die is that he intended to have him murdered. That is why he hurried to London, feigning such concern over his wife's 'disappearance' – he was ready to put his patricide into motion. I hope I am not too late to prevent it."

It was a remarkable conclusion to a bizarre and horrific case. Holmes's message to Lestrade sent the bulldog of Scotland Yard racing to Colonel Jasper's London home, where he found the old man in writhing in pain, complaining of a bad meal. Fortunately, Holmes's information led to a rapid diagnosis of poisoning, and the proper antidote was applied, despite the old hero's objections that he was merely suffering from poor digestion. Neddy Jasper and Namir vanished. The Colonel's servants said they had gone out walking together, just before the Colonel was served his dinner. In a matter of days, when the depths of the pair's depravity became clear via stories in the sensational press, all of London was searching for them. The shock and shame of his son's behavior accomplished what a toxic concoction in his wine had not, and Colonel Jasper was buried at Highgate within a week.

A month later, the body of Edward "Neddy" Jasper was fished out of the Thames, a large Indian dagger protruding from his back. Namir was never apprehended. Perhaps he joined the vast criminal underworld, where a man of his cunning would be highly valued. Holmes grumbled a good deal about having been deprived of the satisfaction of seeing the pair brought to justice.

Unable to let the matter alone, Holmes determined to his own satisfaction, through the research of associates he'd encountered during his Hiatus, that the man known as Neddy Jasper, who had returned to London only to die there, was in fact not the Colonel's true son at all, but rather a disguised imposter who had assumed the prodigal's identity after the real article had died in India – possibly from an illness, or more likely from the sinister attentions of his substitute. But rather than make this fact known, except to me, Holmes chose to keep it secret – for good reason.

It gives me pleasure to add a postscript to my notes, to add a postscript to my notes, courtesy of Miss Anna Moore. Her dear friend Celeste Brown Jasper made a full recovery from her terrible fall and premature interment, and in due time gave birth to the Jasper heir, a little girl who was christened Anna Aarna, after the two women who rallied to her mother's side in her hour of distress. The trio are now happily raising the little miss in London, where her future may never be darkened by the cruel stains of the past.

The Curious Case of the
Soldier's Letter
by John Davis

Rain seemed to presage all of our most intricate cases in that long ago year of 1898. I recall vividly my friend Sherlock Holmes standing at our window overlooking Baker Street. Sheets of gray rain pounded incessantly while he watched the public passing in a parade of umbrellas below. I'd only arrived in our sitting room shortly before our normal breakfast time.

"Watson, have you thought about travel at all recently?" he inquired.

"Not at all," said I, reaching for the newspaper. "Particularly not on a day like this."

"Yet so many in this world seem compelled to do so. Consider the French Foreign Legion."

With that, I put down *The Times* and turned to look at him. "I say, that's a strange speculation."

"Why so? Many's the young man who, facing disaster at home, decides to leave it all and disappear. Scoundrels who've stolen from the family fortune. Good-for-nothings who wish to avoid the raging father of a young girl. Wanderers, dreamers, seekers after adventure."

"What brought to you to this line of observation?"

"I received a peculiar message yesterday, shortly after you retired. It seems we are to receive a visitor today. A French Foreign Legionnaire officer, no less. His inquiry led me to this speculation, although in his case I would imagine that he wasn't among those who sought to disappear."

"And why so?"

"The Legion is officered by either native-born Frenchmen seconded to leadership positions from their own regiments, or naturalized French citizens. They would have no need to hide, one should think."

"Ah, I didn't know. And he left no clue as to the cause of his visit?"

"None at all, but I hear the bell. Mrs. Hudson will doubtless solve this question shortly."

A dashing figure entered our room, shown in by our landlady. Tall, elegantly outfitted in a blue uniform, complete with officer's Kepi, or service hat, was a healthy looking young man about thirty years of age.

"Mr. Sherlock Holmes?" he asked. "I am Captain Jules du Lac, officer in command of a company of French Foreign Legionnaires in Algeria."

"And this is my friend and colleague, Dr. John Watson. Please take a seat, Captain."

"Thank you. I've only recently arrived from Victoria Station."

"Ah, in that case you may join us for breakfast. Mrs. Hudson, would you please be so kind as to add a third plate for our visitor?" With that, she nodded and exited.

"You are too kind, sir. I come to you, gentlemen, with, perhaps, an unusual case. May I proceed?"

"Please," said Holmes. He and I took our places, keen to listen attentively. The officer sat near the fireplace. He seemed straightforward, expansive, and an honest fellow who appeared shocked to reveal his tale.

"Gentlemen, I'm the bearer of news that could affect France, my army, and my career. I regret that what I have to say must come to you, despite the fact it bears upon intrigues in my own country. These French intrigues would prevent – indeed *have* prevented – the truth from prevailing. Indeed, if what I say to you came to light in the wrong hands, justice would be rendered undone, and so made impossible."

"We shall do our best to help," I offered.

"I'm quite tired, unfortunately. I've ridden the train from Marseilles all through the night, through Paris, and ultimately to Calais. My arrival in your country wasn't helpful, as I was then not only tired, but thoroughly wet. Very wet indeed."

"Nothing at all like the weather in Algeria, Tunisia, or dare I add Madagascar, Dahomey, and Mandingo?" Holmes commented.

"You're quite informed, Mr. Holmes."

"You've provided the information through your medals, Captain. Indeed, I see you only recently changed into your uniform, perhaps at Victoria? But alas, your preparations for our visit were hurried because your train was delayed, which you hadn't anticipated. Indeed, that would explain your not having time to adjust your scheduled appointment with us. You were rushed, not allowing your boots to properly absorb the polish, your medals not to be attached in the appropriate sequence, and your kepi to be somewhat ajar. Remembering a scissors, but not having access to a mirror, your mustache is impeccable on the left, but barely askew on the right. A left-hander, which explains your somewhat more-tightened tunic on the left than the right, and which would also explain why you prefer rifles to pistols, not having left-handed holsters.

"Holmes occasionally gets carried away," I diplomatically observed.

Our visitor sat aghast. "Mr. Holmes, I can see now why your reputation precedes you."

"And so to your narrative, Captain."

"I received orders to proceed from my base at Sidi bel Abbes in Algeria to Tunisia, there to contact Lieutenant Colonel Georges Picquart, commander of the Fourth Regiment of *Tirailleurs*, comprised of native French Tunisian infantry. They were located in Fort Zinderneuf, one of the most remote, lonely outposts of the entire French Republic. It sits without any natural shade on a rock outcropping in the middle of the largest desert on earth."

"Good heavens," I exclaimed, "why?"

"It is the only prominence on a long, centuries-old track which has borne traders and camel caravans for ages."

"Indeed. Continue."

"My mission was to visit this Lieutenant Colonel Piquart and discuss with him a joint action to be taken against Berber ruffians of the Butuli tribe. They are mighty warriors, and such a plan had to be well-coordinated before we committed our units to battle. Upon my arrival at Zinderneuf, I was allowed entrance. I'd travelled with a sergeant and three solders. As our horses were led away, I could hear the most remarkable sound that I least expected to hear in the middle of the Sahara. As my men went about their business, I walked to the commander's office. The music, played on a grand piano, was truly wondrous, if not perhaps the saddest, most melancholy tune I'd heard in my life. It was being played by Lieutenant Colonel Piquart.

"He greeted me with a solemn demeanor. After offering me a drink, we sat down. It was then that he told this remarkable tale. I daresay we spoke of nothing else for the next hour, I having forgotten my mission upon hearing his story unfold.

"Piquart said he was sent to Zinderneuf, a career-killing, hopeless outpost of empire, because he spoke the truth. You're familiar with our notorious Captain Dreyfus case, no?"

We both averred that indeed we were. "Dreyfus was the French artillery officer convicted of treason by espionage for Germany. He was disgraced publicly, then condemned to the dreaded Devil's Island in French Guiana, a soulless, body-wracking prison on the coast of South America where horrible criminals are sent to die.

"And how can we help, Captain?"

"Mr. Holmes, I give you this." Captain du Lac took from his tunic a letter. I read it aloud.

Dear Mr. Holmes,

I write you in desperation. Not for myself, but for a man wrongly convicted. I am a serving officer in the French Army.

51

I was recently assigned to French counterintelligence at the General Staff in Paris before my stationing here in French West Africa. My job in Paris was to detect espionage and sabotage directed against our army. As you know, Captain Dreyfus was tried by court martial for espionage, and was found guilty.

But he was not guilty! Through clever means, enemies gave false evidence which convicted him. I took the information I discovered in my own further inquiries to that court after he was sent to French Guiana, but the exonerating information I provided was suppressed, and he remained on Devil's Island. I did my duty by reporting through the chain of command. My reward, for insisting on this retrial, was to be sent to this most remote site, here to conclude my career amid the flies and sand. I send this message with a trusted friend, Captain Jules du Lac, who will explain.

Piquart

Du Lac continued, "Dreyfus was sentenced based on his alleged espionage for Germany. This espionage was supposedly proven by Dreyfus' handwriting on a document which revealed our new artillery designs to a foreign adversary. This damning document was retrieved from the rubbish container of an officer of the German Embassy in Paris by a chambermaid in the pay of French Intelligence. In short, gentlemen, Piquart found out the whole story of this man's conviction was false. He has the documents to prove it."

"They why did he not simply show the military court his information?"

"He did. Piquart was an officer on the French counterintelligence staff. His inquiries led him to concrete evidence that the criminal was not Dreyfus, but another man, called Major Esterhazy. Esterhazy is a French officer who has remained in the background throughout this entire affair. Yet his handwriting matches exactly, his motive was the pursuit of money, which can be proven, and his opportunity to get lots of money for his betrayal was provided by a clever German spy. The spy knew Esterhazy needed money, and offered to provide it. For a price, gentlemen – the price of betraying Esterhazy's country."

"I gather from *The Times* that Dreyfus' conviction is not only about a crime, but a sort of indictment of the French Republic by military reactionaries. Dreyfus is Jewish, is he not?"

"Yes, but gentlemen, he is as French as I am. Loyal, true, and a good officer."

"You are aware," I added, "that a renowned French author, Mr. Emil Zola, has published a monumental denunciation of the entire affair. He accuses the military and some of their government allies in an essay titled, '*J'accuse!*'"

"Indeed I am. For that reason I showed the article to Lieutenant Colonel Piquart in that pestilential hot-box of a headquarters he has at Zinderneuf. He wanted to join forces with the Fourth Estate. However, he believed if anyone can help, it would be you. Sadly, Zola is now condemned for libel. Zola's hope was to accuse the French Government of obstruction of justice and antisemitism by suppressing exculpatory evidence which would have saved Dreyfus. Indeed, the military and government had done just that, gentlemen. By having Dreyfus' second court martial behind closed doors, the new evidence was hidden from the world, and the old lies remained. Zola wanted all the new evidence proving innocence for Dreyfus to come out. So Zola wrote '*J'accuse*' to create a trial for libel against himself! What moral bravery, no? If his appeal fails, he'll go to prison for telling the truth. Thus it is clear why Piquart comes to you. He wanted me to give you these documents."

"Thank you for this narration, Captain du Lac," said Holmes as I took the documents, reading carefully. He continued, "Any true detective cringes when prejudice, preconceived notions, and pride interfere with objective investigation. I shall take your information, review it, and see what we can do to assist in this apparent corrupt practice."

So saying, Holmes bid our visitor welcome to breakfast.

That afternoon, du Lac had gone to his hotel, while Holmes and I discussed the entire affair.

"The French can be stubborn, particularly when it comes to *l'honneur*," Holmes noted.

"Yes but goodness man, a man is suffering unjustly! Surely anyone can admit to wrongdoing, or misunderstanding, if such will resolve the issue honestly – fair play and all that."

"One would hope, Watson, but you are dealing with a decision wrought not through calm reflection, but by zealotry. Whole episodes of French history seem to be under assault in the minds of some of these French perpetrators. These reactionaries won't hear otherwise, despite all evidence. Nor will they change their decision by an iota. They see this case not as one man, Dreyfus. Rather, they view him as representative of those taking their entire world under attack – outsiders, Jews, whomever. Had it not been Dreyfus, it would have been someone else, another outsider, another 'traitor'. Esterhazy, who calls himself a 'Count', and is a French officer with a distinguished name, is, by these reactionaries' lights, not a traitor at all, because someone with his pedigree could by definition not be a traitor. Dreyfus is just a pawn in that game. But to the matter at hand!" Holmes announced, a gleam returning to his profoundly thoughtful countenance. "Watson, go to the Foreign Office. There Mycroft's man Barksdale will assist you. Send a telegram to the British consulate in Marseilles. Inquire of our consulate there whether a German officer at their consulate named von Ruetzel has departed, and if so his current whereabouts. I shall depart for Harpenden in Hertfordshire this very day.

"What on earth for?"

"I've a matter to attend to which shall not interfere with your inquiries."

We rendezvoused at 221b later that evening.

"It seems that von Ruetzel departed the German Consulate at Marseilles some years ago. He'd been assigned in there from 1888 to 1893. He was reassigned to the German London Embassy after that. And then the most extraordinary thing happened. He disappeared from the face of the earth."

"Indeed. Shortly after his arrival, Von Ruetzel established an affair of the heart with an Englishwomen, a Miss Cynthia Bradford. Then, he simply vanished."

"So who was this von Ruetzel fellow, Holmes?"

"He was a German spy, Watson. Travelling under the guise of a German Transportation Ministry representative, he was actually known to our intelligence circles as a spy. Under diplomatic immunity, he recruited people in countries to which he was assigned so that these recruits would serve German interests. He'd been active for several years, when we first discovered him involved in the case of poor Mr. Edward Snoke."

"Poor fellow. I recall that scandal indeed. Von Ruetzel then was the cad who caused Snoke to give away a code we once relied upon?"

"Yes, he was – the same."

I'm now going to pause a moment to set in sequence events only collated later in this intricate case. Let me clarify. After years together, Holmes trusted my judgment, as I his. Holmes mentioned that upon his return from Harpenden, he'd paid another visit to his mysterious stationary brother, Mycroft. From Mycroft's Diogenes Club I received a memorandum that Holmes would be out of touch for some short time. How long was not specified. Let us follow developments from this point.

Holmes left me with this instruction per the memorandum. I was to send a telegram, written in the French language, to M. Etienne du Pont in

Calais, who in turn was to forward the message to M. Andre Fiquelle in Paris. The message was to be signed by Count Martin Voilemont. It read: *"We must meet again. It will be well worth your while. We shall meet outside Le Môle Passedat Café in Marseilles, known to us both, in two days' time. Tuesday, noon. Failing that, one day later, one o'clock. Wait ten minutes only. Urgent."*

With this bizarre errand I was off. Had I only known.

The next morning, at the address to which du Pont forwarded the telegram in Paris, the recipient's shocked look greeted the delivery boy of the telegram I'd sent. Monsieur Fiquelle paled, and seemed about to pass out.

"Are you all right, Monsieur?"

Catching his breath, the man replied, "Yes. Thank you. No reply."

With that, Fiquelle turned and raced, throwing clothing for an overnight train trip into his suitcase. He adjusted his tunic, then military hat, and was out the door. He pounded down the street, running for all he was worth. His destination: The train station, there to depart for Marseille.

The Count Martin Bernard Josef Marie de Voilemont was regal. He sat erect at a table looking out onto the grand harbor of Marseilles. He seemed to belong in the café – indeed, anywhere that one might pass serious time reflecting on the world's events. Tall, a beard and moustache like Napoleon III, sporting a camel hair coat recently acquired from one of the finest salons in Paris, he sipped coffee while poring over *France Soir*, the Paris daily bought at the newsagent. His intense concentration was soon interrupted. He observed a man in apparent distress, glancing feverishly from table to table.

"Monsieur, may I be of assistance?" he inquired of the heavily breathing military man casting his eyes around the room.

The distraught man responded through eyes reddened by sweat, "No, thank you. Err . . . yes!" he mumbled, with a feint sparkle of recognition. "Count de Voilemont?"

"Indeed," the Count responded.

"Oh Count, I thought it was you! It has been many years, no? I barely recognized you."

"Please, take a seat."

The two sat, the discussion turning to years gone by. The Count ordered a coffee for his recently arrived colleague.

"I fear I have some distressing news for you, Fiquelle." There was a momentary flash of fear.

"Oh, yes. Count," Fiquelle said. "Indeed, Count. Pray continue."

"I fear the past has come upon us both. This will not be a conversation you and I shall recall with pleasure as we have of our previous meetings."

55

"Why? Why not?" Fiquelle stammered, as he'd become visibly worried.

"Sadly, your brother officers are making their way through the – shall we say – back window of your house. Your real name is suspected by them."

"But what about Dreyfus? We shifted all suspicion upon Dreyfus. And the second court martial found him guilty again, no?"

"While true, I'm afraid that more came out of that trial than was in the newspapers. Surprisingly, the military court was able to keep secret that another name has come into the picture. That name is, regrettably, yours – *Esterhazy.*"

"Oh my God! What can I do?"

"Do you remember the counterintelligence officer whose accusations reopened the Dreyfus case? Lieutenant Colonel Piquart? Despite being sent to the middle of the desert, there to die as we hoped, he has not. He has prevailed on the French General Staff to investigate you. My staff at the German Embassy discovered this because of another, shall we say, cooperating French officer on the French General Staff who has kept us well informed throughout this entire Dreyfus affair."

Fiquelle/Esterhazy looked like a man afloat, all alone on the sea. "Oh . . .what will become of me?"

"All is not lost. We never forget our friends, and you have been a great friend to us. We greatly appreciate that, as we've shown over the years. That deposit each month of several thousand francs in your secret account has certainly solidified our trust, no?"

"Oh, I'm eternally grateful – "

"And so you shall be," the Count advised. "One last mission for us, and you'll be free of all concern that the French may one day place you in the dreaded prison at Devil's Island."

Bereft of hope, Fiquelle listened to the Count's every word, as if his life did indeed hang upon each one. It did.

"One last mission. If you succeed, you shall have a home only dreamed about by anyone. No French counterintelligence officer can find you. No French law will pursue you. You will be safe in England."

"England? England! But – "

"There is no time to discuss. You are a marked man. One last mission. Go to Paris. Secure a copy of the designs for the French 75-millimeter cannon."

"That is highly protected! Oh *mon Dieu!*"

"With those plans in hand, you will depart for Brussels. There, you'll be met by a man who will escort you to London. You will present yourself at the German Embassy, where I am now stationed. I shall meet you there.

We shall exchange your design documents for a new identity for you, and a secret home that shall be yours forever more. No one will ever find you."

"Oh, *mon Dieu!*" whimpered Fiquelle. "Herr von Ruetzel, you can't imagine how grateful I am to you. Devil's Island. Oh, oh – "

The Count, with a piercing rage in his eyes, passed Fiquelle a document. "Never! Never use my name in public." Voilemont/von Ruetzel whispered. "Here is the location you are to meet our man in Brussels. He will be carrying a cricket ball in his left hand if it is safe to meet. If not, he will carry it in his right, together with a copy of the day's *Paris Match*. You shall attempt to meet again at the same time and place every day thereafter until you can safely depart with this man for England. Memorize this. Then destroy it."

Fiquelle read the document as one might grasp at a fellow swimmer when the waves are pulling him down to drown. "You can rely on me, Count Voilemont."

A couple days later, I had only opened the day's newspapers when Mrs. Hudson knocked at the door. "Doctor Watson, the French military gentleman is here to see you."

"Thank you, Mrs. Hudson. Please show him in."

Du Lac came to inquire after developments. He maintained a proper demeanor, his military bearing not once betraying his intense concern for his friend in the desert, nor the justice he now saw balancing on a thin string indeed.

"Have you had any luck, Doctor? I fear things do not look well for M. Dreyfus. He is being returned to the horror-inducing Devil's Island. Only a pardon can save him, but his pride cannot admit of any guilt."

"Would yours, if you were innocent, Captain?"

"But Devil's Island! Dreyfus was a sickly skeleton when he returned for his second trial. He'll die out there soon."

As we were discussing the case at 221, a meeting occurred at the arrival of the Paris Limited at Brussels' main train station. Under the archway which led to the main thoroughfare, a tall man in a camel hair coat, goatee like Napoleon III, and with a cricket ball in his left hand greeted the man in civilian clothes who got off the train.

"Count de Voilemont! It is you!" cried the arriving traveler.

"Esterhazy, so glad you made it. I knew you would!"

"Names, sir? Should you not – "

"Nonsense, Esterhazy. We are beyond the reach of French law. Here you are as safe as you'll be once we get across the Channel. In fact, we have only to wait another forty minutes for the train which will take us to

Ostend, then over to England. You have the documents we discussed, I trust?"

"Of course," replied Esterhazy, tapping his breast pocket.

"Then we are off."

That day I was to present myself on walkway in the front of the German Embassy in London. Holmes wired me from the Continent that he'd accomplished Mycroft's requirements, and was about to return with a colleague that I did not know. I was to greet him without using his name, and say not a word thereafter. I was further to accept whatever I heard him say with a gruff nod if appropriate. Indeed, I was to accept documents to be handed me by his associate, and then open it, state its contents, and depart, taking the documents with me.

I saw Holmes's figure in the distance, accompanied by another man. This other man was shorter, but wore a distinctly large mustache. Upon their arrival, I noted that Holmes was wearing a camel-skin coat I hadn't seen before.

"Good day, Herr Knoch," he greeted me as they approached.

"Good day." I declaimed.

"My colleague Mr. Esterhazy has something for you." With that, Esterhazy reached into his suit and withdrew the documents. I opened them. I then huffed and hummed, hoping not to overplay my role as I beheld a French military blueprint which revealed the designs of a French cannon.

"Is that what you wanted?" Holmes asked.

I nodded. "Artillery designs."

"Then we can be off. Please take these documents to the Ambassador, Herr Knoch," Holmes concluded.

Once again I nodded, my moment in the London Theater complete.

Holmes departed with his charge toward the train station.

As I returned with my documents to 221b, I found there a message from Mycroft Holmes:

Dear Doctor,

I trust you now have the incriminating documents delivered to you by the man who arrived at the German Embassy gate with Sherlock. Please place them in an envelope, marked for me. Barksdale, my trusted colleague from the Foreign Office, will collect them at 221b later this day. I should like you to proceed to Harpenden immediately,

58

there to meet again my brother and the gentleman accompanying him at the Horn and Post on the High Street.

M

I did so. The train ride was swift, the train having been long in service from London. Upon my arrival, I went directly to the pub. The town through which I walked was a typical English setting, complete with well-maintained homes, quaint small businesses, and a town square. Inside the pub were Holmes (in his disguise) and Mr. Esterhazy. They sat in an apparent purpose-built private side room, unusual for such a public drinking establishment.

"Ah, welcome Doctor Watson!"

A shock of recognition bolted across Esterhazy's face. "Watson? You are Herr Knoch!"

"Sorry Esterhazy, I'm afraid not."

At that very moment, another man – also tall and distinguished, and wearing a Napoleon III goatee and camel coat – entered. Esterhazy stared utterly mesmerized at the two gentlemen before him. Both were to his mind von Ruetzel.

"Oh," said Holmes, "I'm actually Mr. Sherlock Holmes, working on behalf of a Mr. Dreyfus, recently of the French Army. You may know him, Mr. Esterhazy, as the man whom you betrayed in the course of hiding your treason to France. This man," Holmes pointed to the other gentleman in a camel hair coat, "is your former German colleague, Herr von Ruetzel."

Stunned, Esterhazy could only stammer, "How? Who?"

Holmes was apparently enjoying this turn of events. "Herr von Ruetzel, you may recall, was your spy master. It was he who recruited you in Marseilles when you'd gambled away your own and then your wife's fortunes. I must say our German colleagues are very good at discerning weaknesses in men, then exploiting them.

"Who?" muttered Esterhazy. "How?"

"Luckily, we British are also very good at the clandestine arts. We discovered that Herr von Ruetzel had a charming English lady he'd become enamored shortly after his arrival at his new duty station in London. So much so, that we thought some years ago to consider discussing our mutual interests with him. I'll let Herr von Ruetzel continue the story."

"Yes, Esterhazy, everything Holmes has said is true. I'd recruited you to work as an espionage agent for Germany, then left for a new assignment in London. My love affair with Cynthia is a true love. I could not leave her. Then the British intelligence services approached me with an astounding proposal. I could be resettled in the United Kingdom, together with my Cynthia, if I concluded some work for the English intelligence officers. I'll spare the details. They were satisfied with the list of names I provided them, mostly from places I'd worked prior to my assignment in London. The names were of course those of men and women who'd betrayed their country to work for me on behalf of Germany – that is to say, my interest at the time."

"And now the British government offers the same to you, Esterhazy." Holmes said. "I paid a visit to Harpenden, where von Ruetzel was relocated as part of his agreement with the British Government. I did so before coming to see you in Marseilles. I knew Herr von Ruetzel was living here, after he'd 'vanished', so I thought it would be profitable to visit him and discover something about you. Mostly I wanted to find out what he looked like, the better to plan my disguise – the better to deceive you, his former spy."

"Oh, *mon Dieu*! What do you want of me?"

"First we need to be assured you'd prefer not to be sent to Devil's Island, together with other fellow citizens of France."

"Oh, anything but that!"

"Then the following is our proposition to you," said Holmes. "We expect a complete confession. Everything: Dates, places, names. Everyone you betrayed, and everything that you took from your French Military Headquarters over the years since you began spying in Marseilles. Mostly, however, we want to know how you concocted the plot to, as our American cousins so charmingly put it, 'frame' poor Dreyfus, making him look like the guilty party when it was really you."

"Anything. Anything you want," cried Esterhazy.

"There's more. You will not only sign this confession, but have it notarized. We shall deliver it to the French Government. You shall add that your cruel plot against the honest Lieutenant Colonel Piquart was also part of your scheme. You shall admit to everything, naming names of all those who conspired with you."

"And then what?"

"Then you may live here, Esterhazy. This village of Harpenden is not so bad. Of course, you must stay here. You'll never, ever leave. If you depart, even to walk outside the town limits for a short stroll in the countryside, you shall be returned to the tender mercies of your colleagues in France. They apparently provide justice in the terrors of Devil's Island for those they truly despise. Trust me, after your confession, they will despise you."

"Here? How?" stumbled Esterhazy, utterly mystified by the strange locutions happening in his presence.

60

"You will be given a different name, a home here, and since your background is so problematic – oh yes, we know how you gained your French military commission through corruption, and your title of Count Esterhazy is also a fraud – you'll be given a new history. No one will question you, of course, because you will be leading a quiet life in an apartment located above the town bakery. Where you will be gainfully employed."

"Bakery? What?"

"If your establishment is visited by Herr von Ruetzel or his wife, Cynthia, you'll not know them. You will not so much as give a glimmer of recognition. For you see, they live here too. You'll never ask the background of any of your neighbors, in fact. You see, this is a town of secrets. Our colleagues in the British Intelligence Services have persons who can detect anyone here who chances to try our patience with challenges to our rules. Do we understand each other?"

"Indeed we do," said the crestfallen Esterhazy. "What name shall I go by?"

"Why, you can be the Count de Voilemont. This way, it explains your foreign accent, suggests that you have fallen on hard times, which proper Englishmen never inquire too deeply about, and retains your false need to believe you are from the nobility. And you can no longer cook up plots against your fellow man, but perhaps introduce some French pastries to the English countryside."

So did that day come to its dramatic end.

Holmes and I were relaxing in our sitting room at 221b. We'd only a few moments before bid farewell to our French officer of the Foreign Legion. Du Lac went back to Paris, there to report all that he heard. He would pass along the Esterhazy confession to M. Zola and his associates, and to the French government. It would be several more years before Captain Dreyfus would be reinstated – indeed promoted – but the laws of French justice are slow, slow indeed. Lieutenant Colonel Piquart was retrieved from his outpost of loneliness and ignominy on the high Sahara, to be reinstated as a promoted senior officer in Paris. Later he became the Minister of War. Esterhazy remained a baker in Harpenden. He occasionally saw his former *protégé* Herr von Ruetzel, but never once acknowledged him. Von Ruetzel went on to live happily in that obscure town, never asking who his neighbors might be. I believe that Holmes's brother Mycroft possessed a complete list of the strange array of immigrants who dwelt among the British residents of that odd community of the British Secret Services.

Holmes and I received annual letters from the recently promoted Colonel du Lac. He occasionally apprised us of the developments in the life of his friend – and now ours – General Piquart. Both wrote often to express how grateful they were for our efforts on behalf of elementary justice and mercy. I would be remiss if I didn't add that Captain Dreyfus invited us to visit him any time we were in Paris. Hopefully, he asked, he'd like us to join him for his upcoming promotion, with back pay.

And that would be the happy ending, but there is even more good to report. We discovered that a token of the magical British genius William Shakespeare had impacted the case. Du Lac wrote one day and reminded us of the melancholy tune he'd heard then Lieutenant Colonel Piquart playing on his piano in the middle of the Sahara when first they met. It was called *Le Tempeste*. He even remembered the greeting Piquart had given him at that time when that sad officer, those long months before, said "As Mr. Shakespeare said in *The Tempest*, a musical arrangement of which by Monsieur Ernest Chausson I'm playing, '*Hell is empty and all the devils are here.*'

Du Lac wanted to convey to us this message of a complete change of heart, from Piquart: "I can now attest that from out of my despair, you, Mr. Holmes, and your esteemed colleague Doctor Watson, brought me literally back to life. I can now say, quite honestly, as did Mr. Shakespeare in that same play, "*Now I will believe that there are unicorns . . . .*"

The Case of the
Norwegian Daredevil
by John Lawrence

As I review the many adventures in which I was engaged with Sherlock Holmes, I note that I have never before related the strange case of Larsen the Poisoner. The adventure, which occurred in April of 1898, appears in my files under the heading of "*Poison*" between "The Case of the Poisoned Scones" and the misplaced "*Poisson Frêche* Caper", and had several intriguing features which make it a most remarkable example of Holmes's skills.

A cold and blustery winter had left London longing for the gentle rains and bursting gardens of the springtime. Holmes and I sat at breakfast in our rooms at 221b Baker Street. He was deeply immersed in *The Times*, alternatingly sipping his coffee and taking long draws from his new briar pipe, and then filling the air with a stream of acrid smoke. As he threw down sections of the paper, I would pick them up and peruse them for interesting tidbits and potential cases.

"Ah," I said, holding up the newspaper, "do you see here there is some controversy brewing over the treaty that Sir Rennell Rodd signed with Menelik II?" Holmes put down his paper and took a long draw on the pipe.

"No, I wasn't aware of that fact," he archly replied. "Nor is it likely to influence significantly my plans for the remainder of the day."

"Quite significant, I should think," I added. "You realize, of course, that England has joined France in recognizing him. A blow to Italy, I should think."

Holmes put down his pipe and settled his arms onto the tabletop. "Pray explain why you believe I should care about Emperor Menelik," he asked.

"The *second*," I corrected. Holmes raised his hand to his mouth and slowly shook his head in disapproval.

"Or the *fifth,* for all I care!" he exclaimed in a theatrically exasperated voice.

"The Emperor of all the Abyssinians," I explained. "The treaty helps to clarify the border with Somaliland."

"Watson," Holmes began with a fatigued voice, although it was only 8:30 in the morning, "with all deference to Sir Rennell and the Abyssinians, what difference does this triumphant development mean to me? Menelik – the second – the Somalis, and Abyssinians will surely continue to conduct their affairs with no attention from me."

He pushed away the plate containing the crumbs from his breakfast and stretched his long legs under the dining table. He gazed out the slightly opened window to Baker Street, where the carriages were bustling along, their wheels click-clacking on the paving stones.

"Spring is finally upon us," he began.

"And '*a young man's fancy lightly turns to thoughts of love*'," I said, finishing Tennyson's quotation.

Holmes looked disapprovingly at me. "I was going to say, 'and still no problem of interest has crossed our entry way in days.'"

"I suppose one can always hope some heinous crime will make its appearance," I offered hopefully.

"Just so," Holmes replied, missing my sarcasm entirely while continuing to stare out the window.

A sharp rap on the door broke our reverie, followed by the entry of Mrs. Hudson who poked in her head, surveyed that all was well, and then slipped inside, leaving the door slightly ajar behind her.

"There's an officer of some sort here, Mr. Holmes," she said in a hushed tone, looking back over her shoulder towards the staircase. "He is most desirous of seeing you immediately." She looked to Holmes and then back again over her shoulder again. "I must say, he seems greatly agitated!"

Holmes drew in a deep breath and waved towards the door.

"Show him in, Mrs. Hudson," he called. "Show him in, by all means."

She opened the door and beckoned in an officer of perhaps thirty, dressed in civilian clothing and wearing a look of great concern.

"Mr. Holmes, I'm so grateful that you've agreed to see me," he said, extending his hand to Holmes. "I'm Waters, Inspector Roger Waters, of Scotland Yard. A detective," adding tentatively, "like you."

Holmes considered the description for a moment, and then swept his hand towards the basket chair instead of grasping the stranger's outstretched offering. "Please sit down and explain your urgent mission."

"Inspector Lestrade suggested that I come to see you about a most peculiar incident that occurred last night," he began, removing his overcoat and throwing it over a chair before seating himself.

"And yet Lestrade hasn't come himself," Holmes noted. "Indisposed?"

"On holiday," Inspector Waters explained. "He left this morning for Inverness. But he did have a chance before departing to help me with the initial inspection of the premises where the crime occurred."

"How fortunate to know the clues were treated with as much care and attention as Lestrade invariably provides," Holmes murmured. His deprecation was utterly lost on the young detective.

"I scarcely know where to begin," the man said. "Such a peculiar matter."

"Start at the beginning," Holmes urged. "It is invariably the most instructive place." We all sat around the table, Holmes's elbows resting on the surface, his hands folded with his long fingers interlacing each other.

"There has been a most peculiar death at the Great Eastern Hotel," the young man began. "A guest has been found dead in his room, with terrible injuries, but what exactly occurred remains a confounding mystery."

"Certainly you must have learned the man's identity," Holmes said.

"Oh, yes. He was Mr. Meriwether Flicker, an American salesman. And just arrived yesterday."

"An elderly man?" Holmes inquired.

"No, not at all," said Waters. "Rather about twenty-nine or thirty, I would say. He arrived on a ship from New York. My men were summoned this morning when he failed to respond to repeated knocks from the cleaning staff of the hotel. I don't mind telling you they were quite startled when they were finally able to enter the room."

"You say 'finally'," Holmes noted. "I presume, therefore, that access was difficult?"

"Oh, yes, Mr. Holmes, that is one of the mysteries," replied the young officer. "The door was locked from the inside, with a bolt."

"Of course it was," Holmes responded with evident exasperation. "Are there no communicating rooms?" I asked.

"None," answered Waters, shaking his head. "There is but one way in and out of the room, and that is via the door through which the police entered after breaking it down."

"And what did they find?" inquired Holmes.

Waters gave a small shudder. "Mr. Holmes, it was quite horrible. Mr. Flicker was lying on the floor in the middle of the room with terrible cuts on his hands and wrists. The mirror in the lavatory had been smashed to pieces. That was evidently the cause of the lacerations, and there was blood everywhere. It seemed an obvious case – for some reason, the man had shattered the glass, perhaps intentionally, mortally injuring himself."

"And yet," Holmes replied, "you have come to me."

Waters shook his head slowly. "Something doesn't feel right. I find it difficult to understand why Mr. Flicker should travel all the way to London from New York, only to go mad the first night after his arrival, let

65

alone purposefully kill himself by smashing a mirror. And yet, we can find no alternative explanation as to what transpired."

"Might there have been an altercation?" asked Holmes. "Could someone else have entered the room?"

"And locked the bolt behind them? I think not," Waters insisted.

"A window?" asked Holmes.

"Oh, yes, of course, there is a window," agreed Waters. "But Mr. Flicker's room was on the second floor, and there is no fire escape or other way anyone might climb up the sheer wall to enter that window. Quite impossible, I assure you."

"And yet," Holmes replied. I could hear the familiar remark coming even before it escaped his lips. "When you have excluded the impossible, whatever remains, however improbable, must be the truth," he declared for the hundredth time in our association.

"Whatever do you mean?" asked Waters. "Are you suggesting an intruder might've entered through a window located on the second story, accessible only by climbing a sheer wall?"

"Since I don't have all the facts as yet, I cannot say that is what happened," Sherlock Holmes declared. "Never allow theory to run ahead of the facts, Inspector. I'm saying it isn't improbable that it happened as you describe. Why don't we visit the scene of this tragedy and see what clues might still remain that would help clear up this matter?"

"I've given an order that nothing be disturbed," Waters assured. "My cab is downstairs."

We grabbed our coats and hats and descended into busy Baker Street where the police wagon was awaiting us, and soon we were clattering along to the Great Eastern Hotel.

We were met outside the hotel by a distraught gentleman who hurried to our carriage as it came to a stop. "Please, please, I beg of you, keep a low profile!" he urged.

"And you are?" Waters asked.

"Gilleston. The hotel manager," the worried man declared. "Oh, please, can't we keep this as quiet as possible? The scandal!" He looked apprehensively over his shoulder towards the lobby.

"May I remind you that a man is dead in your hotel, Gilleston?" Waters rebuked him. The manager uttered a whimpered groan. "We will have to conduct a thorough inquiry." The remaining color drained from the manager's distressed face.

Holmes stepped forward and put his hand on Gilleston's shoulder. "Rest assured, we will do everything possible to avoid disturbing your remaining, living guests." Gilleston uttered another soft groan.

66

The hotel was a well-known London landmark built in the previous decade on the former site of the mental hospital known as "Bedlam". It was tastefully furnished with plush sofas and chairs arranged around the lobby, flickering gas lamps and muted rugs covering much of the wooden floor. People were gathered reading newspapers and otherwise going about quite normal business, seemingly unaware of what had transpired above them during the night.

"What is the dead man's room number?"

"214."

"May I see the registration materials for that room?" Holmes asked Gilleston, who nodded and handed him a card. "'*Meriwether Flicker*'," Holmes read. "What can you tell me about his movements since his arrival? Think carefully!"

"Well, he arrived shortly after two in the afternoon," Gilleston responded. "He went to his room and remained there until about five-thirty, I believe, when he came down the stairs to have an early supper at our restaurant."

"Did he seem suspicious or wary in any way?" Holmes asked

"Not at all," Gilleston replied. "He was quite calm and polite. He remarked that this was his first visit to London and that he was looking forward to a good night's rest before beginning his sales meetings."

"Did anyone visit with him" Holmes asked. "Did anyone stop to speak with him, or perhaps visit his table? Might a guest have visited him in his room after his dinner?"

"No, no one went to his room, of that I'm quite sure. He seemed a quiet, solitary young man."

"And yet," Holmes mused, turning the registration card over and over in his hand. "And yet."

He slipped the card into his pocket and strode off in the direction of the staircases. None of the patrons in the lobby gave our group much notice at all with the exception of a large older man who moved to block our path.

"Hey, what's going on here anyhow?" he insisted to Waters and Holmes, who led our little delegation. He wore a slightly frayed shirt and inexpensive woolen pants, and he had a small cap sitting back on his head, despite being indoors. The man spoke loudly and his brusque manner clearly identified him an American.

"You guys the cops?" he inquired, employing the curious vocabulary of the States.

Waters regarded the man for a moment and then took his shoulder in his hand and pushed him out of our path.

"Hey! Whatsa big idea?" the man called after us, before breaking into a phlegmatic cough. Holmes had already evaded the intruder and bounded

67

up two floors, heading to the room of the unfortunate Mr. Flicker, and I was in close pursuit. A groan escaped Holmes's mouth as we arrived at No. 214. Several policemen were gathered in the hallway and the door to the room was wide open with additional police inside. I didn't have to ask why Holmes was distraught. Certainly, they had already trampled many of the clues that he might have been able to glean from an untouched location.

Holmes pulled Waters by his arm. "Please ask these men to leave," he urged. "They are doing little here but eradicating any hope of my determining what has happened."

"But they are from Scotland Yard!" Waters protested.

"Precisely," answered Holmes as he eased past the battery of departing police and cautiously stepped into the room. Knowing Holmes's attention to footprints, I carefully placed my feet only where his had already landed and followed him in.

In the middle of the room lay Mr. Flicker, dressed in his sleepwear and soaked in blood. Holmes avoided the corpse as he knelt upon the floor, carefully examining the carpeting, but his dismay was immediately evident. "There might as well have been a herd of cattle through this doorway!" he protested. "Any clues as to who entered or left have been obliterated!"

"But what difference does it make?" responded Waters. "No one could've entered through the locked doorway."

Holmes drew himself up to the detective, looking down his long nose several inches to the shorter man's face. A long, bony finger emerged from his fist and he poked the young man soundly in the chest.

"That is merely your supposition, Inspector Waters," he said sharply. "It isn't a fact. We don't yet know the facts, and thanks to the trampling of this carpeting, we may never know them." He turned and knelt again beside the unfortunate Meriwether Flicker.

"Is this the man who registered as Flicker?" he asked Gilleston. The horrified man couldn't stop staring at the gory scene laid out before him. Rapidly, the manager shook his head up and down to confirm the identification and quickly turned away.

Holmes began to examine the area around the body, again searching for identifiable footprints. Finally, clearly exasperated, he turned his attention to Flicker's corpse.

The dead man lay on his back, his eyes were wide open, the pupils fully dilated, and his mouth hung open. Altogether, his visage was one of utter horror. His hands and wrists were a mass of deep cuts that had bled liberally. Where he had fallen, thick puddles of coagulated blood had pooled under his lifeless arms, which lay stretched out to his sides.

Holmes peered into the man's vacant eyes and placed his nose near the gaping mouth and took a deep sniff. He held each hand, considered the wounds, and examined the blood saturating the carpet. "Look here, Watson," he called, pointing to the injuries on the wrists.

"Yes, I see," I answered. "Severe damage to the ulnar and radial arteries," I affirmed. "He would've bled most profusely without treatment. Unconsciousness would've occurred within a fairly short period, I should say, with death inevitable, absent immediate medical attention."

Holmes nodded his head in agreement. He turned his attention to the dead man's bare feet, which were also a mass of lacerations. Using a pen knife, Holmes dislodged a number of shards of glass from the bloody soles which he held in his palm, regarding them for a moment. Then he stood and walked briskly to the lavatory where a scene of similar carnage greeted him.

Above the sink, the mirror had been shattered into thousands of pieces that now lay on the floor, along with the remnants of a drinking glass. Clearly great force had been used. The effect was obvious: Razor sharp glass had sliced through Flicker's hands and wrists. Prodigious amounts of blood had streamed onto the sink and were flecked around on the walls, and the floor had a path of bloody footprints, streaking back towards the chamber where Flicker had collapsed as his blood gushed from the multiple injuries.

After several moments regarding the pattern of the blood spatters, Holmes returned to the bedchamber and surveyed the room, taking in the doors, the furniture, and the fixtures. Satisfied, he walked over to a small table where there were several small boards with bits of brightly coloured ribbon attached to them, as well as a schedule of appointments in London. The dead man had evidently been reviewing the materials, and his ribbon samples, before going to bed.

"Have you this gentleman's wallet?" Holmes inquired. Waters handed it over and Holmes rifled through it, pulling out some papers and cards. "Mr. Flicker of Paterson, New Jersey seems to have been a seller of silk bows and ribbons," he declared. "Paterson is a manufacturing center known, if I recall correctly, as 'The Silk City of America'. Hardly an occupation one would associate with such business as this."

Holmes poked among the scattered items on the cluttered desk and looked in the trash pail next to it, and then pointed to a small blue bottle, which was next to an empty glass. Beside it rested a note on which had been roughly handwritten "*Welcome to the Great Eastern Hotel!*" and a small envelope in which the note had been enclosed. He picked up the bottle and sniffed it, closing his eyes to blot out other sensory distractions.

"Is this a bottle of spirits which your hotel routinely provides to guests?" inquired Holmes?

Gilleston regarded the bottle curiously. "Why, I have never seen such a thing before," he declared. "We provide no such gift to our guests!"

"And there is no chance someone in the hotel might've come to his room to provide this bottle?"

"Absolutely not. No peddlers or others except registered guests are permitted above the ground floor."

Holmes moved towards the window, taking time to examine the carpeting in that area as well, and then briefly studied the sill with his magnifying glass. Planting his gloved hands on the sash, he pushed it up and stuck his head through the open window, looking up and down the outside of the building and then at the alley that ran around the back of the hotel. Bringing his head back inside, he pulled down the sash and turned triumphantly to face us.

"Well, we have one answer," he announced triumphantly, "and two remaining questions."

"What are the questions?" asked the inspector.

"The questions are 'Why', and 'By whom'," Holmes responded.

"And the answer?" Waters inquired.

"Oh, I would've thought that was obvious," answered Sherlock Holmes. "The answer is that this man was murdered."

A look of astonishment froze the faces of those in the room, myself included. "Murdered?" repeated Waters incredulously.

"Indisputably," replied Holmes.

"Holmes!" I said. "Did the murderer walk into the room, murder Mr. Flicker, then walk out and bolt lock the door behind him? Or perhaps he just scaled the outside wall like Poe's orangutan and came in through the window."

"Yes, Watson," Holmes said. "That is precisely what he did. Obviously neither the murderer nor Flicker could've possibly locked the door from the inside *after* such grievous wounds were administered. Therefore the only remaining possibility must be that the murderer entered here," he said, pointing towards the window. "When we catch him, I must thank him for wearing shoes having such a characteristic sole. By the way," he said to Waters, drawing his finger across the sill and producing a small residue, "here is some dirt that scraped from his very distinct shoe when he climbed through the window."

"How did you find those footmarks?" asked Waters, squinting to see the faint impressions on the carpeting.

"I *looked* for them," Holmes replied. He pointed to the carpeting. "There are impressions – faint, I grant you, but unquestionable – that lead from the window to the desk and back again. Since our unwelcome visitor is unlikely to have walked through the walls, he must have opened the sash from the outside and entered the room."

"But why would he do that?" asked Waters.

"Presumably for the same reason you would do so," said Holmes, "to avoid being observed leaving this room or walking through the hotel." He moved carefully to the window to avoid trampling the barely visible footprints that he'd detected. "For someone to possess the required skill, however, I image it was no more challenging to scale the building and enter the window than for you or I to turn the knob and enter by the door."

"But murder!" Waters persisted. "How do you know Flicker was murdered? Clearly these injuries are self-inflicted as a result of smashing the mirror. Might it not even have been suicide?"

"Well, it is consistent with someone wanting us to *believe* it was an accident or suicide," said Holmes, "but I rather doubt it. The evidence is quite to the contrary." He pointed to the empty bottle on the desk. "Waters, I suggest that the remaining contents of that bottle be analyzed. I would be quite surprised if it doesn't contain a very heavy dose of some drug that can induce the most erratic behavior. I've made a study of such drugs," he added. "Perhaps you recall the paper I published last year on the disturbing effect of mood-altering drugs, in excessive quantities.

"I suspect Mr. Flicker was deceived into drinking the spirits that were in this bottle," he said, pointing to the blue bottle. "No! Don't touch it!" he cried as a policeman who had remained in the room reached for the vial.

"Undoubtedly," Holmes then continued, "he became highly disoriented and erratic after imbibing the mixture and went to the lavatory for water, but became utterly distraught and smashed the looking glass. Whether that was the intended outcome of whoever supplied this concoction, of course, I cannot say. He walked around disoriented and waving his arms, smearing blood from his lacerated feet – that accounts for the splattering of blood and the bloody footprints. Yes, indubitably, there has been bad business here in the night, and it has ended with this man unintentionally taking his own life."

Every mouth in the small room except for Holmes's hung open in astonishment. Finally, Waters spoke. "How can you *possibly* guess such a horrible act?" he incredulously asked.

Holmes stared hard at him and narrowed his eyes. "I *never* guess," Holmes sharply responded. "Facts! The facts lead to the escapable conclusion that a person unknown to us scaled the exterior wall of this hotel, opened that window, and gained access to this room."

Waters and the other policemen looked at Holmes with expressions of mystification on their faces. "And why didn't the murderer simply leave by way of the door, which surely would've been a far easier means of egress?" asked Waters skeptically.

"He might well have been seen," Holmes said, "which would have precluded this crime being dismissed as a suicide or accidental overmedication." Then he added, somewhat ungraciously, "As it evidently *was* before I arrived on the scene. No, no, far safer to depart the way he arrived, by the window, down to the alley, from whence he made good his escape. It cannot have been much more of a challenge for him to descend than it had been to climb up in the first place."

The room grew quiet as the observers contemplated Holmes's words. Finally, Waters spoke up. "But why, Mr. Holmes? Why would anyone commit this terrible crime?"

"That is precisely what I intend to discover," replied Holmes.

We reconvened in the small office of the hotel manager on the ground floor, joined by the housekeeping supervisor, Mrs. McSorley, who had first raised the alarm. "You saw and heard nothing from Mr. Flicker after he had returned to his room for the evening, after dinner?" Holmes pressed. "Not a request, not a call of any kind?"

Mrs. McSorley paused thoughtfully. "No," she said. Then, just as Holmes was about to speak again, she suddenly perked up. "Well, there was one curious thing. Last night, I would say perhaps around ten o'clock, one of the chambermaids was walking on the second floor. She said she heard very loud voices from one of the rooms down in this part of the floor, but she couldn't say which one. By the time she came down to this area, the voice had died down, so she didn't bother to report it."

"Doubtless the effects of the hallucinogen," Holmes declared. "And had Mr. Flicker left his order for his breakfast?"

"Oh yes!" Mrs. McSorley exclaimed, relieved to abandon the earlier topic. "A good breakfast, with eggs and bangers and toast and jelly," she described. She began to weep as she considered the man never had had an opportunity to eat it. "We thought he'd decided to sleep in, and so we returned the breakfast to the kitchen."

The body had been discovered about two hours later, when Flicker had failed to respond to the repeated inquiries from the hotel's cleaning staff.

"And what did you do after making the discovery?" Holmes asked the manager. "Where did you go? To whom did you tell of this unfortunate tragedy?"

"Why, I went to the desk downstairs to alert the police," Gilleston replied. "Of course I didn't want to alarm the other guests and I spoke only to Rufus, the boy who runs messages. 'Go get a constable, on the double!' I told him," the nervous manager recalled. "'There's been a murder in No.

214!' I assumed it was murder. There he is now," he added, pointing to a boy of perhaps twelve or thirteen who had suddenly appeared in the office door, the scruff of his neck firmly in the hand of a policeman.

"I caught this hooligan hanging about," the officer announced. Holmes regarded the boy and then walked over. He then guided him to a nearby sofa.

"Now, then, I'm Sherlock Holmes," he began. "Perhaps you've heard of me."

At the mention of the detective's name, the boy brightened considerably. "Oh, yes, sir," he said, bowing slightly his chair. "I know who you are. A pleasure. My name is Rufus," he offered. "Rufus Janney."

"Now, Rufus, what was the message you received from Mr. Gilleston this morning?" Holmes calmly asked.

"Well, sir," the boy said hurriedly, "he – Mr. Gilleston – said there was an awful bloody mess in No. 214, and that a man was dead, and I needed to go fetch the police right quick

"And what did you do?" asked Holmes.

"Well, I ran down the street to fetch the police," Rufus declared, "just like he asked me."

"And did you encounter anyone on the way?" asked Holmes. "Did anyone accost you and ask about your mission?"

The boy looked wary, his eyes darting. "I – I didn't tell nobody, Mr. Holmes," he said rather unconvincingly. "Really I didn't!"

"Come, come," Holmes said soothingly. "No harm done! We were all once boys, Rufus. I'm sure that with such a juicy bit of information as a bloody corpse in the room, you must have shared it with someone between here and the police station, and perhaps have a shilling to show for it."

The boy chewed his bottom lip for a moment or two and ruminated about the question.

"Well, I did tell one person," Rufus admitted. "An older American who was hanging about in the lobby of the hotel."

"That is the same older gentleman who just inquired about the goings on when we entered the hotel!" Gilleston declared

"I bumped into him as I was running off to get the police," Rufus said. "I bumped into him just outside the front door."

"Did you?" asked Holmes. "And pray, what did he say?"

"Well, he asked what all the commotion was about, and offered me a shilling," Rufus explained. "I couldn't see where there was any harm in letting him in on it, so I said that a man had been killed in No. 214 and I had been deputized to bring the police."

"And what did your new friend say in response?" Holmes inquired.

"He got quite alarmed," the boy said. "'What's that you say? A body in No. 214? Did you say No. 214?' That's what he said. 'Are you positive?' I just answered 'Yes, that was it.' And off I went."

"Is that man a guest at the hotel?" asked Holmes asked, turning to Gilleston again.

The manager licked briefly at the corner of his mouth. "No," he said slowly, "I can't say as he is." He thought a little more, then added more confidently, "No. No, sir. He most certainly isn't a guest. He's just passing time in the lobby, watching the stairs. I presumed he was waiting for a guest to come down."

"Have you seen him otherwise?" Holmes asked.

"Well, I first saw him in the lobby, after the alarm had been given," he offered. "There was quite a bit of agitation as the word spread, as you can imagine. We even had one guest who very abruptly appeared, bags in hand, and declared to me he was leaving the hotel immediately."

"Do you recall who that guest was," asked Holmes.

"Oh, yes, it was Mr. Lewis Ullman, from No. 314."

"Room No. *314*?" Holmes repeated. "Are you quite certain?"

"Oh, yes," said the manager. "He arrived from the U.S. yesterday as well." The coincidence suddenly struck him. "Why, his room was right above the room where . . . ." His voice drifted off. "I wonder if he might've been disturbed by the loud noise during the night."

"So might I," added Holmes. "What else do you know of our late friend in room No. 214? You say he arrived just yesterday. Do you know from where? Did he have kith or kin here in London? Or was he passing through to another destination?"

"He arrived yesterday, on the *Isle of Wight* from New York," said Gilleston.

"Yes, of that much I'm aware," said Holmes. He noticed the curious looks on the faces of the men surrounding him. "The remains of a ship's receipt in the waste can," he quickly explained.

Holmes turned briskly and abruptly walked out the front door of the hotel. I followed as he went around to the alley running behind the building. Locating the window of the unfortunate man's room, Holmes fell on the ground, carefully examining a number of footprints while picking up bits of paper and other detritus on the ground, some of which he slipped into his pocket.

"Very interesting," he murmured, standing up and casting a look the nearly sheer wall. "A most formidable climbing achievement, wouldn't you say, Watson?" He picked up a small amount of the dirt and examined it under his hand glass, and then rolled it thoughtfully between his thumb and middle finger.

74

"The mud on the sill in Flicker's room most certainly originated here," he said assuredly, "in this very path behind this building. And here are more of those marks left by that peculiar shoe."

Back inside the hotel, he asked Gilleston for a copy of the London *Directory*, and the manager soon returned with the thick volume. Holmes sat at a desk in the small room, pouring over the contents. For the life of me, I couldn't imagine for what he was searching, but within a few moments he smiled. He quickly wrote down an address and stood to leave.

"Watson, please do me the favour of conducting some research this afternoon," he requested. "Can you check with the steamship office and secure a list of the passengers who had accompanied the late Mr. Flicker on board the *Isle of Wight*? Let us compare that list with the guest list here at the Great Eastern Hotel. I will meet you at Baker Street by four o'clock with information of my own."

"And where will you be looking for clues?" I asked.

"Oh, I think I *have* the clues," he replied cheerily. "What I'm looking for is a Norwegian daredevil." He gathered up his coat and hat and hurried out the door and into the street.

Waters looked at me with a face filled with puzzlement. "A what?" he repeated incredulously.

"Of course!" I responded, although I was quite as mystified as the detective.

"He seems quite sure of himself based on rather sketchy evidence, if I say so!" the inspector declared as we strode back into the hotel. Accepting a list of the hotel guests from Gilleston, I bid *adieu* to Waters and sped off to the shipping office to secure the list of passengers that Holmes had requested. Acquiring the manifest proved no difficult matter and I returned to our rooms in Baker Street to compare the hotel and ship lists while awaiting Holmes's arrival.

At the appointed hour, Holmes strode through the door to the sitting room. "You were quite right," I called out as I greeted him. "There are several people from the *Isle of Wight* who spent last evening at the hotel."

Holmes took the list from my hand and looked over the names from the Great Eastern Hotel register that I'd circled with a red pencil. "Let me see," Holmes mused. "Mr. and Mrs. Cecil Gladnow of Philadelphia, in room No. 223. No, of no interest," he said, crossing off the Gladnows' names. "Miss Catherine McCliff of Newport, Rhode Island, and Mrs. Emma Staansfield – undoubtedly a young woman of means and her chaperone," he commented, again crossing off the names next to room No. 308. "There is the recently deceased Mr. Flicker in No. 214, and Mr. Lewis Ullman," he read, his eyes narrowing, "who this morning departed room

No. 314. Let us go speak with our friend Gilleston back at the Great Eastern."

We rattled along the streets in our hansom as Holmes explained that he'd made several inquiries of his own that had been proven suggestive. The intervening hours had done little to calm Gilleston, who had spent his day explaining to alarmed guests that "Everything is just fine. Please don't feel it necessary to interrupt your stay." He seemed relieved when we strode into the lobby and motioned us into his office.

"Have you found the murderer?" he anxiously inquired.

"Patience," replied Holmes in a soothing voice. He produced the list of names that I'd acquired from the shipping office and pointed to that of the former inhabitant of No. 314. "Let me ask you about this gentleman, who departed the hotel this morning in something of a hurry," Holmes said. "What can you tell me of Mr. Lewis Ullman?"

"Ah, the *other* American gentleman who checked in yesterday," he said. "He arrived somewhat earlier than Mr. Flicker, and wanted a room for just a single night, but he had no reservation. Mr. Flicker had booked a room for three nights," he added approvingly. Holmes's face noticeably brightened at hearing this piece of news.

"He fairly flew out of the hotel once news of the murder was disclosed!" Gilleston added. "He didn't even wait to pay his bill. He just put two pounds down on the counter and walked out quite briskly. Do you think he might've been involved in the murder?"

"What of the loiterer in the lobby?" asked Holmes instead of answering.

"He stood up when Mr. Ullman came down the stairs, now that I think of it," Gilleston said. "He had a hard look on his face, and he followed Mr. Ullman out the door. I followed to look outside, Mr. Ullman was already quite far down the street and the big man was hurrying to catch up to him." The manager looked mournful and then brightened. "Perhaps they were it in together!" Gilleston suggested hopefully.

"No," said Holmes, "I rather doubt that was the case. Ullman and the stout gentleman certainly are connected, but not associates, I suspect."

"What relationship do you presume?" I asked.

"I think rather hunter and prey," Sherlock Holmes replied.

"But surely Mr. *Flicker* was the prey," I protested.

"I wonder," Holmes replied. "Thank you for your cooperation, Gilleston. Come, Watson, we have a trip to make and it's getting late."

Soon we were rambling in a cab towards East London, where a rougher element made their homes and workplaces. Thirty minutes later, the cab pulled up outside a nondescript stone building. A weathered sign hung over the doorway: "*Saylor's Mountaineering and Expeditionary*

Club". We disembarked and went inside, where we met a tall and lean man, quite as weathered in the face as the sign hanging outside.

"Can I help you gents?" he agreeably asked.

"Thank you, some information, please," said Holmes. "I'm interested in finding out about a hiking trip I'm planning in Kjeragbolten." The man behind the counter looked blankly at him. "In Norway," Holmes explained.

"Of course!" the proprietor exclaimed.

"Perhaps you might know of someone knowledgeable about that region," Holmes continued. "I know I could make arrangements once I arrived there, but I would so much rather do so before my departure. And there is a fat fee for identifying someone who could assist me."

"Well, now, I believe that I can help," the man responded. "It just so happens I know a man from Norway himself, and he's one of the best climbers I've ever known."

"Is he available?" Holmes asked.

"Well, there was another man round here yesterday who went to talk with him," the shop manager recalled. "Asked if we hire any foreigners." He lowered his voice. "Sometimes they're the best, you know. Now, for that fee, of course, I could give you his address and you could go around and see if he might be available for the job."

Holmes quickly produced a five-pound note and laid in on the counter while the man consulted a list of names he kept under his desk, and then dashed up a quick note on a scrap of paper. "There you go," he said. "You go 'round to that address and see if you can find Mr. Dag Larsen."

Holmes thanked his informant and we strode back to our waiting cab, handing the paper with Larsen's address to the driver. "Quick now," he said, "not a moment to lose!"

Ten minutes later we stopped before a row of shambled mews off a main street. Holmes hopped out, checked the address, and walked to the door. I followed. He knocked heavily, but there was no response. Again, he knocked and this time, there was a gruff voice from behind the door, which remained close.

"*Ja?*" came the response from inside.

"*Unnskyld meg, er det Dag?*" [1] Holmes said loudly.

"*Ja! Dette er Dag,*" came the reply. "*Hvem ringer?* [2]

I looked at Holmes amazed. How was he carrying on a conversation in Norwegian with this unseen person, and why?

"*Jeg er så glad for å endelig finne deg!*" Holmes responded. "*Jeg har søkt etter deg så lenge. La meg se på ansiktet ditt, min gamle venn!*" [3]

Behind the door, I could hear the lock being opened and in a moment the door swung open to reveal a man of perhaps thirty, of medium height and muscular build. Seeing Holmes and myself, he quickly tried to shut the door, but Holmes had wedged his walking stick into the jamb and prevented it from closing. With a grunt, Holmes shoved, but the door barely moved.

"Watson! Together now!" he called, and breaking from my astonishment, I leaned my good shoulder into the door as well. Larsen was strong, but not strong enough to resist the two of us, and the door was flung open as he fled back into the small house. Holmes was on him in an instant, however, and the two rolled together in the corridor trading blows until I was able to bring my service revolver down on the man's head with an authoritative "crack". He slid unconscious to the ground and Holmes, pushing the man off him, stood up and clapped me on the arm.

"Good job, Watson! You likely saved me from a much worse altercation with this very strapping young man," he remarked. "Let's get him revived. But first –" Holmes reached into his pocket and withdrew a pair of steel handcuffs. Slipping them on to the inert man's wrists, he leaned him against the wall and brusquely slapped his face.

"Larsen! Larsen! *Våkn opp*!"[4] Holmes said next to the man's ear. "Perhaps some water."

I returned with water in a filthy glass I found in the kitchen. "I'm not sure how good that would be to drink," I admonished Holmes, but he simply looked at me before splashing the water in the face of the mountain climber, who shook his head and slowly came back to life.

"*Hven er du*?"[5] he said, but then, realizing he had been tricked into believing Holmes was one of his countrymen, switched into understandable English. "Who are you, and why have you broken into my room?" he inquired. He looked down at his manacled hands. "Are you the police?"

"No, but we could arrange for them to come and arrest you if you prefer," Holmes responded. "We would like to discuss your recent climbing feat at the Great Eastern Hotel."

His eyes grew wide and he looked from Holmes to me, and then back at Holmes. Then a look of terror crossed his face. "No! No!" he cried. "I did no wrong. I did no wrong! It was the American! I did no wrong!"

Holmes laid his hand on the man's shoulder. "Calm yourself," he said. "I believe that I can be of some help with the police." The man looked horrified but Holmes patted his shoulder and continued. "But I cannot help you if you don't make a clean breast of it. Shall I begin for you?"

The man looked confused, but Holmes's hand on his shoulder seemed to provide him genuine calm, and he nodded his head.

"I believe I'm not the first person to be seeking your services as a climber of late, am I right?" Holmes asked. The man mournfully shook his head affirmatively. "I expect a rather large American recently found his way to the shop to engage your services."

"Yes, that is right," the Norwegian said. "He said, 'Just call me Smith,' but I don't think that is his real name."

"Yes, I have no doubt," Holmes responded drily. And he asked you to deliver a package for him – to a friend in a room at the Great Eastern Hotel, correct?"

"Yes, a bottle and envelope, exactly, to the man staying there," he answered.

"And did you ask why he engaged you to climb that outside wall instead of simply delivering the package by the more conventional way, such as the door?" asked Holmes.

"Oh yes, he said it was a surprise, a joke, and he didn't want his friend to know where the package had come from. He offered me five pounds, and when I'm offered so much money, no questions. He was afraid someone might be seen entering the room by the door," he explained. "He thought it would be a good joke, and it wasn't a difficult climb at all, just three stories."

"Because he told you the man was in room No. 314, is that correct?" Holmes asked.

"*Ja*, I waited behind the hotel for a while for Smith to signal the man had left his room to go to dinner," he continued.

"And you ate a chocolate bar while you waited," Holmes added.

Larsen stared at Holmes. "*Ja*. Then about six o'clock, Smith signaled that the man had gone to dinner. I climbed up to his room and opened the window. The room was empty," he explained, "so I left the bottle."

"On the small desk?" Holmes asked.

"*Ja*, that was what Mr. Smith said to do," he agreed. "Then I climbed back out the window, closed it, and climbed back down."

"Are you aware that the man in that room was found dead this morning?" Holmes asked sharply.

Larsen physically started, and his chin trembled. "Dead!" he cried, rising to his feet. "Dead? No, no, no. This was a joke," Larsen said. "A present for his friend. How is he dead?"

"That isn't important right now," Holmes explained. "What is important is for whom you were working, and what has become of him." Holmes looked intensely into the man's face as the Norwegian pondered his options.

"If you know, Larsen, I cannot implore you too strongly to come clean, " Holmes said, "I might be persuaded to appeal to Scotland Yard and save you from the gallows."

79

Larsen turned as white as a sheet, and I truly believed that he was about to collapse. I reached into my bag and brought forth my flask of brandy, which I held to his lips as he took a long swallow and then shook involuntarily

"*Herregud!*" the terrified man exclaimed. "*Dette er forferdelig!*" [6]

"Yes, quite terrible," Holmes translated. "Come, there is no time to lose. The whereabouts of the portly Mr. Smith who hired you."

"I'm to meet him tonight, at ten at The Prancing Horse to get the rest of my pay," he said, identifying a local pub. "He would only pay me half before the job was done. I told him I needed to be sure he'd show up, so I demanded to hold his pocket watch." Larsen displayed a cheap watch on a chain. "He didn't care for that," he said, "because it belonged to his dead son, but he say all right, and now, I have to be there to get my money and return it."

"Yes," said Holmes. "You will show, but so shall Dr. Watson and myself. We will take you, but if you give him a signal or otherwise double cross us, I give you my word you will not hang because I will instruct Watson to blow your brains out on the spot!"

Although I knew it was false, I was startled to hear such a belligerent tone come from Holmes's mouth, not to mention the idea that I would do such a thing.

At 9:30, Holmes and I were racing with Larsen in a four-wheeler to The Prancing Horse pub, after first stopping to send a message to Inspector Waters. "Now remember, engage in conversation for as long as you're able, and we will handle the rest," he told the Norwegian, who soon disappeared behind the grimy painted windows that sheathed the front of the building. We waited together across the street for a few moments before ambling up to the door.

"Watson, remain here and stay alert," he explained. "I'm going to lock the rear door, and then we'll attempt to apprehend our prey. Should he bolt, it will be through this door, and therefore it's upon you to apprehend him. Do not fail me!"

With that he was gone into a dark alley that ran alongside the pub. I waited for several minutes, occasionally peering through the glass where the paint had worn away. Excitedly, I saw that Larsen had quickly met up with the large American from the hotel lobby. They were sitting at a small table, glasses of some concoction between them, and the heavy man was speaking in an excited manner.

The large man held up his hand to summon the waiter who was meandering through the dimly lit room, and the tall, thin man ambled over to the table. They spoke briefly and then suddenly, the large man jumped bolt upright and pushed the waiter hard on the chest, knocking him backward over some tables, before disappearing into the rear of the pub. The patrons were all on their feet and talking excitedly when the large man came running back into the room and headed for the door near which I was standing. As he ran past me, I stuck my walking stick out and he fell head over heels into the street. Holmes quickly appeared, still dressed in the costume of the waiter the he'd donned inside the pub.

"Nicely done, Watson!" Holmes said standing over the fallen man, who was already attempting to stand. Holmes grabbed his arm, on which already dangled the formidable handcuff that earlier in the evening had been affixed to Larsen. Locking it to the man's wrist, he led the manacled prisoner back inside where he attached the open half of the device to a heavy chair and then pushed the man onto the seat. Momentarily, none other than Inspector Waters came running into the pub and addressed Holmes.

"Move away, move away," he instructed the patrons who were gathering around us with growing curiosity. "Scotland Yard!" The crowd took several steps backward. "See here, Mr. Holmes, what is this message I received to meet you here to take possession of the murderer?" he questioned. The inspector looked down at the groggy man handcuffed to, the chair. "And who might *this* be?" he asked.

"Based on the information from the ship's records, this must be Mr. Drago Szabó of Hazelton, Pennsylvania, who arrived yesterday on the *Isle of Wight* along with the late Mr. Flicker," Holmes declared. "He is responsible for the tragic events at the Great Eastern Hotel last evening." The man stirred further and began a heavy cough that shook his large frame violently.

Holmes turned to Larsen. "Is this the man who hired you?" he inquired.

"*Ja!* *Ja!* That is the man!" the Norwegian said excitedly as Szabó glared at him.

"And who's *this*?" exclaimed the perplexed Waters, jabbing his thumb towards Larsen.

"This is the Norwegian daredevil that I was seeking!" Holmes said.

"The Norwegian . . . I'm so confused!" Waters admitted, putting his hand to his forehead. "Who *are* all these people?" He sat down in a chair next to Szabó who continued to rub his head with his free hand.

"I believe it is quite clear. Szabó hired Larsen to poison Ullman, but the concoction was mistakenly delivered to the wrong room. Mr. Flicker mistook it to be a complimentary welcome gift from the hotel management and drank it, with tragic results. Szabó had arranged to meet Larsen here at The Prancing Horse to finish paying him off before escaping back to

81

New York tomorrow," Holmes explained. Waters' face was a mask of total puzzlement.

"I suggest you gather up these two and take them back to Scotland Yard," Holmes offered. "I will come by in the morning to clear up this entire case for you, which you can then present to Lestrade as your great success."

Waters' face brightened at that suggestion and two officers were summoned to escort Szabó and Larsen to the waiting police wagons. Waters offered his appreciation to Holmes, and then accompanied his prisoners back to central London.

"Holmes, I must say, I'm not much clearer on all this than Waters appears to be," I admitted. "Can you untangle the skein for me and make sense of who hired who to kill whom and why?"

"Good old Watson! Of course, it's admittedly a complex matter," Holmes agreeably said. "What do you say we return to Baker Street and I'll tell you everything over a generous glass of brandy and some shag.

"The key to the case was, as always, answering the question 'Why?'" Holmes began as we settled into our familiar chairs at 221b. A small fire crackled and hissed against the chill in the early spring air, and the brandy proved an excellent relaxant for the day's hectic and confusing events.

"Why, I wondered, would Mr. Flicker – an unassuming New Jersey ribbon salesman who had booked a three-day hotel stay, scheduled a number of business appointments, and ordered a good English breakfast – suddenly go mad, smash the mirror, and cause his own death, probably quite unintentionally? That was the initial question I asked myself. It didn't seem possible that this was the entire set of facts.

"My examination of the room clearly indicated that someone had entered his room via the window and left a bottle of tainted spirits laced with a powerful hallucinogen, complete with a counterfeit welcoming note, had been left where Flicker couldn't possibly fail to imbibe its tainted contents."

"But do you know it was tainted?" I inquired.

"We will know more when we see the results of the autopsy and the analysis of the bottle's contents," he answered, "but I have no doubt an ingredient was added to the spirits to ensure the victim had a very unpleasant experience. Probably a hallucinogen of some type, perhaps mescaline or psilocin. Driven mad by the drug – that would account for the cries heard by the maid in the hallway – Flicker became highly unnerved and doubtless smashed the glass in the lavatory, badly cutting his wrists in the process."

"How horrible!" I replied. "Do you think the intention wasn't to kill him, but rather to have some fun at his expense with the drug?"

"No, I imagine the expectation was that he might throw himself out the window or otherwise do severe damage to himself," Holmes replied.

"But why drug him at all," I asked, "if he was an unassuming ribbon salesman on a business trip to London?"

"Ah, the motive," Holmes repeated, stretching his long legs towards the fireplace. "The motive was to accomplish exactly what occurred. To cause the death of the young American who arrived at the Great Eastern yesterday from the *Isle of Wight*. The problem, in this case, is that the wrong man drank the drug that cost him his life."

"The wrong man!" I cried. "How could you know that to be the case?"

"Well, it is really as simple as *1-2-3*," said Holmes with a slight grin crossing his face.

I threw up my hands in utter vexation. "What on Earth are you saying?" I responded.

"The fact that the entry to the room was through the window was absolutely fundamental to understanding the case," Holmes began. "Once I determined there was an American implicated in the matter – the bellicose gentleman in the lobby who turned out to be Mr. Szabó – I had no doubt that I'd hit on the explanation, which was only confirmed when we learned of the hasty exit of Mr. Lewis Ullman from Hazelton, Pennsylvania from the Great Eastern Hotel.

"Suppose, I thought, the intended victim wasn't Mr. Flicker at all, who seemed to present no reason whatsoever to be murdered, but rather the American in the room directly *above* his, Mr. Ullman, who had arrived the same day and on the same ship," Holmes reasoned. "I imagine Szabó had followed Ullman from the wharf to the hotel and discovered that his intended prey was in room No. 314. The window to that room would've been easily accessible from the alley by a proficient climber.

"But Szabó himself was far too large to ascend such a sheer wall. He must have had an accomplice, someone with considerable climbing skills. There were only tiny irregularities in the stone wall, and the ascent would've been quite challenging for anyone but an experienced mountaineer. That fact was confirmed by my examination of the ground below the window which yielded footprints made by the climbing shoe whose prints I discovered inside the victim's room, including one set particularly deeper than the others."

"And what was the significance of that set of prints?" I asked.

"They were the prints left when the climber jumped down the last several feet whilst descending, of course," Holmes explained. "The prints were familiar to me – I've written several monographs on the soles of various shoes and boots, as you well know – as being typical of a type of climbing shoe manufactured in Scandinavia.

"My suspicions were confirmed by this scrap of paper I discovered not far from the prints," he said, handing me a wrapper with the word "*Freia*" and a picture of a small boy. "Apparently our climber was a Norwegian who enjoyed a chocolate bar while waiting for the signal that it was safe to begin his ascent.

"Where better to find a Norwegian climber than through a climbing club?" he asked. "Thus, our visit to East London."

"But the mistake in the rooms?" I asked.

"Forgive me," Holmes answered. "Yes, a most calamitous error, particularly for poor Mr. Flicker. Having managed to examine the hotel's registration book, Szabó knew his target was in No. 314. He instructed the Norwegian climber Larsen to climb up to the third story, enter the window, and leave the bottle of poisoned spirits.

"But they both made a mistake, and one with tragic consequences for our ribbon salesman. Americans describe the entry floor of a building as the first floor, whereas we in England call the entry the *ground* floor. So, too, does nearly everyone else on this side of the Atlantic. The *first* floor for *us* is the *second* floor for an American, and so on.

"When Szabó told the Norwegian to enter the window of room No. 314 and leave the bottle, Larsen naturally assumed that meant the third floor from the street level, as it would in the US. But the intended victim, Mr. Ullman, was really one floor *above*, on the American *fourth* floor," Holmes explained. "The mistake would have been immediately obvious if the bottle were brought in through the entry door, which is marked with the correct room number, but from the alley, a climber would've no way of knowing he had entered the wrong room!"

"But surely the Norwegian climber would have instinctively gone to the correct floor," I reasoned. "After all, Norway is a European nation. Even if Szabo's instructions were flawed, any European would've automatically selected the correct window."

"True, if that European were from any country but Norway," Holmes said. "I learned a good deal about that country during my sojourn, after my escape from the Reichenbach Falls, as the Norwegian explorer Sigerson. Remarkably, Norway alone among all European nations counts the floors of a building in the same manner as Americans!

"When the clerk at the climbing store confirmed that he had recommended a Norwegian climber to Szabó, I had no doubt I was on the right track," he continued. "My passing mastery of Norwegian was helpful in tricking Larsen into believing I was a countryman of his, and the pieces began to fall into place."

"Remarkable!" I exclaimed. "Szabó must have realized the mistake when he was informed by that ragamuffin that the murdered man had been in No. 214 rather than No. 314, as he had intended."

"Precisely, Watson, well done!" Holmes congratulated me.

"Well, we know 'how' the murder was committed, but there remains the important question of 'why'," I added.

"We can confirm that in a conversation in the morning with Szabó and Larsen, who are fortunately now in the reliable custody of Scotland Yard," Holmes said. "By the time we meet with them, I will have received the information I'm awaiting by wire which, I've no doubt, will clear away the remaining fog of the matter."

Holmes was gone by the time I awoke in the morning, but returned as I was finishing my breakfast and perusing *The Times*.

"Have you the information you were seeking?" I asked.

"Yes, yes!" he excitedly replied. "Right here." He patted his breast pocket and withdrew a sheath of papers that he threw on the table. After pouring himself a cup of coffee, he pick up the papers, and leaned back in his chair.

"The key to the case lies in the bad business in Lattimer, Pennsylvania last year," he began. "The cast of characters had left little doubt in my mind that the origins of this messy business lay on the other wide of the Atlantic. When I determined that the intended victim, Ullman, as well as Drago, were from eastern Pennsylvania, it remained only to uncover what might have recently transpired there that would merit such a trans-Atlantic pursuit. These responses to my wires confirm my suppositions."

"And what were those suppositions?" I inquired.

"Doubtless you've heard of the recent labor dispute involving the anthracite miners in Hazelton?" he asked. I shook my head as this topic was totally unfamiliar to me. "A most unfortunate incident. Twenty-five unarmed miners, mainly immigrants from East European countries, were gunned down by police during a strike at the Lehigh and Wilkes-Barre Coal Company last September. Many more were wounded. There was a report of police shooting wounded strikers as they lay helpless on the ground!"

"Shocking!" I exclaimed.

"Yes," he said, reading aloud the headlines. "'*Dead in Heaps*'. '*The Slaughter Was Terrific*'. And the tragedy continued last month," Holmes recounted. "The sheriff and his officers were acquitted on all charges, despite many eyewitnesses who confirmed their role in the unwarranted massacre.

"A check of the court records confirmed that Mr. Ullman was one of those officers who had been acquitted," Holmes said. "A quick review of the victims also revealed the name of Lukas Szabó, a miner just nineteen years old. I wouldn't be surprised if, following the unsatisfactory end of the trial, the victim's father swore to track down Ullman to seek revenge. Perhaps he even informed the deputy of his intentions, and Ullman wisely decided it was advisable to flee Pennsylvania and even America."

Holmes further perused the wires from America, and we were soon on our way to Scotland Yard, where Waters and several officers were waiting with Drago Szabó, who glowered menacingly at Larsen, the mournful Norwegian climber.

"Good morning to you all," Holmes said with seriousness to the prisoners. "I believe I understand what has transpired here, and I need only a few additional pieces of information from both of you to conclude this investigation."

"Go to the Devil!" spit out Szabó, followed by the same hacking cough we had heard the night before. As a physician, I couldn't help but conclude the man suffered from some serious pulmonary disorder, but for the moment, the focus was on his criminal activities.

"Gracious!" replied Holmes. "I rather suspect it is you rather than I who shall be meeting Lucifer in the near future! But let us clear up the details first, which will explain your actions following the trial in Hazelton."

At the mention of the Pennsylvania mining town, Szabó sat upright and glared at Holmes. "Here," he growled, "what do you know of Hazelton?"

"More than you might think – about the strike, the massacre, and the verdict," said Holmes. "And perhaps even more about the reasons you believed your actions in pursuing Lewis Ullman to London were justified."

"Well, you seem to know all sort of things," Szabó said, settling in his chair. His tone lowered. "I guess I might as well tell you the rest. Yes, you're right, I've been on the trail of Ullman, that murdering scoundrel. It was my son Lukas that he killed – shot him in the back as he lay wounded and bleeding on the ground, helpless as a newborn baby." The man's voice broke, and his shoulders began to heave, and the violent coughing began again. It took several moments for him to regain his composure.

"Those deputies cut the miners down with less regard than if they had they been shooting bottles," he continued. "Do you know what the Sheriff said? 'A little cold lead is the only way to halt these strikers.' And that's what them deputies gave us, cold lead. Twenty-five lay dead, including Lukas, and many more shot in the back and tore up for life. They will never be able to lift a pick or shovel again."

Here he paused for a moment and took a drink of water. His face grew grim as he continued. "And wouldn't you know, the jury let them go, every damn'd one. They walked out of the court laughin' and slappin' each other on the back and forgot all about what they done. But *I* don't forget. *I* don't forget my son, murdered as he lay in the dirt bleedin', beggin' for his life.

"Yes, I resolved to get my satisfaction with this Ullman, and I told him he would never have a day's peace so long as I drew breath." He grew contemplative. "And that won't be long either, as I've got the coal disease in my lungs." Another bout of coughing followed as he tried to clear his throat.

"I learned he'd booked passage to England to escape the punishment he knew I would give him. I sold everything I owned and spent every cent I had in the world to buy a ticket on the same ship, the *Isle of Wight*. I planned to throw him overboard into the ocean on the voyage, but he hardly came out of his cabin the whole trip, and was armed when he did.

"We landed two days ago and I followed him to the Great Eastern Hotel. I knew I couldn't just walk in and shoot him like I wanted, so I came up with the idea of tricking him into drinking a brew that would drive him insane and then kill him dead. I wanted him to suffer before he died, just like he made Lucas suffer on the ground!

"I didn't have money for a hotel, so I spent my time sitting the lobby. I was able to steal a look at the registration book was when the manager went off on his duties. Then I figured out how to get it to his room without being seen."

"Which is where Mr. Larsen enters this disturbing picture," Holmes offered. The Norwegian cast a mournful look at Holmes.

"I don't know nothin' about no strike or shooting!" he pleaded. "I don't poison nobody! He tell me it a joke!"

"I don't know how you know all this," Szabó continued, "but yes, I needed a climber fast and I couldn't very well just walk around London asking for one. So I found a mountaineering shop and asked about hiring a skilled man. When the gentleman told me he knew a Norwegian for hire, I thought, 'What a piece of luck! He will not be reading any papers in English and wouldn't know anything of the strike or the trial.' So I took this man's name and engaged him to climb into Ullman's room and deliver the bottle of spirits that had something extra added to it."

"You brought the drug with you from America?" Holmes added.

Szabó looked amazed at Holmes. "Yes. I had figured I might put it to use. And I gave him a good dose, to make sure he suffered good before he died." His face grew grim. "I told this man, 'Climb into room No. 314.' But I didn't know this man would make a mistake and go to the wrong room!" Another round of coughing exhausted Szabó and he sat back on his chair. I noted some blood flecked the corner of his mouth, which confirmed the he was in the final stages of lung disease and would almost certainly be dead before he faced a hangman.

"I went to the third floor like you said!" Larsen cried.

"But room No. 314 would be on what an American would think is the third floor," Holmes declared, "and so would a Norwegian, because they count floors as they do in the States. And so you mistakenly delivered the bottle to a man one floor below Ullman, the intended victim, who was on the European *second* floor."

Larsen hung his head. "*Ja,*" he said. Then he became more engaged. "But I didn't know anyone being poisoned or killed! I think it a joke!"

"In the lobby," Holmes said to Szabó, "when you heard the dead man had been in room No. 214 and not No. 314, you realized the terrible mistake that had been made."

"Yes," Szabó confessed. "Now there was some terrible luck, and I admit I feel badly. But I still had promised this man his pay and he had my boy's watch," he said, pointing to Larsen. "I didn't need him spilling the story to the police, so I met him at The Prancing Horse as we had arranged." He looked at Waters, who remained impassive. "I thought he'd want to escape any responsibility for what he'd done and use the money to go back to Norway and that would be the end of it. I didn't think anyone could connect him to what had happened.

"As for me, I didn't care no more. I only wanted to track down Ullman and take care of him myself, but this gentleman grabbed me first," he said, jabbing a thumb at Holmes. "Now, I expect that he's got away."

"It is a bad business to take justice into your own hands," declared Waters.

"You talk about *justice!*" the old man roared. "Judge Woodward didn't care about it," Szabó spit back at him, "and my son and twenty-four more are cold and in their graves. So I guess if there's justice to be dispensed, it's up to me that's got to do it." He resettled himself in his chair. "There's not much your courts can do to me that the mines ain't done already," he declared.

Holmes motioned to Waters, who joined us outside the interrogation room.

"A bad business to be sure, Waters," Holmes said. "I think it is fairly evident that the Norwegian Larsen was an unwitting accomplice in this tragedy. Undoubtedly, he must be held accountable for his complicity in breaking into poor Mr. Flicker's room, but it seems clear there was no intent on his part. I would hope that would weigh on you as you make your recommendations to the prosecutors."

Waters regarded Holmes warily. "I don't know, Mr. Holmes, but we shall present the evidence just as it is and let the court make their decision."

"Of course," Holmes replied, adding, "Justice must be blind, but it need not be indifferent. As to Mr. Szabó, while his actions are understandable, he must face serious retribution. If he is telling the truth – and Dr. Watson believes his racking cough suggests he is – he will likely escape the noose through more natural means."

"I have no doubt, "I added. "The man has weeks left at best."

"Well, Watson, I think we've had enough of this business. Let us take advantage of this fine spring day for a brisk walk and then perhaps lunch at the Criterion?" Holmes suggested. "This was a complex and not altogether satisfying case on many fronts, and I'm happy to put the entire business behind us."

And so we did for several weeks. In late May, I rose as usual to find that Holmes had already breakfasted and departed Baker Street. He soon returned with a copy of *The Times*, which he placed before me on the table.

"The long arm of justice, Watson," he said, pointing to a small article on page four:

> *Body of American Tourist Found in Thames* [the headline announced.]
>
> *The body of Mr. Lewis Ullman of Hazelton, Pennsylvania was found Tuesday evening on the Embankment south of the houses of Parliament,"* the story read. *"Ullman had been stabbed in the heart and his body thrown into the Thames sometime in the past two days, according to police. Curiously, a lump of anthracite coal was inexplicably found lodged deeply in his throat. The investigation of his mysterious death is continuing.*

Obviously, the other Lattimer miners had found a means for extracting retribution that some might feel was warranted, but I remained dissatisfied with the resolution of the affair. "Is this justice, Holmes?" I asked. "Or is it wanton vigilantism?"

"A question to ponder, Watson," Holmes replied. "Certainly a question to ponder."

NOTES

1. "Excuse me, is it Dag?"
2. "Yes, this is Dag. Who is calling?"
3. "I'm so happy to finally find you! I've been looking for you for so long. Let me look at your face, my old friend!"
4. "Wake up!"
5. "Who are you?"
6. "Oh my God! This is terrible."

The Case of the
Borneo Tribesman
by Stephen Herczeg

Even though it was heading towards nightfall on that August evening, the dying sun of the day still beat down with a ferocity that had been unseen in London for quite some time.

Holmes and I departed our hansom and stood before the modestly appointed three-storey Kensington abode. From what I knew of our host for the evening, the appointment of the building was more in line with the tastes of his wife, rather than the flamboyant nature of the man of the house. The couple had bought all three connecting terraced houses and made them a single abode, with all décor and modifications left to the wife.

It was two days since the simple but elegant card had arrived, inviting me rather than Holmes to what was coined an "event" at this address.

Our host was adventurer and businessman Sir Tristan Leavins, the head of the London division of the North Borneo Chartered Company. From my own reading, I knew that he spent the majority of his time in the East Indies, coordinating the trading of resources and goods between Borneo and England.

A small handwritten note had accompanied the card and told me more than I could have gleaned from the invitation itself.

It seemed that Sir Tristan was to present to the British Trade Commission a selection of goods from far-flung Borneo to engender a want within them and secure funds for establishing a series of trade routes between the two countries. The gathering was a small but distinct class of attendees.

How I had been chosen to attend was indicated by the signature at the bottom of the letter. The name was Willard Kesson, or as I had known him Lieutenant Willard Kesson, of the Royal Engineers, who fought in the Battle of Maiwand where I was unfortunately injured.

As a postscript, Kesson had noted that he would be delighted to see me again. He also suggested bringing Holmes to add colour to what might be a rather dull affair.

Taking the lead, I approached the door, readying myself to lift the brass knocker to announce our arrival. As I reached towards it, the door was opened wide and we were met by an incredible sight.

Standing in the entranceway was a half-naked, dark-skinned man. He was resplendent in a brightly coloured cloth that wrapped around his waist, with a long section hanging down the front. Upon his head he wore a feathered headdress, with several beaded necklaces that draped down his chest. I was so stunned by the man's appearance that I simply stood with my mouth open.

A bright white smile split the man's dark face. "Good evening, gentlemen. Welcome home to Sir Tristan's." Holmes bowed slightly to the man and introduced us. "Ah, good, good. Holmes and Watson. Yes. I hear that name." He stepped back and bade us enter.

As we passed by, Holmes stopped and spoke. "I can only assume you hail from Borneo. Your headdress and loincloth are reminiscent of the Northern area, or indeed from the island of Labuan."

"Yes, sir. We all from Labuan. Many more inside," he said.

"And what is your name?" Holmes asked.

"Jamal," the man said, bowing before us. "Your service I am."

"*Selamat Berkenalan,*" Holmes said.

"And I pleased meet you too, sir," Jamal replied.

"Your English is quite good." I said. "Where did you learn?"

"The sisters at the Mission." His face went dour at some remembrance. "I was many, who no parents."

"Oh, I'm so sorry, my good man. An orphanage." He nodded. I started to speak again, but another couple arrived at the doorstep. As Jamal attended to the new arrivals, we took our leave and moved into the house.

Looking down the hallway leading away from the entry foyer, we found another similarly dressed tribesman. He shook his head when I asked him a question in English. Instead, he simply held out a hand towards the nearby open set of double doors. Holmes repeated his Malay welcome, to which the man's face broke into a wide smile.

As we stepped through, I was simply awestruck. This would be called a ballroom in a country manor house, but here in a simple terraced house it was something else entirely. The room stretched from the entrance hallway all the way to the far end of the third house. On one side a series of bay windows looked out across the gardens and onto the street, while on the other a succession of small alcoves had been created, with curtains hanging in front of doorways exiting the room.

I wasn't an architect by any measure, but I could see that as part of the expansion, the supporting walls between each house had been removed – something that I presumed would be extremely dangerous to the structural integrity of the floors above. "Holmes?" I asked my friend, turning to find him likewise studying the grand room.

"Yes, amazing isn't it? An incredible feat of engineering. The man responsible must be congratulated."

"I think you are seeing the room differently from me."

Holmes glanced at me for a moment, and upon seeing my slight discomfort, patted me on the shoulder and began to point out certain aspects of the room. "Fear not. If you look along the lines of the original walls, you can see arches built at the extremities. They meet up with sunken iron beams that virtually replace the function of the old bricks-and-mortar walls." He pointed along the length of the room and I could finally see the series of beams that had been added to strengthen the floor. "It's quite a remarkable design."

"Thank you," came a reply from nearby, "Sir Tristan asked me to help the builder with a new style that would enable the virtual disappearance of the load-bearing walls."

We both turned and found my old friend Lieutenant Willard Kesson standing just slightly behind us, a wide grin on his face.

"Willy!" I almost shouted, delighted to meet my old friend.

He stepped forward and thrust a hand out, grabbing mine and shaking vigorously. "John, it's been far too long! So good to see you again." Before I could introduce him, Kesson turned to Holmes and shook his hand as well. "Mr. Holmes, I am so glad you could make it. Even more pleased that you appreciate all of my designs in this room."

"It is a rather remarkable feat, sir," Holmes replied.

"Lieutenant Willard Kesson, here, was with the Royal Engineers at the Battle of Maiwand."

"Willard is fine if you please. John and I met in the field hospital after I also nearly succumbed to my injuries."

"And you've been in Borneo for the last few years?" asked Holmes.

"Yes. I was recruited by Admiral Mayne, one of the North Borneo Company's directors. They needed engineers, and the Admiral wanted servicemen due to their diligence and perseverance. Plus, the warm weather is kinder on my injured leg."

"What have you been doing over there, Willy?" I asked.

"Ah, John, some amazing things. The North Borneo Chartered Company, as it is rightly called, was set up in competition to the East India Company. The Directors have been given the rights to investigate and exploit the resources available in the country."

"I'm intrigued," said Holmes. "What resources exactly?"

"Well, to begin with foodstuffs, and animal and plant goods, but there are moves afoot to investigate any mineral finds that we can unearth." Kesson indicated the room before us. "That's what tonight is all about. A first introduction to some of the produce, animals, and cultural artifacts that are on offer in Borneo. Sir Tristan has brought some of the local tribesmen with him, and a range of foodstuffs and produce to tempt the

93

British Trade Commission, in the hopes of garnering further financial support and setting up future trade routes."

"Doesn't really sound like any of that is within your area of expertise," I said. "What do you do with your time and intellect?"

"That's where it is interesting," Kesson said. "The Admiral sent me out to Borneo with the intention of assisting with a way of bringing fresh food all the way from the East Indies to England. My first stop was in Australia where I met with a man called James Harrison, who had invented an ice-making machine. I brought his design and manufacturing techniques back to Borneo, and using his initial design, I've improved it to a point where we can install the machine onto a ship and create ice at will, ensuring that any food shipped across the globe will be kept frozen or chilled for the entire journey."

"Marvellous," I said.

Kesson indicated the various displays and offerings around the room with a sweep of his hand. "What's on show tonight are some of the tastiest delicacies and intriguing objects of interest that we've discovered so far in Borneo." We stepped into the room, following Kesson as he led us around the various exhibits.

Following his movements, my eyes fell on several distinct areas. In one small alcove, one of the tribesman stood with an orange-haired orangutan on a stand. "We brought in another female," Kesson explained, "as a donation to London Zoo to assist with their breeding program." Nearby was a table with an aquarium sitting on top. Inside, a long blue snake, with black stripes and a tiny swatch of yellow around its mouth, swam around. Its wide black eyes seemed to be fixed on my own as it moved. "This is the yellow-lipped sea krait," said Kesson, leaning in close to the aquarium. The snake jerked back before striking forward and smacking into the glass. "Quite deadly – and aggressive, as you can see. We did bring a breeding pair, but sadly one of them died on the voyage."

Not far from the aquarium was a six-foot-tall cage, with a wide-eyed animal, reminiscent of a small lemur, clinging desperately to a cut-down tree branch. "Ah, this cute little creature is locally called a cuscus. Again, we wanted to have a breeding pair, but thought best to settle this little one in first and bring another on the next journey."

As we stepped away from the cuscus, we were approached by a tribesman carrying a large silver platter, covered in chips of ice and topped with orange-and-white striped morsels of prawn meat. "Now this is special," said Kesson, picking one of the prawns from the tray with his fingers and biting into it with pleasure. "These are a large type of prawn caught off the coast of Borneo. We cooked and then froze them for transportation, ready to be thawed and consumed. You really should try some." He waved a hand at some of the other men holding serving platters. "We also have crayfish meat, brought over the same way, and some wonderful fruits, like jackfruit and rambutans. The fruit itself wasn't frozen, but stored in a chilled room to ensure that it was kept fresh."

I did as Kesson said and, using a small plate and fork offered to me by the tribesman, plucked one of the prawns from the tray and experimentally bit into the fleshier end. The meat was exquisite, the consistency of succulent chicken, but with a saltier, light fish taste to it. The morsel also had a slight smell to it, which remained on the plate afterwards, making me glad I had used the fork. "My word," I exclaimed, "that is indeed delicious."

"So it isn't just the food that your company is promoting," said Holmes, "but also the freezing technology?"

"Indeed it is, sir. The modifications I've made to Harrison's design could revolutionise food transport and open up the world."

Just as I was about to ask another question, a tall, immaculately dressed man entered with a much more demure lady by his side. Holmes leaned in and said, "Our host, I think."

Indeed, Sir Tristan Leavins, with his wife Blanche close by his side, made such a grand couple as they worked their way around the room that I almost forgot about the wonderful fare on offer and the fabulous beasts and items on display.

As they finally approached, Kesson introduced us. Usually upon the mention of Holmes's name, people's faces light up with recognition and they begin to deluge him with questions aplenty. Sir Tristan's face was placid and engaging, but it was as if he'd never heard of Holmes. Lady Blanche was another matter. She gushed with enthusiasm and asked him all manner of trivial questions about some of his adventures. Sir Tristan moved off, leaving his wife to interrogate Holmes for a few moments before finally signalling her to join him and make the acquaintance of a couple across the room.

Turning to Holmes, I asked, "Do you think Sir Tristan was purposely rude, or did he actually not know who you are?"

"Well, given that the man has spent several years in Asia, building up the presence of his company, he may not have had a chance to peruse *The Strand*, unlike his London-based wife."

Nodding, I retorted, "Well, that would be fair. For a moment, I thought my writing had lost its touch." I searched for Kesson and found him munching on another prawn, smacking his fingers afterwards. I started to ask a question when a young man in his early thirties, with the tanned skin of someone that spends much of his time outside, stepped up beside Holmes and spoke quietly into his ear at the same moment. Kesson quickly excused himself, stating that he was needed to see to the ice machine and would return once the problem was resolved.

Holmes and I amused ourselves by trying the crayfish meat and fruits on offer. Each was a delight and pleasure to the senses. Sating our appetite, we moved around the room and examined the special items that were displayed. Most were collections of weaponry, supposedly from the Bornean tribes during their pre-colonial state. One display contained several long wooden spears, and another a collection of short wooden, stone, and even iron knives. One of the most fascinating was a set of blowpipes, ranging in size and intricacy. There were five in all, starting at six inches in length, and growing to almost a yard.

In a small dish below the rack of blowpipes were a selection of actual darts used in the pipes. They were about three inches long, consisting of a slender needle for the most part and a thicker cone-shaped section at the end. I assumed that the thicker part pressed against the sides of the pipe, with the needle penetrating the skin of the animal or man. A small card explained that the darts were generally dipped in poison to incapacitate or kill the intended target.

I turned to ask Holmes's thoughts, but found that he'd wandered away and was engaged in conversation with a couple across the room. Glancing back, I began to examine the longest blow pipe again. I was fascinated by both the simplicity and complexity of such a weapon. As I leaned in to look closer at the mouth piece, a male voice spoke over my shoulder.

"Pick it up if you like," he said.

Standing nearby was an elderly gentleman. Although succumbing to a slight arch in his back, he stood as ramrod straight as he was able. "There's no mistaking a fellow military man," I said, holding out my hand, "I'm Dr. John Watson, formerly of the Fifth Northumberland Fusiliers, and then with the Berkshires at Maiwand."

The older gent took my hand and shook it firmly. A small smile crept to his face. "Rear-Admiral Richard Mayne, formerly of Her Majesty's Royal Navy. Now I simply sit on the board of this damn company."

"Very pleased to meet you, sir. I am a good friend of one of your employees – Lieutenant Willard Kesson."

"Ah, Kesson. Good man. Brilliant mind. I recruited him myself, you know. Was in the Royal Engineers. His superiors were very impressed. Sad that he was injured at Maiwand, though. Has been doing some great things in Borneo the past few years. That ice-making machine is a stroke of genius. His ingenuity will bring millions into the company. He'll be well rewarded for his efforts, but," the Admiral's face turned slightly dour, "I'm afraid that he wants more than just money."

"I don't follow, sir."

"Power, my boy! Power. Too many people want power for power's sake. Kesson will go far, but it will take time. This company has been built on reputation more than genius." Turning, he pointed towards Sir Tristan. "Kesson needs to build up his own status, like Leavins over there. For the North Borneo Chartered Company to grow, we need people who can present to Parliament and Governments around the world. That requires status. We only put Knights of the Realm or highly ranked military men in such positions." He stood for a moment and stared at the blowpipes, gathering both his thoughts and breath. "Kesson has time. His brilliance will shine through. He just needs time."

The Admiral reached for the longest blowpipe and passed it to me. "Though genius can sometimes come undone. Even something as elegant and deadly as this weapon is no match for a good soldier with a gun."

Examining the blowpipe, I was still impressed with the design. Looking down its length, I was unsure whether the tribesmen had hollowed out a straight length of wood or used something of a natural occurrence. It was light, and I could only assume that the length gave the projectile a much truer flight. When I turned back to remark to the Admiral, he was gone, almost as if he had never been there in the first place.

Replacing the blowpipe, I moved past the animals again, smiling at the huge eyes of the cuscus and the ancient looking face of the orangutan before joining Holmes and being introduced to the couple with whom he conversed.

After a few moments of answering questions, I chanced a glance across the room and noticed Sir Tristan and his wife speaking with another couple. They stood in a small alcove on the other side of the room not far from the racks of weapons. As I turned back, my eyes darted to the sharp movement of Sir Tristan's hand as it slapped at the back of his neck. I could have sworn he mouthed the word "Mosquito". At the time I thought nothing of it, amused by the idea that there would be any mosquitoes inside a Kensington residence, but I supposed at the height of summer, with Hyde Park not that far away, it was a possibility.

Re-joining the conversation around me, I found myself once again plied with questions about Holmes's adventures. I was, however, delighted when Kesson stepped up next to me. He leant in and whispered. "John, can you come with me? Sir Tristan has taken ill." I glanced over at the alcove where I had last seen our host and found it empty.

"Do you know what's wrong?"

"He fell faint, and it was only fortunate that another man caught him before he collapsed to the ground. He's been taken into a nearby room and laid on a settee. When I left, he was unconscious."

Holmes noticed our conversation and made his excuses as Kesson and I stepped away, joining us as we exited the large room and came upon the small crowd surrounding Sir Tristan.

I hurried up to the reclining man and ushered the others away. "Please, I'm a doctor. Give this man some space and air to breath." Kneeling down, I felt Sir Tristan's brow. His temperature was elevated, leading to my first thought that he had simply been overcome by the heat of the occasion. Glancing around, I noticed a maid servant standing nearby. I implored her to retrieve a cloth and some cold water.

"Would ice be better?" Kesson asked.

"Much."

"See to it, Gwendolyn." The young girl disappeared.

"What's wrong with him?" my friend asked.

"I think he has simply been overcome. I do wish I had my bag. I'd like to check his heart." Dismissing any propriety, I reached down and undid the neck of Sir Tristan's shirt and loosened his tie. Touching my fingers to his neck, I counted the rate of his pulse. It seemed to be slowing. I hoped that meant that he was relaxing after a mild case of anxiety.

I was so wrong.

Suddenly, Sir Tristan's body arched from the settee. His arms and legs twitched, his eyes snapped open, with the whites showing. Frothy drool gathered at his lips and streamed from his mouth.

Frantically, I glanced around at the nearby audience. "He's having a seizure. I need something small and hard – a spoon, fork, or knife. Quickly now!" It was Holmes that found a letter opener with a thick wooden handle on a nearby desk. Snatching it from him, I tried to prize the man's mouth open, so I could slide it above his tongue, but as quickly as the seizure started it stopped.

It was then I realised the man in my arms was dead.

Checking his pulse again and finding nothing, I dropped my head in dejection. I hadn't realised who was still in the room, but regretted my actions when Sir Tristan's wife cried out in despair. "No! No! Tristan – *No!*"

Kesson went straight to the stricken woman and organised someone to take her from the room. My last sight was of the look of hopelessness on her face as her eyes stared at the corpse of her husband. Others were ushered out until it was only Holmes, me, and the corpse.

"If I'd had my bag," I spat, "I could have saved him." A hand patted me on the shoulder. Turning I gazed up into Holmes's stoic expression.

"You did everything you could, given the circumstances – more than anybody else could do." I realised his eyes lay on the corpse, rather than on my face. As always, he was searching for clews. "I have my opinions, but from what do you believe he died?"

Staring back at the poor dead man before me, I answered, "Until a police surgeon investigates, we won't have a solid answer. It could have been anything – a heart attack. A stroke. An epileptic fit. Perhaps a reaction to something."

"You may be onto something with that." Moving closer to Sir Tristan, Holmes bent over and began examining the corpse.

I must have been weary, as I snapped at him, "Come, Holmes! A man has just died. In all likelihood it was natural. Not everything need be suspicious."

"That may be so, but until everything is eliminated, I will never drop my scepticism." He proceeded to kneel, examining him before gently lifting the man's head to reveal a small, dried blood-spot on the back of Sir Tristan's neck. "Now that is interesting."

Looking with weary eyes, I realised the spot was where I had seen Sir Tristan slap, only minutes ago. "That was where it looked as if the mosquito bit him . . . ." But I was also recalling something else that I'd seen not long before – at the beginning of my conversation with Admiral Mayne.

Holmes glanced around at me, a look of surprise on his face. "Mosquito?" Nodding, I explained what I had observed earlier. His eyes drifted away as some inner thoughts began to run. Reaching into his pocket, he withdrew his magnifying glass. Smiling at my look of shock, he said, "Always come prepared, Watson. Always come prepared."

I thought his comment a little rough, given my wish to have my doctor's bag at my side, but left it at that.

"Help me roll him on his side." I did as asked and watched Holmes study the small blood spot with great interest. "What do you make of this?" he said. He pulled away, leaving his glass hovering over the spot. Leaning in for a closer look, I noticed the blood spot was a lot larger than a simple mosquito bite. There was also a dried crust around the area. It was difficult to tell colour in the dull light of the room, but it looked cream or light yellow in tone. Definitely not a normal bodily fluid from such a wound.

"I have no idea, but whatever that dried substance is, I don't think it came from Sir Tristan."

"My thoughts precisely. Now where was he when you saw the mosquito bite him?"

I described the alcove again – and the fact that there were blowpipes on display. Holmes was away within seconds. I was in two minds whether to follow or stay with the corpse until Kesson returned with help. There was nothing more that I could do for the dead man. Since he was beyond

99

help and wasn't going anywhere in a hurry, I rolled him again onto his back and placed his hands on his chest. To anyone else he would look as if he was simply reposing.

Moving into the ballroom, I was surprised to find it empty of people and animals. I assumed that Kesson had sent word throughout the room that their host and hostess were indisposed and informed all to vacate the premises. I noticed that the racks of weapons remained, presumably to be removed at a later date.

I found Holmes on his hands and knees, studying the floor near where I had seen Sir Tristan supposedly bitten by an insect. "What the devil are you looking for?"

"Clews."

Remaining on his knees, Holmes looked at me and held up a small object. "I don't wish to suppose yet, but I'm beginning to paint a picture in my mind."

"Is that what I think it is?"

Holding the object between thumb and forefinger, he looked at it through his glass. "It appears to be small and cone-shaped, possibly made of wood or bamboo. There is a tiny indentation in the centre of the pointed end."

I noted that it very much resembled one of the darts that had been near the blow-pipes.

"This is where it lay," he said, pointing to a small, discoloured area on the dark wooden floor. From where I stood it was either off-white or a light yellow in colour.

"Is that – ?"

"The same substance as we found on Sir Tristan's neck? It may well be." Holmes leaned in closer with his glass to study the substance again. "We shall need to examine it further, and possibly run a chemical test, but given the colour, consistency, and location, I am fairly certain they're one and the same."

"Any conjecture on what it could be?"

"No, but let us look amongst the weapons." In just a moment, we confirmed that the largest blowpipe was missing.

"The one I picked up and examined," I added.

Holmes gave the vacant spot a cursory glance before picking up one of the darts and holding both it and his prize next to each other at eye level. The small conical object that Holmes had found was identical, although the needle was missing from the base of the dart.

I commented on that fact. "Do you think that it fell out?"

"I didn't find a needle anywhere." He placed the dart in one of the small envelopes that he habitually carried. "I think this is our mosquito."

"Perhaps the needle was caught in Sir Tristan's clothing."

That sly grin grew on Holmes's face. "Perhaps. That would be one answer, but there's another I'd like to investigate."

"These darts are generally tipped with poison. It seems likely that this is what happened to Sir Tristan."

"I'm not prepared to say anything at this stage, but I want to eliminate as much uncertainty as I can." Turning to face me, Holmes asked, "Think back on Sir Tristan's symptoms before his unfortunate demise."

"He fell faint and reportedly passed out."

"Yes, and when you were attending him?"

"He was unresponsive. His heartbeat was slow, but erratic, then finally he had a seizure before expiring. Everything happened so quickly."

"Yes. Not the sort of thing I would have thought could be attributed to a simple heart attack or apoplexy."

"True, but poison? Cyanide or even arsenic wouldn't affect someone in that way. Plus, they are much slower."

"What about some poison that attacks the central nervous system?"

"Well, I suppose, but where would someone obtain something so toxic?"

Holmes pointed behind me. As I turned, my eyes fell on the slowly moving solitary sea krait in its aquarium. "Good Lord? But how? I'm not even sure how to extract the venom from such a dangerous animal."

"Ah, but if you recall, there were originally two."

"Of course. If you removed the poison glands, you could extract the venom, and even concentrate it. That would make it more deadly."

"Something, I think, that the Bornean tribesmen have been doing for centuries."

"What have the Bornean tribesmen been doing?" asked a voice from behind us. We both turned to find Kesson standing nearby.

"Watson and I were just ruminating on the use of blowpipes by primitive tribesman in Borneo."

"That's a strange thing to be talking about moments after a man has died." Kesson's face was stern, almost brimming with anger at our indifference, until his eyes grew wide. "You don't think Sir Tristan was killed by poison?"

I chipped in to try and guide Kesson's thought patterns in a different direction. "We were simply passing the time until the authorities arrive."

It was then that my old friend noticed the objects in Holmes's hands. "Those are blowpipe darts." His eyes rose to Holmes's face, and then to mine. "You *do* think Sir Tristan was poisoned, don't you?" Turning his head, he glanced at the empty spot in the rack nearby. "One is missing. Those cursed tribesmen! I knew they were a foolish idea." Without waiting, Kesson stormed from the room. I started after him, but Holmes placed a hand on my shoulder to stop me.

"Stay, Watson. With the Lieutenant out of the way, we can investigate further in peace."

Understanding my associate's desire, a niggle of doubt surfaced in my mind regarding Kesson's possible future actions. Turning those thoughts more towards things at hand, I glanced around to see what Holmes was up to.

He stood, hands on hips, near the alcove where the blowpipe dart had been found. As I stepped up next to him, he remarked, "I need you to do something for me."

"Yes?"

"Can you stand in the spot that you saw Sir Tristan when he was bitten?"

"Certainly." I stepped back a few strides and studied the area for a moment, whilst replaying as many of my memories of the event as I could. I then strode forward and stood in the posture of our host, as best as I could remember.

"Excellent," said Holmes. "Now stay still for me." He was silent for a while as he continued to stare, first at me, then at the small stain on the floor, before I heard him step away across the room. I chanced a glance over my shoulder to see him searching behind the curtains at the other end of the room. Finally, he expressed an "A-ha!" Checking my position and location, I broke away and hurried to see what had piqued his interest.

There, behind one of the heavy drapes, and propped up against the wall, was the missing blowpipe. I glanced across to where I'd previously stood and judged the distance to be some fifteen yards. "That would be a remarkable shot."

"Yes. I can only presume that whomever made it was quite conversant with the use of these blowpipes and had many years of practice."

"Oh, surely not one of the tribesmen?"

Standing, Holmes replied, "I will wait to answer that question." Pushing aside the curtain, he stepped through the doorway behind. Following, we found ourselves in a small, dark anteroom that led further into the bowels of the house. I pushed on and found an exit door that opened into a passageway leading through to the rear of the building.

Returning, I found Holmes holding a small silver dish. "What have you there?"

Pulling the draw-cord for the drapes and parting them to let light from the main room enter, I saw that the dish held two of the cone-shaped darts. They floated in a small puddle of coloured liquid, along with several chunks of ice.

"These are the ammunition for that blowpipe," Holmes said.

"But aren't those simply the larger cones? There are no needles – they simply wouldn't fly."

"Ah, there are needles – or at least there *were* needles, I believe."

"I don't follow."

"The day has been hot, has it not?" I nodded. "There are small bits of ice floating in this dish of water. I would conjecture that originally the dish was full of small chunks of ice, used to keep something cold – the needles of several blowdarts – perhaps formed of ice themselves."

"Incredible."

"Quite so. And quite ingenious. If one could create needles from ice, they would remain intact for the immediate purpose, and then melt away to nothing more than liquid in a matter of minutes or even seconds. The only remains would be the conical end used to stabilise the dart during flight – something so small and trivial that most people would dismiss one as merely a piece of detritus and not give it another thought."

"Devilish. If the needles were formed from pure venom, then they would be deadly. The tip would penetrate far enough to break off inside the skin and deliver a dose of poison directly into the blood stream. Death would almost be a certainty."

"Exactly."

A voice floated to use from across the room. "John? Are you still here?"

I stepped out through the curtains and found Kesson standing in the alcove leading through to where the unfortunate Sir Tristan lay. "Willard, over here."

"Good, good." He approached, his eyes darting to where the curtains were gently moving after Holmes had dropped them back in place. "The police and the surgeon are here. As you were the doctor that pronounced Sir Tristan dead, they would like to talk with you."

"Of course, of course." I glanced around before following Kesson, but there was no sign of Holmes.

Behind the curtains we found a sorrowful looking man in his late fifties and a pair of young bobbies. All were staring down at the reposing form of Sir Tristan. The older man, whom I guessed to be the police surgeon, glanced across at us as we entered. Kesson quickly introduced us, and the man plied me with questions that I duly answered.

"Hmm," he said. "Based on so little, I can only conclude that it was natural, but I will have to investigate further back at the morgue. Thank you for being so diligent and thoughtful, Doctor Watson. Sir Tristan might have been saved if you'd had your medical bag, but given the rapidity with which he passed, I sincerely doubt it. Death appears to have been sudden, and probable."

"One thing you may wish to undertake is an analysis of the blood."

"What am I looking for?"

"A poison."

"What?"

"Possibly from snake venom."

"Surely you're joking! How would this man have been bitten by a snake in this environment?"

"Well, there was a live sea krait in an aquarium, but we don't believe that's how the venom entered his system."

"We?"

"My associate and I – Mr. Sherlock Holmes."

The old surgeon's eyes went wide. "You're *that* Doctor Watson?" I nodded in answer. "Do strange deaths just follow you around?"

"It does seem that way. Regardless, we have no solid proof as yet, but there are indications that this man has been the victim of foul play. The small mark on his neck. The dry crust around it. The seizure he had just before expiring. Holmes is working on other evidence as we speak, but it would add to our store of knowledge if you could undertake further investigation of this poor man."

He nodded. "I thought this would be a simple case, but you're right. I'll do as you say before writing up the certificate."

"Thank you. I'm sure we'll be in touch if we have anything more, either directly or through Scotland Yard."

Kesson seemed to have lost all interest in overseeing his former employer's corpse and had taken on an air of agitation. Standing in the doorway, he indicated that I should follow. As I joined him in the adjoining corridor, he turned and said, "I think I have our man!"

Slightly stunned, I simply trailed behind him as he wound his way through the house and down into a dimly lit area of the large basement.

There, one of the Borneo tribesmen sat on a straight-backed chair. Another man, apparently some sort of assistant to Kesson, stood behind him, an indifferent look on his face, but bearing a posture said he was ready to pounce if the man in the chair even moved.

The tribesman's face bore all the hallmarks of someone frightened out of his wits. His eyes were wide, and darted between Kesson and myself upon our entry.

Taking a long look at the frightened Bornean, I asked, "Why?"

"What do you mean?"

"Why would this man have killed Sir Tristan? Motive is generally the first thing that Holmes establishes when faced with a puzzle such as this."

Kesson stared at me for a moment and then approached the tribesman. Leaning in he asked a question in Malay, which was followed by a fearful response. Standing, Kesson crossed his arms and glared at the man in anger. "I asked why he murdered Sir Tristan. His response was that we British must be killed because we invaded Borneo."

Leaning in close to the man's face, Kesson spoke another long string of Malay, which was followed by an equally long response, the man's mouth turned down in a grimace of absolute fear. "He is part of a Labuan resistance group who have sworn to destroy our company." Turning towards the man standing nearby, Kesson added, "Anderson, make sure he doesn't move. I'll bring the constables to take him away." Without another word, Kesson stormed from the room.

Standing for a moment, I stared at the poor tribesman for a while. Even though he didn't seem to speak English, his face spoke volumes. To me, this man wasn't someone fighting for a cause. He was simply a lone man, a long way from home, in a truly alien world. Glancing at Anderson, I asked, "Do you believe any of what Willard just said?"

Anderson looked my way, shrugged, and said, "I'm not paid to think, sir. Simply to do. If Mr. Kesson believes this man is responsible for Sir Tristan's murder, then I believe what Mr. Kesson believes."

A very convenient way of thinking.

"I personally don't believe a single word of what your friend said," came a voice from the shadows. The tall form of Sherlock Holmes appeared from the gloom. He still held the long blowpipe, and I noticed the shorter form of Jamal, the man who had greeted us at the front door upon our arrival, appear behind and followed him into the light. The Borneo tribesman still wore his ceremonial dress, but his smile had disappeared to be replaced by a dour look on his face. Indicating the seated man, Holmes said, "This man is innocent."

"How so? What further evidence have you found?"

"I'll get to that, but from what I overheard in the conversation between him and Kesson, I'm afraid that your friend is lying."

"How did you understand what they were saying? I didn't think you spoke Malay."

"Well, I don't very well, but I have studied."

"When?"

"The other night, after you received your invitation. Why? Didn't you?"

I gave Holmes a withering look before noticing movement as Jamal stepped over to the man and said, "Lian?" He followed up with a few words in Malay. Lian, the other tribesman, responded with his own string of sentences.

Finally, Jamal turned towards Holmes. "Lian, my friend here, he says that Mr. Kesson asked him to – how you say? – play a trick on Sir Tristan." Lian spoke further, with Jamal simply listening for a moment. "Yes, it was to show how the blowpipes work. The darts were only ice. Harmless. Mr. Kesson made them."

Holmes addressed Jamal, "I assume that Lian here was asked to hide behind the curtains and shoot one of Mr. Kesson's supposedly harmless darts into Sir Tristan's neck?" Jamal spoke to Lian who simply nodded. "The problem being that Kesson's darts were poisonous."

"What do you mean 'Kesson's darts were poisonous'?"

We all turned to the source of the voice. The man who until that point I had thought of as a friend stood in the entranceway, the two police constables standing behind him.

"Ah," said Holmes. "Just the person, I think."

"Why?" Stepping into the room, Kesson's eyes fell on Jamal. "And what is he doing here?"

"Jamal here has been helping us speak with Lian, your chosen perpetrator."

"What? He can't speak English. None of them can."

"Ah, that isn't quite true, sir," said Anderson, his face a slight shade of red from embarrassment at contradicting his superior. "Jamal's English is quite limited, but effective. That's why I placed him on door duty."

"But he's obviously lying, just like this one," Kesson retorted, pointing at the seated man. "They're all in it together. We've been defending ourselves from their type for years."

"What do you mean by 'their type', Willard?" I asked.

"The insurgents. The resistance. They've obviously infiltrated the locals that we employ in the company, to get what they've always wanted. To kill Sir Tristan – or any of us, for that matter."

Turning towards Anderson, I asked, "Is this true? Have you been struggling against these terrorists?"

Anderson's eyes grew wide. They darted towards Kesson, who scowled at his underling, then to the policemen, then to Holmes, and finally back to me. His head began to shake slowly from side to side. A growl rose from Kesson. "Anderson, remember for whom you work." The younger man's gaze rushed back to Kesson's.

"I'm sorry, sir. I cannot lie. Not about this. Not with Sir Tristan dead. Especially if you are involved."

"Anderson . . . ." Kesson's voice rose in pitch and volume. His face flushed red with anger.

"No. I can't. There is no resistance. We've been at peace with the local tribes for years. They've never had it so good. Our company has

106

furnished them with clothes, food, housing, and employment. Brought them out of their primitive ways and into the Nineteenth Century. They love us." His face turned towards Jamal. "Isn't that right, Jamal?"

"Yes, sir. It is. We would never wish harm on the white men."

All eyes turned back to Kesson. His own grew wide. "What? What am I supposed to have done? I have done nothing. If I have, where is your proof?"

"Ah, proof," said Holmes. "Let me replay the facts for our constables here. One: Sir Tristan Leavins died earlier tonight, from a suspected heart attack, but more likely from the poison of the yellow-lipped sea krait. Two: This tribesman was coerced to unknowingly deliver the fatal dose of poison, using a primitive blowpipe, armed with darts made from frozen krait poison."

"Ridiculous!" cried Kesson. "That would be impossible."

"Except for the fact that you are a genius at ice making and refrigeration," answered Holmes, bringing a small metallic object from his pocket, and holding it before him. He broke the object apart, showing it to be a solid metal mould. "I visited your ingenious ice making machine, and the little work space you created nearby. This was simply sitting on the bench. It is a mould that can be used to create extremely delicate needles of ice." Pointing to a set of small conical cavities at one end, he said, "You can place a cone shaped dart stabiliser in here, then pour liquid here, ready for freezing. And, *voilà*, ice darts ready for use in a blowpipe. Though you must be quick, or else they melt, as Watson and I discovered, when we found a dish with the remains of two darts and the ice that kept them chilled."

"That could have been used to make ice for drinks," Kesson countered.

"Perhaps, but the other mould I found inside a refrigeration unit upstairs would contradict that. It contained three cone-shaped moulds that still had traces upon them of a light-yellow liquid, seemingly formed into highly lethal poison darts."

"What liquid?"

"This liquid," said Holmes, holding up a small glass vial half-filled with a light-yellow liquid, "It was in a drawer attached to the work bench. I'm sure if we have it analysed, it will prove to be sea krait venom."

"Where would that come from?" Kesson demanded.

"From the poison sac of a certain yellow-lipped sea krait that expired on the journey from Borneo, most likely."

"But what possible reason could I have to orchestrate all of this? I was recruited personally to this company. I've worked diligently for years. I'm in charge of the entire engineering team in North Borneo."

107

"I think I can answer that," I said. All eyes turned my way. "I met Admiral Mayne. He was very complimentary of you, but was a little concerned about your ambitions – ambitions that he believed might never be realised."

"What? What do you mean? I was virtually second-in-charge to Sir Tristan."

"From the Admiral's words, it seems that the company only promotes self-made men of station or with high military ranks into the top echelon of the company. He suggested that you could gain a higher level if you established yourself outside of the company or gained a title or honour."

"That old fool! When I was hired, he promised me a long and industrious career. I could take them far. My inventions will open new trade routes and bring millions into the company's coffers. But I can't do that as just as an underling, I need the power to direct the operations of the company. Sir Tristan was a blind fool, with no foresight. The company is better off this way."

"Does that mean you eliminated him for just that purpose?"

"What? No. I had nothing to do with this. Everything you have said is just circumstantial. You have no solid proof."

"Oh, I wouldn't say that," said a familiar voice from the doorway. Glancing across, I saw the short frame of a man whom we knew, filling the doorway. "In fact, from what I've just heard, I think the Yard could build quite a case against you, Mr. Kesson."

"Who are you?" said Kesson, his voice rising close to a yell.

"Inspector Lestrade, Scotland Yard, at your service," our colleague said, with a wry smile on his lips. Turning towards the two constables, he said, "You two, take Mr. Kesson here up to the wagon parked outside. Hold him for murder, and I'll interview him when I return."

The constables, each took hold of one of Kesson's arms.

"Anderson," said Kesson, "I need the company's solicitor. They'll have me out in a moment."

"Yes, sir, but I don't think the board will be very happy. They have very strict rules about the consequences of any improprieties of senior staff members – even where the person has only been charged, but the charges are overturned later. They simply do not tolerate any sullying of a person's reputation."

Kesson's face dropped as Anderson's words sunk in. "No! I've done nothing." The two policemen led him struggling and yelling from the room. I could hear his proclamations of innocence all the way down the corridor and up the stairs to the ground floor.

When all was quite once again, Lestrade turned to face Holmes and said, "I received your message. I'd already heard about the poor unfortunate Sir Tristan, so now you'd better fill me in on the rest of this case."

It was several days later, whilst I was finishing my breakfast coffee and reading the morning paper, that Mrs. Hudson brought Lestrade into the sitting room.

"Good morning, Doctor. I just wanted to drop by and give you and Mr. Holmes an update on this Sir Tristan Leavins business."

"Excellent," said Holmes stepping into the room. "I'd been wondering how you'd got on." He walked across to the table, sat down, and poured himself a cup of coffee. I offered Lestrade a cup, but he declined.

"It didn't take long, but this Kesson fellow broke down after a few facts came to light. The police surgeon was quick. He found traces of poison in Sir Tristan's blood and labelled the cause of death as such. He also identified the liquid in the yellow bottle as krait venom. That, linked to the frozen darts, and a full version of events from Lian, the Borneo tribesman, confirms everything."

"How did you get more information out of Lian?" Holmes asked. "We only had Jamal to translate, and while his English is good, it probably isn't good enough for that purpose."

"There was a Professor of Asiatic dialects at London University who is fluent in Malay. He was good enough to sit in with us and interpret."

"Has Willard been charged with murder then?" I asked, my heart heavy at the thought of Kesson's imminent fate.

"Yes. I know he was an army friend of yours, Doctor, but murder is murder, and it is especially heinous when the reason is for personal gain."

"He'll hang then, won't he?"

"Oh, yes. I can't see any other eventuality than that. Again, I'm sorry."

When the inspector had gone, Holmes glanced my way and spoke. "I, too, am sorry. We make far too few good friends in our lives. To find one that has transgressed the law in such a calculated way and used the ignorance of someone so innocent as a primitive tribesman is especially galling. You have my sympathies."

"Thank you, but I find that with all that we've discussed about this man, I can neither condone his actions, nor indeed regard him as a friend after such. My only hope is that the poor tribesmen that were caught up in this are treated properly and taken home quickly and with a minimum of fuss."

"That would be a proper conclusion to this adventure," Holmes said, sipping his coffee.

The Adventure of the
White Roses
by Tracy J. Revels

"**M**y fiancé tells me that I am being overwrought, perhaps even a bit hysterical, Mr. Holmes. Yet, I know what I saw and what I heard. It is too late to do my poor father, or Mr. Latham, any good – but perhaps you can save their friend, who I believe is in great danger."

These words were spoken by a small, rather plain young woman swathed in mourning. Her raised veil revealed a simple face, with wide eyes and a firm, hard mouth. She had introduced herself as Miss Sarah Gibbons, daughter of the late Professor Sterling Gibbons of Essex College. Though far from beautiful, or even memorable in her face and figure, there was such a determined quality to her words that my friend could hardly refuse to hear her story.

"Your father authored a book on the Great Rebellion in America, did he not?"

Our visitor gave a little smile of pride. "He did indeed, Mr. Holmes. His specialty was the history of the American nation. Father and his friends were in America during that war. Let me show you." She produced a small photograph in a leather frame. It showed three dashing young men lounging around an encampment, smoking cigars and playing cards, as if they were blissfully unaware of the great struggle all around them.

"They do not appear to be soldiers," I observed.

"Mr. Colin Latham was a photographer. My father was a writer, and Sir Howard Blakely was . . . I suppose 'adventurer' might be the word for it. They thought it would be thrilling to see the great conflict at close range. Father hoped to write a book, and Mr. Latham to sell his pictures. Sir Howard?" The lady shrugged. "There was some falling out among them after they returned to England. I have never met Sir Howard, but Mr. Latham lived in a secluded cottage on the ocean, just a few miles from our village.

"Father had retired from his college. Five years ago, he and my mother were in a terrible carriage accident, which she did not survive, and which left Father badly crippled. Shortly afterward, Father was diagnosed with consumption and told he must have sea air to survive. After that, Father tutored a handful of village lads, but otherwise our life was quiet and uneventful. That is, until recently."

The lady shivered, despite the warmth of the rooms.

110

"I have thought of little besides the events of the last months, but I have no wish to recount them unless I am certain that you will hear my case."

"We are all attention," Holmes said.

"It was the first of March when my father received a letter that upset him. It came in the post, but I couldn't tell you anything about it, as I attached no special significance to it. Father was sitting at his desk, working his way through the mail, and I was seated in a chair not five feet away, when I heard him give a horrible gasp. I turned to find his face as pale was death.

"'Papa, what is wrong?' I asked.

"He would not reply. Before I could rise from my chair, he took the letter and the envelope and consigned them both to the fire. He staggered back to his seat and slumped forward on his desk. I was ready to shout for our housekeeper to send for the doctor, but he caught my wrist. His hand was ever so cold.

"'Sarah, no, it is nothing. Now, child, please – bring me some brandy and leave me. I must finish my letters.'

"I had no wish to depart, but he was most insistent. The brandy seemed to restore him, and I removed myself only as far as my room and listened quite intently, so that I could run to his aid if needed. By supper, he was more himself."

"And you never learned the subject of the letter?"

"Father never spoke of it again, though from that day forward he became much more cautious. When we walked to church on the Sabbath, his eyes would dart about, and he was much more nervous than I could ever recall. But I had become engaged the previous Christmas, and there were times when I assumed Papa's nerves were nothing more than distress over my coming marriage.

"Then, in mid-April, Mr. Latham arrived. We had not seen him since New Year's Day. I was just leaving for the market, with a basket over my arm, when he came stomping up the lane like some kind of human locomotive. He was a short, stout man, with great grizzled side-whiskers, and a large high hat. As he drew closer, I saw that his face was red, and he was clutching a letter in his hand."

"'Why, Mr. Latham, whatever brings you here?' I asked.

"'I must speak with your father, immediately. Is he about?'

"I directed him to the study. He rushed by me without another word – he had always been an eccentric, strange man, a confirmed bachelor and a recluse, but on that morning, he was so uncivil that I was left quite astonished. I followed him into the house. He had already gone up the stairs and was bellowing for my father.

"'For God's sake, man, lower your voice,' Father said. 'Do you want the entire village to hear you?'

"With that, the study door slammed. I shooed away our puzzled housekeeper and tiptoed up the stairs, placing my ear to the portal. My father's tone was soft and low, but I distinctively heard Mr. Latham say, 'So you have had a letter too?' After several minutes, I heard, 'And what of this? Look. I found them scattered all about my house, even on my roof. Tell me how! How can this be?' There was furious pacing and more indistinct muttering. Mr. Latham shouted, 'Damn Blakely, it was all his fault!' I had just time to jump away from the door before Mr. Latham threw it open and stormed out of our house, uttering the most terrible oaths. He never saw me in the passage and was gone before I could recover my poise."

I found myself caught up in the drama of her story. It was easy to imagine the old village house, the elderly scholar, the strange friend, and the frightened girl. "What did you do?" I asked.

"I waited a few moments, and then I entered the study. Father didn't see me come in, for he was looking out the window, no doubt watching his friend go down the road. My eyes, however, were drawn to something that hadn't been there before – a single white rose upon my father's desk.

"'I fear we must cease our relations with Latham,' Father said, as he turned. 'The man has taken to drink. I hope he was not vulgar to you.'

"'He seemed very upset.'

"Father nodded. 'He has an idea that he is being persecuted. We must not allow his delusions to intrude upon our happiness. Shouldn't you be at the market already?'

"I pointed to the flower on the desk. Father laughed – I tell you that my blood ran cold, for the sound was nothing like his usual mirth. It was hollow and false.

"'Oh, Widow Grimbly gave it to me this morning. What a silly person she is. I think she has it in her head that I will marry her when you are gone. Now run along, child.'

"I couldn't imagine why my father would tell such an atrocious falsehood, but my nerves were so rattled that I left the house and went to see Eddie, my betrothed. He laughed it away.

"'Old men have queer secrets, Dearest. Don't let it worry you.'

"I tried to follow his advice, but a week later Inspector Callahan of Scotland Yard arrived at our door with terrible news that Father's friend had been murdered. Mr. Latham's body had washed up on the shore some ten miles from his seaside cottage."

"And why was his death presumed to be foul play?" Holmes asked.

"Because it was well known, despite his residence near the beach, that Mr. Latham avoided the ocean. He did not sail or fish or swim. When his body was found, it was fully clothed, though so badly battered by the rocks that it was difficult to state what he had died of – whether he had drowned or been harmed in some other way before he was thrown into the waters. And, stranger still, his wallet was found still tucked inside his breast pocket, filled with notes. The inspector wanted to know if Father suspected anyone in the affair. Father said no, but I knew he was not telling the full truth. I walked with the inspector to the gate. Just as he was about to step into his carriage, he mentioned something that nearly caused me to faint.

"'There was one very strange thing about Mr. Latham's home. The place was littered with withered white roses – a hundred or more of them. He must have been an exceptionally fine gardener.'

"Father's behavior became more fearful afterward. It was all I could do to coax him down to take a meal. My maternal aunt, who resides in London, had arranged for me to spend a week shopping for my trousseau. I was reluctant to leave, but Father insisted that I go. After two days, I couldn't stop thinking about him, and I returned home. Our housekeeper met me at the door.

"'Miss Sarah, you must tell your young man to stop it. I know he means well, but it will kill the professor.'

"'What on earth are you talking about?'

"'The roses, Miss! When we awoke this morning, we found roses scattered all about the place – in the yard, the steps, even some down the chimneys. Lovely white roses. I know that your fellow is very romantic, but –'

"Mr. Holmes, no sprinter ever ran faster than I did. Father was in terrible distress. I shut the door and begged him to tell me what this meant. A few times, I thought he would speak, but then the words choked him into silence.

"That was a week ago. For two days, nothing occurred, and Father appeared to rally. A little fair was opening in our village, which Eddie wished to attend. I tried to get Father to come with us, but he insisted he was too old. It was a beautiful day and we had a grand time, enjoying all the treats. There was a dance afterward, so it was nearly midnight before we returned home. Much to my surprise, Father was not in his room, and the housekeeper was already abed. I was alarmed, but then I recalled how often Father had walked across the lane to our neighbor's house and fallen asleep in a chair beside that kind gentleman's fireplace. I was certain he had done so again, and it seemed better to retire than to knock up another household.

113

"The next morning . . . I was awakened by our housekeeper's scream."

The lady's sudden distress at the memory was evident in her face, which had gone ghostly pale. Holmes raised a hand.

"I read of the event in the newspapers – I shall summarize and you may correct me if I err. Your father's body was found beneath a large oak tree in the yard, in the rear of the house. His neck and numerous other bones were broken. The coroner ruled it was a death by misadventure, that your father had climbed the tree and fallen from its branches."

"As if Father were a schoolboy, scampering up to steal robins' eggs!" the young woman wailed. "He was weak, in poor health, and crippled. He certainly could not have climbed a tree, nor jumped to it from a window."

"And there was another discovery. A great deal of money was found in his pockets."

"Yes, nearly two-hundred pounds were stuffed into his clothing. It was almost all of his savings."

"Did you tell the police about the roses?"

Miss Gibbons nodded. "Inspector Callahan came to investigate. He dismissed the roses as a lark, something concocted by Father's pupils to honor my impending nuptials. Afterward, I looked through Father's papers, but there was nothing in them, except . . . Father had a journal from his time in America. I couldn't find it. The housekeeper told me that, while I was at my aunt's, she saw Father destroy it in the fireplace."

Holmes nodded. "As a consequence, you fear for the safety of Sir Howard."

"It is the only connection I can make. Father had so few friends, and I cannot imagine why he would burn his American diary unless there was something in it that was dangerous. Eddie tells I have no right to bother a man of Sir Howard's status, and that he will think me some kind of maniac. Yet at the same time, I would never wish upon his daughter the sorrow that has come upon me."

Holmes rose, extending his hand. "Leave it to us, Miss Gibbons. I did a service for the Blakely family in the past, enough to gain me admittance to Sir Howard's august presence. I will alert him of the danger he's in, and perhaps unravel the mystery of your father's murder in the process."

"It was murder, then."

"Yes, dear lady, I am certain that it was."

Miss Gibbons left our suite with a sorrowful heart, but expressing her great trust in Holmes to bring her father's killer to justice. As her footsteps faded away, my friend lit his pipe and turned to me.

"What do you make of it, Watson?"

"It is clearly a case of blackmail!" I said. "The money in Gibbons' pockets is proof that he hoped to meet his persecutor while his daughter was away and pay him to trouble them no more. One would have thought the villain would have taken the money."

"That the offering remained in the dead men's pockets – for remember that Latham also had substantial cash upon his body – proves blackmail was never the intention," Holmes corrected. "No, our murderer is not motivated by monetary gain. He is out for revenge. This speaks to vengeance."

"For what crime?"

"That we cannot know without more data. Tell me what you make of the roses."

"A warning, of course. A signal of intent, designed to terrorize the victims."

"Excellent. You scintillate today."

"And white roses are the symbol of the House of York!"

Holmes lifted an eyebrow. "Are you accusing Richard III of this crime as well? Isn't it enough that he must take the blame for the deaths of the princes in the Tower upon his rather crooked shoulders?"

"I only mean that this may be related to Gibbons's profession. He was a historian. Perhaps one of his students is at the bottom of this."

"And I will remind you that he was a historian of the *American* experience, not the British."

"Do you have a better interpretation of their meaning?"

"I have none, beside the obvious one – that the roses were designed to alarm the intended victims, that Inspector Callahan is an incompetent oaf, and that whatever the secret was, Professor Gibbons preferred death to its revelation. A few words to his daughter could have saved him, yet he refused to utter the truth. What could be so horrific?" Holmes rose and knocked out his pipe. "It is too late to start for the Blakely seat tonight, but I shall send a telegram and request an audience for tomorrow. Be ready to start at five, Doctor!"

As we made our way toward the little village that was closest to Blakely Manor, Holmes gave me a quick sketch of the family's history, drawn from his voluminous Index. The estate had once numbered in the thousands of acres, but was now reduced to a single manor and its rents. Sir Howard had few accomplishments, but his daughter was a remarkable beauty. The young lady was currently enjoying a splendid Continental debut, accompanied by her mother. The son, only ten years old, was at Eton.

"This is good fortune for us," Holmes said, as we disembarked. "The presence of the womenfolk might complicate a frank discussion of Sir Howard's past. I doubt he will recall me, as my service – "

"Mr. Sherlock Holmes!"

The hailing cry came from a young blond man in country attire, his boots considerably muddy. He held out a hand to my friend.

"You must be a wizard indeed, sir – and flown in on a broomstick, to have arrived here so promptly. Why, I sent the telegram to you only five minutes ago! I had no hopes of a reply by now, much less your actual presence."

"I fear you have me at a disadvantage, for I possess no supernatural powers."

"I am Constable Byron Price. I've read of your work and much admire it – and I have just sent a message requesting your assistance."

"About a murder?"

"Indeed."

"Of Sir Howard Blakely?"

Price gasped. "Why – yes – though I think I spot your trick. Only the murder of such an important individual would lead to you being summoned."

Holmes raised a hand. "Recently, a letter disturbed Sir Howard and then a shower of white roses occurred on his property."

Price stepped backward so quickly he nearly toppled from the platform. "Sir! Do not dispute that you are magical if you know these things already. You must have the second sight!"

"Allow me to prove I do not. Where was the body found?"

"That is the most baffling aspect of the entire business. Come, I will take you there."

We were soon ensconced in a comfortable landau, making our way out of the little village and toward the manor. The smells of early summer were rich upon the air, and lively noises were rising a country fair being set up in a meadow. Merry birdsong all around us made a strange accompaniment to Price's dark tale.

"Between us, Sir Howard was a disgrace to his title. He neglected his duties to his cottagers and gained a rather black reputation in these parts for dissolute behavior. His gambling debts were substantial. I've heard rumors that he'd begun to sell off some of the family pictures, as well as furnishings that date back to the Tudors."

"So he was a man with enemies?" I asked.

"Many – known and unknown. He was also in regular trouble over women. No servant girl stayed employed for more than a month, he was

116

so odious with them. You see, Mr. Holmes, I already have my work cut out for me, sorting through all the people who could have wanted him dead. Ah, we've arrived. I apologize ahead of time for your shoes. They will probably be quite ruined."

Our vehicle had halted before a newly planted field. The earth was dark and loamy, still wet from the rain of the previous evening. Our guide halted us and pointed to a quartet in the center of the field.

"That's Chapman, standing there with my men. He was passing by at about six this morning with his son, setting out for work at the next farm, when he saw the body in the field. He ran to it, realized that the man was dead, then sent his lad on a plough-horse for us. Here's the devilish part, Mr. Holmes – there are no marks in the field. The earth is perfect for taking footprints or the tracks of wheels or animals, but there is absolutely no impression anywhere around the body! Sir Howard was a bit disheveled, with a broken bone or two, but he died from having his throat cut."

"Indeed?" Holmes asked, as we carefully followed the single trail the policemen had worn into the soil, as a way to reach the body without disturbing the evidence of the immaculate field.

"It seems impossible, but the corpse is nearly drained. There is only a wound on his throat to account for it. Of course, that means he was killed elsewhere and brought here." We reached the body, which lay upon its back. Sir Howard had been a handsome, silver-haired man, with a robust physique. His clothing spoke to a privileged life. A diamond stickpin glittered amid the gory bloodstain on his ascot, and a gold watch dangled from his silken waistcoat.

Holmes knelt, subjecting the body to a quick and intricate inspection. "Robbery does not seem to be the motive. I perceive that, along with his other accessories, he has maintained at least three gold rings on his fingers."

"And this was in his pocket," Price said, holding out a black velvet bag. He emptied the contents into his own palm. I counted a half-dozen pearls, easily worth a thousand pounds or more.

"I doubt that his wife would have approved of him robbing her jewel box so flagrantly," Holmes said, rising and making an attempt to brush the muck from his trousers.

"Lady Blakely has a temper, she does – my missus used to work for her," one of the policemen volunteered. "Sir Howard better be glad he got himself murdered."

"That's enough out of you," Price warned. "Mr. Holmes . . . I confess I am out of my depth here. Most crimes in our little village involved stolen apples or pilfered pears. What should I do?"

117

"You must follow procedure," Holmes said. "You have already spoken with the household staff?"

"Only briefly. The butler mentioned that his master had recently been disturbed by a letter, and that white roses had fallen on his house. That is why I believed you were clairvoyant."

"Continue with your interviews," Holmes said. "If possible, keep the news of Sir Howard's death confined to yourself and your men until tomorrow."

The officer nodded eagerly. "And what will you do, sir?"

"Doctor Watson and I have not enjoyed a day in the country in a very long time. I believe we shall go to the fair."

I was baffled as to why Holmes hadn't also chosen to retire to the manor, to poke around the grounds or ask questions of the servants, but there was little I could do except conform to his will. The fair was brimming with all the simple recreations rural folks enjoyed. Children danced around a maypole while a brass band tooted and honked in enthusiastic, if rather tuneless, accompaniment. Pies, flowers, and pigs were being judged. A variety of games were set up, to test one's skill at knocking down milk bottles or popping balloons with darts. Holmes insisted that I enter a shooting match, since I had my service revolver with me, and I'm proud to write that a lovely village maiden pinned the second-place red ribbon to my jacket. There was a Punch-and-Judy show, a carousel, even an elephant and a clever little monkey on exhibit. After a few hours, I found myself caught up in the laughter of the children, the general gaiety of the crowd.

The afternoon was drawing to a close, and most of the townspeople were beginning to depart, when Holmes drew my attention to the attraction at the corner of the fair. It was a large balloon with a wicker basket. Much to my surprise, it was painted not with a Union Jack, but with a crude approximation of the American Stars and Stripes. A sign announced that an ascent of a half-hour, courtesy of Professional Aeronaut Theodore Vance, was available for six shillings per passenger. The aeronaut, a trim and handsome man with a slender black mustache, was making some adjustments to the moorings as we approached.

"Is it too late to go up?" Holmes asked. I can only imagine the look I must have given my friend as he made this request. I don't consider myself a cowardly fellow, but I have no great love of heights, and the very thought of dangling above all of creation in a tiny basket made my head spin and my stomach pitch.

"I'm sorry, but I'm done for today."

118

"It wouldn't take long," Holmes said, with the air of an annoyed tourist, "and I can pay handsomely for the privilege. Of course, I would need to be careful, as you do have something of a habit of throwing your passengers overboard."

The man had crouched down to secure a knot, but he rose suddenly, spinning around with a fiery expression. "My vehicle is perfectly safe, and I've had no complaints."

"Dead men tell different tales." Holmes reached into his coat and pulled out a single white rose that he must have purloined from one of the stalls. "Your calling card, Mr. Vance."

The effect was astonishing. The aeronaut drew back, his face going pale, his teeth bared at us. "What is the meaning of this?"

"Murder. And I would like to know why."

"You're a funny kind of policeman."

"I am not the official forces. My name is Sherlock Holmes, and I am a consulting detective. The daughter of one of your victims has engaged me."

"Am I under arrest?"

"You will be, very soon."

"Then perhaps I have time enough for a drink? I'd prefer not to be dragged off to prison thirsty."

Holmes made an elegant gesture, and we found ourselves walking beside the man into the local public house, which was doing a brisk business. Holmes signaled for our quarry to be seated with his back to the wall, which he did with no protest. He accepted a mug of ale with a quick salute.

"You wish to hear my story? Well, it is worth hearing." He drank deeply. "I was born in Virginia in 1847. I had a twin sister, Barbara. Our parents were poor, honest people, but they perished in a cholera epidemic when we were only four, and a judge gave us to a wretched tavern keeper in Fredericksburg. We were told we must work for him until we were both twenty-one. We were treated much like the Negro slaves, forced to labor night and day, wearing ragged clothes and never having enough to eat. When the war came, I swore that I would run away and join the Union Army and kill every man who took another man's freedom. But I was too young, and I was small and underfed, so that I appeared even younger than my years.

"In December of 1862, our small town was the focus of both armies. The Confederates took to the hills, and the Union men marched through in pursuit of them. Our master fled to the plantation of a friend, but we were left behind and told to guard the tavern. What chance did children have

119

against armies? Both sides came through and plucked our establishment bare.

"That day, as the terrible battle raged just beyond the town, three men came into our tavern. It was obvious that they were not soldiers. Their voices betrayed them as foreigners. The one they called Blakely was clearly wealthier than the others. He wore a fine coat, had a diamond stickpin in his tie, and generally told the others what they should do. He demanded we serve them dinner and offered to pay us in gold. We scratched up what provisions we could find, and poured the single bottle of whisky that was left to us. The men talked and smoked, and we hoped they would pay us and go about their business.

"Then Blakely cast his evil eyes upon my sister. He began to speak to her in vulgar ways, and when she ran out of the room in mortified tears, I told him to leave. He merely laughed at me and called to his friends to 'Hold the lad!' The one they addressed as Latham was a stout man. He knocked me down, kicked me until I coughed up blood, and then knelt upon my back, nearly crushing me. Blakely left the room, and I heard my sister screaming. I fought and kicked, but the man atop me was too heavy to be dislodged. The third man, the one they called Gibbons, stood in the doorway. He averted his eyes from the scene. He would not come to my aid or my sister's.

"It seemed like an hour passed. Finally, Blakely came back into the room, smirking. Our tavern was called The White Rose, named for the flowers which grew on a trellis beside the door. He had plucked one, which he threw at me."

Vance took up his glass again, but only stared down into it.

"There was no doctor to come and tend Barbara's wounds. She took a fever. Before a week passed, she was dead. Over her grave, I vowed eternal vengeance."

"How did you come upon your singular career?" Holmes asked.

"After I buried my sister, I ran away to the Union lines, thinking that perhaps I could become a camp servant or cook, if not a soldier. The army had observational balloons, and I was fascinated by them. A friendly officer saw my wonder. He took me on as an assistant and taught me everything there was to know about being an aeronaut. After the war, he adopted me as a son, and I was as loved by his wife and children as I had been despised by my former master. We toured the country with his balloon, performing ascents at hundreds of fairs. It was a fine life for many years, but I remained haunted by Barbara's fate. I saved all the money I could, and when at last I had enough, I said goodbye to my friends and came to England.

120

"For the last five years I have devoted myself to finding the evil men who killed my sister. I invested in a balloon and established myself in the circuit of rural entertainers. At last, this spring, I saw my opportunity. First, I sent each man a letter, telling the offender that the hour of reckoning had come. Then I went above and showered his dwelling with white roses. Afterward, I sent him a note saying that he might purchase forgiveness if he would meet me in a private place of my choosing." Vance looked up with a snarl. "I did not want money. I only used it as a lure, to convince them to meet me – to lull them into thinking they would survive the encounter. I did not steal so much as a penny. I killed each man and took his body aloft, to leave it in a place that would strike fear and wonder into those who might find it. But I see my little trick of dropping Blakely's corpse in the field did not fool you, sir."

"It was impossible for his body to have been placed there in any other manner," Holmes said. "It was the singularity of the thing that made the method clear."

Vance nodded. "My vanity was my undoing. I do not regret killing them, even if I hang for it. But I am not a thief, nor do I bear any ill will against their families. My job is done. My sister's soul can rest. So often I have felt her presence beside me, in the basket. Last evening, when Blakely was slain, I sensed her spirit flying up into the heavens, to reside with the angels."

At just that moment, a shout – more of a war cry – erupted from the bar. A massive, red-headed man swung his meaty fist at the equally large man beside him, who retaliated by grabbing a bottle and breaking it over the assailant's head. The entire room was thrown into chaos as men leapt up, shouting encouragement, some of them eager to join the fray, others trying futilely to halt it. Vance abruptly hurled his mug at my friend, nearly crashing it into his skull. Before I could react, the American, who was clearly much stronger than his trim frame suggested, had flipped the table over. We toppled to the floor. Vance disappeared into the crowd of writhing, struggling bodies.

"Holmes!" I called. "Holmes, hurry!" I gained my feet and darted forward, but when I looked back, Holmes was casually brushing off his coat. "He will escape!"

"That is certainly his intention," my friend said. Police whistles sounded, causing the knot of fighting men to untangle, and at last we were outside.

"Where would he go?" I said.

"His route is obvious. Let us return to the fairground."

We broke into a run, reaching our destination in a matter of minutes. Vance had already cast off all but one of his moorings. As we ran up, he sliced the final rope with a knife and the balloon began to rise. I drew my pistol from my pocket.

"Watson, no!" Holmes yelled, slapping the weapon away.

"I could have stopped him!" I protested, watching helplessly as the balloon went silently away into the night's clouds.

"What goes up must come down," Holmes replied. "If you had injured or killed him, it would trouble your conscience. Come – let us see if we can find a room at this hour."

The next morning, Holmes sat smoking at the breakfast table of the little hotel where we had retired. He had been silent all evening, making no further comment upon the investigation or the remarkable story we had heard from the murderer. At last, he pushed his plate away and tapped out his cigarette.

"Watson, you have frequently commented on my propensity to play judge and jury, or perhaps even God. But I am troubled by this case. My responsibly to the law lies in one direction, my duty to justice in another, and my obligation to my client in a third.

"Hear me out. Theodore Vance is a confessed murderer. By the laws of England, he should be tried and hanged. Yet upon hearing his story – and there is no doubt in my mind it is a true one, for what other motive could this man have possessed? I am inclined to think that justice has been served. Clearly my client is in no danger, but she is owed the truth about her father's demise. However, it is impossible to explain the murder without engaging with the motive."

"It will break the young lady's heart," I said. "She clearly adored her father."

"Indeed. And one must ask, what good will come of this? This revelation might put a strain upon her engagement, or even her marriage. Is it right to steal happiness from her?"

"She asked you for the truth."

"And she deserves no less. Ah, but here is Price – looking rather distraught, I think."

The constable's face was drawn and pale. His hair was uncombed, and he had clearly not paused to shave. He collapsed into a chair.

"Troubles come in threes, do they not? First the murder of Sir Howard, then the brawl at the pub, and now our poor balloonist, who vanished in the night!"

"What has happened?"

"I just received a telegram. His balloon was spotted in the waves off Dover. The basket was smashed upon the rocks. They are still looking for his body."

Miss Sarah Gibbons's eyes were damp with tears, but she quickly mastered her emotions. She seemed satisfied with Holmes's explanation that her father's murder was connected to an American tragedy, decades in the past.

"It is a sad story, but one that has been concluded," Holmes said. "Do not allow it to affect your happy memories of your father or cause you to fear for your future."

"You have learned evil things that you do not wish to tell me," she said.

Holmes nodded solemnly. "You are very perceptive. I would ask you to allow me to serve as a guardian for these unpleasant facts and hold them in a kind of trust for you."

The lady smiled. "I have lived a sheltered life. Father – *Papa* – was always so protective of me. He said the world was wicked, and he was far from perfect, but he would shield me from all harm, as long as he lived. You are clearly a man of wisdom and experience, Mr. Holmes. If you are satisfied that my father has received justice, I will ask no more. Perhaps in the future, when my feelings will not matter, Doctor Watson might record this story for posterity. Thank you, sir, for finding the truth."

Miss Gibbons took her leave. She went on to marry and lived a happy life, but a few weeks ago we received a note from her husband, saying that she had perished from influenza. Poor Constable Price never solved his case, and some of the more sensational newspapers had a field day speculating that Sir Howard Blakely had fallen victim to the legendary leaping demon named Spring Heeled Jack.

A month after Vance disappeared, Holmes and I were walking through Regent's Park. Two children, a boy and a girl so alike they might have been twins, skipped by, towing a single red balloon between them. Something in the image sparked a thought.

"Vance is not dead," I murmured.

"Assuredly, he is not," Holmes answered. "He was a master of the art of navigating the air. It would have been simplicity itself to bring his device to the ground and then abandon it, allowing it to soar unguided over the Channel. He is doubtless on his way back to America. One day, he will face a higher judge than any in this empire and we, perhaps, will receive credit for our measure of mercy."

Mrs. Crichton's Ledger
by Tim Gambrell

I find I am minded, at times, to revisit some of Sherlock Holmes's investigations that were quietly set to one side at the time of their occurrence, over concerns that they were perhaps a little too *personal* in their subject matter. Not personal to Holmes nor me, necessarily, but likely uncomfortable to those whom the investigations concerned, even if the names were changed. And, it must be said, those more personal or domestic stories were often of a less overtly sensational nature. Holmes was wont to accuse me of embellishing our adventures with additional dramatic flourishes to titillate the reading public. Whether that be the case or not, I have always striven to ensure that I do not pander to any of the more unprincipled elements out there.

Thankfully, I've always kept meticulous notes – a practice drilled into me by both my medical and military training. Some years having now passed, and the lives of those concerned having moved on, I occasionally consult these notes at my leisure. More often than not, I'm pleasantly surprised at how much of the detail I've retained in my memory. It gives me much joy to relive those years of my prime, and to commit further tales of Holmes's exploits to the printed page.

One such case in point concerned a lady likely known to many readers, the noted Bluestocking, Mrs. Amelia Crichton. She called upon us one balmy afternoon in 1898, towards the end of August. There were the usual niceties and conversational preamble, wherein we offered cool refreshments on such a warm day and she, accepting our offer, held forth regarding her next series of church hall lectures to aid female literacy. As we settled down to discuss the matter of her visit, Mrs. Crichton produced her housekeeping accounting ledger from within a voluminous bag by her feet. I had seen plenty suchlike books before and had often been asked to record my own fees within their pages. Neither Holmes nor I were in any way accounting specialists, our experience extending little beyond the maintaining our own purely domestic matters. I wondered, briefly, if the lady had ventured upon us in error. Such thoughts were quickly corrected.

Mrs. Crichton advised that her ledger had been interfered with, but not specifically to what end. With his expression unreadable, Holmes motioned for her to continue.

"I am, as I'm sure you know, a very precise and particular woman, with a keen eye on helping others."

124

Her reputation preceded her, and I was happy to confirm this. She continued.

"My husband, Colonel Crichton, and I keep a pot of money in our quarters. For domestic purposes. My husband replenishes it, and I draw down against it for the housekeeping, which is then passed to Mrs. Crick, the housekeeper. We maintain only a modest household on the Colonel's pension, and we have found that this method is our surest way of living within our means. It came as some surprise to me recently when the pot was found to prematurely run dry for the month."

I took the opportunity of a pause in her narrative to clear my throat. "Stolen?" I enquired, when she didn't automatically continue.

"Spent, Doctor Watson. And yet not spent." Mrs. Crichton replied, bewilderingly. "Initially, I was made to endure some cruelty at the hands of my husband, accusing me of being profligate and not keeping an adequate or accurate account of expenditure. To this, of course, I showed him the accounts. I have always kept a very close eye over them. The Colonel maintained his stance, so I reviewed the entries myself. I was very surprised to find that, for the previous three weeks, what was recorded did not match my recollection of the sums I had requested from my husband."

"And your memory for such matters is sound?" Holmes asked.

Mrs. Crichton was a woman of upwards of forty years of age. Holmes was met with a look that would undoubtedly have turned The Medusa herself to stone.

"I remain in perfect command of my faculties."

"I am glad to hear it," he replied with a dazzling smile. "Please, do go on."

She puffed out her cheeks. "Well, frankly, Mr. Holmes, I'm not sure there's much else to tell you."

"I doubt that most sincerely," he said, bounding from his chair. "You've given me virtually nothing to go on. However, I've solved crimes with less. First off, let's see what secrets this ledger of yours is concealing." He reached out to take it. "May I?"

I watched the dynamic between the two of them as the accounts were handed over. A look of doubt flash across Mrs. Crichton's eyes. She was a very proud and intelligent woman, who would certainly not have come to see us if she could have managed the matter herself, within the confines of her own four walls. I couldn't help but have the utmost respect for her, and pity for the predicament in which she found herself.

Holmes opened the pages and began to pace, pursing his lips as he read. I noted how he didn't turn immediately to the most recent entries but started at the beginning. No doubt this was to familiarise himself with aspects of the accounts, so that when he looked for changes or errors, they would stand out more starkly. *A keen eye only notices difference once it has first established normality,* he once told me.

He continued to flick through from page to page, his face hardly moving but his keen eyes darting up and down each time, absorbing, cogitating, deliberating.

I, in turn, observed Mrs. Crichton. She was never unnecessarily demure or subservient in her behaviour. I was conscious that she was studying Holmes almost as intently as he studied her ledger.

"Tell me," Holmes asked after a while. "How many are there in your household at present?"

"Besides the Colonel and me, and our youngest son Frederick, who's home from school for the summer, there are four: Evans the butler, Mrs. Crick the housekeeper, Dilys the cook maid, and Mavis, my lady's maid. As I said earlier, we keep only a modest staff."

"And your household arrangements are happy and settled?"

"Well, erm . . . ." Mrs. Crichton cleared her throat a little forcibly. "There has been a little upheaval of late, I can't deny. Mavis is with child and unmarried. She won't reveal the identity of the father."

"I see."

Mrs. Crichton was quick to continue. "To my eternal shame, I was rather hasty in responding to the news."

"Many would have let her go without further ado," I stated.

Mrs. Crichton smiled awkwardly at me. "I'll come to that. Firstly, I mistook her stubbornness to be an indication that she was protecting one of the household. I have often noted a familiarity between Mavis and Evans. Perhaps that familiarity was of a more parental nature than lustful, but my hasty thoughts immediately ran to him being the father, and interfering with the housekeeping accounts to obtain funds for Mavis's laying-in."

"He is unmarried, then?"

"And old enough to be the girl's father, too. Evans was my husband's batman in the Crimea and has served him ever since. He was already butler to the household before I became Mrs. Joshua Crichton. I should have realised at once, of course. Evans is totally dedicated to us. To the Colonel. But instead, I foolishly challenged him. His shocked reaction will stay with me for a goodly while. Of course, he complained bitterly to my husband and threatened his resignation." She paused. "How do you do it, Mr. Holmes? How do you weigh up the evidence and single out your villain without embarrassing yourself with false accusations?"

Holmes considered for a moment, before answering. "A wise detective somehow allows his culprit to reveal him or herself, Mrs. Crichton."

She nodded. "I see. Well, I'm sorry to say that I'm now forced to suspect that the Colonel may have had something to do with Mavis' situation, even at his age."

"Indeed, Mrs. Crichton. Perhaps you could explain your reasoning?"

"To hark back to Doctor Watson's point a few minutes ago, the Colonel initially ordered Mavis to be dismissed – an action I had intended to take anyway. But immediately after, he sent word that he'd changed his mind. He stated that she should remain under our roof so that we could protect the young girl's honour, prevent her from descending into prostitution and suchlike."

I commended such noble sentiments. "Those in more comfortable situations are wont to judge hastily against the poor and common classes, and often cause them more grief in the long run."

"That's all well and good, Doctor Watson. But could it not as easily be that he wants his whore close at hand for further pleasures?"

I felt the crimson rise to my cheeks. I wasn't used to such forthrightness from one of Mrs. Crichton's standing.

"Please, Mrs. Crichton," said Holmes, urgently. "Calm yourself. I fear this line of reasoning will add nothing but further pain to your troubled heart."

She cast her eyes to the floor and Holmes drew a deep, calming breath.

"Besides which," he continued, "I've made a discovery."

Mrs. Crichton looked up again immediately.

"It was the most recent three weeks over which you raised doubts, did you not?"

"Indeed."

Holmes turned to me. "Watson, would you mind asking Mrs. Hudson to step in and remove the tray?"

I did as requested, and very shortly after Holmes was able to place the open ledger on the now empty table for all to see.

"Talk me through the process, if you wouldn't mind, Mrs. Crichton. How do the figures recorded here transform themselves into money?"

"It's all on credit, Mr. Holmes," she replied. "I make a note of the sums we owe day by day. At the end of the week, Evans takes the ledger up to my husband. We have our monthly pot, based on an average spend, and the correct money, or thereabouts, is sent back down with Evans. The due bills are then paid, usually by Mrs. Crick. It's as simple as that."

"So the active players in this are Evans the butler, Mrs. Crick the housekeeper, yourself, and the Colonel – your husband?"

"Indeed, yes."

"And where is the ledger kept?"

"In my *escritoire* in the drawing room."

"Locked away?"

"Until now there has been no need."

Holmes's eyes sparkled. "You say that, Mrs. Crichton, but there are plenty of instances of earlier interferences and alterations."

The lady looked completely shocked.

"Forgeries?" I asked.

"I'm not entirely certain at present, Watson." He turned to our guest. "You are not in the habit of amending figures after the event, are you, madam? There are plenty of pages with no changes."

Although this was posed as a statement, not a challenge, Mrs. Crichton took a moment to collect herself. "Certainly not, Mr. Holmes. I take a great deal of pride in the accuracy of my bookkeeping."

"And you always use the same pen and brand of ink."

"I do. The pen was a present on my wedding day."

"Spencerian steel – am I right?"

"Why, Mr. Holmes, you are." Mrs. Crichton looked very impressed. I had a feeling the best was yet to come.

"And Carter's Ink? Imported from Massachusetts by the stationers on the Edgware Road, if I'm not mistaken?"

The lady's eyes widened in amazement. "How could you possibly know that?"

Holmes gave one of his most genuine smiles. "I have studied these things at great length. Watson can draw your attention to my monograph on the subject. However, for the moment we still have a mystery to solve. And may I say for starters, Mrs. Crichton, you were correct to bring this ledger to us. I'm not entirely sure that an accountant would have seen anything amiss – or at least nothing that goes against received practice. Figures have been altered after the event. Very surreptitiously, too. But clues remain – not the least of which are the fact that a different pen and brand of ink was used to record the changes." Holmes grabbed a nearby letter opener and brandished it as a pointer. The three of us gathered in around the open pages.

"You can see, on this page alone – here, here, and here," he indicated, "the velum has been very carefully scraped to obfuscate your original figures. The fibres were then smoothed – although not completely – and new figures entered." He held the book up so that the sunlight from the window hit the page at a particular angle. "The difference in ink is more obvious to the untrained eye when light is played across the page. Do you see? The ink used for the replacement figures, although blue like yours when looked at face-on, has a different reflected hue when sunlight shines upon it."

I could plainly see that the colour reflected under sunlight was more purple than blue, whereas the ink from Mrs. Crichton's pen had a greener hue under the same conditions.

"Is that not just down to the thickness of the ink on the page?" Mrs. Crichton asked.

"It stems from the manufacturing process, I can assure you. This ink was manufactured differently and therefore has a different quality. Also, this sum: Fourteen shillings, four-pence-three-farthings for boot blacking. Utterly ridiculous."

"I see that now." The lady sounded resigned. "And such things have happened before, you say?"

Holmes turned back towards the beginning of the book.

"I must say," the lady mused, "it didn't occur to me to check whether this had happened before or not."

"It wouldn't," Holmes confirmed. "The earlier alterations were only for small amounts – a few shillings here and there at most. Likely that this was easily accommodated within whatever rounded-up sum was sent down by the Colonel that week."

"Is it all the same hand? Can you tell?"

"Oh, indeed. There are clues aplenty. I perceive the forger to have been left-handed."

"Oh, good grief!" the lady burst, her face expressing a curious panoply of emotional states. She calmed herself and continued. "I must apologise, gentlemen. Left-handed you say, Mr. Holmes? How so?" I detected an edge of worry to her voice.

"The figures, brief as they are, show a very slight leaning to the left on the upward sweeps."

I peered closer. "By Jove, I see it."

"Whereas your own handwriting curls away gently to the right, madam."

Concern was firmly etched on her face.

"Further, if we turn to the first of the recently forged pages, you will note some light marks and smudges."

The markings were very minor. One had to look very closely to spot them. But also, I knew from experience how easily this was done. I ventured that, surely, this was a likely occurrence within a book so frequently used. It seems I was mistaken.

"Mr. Holmes is correct to draw attention to the fact, Doctor Watson," Mrs. Crichton countered. "I can assure you that the greatest of care is always taken when I complete the ledger. My figures are correct and you will find no misplaced marks, blots, or smudges elsewhere within the pages."

Holmes agreed. "And I believe that here, our forger was careless. Whatever he or she did on this page, extra care was taken not to repeat the error with further amendments."

"Hang on," I said, interrupting. "You said changes had already been made earlier in the book."

"Very minor. Often the existing figures are tweaked, that's all. The difference here with the most recent pages is that the forged amounts are much larger. Pounds, not just shillings or pence. I think the forger was nervous because of the increase. This caused him or her to be clumsy at first."

He looked at us. We had nothing to say, so he continued.

"These ink marks, then. If one takes them to have come from the side of the hand which rested on the page, thusly." He placed the edge of his hand on the page, as one would when one is writing. "You see, the smudges here and here – " Again, he indicated with the tip of the letter opener. " – would coincide with the figures entered here and here."

"Except they don't," I pointed out. "At least not on your hand."

He held up an extended digit to me. "Capital, my friend. Which shows that our culprit had smaller, or stubbier, hands than me. You'll notice as well that he or she learned the lesson. On the remaining pages, the figures were entered in a different order to avoid placing a hand back on the page where he or she had already written – a common dilemma for a left-handed person amending a right-handed person's work. Or *vice-versa*."

Mrs. Crichton was sombre. "This can't have anything to do with my maid, then. I know for a fact that all those within the household who can write or use numbers are right-handed, with one exception – my young son, Frederick."

"Where does he school?" I asked.

"Winchester," she responded proudly.

"What about ambidexterity amongst the others?" Holmes asked.

Mrs. Crichton glanced at us both, enquiringly.

"Anyone able to use both hands with equal skill?" I clarified.

"Not that I've ever witnessed," she replied.

I sat back in thought, and Holmes steepled his fingers to his lips. Mrs. Crichton snapped the ledger shut and returned it to her voluminous bag, muttering about it being a "thorny situation" all the while. Then she stood and fixed us both with look that contained a mixture of respect and regret. "I thank you, gentlemen, for your time and assistance today. I shall ask my husband to send you something to show our gratitude. But now I feel I should return home and speak with young Frederick. I need to get to the bottom of this before he returns to school in a few days."

Holmes once again burst forth with sudden urgency. "Mrs. Crichton, did these most recent accounting forgeries only appear after it was known that young Mavis was with child?"

"Yes, Mr. Holmes. The following week, in fact. But I hope you're not suggesting that my Frederick is responsible for her condition. He's only fourteen."

"Nothing of the sort, I can assure you. But I am concerned that the matters are somehow connected. And it's clear what pride you take in your family and your household. I should like to propose that Doctor Watson and I accompany you home and then, within the discretion of your four walls, I firmly believe we can solve the mysteries currently facing you."

It was only when I saw the lady's shoulders drop that I realised how physically stressed she'd been. She was clearly putting herself under considerable strain.

"If that wouldn't be imposing upon you too much," she replied, "then I should be very grateful. Thank you."

"Think nothing of it."

And with that we left, grabbing only our jackets, for the day was still very clement.

A short cab ride was all that was required. The Crichtons lived nearby on Bryanston Square, and if Mrs. Crichton hadn't been with us, we would likely have walked. I couldn't help but notice the look on the stiff-backed butler's face as we entered. Mrs. Crichton endeavoured to hide her embarrassment from us. It would clearly take some time for Evans to forgive his mistress over her accusation.

The Colonel was in his study and soon to leave for his club, where he was due to dine later. Holmes preyed upon Evans to request a few minutes of the officer's time first, to help clear up a "thorny domestic matter", as he put it. Casting a sidelong glance at Mrs. Crichton first, Evans did as he was bid, and very shortly after Holmes and I were announced.

Like many a retired colonel, Crichton showed evidence of having been an imposing figure in his prime, but was now turning somewhat to the rotund in his advancing years. And, whilst by no means being a child bride, it was clear that there was quite an age gap between Mrs. Crichton and her husband. Indeed, they appeared to have separate suites of rooms on the first floor, presumably only coming together for meals and social occasions.

I surmised that he had already retired from military service and taken up residence here, in London society, before taking himself a wife and starting a family. The Colonel being roughly sixty years of age (according to my practiced eye) and the children being older and away at school undoubtedly allowed Mrs. Crichton the freedom she cherished to be a lecturer and political activist – activities for which she was widely renowned.

"No matter for the police, this, surely?" said the old man gruffly as he finished his drink. The fact that he didn't offer one to Holmes or me, or greet us in any way, indicated that he wasn't prepared to compromise over his scheduled plans. His ruddy complexion betrayed a man who drank regularly.

"We are not the police, Colonel," Holmes responded sharply. "But your wife is in some distress and has sought our assistance."

"Woman just got her figures wrong, that's all."

"And Mavis?"

"What the deuce – ? Sort of thing happens all the time. Girls get themselves into trouble. What business is that of yours? Unless you're the father."

Holmes didn't even flinch at the rudeness. "You've been very generous in allowing her to keep her position."

"Yes, well. The dame likes her, and she does a good job, by all accounts. I don't want her falling into disrepute. If she stays on here, maybe the wretch who got her into that situation will make an honest girl of her. Or she'll find a decent chap to take her on. Not likely to happen if we send her back to her parents in that state. She'll end up working the docks."

"You don't think it might have been someone here in the household?"

"What's the dame been telling you? Evans is a man's man, dedicated to me. Always has been. Splendid chap. Don't have a footman anymore. There's no one else except my boys. George is away with his regiment. Frederick's still a lad."

"You haven't seen George for some time, then, I presume?"

"Easter. Had the weekend off. That's it all year. Cut the apron strings. Do him good."

I studied the Colonel. I couldn't detect any duplicity or hidden agenda behind the old cove's bluster. No doubt Holmes would have picked up on something, though – the untimely flick of an eyelid or suchlike. We didn't get much further with the interview. A carriage was waiting, and the old man wouldn't be delayed.

Similarly, we didn't get far when we spoke with Evans immediately afterwards. He had already taken against us for being associated with his mistress. Beyond his military service and his dedication to the household, we got very little out of the man. But Holmes didn't seem bothered at all.

"We're getting a lot of clues here," he said, his eyes gleaming. For my part, I could only nod encouragingly whilst inwardly shrugging.

132

After Evans pleaded his duties and quickly left us, we appeared to have the freedom of the house. We encountered Mrs. Crick, the housekeeper, in the hallway by the front door as we descended. She was a middle-aged woman with a matronly bearing. She had plenty to say on the subject of Mavis – all of it unbidden, most of it apocryphal (or at least wildly unlikely), and hardly any of it applicable to our investigation.

Holmes dismissed the housekeeper as soon as he could get a word in edgeways, and we agreed to file her evidence under "gossip" of "questionable integrity". She did, however, indicate that we would find Mavis in Mrs. Crichton's rooms upstairs, so that was where we headed next.

Mavis was indeed there, folding laundry. Her circumstances were very much visible by now, and I could see that she was a comely wench. She was also no fool. Like Evans, the butler, she was fiercely protective of her position and the household as a whole. All we got from her was her surname, Hawkins. Otherwise, her stock answer to everything else was "I'd rather not say, sir," even when assured that anything she told us would be in strict confidence.

At the first lull in Holmes's questioning, she gave a brief curtsey and excused herself. I was beginning to feel exasperated. What a household!

"How far gone would you say Mavis is?" he asked as we headed back down the stairs.

I pondered. "Difficult to say precisely without an examination, of course, because the visible signs can vary a great deal. But I'd say she looked about halfway to a full term, maybe four or five months."

"Thank you."

"Are you frustrated? I don't really feel that we're getting anywhere."

"Not at all," he replied, before turning and rewarding me with a hearty slap on the upper arm. "This has all largely been preamble, anyway. It's young Master Frederick with whom I really want to speak. I think he'll hold the answers to my remaining questions."

Mrs. Crichton intercepted us to ask how we progressed. Holmes merely enquired if we could speak alone with Master Frederick. Mrs. Crichton wished us the best of luck. The young lad was in the drawing room, about some quiet study. She said she had been trying to get answers out of him since we'd arrived, but all to no avail, the stubborn lad. We were told we were welcome to interrupt him and continue the questioning if necessary.

The drawing room was very elegant, boasting a proud view out onto Bryanston Square. In its successful combination of comfortable style with military memorabilia, it somehow managed to reflect both Colonel and Mrs. Crichton perfectly.

Young Frederick was the image of his mother. Having met his father, I decided this was undoubtedly in the boy's favour. He was sitting at a desk to one side, reading Tennyson. I thought how much of a relief I'd have felt being interrupted at such a task had it been me. Not so Freddie Crichton, it seemed. He didn't acknowledge our greeting or our presence. This had clearly been his mode of resistance against his mother's approaches. Holmes and I pulled up some chairs and seated ourselves on either side of the boy.

We fired a few questions his way about school and sports in an attempt to find a point of connection. Holmes had a stroke of luck when he hit upon boxing. Young Freddie was a keen boxer, it seemed, and had hopes of representing his school. Holmes responded with great encouragement. They were both looking forward to the Sullivan-Smith bout scheduled for New York a few weeks later. Hereafter, the boy began to open up to us. He even indicated he'd read some of my reports of Holmes's exploits, and I couldn't help but be a little flattered by this. I laughed when he informed us that the school didn't approve, so the copies had to be passed about the dormitories in secret.

As the mirth died down, Holmes suddenly asked Freddie when he'd last heard from George. The boy blanched. He clearly hadn't expected to be questioned about his brother and, unwittingly, his face appeared to tell Holmes everything he wanted to know in an instant. I glanced at my friend and he nodded, indicating that I should check all the doors into the room, which I did. They were secure and no one was listening outside.

"Come, Freddie," Holmes said, gently. "There's no one else around, and you can trust Doctor Watson and me to act with the utmost discretion. You've been receiving weekly letters from him of late, haven't you?"

The boy nodded.

"Because George is the father of young Mavis' baby."

I nodded. "Easter."

"Exactly, Watson. The Colonel said that's when George was last here. You recall the date?"

I did indeed. "Easter Sunday. Here we are, late August, nearly five months later." I realised instantly the importance of what Holmes had asked me on the stairs a short while earlier.

"Please don't tell mother and father," bleated Freddie. "They'll kill him."

Holmes smiled. "I doubt it would be as severe as that," he said gently. "But I do need you to tell me why you've been falsifying your mother's housekeeping ledger, and what you've been doing with the money."

Young Frederick stood and walked to the bay window. He'd make quite the dapper gentleman when he came of age, that much was clear. He bowed his head and sighed in the late afternoon sun before turning. It was with a measure of resignation that he passed onto us the knowledge we sought.

George Crichton had had his eye on Mavis for some time, and that April, when he was home for the Easter weekend, she'd finally given in to his advances when he promised to marry her. Some four months later, when the results of their encounter were evident to all, Mavis wrote to George at his regiment, but he refused to come home and do the honourable thing. By then, Mavis' family also knew what had gone on. Her brother, Jeremiah, had become incensed. Initially, it seems, he wanted to confront Colonel Crichton and demand he take action with George. According to the second letter Mavis wrote to George, she managed to talk Jeremiah down from this endeavour, fearing that nothing but ruination would come of it for any of them. But she feared Jeremiah would attempt some action or other, regardless of the consequences, unless George proved good by his word and took Mavis to be his wife.

The next letter that George received was from Jeremiah himself, threatening to reveal all unless George married Mavis or made it financially worth his while to keep quiet. From what Holmes and I eventually saw of this correspondence, some weeks later, it certainly wasn't clear if any of this blackmail money would actually go to Mavis or assist with her circumstances. George then wrote to young Freddie and asked him to pay off Mavis' brother, keeping their parents in the dark on the matter.

It was Holmes's view that this was the worst thing the brothers could have done, acceding to the blackmail. But, then, they were both young and inexperienced. George, for all his paid commission, had still only just reached his majority. Holmes nodded sagely as Freddie outlined how the demands from Jeremiah, and the resultant requests from George kept coming week after week.

Freddie, being underage, didn't have access to any funds other than a small weekly pocket money allowance. This was more than sufficient at first, but as the weeks went on the amounts increased and, more recently, they had reached beyond his means. He couldn't ask his parents for more for fear of revealing all. But what he had done in the past was to amend his mother's housekeeping ledger and pocket the resulting odd few shillings for a bit of extra spending money. Boyhood jinks, nothing more. All he could think of doing to comply with his older brother's instructions was to repeat this trick. But the demands continued to increase, of course. Jeremiah Hawkins had realised that he was on to easy money with this

135

endeavour. Alas, it was inevitable that Freddie's actions would be detected at some point.

"George has written to me again today," the boy revealed at the end of his tale. "Another demand from Hawkins. And now I don't know what to do, Mr. Holmes. The housekeeping has run out, Mother has discovered that her figures have been falsified. And the amount that Hawkins wants this week is beyond those means anyway. Maybe this is it – George's whole mess is going to get revealed to the world and we'll all be ruined."

"Freddie," said Holmes, holding the boy by the shoulders and peering into his face. "Calm yourself. Doctor Watson and I are here to help – and help you all we shall. Now you run along to your room and await my instructions. Understand?"

He nodded. "Yes sir. Thank you, sir." He looked at me, too. "Sirs." And with that, he was off. I watched the lad leave the room and then turned to Holmes. My friend was nodding to himself as he examined a silver-framed photograph on the mantelpiece. A handsome young subaltern: Presumably George Crichton.

"Poor Mrs. Crichton," I said.

"Indeed. But there is much still to do, and delicate work, all of it." He strode over to the bell and rang. A few minutes passed, and then the final member of the household appeared through the door: Dilys, the rosy-cheeked cook-maid. She curtsied and asked, with profoundly blocked adenoids, what we gentlemen wanted.

"Dilys, isn't it?" I said.

She curtsied again but spoke not this time.

"Please send Mavis to us," said Holmes. "Thank you."

Dilys stared at Holmes as if she'd expected me to do all the talking and he was breaking protocols. Then she appeared to remember her manners, or perhaps her instructions sank in, and she gave a third curtsey before turning and leaving the room – pausing midway through the door to give us a final curtsey.

Holmes and I grinned at the poor flustered girl's efforts, but we didn't have long to ourselves before Mavis entered.

Mrs. Crichton's lady's maid could barely conceal her annoyance at having to come before us a second time. Holmes smiled at her, generously and indicated that she should be seated. She complied, but I noticed this did not appear to improve matters.

"My dear Mavis," he said, after a few moments. "You need not worry. We now know everything, but discretion is our watchword."

Mavis clearly hadn't a clue what to say.

"Only tell me this, did you know that your brother is still blackmailing George?"

The effect of his words was immediate and pronounced. The poor girl fainted clean away before us. Thank goodness she was already seated. I rushed to attend and make her comfortable, whilst castigating Holmes for his lack of tact when presenting a shock to a woman in her condition. *Delicate work, indeed!* I was furious.

Mavis was carried out and taken to her bed, where she very soon recovered consciousness. A cursory examination was all that was required to convince me that both she and the baby were fine, although I instructed Mrs. Crichton to keep Mavis at her bed for the remainder of that day at least.

"Please, mister," Mavis hissed at me as Mrs. Crichton left us. "I didn't know nothing about our Jemmy blackmailing George. Will he be arrested? What's to become of me now? Are we all ruined?"

"Calm yourself, Mavis," I said. "All will be well, don't worry." I felt it best to give her a mild sedative, common to most kitchens, to aid her recovery. Very soon she was in a perfectly natural slumber, to which I left her.

I found that Holmes was still in the drawing room, now accompanied by Mrs. Crichton. The dear lady held a handkerchief to her nose, and it was clear in an instant that Holmes had been revealing the whole sorry affair to her. He looked up at me as I entered.

"Did you get an answer?"

I rolled my eyes at his continued lack of tact and indicated the lady.

"It's all right, Mrs. Crichton knows everything now, but an answer to my question is *vital*."

"Mavis is sleeping, but she told me that she didn't know anything about . . . ." I tailed off, not wanting to mention such things in front of an already tearful Mrs. Crichton.

"The blackmail," Holmes finished for me, regardless of the lady. I held my hands up in despair. "Good," he said, with a nod. "Will you remain here with Mrs. Crichton and give her any assistance she requires? I need to arrange an appointment."

I was incredulous. "An appointment? Now?"

"Yes." He approached me, confidentially. "You have appointments too, from time to time."

"I know that, but Holmes – there's a time and a place and all that."

"Indulge me," he said, with a wink. I knew at once that he had a plan of which my part was to keep the lady in good company and at ease. It was, as always, both my duty and my honour to assist Sherlock Holmes in whatever way he required. I set my jaw and nodded my acquiescence.

"It might be best for me to stay around, in case Mavis takes a turn for the worse."

Holmes nodded. "Sound reasoning, my friend. Await my return."

"Take good care," I told him.

"Without you to watch my back, Watson, I shall be extra cautious. I shall be taking young Master Frederick along with me, as well. The experience will do him all manner of good."

And with that, he left.

Mrs. Amelia Crichton was quite a remarkable woman. I've known many of the fair sex who would have been left inconsolable by the news she had received, but very soon she had composed herself and was playing the perfect hostess once again. I told her as much, but she brushed off the compliment with elegant grace, saying that the world needed more women who were literate, independent, and strong. I couldn't help observing how she wasn't independent. Mrs. Crichton, in turn, pointed out to me that she *was*. One of the main messages she passed on to women – particularly poorer women – was how to fulfil that independent role within the strictures of a male-dominated family unit and a male-dominated society.

"It won't always be this way, of course," she told me. "But, as they say, Rome wasn't built in a day."

I could imagine her holding forth about such ideological matters to a group of ladies in a church hall. Her personality and charisma were strong and persuasive.

Dilys interrupted us with some fresh tea, which was very welcome. Mrs. Crichton asked me if I'd care to dine with her that evening, since everyone else appeared to be out. I graciously accepted. I had, after all, agreed to wait there for Holmes, so why not do so on a full stomach?

"Tell Mrs. Crick that we're just two for dinner this evening. That'll be all, thank you, Dilys."

"Ma'am." Dilys curtsied and left.

"There is something about Mr. Holmes," said Mrs. Crichton, as she poured us each a fresh cup of tea.

All at once I feared that I was going to have to defend Holmes's manner – something I had done on many occasions and would continue to do for the remainder of his and my acquaintance. But I was mistaken, this time.

"He has an admirable ability to inform one of the greatest personal disasters, but in such a skilful and straightforward way. There is no mollycoddling, no sugar-coating. It encourages one to accept the news without question or complaint. Too often, Doctor, we are expected to endure bad news with an unnecessary touch of the hand and a gentle voice.

Evasiveness does not equal kindness, and I am most grateful for his plain and simple manner."

"Will this change anything with regard to Mavis, do you think?"

"Yes, and no," she replied. "My husband has taken a commendable line with regard to her honour – even more important now we know that George is the father. I will arrange to have Mavis moved to the household of my elderly aunt, in Suffolk, until George is in a position to do the honourable thing by her."

"You will not stand in the way of marriage?"

"Heavens, no. He will stand by his word and do the honourable thing by that poor girl or he won't again be welcome within these walls, Doctor Watson. And I know that his father will insist likewise. The Colonel."

I was impressed to find such a progressive, levelling attitude, considering the gulf between George and Mavis imposed by the British class system.

Dinner was a little side of beef, dressed with a French wine and mushroom sauce, and served with seasoned vegetables. It was pleasant enough, although I suspected Mrs. Hudson would have something waiting for us at Baker Street when we returned later, too. We saw only Mrs. Crick. Evans was keeping away from his mistress as much as possible. It pained me to witness it, and it clearly pained Mrs. Crichton even more to experience being avoided in such a blatant way by a member of the staff. I feared his position had really become untenable, and I hoped it wouldn't put an unnecessary strain on the Crichtons' marriage.

We talked further and played at cards. I was most intrigued to learn how much she, and other Bluestocking ladies like her, had helped and improved the lives of so many working-class women. Despite my interest, and Mrs. Crichton's obvious oratory skill, I fell asleep in the drawing room and woke some hours later when Holmes finally returned. He had with him the old colonel and young Master Frederick in tow. All were in jubilant high spirits as they joined us.

The young lad placed a leather purse of before Mrs. Crichton. The contents jangled as he did so.

"Your missing housekeeping money, Mother – or as much of it as remains unspent."

Mrs. Crichton's face lit up. "Freddie! Oh! My boy. How did you ever – ?"

"I didn't, Mother, but Mr. Holmes did. He's saved George, and he's saved the family name, I shouldn't wonder."

"I'll say he has," slurred the Colonel as he tried to undo his jacket buttons and ended up loosening his trousers instead. "Saved our name and boxed seven shades of . . . something or other out of the villain, by all accounts." The old man then collapsed onto a *chaise longue* and promptly began to snore.

"I feel I must apologise on my husband's behalf, sirs. Freddie, please call Evans for me."

"Is he often like this?" I enquired as Freddie moved to the door.

Mrs. Crichton's mouth curled at the edges. "It's his standard routine after a visit to his club these days, isn't it, Freddie?"

Young Frederick looked back at us and nodded. I, in turn, looked at Holmes with an expression which told him full well that I was awaiting an explanation as to their disappearance. Holmes nodded.

"Jeremiah Hawkins, Watson. I recognised the name immediately, but I suspect you probably didn't."

This was true.

"He's a boxer of some repute within certain circles here in the city. I knew the best way to stop him continuing to blackmail George was to challenge him to an underground boxing match. The winners dictate the prizes under such conditions, and sometimes these bouts can make or break a man. So I challenged him, and he accepted. I gave young Freddie here a little extra tuition while we waited for our turn. He is already very accomplished, Mrs. Crichton. You should be very proud of him. He then acted as my second in order to study the fight at close range."

Only now did I spot the marks and abrasions on Holmes's face and the way he nursed his right arm. "I assume, from what the Colonel said, that you won?"

"He felled the blighter in the second round with an uppercut to the jaw!" confirmed Freddie. "Never seen the like before. It was beautiful!"

"Can he be trusted to keep to his word?" asked Mrs. Crichton.

"Oh yes. There is much honour amongst thieves and brigands. If he steps out of line now, he'll know about it."

There was more congratulating.

"Where did you fight?" I asked.

Holmes smiled and tousled Freddie's hair. "There are plenty of places for this sort of thing, if you know where to look."

That told me everything and nothing.

Mrs. Crichton gestured to the slumbering form of her husband. "And how does the Colonel come into all this?"

"We picked him up wandering the streets on the way home, Mother," Freddie told her. "He must have got confused and asked his own cabbie to drop him off a few blocks too early. We told him what we'd been up to during the brief remainder of the journey."

At this point Evans knocked and sombrely entered, and the company split. In the interest of the Colonel's health, I assisted the butler to support him up to his rooms and put the bluff old cove safely to bed. He'd sleep the evening off well enough.

Evans thanked me for my assistance. I told him we could do him a further assistance. He resisted at first, but when he saw that I wasn't going to back down, it was clear that he was obliged to obey. We returned to the drawing room, where Holmes awaited us.

Much later that night, I was in our sitting room back at Baker Street, nursing a glass of brandy. I had tried to sleep, but unassisted, it evaded me.

Holmes entered. It was normal that he should be up until all hours, but tonight he had the added task of tending to his minor wounds from the boxing match – something he rarely let me assist with.

"Not tired, Watson?"

I suspect my eyes provided sufficient indication that I was physically exhausted, even if my brain was too active to rest.

"What troubles you, my friend?" he asked, seating himself opposite.

I explained how I had been running over in my head what had transpired after we'd spoken with Evans, the butler, at the end of the evening earlier.

"You're a man of the world, Watson," Holmes replied. "Surely you must have realised by now that love comes in many ways, and strikes in many forms?"

He was right, of course. And if he could willingly overlook such impropriety, why couldn't I?

I ran through those final events in my head once again. Evans had remained rigid and tight-lipped when I'd escorted him from the Colonel's chambers into the drawing room. But he gradually mellowed as Holmes and I carefully explained to him what had happened with regard to Mavis, and who else was involved. I'd noted at the time his somewhat paternal attitude when discussing both the Crichton sons, which I'd put down to his long service in the family. Evans' obvious disappointment at George's actions was quickly replaced by anger at those of Mavis' brother. Holmes impressed upon the butler as strongly as he could that Jeremiah Hawkins' extortion days were at an end – on this matter, at least.

If we'd planned the subsequent encounter with Mrs. Crichton, we couldn't have stage-managed it with more perfection. The lady entered just at the end of our conversation, with Evans thoroughly moved. The two of them shared a look which lasted longer than was rightly courteous. No words were spoken, but a story laid itself out very clearly, writ large on their faces and in the awkwardness of their movements. I felt thoroughly uncomfortable. Holmes turned to me, flashing a sly grin. I didn't reciprocate. Instead, I cleared my throat and backed away a few paces.

This appeared to break the moment. Mrs. Crichton touched her hair and asked us if all was well.

I could not speak, but Holmes replied that everything was in order and that it was probably time we left the household to its business. Mrs. Crichton thanked us again with all her heart and instructed Evans to hail us a cab, as the hour was so late.

"Doctor Watson," Mrs. Crichton said, touching my arm. "Would you mind calling by tomorrow to look over dear Mavis once again?"

I smiled as best I could and nodded.

"I know I can count on your discretion."

And therein lay the cause of my disquiet. Did she mean professional discretion or personal discretion? How could I return to the Crichton household, knowing that a bond – a relationship – existed between the good lady and her butler above and beyond that which should exist between mistress and servant? A relationship that flew in the face of the sanctity of marriage. A relationship that flourished under the same roof as lived her husband, the butler's ex-commanding officer. Was this not as great a crime as that over which Mrs. Crichton had originally consulted us?

I dragged my hands down over my face. Holmes looked at me with an expression I took at first to be supercilious, but on reflection it was simply symptomatic of his facial injuries.

"Who suffers? Who is hurt or damaged by any of this?" he asked.

"It's not a question of *who*, Holmes," I retorted. "This is about morality, about honour, about right and wrong. If word of this got out – "

"And why should it?"

I opened my mouth but could find no voice with which to respond.

"There is no reason to assume it would," he continued. "And things have clearly been going on for some time. Young Frederick is, what, fourteen years of age?"

"Frederick!" I gasped, incredulous.

"When you pay your return visit tomorrow, take a good look at his eyes. You will see they are Evans' eyes, for sure. Otherwise, like his older brother – he seems to have inherited his features mainly from his mother's side. I had an inkling that something was not as it should be from the start."

I held my hands up in resignation.

Holmes continued. "Take, for example, the suppressed jealousy with which Mrs. Crichton accused Evans of dallying with Mavis, when she told us her tale. The relief that flashed across her features when I announced that the forger was left-handed. Then there was the tension between the

142

lady and her butler as we entered the house. That was far more than you would expect between a disgruntled servant and his mistress."

I had missed all of this. "But what of young Frederick, then?" I asked. "Is it not right that he should know who his father is?"

"That is not a matter for us to judge, or even comment upon. Maybe he will, one day. Of one thing, however, I am certain: He will have more opportunities in life and a better standing in society as the son of Colonel Crichton than he would that of Evans the butler. Surely you wouldn't wish to deprive him of that?"

"No less than I would wish him the care of a loving father."

"My friend, the Colonel may be a drunken old cove, but he dotes on his sons – that much was evident from the brief cab ride we shared. I don't believe there is any reason to concern yourself on that account. Think, instead, on poor Mrs. Crichton. The Colonel and she live almost totally independent lives, it seems. Joined by name and financial dependence only. The Colonel clearly shows little in the way of affection for his wife. I am not judging, as I do not know the circumstances under which this . . . arrangement, if you will, came into being. However, as you well know yourself by now, humanity requires companionship, attention, someone with whom to share thoughts, experiences. And someone to whom we can unburden ourselves from time to time. Would you then disavow Mrs. Crichton of that opportunity, if her husband chooses to shut himself away in his own bubble of fading military glory?"

"But her friends, her work – ?" I countered.

He would hear nothing of it.

"For some, Watson, work is not enough, no matter how noble or just the cause. And I say this as someone for whom work is *everything*."

This much was certainly true. I thought of the plentiful times I had witnessed Holmes between cases, listless, seeking solace in a syringe. If I could accept him for his ways, it seemed hypocritical of me not to do the same for Mrs. Crichton.

"Allow the lady some affection. Some attention. Allow her to love and be loved. Of course, I speak as someone very much on the outside looking in, in such cases. But although I cannot *feel* in that way, I can understand what those feelings mean to a person."

I had to smile, in spite of myself. Here I was, getting a lesson on the human condition from Sherlock Holmes, of all people!

"With acceptance comes understanding," I told him. "Thank you, Holmes. You are a true friend and *confidante*."

"Likewise, my dear Watson," he replied. "And now, if you'll forgive me, I'm not sure I don't feel a little sleep beckoning, for once. Probably the exertion of the bout. Good night, my friend." And he left.

143

A weight had lifted from my conscience. I felt at last that I could not only face sleep, but I could also face the Crichton household again on the morrow – or in fact today, as the mantelpiece clock chimed two in the morning. I extinguished the lamp. It would not be an early start, I decided.

The Adventure of the
Not-Very-Merry Widows
by Craig Stephen Copland

"Well, if you must know, Mr. Holmes, I can tell you that at ten minutes past seven on Tuesday morning, I was part-way through the lovely full English breakfast my maid had prepared for me, and the very idea that I would get up from my table and allow my sausage and eggs and fried bread to become stone cold while I traipsed next door to Mrs. Chowser's house, found and loaded a shotgun, inserted the barrel into her mouth, and blew her head off, is utterly and completely absurd. Total lunacy and entire nonsense.'

"And your maid, Mrs. Blimber? Will she vouch for you?" said Holmes.

"She will. I never left the house, and she was with me throughout, and I am outraged at the suggestion made by that idiot police inspector that I am considered a suspect."

"He was informed by your neighbors that there was, shall we say, an intense animosity between you and Mrs. Chowser. Is that not true?"

"Of course it is true. And I was not alone. Nobody liked her. Well, to be more specific, as you are likely to discover anyway if you are as good a detective as they say you are, I used to be one of her friends. That ended almost a decade ago."

"Did it now? What happened?"

"What has that to do with anything? It was years ago and is nobody's business – including yours, Mr. Holmes."

"Madam, allow me to remind you that Dr. Watson and I have come to your home at your request and that you are wishing to contract for my services to help find and arrest the true killer – "

"That is exactly what I want you to do, Mr. Holmes. The sooner this dreadful nuisance is over, the better."

"Very well then, please understand that my part in it will be over immediately if you do not answer my questions and agree to have me undertake whatsoever tasks I choose without question. It is your choice, madam."

"Fine, if you are going to be that way about it. You may record that I have been furious with Henrietta Chowser for the past nine years because ten years ago last month – that would be November of 1889 – her husband died, and a year later, she stole mine away from me. That summer, she

145

enticed him on, for lack of a more vulgar word, a *rendezvous* to Brighton and insisted on the two of them going sailing. Being the clumsy oaf she is, she almost capsized the boat, causing my husband, Elmore, to fall out, and since she was useless as a sailor, she could not rescue him, and he drowned. Is that a good enough answer, Mr. Holmes?"

"It will do."

"Fine. Then kindly get to work and find who did it. Now, allow me to excuse myself. I have a busy day ahead of me."

Mrs. Arabella Blimber stood up and walked out of her parlor, leaving Holmes and me alone. We looked at each other, shrugged, got up, departed the house, and began an unusual inquiry into a strange case that had its genesis thirty years earlier.

Coming to meet Mrs. Blimber in her home was the easiest part of the case. She lived in Baker Street. Her home was several blocks south of 221b and close to the intersection with Oxford Street. It was in a short row of new terraced houses, all quite modern in design and built mostly of cinder blocks with a minimum of wood. According to the advertisements, that made them fireproof. They were not of the same caliber as houses in Mayfair or Belgravia, but not all that far behind. I was somewhat surprised at how tastefully the interior was furnished and impressed with her collection of prints of classical Spanish painters, and plates and ashtrays made of black slate and inlaid with gold filigree.

I would guess, being generous, that her age was about forty. She was what people might describe, when speaking charitably, as having an attractive face but being otherwise strapping, or as looking like a farm-girl from Freesia, when not.

On the morning of Tuesday, 19 December, several neighbors reported hearing a loud bang that they took for a motorized lorry backfiring. At nine o'clock, Mrs. Henrietta Chowser's maid entered the house and found her dead in her bed, the back of her head having been blown away by a shotgun. The gun was lying on the floor at the end of the bed, creating the immediate impression that the lady had taken her own life. However, it took Inspector Lestrade less than a minute to discount suicide, seeing as the barrel of the shotgun was too long to permit the deceased to put one end in her mouth and still reach the trigger with her hand. As her body was completely covered with a blanket and a quilt – it being winter – there was no way, according to the inspector, she could have contorted her leg and used her toe to fire the gun.

Lestrade immediately pronounced it a case of murder and began questioning the neighbors.

In spite of his determination not to allow his emotions to go on display, I could tell that Sherlock Holmes was impatient to be brought into the case. After all, the murder had taken place on the very street where England's most famous detective lived, a fact the sensationalist Press had been eager to point out.

But no request had come. Therefore, he readily agreed to offer his services to Mrs. Arabella Blimber when she summoned us to her home on the morning of Friday, 22 December.

It was going to be a busy Christmas.

As we stood on the pavement of Baker Street, Holmes lit a cigarette and gazed up into the cloudy sky, apparently oblivious to the cold. I, on the other hand, could feel the chill of the solstice wind and was not in the mood for standing still and freezing.

"What say, Holmes?" I asked, prodding him. "Shall we begin with the old *cui bono*? Who gets rich off the death of the widow?"

"Not a bad suggestion, Watson. Yes. A good place to start. She had two sons, both of whom work in The City and belong to Boodles. It is a Friday afternoon, and I expect that they will come to their club for drinks before going home for the weekend."

Boodles in St. James is one of the oldest and most prestigious clubs in London. It has been around for well over a century, and its members, past and present, include royalty, aristocrats, esteemed philosophers, and captains of industry and commerce. Amongst those of us who would never be invited to join, however, we could not walk past the door without recalling Charles Dickens's ridiculing it with his recounting the silly goings-on of Lords Boodle and Coodle, Sir Thomas Doodle and the Duke of Foodle, along with Goodle, Hoodle, Loodle, and Noodle.

Nevertheless, I felt somewhat intimidated as we approached the door.

"These sons of the widow must have done quite all right for themselves to belong here," I said. "We certainly do not fit in."

"Nor should we ever want to," said Holmes as he banged on the iron ring door-knocker. "Most of the members of these clubs owe their being permitted to join to nothing more than a fleeting moment of intimacy between their mothers and fathers and their resulting birth into wealth and title."

There was no respect of persons with either God or Sherlock Holmes.

In response to Holmes's request to meet with either Mr. Collingwood Chowser or Mr. Cranleigh Chowser, the porter disappeared into the bowels of the club and reappeared five minutes later with two tall, good-looking young chaps, dressed from Savile Row.

147

"Mr. Sherlock Holmes, is it?" said the first, extending his hand and smiling widely. He introduced himself and his brother and, gesturing to the hallway behind him, invited us to join them in the Beau Brummell Room.

After the necessary brief chit-chat about the weather in December and asking the staff to bring in some sherry, Mr. Collingwood Chowser, apparently the older of the two, came directly to the point.

"We assume that you are here regarding the death of Henrietta. We've already spoken to one of Scotland Yard's inspectors and tried our best to tell him everything we knew. Are you assisting him? Not that it matters all that much. My brother and I are delighted to meet the famous Mr. Sherlock Holmes and England's most popular writer, the esteemed Dr. Watson, regardless of the circumstances."

I thought he seemed awfully chipper for a young man whose mother had had her head blown away only three days earlier.

"My condolences," I said, thinking it only appropriate, "on the tragic passing of your mother. It must have been – "

"*Not* our mother, Doctor," said Collingwood. "Terribly sorry to rudely interrupt, but Henrietta was our *step*-mother, and we may as well be frank . . ." He glanced at his brother, who shrugged and nodded. "We are horrified with the attaching of such a bloody crime to the history of the family, but otherwise not at all grief-stricken. Frankly, we must confess that we were both somewhat happy to see the end of her. Isn't that right, Cran?"

The younger brother grunted in the affirmative.

"Were you now?" said Holmes. "Then please be more precise than *somewhat*. How *financially* happy were you with your step-mother's death?"

"Oww! Well now . . . we had read that Sherlock Holmes was economical with his questions, but that one was rather blunt, sir."

"A blunt answer then would be in order."

"My brother can answer that better than I can. He's the numbers man between us. What do you say to Sherlock Holmes, Cran?"

"Honestly, sir, we do not know," said Cranleigh Chowser.

"Honestly, sir," replied Holmes. "I find that hard to believe."

"As would I, if I were the famous Mr. Sherlock Holmes. So here is the most precise answer we can give you at present: We assume that there is little cash left in the estate. No more than five-hundred pounds. Our father transferred fifty-thousand pounds into a trust for the two of us whilst we were both still at Cambridge. Obviously, Henny had more than enough to live on and live well she did, but she did not have a fortune from Father."

"What about the house in Baker Street? And I believe there is also some property in Sussex, is there not?"

"Ah, you are indeed quite the detective, sir. If you have found that out already, then you can no doubt also find out how much equity there is in the two properties. We do not have exact current numbers, but we understand that Henny hypothecated them to give herself more cash. We have wondered what she was going to live on when she reached the limits of the collateral value. We now take title to the house but, frankly, we do not expect more than a net of two-hundred-and-fifty pounds from the sale."

Holmes paused for a minute, took a sip of sherry, and lit a cigarette.

"Allow me then to pursue a different tack."

"Go right ahead, Mr. Holmes," replied Cranleigh. "Ask us anything you want. If we can help you and Scotland Yard find out what happened, we don't mind sitting and chatting for as long as you wish."

"Thank you. I shan't detain you much longer. Tell me – why did you dislike your step-mother? Did she interfere in your father's marriage? Was not your mother dead and your father a widower before he met Miss Henrietta?"

The younger man looked at his brother, who nodded in return.

"To be candid about it," said Collingwood Chowser, "I suppose you could say, "that *the funeral bak'd meats did coldly furnish forth the marriage tables,* if you know what I mean, sir."

"I do. How long was it?"

"Two months from the day Mum died until Father remarried. I suppose we should have been happy for him, but it was disturbing for both of us." His voice faltered ever so slightly. "Right, Cran?"

"Umm, right."

"Quite understandable. Then just one more issue for the moment, if I may."

"Like I said, sir," said Cranleigh. "Ask away."

"Thank you. Very well, then. Ten years ago. How and when did your father die?"

The casual confidence that both of them had exuded up until that time vanished. A cloud came over both of their faces, and it seemed that they had not expected such a question, nor welcomed it.

"It was a decade ago, sir," said the older brother. He paused and took a deep breath. "It was terribly painful for both of us. Is it truly necessary to drag it back up? Does it really have anything to do with a murder that took place three days ago?"

"I am sorry," said Holmes. "I can see that I touched upon a sore point. However, let me remind you that I am investigating the murder of your step-mother and no data, regardless of how remote it may seem, is inconsequential. Please answer my question."

Collingwood Chowser took a deep breath and blew out through pursed lips.

"Sir . . . if I were to state the address . . . 19 Cleveland Street . . . would that mean anything to you?"

"It would. Go on."

"We found it hard to believe – indeed we still do – but our father's name was found amongst the patrons of that house. In the autumn of 1889, Inspector Abberline and the Crown Prosecutor, Charles Russell, came to our home and told Father that he was going to be charged along with all the other perverts and loathsome creatures, and . . . he could not bear to face the humiliation and shame . . . and he took his own life."

"How?"

In a halting voice, the older Chowser continued. "He went out into the yard behind the house and shot himself in the head."

"Were you in the house at the time?"

"No, we were away at school. When we came home, Henny told us what had happened."

"Did you believe what you were told?"

"Not at first. Father never gave any inclination of being inclined in that way. Quite the opposite. But Scotland Yard gave Henny the file of all the notes and correspondence and receipts they had collected that led them to charge Father. Doing so was in violation of police practices, but decent of them all the same. They said they had no further use for any of it, and it would be best if it were destroyed."

"And was it?"

"We burned it. But every word we read is burned into our memories . . . Can we please move on to any other topic, Mr. Holmes? Please."

"Those are quite enough questions for the day. There is only one misconception that I must clear up before leaving: I have not been contracted by Scotland Yard to investigate this case. I have been contracted by Mrs. Blimber."

"Her?" said Cranleigh. "What for?"

"Some parties added her to the list of suspects, and she has requested my services to find the murderer and allow all suspicion to be lifted from her. I'm sorry . . . do you find it objectionable that I would be working for her?"

The older brother then resumed responsibility for the conversation. "No . . . no, not really. We have very little to do with her. All we know, I guess, is that she and Henny hated each other, and as we were not very fond of Henny then – well, as they say, the enemy of my enemy is my

150

friend. Frankly, we bear her no ill will, and it makes no difference to us if she is paying your tab."

"Excellent," said Holmes. "And a final request: As the house in Baker Street is now your property, may I have your permission to enter it?"

"By all means. Do you want the key?"

As it is likely that some readers are not aware of what came to be known as the Cleveland Street Scandal, allow me a circumspect explanation. In the summer of 1889, the police arrested a fifteen-year-old telegraph boy who had far too much money in his pockets. He led them to a homosexual brothel on Cleveland Street in which many young boys worked as prostitutes, serving the licentious practices of a long list of wealthy men, many of them titled and a few connected to the Royal Family. The government attempted to hush it up, but word inevitably made its way into the public square. It was understandable that an otherwise honorable man might prefer to end his own life instead of enduring the disgrace of being identified with the sordid event.

I was not surprised at the reticence of the brothers to speak about it.

As soon as we were out of Boodles and standing on the pavement of St. James Street, Holmes, holding a key in his hand, lit a cigarette and stood like a statue in the cold.

"Well, Holmes," I said whilst I could still speak before my teeth began to chatter. "A penny for your thoughts."

"Hmm? Oh, yes, well, I suppose that I am thinking that, frankly, any man who repeatedly insists that he is speaking to you *frankly* . . . isn't."

During the week leading up the Christmas, the sun sets before four o'clock in the afternoon. As we stood in the dark after our time in Boodles. I was more than ready to return home and sit in front of the hearth with a hot toddy.

Holmes was not.

"*Tempus fugit,* my dear doctor. It is only a few minutes back to the location of the crime." He waved at a cab as he spoke.

We quickly returned to Baker Street. The house in which the murder had taken place was immediately adjacent to the one in which our morning had begun.

A uniformed constable stood on the pavement in front of it, barring any entry to the house by the curious and prurient.

"'Ello there, Mr. 'Olmes," he said as we approached. "The inspector 'adn't told me you would be stopping by. I assume you're working on this case, eh?"

"Right indeed, sir," said Holmes. "Your dear Inspector Lestrade forgets to tell me things all the time too. All I got was the key."

He held it up, and the constable smiled and stepped aside. "It's all yours, sir. The switch for the electric lights is to the left, just inside the door."

Like that of Mrs. Blimber, the house was of a new design with all of its walls, both interior and exterior, made of concrete blocks stacked on top of each other. The bare concrete had been covered with a parging and a coat of plaster. This practice may have meant that the house was cozy and safe, but it was impossible to tap a nail into any wall if one wished to hang a painting or photograph. Owners were forced to glue small blocks of wood to the plaster and then tap the hooks into them.

Mrs. Chowser must have mastered the technique, as she had hung many prints of paintings that were remarkably similar to those next door. So also were the Spanish curios and pieces inlaid with gold filigree. The only major difference between her walls and those of Mrs. Blimber was the additional presence of pictures and objects with a religious significance. I noticed scenes from Bible stories, plaques inscribed with verses of Scripture, and a half-a-dozen printed portraits of Pope Leo XIII, every one in a slightly different pose but all with his hand raised, blessing the faithful with the two-up-two-down fingers. Crosses were ubiquitous.

"What are we looking for?" I asked Holmes.

"Ignore the obvious. Lestrade and his men are perfectly capable of looking there and most likely already have. Give priority to those places where things can be hidden – under loose floorboards, behind wainscoting, under the eaves on the upper floor, hiding behind jars and under sweaters. I suggest you start with the lavatory."

There was nothing hidden there. Everything of interest was staring me in the face. On the dresser was a pair of quart jars of laudanum, one of which was nearly empty. In the drawer beside the hand basin were the syringes and vials of seven-per-cent, and stronger solutions of mind-numbing pharmaceuticals.

"This woman," I said to myself, "had a serious habit of dulling her physical and emotional sensations."

I moved on to her dressing room and went to work immediately on the score of hat boxes, reputed to be favorite places for women of a certain age to keep items they wished to hold on to but never to be seen by others.

The first six boxes contained hats, most of which had passed out of fashion a decade ago. The seventh was considerably heavier and revealed a trove of letters, photographs, certificates, postcards, and the like. Holding the box as if it were a prize cake, I strutted back to the hallway.

"Holmes! Where are you?"

"In the middle room," came the reply. I went there, box in hand.

"What are you doing in here? This looks like a dressing closet?"

"It is. It is also where the lady slept and where she was shot."

"In here? That's odd. It's cramped and rather unappealing compared to the master bedroom. Not even a window. Are you sure?"

"Yes," said Holmes. "As you can see, the cot has been stripped and the bloodied sheets, blankets and pillows taken away. And then some service has come by and cleaned up the entire bloody mess. As to why she preferred this room to the master bedroom, who can say. Single women of a certain age develop habits that suit them for reasons unknown and inexplicable to men. Perhaps it was warmer and away from the street, and she slept more soundly. Who knows?"

Who knows, indeed, I thought. The bed was only a single cot, but had a thick mattress and was now bare, except for a thick quilt that must have survived the horrible event unpolluted and lay folded-up at the end of the bed.

"Carry on, Watson. We can take that box back with us and look at it later."

"Isn't that removing evidence from a crime scene? That's against the law, is it not?"

"If Scotland Yard left it behind, then they must not have considered it to be evidence."

"But they did not even find it. I did."

"I shall recommend that they hire you as a house-searcher extraordinaire. Kindly keep searching. An hour more should do the job. By then, Mrs. Hudson should have supper ready for us."

I poked my way up and down and all over several more rooms on the second floor and climbed a ladder into the small attic. Nothing more of singular interest presented itself. At the end of an hour, I met Holmes in the parlor. He had a cloth bag over his shoulder and a porcelain serving plate in his hands. With a flourish, he flipped it over and displayed the surface of the plate to me. It was fine, white china with a stylized drawing of a tree in the middle of it, surrounded by words in Latin that I couldn't read from where I stood.

"Why do you want that?" I asked.

"Because our client, Mrs. Blimber, had one exactly the same on her coffee table. Did you not notice?"

Apparently, I had not.

"Come now," he said. "We can walk home in ten minutes."

"Holmes, stop. There's a constable out there. You cannot expect him to let you walk out of here carrying a load of property."

He paused. "An excellent observation, Watson. I suppose I could come up with a plausible reason for taking all this, but it might be easier if we were to leave by the postern door and deposit the goods in the alley and then come back and fetch them."

"Much easier," I said.

The kitchen had a door that opened to a small back stoop and into the back garden. There was sufficient moonlight for us to step down into the garden and start toward the back wall. I was leading the way when Holmes whispered to me to stop.

"What for?"

"Hold these," he said, and I soon found myself holding the hatbox, the cloth satchel, and a porcelain serving plate. He stepped through a garden bed to the wooden wall that separated Mrs. Chowser's back garden from that of Mrs. Blimber's. As I watched, he lit a match, blew it out, and then lifted a metal latch and opened a small door in the wall. He stepped through it, vanished for several minutes and then returned.

"Holmes," I said in a stage whisper. "Enough. It is below freezing out here, and my fingers are turning to icicles. Take your evidence and let us get home."

To my relief, he complied.

All through supper, he perused the contents of the hatbox and said nothing. I went to bed early and left him to his task. I expected that he would be up all night.

At seven-thirty on the morning of 23 December, I descended from my bedroom to find Holmes already at the breakfast table and juggling a cup of coffee, a sheaf of papers from the hatbox, a fork with a chunk of sausage attached, and a cigarette.

"Watson, before you sit down, please take a look out of the window to the pavement below. But keep yourself hidden."

"What for? Is someone about to attack us?"

"Do you see the man pacing back and forth in front of our door?"

I slipped one eye past the window frame and looked down. It was still dark and gloomy, and the only light came from the nearest street lamp.

"Yes. I see him. What about him?"

"Can you see what he is wearing?"

"A winter coat and hat. What would you expect?"

"Look closer. Below his coat."

"Is that . . . is he wearing a skirt? Oh no, it's a cassock. He's a priest. What in the world is he doing?"

154

"He has been there for the past ten minutes, and he appears to be debating whether or not to knock on our door. Would you mind going down to the street and quickly accost him and drag him in here?"

"What for?"

"Because he must have a reason for coming here, and I want to learn what it is."

"Oh, very well then."

I walked down the stairs and, in a quick set of movements, I opened the door to Baker Street and walked toward the clergyman.

"Good morning, Father. I have divine orders to bring you in from the cold so you can enjoy a hot cup of coffee and a chat. Do come."

The poor fellow was thoroughly nonplussed. I didn't give him time to recover but slipped my arm through his and encouraged him, bodily, toward the door.

"Right up the stairs, Father. Mrs. Hudson will take your coat and hat, and Sherlock Holmes is ready to listen to whatever you are bursting to confess to him."

He moved slowly and hesitantly up the first five stairs, then stopped, shrugged, and clambered up the rest of the flight. Mrs. Hudson greeted him as he entered our sitting room.

"Oh, my goodness!" she said. "It's Father Flanagan. Welcome, Father. I hope you've come to bestow a Christmas blessing on my house. There's no telling what little devils have crept in this past year with these two scalawags coming and going."

"You two know each other?" I said, rather stupidly as the answer was obvious.

"This is Father Michael Flanagan," said Mrs. Hudson. "He the parish priest at St. James Spanish Place. Our women's guild at St. Monica's and the St. James ladies get together every quarter. They are very proud of their beautiful new church, as they should be. Right, Father?"

She took his hat and coat while Holmes poured a hot cup of coffee from the carafe on the table.

"Uh, oh, yes, right, yes of course, right. St. James is indeed a beautiful new edifice."

He sat down, but looked more than somewhat confused and averted his eyes by concentrating on blowing into the not-particularly-hot cup of coffee to cool it off. He was a man about the same age and shape as myself, but with a distinctly Irish complexion.

"Beautiful new Gothic church or decrepit old chapel, it matters not," said Holmes. "I am grateful for your visit. Am I right in assuming that your doing so is in some way connected to the tragic death of one of your parishioners, Mrs. Henrietta Chowser?"

He was startled by Holmes's question but recovered his wits immediately. "Yes, that is why I have come. I learned that you are working on the case."

"You learned, you say? And might you have learned of my involvement from another one of your parishioners, Mrs. Arabella Blimber?"

"Yes. She has informed the entire neighborhood that she believes Scotland Yard to be incompetent imbeciles and that she has hired the detective, Sherlock Holmes, to find the killer."

"Has she now? And for some reason, knowing *that* has brought you to my door the next morning. And that suggests to me that you are in possession of either an unholy curiosity about the murder, or you know something about it which you believe you should make known to me. One of the two, Father. Which is it?"

"The latter."

"However, you hesitated before knocking on my door, which suggests that you are troubled about imparting that data to me. Data germane to a murder investigation should, of course, be readily turned over to the police, and yet you have not done so. That must be because such data was revealed to you in the context of a confession and, as such, is subject to the sacred vow, the Seal of the Confession, demanding that confidentiality never be violated. Is that correct?"

He gave Holmes a sidewards look. "Correct."

"You have acknowledged that both Mrs. Chowser and Mrs. Blimber are members of your parish. Or, in the case of Mrs. Chowser, *was* a member. As Mrs. Henrietta Chowser was by far the more devout of the two, it is safe to assume that it was she who regularly confessed her sins and not her neighbor. Also correct?"

He took several seconds before answering. "I cannot reveal anything concerning confession, but I am free to tell you that she began six months ago to attend Mass every morning."

"And Mrs. Blimber?"

"Mass at Christmas and Easter only."

"Ah yes, one of those. Now, then, Father Flanagan, you know of my reputation as a detective, so there is nothing to be concerned about if such knowledge as you have acquired during the sacrament of confession is something you assume I would discover in the course of my investigation. On the contrary, it must be something which you are quite sure I would never discover. Is it?"

"I am sorry sir, but as much as I feel compelled to help you, I cannot violate the Seal. Not even after the penitent is dead."

156

"Of course. As I have the highest respect for your vows and would never think of asking or coercing you into violating them, we need to find a way for you to impart such important data to me without offending the Almighty – to say nothing of your bishop."

"That would be. . .very useful, Mr. Holmes."

"Very well then. What say you do not tell me what it is that you know, but only give me some clue, a hint as to the direction I must pursue in order to discover the facts myself. Might that solution be acceptable to you?"

"It might. No . . . it would. Yes, it would. I believe I could do that."

"Brilliant. Then kindly provide me with such a clue."

The Reverend Michael Flanagan was silent for several seconds before breaking into a satisfied smile.

"Brighton."

"That's all?" said Holmes. "Just one word. *Brighton.* Oh my, you are going to make me sing for my supper, aren't you?"

"From what I have heard about you, Mr. Holmes, I doubt it will take you long."

"Do you now? Brighton, you say. Perhaps the tragic sailing adventure in which Mr. Edmond Blimber drowned and Mrs. Henrietta did not?"

That brought a startled look to the face of the clergyman. He nodded and replied, "It will not take you long at all. Brighton is where to start. It is not where to end. And now kindly allow me to extend warm best wishes for the Christmas season, and I shall be on my way."

He stood, and Mrs. Hudson, who had been watching and listening throughout, assisted him with his coat. As he was about to leave the room, he turned back to Holmes.

"There is a train to Brighton leaving within the hour from London Bridge. I suggest that you be on it if you wish to meet with the necessary people before they vanish over Christmas."

Then he turned to Mrs. Hudson, smiled, faced the room, and made the sign of the cross over it. "And a blessing on your house, Mrs. Hudson, and prayers for your . . . what did you call them? Scalawags?"

With that, he descended the stairs back to Baker Street.

Holmes gave me a look, and I knew what was coming.

"Watson?"

"Right, Holmes. I shall be ready to depart in ten minutes."

Within forty-five minutes, we were at London Bridge Station and in a cabin bound for Brighton. Expecting that I would have an hour of undisturbed time to write, I brought my notepad and pencil.

Holmes had other ideas.

"Please read these," he said, handing me several files. The contents I recognized as having come from the hatbox I had discovered the previous day.

"What am I looking for?"

"Anything that doesn't appear to fit with the devout Christian character of the deceased."

"Has it occurred to you, Holmes, that the onset of serious piety may be of recent history? Any priest, physician, or even a husband for that matter will confirm that women of a certain age are known to experience soul-altering epiphanies from which they never recover."

His face acquired a blank look for several seconds before he responded.

"That had not occurred to me, and I acknowledge that the fairer sex is your department. Very well then, look for something . . . anything . . . that strikes you as interesting."

"Oh, such as any indication that the deceased might be having an affair with the bishop, who had secretly fathered a child in Boston? Something vaguely like that?"

"Precisely."

"Before I start, would you mind telling me how you are going to go about finding out anything about her whilst in Brighton?"

"All men who operate rental businesses have remarkable memories of the day when one of their customers died. In our case, the man who rented the sailboat to a couple and had it returned minus one passenger will have a very clear memory."

"Ah, yes, of course. But would you mind telling me how we're going to find him? There must be a dozen such chaps in Brighton that rent boats to vacationers from London."

"We shall inquire at the newspaper. Editors also remember stories that had even the smallest hint of scandal. Indeed, they are very fond of such stories, as they do wonders for the sale of newspapers."

For the remainder of the journey, I looked through letters, postcards, photographs, and newspaper clippings. None struck me as interesting in the least, and it was not for lack of diligent searching. Anything beyond the trivial and mundane would have relieved the boredom, but no such account could be found. Looking across at Holmes from time to time, I concluded that he was encountering the same.

The Evening Argus provided the daily news to the good citizens of Brighton and Hove. A copy purchased at the station gave us its address and the name of the editor. It was a fifteen-minute walk from the station to the *Argus*'s office on Manchester Street, and during the summer months, with a breeze blowing in from the ocean, it might have been pleasant. In late December, it was not.

"Might we have a word with your editor, Mister Harry Heaver," Holmes said to the young chap who manned the front counter of the newspaper.

"Is there no one else who can help you, sir?"

"What's wrong with him?" asked Holmes.

"There's nothing wrong with him, sir. But there might be with you after I disturb him. He's a bit tetchy when we're trying to get the paper put to bed. Doesn't take kindly to being distracted."

"Tell him that Sherlock Holmes wishes to speak to him and that I shall not need more than five minutes of his time."

"You're really Sher – "

"I am. Please assist me and find Mister Heaver."

The young chap scampered off, and three minutes later he reappeared, followed by a thin, stooped man of about my age who gave one the impression of having been messing with printer's ink every day of his life since he was born.

"You say you're Sherlock Holmes, do you?" he said as he approached us.

"I do and I am."

"Yeah, well that makes me the Queen of Sheba. What do you want, whoever you are?"

This was not the first time that someone had refused to believe that Sherlock Holmes was indeed Sherlock Holmes. I had come prepared with an old copy of *The Strand* magazine in my portfolio case that Mr. Sidney Paget had illustrated with a very fine drawing of Holmes. Without saying a word, I extracted it, walked over to Mr. Heaver, and held it up in front of his nose.

"And I suppose," he said, "that makes you Dr. Watson, the writer who has become filthy rich penning all those sensational stories whilst the rest of us scribblers slave away every day and get paid a pittance."

"It does," I said. "Now sir, may we please have a moment of your time? Mr. Holmes is working on a murder case, and we are in need of your knowledge and advice."

A humble and sincere request for advice is one of the surest ways on earth to get a busy man to take the time to have a word. It worked again.

"What do you want?"

"Thank you, sir," said Holmes. "Could you kindly turn your mind back to the summer of 1890? Might you remember a couple, a man and a woman who came to Brighton but who were not married to each other – "

159

"Ha! You'll have to do better than that, Mr. Holmes. That describes half the Mr. and Mrs. Smiths who find Brighton a fine place for trysting. There's a better chance of my remembering any couple if you said they truly and legally *were* married to each other."

"The man's name was Elmore Blimber, and the woman was a widow, Mrs. Henrietta Chowser. They went sailing, and he drowned."

"Is that so? Well, it so happens that I do remember that day. Remember it rather well, in fact. We had a nice short article ready to run about it, and we never did. So, don't be asking me to go looking for it in our archives. It's not there."

"Do you remember why it was not reported?"

"For the most honorable reason, Mr. Holmes: Somebody paid us not to. In keeping with the high standards of the members of the Press of Great Britain, we took the money and spiked the story. And don't ask me who paid us, because I don't know."

"But you do know, I am sure, who it was who provided you with the information that was used to write the story."

"That I can help you with. It all came from Captain Dudly Duff. He runs the shop that rented the boat."

"And what shop might that be, sir?"

"Called *Rigged Out Rentals.* About two-hundred yards east of the pier. But you won't find him there now."

"And why might that be?"

He uttered a colorful oath and said, "In case you had not noticed, Mr. Famous Detective, it's the middle of winter. No one, not even American tourists, rent boats this time of year. His shop is closed until May."

"Does he live in Brighton all year?"

"That he does. I can give you his home address, but it won't do you any good right now."

"And why not, sir?"

"Because Dudly is bound to be sitting in The Pump House Pub getting three sheets to the wind. You can go and talk to him there, and if he is still sober enough to utter a sentence, he can tell you all about it. But let me warn you: When you walk in there, you might be mistaken for a bounder from the Board of Inland Revenue, and that might shorten your pleasant morning. So, good luck to you, Mr. Holmes."

He turned away from us and retreated behind the front counter and down the hallway.

The Pump House Pub was in the old town center of Brighton, and a sign above its door proclaimed that it had been in operation since 1776. The door was closed to keep out the cold, but we could hear laughter and

160

singing coming from inside as we approached. Within ten seconds of our entering, the place fell silent, and some twenty pairs of eyeballs were glaring at us.

"Gentlemen!" said Holmes in a loud voice. "Not only am I *not* from Inland Revenue, but I have come enjoy Christmas cheer in this fine establishment. My friend here has offered to buy a round for every man in the house."

A cheer went up from everyone except me. I grumbled and walked to the bar to pay for the round.

"And what is it," asked the barkeep, "that brings you to our pub so close to Christmas? I can see you're not from around here."

"We are here on a private matter," I said, "and we need some advice from a chap named Dudly Duff – *Captain* Dudly Duff. Might we find him here?"

I had dropped my voice to a whisper and held a finger to my lips as soon as I had uttered the man's name. The barkeep whispered in return.

"Back to the wall. Captain's cap. Under the ship's wheel. That's Dudly."

"Thank you, my good man. You might just see a cheerful reference to this pub in *The Strand* magazine someday."

I gestured to Holmes, and the two of us made our way through the cluster of boisterous men to the back of the pub. As soon as Dudly Duff caught our eye contact and concluded that we were coming for him, he stood up. He was a powerful man, still trim for his sixty or more years. His thick forearms covered with tattoos and his trimmed beard and captain's cap all said *Her Majesty's Royal Navy*. He must have entered the boat rental business after retiring from a life before the helm.

"Captain Dudly Duff?" said Holmes.

"That depends on who it is that's asking."

Holmes handed the fellow his card. He looked at it and shouted to the barkeep.

"George! I need a coffee and leave the pot on the table." Then he looked at Holmes. "I'll be back in three minutes."

Leaving his coat draped over the back of the chair, he walked out of the bar in his shirtsleeves. Three minutes later, he returned, his face flushed from the cold.

"Nothing," he said, "like a cold blast off the ocean to sober a man up. Follow me. We can talk in the back room. George! Bring the coffee into the back, will ya? Thanks, mate."

The three of us sat around a small table in a private room, and before Holmes or I could say anything, he looked right at Holmes and said, "Aye, it's about that Chowser woman, isn't it?"

161

Sherlock Holmes is seldom if ever surprised, but this caught him off-guard.

"It is, but may I ask – "

"Read about her in the paper last night. Always wondered how long it would be before someone wanted to know more about what happened. So, when Sherlock Holmes shows up the next day and wants to talk to me, what else could it be? Logical, right, mate?"

"Very. So, what can you tell me about her sailing adventure during the summer of 1890?"

"If you are referring to Sunday, the eighth of June of that year, where do you want me to start?"

"At the beginning. Kindly be precise and concise, but omit no significant detail, and forgive me if I interrupt from time to time for clarification."

"Aye, aye, Mr. Sherlock Holmes. So, what my boys and I got to calling the Anne Bonny incident – she being a famous pirate who disposed of unwanted men on her ship, you know."

"I know. Continue."

"Well, it was around eleven in the morning, and it was as fine a morning as one is likely to have and for which sailors say a prayer of thanks to the good St. Brendan, seeing as the sun was warm and shining and the breeze was light and steady from the west, and just one of those jolly good days for a man to be at sea."

"It was a pleasant day, I understand. Please continue."

"Aye, so there I was with my boys setting out the boats for the day for the vacationers who had come down from London for the weekend, and along comes this fine-looking couple. Not old but not young either, but well-dressed, except that the gent had his hat pulled down to hide his face, and the lady had a full bonnet for the same reason, and I reckoned straight away that they were not a husband and wife but had come to Brighton for a bit of the you-know-what, from which we have sons-of-guns in every port of England. None of my business, of course, so I turn a blind eye and rent them the fat tub of a sixteen-foot dinghy, the one my boys named after a couple of those Greek gods they learned about in school, the two who always chummed around together."

"Oh," I said, "you mean Zeus and Mercury?"

"No," he replied, keeping a blank face. "Titan and Uranus."

A second later, Holmes guffawed. The captain joined him. I did not. For the life of me, I could not understand what was so funny.

"I can see, Mr. Holmes," he said, "that you appreciate a sailor's sense of humor. You'll have to join us on board someday."

"I would enjoy that, as long as it is not on that boat," said Holmes.

He and the captain both laughed heartily again, for a reason that I, to this day, still do not see.

"It was just one of the boats we rent to folks who look like they can't tell a rudder from a rat line, because it's nigh on impossible to capsize them, if you know what I mean."

"I do. Is it your practice to let people with no skill in sailing take boats out on to the ocean? What if there was a storm?"

"If there's a storm coming in, we don't rent to nobody, as doing so would be madness. But on a day like that one, anyone could have smooth sailing. So off they went. And blow-me-down if the woman don't look like she's an old hand, and she's tells the gent to man the jib sheet whilst she holds the mainsheet and tiller and off they go. Once they are far enough out to sea and past the end of the pier, she tacks starboard and sails off to the west, and I tend to the next set of customers."

"How long did they book the rental for?"

"They set sail that day for a three-hour tour. But after one hour, one of my boys, young Maynard with his eagle eyes, comes to me and says, 'Captain, you might want to take a look at the *Titan*.' So, I take my glass and looked, and about three-hundred yards out from the shore is the boat we rented to that couple, but I can see only one person in it. And it's the woman. And she's sailing it all by herself and doing just a fine job. When she is within a hundred yards of our dock, the boat goes into irons, and the sails start fluttering, and she starts waving her arms and screaming for help."

"With no sign of the man?"

"Aye. So, I tell Maynard to fetch his brother and take the two-man skiff and row out to her, which they do, and they tow her back in to the dock. And she's hysterical and sobbing and crying and says that her Jack fell overboard and drowned. So, we brought her inside and asked the woman who ran the stall selling meat pies to come and sit with her."

Here he stopped and poured himself a cup of hot, black coffee.

"Surely, that was not all you did," said Holmes.

"Of course not. I set off the alarm, which is what is done in Brighton and Hove when any tragic event takes place, and within ten minutes every boat up and down the shore was out on the water and conducting a search, hoping they might find a man who was still alive. Three hours later, they called it off. A full set of clothes and boots may as well be a layer of cement in the water. Unless you're a strong swimmer and can shed them quickly, you're going down. And in June, the North Atlantic is still bloody cold, and if the boots and coat don't take you down, the cold will get you an hour later."

"Did his body ever emerge?"

"Almost all bodies come back to the surface sometime. In warm water, they'll be back up in a few days. In cold water, it takes longer. Ten days later, some fishermen from Eastbourne pulled him out."

"I assume there was an inquest."

"There was. But there were no witnesses, and either Mrs. Chowser or the widow of the man who died or maybe both pleaded with the presiding judge and the press, or maybe paid them off, and it was all swept off the back of the poop deck. There was no reason anyone could find for her to do away with him. All she got out of it was a boatload of grief and the nuisance of the inquest, but not a farthing. Inquest was over in a day. Ruled accidental."

"But, as I sense from your manner of speaking, Captain, you thought otherwise."

"As soon as we helped her out of the boat, young Maynard comes to me and says, 'She could have turned that dinghy around and been back to him in a minute.' And I did not say anything, but in my mind, I agreed with him. I may have said a thing or two in the days following whilst I was in the pub, and soon all of us seamen were of the same mind, and we started referring to her as Anne Bonny, but that was a decade ago and mostly forgotten now."

"Did Mrs. Blimber come to the inquest?"

"She did, but all she did was sit by herself and weep, except for the times she was staring daggers at Mrs. Chowser – with good reason, mind you."

During the hour or so it took to return to London, Holmes sat in silence, his motionless body shifting only slightly to accommodate a few minutes of puffing on his pipe. As we were passing through Croydon, he muttered something that I shall not record and then added, "It makes no sense, Watson. We may have discovered that the victim was herself suspected of killing a man, or maybe even two, but she is herself now dead. The only one we know of with a motive – a decade old one at that – has an ironclad alibi. The step-sons had nothing to gain and far too much at risk. Who does it leave?"

"Well, there's the maid, and maybe a neighbor we have not met, and the priest."

"All highly improbable."

"When you eliminate the impossible, Holmes . . . ."

"Thank you, Watson. I am familiar with the maxim."

It was after four o'clock by the time we returned to London, and the sun had already set. On the ride back to Baker Street from London Bridge,

164

I couldn't help but notice all the lights and decorations that had been set out for Christmas. Several groups of carolers dotted the corners of the intersections along Holborn and Oxford Streets, and merchants with food carts offered hot snacks, Christmas pudding, and all manner of intoxicating beverages. Had Holmes not been so morose, I might have suggested that we get out of the cab and walk home.

We had been back in 221b for about half-an-hour when someone knocked on the door, and Mrs. Hudson offered to respond. A well-dressed gentleman of about sixty years of age entered and greeted both Holmes and me by name.

"Ah, Inspector Abberline," said Holmes, hopping to his feet and extending his hand. "So kind of you to come. A brandy, perhaps, on one of the longest nights of the year."

"Happy to oblige and don't mind if I do. I was here in London shopping for a Christmas present for my dear Emma. It has been several years since I retired from the force, and receiving a request from Sherlock Holmes rather made my day. Bournemouth is dull on the best of days and deadly boring this time of year. How can I help you?"

Holmes pored three brandies from the snifter on the mantel and we sat down. After a few sips, Holmes said, "I need to draw on your memory from the year 1889."

"Oh no, you're not dragging up Jack the Ripper again, are you? I thought I might be finally done with him. For three years after the murders, I chased down every tip and possible lead that came to us. All for naught. Do you have a new theory, Mr. Holmes?"

"No, and I have no interest in that case at all. Another case, sir."

"Ah, well that's good to hear. Which one?"

"19 Cleveland Street."

Inspector Abberline scowled. "That mess? Yes, I remember it. Last major case I worked on. Turned me right off police work, it did – the way everyone up the ladder obfuscated and covered up to protect all those toffs and nobles and princes. If you have some new evidence that would put the true culprits behind bars like they did with Oscar Wilde, more power to you, sir. But I have to warn you: There are powerful men who were involved and who will do whatever it takes to keep you from breaking the case open."

"I am only interested in one man, sir. His name was Elmore Blimber. Kindly tell me, and please, with the unvarnished truth that can pass between two honorable detectives, what you remember about him."

The retired inspector gave Holmes an odd look. "The unvarnished truth is that I've never heard of him."

165

"But you and Charles Russell either charged him or were about to charge him when he took his own life to avoid the scandal."

"Like hell we were. I can tell you the name of every man we investigated, including the ones who we were told we could not identify publicly, and there was no Elmore Blimber on any list. Like I said – never heard of him."

"I was recently informed, sir, that you had a file of evidence proving his guilt and that you, or someone either from the police or the courts, gave the file to his wife after his death so she could destroy it."

"Who in the blazes told you that?"

"His sons. They saw the file and were present when it burned."

"It looks to me, Mr. Holmes, like you have a case on your hands in which someone is stringing you a line. We never give away files of evidence to anyone to destroy, and we certainly did not give one concerning a Mr. Elmore Blimber, since no such file ever existed. My suggestion, sir, from one detective to another, is that you investigate the widow. She's lying about Cleveland Street, and my instincts would lead me to think she might be lying about her husband's suicide as well."

Holmes took a slow sip of brandy. "I fear you may be right, sir. And I fear I cannot interrogate the widow."

"Why not? There's no law that says widows cannot be given the third degree."

"I cannot, because she's dead."

"Well then, you do have a case on your hands, Mr. Holmes. I'm in no hurry to get back to my hotel, so why don't you pour another round and tell me all about it."

I certainly knew of Frederick Abberline. When he retired from the Metropolitan Police Force after thirty years of service and, having received several score of commendations and awards, he was honored as one of the finest men ever to pass through the halls of Scotland Yard. Unlike the way Holmes thought of so many other police inspectors, he treated Inspector Abberline with great respect and deference.

For the next two hours, Holmes explained every conceivable detail of the Chowser case, and the inspector quizzed him on no end of fascinating and imaginative possibilities. It was approaching seven-thirty when Mr. Abberline indicated that he would have to go and meet his wife and friends for dinner at their hotel.

"Anything else, Mr. Holmes?"

"Just one small item, and it may have no significance at all. Please take a look at this serving plate. I removed it from the Chowser residence, having seen an identical one in the home of Mrs. Blimber. Do you recognize it?"

"I do recognize it. It bears the symbol and the motto of Badminton School in Bristol. Do you know it? It's quite the select school for girls. Not necessarily known for the richest of the rich, but certainly for the brightest of the bright. You say both of these women had one. The same plate?"

"They did."

"Then they both went there. A few decades back. I suspect that that's where they met each other and where whatever has gone on between them started. And if I were you, Mr. Holmes, I would be on a train tomorrow morning to Bristol and start asking questions."

"But," I protested, "tomorrow is not only Sunday, it's Christmas Eve. The school will be closed."

"There will be people around, Doctor. The international girls cannot go home, and the staff make sure that they have a Christmas as well. Give me a moment, and I'll think of a name."

He closed his eyes and tented his fingers under his chin. The similarity was uncanny if not unnerving.

"Arleigh Eisenberg. Yes, Miss Eisenberg. That's the one. She'll be your best bet. Ask for her."

"Will she be there?" I asked. "At the school?"

"Not likely. She'll be retired by now. But all those retired spinsters who taught at girls' schools their whole lives have no other life. So they find a place to live nearby and then find excuses to keep coming back. Arleigh Eisenberg was head of the girls' sports programs for forty years. The sports teachers always know the most. Ask for her. Tell her I sent you."

As soon as he had departed, Holmes turned to me with that all-too-familiar look on his face.

"Watson?"

"Right. I'll be ready by six tomorrow morning."

"Wonderful. Perhaps seven for breakfast and seven-thirty to depart. After all, it's Christmas Eve."

At seven-twenty-five the following morning, Holmes and I were finishing our last cups of coffee and about to don our coats and hats and head off into the winter gloom when a loud knock came to the door.

I went down the stairs to answer it, and Inspector Lestrade barged past me and charged up the stairs.

"Mr. Holmes!" he said as I followed him into our front room. "You're still here? Good!" Without taking his coat off, he pulled up a chair and sat down at the breakfast table.

167

"Mrs. Hudson," he said, "would you mind? A cup of coffee, if these two haven't finished the pot."

She poured a full cup for him, and he helped himself to a generous slice of Christmas cake. After sloshing it down, he looked at Holmes.

"I had a wonderful dinner last night with my old friend Fred Abberline and his wife at the Langham. He tells me that you're working on the Chowser case. That was news to me, but he said you were doing a fine job even if you had been removing evidence from the lady's house. Now, I should have you put into irons for doing that, Mr. Holmes, except that you might be on to something and someone else is paying your tab."

"How thoughtful you are," said Holmes. "The Christmas spirit must be getting to you."

"Don't count on it. All right, so Fred passed along everything you had told him about the case, and it seems only fair that I bring you up-to-date on what we've found out."

"Definitely the Christmas spirit thee hath in thrall."

"Don't you wish, Mr. Holmes. Anyway, before you head off to Bristol, I thought you should know what we learned about the two sons, the ones you met at Boodles. It's just one of those things that methodical, plodding police work turns up, and is therefore likely unknown to Sherlock Holmes."

"I am all attention."

"We start by asking *cui bono*. That's Latin for *who benefits*."

"You are truly a font of knowledge."

"We discovered that Messrs. Collingwood and Cranleigh stand to benefit substantially from the death of their step-mother."

"Do they? I was led to believe – and I confirmed the same – that there was very little money left in the estate, and that properties and been pledged against a large loan. Wherein is the benefit?"

"In the firm."

"And what firm might that be?"

"A-ha! That's what you would have learned if you kept asking questions like we regular policemen have to do. The company is called Imperial Manufacturing Limited. It was established by the father and, upon his death, the shares were divided amongst the two boys and the step-mother."

"Were they? Pray continue."

"And do you want to know what that firm makes?

"Most certainly."

'Nothing."

"Nothing? Then wherein is your benefit to Mrs. Chowser?"

"It doesn't make anything, and it doesn't do anything, but it owns a whole lot of things. Mostly licenses, copyrights, options, rights of first refusal, mining rights . . . you name it. Most of those things are static, meaning they aren't generating any cash, but all together, they are highly valuable. Well, it seems that the boys had no interest in actually doing anything with all those assets, seeing as they were too busy with their careers and making substantial money in the City, but they wanted to sell it off. Wicked step-mother didn't want to, and had enough shares to block the sale. The day after she dies, the firm is on the market. Don't know for how much. Very hush-hush and confidential, but getting interest all through the City. So, I don't know about you, Mr. Holmes, but that puts those two toffs right up to the top of my suspect list."

"And rightly so."

"So when you get back from Bristol, I suggest you get to work looking into them more than you have. Oh, I suggest you can take Christmas Day off. Good for the soul. Now, if you will excuse me, I'll be on my way back home. And a Happy Christmas."

"And to you as well, Inspector."

He rose, smiled smugly, put another slice of Christmas cake in his pocket, and departed.

"Merciful heavens, Holmes," I said, "that changes everything. You don't still want to go to Bristol, do you?"

"Indeed, I do. There's a GWR train leaving from Paddington at 8:15. If we move smartly, we can make it in time." He had already started pulling on his winter coat.

The sun had not yet risen, but the gloom of night had passed, and a bright, cold Christmas Eve Day was dawning. Cabs were few and far between on a Sunday, the day before Christmas, and we elected to employ Shanks Pony. Twenty minutes of a forced march brought us to the platform in Paddington with less than five minutes to spare.

"My present to you," said Holmes as he handed me a first-class ticket.

"Thank you. And now who is it that has been seized by the Christmas spirit?"

"I assure you, my friend, I will have recovered by Tuesday."

On a Sunday morning, it was a fast, direct run to Bristol, and we arrived by ten. Fortunately, there was a handful of cabs in the queue, and we entered the gate of Badminton School for Girls on Clifton Road by half-past-ten.

There was no one to be seen. That wasn't overly surprising as it was a cold morning, and sensible girls, especially those who hailed from the warmer climes, would be inside and not risking their delicate lungs in the

169

freezing air. In response to our knock on the door, a lovely young lady from the lands of the Raj opened it and graciously welcomed us. She quickly fetched one of the teachers who had the look of a youngish woman destined to be a headmistress two decades from now.

Yes, she did know Miss Arleigh Eisenberg. If we could come back tomorrow, she would no doubt be spending her Christmas Day at the school with the dozen or so girls who had no homes in England to go to over the holidays. When we explained that we had to see Miss Eisenberg *today*, she was hesitant to give us the home address, but succumbed to Holmes's concocted explanation that I was a writer with *The Strand* and was carrying out research on the splendid history of the school.

"Miss Eisenberg lives quite close by," we were told. "She has a very nice house overlooking the river on the far side of the bridge. You can walk there in ten minutes. There's no wind today, so the bridge should be safe."

She gave us directions, and we started walking.

"Why would she be worried about the safety of the bridge?" I asked.

"You'll see," said Holmes.

I saw.

The bridge we had to cross on foot was the magnificent Clifton Suspension Bridge across the Avon River Gorge. When it was opened twenty-five years before, it was the largest bridge in the world. In length, it was over one-thousand feet, and the height from the roadbed to the river below was nearly two-hundred-and-fifty feet. The architect and engineer who designed it, Mr. Isambard Kingdom Brunel, went on to become one of the most famous engineers in the world.

Half-way across, I stopped and gazed into the gorge below and felt my knees becoming like limp rags.

Sad to say, this brilliant structure had also become a magnet for those who wished to end their own lives. Every year, far too many people leapt to their death. The height of the bridge above the river and rocks below made it almost certain that no one could ever survive the fall.

I vanquished that thought from my mind, and we completed our crossing and went in search of Miss Arleigh Eisenberg. We found her in a small but modern home on the far side of the bridge and adjacent to the railway tracks. It was perched at the edge of the gorge and afforded a stunning view of the river and the bridge. Like the terraced houses on Baker Street, it was also constructed of cinder block covered by a sealant parching and stucco.

In response to our knock, a woman opened the door. Her grey hair and lined face suggested that she was near to seventy years in age, but she was tall, broad-shouldered, and remarkably slender and erect for her age.

170

"Yes, gentlemen?" she said.

"Miss Eisenberg," said Holmes, "my name is Holmes, Sherlock Holmes – "

Our conversation was interrupted by the passing of a train. At first Holmes tried to raise his voice to be heard but was drowned out by the roar. For two minutes, the three of us stood there, saying nothing, until the brake van had vanished across the gorge. Only then could Holmes continue.

"We have been directed to you by Inspector Frederick Abberline, formerly of Scotland Yard, and we seek your advice and assistance. May we have a few minutes of your time?"

To my surprise, she laughed. "Good Lord, what is Freddy up to now, sending Sherlock Holmes to my door? Well, come on in. I've been baking some treats to take to the girls tomorrow, but I'm sure they can spare a few. Sit down. I'll be with you in a minute."

She re-appeared soon, carrying a tray that bore a plate of shortbread biscuits, a pot of tea, and a set of cups and saucers. She poured the tea, and I helped myself to one of the biscuits. In removing it from the plate, I exposed a section of the same stylized tree and Latin words we had seen in the houses on Baker Street.

"We have come, madam," began Holmes, "because we're investigating a case that involves two women who we have reason to believe are Old Girls of the Badminton School, and anything you can tell us about them whilst they were here may prove useful in resolving the serious concerns the case has raised."

"From which decade? The two girls?"

"They are in their mid-to-late forties now. So around thirty years ago."

Miss Eisenberg laughed. "Oh, come, come, Mr. Holmes. I taught several thousand girls during the four decades I served at Badminton. Most of them beyond ten years ago are a blur. The few I remember were either the superb athletes, those with truly brilliant minds, the trouble-makers, and the ones who were odd and strange beyond reason. Unless the two you're asking about fall into one of those baskets, I doubt I can help you. What were their names?"

"Their maiden names were Henrietta Langhorn and Arabella Cronfeld. Their married names became Henrietta Chowser and Arabella Blimber. Do those names ring a bell in your memory?"

Miss Eisenberg took a slow sip of tea and placed her cup back on the table.

"Yes. They do. They – " She stopped speaking and gasped. "Arabella became Arabella Chowser? That name was in the newspaper yesterday. A woman was murdered in Marylebone. Was that Arabella Cronfeld?"

"It was."

Her hands and lower lip began to tremble. Twice she tried to take a deep breath and regain control of her emotions, but then she stood and quickly walked out of the room. Five minutes later, she returned and sat down calmly.

"Forgive me, gentlemen. Arabella and Henrietta were two of the worst trouble-makers who ever attended Badminton. But it pains me terribly when I think of any of our girls coming to a tragic end, and that news came as a shock. But please, continue with your questions. I will do my best to answer them. I remember the two of them very well indeed."

"What is it you remember most about them? Perhaps you could start with the most striking memory and go from there," said Holmes.

"I shall leave the most powerful memory for later and start with their arrival at Badminton. They both came from farm families in the North. They grew up as neighbors, and must have spent every day of their lives together from the time they were five years old. The families were not at all wealthy, and they came on scholarships."

"Ah, so they must have been on the brilliant end to earn that," said Holmes.

"You would think so, but they weren't. Academically, they were average and, as you are conducting an investigation, I have to admit that there was always suspicion that they had cheated on the entrance examinations. For that matter, there were rumors during the entire time they were here that they either paid other girls or bullied them into helping them pass all their grades."

"And how did they get along with the other girls?"

"They didn't. The two of them stuck together as if glued together at the hip. The other girls, who came for the most part from wealthy families, many of them nobility and landed gentry, may have said horrible things about them behind their backs, but they did not dare show any disrespect to them to their face. They were afraid of them."

"Afraid of what?"

"It began the very first week. They arrived at the start of the Michaelmas Term when they were fourteen. A few of the girls from the richest families thought it their divine right to give orders and expected all the other girls to obey them. One morning, those rich little snobs came to breakfast either with a black eye or a cut lip and badly bruised. They were too proud to say what happened, but the word was that they had tried to

172

lord it over Arabella and Henrietta and paid the price for it. And that was the end of that."

"And other incidents?"

"Too many to recall, but none crossed the line to have them sent down. They always managed either to avoid getting caught or to talk their way out of it – lying through their teeth if they had to. Or they might bully some of the other girls to lie for them and give them alibis. In their final year, there were some serious incidents. As older girls, they had less supervision and were constantly sneaking out at night and going into town to meet local boys and young men at the bars – their preference was for soldiers."

"Surely they must have been caught at least once."

"Oh, they were. But it was after Christmas and they were threatened that if there was another incident, they would be expelled. After that, they behaved and secured scholarships to the Ladies' Department of King's College. We all assumed that they had no interest in acquiring a Bachelor of Arts degree. They were aiming for good marriages, and both of them graduated with honors."

"And was that the most powerful memory you had of them to which you referred earlier?"

"No. There was another event later that final year. A terribly tragic one."

"Yes, madam?"

She was about to begin her account when another train passed by. Even inside the house, the noise made conversation impossible. We had to be content to sip our tea and indulge in the shortbread until quiet returned.

"It was also during their final year," she said, "toward the end of the Summer-Term. A new girl had enrolled that year. Rose-Anne Sykes. She was an exceptional young woman. Tall – nearly six foot. A brilliant scholar and an outstanding athlete. Beautiful beyond words, and fearless. Her older brothers were in the Royal Marines and had taught her hand-to-hand combat. Yet she was not in the least snobbish or bullying. On the contrary, she was kind and generous and encouraging. All of the girls in the senior year adored her. All that is, except Henrietta and Arabella. Unlike the rest of the students, Rose-Anne had no fear whatsoever of those two. I do not know how it started, but one night there must have an altercation between the two of them and Rose-Anne. The next morning, Arabella appeared at breakfast with two black eyes and Henrietta with a cut and swollen lip. Rose-Anne had put them in their place.

"On a Friday evening during the first week of June, the two of them somehow convinced Rose-Anne to join them on an illegitimate outing to the town and going dancing in one of the bars. Rose-Anne was always

173

ready for anything she thought might be a lark and went. By ten o'clock that night, she was dead. Arabella and Henrietta claimed that she had become very drunk whilst at the bar and that the three of them had taken a walk to the bridge to try to sober up before coming home. Rose-Anne was said to have been foolish enough to try to climb the great steel cable up to the tower, got part way up, and fell off. She fell all the way to the bottom of the gorge. The other two came screaming back into town, shouting for help, but she had landed on the rocks and was dead.

"There were no witnesses to the fall, and the other patrons of the bar testified that Rose-Anne had indeed been drinking, but that Arabella and Henrietta had not, so no one could dispute the account given by the two of them. They responded to all the questions from the police as if they had the same mind, and their accounts were identical. Yet there was immediate doubt, and a surprising number of the staff and the students suspected that Rose-Anne hadn't just fallen off.

"That was the powerful incident, Mr. Holmes. I was glad to see the two of them leave. They were loyal to nothing except each other, and were ruthless in their joint pursuit of a better life for themselves."

"Were you aware," said Holmes, "that a rift emerged between them starting ten years ago, and they have refused to have anything to do with each other since that day?"

Miss Eisenberg looked very puzzled. "No, I was not. And forgive me if I seem to doubt what you have just said, but I find it very hard to believe. The two of them were like one person, incomplete without the other. A rift, you say? Unless some miracle brought about a change in their souls, my immediate suspicion is that it was another one of their acts."

Now Holmes looked puzzled. "An interesting insight. Indeed, a new and significant piece of data. Would you say – "

He had to stop as yet another train rumbled past the house. When it had passed, I could not help but comment.

"My goodness, Miss Eisenberg. You must get terribly tired of those things."

"Oh, not really, Doctor. I knew when I bought this lot – it was the only one I could afford – that the trains passed by every few minutes. But my little library is at the back of the house and not nearly so noisy."

"But they must continue twenty-four hours a day. How do you sleep at night?"

"It's not so bad. I have a dressing room beside my bedroom, and it has block walls and no windows. I have a cot in there. It is nearly silent."

"Ah yes," I said. "Coincidentally, that is exactly what Mrs. Chowser did in her house. Maybe something of you rubbed off on – "

174

"Watson!" Holmes cut me off. He had grabbed his watch. "Come. We have to go. Now!"

He was on his feet and looked at Miss Eisenberg.

"Thank you, madam, for your hospitality and information. Unfortunately, we have to leave straight away. Happy Christmas."

He was already walking toward the door and I stumbled after him whilst pulling on my coat and had to run a few steps to catch up.

"Good heavens, Holmes. What is it?"

"Never mind. Just hurry. There's a train back to London in half-an-hour. Stop the first cab you see. We won't be able to make it in time on foot."

"What's the rush?"

"I'll tell you once we get on the train. Just hurry, please."

At noon on Christmas Eve, cabs are as scarce as hen's teeth. We were already on the other side of the Clifton Suspension Bridge when one trotted by, and I had to jump in front of it to make sure he stopped.

"Come on there, lads," shouted the driver. "I'm done for the day. It's Christmas Eve."

"Two pounds if you'll take us to the station," I shouted back. "You can stop and buy another present for the missus on your way home. But you'll have to hurry."

"All right. Get in."

The roads were empty, and he galloped his horse any time a straight stretch opened up in front of us.

We made it.

"Now, Holmes," I said. "What has gotten into you?"

"She lied to us."

"Who? That Miss Eisenberg lady? She was the soul of honesty."

"No. My client. Mrs. Blimber."

"About what? How can you be sure of that?"

"I'm not. But I will be as soon as we get back to Baker Street. Kindly do not disturb me until we get there."

I shrugged my shoulders, sighed, tipped my head back on the back of the seat, and promptly fell asleep. As we pulled into Paddington, Holmes gave my foot a solid kick and I woke up. Once again, I had to hurry to keep up with him as he rushed toward the cab queue. He shouted to the driver to take us home to 221b. That made no sense to me, as Mrs. Blimber couldn't possibly be there to confront and accuse of lying.

As we pulled up to our front door, Holmes sat back and motioned for me to get out.

"Please, Watson. Run in and get your service revolver."

"What in the world – "

175

"And do you still have any of the blank cartridges?"

"Well, yes, a few. I – "

"Bring them. And please hurry."

I ran in, found my gun, and then, after a few minutes of searching through my cabinets, found some blank cartridges and scampered down the stairs and back out to the cab somewhat more quickly that was safe for a man my age.

"Excellent!" said Holmes. Then he shouted to the driver to take us to the houses occupied by Mrs. Chowser and Mrs. Blimber.

As we bounced along, I loaded the blanks into the chambers of my revolver. As soon as I snapped it closed, Holmes reached over and took it from me.

"I will enter the house. You need to stay outside and chat with the constable. When you hear a gunshot, and there may be up to three of them, just say something to the constable about those bloody noisy new lorries. I will return in five minutes."

When we reached the houses, Holmes jumped out and told the constable that he needed to make one quick check and would be right back. I immediately engaged the fellow in conversation about the weather, and Christmas, and his family up in Banbury, and I was about to launch into the prospects for our favorite football teams next year when *Bang!*

Both of us jumped. I was so startled that I almost shouted at him to get down because someone was shooting. But then I recovered and uttered a few chosen words about those new motorized lorries, and making such a racket on Christmas Eve of all things.

Holmes re-emerged, walking casually, bade the constable his warm best wishes for the season and the coming year, and started to walk back up Baker Street.

"You frightened me half to death. And that poor policeman nearly jumped out of his skin."

"How many times?"

"What? Just once, that was enough."

"I fired three shots."

"You did nothing of the sort."

"Oh, yes, I did. The first two were inside Mrs. Chowser's dressing closet where she slept, with a quilt wrapped around the revolver. The third, which you heard, was when I held the gun next to a window I opened in the front room."

I was at a complete loss as we walked north on Baker Street. As we approached Marylebone, a light illuminated my brain.

"Mrs. Blimber said that she and the whole neighborhood heard a gunshot at a quarter-past-seven."

"Correct."

"But the room in which Mrs. Chowser was murdered was nearly soundproof – especially if someone wrapped a quilt around the shotgun."

"Brilliant, Watson."

"So whoever killed her could have come into the house before seven, shot her with no one hearing anything, and then fired another shot at seven-fifteen."

"Precisely."

"But who killed her?"

"Most likely my client, Mrs. Arabella Blimber."

"That's . . . that's beyond belief. Why? What possible motive?"

"That I do not know. Not yet. However, the Blimber house is of the same design as the Chowser house. Mrs. Blimber knew that a gun fired inside the small interior room could not be heard. Miss Eisenberg's observation that the animosity must have been a blind was most instructive. It helped explain why the path leading through the gate in the garden wall was well-trodden. The two of them visited together regularly. Why they chose this strange behavior, we do not yet know. Possibly to keep anyone from thinking that they colluded in the deaths of their husbands. That can now wait. She isn't aware that I am on to her, and between now and Boxing Day, I can work with Lestrade to assemble all the data before arresting her."

"What about the sons? And that firm they wanted to sell?"

"Worthless."

"You knew about it?"

"Please, my friend, give me some credit for knowing how to conduct an investigation."

"But Lestrade said the firm owned all those rights and licenses and first refusals and such."

"And the one thing almost all those assets have in common is that they expire. Most were acquired well over five years ago and are now meaningless. Possibly Mrs. Chowser wanted to hang onto them for sentimental reasons. We shall never know, but there isn't more than a hundred-pounds value. The annual filings must have become a nuisance for the sons, and they merely wanted to get rid of it."

His pace had slowed down, and he became relaxed for the first time that day.

"It's Christmas Eve, my dear Doctor. I think it would be appropriate to have Mrs. Hudson prepare a fine dinner for us, which we can enjoy as we contemplate the good fortune that has been bestowed upon us. What do you say?"

It seemed so utterly out of character for Holmes that I agreed straight away, fearing that such a moment might not come again soon.

By ten-thirty that evening, Holmes and I were sufficiently fed and mildly inebriated, and we sloped back into our familiar armchairs like a pair of beached walruses. Holmes was staring into the lovely fire in the hearth and began to reflect.

"There is a phrase, Watson, that comes to mind at a time like this," he said as the glow of the flames made shadows dance across his narrow face. "*Benigno numine.* Roughly translated, it means '*Blessed by the Divine*'. It is the way I feel when what seemed to be a challenging case has been solved and that the villain is on her way to her just reward. I confess that there may be an additional element of satisfaction when I recall that she tried and nearly succeeded in misleading me by hiring me to work on her behalf, and in doing so, knowing that I would not then be working for Scotland Yard. There is a reason that I was given such a singularly unique mind and called to use it for the pursuit of justice and – "

The bell rang and Holmes stopped speaking. He appeared to be a little annoyed to have had his reveries disrupted.

"Watson, would you mind?"

I got up and walked down the stairs to the door. A bicycle delivery boy stood there proffering a large, thick envelope and shivering.

"Ss. . .ss. . .sorry to coming so late, sir. Bu . . .bu. . .but Scotland Yard gave me a large bag of items to deliver and demanded that they be all done before midnight. Yours is the last one. So sorry to disturb you on Christmas Eve, sir."

"Good heavens, young man. Get inside out of the cold. Let us get a cup of hot cocoa into you before sending you out again, and here. You've earned it."

I took three shillings from my pocket and gave them to him. He thanked me profusely before I handed him off to Mrs. Hudson to fuss over.

Back in the front room, Holmes was still gazing intently into the hearth. I sat down beside him and as the package bore both his name and mine, I opened it."

"It's the autopsy report on Mrs. Chowser," I said.

"Now that is a useless document if ever there was one. What is in it? One sentence? '*The back of her head was blown off, and this brought about her death.*'"

I glanced at the report and stopped at the third paragraph.

"Holmes . . . you should see this."

"What? They added an entire section about damage to her dentures?'

"No, it says that when the pathologist inspected the rest of her body, he discovered that she was riddled with cancer. It had spread into several of her organs and her lungs, and that she had no more than a week or two to live."

That got his attention. He reached over and I handed him the report. For the next ten minutes, he read through it and then laid it aside.

"Her approaching death would account for her recently acquired devotion to the Church and fervent faith. I suspect that we will find that she made significant donations to St. James in an attempt to persuade God to grant her an indulgence."

"You are terribly cynical, Holmes. Father Flanagan told us that she came daily to Mass. She most likely got around to confessing whatever happened all those years ago in Brighton and Bristol and to her husband. I imagine that Father Flanagan knew Henrietta Chowser's entire criminal past."

"And," said Holmes, "by extension, that of Arabella Blimber. Yes, Father Flanagan came to know everything about both of them. The next likely stop on Mrs. Chowser's confessional pilgrimage would be the police. Mrs. Blimber could not allow that to happen. So, knowing that her dearest friend was going to die soon anyway . . . she shot her. And then, quite cleverly, I must say, she attempted to best me by hiring me to protect her and find another suspect or two. Very clever, indeed."

He returned his gaze to the fire and smiled, a little smugly.

"Holmes, is there any chance that Father Flanagan might be in danger? You say he now knows everything."

"My dear Watson, it's Christmas. Priests are confined to their churches until Boxing Day, and we shall have her arrested by noon. He will be safe. Did not the Father say that Mrs. Blimber never attended church?"

"Yes, only at Easter and Christmas."

He continued gazing for a few more seconds, and then his head jerked up and he leapt to his feet.

"Watson! What time does the Mass end this evening?"

"Good heavens, Holmes. It will be over soon. It always runs from ten to eleven. The end is usually quite inspiring. After the final blessing and being sent forth into the world, the organist pulls out all the stops and plays 'Joy to the World' and 'The Hallelujah – '"

"Watson. Get your service revolver. And real bullets this time. And hurry! We can make it to St. James before it ends. Please. *Now!*"

He was on his feet and pulling on his coat. I ran up to my bedroom, loaded my revolver, and ran back down. Holmes was already on his way out to Baker Street. By the time I joined him out on the pavement, he was shouting for a cab.

There are no cabs on any residential street in London late on Christmas Eve – "

"We'll have to run," he said. "We can make it in fifteen minutes."

I am now of the age when I am unaccustomed to placing a tax upon my legs. I strove to keep up with him, and to my relief, after years of using tobacco much too often, he was no more prepared to run all the way to St. James Spanish Place than I was. We ran a half-block and then caught our breath whilst walking and then ran another half-block and walked again.

As we ran along George Street, I could hear the strains of Isaac Watts's great Christmas anthem streaming from the opened doors of the church. We ran up the stairs and entered. There must have been over five-hundred worshippers crowded into the sanctuary. A few of them were departing, but most of them were standing in the pews, along the aisles, and at the back of the nave, looking rapturous as they listened to the massive pipe organ. When "Joy to the World" ended, there was a murmured cheer when the organist launched into "The Hallelujah Chorus".

"Where will he be now?" Holmes shouted to me as we elbowed our way up the crowded aisle toward the altar.

"Likely the vestry. The door is at the end of the west transept."

By the time we had pushed and shoved and excused ourselves all the way to the altar, the west transept had cleared. We ran along it and through the door to the vestry. As we approached the closed door, over the strains of the organ I could hear a man's anguished voice shouting.

"Do not do it! Don't! Please – think of your eternal soul!"

I had my revolver in one hand and tried the door handle with the other. Locked. I stepped back and, with all my strength, raised and smashed my foot against the door. It crashed open.

I leapt inside in time to see Mrs. Arabella Blimber pointing a gun at Father Flanagan, who had his back to the wall, his hands up in front of him, and a look of terror on his face.

Mrs. Blimber immediately swung her arm around and pointed the gun at me.

If there is one thing one learns whilst serving in the army, it is that when two enemies are pointing guns at each other, the one who chooses not to shoot first loses.

So, I shot her.

I aimed for and hit her shoulder. She screamed in pain and fell back. Holmes leapt on to her arm and removed the gun. Father Flanagan staggered to a chair and collapsed onto it.

At one o'clock in the morning of Christmas Day, Sherlock Holmes, Inspector Lestrade, Father Flanagan, and I sat in the parlor of the St. James Spanish Place manse. An ambulance had come and taken Mrs. Blimber to hospital, accompanied by a pair of police officers. Inspector Lestrade had been summoned from his home and had appeared before midnight.

"I suppose, Mr. Holmes," said Lestrade, "that I should be bloody annoyed with you for dragging me away from wife and family late on Christmas Eve."

"Terribly sorry about that, my dear Inspector. There will still be time for you to dress up as Father Christmas and fill the stockings before the grandchildren wake up."

"Enough of your sauciness, Holmes. I was about to say *well done*. You appear to have accomplished clever work one more time and saved Father Flanagan here from becoming the next victim. Now, are you going to tell me how you sorted it all out, or are you now going to claim that because a priest and the sacrament of confession were involved, you are under some sacred vow of confidentiality?"

"Not at all, Inspector. Father Flanagan maintained his confessor-penitent vow, but I was able to discern such data as I needed. Is that fair to say, Father?"

"It is," said the priest.

"I was able to deduce that when Henrietta Chowser learned that she had only a few more months to live, she started attending church regularly, and over the past two weeks, as she knew her death was imminent, she likely confessed to the murder of a girl at the Badminton School, to the deliberate drowning of Elmore Blimber, and to her part in the staged suicide of her own husband. The evidence of his involvement in the Cleveland Street affair was concocted to keep the sons from suspecting anything, as was the ruse of the animosity between herself and Arabella Blimber."

"So, the friendship was never at risk, was it?" said Lestrade.

"No. Never. They became friends as children and they made a pact between them that they would be masters of their own fates, live well, and all be fiercely loyal to each other. Husbands were stepping stones to complete financial freedom, to be acquired and disposed of as necessary. All was going as planned up to the point that she became ill."

"Then, did she tell her dear friend that she had confessed everything to her priest?" I asked.

"She must have," said Holmes. "Arabella knew that the truth would out eventually, and she couldn't allow that to happen. So on Tuesday morning, she rose early and walked next door through the garden. She knew her friend would have taken several doses of laudanum during the

181

night to dull the pain and would not wake up. She loaded one of Mr. Chowser's guns, took it up to the interior bedroom, wrapped it in a quilt, and shot her friend. I suspect she justified such a crime by telling herself that she was putting her lifelong friend out of her pain and merely hastening an otherwise horrible, slow, and painful death."

"Right, Mr. Holmes," said Lestrade, "but as much as I hate to hear what it was that you noticed that my men and I failed to, you have to tell me: What was it?"

"No one thing, Inspector. Rather a sequence of items that didn't add up. The first was the collection of Spanish prints, curios, and expensive gold filigree that were present in both houses. They were remarkably similar in age and design, and gave the impression of having come from the same shops in the same villages around the same time. That suggested that they had vacationed together several times to Spain. That isn't something that two women do who hate each other."

"Right. Go on."

"The two sons were altogether too eager to help and too grief-stricken over the death of their father, now almost a decade in the past."

"You're not saying," said Lestrade, "that they had anything to do with the murder of their step-mother, are you?"

"Not at all. They honestly believed the doubtful story that Scotland Yard had handed over a file of evidence. What I suspect is that they are involved in some other sort of criminal enterprise in the City and didn't wish to have me or Scotland Yard thinking that they had something to hide. Thus, they erred the other way and were far too happy to see us when anyone else at Boodles would have found reason to shoo such undesirables as Watson and me out the door."

"Come, now, Holmes," I said. "I'm sure we would make excellent members. Do you honestly believe that all those fine toffs and snobs would mind having a famous detective overhearing all their conversations and learning all their secrets?"

That brought a short chuckle from the other two. Holmes carried on.

"The serving plates, the help from retired Inspector Abberline, the hints from Father Flanagan, and the information given by Miss Eisenberg and Captain Duff led to the conclusion that the two of them colluded together for years and that my client was herself the killer. Had it not been for Dr. Watson's diligent reading of the autopsy report, sent by you Lestrade, I fear we wouldn't have made it to the church on time. The loud organ, the crowd, and the occasion of the Christmas Eve Mass all provided Mrs. Blimber with an opportunity to shoot the only person who now knew everything about the past crimes and exploits of herself and her friend and to escape unseen."

"Right," said Lestrade. "Anything else?"

Holmes paused for several seconds and then smiled at Lestrade. "Only to wish you a Happy Christmas, my dear Inspector."

"Right. And a Happy Christmas to you too, Mr. Holmes."

The Son of God
by Jeremy Branton Holstein

As Sherlock Holmes's long-time companion and biographer, there is an assumption amongst my readers that I know all that there is to know about the man, yet I assure you that is far from the truth. There is much that Holmes either kept private or never revealed during our long association, preferring our relationship to focus around those little problems which fascinated the readers of *The Strand*. Even today I am peppered with questions about Holmes's feelings toward the opposite sex, his political affiliations, and his religious beliefs. I decline to answer all of these questions, preferring instead to let his adventures speak for themselves, rather than to make bold assumptions. If Holmes wants to provide answers, he can do so himself.

Still, there are investigations that we shared together which can provide some insight. "A Scandal in Bohemia" is perhaps the best answer I can provide for Holmes's feelings towards women. There are numerous instances where we dealt with royalty and politicians. But there is one case in particular which I feel serves best to attempt to answer the question of Holmes's religious nature.

It was a Thursday afternoon in the fall of 1901, and I hadn't seen Holmes for some days now, but this was hardly unusual. It was therefore little surprise, while I was out and about my on my constitutional, when a carriage pulled up beside me on the road and a familiar voice emerged from within.

"Ah, Watson!" said Holmes. "Fortune favors us with this chance meeting."

"Holmes!" I said. "Where have you been? It's been days."

"That story must wait until a later time," he said, "for at this moment I have need of your assistance."

"Oh?" I said. "Whatever has happened?"

"Climb in, dear fellow," said Holmes. "I will explain on the way."

Soon we were rattling through the London streets, moving from Regent's Park toward Bloomsbury.

"Tell me," said Holmes at last, "have you ever heard of Christ's Heralds?"

"I cannot say that I have," I answered.

"Aye, and that's the wonder of it all!" said Holmes. "They are one of the most powerful churches in Europe, yet few outside of their own congregation have ever heard of them! That in itself is a miracle, even if their charter seems based upon a false pretense."

"You intrigue me."

"As intended," said my friend. "The church was formed, you see, to bring about the long foretold 'Second Coming'."

"Of Christ?" I said. "That seems folly, for man is not meant to alter the will of God."

"Yet that is precisely what the church has been attempting to do for the better part of a century," said Holmes. "Their founder, a Scots clergy by the name of McAdams, longed for the days of the Crusades, with Christian soldiers carrying the word of God into heathen lands. But his ambitions didn't stop there, Watson. He wanted to engineer the event the scriptures call the Rapture, and to ensure the return of the Son of God to the mortal world. To this end, he formed the Christ's Heralds and delivered to his flock a prophecy."

"Prophecy is not a word I associate with the church," I said. "I think of it more as being the tool of charlatans or witches."

"Yet McAdams was no charlatan," said Holmes, "at least not as far as my research can determine. He truly believed in his cause, and was able to inspire the faith of thousands."

"What was his prophecy?"

"That he was to appoint twelve mortal Angels, and that the Son of God would return to Earth after the last Angel returned to Heaven."

"And how many of these so-called Angels remain?"

"Only one," said Holmes. "We are en route to see him now."

Our carriage turned a corner and pulled through a wrought-iron gate. Beyond lay a house of worship constructed from the uninspired industrial brickwork so common in our cities. The only distinguishing feature of its main wall was an enormous stained-glass portrait of a man gazing upward toward heaven. Holmes gestured toward it.

"There, Watson," he said. "That is McAdams, the founder of this church's peculiar faith."

"I thought sacred images were prohibited," I said.

"In some religions, yes," said Holmes, "but this is no ordinary religion. Pay the driver, won't you?"

I did and we were ushered inside by a prim white-haired woman in dark dress. Holmes presented his card.

"Ah, Mister Holmes," she said. "My husband is expecting you. This way, please."

She guided us through an enormous sanctuary filled with pews, its pulpit loomed over by the stained-glass portrait we had seen outside, and finally into a dim chamber just off the main hall. Lit only by candles, the space was dominated by an enormous bed, leaving little room for furniture or visitors. On the mattress lay a frail, elderly man, his body propped up by mountainous pillows, his eyes closed, seemingly asleep. Around the bed four men in robes knelt, their heads bowed in prayer. So engaged were they that no one seemed to notice our entrance.

The woman bent low to whisper into the ear of the elderly man, who opened his eyes and smiled at us.

"Ah," he said. "Sherlock Holmes. Thank the Lord you are here at last."

The quartet of robed men looked up at the mention of my friend's name. "Sherlock Holmes?" said one with a tone I judged to be surprise, but with an odd tinge of fear.

"Indeed," said the elderly man. "He is here at my invitation. Now, my deacons, please – if I might have a moment of privacy with our guests."

One of the deacons took the hand of the bedridden man. "Are you certain, Angel?" he said. "He is not of our faith. Would it not be better if we remained with you?"

"This is a private matter, Mathew," said the elderly man.

"There is nothing private about it," responded Mathew. "We all know why he is here."

"Brother Mathew is right," said a second of the robed men. "You might as well just come out and accuse us all."

"I am still your leader, Joev," said the elderly man, "and until I join the other Angels in Heaven, you will both honor and obey me."

The robed man's pain was clearly written in his eyes, but he still stood and took his leave, the other deacons filing out after him. The white-haired woman kissed her husband upon his forehead and then also departed, leaving us alone with our client.

"The folly of youth," said the man. "We love them, but they will be the death of us all one day." His eyes drifted toward me, regarding me with not unfriendly dispassion. "Doctor Watson, I presume," he said.

"I have that honor," I replied. "Although I don't believe that we have been introduced."

"How rude of me," he said. "You must forgive me, Doctor, for I am intimate with most who enter this room and I clearly have become lax in my manners. My name is Martin Tyrell, and I am the last living Angel on this earth."

"Mr. Tyrell, you are clearly in some distress," I said. "May I examine you?"

"Ever the medical man," said Tyrell. "Do as you must, Doctor, but know that I am beyond earthly assistance. Only God himself may save me."

186

I nodded, and began my examination.

"Your telegram asked for my assistance," said Holmes, "not God's. If there is nothing to be done, then why am I here?"

"Are you a believer, Mister Holmes?" asked Tyrell.

"I believe in what I can prove," said Holmes.

"That is not an answer," said Tyrell.

"It is the only answer I can give you," said Holmes.

"Then it will have to do," said Tyrell. "I did not summon you here to save my life, for I can feel in my bones that my time on this earth is almost done. My heart knows that I will soon die, and I am at peace with that fate. It is, after all, what McAdams himself foretold, oh so many years ago."

As Holmes and Tyrell verbally sparred, I continued to study Tyrell. His skin was discolored and blotchy, his movements lethargic. My conclusion seemed inevitable. I stood and looked at Holmes. "Arsenic poisoning," I said. "No question about it."

"Delivered in small doses over a long period of time," said Holmes. "Yes, I suspected as much."

"As had I," said Tyrell, "although I am at a loss as to how. I share the same meals nightly as my caretakers, yet I am the only one who has sickened."

"Perhaps it is God's will," said Holmes.

"Holmes!" I hissed, but Tyrell was not offended. Indeed, he laughed, uttering the thin raspy chuckle that only the dying possess.

"I am surprised that you, Sherlock Holmes, would offer a divine explanation," he said, "but I agree that a mortal agency is at play here. That is why I summoned you. There is a mystery before us, and before I leave this mortal plain, I can think of none better than Sherlock Holmes to unravel it."

"You want to know who has murdered you," said Holmes, "and why."

"Oh, the why is no mystery," said Tyrell. "My death will signal the return of Christ and usher in the next age of humanity. There are many in my flock who are willing to sacrifice their very souls to hasten his return."

"Very well," said Holmes. "Pray, give us all the details of your case."

"You speak as if you know much of my history already," said Tyrell. "And is that not your reputation? That you can tell everything about people from just a quick glance? From the dirt on their trousers, or the stain of ink on their fingertips?"

"You give me too much credit, Mister Tyrell," said Holmes.

"Angel," said Tyrell. "My title is Angel."

"It is true," he said, "that I can deduce some truths from the tell-tale traces on a person, but you, sir, have not left your bed in some time due to

187

your weakened condition, so I am robbed of evidence. It is clear that you are a scholar – the calluses on your writing hand are most distinctive, as are the marks on your nose from wearing *pince nez* for much of your adult life. But really, both conclusions are obvious considering your station and . . . " Holmes hesitated, then concluded, " . . . your *title*."

"All that you say is true," said Tyrell. "I was a scholar, and had even achieved a chair at a small university before McAdams changed the course of my life and revealed to me my grand destiny."

"Leave the dramatic flourishes to the Doctor," said Holmes. "Facts only, please."

"But you do not understand, Mister Holmes!" said Tyrell, color flushing to his cheek for the first time since we had entered the room. "McAdams was a man, yes, but his words were sent from Heaven itself. This is fact."

Holmes sighed. It was clear that he would not be able to avoid Tyrell's dramatics, for he considered them to be truths. "How did you meet McAdams?" asked Holmes.

"He came to my University to spread the word of the Lord," said Tyrell. "I was a man of science, but McAdams opened my eyes and soul to the world and word of faith. Soon I had abandoned my studies and joined McAdams' flock. My timing was blessed, for shortly after I became a believer, McAdams had his divine vision."

"The vision of the Second Coming," said Holmes, clearly impatient.

"Yes," said Tyrell. "One morning McAdams sent for me, and eleven others of his most devoted. He gathered us in the chapel and told us that the night before he had been blessed by a communication directly from the Holy Father, who told him he was to appoint his most devout followers as Angels and charge them with restoring faith to this forsaken land. If we were successful, we would be rewarded with the return of Christ himself before the last of us entered Heaven's gates. From that day to this, I have worked tirelessly to further McAdams' vision."

"What happened to the other Angels?" I asked.

"They all took a similar path. We scattered across Europe to establish our congregations, thus maximizing our ability to encourage the unbelievers to accept the truth of his word. I do not believe I have seen any of them in person for almost forty years, not since McAdams' funeral. It all seems so long ago."

"How long have you been ill?" asked Holmes.

"Just under six months," said Tyrell. "First I began to suffer bouts of nausea and exhaustion, followed by welts upon my skin. I did my best to continue my ministry, but while the spirit was willing, my body became

188

weaker and weaker and I was forced to withdraw. I have been bedridden for almost three months now. I do not expect to see in another year."

Holmes looked at me for confirmation, and I offered a small nod to confirm Tyrell's supposition.

"Do you have any suspicion as to who is poisoning you?"

"I wish I did," said Tyrell. "I have lived what I believe to be a holy life of service to God. I cannot think of anyone that I have wronged."

"Is it possible that someone is killing the Angels?" I asked. "Did any of the others die under suspicious circumstances?"

"I do not believe so," said Tyrell. "The first Angel died not long after McAdams, and the eleventh only last year, all of natural causes."

"The four men who were here when we first arrived," asked Holmes. "They are part of your congregation?"

Tyrell nodded. "My deacons: Joev, Adam, Bassick, and Mathew. All devoted members of my flock, and all above suspicion."

"But that is not entirely true," said Holmes. "I believe I recognized at least one of your deacons, and know him to be a convicted felon."

Tyrell nodded. "In a past life, perhaps, but they have all sought redemption in our faith and have been reborn. They now live lives without sin, and have been an essential aid to my wife, helping her with my care. They feed me, bathe me, provide me with fresh linens every morning and candles every night. I could not have asked for better caretakers. Whatever their past, they are now holy men."

Holmes mused silently for a moment. "You have not given us much to go on," he said at last.

"I realize that," said Tyrell. "But I've read of your exploits. I know you have worked miracles before."

"Never miracles," said Holmes. "I will see what I can do, Mister Tyrell. I have one or two other matters that I must attend to, but I shall return here soon to begin my investigation."

"Bless you, Mister Holmes," said Tyrell.

Holmes seemed uncomfortable with Tyrell's words, and so merely nodded as he left the room. I uttered a short prayer for Tyrell's recovery, and then followed.

As soon as we emerged from Tyrell's chambers, we were accosted by his deacons.

"Mister Holmes," said the black-haired deacon Tyrell had referred to as Mathew. "I must insist that you leave this sanctuary and never return. Your interference is not wanted here."

"On the contrary," replied Holmes. "I think it's very much evident that my interference is desired. I am, after all, here at Mister Tyrell's

189

request. Still, if you will consent to answer one of my questions, I shall endeavor to leave here post-haste. This is, after all, a fool's errand."

"What do you mean?" asked Mathew with obvious suspicion.

"Come now, sir," said Holmes. "We both know that Mister Tyrell is addled both in body and mind. His suspicions are little more than a symptom of his disease."

I started at this, but a warning glance from Holmes silenced me before I could protest. This was clearly a gambit of some kind, although its goal escaped me.

"Aye," said Mathew. "That's true enough. He has become more secretive since he took ill."

"He is a man living on borrowed time and as a result sees devils everywhere," said Holmes. "I will go through the motions of an investigation to assuage him, but we both know there is nothing for me to find."

Mathew relaxed visibly, his stance backing away from aggression. "I misjudged you, Mister Holmes," he said. "You are clearly more sensitive to the nuances of the situation than I thought. Ask your questions."

"I have but one," said Holmes. "Upon Mister Tyrell's death, who will take his place as the leader of the church?'

"That," said Mathew, "has yet to be determined. The congregation will choose his successor, but only after we have given him a proper burial."

I noticed something odd in that moment, the way the three unnamed deacons pulled their hoods low around their heads as if seeking anonymity from my friend's probing gaze. An odd behavior for any innocent man, let alone a member of Tyrell's clergy. Perhaps their sins were not so far in the past after all.

Sherlock Holmes nodded. "As it should be," he said. "Well, gentlemen, I've taken enough of your time. Good day. Come, Watson." And, together, we left the sanctuary.

Our return journey to Baker Street was a silent one as Holmes pondered the problem. Upon reaching our destination, Holmes tore into his index, his system of docketing information concerning men and other things, and spent several hours in research. I spent the time beginning to record my notes upon the case.

That evening we dined over an excellent meal prepared by the always reliable Mrs. Hudson. We then retired to the fireside, where Holmes retrieved some tobacco from the Persian slipper and lit his pipe.

"What do you make of it?" he asked.

"The facts seem straightforward," I said. "Tyrell is being slowly poisoned, and only four men have regular access to him. Therefore, the poisoner must be one of those individuals."

"Five, you mean," remarked Holmes. "You overlooked his wife."

"That seems rather cynical," I said. "She seems to love him."

"Women can bury cruel intent beneath a sweet exterior. It is one of the skills of their sex. You should know this."

Holmes and I have often disagreed as to the nature of women, and I was eager to discuss the case at hand, so I didn't take his verbal bait.

"But otherwise," continued Holmes, "your reasoning is sound."

"I assume," I said, "that is what you have been researching in your index. You wished to discover any record of the four deacons."

"Indeed," said Holmes. "And may I say, Tyrell has gathered about himself a fascinating group of sinners."

"They are known to you, then?"

"I confess I didn't recognize them all at first glance, but records rarely lie. Three of them have served time in the Old Bailey, two for capital crimes. One we have even encountered before."

"I didn't recognize any of the gentlemen."

"He is much changed from when we last saw him. The man referred to as Joev? His real name is Joseph Anton."

"Not the man behind the Giant Rat of Sumatra!"

"The very same. He has lost three stone since our encounters in the sewers beneath London, and now bears a scar on his right cheek. But it is him, Watson. I'd swear it."

"Then we have our man," I said. "Anton is a known poisoner."

"He is certainly chief among our suspects, but let us not discount the others. Adam Enberg, for example, the red-haired deacon. He was convicted of fraud and bank robbery in 1887, narrowly avoiding the hangman's noose thanks to the extraordinary efforts of his solicitor. He served his time quietly and was released only a few years ago. The story of how he went from prisoner to clergy was not present in my index, but we may theorize that he needed a home and found it in the church. Then there is Bassick, who was once an associate of none other than Professor Moriarty."

"You are making this church out to be a den of murderers and thieves," I said.

"Bassick never rose high in the ranks of the Professor's organization, but was often called upon when a strong arm was deemed necessary. Upon Moriarty's death, Bassick lost the protection he had enjoyed and was soon thereafter convicted of assault. He too was recently released from prison, and is now a member of Tyrell's congregation."

191

"And the last of the quartet?"

"Ah, yes. Mathew," said Holmes. "It might interest you, Watson, to know his full name."

"Which is?"

"Mathew Tyrell."

"Tyrell's son!"

"*Adopted* son," corrected Holmes. "Mathew's mother died in childbirth, so Tyrell took him in and has raised the boy on his own, although he has for some reason kept their familial link a secret from the congregation. Still, it seems only natural that he should follow in his father's footsteps and become a member of the church."

"It would also follow that he is Tyrell's logical successor."

"Which is as good a motive as any, wouldn't you say?" said Holmes. "We're dealing with a clever adversary, who has surrounded himself with a veritable rogues gallery of suspects to choose from. Yes, I fancy it is a three – perhaps even a four – pipe problem."

"Indeed. Who is poisoning Tyrell? And how is he being poisoned?"

"Oh, the method of poisoning is obvious," said Holmes. "A child could deduce it."

"Then I must be a child," I said, "for I didn't see anything."

"As always, Watson," said Holmes, "you saw everything, but you failed to observe. Now, please. I need some time to consider how to proceed."

At which, he sat back into his armchair and began to lazily smoke his pipe, gazing deep into the flames. I knew from experience that it would be several hours at least before he spoke again, so I took my leave and retired to bed.

The next morning I awoke to discover Holmes gone, leaving no note behind. Regardless of my curiosity toward the Tyrell case, I still had my rounds to conduct, so I made my way across London, consulting with three patients all suffering minor maladies. That evening I returned to Baker Street, hoping to find Holmes smoking by the fire, but there was no sign of him nor any instruction or telegram. I passed the time writing out some additional notes on the case, and, after waiting some hours, finally turned in for the night, hopeful that the next day would bring about revelations. I was not to be disappointed.

The following morning, Holmes still hadn't returned. I questioned Mrs. Hudson over breakfast, and she confirmed that he had left early the previous morning but she hadn't seen hide nor hair of him since. This in itself was not unusual, so I contented myself to read the morning paper by the fireside. I was just turning the final page when Mrs. Hudson entered the sitting room.

"A telegram for you, Doctor," she said.

"From Holmes?" I asked.

"Naturally," she said. "Not that I peeked."

I took the telegram and read it.

Events have reached a crisis. Come to Tyrell's home as soon as you can. Stay close to the man, no matter what happens.

Within minutes I had located a cab and tipped the driver an extra fiver if he could get me to Tyrell's chapel before the hour turned ten. By not sparing the whip he made it with minutes to spare. I threw my fare at the driver and dashed toward the front door. When his wife greeted me, I could tell from her ashen expression that something was very wrong.

"It's Martin," she said, wiping away a stray tear with her sleeve . "He passed away in his sleep last night."

I stammered in surprise. "I am . . . so sorry to hear that." I said.

The woman bowed her head gravely. "I thank the Lord for an end to his suffering, but I weep that he is gone. My life will never be the same." She dabbed another tear, then straightened herself up into a professional stance. "I'm sure you are here looking for your companion, Mister Holmes."

"I am."

She nodded. "He came here late last night, and he and Martin were still discussing the details of the case when I retired. But when I woke up this morning I discovered . . . ." She trailed off, her voice thick with obvious emotion. "I do apologize, Doctor Watson. I am still recovering from the shock of finding my husband's body."

"I quite understand," I said. "I presume that Holmes isn't still here?"

"I haven't seen him here this morning, nor do I know where he has gone."

"May I come in to offer my respects?"

She shook her head. "I don't think that is appropriate, sir. The deacons have gathered, and are preparing for Martin's memorial. Outsiders are not permitted during this time. I'm sure you understand."

"Of course," I said. "And when is the service?"

"This very evening," she replied, "as is our way. Seven o'clock in the chapel."

I thanked the grieving woman, again bid my condolences, and departed, unsure of how to proceed. Holmes's message had told me to stay close to Tyrell, but how was I to stay close to a man whose soul no longer resided on this earth? What of the church itself? Surely the poisoner was inside, using the day of mourning to cover his tracks. And what of the prophecy, that Tyrell's death would usher in the return of the son of God? How did it all fit together? I confess I felt myself at sea.

I returned to Baker Street, hoping for another message from Holmes, but no new missives appeared. I rang Mrs. Hudson, but she said she was busy entertaining a visitor and was unavailable.

It would seem I was on my own.

At least I knew where I could find Holmes. He would be at the memorial tonight. That seemed the logical conclusion.

I dressed in my best suit and, at the appointed hour, made my way back to Tyrell's chapel.

For good measure, as I was entering a cathedral of both saints and sinners, I also brought along my revolver.

A crowd of mourners had congregated outside the doors, slowly making their way into the sanctuary. An air of solemn grief hung over the throng as I joined their slow march inside.

The pews were already nearing capacity as I made my way down the aisle. On the altar had been placed an open coffin, the light from the stained glass bathing it in colored beams of illumination. I could see within the familiar face of Martin Tyrell lying in state, his features bearing the serenity and stillness that only death can bring. The four deacons stood by the coffin, acting both as mourners and guardians of their fallen leader. A line of well-wishers waited to offer condolences to Tyrell's widow, yet oddly they were not permitted to approach his coffin. Another eccentricity of this strange religion.

I took a seat at the end of a pew near the front that I deemed inconspicuous and studied the assembled crowd. Holmes was here – I could feel it in my bones – but for the life of me I couldn't see him. No doubt he was in disguise. Could he be that academic fellow who was even now, at this most inappropriate time, taking studious notes on a sheet of paper? Or was he the burly man sitting by himself in the second aisle?

Then my eyes alighted on a gentleman who, against all protocol, was wearing a low slung hat within the sanctuary. This gentleman noticed my attention, and quickly turned away. I smiled. Holmes may have the rest of them fooled, but I had years of experience seeing through his elegant disguises.

One of the deacons signaled that the service was about to begin, and everyone took their seats. This same deacon then walked up to the pulpit, pulled back his hood, revealing a familiar face.

"Thank you all for coming," said Mathew, smiling down at the assembled congregation. "Be not sad, my brethren. This is not a time for tears, but celebration! A celebration of the rich and full life of Martin Tyrell, but also a celebration that the culmination of McAdams' Prophecy is finally at hand!"

The congregation rose to their feet in fervor, crying out a chorus of short prayers and hallelujahs. The atmosphere of grief that hung over the chapel began to break.

"Yes, my brothers and sisters," continued Mathew. "Martin Tyrell was the last of McAdams' Angels, which began with twelve in number on earth and now has twelve in heaven above. As sad as we are to have lost brother Tyrell, we rejoice for we have gained resurrection. We, brothers and sisters, have brought about the Second Coming of the Son of God!"

The fervor of the crowd broke forth into cheers, and Mathew reveled in their adulation.

"Our time has come!" he cried. "Today shall be a day of truth as God at last reveals to us his divine plan. And I, your brother Mathew, am humbled to be his instrument."

The cheering of the congregation broke down into a storm of puzzled murmurs.

"Yes, it is time for truth," continued Mathew. "The man who lies in state behind me, the man you all knew as Martin Tyrell, bore another title that only a select few knew. That title, as you might have guessed, was father – for I am his son."

A collective gasp hushed the astonished throng.

"Indeed, I hold that title not once but twice! For not only am I the son of Martin Tyrell, but I am also the fulfillment of our founder's Prophecy. Brothers and sisters, I come before you as Christ reborn. I am the Son of God, restored to this earthly plane once more!"

Shrieks began to echo through the chamber, but they were not for the blasphemous words that deacon Mathew had uttered. Unseen by Mathew, the body of Martin Tyrell was, astonishingly, unbelievably, rising from his coffin, ascending slowly into a sitting position. The three deacons who were, no doubt, accomplices in Mathew's scheme, backed away in disbelief, while the woman to my immediate right fainted dead away at the sight.

Mathew, however, was oblivious to the miracle occurring just behind his back. He was caught up into a fervor by his revelations, and convinced that the congregation was responding to his dramatic proclamation, not to the impossible resurrection occurring before our very eyes.

The figure in the coffin pushed himself upright with his hands until he was standing, his feet planted within the coffin's velvet lining. He extended a long, bony finger, and pointed it accusingly at his son.

"Mathew," he said, his raspy voice silencing the church immediately. Even Mathew let his proclamations die mid-sentence, and spun around like a hunted animal.

"No!" cried Mathew. "You're dead! You're dead!"

"And you were the one who killed me," said Martin Tyrell with an even tone that did not seem possible given the circumstance.

"I had to!" cried Mathew. "The Prophecy . . . The Prophecy required . . . ."

No one spoke. No one dared to break the silence between father and son as the patriarch stared in judgement upon his heir.

And then the man's posture changed somehow, relaxing, his shoulders dropping into a much more familiar stance.

"Well," said a different but all too familiar voice, "that proved easier than I expected."

"Holmes!" I cried in astonishment.

The man who had been Martin Tyrell only moments ago reached up and withdrew a wig from his forehead, prying a rubber nose from his face. "Did you get all that, Lestrade?" he said.

"I did, Mister Holmes," said the man in the low slung hat. He stood and removed his adornment, revealing the familiar face of Inspector Lestrade. "I'd call that a confession, I would."

"As would I," said Holmes. "And no lack of witnesses either. Do your duty, Inspector."

"You devil!" said Mathew, still drawn back against the pulpit, hunched over in his robes like a cornered tiger. Neither Holmes nor Lestrade could see his right arm reach deep into the folds of his robe, but I could and cried out in alarm.

"Holmes, watch out!" I shouted even as Mathew drew forth a revolver, even as I drew my own. An instant later we both fired in tandem. The sound of gunshots in the chapel was deafening.

Mathew's shot went wild as Holmes's lightning reflexes allowed him to heed my warning, ducking low to avoid the bullet. My own shot, however, was true, striking Mathew in the shoulder. The bullet passed through his body, piercing the stained glass behind him. Mathew dropped his weapon and fell to the floor, cradling his shoulder, even as Lestrade moved in to make an arrest.

But before Lestrade could accost the fallen deacon, there came a terrible sound. The stained glass, now compromised, was radiating a spider web of cracks from my gunshot. Glass popped and snapped as the metal frame began to buckle, threatening to collapse under its own weight. The three deacons and Tyrell's wife could sense the coming catastrophe and fled the altar, even as the congregation began to back away in fear. Holmes saw what was happening and sprang to aid Lestrade with the wounded Mathew.

"Hurry, everyone out!" he cried, his booming voice echoing through the chamber, causing what had been a slow retreat to evolve into a full-out stampede as the congregants crowded the aisle in an effort to flee. Holmes threw his shoulder around Mathew and, together with Lestrade, they began to usher the wounded man off the dais. Unfortunately, their efforts were too late.

With a mighty crash the stained glass shattered, exploding into the sanctuary, raining colored glass and metal down upon all within. I sheltered my head with my arm, struggling to push forward through the remaining congregation to discover the fate of my friend and the others.

"Holmes!" I cried as the cacophony of shards began to ease around me, replaced instead by the groans of the wounded. "Holmes!"

I found him a moment later, blood seeping from a gash on his forehead, but still conscious, still moving to guide Lestrade and Mathew Tyrell toward the exit at the other end of the sanctuary.

"I'm all right," he said.

"You're bleeding," I said.

Holmes touched his hand to his forehead, his fingers coming away stained with blood. "A superficial wound at best," he said.

"I should look at it," I said.

"There are others here who need your assistance more than I do," said Holmes. He looked at me, and I could see the sharp clarity in his eyes. I knew then and there that Holmes would be all right.

My fears assuaged, I set about aiding the congregants injured in the calamity, while Holmes and Lestrade guided Mathew Tyrell out of the sanctuary and to justice.

It was several hours before I returned to Baker Street, exhausted from treating countless lacerations and flesh wounds. Miraculously no one had been killed, and the wounds all proved superficial, thank the Lord. I found Holmes seated by the fireside. Outside of a bandage affixed to his forehead, he looked very much himself.

"Ah, Watson!" he said. "You played your role beautifully. Grab yourself a brandy and join me by the fire."

I poured myself half a glass and took the proffered seat. We sat together in comfortable silence, until I could contain my questions no longer.

"Holmes," I said at last. "Where have you been?"

"In a coffin for the better part of a day," he said. "Impersonating the dead is not as easy as you might think. It is only by utilizing meditation techniques that I acquired during my time in Tibet that I was able to fool Tyrell's deacons."

"And his wife," I said.

"Oh, Watson," said Holmes. "You of all people should know of the intuition possessed by the fairer sex. I might have been able to deceive some members of Tyrell's congregation, but his spouse? No, that was too great a risk. She was a hesitant participant in our trap, but her participation was essential to its success."

"And your trap was to impersonate a dead man."

"It seemed the most prudent way to smoke out the poisoner," said Holmes. "It was a case of too many suspects, and not enough time. All four deacons stood to gain from Tyrell's death, so it seemed only logical to let that death occur and observe the results. Tyrell was surprisingly agreeable to my plan."

"And where is the real Martin Tyrel?"

"Currently? He is in a cab, being shepherded to Scotland Yard, where Lestrade will reunite him with his wife and son. I dare say it will be an uncomfortable reunion. Still, one should never bait a trap without being prepared for unexpected prey. "

"And where was he whilst you had taken his place?"

"Here," said Holmes.

"Baker Street?" I said in amazement.

"Indeed," said Holmes. "I spirited him out of the sanctuary in the dead of night and placed him under the care of Mrs. Hudson, after luring you away with a telegram."

"You felt you could not trust me with your secret," I said.

"Oh, Watson," said Holmes, "you know that isn't true. I trust you with my life, but I also needed your grieving face in the chapel to complete the illusion. Do forgive me."

I sighed. "I do. You know I do."

"There is precious little else to tell. Once Tyrell was gone, I took his place in the bed, after carefully replacing all the candles in the room."

"The candles?" I said, bewildered.

"Of course," said Holmes. "It was the candles that were slowly poisoning Martin Tyrell. As soon as we entered, I noticed their unusual scent permeating the room. Do you remember what he told us during our interview?"

"About the candles?" I said. "I believe he said that they were replaced nightly along with the linens."

"Precisely," said Holmes. "Consider the problem. Food and drink could be eliminated as the poisoning method because Tyrell shared his food with others. Poisoning by linen seemed exceedingly unlikely, given that the linens were laundered nightly. But the candles? Those could be treated and controlled by a few hands at most, and by infusing the wax with arsine, Tyrell would be exposed over time as they burned. In small doses, the candles would be harmless, but sustained exposure, say overnight while sleeping – "

"Fatal," I said. "Absolutely fatal."

"An ingenious method of assassination," said Holmes. "It reminds me of the case involving the Devil's Foot Root, although the poisoning in that case was much more potent. I shall have to give the matter further study when time permits."

"Then McAdams' Prophecy is still unfulfilled," I said. "The final Angel is still alive."

"We have only forestalled Tyrell's death," said Holmes. "And what shall happen after death is a mystery even I cannot solve."

"But what is it you believe?" I asked.

Holmes drew thoughtfully on his pipe before answering. "I believe in what I can prove, Watson," he said at last. "No more, no less."

The Adventure of the
Disgraced Captain
by Thomas A. Turley

How does one sum up a marriage? I, if anyone, should know, having been wedded and widowed three times in my long life. Since my most recent marriage (like the others) ended in tragedy seven years ago, I have pondered whether it was, in truth, a happy one. On the two previous occasions, such a question would have been superfluous, although the answer would have differed in each case.

Of the three, my third marriage was undoubtedly the most surprising. It came at an age when I had ceased to imagine the possibility of a new wife. Moreover, as much as I admired and came to love Priscilla Prescott, I never experienced with her the passion that had driven my ill-fated infatuation with young Constance, or the harmony of two souls perfectly attuned, which I had known – all too briefly – with dear Mary.

Because our relationship had begun on a professional level (first as patient's wife and doctor, then as Great Detective's client and associate), Priscilla and I knew each other well by the time our feelings ripened into intimacy. If neither passion nor harmony was initially in evidence, each of us brought to the marriage something that the other needed. I acquired a lovely, intelligent companion blessed with the children I had always wanted. For the widowed mother, I provided financial security and an acceptable role model for her son. Quite soon, our union evolved into a partnership that brought us both stability and happiness. The fact that tragedy eventually befell us – as it had my first two marriages – was due in part to circumstances beyond our control. Therefore, despite the guilt and grief that clouded its last years, despite the sudden, fatal illness that thwarted the full reconciliation I had so desired, I have concluded that my last marriage was by no means the least successful of the three.

200

W hen the South African war broke out in 1899, my first thought was to rejoin my regiment in my former role of army surgeon. [1] However, it was intimated in answer to my tentative enquiry that my slight lameness and advancing age, as well as the long interval since my last posting, left me unfitted for service at the front. No one at the time expected the war to last more than a few weeks, so the high command could afford to pick and choose. After the disasters of "Black Week" revealed the Boers to be more formidable than they appeared, my literary agent, Conan Doyle, made his own way to South Africa. There he volunteered for several months at the Langman Field Hospital in Bloemfontein. More importantly, he began to compose a history of that dismal conflict that would eventually earn for him a knighthood. [2]

Long before its publication, I had settled into an adjunct post at Barts. I might have contributed more productively to the war at Netley, where a great many wounded soldiers convalesced. Remaining in London, however, allowed me to maintain my residence in Baker Street, where I continued to assist my mentor in detection, Sherlock Holmes. Most uncharacteristically, Holmes had made clear his disapproval of any fuller participation in what he considered an unjust, unnecessary war. His opinion would not have deterred me had I been allowed to serve. As matters stood, my scheduled hours at the hospital were less disruptive to our usual routine than the uncertainties of private practice. To my old friend's satisfaction, if not altogether to my own, the Great Boer War remained a passing cloud upon our shared horizon.

Among my patients in the latter months of 1901 was a young officer who had been invalided home with a severe head wound. Captain Giles Prescott's company of mounted infantry had been caught in a Boer ambush, and he was shot in the skull with a revolver. The bullet proved too delicately situated to remove, and transferring him to the divisional hospital had taken several days. The result was prolonged swelling of the brain. Although expert treatment enabled Prescott to survive [3], it was apparent from my first examination that his prospects of recovery were nil. During the time he spent at Barts, the Captain was conscious only intermittently and often incoherent. The best we could do was keep him comfortable while he slid irretrievably towards the abyss.

I was puzzled by the medical staff's perceptible reserve in dealing with this patient, and by the lack of visitors other than his wife. Their absence was surprising, for I knew the Prescotts to be an old and honoured military family. When I enquired as to the reason, my colleague, Dr. Clarke, reluctantly revealed that the Captain was rumoured to have shot himself after exhibiting cowardice during the attack. From a medical standpoint, I found this rumour suspect. The entry wound was relatively high upon the right parietal bone, whereas self-inflicted gunshots are typically found in the skull's temporal area. Moreover, its trajectory indicated that the shot had come from longer range. An X-ray of the .455-calibre bullet, which I found inside the patient's file, could not resolve the issue. The Webley Mk IV that must have fired it could easily have been Prescott's sidearm, but captured Webleys were employed by the Boers as well.

My doubts about the Captain's wounding were shared by Mrs. Prescott, who came to the hospital on an almost daily basis. She assured me that her husband was incapable of cowardice or suicide. His character and his family heritage precluded either course. Naturally, I had cast no such aspersion. She had found it implicit in an ambiguous letter from the War Office. Lest the reader ask how I came into her confidence, we were much thrown together during the weeks I treated Captain Prescott. His wife's visits in the early morning or late afternoon often coincided with my duty hours. The fact that I had been a soldier assured the lady of an informed, sympathetic listener if she chose to share her woes. My motives, I admit, were not entirely altruistic. Priscilla Prescott was something of a beauty and only twenty-seven, the same age as my beloved Mary when I met her. Because she and the Captain had married very young, I knew that soon she would be left alone with two small children. In those days, of course, I had no thought of offering myself as a replacement. Nevertheless, the heartbroken wife's loyal defence of her dying, disgraced husband, and the courage with which she faced a sad, uncertain future, stirred in me protective instincts I had not felt for many years.

Those instincts would be tested on a night in mid-December. Over the past week, Captain Prescott's condition had deteriorated rapidly. When I came onto the ward, my predecessor warned me that the end could come at any time. After charging the attendant to build up the fire, I made my normal rounds, confirming that my other patients were progressing satisfactorily. The Captain awakened shortly before nine o'clock, seemingly in possession of his faculties. His eyes, I noticed, followed me beseechingly as I moved about the room. When I approached his bed, I saw immediately that the poor man would not live till morning. Equally apparent was that he had something urgent to communicate before he died.

It is with reluctance that I recount Giles Prescott's story. I have waited over twenty years to write it down, and many more shall pass before it sees the light of day. It will impugn the honour of two men who died heroically during the Great War, one the most venerated soldier our empire has produced since Wellington. Yet, fantastic and repugnant though the story seemed, I never truly doubted its veracity. I shall not attempt to replicate the manner in which Prescott told it. Although his mind was clear, his physical stamina and powers of expression were almost at an end. The account went on deep into the night, with frequent interruptions when the Captain's strength failed or I was needed to attend another patient. It was after midnight when I returned to his bedside the last time. The lamp I had placed upon the windowsill cast its glow upon his pallid countenance, and I realised that the haunted eyes saw nothing more. The awful tale was told. I was left to ponder what to make of it.

Prescott's company had been part of a mobile column pursuing Boer commandos across the western Transvaal. After a sharp fight in September, he had been delegated to carry despatches to Pretoria, headquarters of the high command. When he arrived there to report, the Captain inadvertently witnessed (here I must sacrifice propriety to fact) an act of sodomy between a staff lieutenant and a senior officer. [4] In a fit of outraged rectitude, he had declared to Lord Kitchener's aide-de-camp (an officer known to his colleagues as "The Beast" [5]) his intention to report the incident. The ADC attempted to dissuade him, but Prescott refused and soon returned to his command.

A few days later, the Captain's mounted infantry were joined by a party of National Scouts, Afrikaners recruited by Lord Kitchener to fight upon the British side. As their appellation indicates, they were especially useful in tracking down the enemy's guerrilla forces. Prescott's orders stated that these troops would guide his horsemen to a certain farmhouse far out upon the veldt, where they would trap a contingent of De la Rey's commandos. Instead, his force had been ambushed by the Boers en route. To the best of his hazy recollection, Prescott had been riding at the left side of the Scouts' commanding officer when the shot unhorsed him. As I was thoroughly familiar with the bullet's track, I confirmed that it must have come from that direction.

While my assurance provided comfort to the Captain as he died, his appalling story left me in a quandary. I did not reveal it to his widow or to Holmes, instead consulting an acquaintance who had served with Kitchener in Egypt. My source refused to discuss the proclivities of individuals, but he did acknowledge that sodomy was not unknown in the Egyptian Army, particularly among officers who had served on the station for some time. [6] As a soldier, I found this information most unwelcome. Not merely for its prurience, for my years as a physician had convinced me that the "evils" of this "vice" were largely due to its suppression. My dismay was that a King's officer had conceivably been murdered by his fellows.

Even so, I found myself unwilling to pursue the matter. A scandal of the kind would have had the worst possible effect upon the British Army, and even more the British public, in the midst of an unpopular and seemingly eternal war. I told myself that the vague suspicions of a brain-damaged, dying patient could not be considered seriously. Moreover, the events had taken place three months before, upon another continent. What reliable proof could be discovered at so late a date? What real hope was there of bringing retribution to the guilty – if guilt, indeed, there was? So I reasoned, ignoring the fact that a brother officer had placed the salvation of his honour in my hands. Ignoring, too, the feelings I had begun to develop for his widow, whose grief I could assuage, and financial security assure, by restoring her late husband's reputation. And ignoring, most of all, my knowledge that if any man in the empire could solve such a puzzle, it was my friend and colleague Sherlock Holmes. Yet, out of a misguided sense of loyalty to my old service, I did nothing. Looking back on it today, I am ashamed to write that the test Giles Prescott set for me I ignominiously failed.

Fortunately for my conscience and my future happiness, I was soon granted another opportunity. Early in March 1902, Holmes and I were finishing a leisurely breakfast when Mrs. Hudson brought in the morning mail. My friend had just returned from a visit to Vienna,[7] while my duties kept me occupied at Barts. Amid my correspondence was a letter that I opened with some trepidation. It was dated the previous day.

Dear Dr. Watson:

> *I hope you will forgive my troubling you, but I did not know where else to turn. Yesterday, I received a parcel containing two documents that I hope will restore my husband's honour. One is his journal from South Africa, which was missing from his kit when he arrived in London. The other is a letter from the sender, a lieutenant in the 17th Lancers whom I do not recall Giles mentioning in any of his letters. Indeed, it seems they did not know each other.*
> *I am perplexed, Doctor, as to how I should proceed. May I visit you and Mr. Holmes and obtain your advice? I have not forgotten your great kindness during those long, sad weeks Giles spent in hospital. Now I beseech you to help me clear his name.*

> *Your sincere friend,*
> *Priscilla Prescott*

P.S. I could come at two o'clock tomorrow afternoon if it would be convenient.

"And how is Mrs. Prescott, Doctor?" enquired Holmes blandly.

"It seems she has received – " I began, before breaking off in irritation. "How did you know this letter came from Mrs. Prescott? From where you're sitting, you could not have seen the writer's name."

"After all these years, old friend, your visage is an open book. As I watched you tear into that black-bordered envelope, blushing like a schoolgirl, I remembered the dying captain's wife you extolled excessively throughout the autumn. A child – or even the youngest Scotland Yard detective – would deduce that his widow is your correspondent. Would it be indiscreet of me to ask to read her note?"

"I suppose not," I grumbled, handing him the letter and (after an impatient gesture) the envelope as well. "As you see, she wishes to consult us."

"No doubt," Holmes murmured. A gleam of interest, I was pleased to see, had come into his eye. "She writes with a firm hand. A woman of strong character, if impulsive and a little nervy . . . Excellent-quality note paper. I see there's money in the Prescott household."

"The Captain's father is General Sir Arthur Prescott. I served with him in India."

"A distinguished soldier but, so I am told, a proud, forbidding man. And it appears," he added thoughtfully, "that his son has compromised the family honour. Obviously, it is in Mrs. Prescott's interest to restore it, if her children are to prosper."

"I hope you aren't suggesting a pecuniary motive," I objected. "To judge by what I learned from her late husband, her faith in him is fully justified."

"And what might *that* be?" my friend demanded tartly. "If I am to advise this lady, Watson, it is essential that I know all the facts."

Having blundered into a confession, I was forced to relate in full the Captain's story, along with the Egyptian evidence supporting it and my decision to suppress the matter. The detective heard me out impassively. Afterwards, he merely sat and sipped his coffee, while I waited in uneasy silence.

"You're certain that Prescott was in his right mind when he told this sordid tale?" he asked at last.

"He was very weak, but seemed perfectly rational. It wasn't delirium, for he had no fever. Apart from struggling to express himself, he was as coherent as I'd ever seen him. It's not an uncommon phenomenon among

205

the dying, Holmes. Given enough motivation, the body marshalls its waning resources in a last, terrific effort."

Holmes grunted with what I took for scepticism. "Did you believe his story?"

"I didn't like to," I acknowledged, "but it had the ring of truth. Why should he lie to me with what he knew to be his dying breath? In Prescott's condition after being shot, he could not have invented so elaborate a falsehood. No, I feel quite sure the Captain was attempting to explain that he'd been murdered."

"And yet, you said nothing to his wife, nothing to absolve the man she loved from cowardice and suicide? Nothing to *me*, the man best suited to investigate the matter? It seems to me, Watson, that you have much to answer for!"

"I'm aware of that," I peevishly admitted. "You can't blame me more than I have blamed myself. Blast it, Holmes, I couldn't accept that British officers were capable of so despicable an act!"

"You *do* recall meeting Colonel Sebastian Moran?"

"And how are we to prove it?" I continued, ignoring his sarcastic query. "It was a renegade Boer who did the shooting. You can be sure the true culprits have their tracks well covered by this time. It's been six months since Prescott's wounding."

"Well, let us not despair," my friend advised, "before meeting *Mrs.* Prescott. She seems to have found hope of vindication in her husband's journal. Until we know what it contains, your question is irrelevant. If you would be so good, please write a note to the widow confirming her two o'clock appointment. I fear that you will have to post it, for Billy is on holiday. Are you not due at Barts?"

"Not until next week. I had intended to spend the morning at my club."

"While you are out, then, I shall peruse the morning papers and those from earlier this week. If you will return half-an-hour before our visitor is due, I shall be happy to discuss my preliminary impressions of the case."

I curtly acquiesced, and Holmes rose from the breakfast table. Stalking to the bow window, he stood looking down upon the morning throng while I scribbled a note to Mrs. Prescott. In this atypically cool manner, we temporarily parted company.

Thankfully, the frost had melted when I re-entered our sitting room at half-past-one. The detective, ensconced on the settee, ruffled through a pile of newsprint and pulled out Tuesday's edition of the *Times*. "Second column on the right, Doctor," he directed, "half-way down the page."

There I found a brief notice headed "*Boer War Veteran a Suicide*". It reported that a lieutenant of the 17th Lancers (whom I shall call "Lieutenant

Smith") had shot himself at the family home in Salisbury while his parents and sister were away. The officer had taken leave upon returning from South Africa, where he had served most recently on Lord Kitchener's staff. His heartbroken father admitted that the young man had seemed depressed for several weeks. It was anticipated that the impending inquest would return a verdict of *"suicide while the balance of his mind was disturbed"*.

"There is the lieutenant of Lancers who is Mrs. Prescott's correspondent," Holmes pronounced. "I think we may take for granted that he is also the lieutenant whom Captain Prescott discovered in *flagrante delicto* with his superior. Obviously, the young man was determined to square accounts before he died."

"How terrible! The poor fellow's humiliation must have been too much for him."

"I should imagine, Watson, that his involvement in a murder – even if unwittingly – was likelier the fatal blow. No doubt we shall learn more from the late captain's journal. Let us hope it provides the evidence we need to bring his murderers to justice."

His hope was soon rewarded. Hard upon the stroke of two, a beaming Mrs. Hudson showed Mrs. Prescott into our sitting room. Holmes and I both rose. My friend (at his most courtly) directed our client to the armchair facing the bow window. I took the basket chair beside him. With a nod of approval, our landlady departed.

I was struck anew by Priscilla Prescott's beauty. Naturally, she wore full mourning, the sombre apparel contrasting with her chestnut hair, green eyes, and pale complexion. Moreover, she exhibited both grace and dignity that brought back my dear Mary, now many years in her grave. I was fairly smitten, and I could tell that Holmes was more attracted than he wished to show. As always in such instances, he took refuge in abruptness.

"I observe, Mrs. Prescott, that you have brought the items referred to in your note. That bulging reticule surely contains your husband's journal."

"Yes, Mr. Holmes, as well as the letter that accompanied it. I shall be happy for you to examine them, but would you not first like to hear my story?"

"Of course," my friend said quickly, recollecting – to my great relief – that Mrs. Prescott would be unaware of his prior knowledge the matter. With admirable clarity and self-control, she recounted what she knew of her husband's wartime service, wounding, and disgrace.

"No one who knew Giles, Mr. Holmes, would ever believe him to be a coward. The letter and journal I received on Tuesday can be used to restore his reputation, for they prove conclusively that he was murdered!"

"One moment," interjected the detective. "This parcel containing Captain Prescott's journal arrived, you say, on Tuesday. Yet, you waited until yesterday to write to Watson. Why delay?"

Our visitor flushed prettily. "My first thought," she admitted, "was to consult Sir Arthur – General Prescott, my husband's father. I telephoned the house, but unfortunately he would not see me. We have had no further contact since my husband died. Because of the rumours surrounding Giles's wound, his parents did not attend the funeral."

"That is more than unfortunate," responded Holmes. "It is unconscionably heartless. Well, let us examine these documents, Mrs. Prescott. The letter first, I think."

The lady passed it over for inspection. The envelope, I saw, was blank. Evidently, it had been included in a parcel with the journal. The detective sniffed the contents as he opened it, then took out the missive. I anticipated his usual running commentary, but after perfunctorily noting the date ("*Sunday night*"), he read on in silence. Dissatisfaction became ever more apparent the farther he progressed.

"I am afraid," Holmes sighed, "that this will be completely useless. It is an exercise in puerile melodrama, without imparting any useful information:

"*Dear Mrs. Prescott,*' he sententiously intoned, "*Your husband died because he intruded on a private moment. Although I was one of those involved, you must believe I had no part in his murder. I was ordered to destroy his journal. Instead, I am sending it to you, in hope you may use it to avenge him once I pass beyond the army's retribution. I shall have sins enough upon my conscience when I meet my God, but murder is not one of them.*' Bah! Not a word to explain who *was* to blame for your husband's murder, or even a clear indication of what your husband saw. He names no names. He offers no particulars. Why, the murderer himself might have written such a note without self-incrimination. What a lily-livered weasel!"

He scornfully tossed the letter towards the fire. I hastily retrieved it.

"What about the journal, Holmes?"

'Ah, indeed, the journal. Let us hope *it* is worth reading." He held out a hand to Mrs. Prescott, who was eying him with indignation. "I trust you will treat my husband's words with more care, sir," she admonished.

"My apologies," my friend muttered, accepting the small, leather-bound volume. As he leafed through it, the widow went on speaking.

"If you will examine the entry for the eighteenth of September last," she suggested, "you will find that Giles's account is *quite* specific. He describes witnessing a . . . a homosexual encounter between Lieutenant Smith and – " She named the senior officer in question. Quickly locating the relevant page, Holmes smiled with satisfaction to see the name recorded there.

"Thank you, Mrs. Prescott. This is precisely the confirmation Dr. Watson and I have been seeking." Realising his error, the detective blanched, as Mrs. Prescott stared at me in consternation. "You *knew* about this, Doctor?"

It was the most humiliating moment of my life, and I still marvel that I did not lose my future wife forever. Left with no alternative, I confessed my knowledge and belatedly retold the Captain's story. His widow listened in shocked silence, at the end remarking bitterly: "All this time, I had feared my husband died a suicide. Why didn't you *tell* me?"

"He has been awaiting proof," Holmes intervened, "which you have now provided. Sadly, written proof is a necessity, for your correspondent is no more. Lieutenant Smith's suicide on Monday was reported in *The Times*. After posting your parcel, he returned home and shot himself."

"Is there no end to this horror?" Mrs. Prescott cried. "Well, gentlemen," she added angrily, "you have your proof at last. What do you intend to do with it?"

"*That*, dear lady," replied the detective, "depends in part upon your own intentions. Do you desire only to salvage Captain Prescott's reputation, or also to bring retribution to the guilty? I believe I can promise you the first. The second may be more problematic."

"I assure you, Mr. Holmes, that restoring my late husband's honour, and assuring a decent inheritance for our two children, are my paramount concerns. If you can bring his murderers to justice, I shall not stand in your way. What steps do you propose to take?"

"I have already taken the first," Holmes responded, "and that is to consult a certain gentleman in Whitehall who has influence in the War Office. In fact," he added, rising, "we are scheduled to meet in fifteen minutes. I have taken the liberty, Mrs. Prescott, of asking our good landlady to provide tea to you and Dr. Watson. You will hear from me again within the next few days."

Our client was given no opportunity to refuse this invitation, for as Holmes exited the sitting room Mrs. Hudson entered it, bearing a sumptuous tea that surpassed even her usual high standards. After serving us impeccably, she tactfully departed, but looked in often enough thereafter to maintain propriety. During the interims, I was left to offer Mrs. Prescott a profound apology.

I shall not regale my readers with the first intimate conversation between my third wife and myself. Naturally, I sought to justify my conduct in withholding information she had every right to know. I spoke of my reverence for King and Country, of the wound I had received at

Maiwand, and of the loyalty I still felt towards my old service – a loyalty I knew her husband shared. Having mouthed these platitudes, I acknowledged them to be self-serving, a dereliction of my duty to a fellow officer and a patient's wife. Priscilla did not sanction the decision I had made, but she accepted my contrition. By the time the pot was emptied, the two of us were on a different footing. When Captain Prescott's widow said goodbye to me that afternoon, she called me "John".

It was nearly ten o'clock when my friend returned from the Diogenes Club. Noting my beguiled demeanour, he enquired with a smile if the "arrangements" he had made had pleased me. I asked, in turn, whether Mycroft had been willing to assist us.

"My brother, when I left him, was not a happy man," replied Sherlock Holmes. "As you know, since the Fawcett Report, Milner's administration in Johannesburg has again come under fire for conditions in the concentration camps. [8] With the war winding down at last, His Majesty's ministers are terrified of any untoward event that might jeopardise the chance of peace. It is to their discomfort, I was told, that Lieutenants Morant and Handcock owe their executions. [9] Kitchener and most of his staff will remain in Pretoria until a treaty has been signed. However, Mycroft revealed to me that one of the aides-de-camp is now in London. That officer is none other than the one Captain Prescott heard referred to as 'The Beast'. After considerable browbeating and eight telephone calls, my dear brother arranged for us to call upon the gentleman tomorrow morning."

To my surprise, Kitchener's ADC was residing at the Langham, once the London abode of our old client the King of Bohemia. For a captain in the military forces of the Raj, such accommodation argued either for substantial private means or another source of income beyond his army pay. However, Mycroft had informed us that this officer was hardly "to the manner born". The son of a shopkeeper in Bristol, his lineage was no more aristocratic than my own.

As Portland Place is but a short cab ride from Baker Street, Holmes and I were easily on time for our ten o'clock appointment. The Beast's lair proved to be an elegant suite on the third floor. Our host received us in his dressing gown. He was approximately thirty, with dark hair parted centrally (a style prevalent among our officers in those days) and the obligatory thin mustache. The careless demeanour he affected reminded me of a messmate in Afghanistan, whose atrocious conduct towards young women had resulted in my brother Henry's downfall. [10] Despite the fearful appellation of the officer before us, I surmised that with him young women were relatively safe.

210

Our arrival seemed to gratify The Beast. "You fought at Maiwand, Doctor, didn't you?" he welcomed me. "Bad show, that. Bit before my time, of course. Naturally, I've heard of *you*, Mr. Holmes. Been reading the Doctor's new one in *The Strand*, the tale featuring the fiendish Hound.[11] That's *you*, isn't it, out there on the tor? Ha! Thought so."

His breezy patter died away, and he regarded my friend doubtfully. "I was surprised you wished to see me, Mr. Holmes. How can I be of assistance to you gentlemen?" He waved us to a well-upholstered sofa and ambled towards the sideboard. "Coffee?"

After declining this offer, the detective was unusually direct. "We are investigating the deaths of two officers whom I believe are known to you," he answered. "One of them, Lieutenant Smith, served with you until recently on Lord Kitchener's staff."

"Smith?" our host repeated. "No mystery there. Poor chap did himself in. I saw it in *The Times*."

"More specifically," said Holmes, "he shot himself the day after the two of you had spoken at his parents' home in Wiltshire. Perhaps you would care to enlighten us as to the subject of that meeting?"

"Or perhaps not," The Beast rejoined, his affability abating. "How do *you* know I was there? Surely, a great detective has more to do than shadow an officer taking a bit of well-earned leave."

"Quite so, Captain. While you were visiting Salisbury last Sunday afternoon, I was reviewing the works of a neglected composer in Vienna. But surely you must realise that the movements of Lord Kitchener's staff are of interest to the War Office, even while they are on leave. As it happens, I have connexions there. You unquestionably took the train to Salisbury."

"Let's just say I went to visit the cathedral."

"Forgive me, but you hardly seem the type. No, your visit was intended to assure yourself – and others – that Lieutenant Smith had carried out his orders by destroying a journal that contained incriminating information. A journal he later forwarded to Captain Prescott's wife, along with a letter confirming that same information. Both documents are safely in official custody, where they can be used in evidence against you – and others – involved in Captain Prescott's murder."

The Beast's face paled, but he laughed heartily. "Really, Mr. Holmes, you should let Dr. Watson write the stories. That's the biggest ball of dung I've encountered since I left South Africa. Bring on the dung beetles!"

Faced with our long silence and impassive stares, his bravado faltered. "Very well, gentlemen. As it happens, I *did* visit Smith on Sunday. The poor boy was as unsteady as a broken reed. That's what we called him in Pretoria – 'The Boy' – and, sadly, that is all he was. If you must know, his veneration for The Chief seemed a bit . . . *unnatural.*"

"So Captain Prescott discovered," I reminded him, "and he told you of his intention to report an offense against British law and military regulations. A few days later he was dead – dead, as I shall testify as his last physician, at the hands of an Afrikaner mercenary despatched from Lord Kitchener's headquarters. Do you deny having met with Prescott, Captain?"

Our host reverted swiftly to evasion. "All sorts of people pass through HQ, Doctor. One can hardly be expected to remember all of them. I'm not the only ADC on staff. It could have been 'Handsome Hammy' [12] or 'The Brat' [13] who dealt with Prescott."

"Oh, no," said Sherlock Holmes. "The late captain's journal clearly referenced an officer known as 'The Beast'. *Your* nickname on the staff, as I have on good authority. I shall not bother to ask how you acquired it."

The captain sprang from his chair, venting an oath that I shall not repeat. He strode to the sideboard, poured out a whisky, and quickly drank it down. When he turned back to us, all friendliness had gone, and he launched into the following tirade:

"I shall not tell you, Mr. Holmes, what it was that Prescott thought he saw. Nor can I explain how that young idiot Smith came to believe there was a plot among the staff to murder Prescott. The idea is ridiculous! The C-in-C may have a bit of a vindictive streak, but at heart he's an old softie. You should have seen him blub when he signed the death warrants for those three Australian chaps. He even let the youngest fellow off with life imprisonment!

"I *can* tell you that our report from the field stated unequivocally that Giles Prescott put a bullet in his own head, out of shame that he'd turned tail when his command was ambushed. Now you say it was one of those d----d Scouts we sent to reinforce him. It could well have been! I've always thought it was bad policy to trust those turncoats. You can never be sure which side they're really fighting on."

He paused for breath, while we did our best to look encouraging. "I will even tell you, gentlemen, that it was *I* who ordered Smith to destroy Prescott's journal when we sent the blighter home. And, yes, I visited him on Sunday to confirm that he had done so. You can understand that Prescott's scribbles weren't the sort of thing we'd want hawked about. Smith swore when we met that the d----d thing was a pile of ashes. So he was a liar as well as a fool! And in case you're thinking I went back the next day and shot him, I was at Netley on Monday visiting a wounded chum. Half-a-dozen staff and doctors there will back me up."

"Anything else?" my friend enquired admiringly.

212

"Only this. If all your brilliant 'deductions' are based on such prodigious bluff, I must conclude that Dr. Watson is simply a bad novelist and *your* reputation is completely undeserved. What evidence do you have to prove your little fable? Two dead witnesses and a diary anybody could have altered! Well, it won't wash, sir – not to bring down the most famous soldier in the British Empire. And I daresay the rest of us have enough VC's, CB's, and DSO's to hold you off. Do you recall Lord Melbourne's advice to his Cabinet, Mr. Holmes, when they found themselves in Queer Street? 'It doesn't matter what we say, so long as we all say the same thing.' Well, you can be d----d sure that every member of Kitchener's staff will sing from the same songbook. And we won't say one d----d word to implicate The Chief!"

The detective smiled resignedly at his interlocutor and rose, nodding to me to follow him. "In that case, Captain, I see no point in subjecting you to further indignation. Do not assume, however, that the matter will rest here. Meanwhile, allow me thank you for an exceedingly amusing hour. I am no longer in doubt as to how your 'beastly' appellation was acquired."

We were halfway back to Baker Street before Sherlock Holmes broke his thoughtful silence. "Well, Doctor," he laughed ruefully, "I don't believe I have ever been rebuffed quite so eloquently in an interrogation. Whatever else one may think of him, The Beast possesses gall."

"He was certainly vehement. How much of his account did you believe?"

'Oh, he answered us honestly when pushed into a corner, but I am sure there was much he did not tell. All the rest was merely bluster. Yet, he was absolutely right! Our entire case consists of circumstantial evidence and bluff. In the unlikely event we ever set foot in a courtroom, a clever counsel would tear it all to rags."

"I was surprised you knew so much about his movements."

"That, my dear Watson, was the bluff! I learned from Mycroft that his agent saw the Captain board a train for Salisbury, but there was no proof that he had visited Lieutenant Smith. I took a shot in the dark, and luckily it hit the target. Even so, it was the obvious conclusion once I knew The Beast was back in England."

"He admitted young Smith's infatuation with Lord Kitchener, and his own attempt to destroy Prescott's journal. Those facts confirm our other evidence."

"Yes, but he gave away nothing that bears upon the murder. The difficulty is that we cannot link the treacherous Afrikaner Scout either to Kitchener or to a specific member of his staff. The Chief, for all his peccadilloes, seems to command intense loyalty among the officers who serve him. So long as they present a solid front, no one takes responsibility, and the man behind them is invulnerable."

"What shall we do? We cannot admit defeat to Mrs. Prescott."

"Have no fear, my friend. I shall not leave your beleaguered lady in the lurch." He smiled reassuringly and dismounted from the cab, which had drawn up at our doorstep. "While we lack enough evidence to convince a court-martial, we can easily make certain people's lives uncomfortable. One of them is Brother Mycroft. I shall visit him again this afternoon. Thank you, cabbie."

"Shall I accompany you?" I suggested as we shut the door behind us.

"No, in this instance I think my brother is better left to me. Your mission will be to enlist a powerful new ally in Mrs. Prescott's cause. Let us see if we can persuade our dear landlady to provide an early luncheon."

Sir Arthur Prescott had returned from India as a nabob, a fact demonstrated when I arrived at his imposing house in Kensington. I was admitted by a grey-bearded, turbaned native servant. After climbing a stairway to the first floor, we entered a splendid drawing room full of Oriental curios and weaponry. Above the mantel hung a portrait of Ensign Arthur Prescott, wearing a bottle-green uniform contemporary with the Mutiny. He had married, I remembered, very late in life, and the Captain had been his only child.

It was ten minutes before Sir Arthur joined me. I occupied myself by admiring his collection of antiquities. At last, the General marched into the chamber as if on parade. "Whisky?" he barked, and, taking my consent for granted, added soda to two tumblers. Though his bearing remained soldierly, Prescott was now white-haired and portly, with a distinctly bilious look. I recalled him as a martinet, although I never served directly under him. My old friend Colonel Hayter had despised the man.

Handing me my glass, my host eyed me sternly.

"I agreed to see you, Doctor, because I would not turn away a Fusilier or any other soldier formerly under my command. However, the call I received from the War Office stated that you wish to discuss a matter related to my son. I warn you that that subject is forever closed. I shall not take the slightest interest in anything you have to say."

"I have come here, Sir Arthur, partly as an emissary of Mr. Sherlock Holmes." This admission was an error, for the General's frown deepened.

"So you are *that* Dr. Watson. I have no sympathy, sir, with amateur busybodies who undermine the work of the police. The fact that you trumpet the exploits of a mountebank does not assist your cause."

It occurred to me that a retired soldier no longer had to tolerate such insults. "Would it interest you to know, Sir Arthur," I asked him coldly, "that the 'cause' Mr. Holmes and I espouse is to restore your family's honour?"

I shall spare my readers most of the conversation that followed. As I rehearsed again the grim events set forth in this narrative, Prescott's remarks progressed from "How *dare* you, sir?" to "Those d----d Egyptians always were a pack of sodomites!" to "I'll have that scoundrel broken to the ranks!" (this in reference to The Beast) before ending with: "My boy. My poor, poor boy." At which point, Sir Arthur astonished me by bursting into tears. By the time I left, he was assuring me that "I am forever in your debt," and that he would visit the War Office the next morning. "Tell dear Priscilla," the General entreated me in parting, "that Lady Prescott and I shall call upon her and the children whenever she is willing to receive us."

It was with satisfaction that I regressed to 221B Baker Street, where I learned that the detective's interview had been far less rewarding. "I fear my brother is intransigent," he sighed. "He is unwilling to take action without irrefutable proof that Lord Kitchener's staff was involved in Prescott's murder. There is no question of proceeding against the man himself. With the 'mob' (as Mycroft called them) incensed by the two Australians' execution and the awful death toll in the camps, any new scandal would be absolutely ruinous to the present government."

"And what of British justice, Holmes? Is a King's officer to be dishonoured, and his murderers go free, so that a handful of politicians may remain in office?"

"You know as well as I do, Doctor, *precisely* where ministers' priorities will lie. It is so with any government, from the vilest Oriental despotism to a democracy supposedly as free as ours. There are moments when I despair entirely of the human race!"

"Then what are we to do?"

"For the present, there is nothing we *can* do. You say that General Prescott will visit the War Office tomorrow. Let us see whether his initiative bears fruit, and meanwhile trust that some unforeseen event will turn the situation in our favour. That is the only plan that I can offer you, and I am sorry it is not a better one."

And yet it worked! The next day's *Times* carried the account of a new disaster in the Transvaal, in which De la Rey had routed an entire British column and captured General Methuen. So demoralising a defeat, coming at so late a date, dealt a heavy blow to the prospects of an early peace. It was reported that Lord Kitchener had taken to his bed. [14] For once, I was almost thankful for a reverse to British arms. My friend immediately demanded another interview with Mycroft. By the time we met with him, he had learned that General Prescott, after a contentious morning at the War Office, had all but offered the responsible minister pistols at dawn. He had also threatened to inform the press unless his son's name was cleared in full. Consequently, we found the King's advisor in a more tractable mood than on the last occasion he had met with his cadet.

After two gruelling hours of discussion, the Holmes brothers reached a compromise. The War Office would state publicly that after an enquiry, it had been proven that the late Captain Prescott was mortally wounded by a Boer during the attack upon his company. Thus, he would be officially exonerated from rumours of cowardice or suicide. In return, Mycroft insisted that all efforts to uncover the alleged role of Kitchener, or any member of his staff, in Prescott's death would be abandoned. All speculation on those lines, or in regard to sodomy, would cease forthwith. After the War Office's statement, no further publicity would be given to the case. I was therefore forbidden to add it to my chronicles, a prohibition lately disregarded (with the permission of both brothers) on the understanding that this account will not be published in the present century.

We explained these terms to Mrs. Prescott on the following evening, at a dinner held in Baker Street. As we had expected, our landlady excelled herself for the occasion. Mrs. Hudson's Beef Wellington was an occasion in itself, and Mycroft Holmes sent over two bottles of the finest Bordeaux in the Diogenes Club's cellar. Even so, the gathering was not intended as a celebration. Holmes was grimly apologetic for his inability to bring the murderers to justice, and our client, while appreciative, was not altogether pleased. She rejected the offer of a posthumous decoration for her husband, an idea imposed upon the War Office by his father.

"Why should Giles receive a medal for being shot by a traitor?" fumed his widow. "When he was alive, he was twice mentioned in despatches and recommended for a DSO. No, I shall not allow the generals and politicians to salve their consciences so cheaply. Should I tell Peter and Emily one day: 'This is the medal your dear father won for getting himself murdered?'"

"I cannot blame you, Mrs. Prescott," Holmes replied, "and I regret exceedingly that those responsible will not pay the price. Unfortunately, it proved impossible to trace the root of the conspiracy and assign culpability to individuals, now that we are six months beyond the facts and seven-thousand miles away."

"I know that, Mr. Holmes, and I know soldiers well enough to understand that they will always close ranks in times of trouble. Why, even Dr. Watson has informed me that despite our friendship, his first instinct was to protect the army, not the interests of his patient or his patient's wife." Priscilla said this with a smile, but it was not a pleasant one. I realised that my misplaced loyalties would always lie between us.

"I am ashamed of that decision," I admitted, "but it was a hard thing to accept that my old service had been tainted by conspiracy and murder. I'm not sure *why*," I added ruefully, "for I saw worse things in Afghanistan." I was thinking of my brother Henry, and of an officer compared to whom The Beast and the Afrikaner Scout seemed virtuous and honourable men.

"Nevertheless, Mrs. Prescott," I addressed my future wife, "I hope you can forgive me. If not tonight, perhaps, then soon."

"I hope so, too," Priscilla smiled – as did, more knowingly, my old friend Sherlock Holmes.

For that night was truly the beginning. As the spring advanced, I continued to see Priscilla Prescott. By early May, our friendship had become romance. I offered the lady marriage on the night the Boer War ended. Given its significance in our relationship, my intended bride imposed a test before accepting my proposal.

"If we are to marry, John, there is something you must promise me."

"And what is that, my dear?"

"As a mother, I never want to face again the anxiety and heartbreak I felt when my husband went to war and returned to me dying and dishonoured. I lost one man I loved to your sacred British Army, and I have determined not to lose another. The army has proven to us both, I believe, that it did not deserve the sacrifice I have already made. You must promise that insofar as it lies within your power, you will never allow my son Peter to become a soldier."

"I am not certain I can promise that, Priscilla," I answered with dismay. "Peter is the son and grandson of British officers. His grandfather will have an influence on his choice of a career. Besides, there may come a day when our country is faced with a great crisis, a greater war that no man fit for military service can honourably shirk." The widow was regarding me with sorrow. I knew our future would stand or fall on my next words.

"But I *can* promise you," I continued, less portentously, "that if war should come I shall not attempt to influence Peter's decision, not unless he asks for my advice. Nor shall I encourage him, in time of peace, to accept the King's commission – which, had you not spoken, I might easily have done." Still Priscilla looked dissatisfied, but my persuasive locker contained a final shot.

"Finally," I added with my most winning smile, "I promise to do everything I can to help Peter become a man of whom we can all be proud,

217

the sort of young fellow who could redeem the army in which his father served. If you and I succeed in that, I shall have no fear for him, whatever course he chooses for his life."

A long moment passed before the woman I loved returned my smile. "Very well, John," she replied, "then I shall marry you."

And there the matter of Peter Prescott's future stood for eleven happy years. I took a house in Queen Anne Street and rebuilt my long-neglected practice. We married in the autumn – a mere nine months since Captain Prescott's death – but a social scandal was averted when his father gave the bride away. As with my earlier two weddings, my former fellow lodger served as my best man.

It was not a perfect marriage, and early on we had our share of quarrels. My new wife exhibited more jealousy of Sherlock Holmes than Mary had. After a three-week-long case in Serbia [15], I promised her that my family's interests would henceforth come first – a promise aided by my friend's ostensible retirement towards the end of 1903. For my part, it was not always easy, as a man of fifty, to adjust to living with small children. While indisputably delightful, Peter and Emily were initially but six and three. Nevertheless, I can confirm without reserve that the experience of fatherhood, even as a surrogate, was undoubtedly the most rewarding of my life.

All went well until my stepson reached the age of seventeen, during his last year at Eton. By that time (1913), the clouds of the Great War loomed on the horizon. While on a visit home, Peter informed us of his desire to attend Sandhurst after university. He had written to his grandparents, and old General Prescott was in full support of the idea. My wife was devastated. The most she could achieve, even with my reluctant backing, was to postpone Peter's decision until the time for it had come. Alas, the time came far too soon. Despite Britain's quarter-century of trying to avert it, the Crowned Heads of Europe had determined upon war. Just as Peter turned eighteen, the shots rang out in Sarajevo.

Even then, Priscilla tried to stave off the inevitable. She assured her son that (as we all hoped then) the war would end by Christmas. Persuaded to matriculate to Cambridge, he joined the university's Officer Training Corps. This solution bought us several months, and at least protected Peter from receiving a white feather on the street. But early the next year,

218

another trainee (also the scion of a military family) sneered at Cadet Prescott: "You must be a coward like your father was." After such an insult, Peter would delay no longer. With little time to call in favours, his grandfather secured a commission for him in a battalion of Kitchener's "New Army". It was an irony not lost on either of us. Three months after his nineteenth birthday, Second Lieutenant Peter Prescott departed for the Western Front. He survived for over a year, dying, as a captain, on the Somme.

His mother never recovered. She stopped speaking to the Prescotts, and I received my share of blame. In her extremity of grief, she railed at me: "You always chose your precious army over us, John, always! The army and Mr. Sherlock Holmes." In time, Priscilla said that she forgave me, but the light in her had gone. At last, during the spring of 1920, she began to rediscover joy while planning the June wedding of her daughter Emily. After a companionable autumn, we decided to spend December visiting America, which my wife had never seen. A few days of sight-seeing in Boston and New York did much to revive Priscilla's spirits. I had planned to travel on to Tennessee, where one branch of the Watson family had emigrated many years ago. [16] Unaccountably, however, my wife's energy suddenly began to fail. We took an early steamship home, arriving back in London on December twenty-third. After a quiet but loving Christmas, I insisted that she consult her own physician. The diagnosis was inoperable cancer, and from that day my beautiful Priscilla faded swiftly. She left us two months later, but Emily and I agreed that her mother's heart had died in France.

In the years afterwards, I have pondered whether my wife's embittered words were just. Even now, in my mid-seventies, I still take pride in my youthful service to the Queen. But the army left me maimed, and it cost me my brother Henry. It cost my dear Priscilla a good deal more than that. Having lost Peter to the senseless slaughter of the trenches, I have little sympathy today with the generals and politicians who send young men to war. However, I must not write more in this vein, or I shall begin to doubt the British Empire. And that, as Mr. Sherlock Holmes would say, will never do.

NOTES

1. It is unclear whether Watson refers to his original regiment, the 5th (Northumberland Fusiliers) Regiment of Foot, or the regiment to which he was attached at Maiwand, the 66th (Berkshire) Regiment of Foot. The latter had amalgamated in 1881 with another regiment to form what became Princess Charlotte of Wales's Royal Berkshire Regiment. Both it and the Northumberlands served in South Africa during the Boer War.

2. *The Great Boer War*, first published by Smith, Elder & Co. after Doyle's return to London in 1900. He continued to update the book, through sixteen editions, until the war's end in 1902. In October of that year, ACD was knighted by King Edward VII. Text of *The Great Boer War* has been made available by Project Gutenberg at:
   https://www.gutenberg.org/files/3069/3069-h/3069-h.htm#link2H_PREF

3. For an account of the excellent quality of British medical services during the South African war, see Chapter 3 of Emanoel Lee's *To the Bitter End: A Photographic History of the Boer War, 1899-1902* (Harmondsworth, Middlesex, England: Penguin Books, Ltd., 1985), pp. 66-84.

4. Although Watson could not bring himself to identify the senior officer, he had compromised him earlier by referring to "*the most venerated soldier our empire has produced since Wellington*". That would almost certainly be Lieutenant-General Lord Kitchener (1850-1916), then Commander-in-Chief of British forces in South Africa. Kitchener was already famous for conquering the Sudan in 1898 while in command of the Egyptian Army. He later served as C-in-C in India, and in 1909 was promoted to field marshal. It was Earl Kitchener's face which adorned the iconic recruiting poster that sent the British Army into World War I. He and his last aide-de-camp, Captain Oswald Fitzgerald, died when *HMS Hampshire*, the ship on which they were traveling to Russia, struck a mine in the North Sea. Whether Kitchener was actively homosexual has been much debated. Jad Adams' 1999 article in *History Today*:
   https://www.historytoday.com/archive/ was-kitchener-gay
   which summarizes historians' opinions, is available behind a paywall. See also Rictor Norton's review of John Pollock's biography of Kitchener:
   http://rictornorton.co.uk/reviews/kitchen.htm.

5. There is confusion or deception at some level here. Throughout his career, Lord Kitchener maintained a "band of boys" – young, handsome, and unmarried junior officers, all with "*nicknames such as Conk, the Brat, Brookie, Marker, and Hand-some Hammy*" – as aides-de-camp. (See Norton's review of Pollock, cited above.) None of the sources I consulted mentioned an ADC known as "*The Beast*". Perhaps Captain Prescott, who visited Kitchener's headquarters only briefly, mistook the moniker of the officer with whom he spoke. More likely is that Watson intentionally obfuscated to protect the real ADC's identity.

6. According to a Reuters representative, A. E. Wearne, *"Kitchener had the 'failing acquired by most of the Egyptian officers, a taste for buggery.'"* Quoted in a blog post entitled "Jalapeno in the Eye" among other sources. *https://jeanfi vintage.tumblr.com/post/187535224275/howdoyoulikethemeggrolls-gareleelove-lord/amp*

7. Holmes's visit to Vienna, where he conducted an investigation for the composer Gustav Mahler, is recorded in "The Solitary Violinist," found in *The MX Book of New Sherlock Holmes Stories, Part XVIII: "Whatever Remains . . . Must Be the Truth (1899-1925)*, (London: MX Publishing, 2019) pp. 212-242. The story also references events in "The Adventure of the Inconvenient Heir-Apparent" from the forthcoming collection *Sherlock Holmes and the Crowned Heads of Europe*.

8. Kitchener's strategy, approved by High Commissioner Sir Alfred Milner, was to deprive the Boer commandos of supplies by burning their farms and placing their women and children in refugee camps. Well over 20,000 internees died. The report of the Fawcett Commission (December 1901) confirmed Emily Hobhouse's earlier findings of dire conditions in the camps. Public horror in Britain led the Liberals' Sir Henry Campbell-Bannerman to condemn the government's *"methods of barbarism"* in South Africa. Due partly to the Fawcett Commission's recommendations, the camps began to improve by the end of 1901. See Lee, pp. 162-190, and Thomas Pakenham, *The Boer War* (New York: Random House, 1979), pp. 536-549.

9. The trial and execution of Lieutenants Morant and Handcock of the Bushveldt Carbineers, who were convicted of shooting Boer prisoners and a German missionary, is the subject of Australian director Bruce Beresford's film *Breaker Morant* (1980). Lord Kitchener commuted the death sentence of a third officer, Lieutenant George Witton, to life imprisonment.

10. Marcia Wilson wrote of the Watson brothers' service in Afghanistan in her excellent series of fan fiction novels, particularly *A Sword for the Defense* and *A Fanged and Bitter Thing*. Henry Watson's subsequent life in San Francisco is recounted in "A Ghost from Christmas Past" from *The MX Book of New Sherlock Holmes Stories, Part VII: Eliminate the Impossible*, edited by David Marcum (London: MX Publishing, 2017), pp. 130-152. An illustrated version, featuring an original painting by artist Nuné Asatryan, was published in *The Art of Sherlock Holmes: West Palm Beach Edition*, curated by Phil Growick (London: MX Publishing, 2019), pp. 196-211.

11. *The Hound of the Baskervilles* was originally serialized in the Strand from August 1901 to April 1902, prior to its publication in book form. It was the first adventure since "The Final Problem" (December 1893) concluded with Holmes's apparent death at the Reichenbach Halls. Only after the detective's supposed retirement in October 1903 was Watson permitted to resume his publication of short stories with "The Adventure of the Empty House."

12. Colonel (later Major-General) Hubert Ion Wetherall Hamilton CB, CVO, DSO (1861-1914) was Lord Kitchener's military secretary from late 1900 until the end of war. He later commanded a division in France and was killed in action during "*the Race for the Sea*" in October 1914. In the movie *Breaker Morant*, Colonel Hamilton sacrifices his honor by lying on behalf of Kitchener about the high command's order to shoot Boer prisoners.

13. Captain (later Brigadier-General) Francis Aylmer Maxwell, VC, CSI, DSO & Bar (1871-1917) This young officer, whose cheekiness with Kitchener earned his appellation, had won his VC against the Boers in 1900. Maxwell's letters (several of which are quoted by Pakenham) offer entertaining insights on the C-in-C. They were later collected and published by his wife. Brigadier Maxwell was killed by a German sniper in 1917. *https://babel.hathitrust.org/cgi/pt?id=yale.39002040678246&view=1up& seq=9*

14. The Battle of Tweebosch, March 7, 1902. It took two days for "*The Brat*" to persuade the C-in-C to leave his bedroom. Despite Kitchener's despondency at the defeat, a fortnight later a Boer delegation arrived in Pretoria to open peace negotiations. See Pakenham, p. 583.

15. A case recounted as "A Scandal in Serbia" first in Part VI of *The MX Book of New Sherlock Holmes Stories: 2017 Annual* (London: MX Publishing, 2017), pp. 545-572. The story is also included in the forthcoming book *Sherlock Holmes and the Crowned Heads of Europe*.

16. In May and June of 1921, Watson returned to the United States, in company with Sherlock Holmes, to carry out his genealogical explorations in eastern Tennessee. David Marcum recounts their time there in "The Affair of the Brother's Request" and "The Adventure of the Madman's Ceremony" from *The Papers of Sherlock Holmes*, Volume One and Volume Two (London: MX Publishing, 2014), pp. 156-216.

The Woman Who Returned
from the Dead
by Arthur Hall

I reflected, one fine early summer morning as we left the breakfast table, that it was probably possible to accurately gauge the mood of my friend, Mr. Sherlock Holmes, by the amount of time elapsed since the conclusion of his previous case.

Three weeks had passed since he was finally able to hand Inspector Lestrade the full facts of the Creighton affair, which would undoubtedly result in Fergus Colloway ending his days on the gallows, and since then I had been able to observe with interest the slow deterioration in Holmes's temperament.

The pattern invariably began with a marked reduction of our exchanges at mealtimes, culminating with barely a word passing between us. When we sat at our ease, in our usual armchairs around the fireplace, he rarely lowered his newspaper, save to listen to the sounds from outside floating through the half-open window in the hope that they brought him some new problem. He would come and go, unexpectedly and abruptly, hardly acknowledging my presence or that of our good landlady, Mrs. Hudson. At times this became unendurable, and the frequency of my solitary afternoon walks around the streets of the capital increased sharply.

This particular morning, to my great relief, was to see an end to this ordeal. Holmes had placed the early edition of *The Standard* on his lap, and was in the process of filling his old briar with tobacco from the Persian slipper, when he suddenly stiffened like a hound on the hunt.

I looked at him, over my book. "What is it?"

"A carriage has come to halt beneath our window." He inclined his head, to listen further. "I hear the cabby assuring his passenger that he has arrived at the address he seeks. Watson, I do believe that we are to be presented with a new problem."

His expression lightened, as when dark clouds give way to sunshine. I watched as he seemed suddenly filled with energy and anticipation. The Holmes with whom I had shared so many adventures was reappearing before my eyes, and I felt my own spirits lift.

The doorbell rang and soon we heard our landlady answer. A short, muted conversation was followed by footsteps upon the stairs, and not long after she ushered in a stocky man of about twenty-six years.

We got to our feet and Holmes dismissed Mrs. Hudson with a gesture. For an instant I wondered that he had not requested tea or coffee for our guest, until I saw that the young man's expression was one of profound grief. His eyes, in particular, testified to his disturbed condition.

"Come, sir," Holmes invited. "Allow me to take your coat and sit here with us." He guided our client to the basket chair and ensured that he was seated comfortably. "Watson, pray pour a brandy for our guest."

I did so and it was consumed rapidly. I retrieved the glass, and I made to pour another, but a hand was held up in refusal.

"No, no thank you, sir. Your kindness is deeply appreciated, but drink will not cure the heartbreak that is blighting my life."

Holmes leaned forward in his chair, as I returned to mine.

"I see that you are most distressed," he said in his most gentle tone, "and breathing heavily because of your agitation. Take some time to calm yourself. Then, when you are ready, we will hear what brought you to us. There is no need to hurry, and we are ready to help if it is at all possible."

Our visitor closed his eyes and sat with the air of someone in great pain. I noted that there appeared to be no physical symptoms, since his movements weren't consistent with those of one who suffers agonising spasms. The outward signs of his distress were contained in his face, which was as pale as that of a dead man. The remainder of his appearance was conventional – his well-tailored suit was of good cloth and his boots of fine polished leather. I concluded that, whatever the nature of his difficulties, they were unlikely to be financial.

"Forgive me," he finally stammered, "and thank you both for your patience. Just a moment longer, and I will be myself."

"Allow time for your tensions to subside," Holmes advised, "for it is clear to me that you have suffered much over the past few weeks."

"How can you possibly know that, Mr. Holmes, for I have as yet revealed nothing?"

"There is surely no mystery about it. When I see how your hands tremble, which is doubtlessly the reason for the several cuts upon your face sustained during shaving, and then I observe other cuts which are in the process of healing, it is no great feat to deduce that your difficulty has not arisen recently. Also, you have neglected to trim your moustache or ensure that your tie is positioned correctly, and as you appear fastidious in your dress otherwise, these, too, suggest that you are troubled."

Our client leaned forwards, his head in his hands, before seeming to gather himself enough to sit up straight. His eyes glistened, I noticed, as he spoke.

"Troubled indeed. Yes, gentlemen, that I certainly have been. I am Mr. William Jeavon, of Fallon Square, near Cheyne Walk, Chelsea. I have been the manager of the local branch of the Millworkers and Miners Bank for the last five years."

"You are young to have attained such a position," Holmes observed.

"I am aware of it. It came about because Mr. Griswolde, my predecessor, died suddenly while performing his duties. I was the senior member of staff who took over his post temporarily, but our superiors were satisfied with my performance to the extent that I was invited to assume it permanently."

"Your problem then cannot be a financial difficulty, unless it is concerned with the bank itself. I'm inclined to think, however, that it concerns someone close to you."

"It does indeed, sir. I must tell you though, that you will find my story difficult to believe."

"We have heard much that is strange and unconventional in this room before now."

Mr. Jeavon nodded but hesitated. There were a few moments of silence, unbroken but for the cries of distant costermongers selling their wares along Baker Street.

"It was two years ago," he began, "that my beloved wife and I walked along Tottenham Court Road one summer evening. I recall that, a moment before disaster struck, it was in my mind that, being financially secure and having a pleasant and beautiful wife, I am indeed a most fortunate fellow."

His speech faltered at the memory, and Holmes and I waited.

"Then Priscilla, for that was her name, saw an urchin begging on the opposite side of the street. Knowing her kind and generous nature, it didn't surprise me that she at once resolved to give the poor child a few coins, but I was unprepared for her immediate intention to approach him."

"She stepped into the middle of the road," I ventured.

"She did, and since we were arm-in-arm, she almost pulled me after her. As it was, I realised that a speeding coach was bearing down on us and instinctively resisted, with the result that she fell headlong into the path of the carriage. There was no question that she would survive."

The cause of Mr. Jeavon's grief was therefore clear, though some time had elapsed. We expressed our condolences before he continued.

"The occupant and owner of the coach was the Member of Parliament, Sir Cedric Wheeler. He was most courteous, making no criticism of my wife's sudden dash, but hailing a constable to fetch an ambulance. We stood together, with him sympathising and offering me brandy from his flask until help arrived – not that anything could be done for her, of course."

225

"Most regrettable," added Holmes to our already expressed sensitivities towards our client. "But tell me, Mr. Jeavon, was Sir Cedric alone in the carriage, or was there another witness to this tragedy?"

"I had assumed that he was unaccompanied until, while we waited, I saw that a lady sat within the dark interior. She leaned out to speak to the coachman, who replied with words I couldn't hear, before looking at Priscilla's body in a most curious way. She didn't display surprise, for the accident had occurred about half-an-hour previously, or horror. It was an expression akin to recognition, or familiarity of some sort that I was at a loss to identify. Not that this has any connection to what I am about to tell you, for the lady did not utter a word to me."

Holmes nodded. "Pray proceed."

"After she was struck down, Priscilla did not die immediately. As she lay in my arms, quickly fading, she told me clearly that she would somehow find me again, that this was not the end of our union. Then she expired."

"She was undoubtedly sincere and hopeful," Holmes acknowledged. "But you must not torment yourself. The dead do not return."

"You do not understand, Mr. Holmes!" Our client's voice was full of emotion. "Priscilla and I enjoyed a degree of intimacy such as I would never have believed could exist. The trust and closeness between us was absolute to the extent that, at times, it was almost as if we could read each other's thoughts. It was as if we were the same person."

I could to some extent understand Mr. Jeavon's feelings, having once experienced such a connection, but I saw that my friend was unmoved. Our visitor suddenly plunged his hand into the pocket of his morning-coat and produced a photograph which he held up for us to see.

"Is she not beautiful?"

"Undeniably," I agreed.

"A handsome woman," Holmes commented with less enthusiasm.

Mr. Jeavon looked longingly at the portrait once more before returning it to his pocket.

A cart with a heavy load, probably barrels of beer, passed along Baker Street, the accompanying noise making conversation difficult. When silence returned, Holmes looked at our visitor with a sympathy I have seldom seen in him.

"Mr. Jeavon, we are indeed sorry to learn of what befell your wife, but I cannot see how we can help you. A priest, surely, would be more able to provide comfort than either Doctor Watson or myself."

Our client shook his head. "I have met with my priest regularly, since shortly after Priscilla was taken from me, and Father Pelham has been very kind. But there is more to this. I have said that I expect you to find my narrative an unlikely truth, and the remainder may strike you as such."

"Very well. Pray continue, omitting not the smallest detail. If there is anything requiring investigation, be assured that we will pursue it."

"As you may have gathered, it has taken me these two years to begin to come to terms with Priscilla's death. The pain began to lessen, and I felt that at last I could face up to life again in a normal manner. Then, about six weeks ago, a frantic knocking on my front door brought me out of my study to answer. I should mention that I was quite alone, as my housekeeper had fulfilled her duties and left. I opened the door to be confronted by a woman soaked to the skin by driving rain. I couldn't guess at the reason for her presence, of course, but seeing her plight, I invited her in. Her long hair had been blown across her face, so that her features were hidden from me, but imagine my surprise, no, shock, when she cried out: 'William, let me in, before I catch my death of cold'."

"A previous acquaintance then," I assumed.

"Not at all. She was *Priscilla*. I felt my heart pumping in my breast, and closed my eyes in an attempt to dispel this fantasy, but I opened them to find her still standing before me. I was frozen with astonishment, and when she calmly requested to be allowed to dry herself and change her clothes, I could do no more than grant permission with a nod of my head. I was speechless."

"That is hardly surprising," Holmes interrupted. "But tell me, did she ask the way to her room, or wherever she needed to go to obtain a dry towel?"

"No, she did not hesitate for an instant. She knew the way."

"And your housekeeper – has she been in your employ for long?"

Mr. Jeavon appeared confused. "She has been with me only three months, but she is a most conscientious woman, with excellent references. She did not know Priscilla, so how could she be connected?"

"Perhaps she is not. I presume she has a predecessor?"

"She did, who served both Priscilla and me well. Poor Mrs. Wandrill was discovered badly injured on Hampstead Heath, probably on her way home from her duties, some months ago. She died the following day."

Holmes nodded. "Did the official force discover the cause of her injuries?"

"Scotland Yard suspect that she was tortured most brutally, but her assailant was never found."

"And the resurrected Priscilla? How did she explain her reappearance?"

"For days, I could get little conversation from her. She appeared as bewildered by the situation as I. Eventually she was able to remember

227

wandering in Hyde Park for a few hours before appearing at my house. She explained that a kindly cab driver took pity on her and delivered her to my home."

"She has no memory of anything since the accident, until then?"

"None. When I pressed her, she grew agitated, and told me that I should accept that my prayers have been answered, that I should consider her reappearance as a miracle and be grateful for it. She would say nothing more."

"How then, has the relationship between you progressed during the subsequent weeks?" Holmes asked.

"She is a little hesitant, unlike the way she was before. She insisted upon occupying a separate bedroom, saying that it would take time before she was ready to resume normal married life. She dismissed the new housekeeper, insisting that she intended to assume the running of the household."

"Has she asked for anything which struck you as extraordinary?"

Mr. Jeavon considered for a moment. "There was one request that I found very strange, considering their previous affection for each other. Priscilla made me promise that, for the present, I would not disclose to her mother that her daughter had returned."

"Has she acted in any other way different to before the accident?" I enquired.

"She has indeed." He swallowed nervously, and his expression again became that of one who suffers. "In fact, her uncharacteristic ways were the reason I am here today. Priscilla is left alone in the house during the hours when I am obliged to pursue my employment. I keep a small amount of money in my room, for unexpected expenses, and this is now nowhere to be found. Tradesmen have sent me bills for purchases about which I know nothing, on one occasion calling personally to demand payment. But the worst of it was yesterday, when I began to feel some discomfort at the bank. This curious situation had begun to tell upon me, so that I felt oppressed while working at my desk. Thinking that the open air would clear my head, I informed my senior clerk that I would be unavailable for half-an-hour and set off on a brisk walk. After about a quarter-of-an-hour I felt much improved, and made my way back to the High Street. I was still some way off when I passed a rather rowdy tavern in the back street which I had taken as a short cut. Hearing the commotion within and seeing the violence brewing among the loafers lounging outside of the place, I crossed to the opposite pavement and hurried on my way. I chanced to look back after covering a short distance, to be utterly astonished by the sight of Priscilla emerging arm-in-arm with a rather rough-looking man whom I had never seen before. They turned in the opposite direction, not

228

having seen me, and it was some little while before I could continue. I could not – cannot – understand how she could find it in herself to treat me in such a fashion."

Holmes remained still for so long that Mr. Jeavon began to look at me with a querying expression. I was about to explain to him that my friend was analysing what he had learned, when the reverie came to an end.

"Which would you prefer me to investigate first, Mr. Jeavon?" Holmes asked. "The mysterious return of your wife, or her association with a class of citizens with whom you are unfamiliar? I should tell you that, although I may be able to throw some light on the first, I have little experience to qualify me for the second."

Then he added in a milder tone, "You must realise, sir, that the essence of all this is that you have been cruelly tricked. This is far from the first time that I have been confronted with a case that appears to have its roots in the supernatural, but I have yet to discover proof that there is any world but this one. Always there is a rational explanation in the end, no matter how well hidden. The dead, I am convinced, have never returned to haunt us or for any other purpose. I am truly sorry to dispel your illusion that your wife is with you again, but I believe that in your heart you knew this could not be."

Our visitor nodded sadly. "You are right of course, Mr. Holmes. I still miss my Priscilla so much that I had become like a drowning man – reaching for anything that would help me from my predicament. This woman looks so much like her! In any other circumstance, I would never have allowed myself to be so deceived."

"I'm sure of it. But now we are left with the task of exposing the tricksters who have brought all this upon you. For what purpose, I wonder? Pray tell me, as the manager of a prominent bank, would you describe yourself as a rich man?"

"Not excessively. I have my home and want for little. I am secure."

"You have not received, or are about to receive, an inheritance?"

"Not at all."

"Have you recently made any investments?" I enquired.

Mr. Jeavon shook his head. "I have some South African bonds that I bought years ago, but nothing more."

"That could be what is behind all this," I said. "I see from this morning's paper that there has been a sharp rise in their value for a second time. The Kimberly diamond mines have yielded much in the last few months."

"Thank you, Doctor. I confess to not having kept track of foreign financial matters to the extent that I would normally, because of my preoccupation with my own affairs."

"That is at an end now, my dear sir," Holmes assured him. "Before long, we will show this matter in its true light."

Mr. Jeavon's eyes widened momentarily, as if he had remembered something important. "But we haven't discussed payment, Mr. Holmes. If you will name a figure, I will be glad to write a cheque here and now."

"That will not be necessary. As I have explained to many before you, my fees are on a fixed scale and do not vary save when I remit them altogether. Largely, the work is its own reward and, in this instance, the satisfaction of relieving you of deep worry and concern will serve as ample recompense. If you will kindly furnish Doctor Watson with your address, that of Sir Cedric Wheeler if you have it, and of your late wife's mother, I believe that I can safely assure you that you will hear from us before long. Also," he added as an afterthought, "the names of both your housekeepers would be helpful."

I wrote down the details to Mr. Jeavon's dictation, before he thanked us both effusively and departed.

"Extraordinary," I mused then, "what a man will allow himself to believe to allay his grief."

Holmes lit his pipe and exhaled a plume of fragrant smoke. "Grief is an emotion, Watson, and I have commented before now on how misleading such impulses can be. Somewhat sadly, there are those who recognise the signs displayed by the affected, and are willing to turn them to their own advantage."

I nodded. "When will you begin your enquiries?"

"If you would care to accompany me, we can proceed as soon as luncheon is over. I believe I hear Mrs. Hudson on the stairs at this very moment."

An hour later we found ourselves in the cluttered office of Inspector Lestrade. When we were seated and had refused the appalling tea which Scotland Yard allows its detectives, the good inspector asked how he could assist us.

"I understand that a lady by the name of Mrs. Bertha Wandrill was recently discovered badly injured and later died," Holmes replied. "Apparently she had been cruelly treated. I would very much appreciate it, Lestrade, if you would make the file available to me for a few minutes."

"Certainly, Mr. Holmes, but a few minutes is all you will need, I think. As I recall, the unfortunate woman was indeed badly injured, and it was no accident." He went to the door and shouted into the corridor for a constable. A young man appeared and set off at Lestrade's bidding, to return quickly bearing a slim folder. The inspector dismissed him and extracted a single sheet, which he handed to Holmes.

"The coroner's report states that this woman was tortured by burning and partial asphyxiation," my friend read. "Were the perpetrators identified?"

Lestrade shook his head. "There was very little to assist us. The poor lady could barely speak, and so we learned nothing. She died a few hours after she was discovered."

"Most unfortunate. However, I have every reason to hope that my present enquiries will shed some light on this matter. My thanks to you, Lestrade. You have been instrumental in pointing me in the right direction to a promising solution."

We left with the inspector looking rather confused, as our visits seldom ended so abruptly.

"Could the new housekeeper have had a hand in this affair, do you think?" I asked when we had left the building.

"That is unlikely, since Mr. Jeavon's resurrected wife quickly dismissed her. I sought confirmation that his understanding of the fate of the former housekeeper, Mrs. Wandrill, is accurate, for this explains how the returning 'Priscilla' was able to usurp his wife's place so easily."

"Ah, you mean that poor lady was tortured to extract the information about Mr. Jeavon and his wife, and the details of their house?"

"Precisely. You continue to improve, Watson."

"This is diabolical!" I cried.

Holmes nodded. "Now, I see that a hansom has delivered its fare just ahead so, as dinner is as yet some way off, we have time to visit Sir Cedric Wheeler in Mayfair." With that, he hurried to secure the cab before it could be driven off or be approached by another fare. According to my recollection, Holmes spoke to me only once during the journey.

"I fear that we may cause Sir Cedric some embarrassment, but it cannot be helped in the circumstances."

"Because his coach ran down Mr. Jeavon's wife? Surely it was never considered to be anything but an accident."

"That, at least, seems to be beyond dispute," he murmured.

On our arrival at Sir Cedric's home, an impassive butler took Holmes's card to his master while we waited in a foyer adorned with portraits of former government ministers. We had little time to give them any attention, however, as we were ushered without delay into a spacious sitting room with tall windows looking out on an impressive display of white roses.

The stocky man with a bristling white moustache who had observed our entry approached us with an outstretched hand.

"Mr. Sherlock Holmes and Doctor Watson! I am delighted to meet you. I understand that you have been of considerable assistance to Scotland Yard on a number of occasions, and that is admirable, sir, admirable."

"You are most kind, Sir Cedric," Holmes responded.

Our host indicated that we should sit with him on the comfortable armchairs surrounding the fireplace, where kindling had been prepared in anticipation of the occasional cool evening that still persisted. He poured glasses of a fine oloroso from a crystal decanter.

When we had settled ourselves and sipped our drinks, Sir Cedric regarded us both earnestly.

"Well gentlemen, it is clear to me that you would not be here if you didn't require information of some sort. If it is of a political nature you will appreciate that my response may be limited, unless it is to add to your understanding of something already made public. Apart from that one exception, I am at your disposal."

"My thanks to you," Holmes replied, "but the matter I am currently investigating concerns yourself only. You will, I am sure, recall the tragic occurrence of two years ago, when Mrs. Priscilla Jeavon was accidentally killed."

Sir Cedric's expression became one of profound sadness. "I do of course. It is not something that I shall ever forget. The unfortunate lady stepped into the path of my carriage, and the horses were upon her instantly. But how is it that you are looking into this now, Mr. Holmes? Is Mr. Jeavon attempting to take me to the courts? If so, I cannot imagine why, since I have several times offered my help, despite the fact that no blame was ever attached to my coachman or myself."

"There is no question of that. I am enquiring into a quite different outcome. I understand that Lady Wheeler accompanied you and recognised Mrs. Jeavon, or appeared to."

"That is most unlikely. If Hyacinth was acquainted previously with that poor lady, she would undoubtedly have mentioned it to me. There, I fear, I cannot help you."

"Perhaps then, her Ladyship was aware of some significance in Mrs. Jeavon's last words," I ventured.

A moment of silence passed, during which a mild breeze stirred the roses at the edge of the garden.

Some of the warmth had left Sir Cedric's smile, and I noticed a furtive glint appear in his eyes.

"Of that I have the greatest doubt," he said guardedly, "and to anticipate your next question, gentlemen, I cannot allow you to interview her. She has just returned from a short stay at her sister's home in Norfolk, and has retired to her room. My poor wife is exhausted from the journey."

To my surprise, Holmes did not press our host, but thanked him before making a gracious exit. The butler showed us from the premises, and it was after the door had closed behind us that we found ourselves alone in the courtyard.

"It was obvious that Sir Cedric was concealing something," said I. "It is most unlike you not to have continued to question him."

"I had intended to, had not your interruption put him on his guard," he glanced at me disapprovingly. "But no matter. I saw the next possible source of information appear briefly as I allowed my eyes to dwell for a moment on that splendid display of roses. We should have no difficulty in seeking him out."

"To whom do you refer? The gardener?"

"The coachman."

Fortunately for our purpose, the stables at the rear of the house weren't visible from the room we had just left. As we approached, I saw that four fine stallions stood watching the coachman from their stalls, while he cleaned and inspected an already-gleaming landau.

The fellow was tall and well-built, red-faced and with a ready smile. Holmes introduced us and the fellow told us in a broad Irish accent that his name was Thomas Burns.

"I understand that you drove Sir Cedric's coach – this one, perhaps – when a lady was unfortunately killed, about two years ago." Holmes began, watching the man's face carefully.

"That would be me, sir. I have been Sir Cedric's coachman for five or six years now. And yes, this is indeed the same carriage. It was an accident though sir, I swear it. There was never a suggestion of carelessness on my part."

"Of that I am sure. There is no question of apportioning blame. What I am interested in is the apparent recognition of the dying woman by Lady Wheeler. Doubtlessly you noticed something of the sort, yourself?"

Mr. Burns cast his eyes to the ground. "It is not for me to comment on the actions of my employers, sir."

But there was something in his voice which lent an element of insincerity to the remark, and I saw without surprise that Holmes had not missed this.

"It is quite obvious that you are a most observant fellow, and I feel sure that you will have seen something which will aid me in my investigation."

"How have you arrived at such a conclusion? I am simply a coachman."

"A little more than that, I think. I see how you have cleaned this carriage, reaching nooks and crannies that many would have missed or ignored. A man as observant and conscientious does not have his eyes closed at a time such as that we are discussing. If I might stimulate your recollection, somewhat."

I saw the glint of a gold sovereign as it changed hands. The coachman glanced around him and, seeing that we were not observed, lowered his voice nevertheless.

"The fact is, sir, that Lady Wheeler was not in the coach with Sir Cedric. He was accompanied by a woman who he saw regularly until recently. Her Ladyship spends much of her time in Norfolk these days, for she and her husband are no longer content with each other."

"But this woman did appear to recognise Mrs. Jeavon?"

"Indeed she did, and I thought that most peculiar at the time, since they were certainly not of the same class." He hesitated, and lowered his tone further. "She was, if you'll excuse me saying so sir, a lady of the night."

I saw from Holmes's gratified expression that this was what he had expected.

"Do you, by any chance, happen to know the name and whereabouts of this woman?" I enquired.

"Indeed I do, sir." At his hesitation, another coin found its way into his hand. "Miss Annie Thurlock is quite notorious in certain quarters, and I was not alone in my surprise when Sir Cedric took up with her. I believe that, since the beginning of his patronage, she has moved to an address in Kensington, near St. Mary Abbots Church. It is 11, Normanton Gardens, one of several houses situated off the High Street in an adjoining square."

Holmes nodded. "My thanks to you, Mr. Burns. I wish you every success in your quest for a new position."

The coachman stared at him aghast. "But, Mr. Holmes, how did you know . . . ?"

"Good day to you," my friend said as we turned away.

We were fortunate in finding a hansom nearby. By the time we were settled and on our way back to Baker Street, I could contain my curiosity no longer.

"It is quite clear now why Sir Cedric was so sparing with his assistance," I remarked. "But I cannot imagine how you deduced that Mr. Burns is seeking other employment."

Holmes leaned back in his seat. "I induced him to be indiscreet so easily, that something in the present arrangement was obviously amiss. I would speculate that Sir Cedric treated his coachman well once, since they had been together for some years, but of late this has changed. Possibly

Sir Cedric's deteriorating relationship with his wife has affected his disposition. At any rate, Mr. Burns did not strike me as a man who would put up with indifference for long, if an alternative could be found."

"As always, you make it appear so simple," I said as our cabby brought us to a halt outside our lodgings.

Mrs. Hudson excelled herself with the steak pie she served for our dinner. Holmes, of course, did not do it justice, but barely sampled the dish as he moodily reflected on our situation. Unlike myself, he waved away dessert but shared the contents of the coffee pot before he raised his head and fixed his eyes upon me from across the table.

"No doubt you were expecting to spend this evening reading, or attempting to extract details of past cases from me, Watson, as you do when your publisher is hounding you for more material?"

"That had occurred to me as a possibility, unless we receive unexpected visitors."

"If we do, then they will have to wait or make another appointment. Tonight, if you are prepared to accompany me once more, we are to search for ladies of the night."

"One in particular, I think: Miss Annie Thurlock."

"Precisely." He replaced his cup in its saucer. "She was present at the death of Mrs. Jeavon, so we will see what she has to tell us."

About two hours later we stood in Normanton Gardens. The shadow of the ancient church spire lay long upon the lawn around which the semi-circle of houses stood, although darkness was not yet complete. We had seen no activity anywhere, although several windows glowed bright with lamplight.

"It doesn't surprise me," Holmes said in a low voice, "that we have seen nothing of Miss Thurlock as yet. Her profession is of necessity conducted after dark, not least because she will not want her neighbours to discern how she earns her living. This is a highly respectable district, and she will not wish to incur the disapproval that she certainly would if her activities became known."

"I would have thought Sir Cedric alone would have provided ample means of support."

In the rapidly fading light, I saw him frown. "Perhaps she aspires to greater things, or is simply a greedy woman. In any event, there is nothing to suggest that he is her only client, still less her first."

"If he believes either situation to be the truth, he is surely deluding himself."

Before my friend could reply, the light in the window of Number Eleven was extinguished. A moment later, the door opened and a tall woman, in a costume that I could just make out to be of vivid blue, stepped out of the house. When she approached the tree that concealed us, we stepped forward.

She stopped instantly, perhaps mistaking our intentions. A welcoming smile instantly lit up her face, mask-like in the light from the lamp-post nearby. I saw that she was, or had once been, a handsome woman indeed, but the weariness of her profession had taken its toll.

"Miss Thurlock?" Holmes asked unnecessarily.

"Yes." Her expression changed immediately to one of surprise.

"Kindly excuse this intrusion. My name is Sherlock Holmes, and this is my friend, Doctor John Watson."

"And what can I do for you gentlemen?"

"We are enquiring about an accident which you witnessed, about two years ago. A lady was run down by a coach in which you were travelling with Sir Cedric Wheeler. Doubtless you will recollect the incident?"

Her expression hardened at once. "You are mistaken, Mr. Holmes. I can recall no such occurrence, and neither am I acquainted with the person you describe. Now, if you gentlemen will allow me to pass, I have an appointment which will not wait."

Two men, one much younger than his companion, had entered the enclave and were regarding us curiously as they walked by. Miss Thurlock was visibly uncomfortable, until they entered an adjacent house.

"Good night to you gentlemen," she said as she walked away hurriedly.

I started in pursuit, but my friend placed a restraining hand on my shoulder. "No need, Watson, I have seen all that is necessary."

We waited until she had passed out of our sight, and then struck out for the High Street in search of a hansom.

"We have learned nothing," I protested.

A quick smile crossed his countenance. "Much to the contrary, I now know that the supposition I had formulated is most likely to be correct. Everything will become clear to you, the moment that you realise that this affair is about family resemblances, as I suspected when Mr. Jeavon began his narrative. However, there are still certain points on which I must have confirmation, but they will wait until the morning. On our way back to Baker Street, I must send a telegram to Barker, our friend the private enquiry agent, requesting that he watch Miss Thurlock's house and follow her should she leave it after tonight. As for now, I see that a rather tired-looking cabby has seen us and is obligingly bringing his conveyance to a halt."

Holmes said little at breakfast next morning, abandoning his bacon and eggs as a rather large post arrived. When he had tossed the last letter aside, seemingly considering all of them to be of little significance, he spent a few moments in contemplative silence before regarding me steadily.

"I think, Watson, that the time has come to visit Mrs. Ellen Danbury."

"Mr. Jeavon's mother-in-law?"

"Indeed. I confess to a certain trepidation, for I have no desire to increase the lady's grief, not least over the loss of Mrs. Jeavon."

I was unsure of his meaning, but I knew at a glance that it would be useless to ask for an explanation. As on many previous occasions, Holmes would tell me of his theory and conclusions when he was ready to do so.

"Very well. If you would care to finish your coffee, I will summon a hansom."

I put on my hat and coat and went out into Baker Street, where my friend soon joined me. We hailed a passing conveyance and arrived before long in a tree-lined street near Hyde Park. Holmes rapped on the roof with his stick and the cabby brought us to a halt before a Georgian town house which appeared to be in need of some repair. As the hansom left us, only to be immediately procured by a well-dressed gentleman from a neighbouring house, we approached Mrs. Danbury's residence and I made use of an elaborate brass door-knocker in the shape of a bear's head.

After a moment the door swung open and a middle-aged woman in nurse's uniform confronted us.

"How may I help you gentlemen?"

"We have called to see Mrs. Danbury," Holmes answered, "if that is at all possible."

The nurse frowned. "She rarely sees visitors. Have you an appointment?"

"No, but my business with her concerns her daughters."

She immediately appeared confused, as was I to some extent.

"I will see if she is well enough to receive you. What names should I give her, sir?"

"I am Sherlock Holmes, and this is Doctor John Watson."

She nodded and took his card, returning after several minutes.

"Mrs. Danbury will see you, sir, but I must make you aware that she is very frail. Also, and for that reason, I must request that you see her alone, since the presence of more than one person at once has proven too much for her before now." She looked at me apologetically as Holmes entered the house. "I am sorry, sir. But I am sure you understand."

I affirmed this and, after the door closed, resigned myself to a possible long wait.

As it turned out, Holmes returned within a short time. The nurse stood watching as we left, her eyes blazing with anger.

237

"Holmes," I began as we made our way back to the main thoroughfare, seeking a cab. "What occurred in there? That nurse appeared furious with you."

"I fear that she was, old friend. I put my questions to Mrs. Danbury as delicately as I could but, alas, I was unsuccessful in preventing her from becoming agitated. However, my suspicions were confirmed in every respect."

Again, the tone of his voice told me that to ask for an explanation would avail me nothing. We turned a corner and saw at once a waiting hansom that we immediately procured. I heard Holmes give our destination to the cabby, but did not recognise it.

"Who is this Doctor Appleton?" I asked him.

"The physician who has attended Mrs. Danbury for most of her life – so she informed me. Unless I am much mistaken, he is the last piece of this puzzle, though he also is elderly."

"And yet he remains in practice?"

We steadied ourselves as our driver rounded a bend without reining in his horse sufficiently. Holmes scowled in his direction.

"Apparently so, although he is to retire before long. I regret, Watson, that we will have to forego our luncheon for now."

We eventually arrived in Harley Street and alighted outside a narrow, red-brick house that stood almost at the junction with Portland Place. The brass plate that proclaimed the doctor's name and profession was slightly tarnished, and the aged receptionist that answered Holmes's ringing of the door-bell appeared surprised.

"Yes, gentlemen?" he asked in a quavering voice.

"We would like to see Doctor Appleton, if he is available."

The elderly man shook his head. "I am sorry to tell you, sirs, that the doctor no longer accepts new patients. Only a few who he has attended for many years are seen by him now, since he is to retire from the profession at the close of the month."

"The matter which we wish to discuss with him concerns one of those patients," said Holmes. "Pray be good enough to take him my card, and to inform him that our visit is in connection with the children of Mrs. Ellen Danbury."

We were allowed into a small foyer, while the receptionist presented the card to his master. A few minutes passed, during which the only sounds were the ticking of the large casement clock that stood near the inner door, and the clatter of hooves as hansoms and carriages passed along the street. Then the receptionist reappeared to show us into the surgery with a polite bow.

I recognised at once the lingering smell of ether, and the lesser scent of familiar herbs. The room, having but a small window, was half in shadow, so that I could make out the labelled bottles and the stethoscope among the papers on the desk only with some little difficulty. The man who rose to greet us was, as I expected, grey-haired and pale – one of those physicians, I discerned, who had pursued his profession until he could do so no more. He bade us sit upon well-worn chairs which were upholstered in cracked leather and resumed his own seat behind his desk.

My friend made to explain our presence, but Doctor Appleton held up an unsteady hand and spoke in a surprisingly clear voice.

"Elaboration is quite unnecessary, Mr. Holmes. I have read of your exploits, as related by the good Doctor Watson here. As soon as my man Collier informed me of your purpose regarding Mrs. Danbury, I knew that the day I have dreaded for years had finally arrived. I must confess that I always imagined that it would be Scotland Yard that confronted me in the end, but it may just as well be yourself."

Holmes's face remained expressionless. "Pray tell us then, what it is that you have anticipated for so long."

I leaned forward in my chair, so that I might miss nothing of the doctor's narrative.

"You are here to determine the truth about Mrs. Danbury's girls, are you not? I imagine that the surviving twin is once more in some sort of difficulty, likely with the law."

"You have perceived correctly," Holmes answered, "although Mrs. Danbury was too perturbed to reveal much to me, other than the connection with yourself."

Doctor Appleton nodded slowly. "She was always prone to excessively emotional responses to her misfortunes, although heaven knows that she has had enough of them. She married very young, and her husband left the family home soon after the birth of the girls, never to return. Mrs. Danbury never really recovered from his desertion, and she was left with two young children and no means of support. This situation did not last however. Soon after, one of the girls, the elder by twenty minutes, was brought to my surgery with breathing difficulties. In those days my practice was much larger, and I maintained a small ward where I was able to treat urgent cases without referring them to hospital. The Danbury girl was soon beginning to recover, and would have been well enough to return home before long, were it not for a visit I had from a local criminal late one evening."

"Doubtlessly that would be Albert Birchett," Holmes ventured.

The doctor looked astonished. "How did you know that, Mr. Holmes? I have carefully hidden my shame for many years."

"It is my business to know such things. In the course of my enquiries, I learn much."

"Of course, such is the nature of your work. At that time I was heavily in debt, because of my addiction to gambling which, thankfully, I was eventually able to rid myself. Albert Birchett informed me that his family had assumed my debts among others, and demanded immediate repayment. I informed him that this was quite impossible, and he responded by insisting that I escort him on a tour of my property. I tell you, gentlemen, I was in great fear of losing the roof over my head, as well as everything else that I own, because Birchett began to talk of payment in kind.

"When we reached the ward, which then contained only the recovering Danbury girl, his behaviour changed suddenly. He spent a few moments in apparent contemplation before announcing that my debt would be erased, on the strength of a single payment. My assumption was that he wished to assume control of part of my premises, perhaps for storage, but he went on to horrify me by picking up the child from her bed. In answer to my protests he reminded me that my debt was now cleared but if I breathed a word of this to anyone, particularly the police, then my life expectancy and that of my wife-to-be would become very short indeed. I could not believe that any man would conceive of such a bargain, but I saw in his eyes that he was totally serious. I had no choice but to allow him to leave with the child."

I was so outraged and appalled by this man's conduct that I could not find words to express my feelings. When I felt I could speak, I was about to impress on Doctor Appleton my disgust at his abuse of his position and of my intention to report his actions to the Medical Council, but a look from Holmes silenced me at once. I perceived that my friend didn't want this affair complicated by the past crimes of this man who had betrayed the public trust. At least, not yet. I struggled with my conscience and my sense of justice, but said nothing.

"No doubt you informed Mrs. Danbury that her daughter had died." Holmes's voice betrayed no emotion, but I could sense that he was affected similarly.

Doctor Appleton nodded and I saw that his eyes glittered with unshed tears. "I received help in the deception from the Birchett family, and I issued a death certificate. At the burial the coffin contained the body of an urchin, retrieved from the Thames. I was driven by conscience to assist Mrs. Danbury with the expense, although I understand that she was rescued from poverty some months afterwards by a bequeath from the will of a distant cousin. As for the child, I was to hear little of her for years,

240

until one of the Birchett's aging henchman came to me for treatment to cure his rheumatism."

"Are you aware of what became of Mrs. Danbury's other girl?" I interrupted, keeping anger out of my voice with difficulty.

"I believe that she married an employee of one of the city banks, and had a good life until she was killed in an accident, some time ago."

"Pray continue with your account," Holmes said then. "What did this associate of the Birchett family tell you?"

"It was apparent from the first that the man was fully aware of what I had done in the past, and he proceeded to inform me, almost proudly, that she had been brought up in the Birchett tradition. By then I had known for some time that the family had connections or interests in many unlawful activities. As Albert Birchett was childless except for his son, Jake, it was decided that the Danbury girl, now called Margaret, would be treated as his daughter. I have no doubt that she has participated in crimes without number, and I bear the burden of all of them, to this day."

"Indeed you do," Holmes confirmed.

Doctor Appleton's confession had run its course. He now stared fixedly before him, a picture of misery. I felt that he expected some form of absolution to lighten his conscience, after relating the story of his appalling crime, but he had received none. As we left his surgery, it seemed to me that he was hardly conscious of our departure.

"A doctor he may be, but he is among the lowest of men," I remarked as we walked along Harley Street. "You can be sure, Holmes, that I shall ensure that this is known in the profession. The notion that he could retire with honour is abhorrent to me."

"And to me, old fellow. But be good enough to restrain yourself until I have concluded this affair. On our return to Baker Street, I expect to hear from Barker."

A telegram did indeed await us.

"Barker has done well," Holmes said as he settled himself at the table. "He followed Annie Thurlock to a tea-shop where she met, doubtlessly by appointment, none other than Mr. Jeavon's resurrected wife. He overheard their conversation, much of which consisted of references to a plan to rob the Millworkers and Miners Bank with the assistance of members of the Birchett family. The so-called Mrs. Jeavon has, it would appear, learned much from her time alone in the Jeavon house – I have not the slightest doubt that she has used her acquired skills to open the safe in her husband's absence, in order to gain access to private documents and information. It seems that she is to finally take her leave tonight, when Miss Thurlock will be waiting with a carriage."

"When we also will be present," I anticipated. "They have certainly caused Mr. Jeavon great distress with all this."

"Had he not been so disturbed by the death of his wife, even after so much time had passed, the concept of her return would have appeared ridiculous to him. The extraordinary closeness of the couple helped to make this appear possible. You will recall, Watson, that the true Mrs. Jeavon's dying words betrayed the belief that she and her husband would meet again."

As he finished speaking, Mrs. Hudson entered, bearing plates of roast partridge. Having missed luncheon, I attacked the meal with enthusiasm. As I ate I reviewed my understanding of the case, and found it wanting. There was much that was still far from clear to me.

"I would be obliged, Holmes," I said as I paused to drink from my water glass, "if you would be good enough to share with me your deductions regarding this affair. Clearly there is much that I have missed."

"Indeed there is, since I haven't explained my observations. When we have disposed of this excellent partridge, I suggest that you accompany me again to the telegraph office, where I will send a message to advise Lestrade of our intentions for later. Then we can return here to enjoy a glass of a fine cognac which I have recently procured, before I explain all to you. Barker has specified that the rendezvous between Miss Thurlock and her accomplice is arranged for ten o'clock, which gives us ample time."

Our excursion to despatch Holmes's telegram was lengthened slightly by a brief but heavy shower. We arrived back in Baker Street with soaked umbrellas, and wasted no time in repairing to our usual armchairs.

"I shall be surprised if this isn't to your taste." Holmes handed me a crystal glass of amber liquid.

We held up our drinks in a toast to the King and sipped.

"This is excellent," I acknowledged. "Where did you get it?"

"The owner of a wine shop in Hackney pressed it upon me, when I informed him that I would require no fee. His problem was a trifling one in any case, and the poor fellow had lost half his stock to burglars."

"I trust that Mr. Jeavon's case will conclude as successfully."

He placed his glass on a side-table. "The most unfortunate aspect, as I have said, is the anguish that our client suffered. From the outset, I discarded the notion that anything supernatural was involved for, as you know, I have yet to find a situation that cannot be explained rationally. I was left therefore, with two possibilities concerning the new Mrs. Jeavons: Either her appearance had been altered to resemble her predecessor, or she was an identical twin. The fact that Miss Annie Thurlock appeared to recognise the dying Mrs. Jeavon suggested the latter, and I confirmed the existence of twins with their mother, much to her regrettable distress. Until our interview with Sir Cedric's coachman, I had assumed that the connection was with Lady Wheeler, but as it was, it had to be with Miss Thurlock. When I set eyes upon her, I knew at once that we were on the right track, since her resemblance to other members of the Birchett family, who I know of old, was apparent. I would speculate that she is a cousin. I'll wager that the new Mrs. Jeavon – in actuality the widowed Margaret Birchett – and Miss Thurlock, grew up together within the bosom of the family – hence Miss Thurlock's surprise at the time of the accident. She was clearly unaware that her friend had an identical twin sister. Sometime later the scheme was hatched, either by Miss Thurlock or some other member of that criminal family."

"Surely, Albert Birchett must be very elderly, by now?"

Holmes shook his head. "He died some years ago. We are dealing with his son, Jake, who is in every respect his father's son."

"It is still difficult to believe that Mr. Jeavon could have been deceived so."

"I agree," said Holmes, "but as I have stated, his most intimate relationship with his wife, his grief, and his natural disposition are all factors in the situation. In addition, I suspect that Margaret Birchett has administered regular doses of an opiate to him, with the intention of making him more susceptible by dulling his senses. You will doubtless recall the curious expression in his eyes during his visit."

We continued to talk of the affair for some time, Holmes concluding by expressing the opinion that this had not been a memorable case and stating that I was free to submit an account of it to my publisher if I so desired.

"That is, Watson, if you believe that your readers will find sufficient interest in the tale."

A glance at the clock on the mantelpiece told us that the time had arrived for our departure. In less than ten minutes, we found ourselves settled in a hansom, and on our way to Fallon Square, a small enclave leading off Cheyne Walk, Chelsea. Holmes said nothing, his head upon his chest.

Upon our arrival, the rattling of the cab died away, as we stood in silence.

"If Miss Thurlock is punctual, she will be here in ten minutes," Holmes whispered.

I let my eyes rove around Fallon Square. It resembled a courtyard, with fine two-storey houses on three sides. Some of the windows were lit, the only illumination other than that from the single lamp-post a short distance away. I saw that a swarm of insects surrounded it, attracted by the

243

muted glow. Trees stood regularly spaced in front of the houses, and the movements and occasional cries of roosting birds was all that broke the silence.

Several minutes had yet to pass before ten o'clock when a brougham appeared at the entrance to the square. The coachman was clad in a black cape, despite the warmth of the evening, and his wide-brimmed hat kept his face in shadow. For some moments everything was still. Then the sound of a door opening reached our ears. A young woman carrying a heavy bag appeared on the pavement and proceeded to hurry, so that she was intermittently screened from us by the trees. At one point she passed quite close, before approaching the brougham.

"Mr. Jeavon cannot be at home," Holmes said in a voice so quiet that I hardly heard. "Or else she has drugged him."

"Holmes, if we do not move quickly, they will escape."

"I think not, but by all means let us draw nearer."

We emerged from concealment and approached the brougham. The woman, who I could now see did indeed bear a striking resemblance to the photograph of the late Mrs. Jeavon, came to an abrupt halt. From within the coach a female voice, alarmed and urgent, instructed her to throw in her bag and enter immediately.

"Give it up, Miss Thurlock," Holmes called. "All is known. There is no escape."

I saw that three burly constables had appeared at the entrance to the square, their shadows cast before them. The coachman quickly produced a weapon and levelled it in our direction, but a shot rang out and the echo faded as he fell to the ground.

"My thanks, Inspector," Holmes said as Lestrade emerged from a pool of darkness near the first house with a smoking pistol in his hand. "An excellent shot."

"Always glad to be of service, Mr. Holmes. I received your long and most interesting message. The only thing that was not clear to me at first was why the Birchett family waited for two years after Mrs. Jeavon's death."

"That puzzled me also," I recalled.

"The governor of Holloway Prison supplied the answer. The prisoner Margaret Birchett was released only recently." Lestrade approached the body and turned it over with his foot. "Likely we'll have no more trouble from these, now that Jake is with his maker. These two women will be residing as guests of His Majesty for the next few years I'd say, on several charges. Conspiracy, intent to rob, and burglary will do for a start."

"Let us not forget the murder of Mr. Jeavon's housekeeper," my friend reminded him, "although it isn't yet clear which members of the family were responsible."

"That will of course be determined by the investigation." He regarded the two women. The one who had posed as Mrs. Jeavon now had a resigned air about her, while Miss Thurlock murmured oaths most unbecoming of a lady. "One of these constables will drive this carriage to Scotland Yard, where you will both be charged with various crimes pending investigations into others of which you are suspected." He called a constable forward. "Redding, make arrangements for the removal of the body of Jake Birchett when we get back to the Yard. Turner will stay here with it until it is collected."

"Most efficient, Inspector," Holmes commented. "As for Watson and myself, we will pay a short visit to Mr. Jeavon to ensure his safety before returning to Baker Street. The poor fellow can now be assured that his wife rests peacefully, and his memories of her will remain unspoiled."

The Farraway Street Lodger
by David Marcum

It was a curious sort of party.

I had been to tea at the Langham on countless previous occasions, ranging from when I was feeling flush as a medical student, unwisely spending what I could not afford, to occasions in the early eighties when I had something to celebrate – sometimes a win on a horse race, a vice that I'm happy to say has long-ago tempered itself with age and acquired wisdom. My friend Sherlock Holmes and I have stopped there on many an occasion, often to meet with a client, or sometimes encountering a new one in the midst of our repast.

In mid-1902 I decided to remarry, having found the ideal woman to join me on the journey through my middle years and beyond. By mid-June of that year I'd found a steady and reliable medical practice in Queen Anne Street, and in mid-July we were wed. September found us both already quite settled into a regular routine. Knowing that the Langham was just a very few short streets away became a special treat to us both – any excuse and we would step over for afternoon tea or perhaps a small lunch made more special by our surroundings.

While my knowledge of London is not as exact as that of Sherlock Holmes, I do have an extra awareness of the various byways that exceeds what most folk have learned about just the half-a-dozen streets in any direction from their own domiciles. And so it had been apparent to me from the first that my new Queen Anne Street home was only a few hundred feet from the Langham – and less if we chose to exit our back door and pass through the mews into Chandos Street. Why, I might have been able to see the place from my highest window if not for the corner of an intruding building.

When I settled into my new practice, it wasn't without some adjustments – although I kept that knowledge to myself. I'd had my own practices before, in Kensington and Paddington, so the routine wasn't new to me. But two things had been different in those later days – I had been younger, and as such I tended to get out and about much more often than the Queen Anne Street routine required.

I had also spent much of the last decade quite active in Holmes's cases, ready to participate in them at a moment's notice, and serving as something of a partner in his agency, sharing in the fees in those matters in which I was involved. I had continued to serve as a doctor through those years – as a *locum* when needed and at hospitals such as Barts, along with the occasional stint as a police surgeon, as well as often patching up those who were injured during the course of Holmes's investigations. That wasn't the same as sitting in an office, with the only change to one's perspective being the arrival and short consultation with the next patient.

Because of this, it was all too tempting to slip away to the Langham in the afternoons, and after finding more opportunities than I should have over the course of several weeks, and realizing that I was becoming a regular patron, welcomed by name and offered the same thing every time because I'd had it the last time, I decided to pull back on the reins, so to speak, and limit my visits. My wife was understanding. Thus, I hadn't been there in a week or more when I was invited to join a small celebration on the afternoon of 13 September.

That morning, Harry Jackson, a middle-aged laborer who had already spent time earlier that year in prison, was convicted in court for burglary and sentenced to seven years. What made this unique was that it was the first time in Britain that anyone had been convicted on fingerprint evidence – a precedent had been set.

Jackson had burglarized a house in Denmark Hill, foolishly leaving his finger-marks impressed into a freshly painted windowsill. These had been compared to those officially collected by the Metropolitan Police and, using the system developed by Holmes and Edward Henry, an initially skeptical judge and jury were convinced to convict, under the skilled trial management of prosecutor Richard Muir.

Holmes had been instrumental over the last few years in working with Henry to develop the successful system for analyzing and classifying fingerprints, as well as experimenting with ways to record them as evidence – highlighting them with refined powders, for instance, and the use of specialized photography. It was with this in mind that he and I were invited to join the victorious team in the Palm Court of the Langham.

Edward Henry was there, along with Muir and a couple of his assistants. Several other involved functionaries whose names escaped me settled around the periphery. Also included were Doctors John Thorndyke and Christopher Jervis, as Thorndyke's work the previous year in the matter now widely known as "The Red Thumb Mark" – both the investigation and subsequent court trial – had paved the way for the Jackson conviction.

The gathering reached that recognizable point where there was nothing left to discuss and recollections of other duties and obligations began to intrude upon one's thoughts. Finally, Holmes and I were left alone at our table – but only for a moment, for even as I took a sip of tea and started to ask about the resolution of the Paddington Old Cemetery

247

vandalism, and the curious abuse of Norman Kerr's grave, I noticed that someone was approaching the table – Steven Pearson, one of Muir's clerks.

"Mr. Holmes? Doctor? May I join you – rejoin you, that is – for a few minutes? Mr. Muir has graciously given me leave to discuss a small matter with you.

Holmes nodded, although I could sense that he had been readying himself to depart as well. I knew that he had unfinished business in regard to an ongoing matter of document forgery at the Capital and Counties Bank. I signaled the waiter for more tea. A new cup was placed before Pearson, and while fixed it to his liking I had a chance to observe him. He was only twenty-four or -five, several inches below six feet, and solidly built. In my younger days, I might have asked him if he played rugby, hoping to recruit him for my team. He had brown hair and eyes, and wore clothing that was neither shabby nor ostentatious – just what one would expect from one of Muir's young employees.

"I have worked in Mr. Muir's office for nearly two years," he said when his tea was ready, "and I believe that I've done well at what was required of me, while in the meantime studying so that one day I can become an attorney before the Bar. My background is modest, and I might not have had the chance to take this opportunity, except that my uncle – my mother's brother, Claude Akins, who just departed with Mr. Muir – is the Head Clerk in the office, and he vouched for me and helped me to obtain the position.

"It's because of my mother that I asked to speak with you. She is Mrs. Elizabeth Pearson, a widow who owns a boarding house near Paddington. She is having . . . difficulties with a most peculiar tenant, and had asked both me and my uncle for advice, but we were at a loss as to what to recommend. It was when we saw you here today that we both conferred, deciding to seek your assistance. My uncle couldn't stay, so I was deputized to speak to you – and as the affair concerns my mother, and the house in which I grew up, he felt that I would be better able to provide an explanation."

Holmes nodded, although I could see that he would have preferred to be consulted in his own Baker Street rooms, in his comfortable and well-worn chair, surrounded by his familiar possessions, and with his client placed facing the window so that nothing in his expression could be hidden.

Pearson took a sip of tea. "My parents acquired the lease of the house before I was born. My father worked at a bank, and had a bit of money set aside from a small inheritance, so they were able to set themselves up better than might have occurred otherwise. Eighteen years ago, when I was a small boy, my father died of a sudden illness, and my mother, upon consultation with my uncle, consolidated our living space and rented the first and second floors to lodgers. Since that time, our circumstances have been modest, but we've lived comfortably enough.

"As I said, two years ago I began to work in Mr. Muir's office, and one year ago my circumstances were such that I was able to afford my own rooms, closer to the Royal Courts and the workings of my profession. After moving out, I've continued to visit my mother several days per week, and to help with any little thing that comes up.

"About six months ago, the married couple who had occupied our rented rooms moved to America, the man accepting an overseas position with the firm in which he was employed. It was rather a disruption to my mother, as this couple had occupied the two floors for a number of years, and in some ways had become like family to us. However, there was no question as to whether new tenants would soon be found, as the demand for lodging in that quarter is always high. And in fact, within just a day or so of my mother posting information that she had rooms available, she was approached by Mr. Lucius Newbiggin, a retired scholar, in London to do research for a book he was writing.

"My mother is a very capable woman, and as she had no qualms at taking on Mr. Newbiggin as a lodger, I had no objections. I met him a few days later, when I stopped by for a visit after work and he was taking the final steps toward settling in, the last of his possessions having just been delivered and carried up to his sitting room.

"He is an exceedingly thin fellow, probably in his forties, with dark hair and very deep-set eyes. He has a very low voice and a pronounced way of speaking that makes whatever he says, even saying hello to me for the first time and indicating that it was nice to meet me, have something in the way of being a dramatic pronouncement. I had gone upstairs to introduce myself, and I could see that his sitting room was filled with boxes, and that there were already a great many books unpacked and arranged on some shelves that came with the rooms, and also stacked on the dining table, the desk, and in the chairs.

"I've only seen him a couple of times since then, when he was arriving or leaving as I stopped in for a visit. I understand from my mother that he rarely goes anywhere, instead preferring to remain inside, where he is working on his book.

"Two days ago – that is, on the eleventh, my mother informed me that there was a knock on the door. She answered it to find a couple of men who asked to speak with Mr. Newbiggin. She said that there was nothing special about them – just two fellows in suits. She thought that they might be friends of her lodger, or perhaps related to his research. It was curious, as Mr. Newbiggin had never had visitors before, but there was no reason that he shouldn't. Knowing that he was at home, she left them outside and climbed the steps, where she knocked on his door. There was no answer, so she went up one further flight to the rooms that he also rents, and which have been arranged over the last few months as something of a library annex to the volumes that are in his sitting room. He wasn't there either, so she returned to the first floor and knocked again.

"A part of his arrangement is that my mother acts as something of the man's housekeeper as well as landlady – providing meals and so forth, going in and out to retrieve dirty dishes, to dust and to tidy – and as such she has access to his apartment. Thus, she knocked again and entered, thinking that the uniqueness of him having visitors for the first time was worth the extra effort taken to notify him. She entered the sitting room to find it empty – he wasn't there, nor was he in the adjacent bedroom that looks out on the back of the house.

"Certain that he couldn't have left the building, she was quite puzzled, but not knowing what else to do, she returned to the front door, explaining to the men that Mr. Newbiggin wasn't home after all.

"They glanced at one another, and one seemed to become angry, acting as if he intended to disagree, but the other laid a hand on his arm. 'We'll try again another day,' he said.

"'Would you like to leave a card?' my mother asked.

"'Not necessary,' was the reply. Tipping his hat and giving a pull to the other man's arm, they turned and departed.

"After they left, my mother, feeling a bit uneasy, locked the door and then set about searching more thoroughly. She enlisted the aid of Trudy, the girl who helps her around the house, to stay downstairs and make sure that Mr. Newbiggin didn't pass her in order to leave while my mother was upstairs, or to notify her if he came in. My mother was certain that he couldn't have gone anywhere, but just in case, she wished to know if he returned during her search. Then she started at the very top of the house, used for storage, and worked her way down, checking more thoroughly the man's make-shift second-floor library, looking behind stacked boxes, and then through the first-floor sitting room and adjacent bedroom. Not finding any signs of him there, she next looked in her own rooms – however unlikely it would be to find him there – and then on to the basement, even going so far as to unlock the door to the areaway – which is always shut tight with several locks to which she and I have the only keys – and the locked storage areas that run underneath the street. Mr. Newbiggin was not in anywhere in the building.

"She and Trudy returned to their normal routines, but as you might imagine, she kept an ear out for Mr. Newbiggin to return, and to make sure she knew when it happened, she put the front door on the chain so he would have to ring the bell. He never came back that day, and she told me all of this when I visited that night.

"It was the next day – yesterday – that she felt more nervous than before. Mr. Newbiggin still hadn't returned – the door had remained chained, she had checked to make sure – and she noticed when sweeping the front step that one of the two men from the day before – the one who seemed inclined to become angry – was loitering in a doorway down the street, watching her. Throughout the day, her lodger never returned, and the man across the way remained in place whenever she happened to look, except for early afternoon, when she suspected he'd gone to find something to eat. He was soon back in place.

"When her friend Mrs. Thrush stopped in for afternoon tea, Mother explained her concerns, and – afraid to leave the house unattended except for Trudy, she had Mrs. Thrush send a note 'round to my uncle and me. We both stopped by after our work was finished, and she told us about what was occurring. My uncle's first thought was to look outside, but the man, whomever he is, was no longer at the station he'd manned since that morning. Then, in order to satisfy himself, my uncle made his own pointless search of the house, but he also found that the mysterious Mr. Newbiggin had vanished. It was then that my uncle, recalling that we would see you today at the trial, suggested speaking to you to see if you can stop by my mother's residence and offer an opinion."

It seemed like a simple-enough affair – too simple for the likes of my friend Holmes, who at that point had built a rather well-known practice and was consulted by many notables throughout both the Kingdom and the Continent. Yet he was never one to ignore a puzzle, and young Pearson's sincere entreaty seemed to do the trick. He looked at me. "What say you, Watson? Are you up for a visit to your old Paddington stamping grounds?"

Always happy for an excuse to slip the leash of my Queen Anne Street responsibilities, I agreed quickly. Obtaining his mother's address from Pearson, who needed to return to his place of work, and with the promise that we would inform him of what we discovered, we settled up and exited the Langham, with Pearson walking off to the east, and Holmes and I entering a hansom hailed by a hotel employee. Within moments we were swiftly traveling west along Wigmore Street. "Perhaps," I said, "you heard something of special interest in Pearson's story that escaped me."

Holmes smiled. "You know me well. I did, and I could tell that whatever else we need to know can better be discovered at the source, rather than second-hand by way of the little that he learned last night from his mother."

"You recognize this Newbiggin fellow, then?"

251

He nodded. "The name itself is rather unusual and stirs the faintest memory. There was an entertainer who used to bill himself as 'The Great Lucius' – a magician of noted lean and sinister appearance who performed at various music halls along the circuit during the late eighties. I rather lost sight of him during the early nineties when I was out of the country, and in truth hadn't given him much thought since then. I initially became aware of him by his rumored connection to some country house burglaries. All indications were that he was a low-level cog in Professor Moriarty's organization. I supposed that he'd either been caught up in the arrests and imprisonments that followed the destruction of that machine, or that he'd managed to slither away and had since kept his head down, fearful and lucky to have escaped."

Abruptly he raised his arm and knocked with his stick to attract the driver's attention. "Stop at the Post Office," he said and, as we were nearly there, it was but a moment for us to pull up at the edge of the street. Holmes jumped down, dashed across and through the traffic with a nimbleness that did not reflect his forty-eight years, and returned in just a moment, whereupon he instructed the driver to continue toward our destination.

"I sent a wire to Patterson," he said. "He was more involved than the rest of the Yarders back in '91 during the actual arrests of the Professor's agents. I asked if he'll send any information about Newbiggin to Baker Street. Perhaps we'd be better served to go to the Yard first and ask – getting our ducks in a row, so to speak – but I don't believe it will prevent us from carrying out an initial investigation."

I wanted to question him further about Newbiggin, but I was aware of Holmes's general wish not to speculate before actual data could be accumulated, so instead I changed the subject, back to what I'd originally intended to discuss before young Pearson joined us in the Palm Court of the Langham. He was still telling me of how he'd deconstructed the code hidden in the markings chalked onto the stones of the Paddington Old Cemetery when we arrived at our destination, not far from Paddington Station, on a narrow lane running east of the Edgware Road.

No. 14 Farraway Street was a typical building of that block, identical in many ways to its neighbors – and in fact, for those who have rarely visited London, it was similar to a vast number of similar structures throughout the capital. Made of solid brick formed and fired from the local clays so abundant around us, it was a four-story structure of plain solidity. In truth, it was very much like 221 Baker Street, although the brick here was a shade more reddish when compared with the lighter and somewhat yellower brick of the houses in Holmes's row. It was about twenty or so feet wide, with a door and window on the ground floor, and two windows apiece on each of the three floors above. I knew that the layout inside

252

would also resemble those quarters in Baker Street where I had resided for so many years, beginning not long after my return from Afghanistan.

As our cab pulled away, I glanced around, but there were no lurkers within sight. I saw Holmes making the same examination, and he said in a low voice, "Either they've given up – for good, or long enough to find something to eat, as was theorized when the lurker left yesterday – or they've upped their game and rented a room to keep watch. In any case, let's get inside, shall we?"

We stepped onto the small stone platform before the door and Holmes rang the bell. It opened very shortly to reveal a woman in her early forties, rather plump, and with what would have been a pleasant expression if her brow wasn't marked by frowning worry lines. She looked back and forth, and then seemed to recognize my friend.

"Mr. Holmes? Doctor? My brother said that he was going to see if you could stop by."

"Actually, it was your son who spoke to us, not long ago. May we come in?"

Her eyes darted to our left, past us and looking across the street. "It's all right – he left about twenty minutes ago. He does leave sometimes, but he'll be back soon. It's fortunate that you arrived here when you did." She stepped aside and let us pass.

Mrs. Pearson took our hats and sticks and then led us into a parlor located to the right. The dimensions and layout of the room were identical to those of Mrs. Hudson's, located a mile or so to the east, but the furniture and decorations were of course much different. Mrs. Pearson seemed to favor a more Continental type of ornamentation.

After we declined her offer of tea or something to eat, Holmes began to question her regarding the curious disappearance of her lodger.

"He answered my advertisement about six months ago – in the spring. He said he was working on a book and needed somewhere to assemble his research and write in peace. I remember wondering why he settled here, instead of nearer the Library or the Museum, but it was his business, not mine. I thought that he might know someone around here that he wanted to be close to, but then he hardly ever went out. Weeks might go by before he'd cross the doorsill – and then, you'd think that he was freezing cold, in spite of it being in the hottest part of summer. He'd pull his hat low, and wrap a scarf around the lower part of his face, and wear a long overcoat."

"And he's had no visitors – not even once."

"Not even once. I suppose that's not as unusual as it seems, but I'd been used to having more people in and out with the previous lodgers, before they moved to America. Mr. Newbiggin seems happy enough on

253

his own, I suppose. That's why it's so unusual that he vanished on the first occasion when someone showed up to see him."

"Yes. Tell me about these two visitors."

"They were of the same type, I suppose. Big men, each around forty. They looked like one another – dark features, and rough, as if they've done work before."

"How were they dressed?"

"Well enough – suits that weren't too shabby, and nice hats. Like the one the doctor was wearing a few minutes ago. But there was something about them in those outfits that didn't look right – as if they would be more comfortable in working men's clothing."

Holmes nodded. "And how would you describe Mr. Newbiggin?"

"Thin – even thinner than you. And a little taller too. His skin has a grayish cast, as if he's been unwell, and there are always great circles under his eyes, as if he isn't sleeping properly. He eats well enough, but he certainly never gains any weight, even when I give him rich foods to fatten him up a bit."

"And how old is he?"

"About your ages, I suppose. Fifty, I'd say. But his hair is odd – it was black when he arrived here, but as time has passed, it has become more brownish-gray where it meets his scalp."

"As if he'd dyed it black in the past, and now it's growing out?"

She nodded. "That's it. And the same for his mustache and beard. Both were black to begin with, and they've gradually lightened as time has passed."

"What sort of beard and mustache are they?"

"A goatee, but trimmed very thin – the mustache is only a thin line across his lip, and there are very narrow lines of hair on either side of his mouth, running down to some pointy whiskers on his chin. Even as his hair has become lighter, he has kept the beard in that same shape."

"Your son told us how you searched the entire house, with the help of your girl, Trudy, and then how it was searched again when he and your brother were here yesterday. Have you looked around any further?"

"No, I haven't. In truth, something about this has upset me. I don't know how he could have disappeared. I *know* that he was upstairs before those two men came knocking – I had just been up there. In fact, I was in his sitting room when the bell rang, and he knew that I was going down to answer it. Trudy was in the kitchen, so he couldn't have left by the back way, and the only other exit, by way of the areaway from the basement, is kept secure with several very good locks, and only my son and I have the keys. When I checked later, they hadn't been opened. Likewise, the ground floor windows have locks on them too – this isn't the safest part of the city, and people can get in anywhere if they have a mind, so I keep things tight. That's the way my husband fixed it up, and I've seen no reason to change it."

"So Mr. Newbiggin couldn't have simply walked out."

"No, he could not have," she replied resolutely.

"And the two men – your son described how they asked for Mr. Newbiggin, and then one seemed more upset at being told he wasn't here."

"As if he didn't believe me – and as if he was going to search himself. He's the one I've been seeing across the street. Both of them looked alike, but this one has a wider face – there's something savage about him that putting on a suit doesn't hide." She twisted her fingers, the first sign of nervousness that I'd observed. "I don't know what Mr. Newbiggin has brought to this house, or why he's left me to face it when it got here."

"Perhaps we'll be able to find some answers," replied Holmes. "May we see his rooms upstairs?"

"Of course." She led us back to the entryway and up the stairs – seventeen of them, I noted with a smile – and so into the sitting room along the front of the first floor. In area it was a duplicate of Holmes's sitting room in Baker Street, but the arrangement of furniture and possessions was disconcertingly wrong. I had the sense of what it would be like to visit 221b someday after Holmes had retired – something he threatened to do more and more with the passing years – and finding that someone else had moved in.

There was a single chair and small side table before the fireplace. A dining table was placed centrally between the two windows, and a couple of sturdy bookshelves were along the wall to our right. The fireplace mantel was lower than that of Holmes's sitting room, and of a more intricate design. What all of these objects had in common was the vast number of books stacked and piled upon each of them. They were on the mantel and the tables. They were in the seat of the chair. The shelves were stuffed full, with more books on top, and also on the floor in front of them.

In a small cleared space of the dining table was a mound of papers, stacked somewhat neatly. Mrs. Pearson followed our gazes. "He used that as something like a desk, where he could write. That's what he called his 'manuscript', or sometimes his *'Magnum Opus'*. He ate on a tray across his lap, sitting there in front of the fire. He would move the books there to sit down, but at some point they would always get moved back." She shook her head. "Listen to me – saying he 'used that' or that he 'would move the books' as if he's dead and gone, instead of just missing for a couple of days."

I smiled politely, but Holmes didn't seem to have heard. Seeing that he wanted to investigate in earnest, I suggested that Mrs. Pearson might make that tea after all – but I assured her that we'd had plenty to eat at the Langham, and no further comestibles were required. With a look that indicated she was a bit leery to leave us alone, she nodded and went downstairs. I was uncertain as to whether she'd rejoin us at any minute, by simply instructing the girl Trudy to make the tea, but she stayed downstairs.

I puttered about, trying not to disturb anything while staying out of Holmes's way. He was this way and that, going into the missing man's bedroom several times, looking here and there without comment before returning to do the same in the sitting room. At one point he went upstairs, presumably to examine the other rooms leased by Mr. Newbiggin, but he soon returned. After he came down, I went up myself to find both the front room on the second floor and the bedroom in the rear – which perfectly matched my old Baker Street bedroom – to be filled with books, even more shambolic than below – mostly stacked on the floors in leaning piles, but with some others on the few tables that were placed up there.

I took a moment to flip through the various titles, initially amazed to see that every one that I examined had something to do with the practice of stage magic – tomes about how to do tricks, and arrange stage lighting, and guides to famous illusions of the past. Wherever I looked, each of the volumes had a similarity of theme. I had no idea that there were so many books on that subject in the entire world – and it seemed as if Newbiggin had assembled the greatest collection of them ever in one place. I wondered at the amount of time and effort – and especially expense – involved in such a task.

I saw no need to explore the top floor, which was used by our host. Instead, I returned to the sitting room, where I found the door to the bedroom closed. Assuming that Holmes was inside, still searching, I stepped to the dining table that served as the missing man's desk and examined his manuscript. It consisted of a hundred or so densely handwritten pages, and seemed to be some sort of introduction to a general survey of literature related to magic and the art of illusion. An ambitious task, I thought, verifying that the nearby books also related to stage magic. It looked as if Newbiggin felt that he could somehow boil down what was in these hundreds – thousands? – of volumes into a work of his own, something of a Whole Art of Magic. I shook my head at the folly of it – or so it seemed to me, who had no understanding of whether he was in fact capable of achieving such an aspiration.

It was at that moment the front doorbell rang.

I stepped to the window – that which was equivalent to the one in Baker Street that was located there beside Holmes's chemical table – and surreptitiously looked down at the front door. It was a skill I had mastered over twenty years earlier. I could see two men in dark suits and hats standing there. Even as I watched, one raised his arm and rang the bell once again.

The door to the bedroom opened abruptly and Holmes looked my way with urgency. "I believe it's the men who were seeking Newbiggin," I explained. He nodded and rushed toward the door to the landing. He then descended to the ground floor at great speed, but he made no sound. The bell rang a third time.

In just a moment Holmes had returned. Downstairs, I could hear Mrs. Pearson speaking to the men, her voice raised, apparently to be heard through the closed door. Holmes walked quickly toward the bedroom, summoning me to follow

It was a dark chamber, with the walls painted some greenish color that made it feel like entering a cave. This illusion was greatly heightened by an unpleasant odor which seemed to hang in the room – musty, with hints of something worse. The room was quite bare – a bed that was little more than a cot, drapes pulled shut, and a cold fireplace. Strangely, this was the one room occupied by Newbiggin that had no books.

Holmes was donning one of Newbiggin's dressing gowns over his regular clothing, adjusting it while simultaneously pulling a case from underneath the cot. He then knelt beside it while saying, "Mrs. Pearson will delay them for a minute or so – as long as she can – before letting them in. She will tell them that Newbiggin has returned, and then show them upstairs. You will hide in here, and I'll speak with them in the sitting room, and see if we can get them to reveal what business they have with our missing magician."

The opened case revealed a cluttered plethora of theatrical makeup. Holmes pushed it around with a long finger before seeing what he wanted – a bottle of some sort. While he shook it to make sure its contents were still liquefied, I held back the curtain to provide more light from the northern-facing window. Pulling out his handkerchief, he opened the bottle and poured some of the contents into it. Then, leaning down toward the small mirror fixed in the case's lid, he began to dab it on his hair, cleverly dying the lower half away from the scalp to resemble how Newbiggin's hair had been dyed. He finished with that in an amazingly short amount of time, looked elsewhere in the case, and pulled out some strips of false hair. With a stick of spirit gum, he quickly applied patches of it around his mouth, making a crude approximation of a goatee. Wiping his hands on the bedclothes, he finished by finding a small rouge pot and rubbing some underneath his eyes and beneath his cheeks, adding deep hollows where none had existed. A quick rearrangement of his hair, brushing it forward, and he stood, looking nothing like Sherlock Holmes, except in terms of his lean figure.

We heard footsteps on the stairs.

"Stay here and listen," he said, dashing into the sitting room. I dropped the curtain, plunging the bed chamber back into darkness, and then walked to the doorway, pushing the door shut to just a crack. Holmes was standing at the mantel, turning down the gas. He had already managed to jerk the front curtains shut, and now the room was quite dim indeed. He was leaning against the mantel when the door opened and two men entered the room.

In the near darkness, it was hard to see their features. They were both bulky, but they moved as if their mass was muscle and not inactive fat. Upon seeing Holmes standing across the room from them, one gave a growl and immediately leaned forward, as if intending to accelerate and charge, but the other laid a restraining hand on his shoulder and pulled him back. The first fought it for just a second, but ended his resistance when the second one spoke.

"You didn't expect us to find you."

It wasn't a question – rather a statement as preamble to a threat.

"Gentlemen," said Holmes, his voice with a quaver, but deep, quite deep. I recalled that Steven Pearson had mentioned Newbiggin having a low and theatrical way of speaking. Holmes, having no idea of the specific way that the missing man sounded, had adjusted by making him sound ill and somewhat feeble. But the theatricality was there as well. "I must say," he continue, "that in truth, I did not expect to encounter you here in my *sanctum sanctorum*."

The first man growled, as if simply hearing Newbiggin speak made him angrier, but the second raised a hand.

"You knew we'd never stop looking – and you were foolish not to change your name. But then, you always were the vainest man I've ever known. What did you think you'd do with it? Sell it to Waybrother? He knows better. Or the Freeman brothers? They might be stupid enough to buy it, but they would have told us who sold it to them – leading right back to you." He stepped closer. "Or maybe worst of all, you had a change of heart? Maybe you intend to share it with the police?"

"Where is it?" snapped the angry one. "Why are we wasting time talking to him? He'll tell us. He'll tell *me*, by God!"

"Enough!" said Holmes, raising a hand, his voice taking on a commanding tone. "Do you think your secrets are the only ones that I hold? I have been busier than you realize – busier and more clever. Why do you think I came to London? Clayton Drummond was happy enough to talk to me."

258

This was a name that I recognized. A self-styled criminal mastermind who was not one-tenth as clever as Professor Moriarty, Drummond had muscled his way into a seat at London's criminal table a half-dozen years before. Holmes and the police were content to leave him in place, as his clumsiness allowed information about other plans to leak out when otherwise it might have been kept secret, and he served to fill a place very poorly that might instead have been occupied by a much more effective criminal.

"Why would you go to him?" snapped the angry man. I realized that his voice and accent – Manchester, I believed – was very similar to that of the other man. Brothers, perhaps? A closer look at their faces would give a better indication.

Holmes waved his hand. "You can see that I'm well set up here, and that I'm under protection. Do you think that I haven't let them know that you've followed me here? You've put your heads into your own nooses."

There was silence while the two men pondered what they had heard. It seemed to make more sense to them than me. Holmes's mind was certainly racing, trying to sound knowledgeable, but just vague enough that he wouldn't reveal the fact that he wasn't Newbiggin. I thought that his introduction of Clayton Drummond into the conversation had been a brilliant way to divert the direction of the conversation onto a new track from what the two men expected.

But the gambit apparently failed. "I don't think that anyone is protecting you," said the second man. "I think that Drummond is too canny to get tied up with this." He looked around at all the books piled around the room. "You were stupid to leave, and you were more stupid to take everything with you. That's the first thing that I thought of – trace how and where you moved all of your collection, and you won't be far away."

"You weren't that smart," replied Holmes. "It took you six months to find me."

"Smart enough. We're here now."

"Where is it?" rumbled the other, stepping forward. I suspected that if he were given an answer at this point, he'd still erupt into violence. Holmes seemed to know it as well. He reached inside the dressing gown and withdrew something from his pocket.

"What's that?" asked the angry man.

Holmes didn't answer. Instead he placed the shiny tube to his lips and blew – a constable's whistle.

At that moment, I stepped out of the bedroom, correctly understanding that Holmes had decided there was no more information to be learned just then from the two men. I had my service revolver drawn, having long ago learned to never be without it. From outside the room, I

259

could hear the pounding of several sets of heavy feet ascending the stairs. It sounded the same as when that noise was made in Baker Street. Apparently Holmes had instructed Mrs. Pearson to summon the police as soon as she let the two men go upstairs.

With an animalistic instinct upon realizing that they were caught, the two men – whom I could now see did resemble one another enough to be brothers – each had a different reaction. The second man to speak, he who had remained more calm throughout the short interview, simply looked this way and that, as if to determine where a profitable bolt hole might be found. But the police were about to come through the door to the landing, and I stood before the bedroom door, gun drawn. He considered the windows, but was apparently unwilling to plunge through the glass and then land in the street below.

The angry brother, meanwhile, resorted to blind rage, intending to use his last seconds of freedom to punish Holmes, whom he rightly recognized as the cause of his dilemma. He ran forward with a guttural cry, his arms outstretched. Holmes deftly stepped to one side, locked his foot in that of his attacker, and taking hold of the man's arm, helped use his own force and speed to send him headlong into the mantelpiece. The impact shook the house, and several books toppled onto the broken features of the man lying unconscious, his head across the blackened andirons of the cold fireplace. He was lucky that his neck wasn't broken – but that only delayed its breaking for a few months, until his appeals ran out and he was led to the scaffold permanently erected inside the execution shed at Manchester's Strangeways Prison.

The two men were quickly taken into custody, and an ambulance was summoned for the injured man. A couple of the constables knew us, and it wasn't long before we were joined by Inspector Lanner, an old friend. We explained the little that we knew, and the two assailants were taken away, one cursing in handcuffs, and the other on a stretcher.

I had been correct in my assumption that they were from Manchester. We were to learn that they were Vincent and James Croughton, both trusted lieutenants in the Brigantes Gang which held such influence there. They had apparently been in the process of setting up their own organization, with plans to mount a revolution against the established criminal hierarchy, and had gathered a handful of like-minded villains to their side. Among them was Lucius Newbiggin, who had moved there following the destruction of the Moriarty organization in 1891. As we were later to confirm from the notes delivered to Baker Street by Inspector Patterson, and interviews among several Manchester criminals, his career as a performer had been intermittent, and it wasn't long before he returned to criminal endeavors, this time finding a place within the plans of the Brigantes.

His rather unique skills had been quite useful, and he had earned something of a position of trust within the gang's councils. It was his awareness of certain documents that had made him an equally valuable recruit to the Croughtons. But after he had been able to abscond with these papers, journals, notebooks, and financial records – which could be used by the new criminal leaders to break and defeat the Brigantes – he had fled. As James Croughton had stated, it was his vanity in retaining his own name, as well as his inability to abandon his collection of books related to magic and performance, taking care to surreptitiously ship them to his new home, that had eventually led to his being found in London.

"But where did he go?" I asked, when it was just Holmes, Lanner, and me left in the missing man's sitting room. "How did he leave the house? Is this one of his magic tricks?"

"And where are the documents that the Croughtons so desperately wanted?" added Inspector Lanner.

"He never left," said Holmes, a strange look on his face.

"What do you mean?" asked Lanner, but I suddenly and unexpectedly had a strange understanding.

"The odor," I said.

Holmes nodded.

"What odor?" queried Lanner.

"He is – *was* – a magician. Did he fix up a hidey hole?" I asked. "In the six months that he lived here? Under the floorboards, perhaps?"

"It's more elaborate than that," said Holmes, leading us toward the bedroom.

While Holmes opened the curtains to the light shining in from the rear of the house, I explained that I'd noticed the unpleasant odor on the first occasion that I entered the bedroom. Lanner now perceived it as well, although it was greatly reduced from what I'd initially encountered, and he also recognized it. "Where is he?"

"He was living here in fear," answered Holmes indirectly, "but he wasn't very good at this sort of thing. He made no real effort to disguise himself, and he foolishly didn't use a false name. Perhaps he thought that those in Manchester would never find him here in this little corner of London. He kept to himself, and covered up whenever he went out. And he wanted to be prepared, should someone some seeking him.

"He was a magician, and seeing the many volumes he'd accumulated, knowing that he was writing a substantial treatise about all of them, one can assume that was clearly an expert. Surely amongst all these books are tomes about constructing devices such as disappearing cabinets and the

261

like, in addition to the trite card tricks and disappearing coin illusions practiced by so many lesser magicians.

"When I was searching earlier, I too noticed the unexpected odor of decay in this room. It didn't take long to find signs of new construction – in spite of how well they had been concealed. Mrs. Pearson said that Newbiggin occasionally went out. I suspect that he did so to purchase a few tools, and a little paint and plaster as well, to cover help him accomplish his goal, and to hide what he'd done."

He walked over to a spot on the wall, along the outer wall of the building near the door from the bedroom to the sitting room. We followed, and illuminated in the dim light from the window behind us, we could see a very thin line in the wall, stretching some five feet from the floor to a spot even with our shoulders. It then turned and ran horizontally across to the corner next to the sitting room door frame. Holmes pushed on the wall near the vertical line, and there was a faint click. The wall at that spot pivoted out like a door, a thin construct of plaster and lathing, revealing a narrow cavity behind it.

The smell of death was suddenly much worse, billowing out into the small bedroom, and Lanner gagged, while I coughed and held my handkerchief to my face.

Holmes tightened his lips and pointed toward the dark space revealed to us. "You can see that the joists in the wall's framing have been carefully sawn away, leaving an open space about a foot or so deep between the plastered wall of the room and the brickwork of the outside of the building – which itself abuts the bricks of the neighboring structure. With my pocket torch, I was able to see that further joists in this narrow corridor have all been sawn away the same manner – leaving a very narrow and tight path between here and the front of the building. I suspect if I were to follow this space between walls all the way around, it would lead to an exit – either in one of the other rooms in the house, or possibly through the brickwork into one of the next-door buildings – though I doubt it.

"In any case, I didn't get far into the passage during my initial exploration before I found him – Newbiggin – still clutching a leather attaché case, containing a bundle of documents. They are almost certainly those sought by the Croughtons."

And so it proved. Rather than locate a member of the force slim enough to re-enter the passage, Holmes himself went back in, first returning with the attaché case, and then going back for the more odious task of retrieving the body. We stood around the poor fellow as he lay upon his bedroom floor, only a few days dead, but his eyes sunken but still locked in that terrible and flat gaze into eternity.

"It sounds as if he was in poor health," said Holmes. "He must have seen who his visitors were from the window when Mrs. Pearson went down to answer the door. The strain of being discovered, and then hurrying into the wall, overcame him, and he died there – probably almost as soon as he was hidden."

"How – after just a couple of days – is the odor of decomposition so strong?" asked the inspector.

"Perhaps whatever illness he had," I answered, "combined with the stress of hiding from the Croughton's, caused his unexpected death, as well as accelerating the breakdown of his body. No two cases are alike."

Holmes nodded. "I suspect that another factor is that he died adjacent to the passage he excavated around the chimney, which is rather warm from Mrs. Pearson's fire downstairs. No doubt that extra heat radiating from the brickwork accelerated the objectionable condition of the body."

Holmes bent forward, looking again into the passage between the walls. "Ingenious. As I recall, Newbiggin was implicated in a number of country house burglaries while in Moriarty's service. If he was able to move about in such a way – through the walls and under the floors – of those houses, his skills would have been invaluable."

That night, I related a suitably edited version of the events to my wife, and she was more worried about Mrs. Pearson than anything. In the morning, I accompanied her back to Farraway Street, where she offered comfort to the still-distressed landlady. They ended up becoming good friends, which is how I was able to recommend Mrs. Pearson to a friend of my own who needed rooms some years later, after the fellow came to London following his emmigration from Belgium during the War.

Holmes, in the meantime, seemed to take a lesson from Newbiggin's curious method of hiding and escape. He spent much of the following fall and winter burrowing through the similarly built walls of Baker Street – without Mrs. Hudson's knowledge! – constructing his own passage of similar claustrophobic tightness but much safer transit, leading first from his bedroom, its entrance in the same spot as Newbiggin's, around and over the rear of the fireplace, and then across the front of the building to a spot along the front windows. It was of great use to him the following year during the trapping of Count Negretto Sylvius, and I have no doubt that he would have kept going, honeycombing the entire structure with passages reminiscent of some medieval castle, if he hadn't abruptly departed London October of 1903, ostensibly retired, but in fact spending most of his time at the service of his brother, Mycroft, in preparing for the Great War.

I recalled these events just last week, when Steven Pearson, now a prosperous middle-aged lawyer, visited to thank me for my condolences

263

following the recent passing of his mother. We discussed the case which led to our first meeting, and how his mother had never bothered to remove the entrance to the secret passage into the walls. He asked me what he should do about it now, as he intended to sell the lease on the property. We discussed the idea of liability should someone enter and become trapped, and agreed that it should be closed up. And yet, a part of me – that young chap who still reads sea adventures and remembers all those many escapades with Sherlock Holmes – seems to regret the loss of such a place. There is a joy in knowing that they exist. But even though the one at Farraway Street shall vanish, I can take comfort in knowing that Holmes's passage still exists in Baker Street, for those who know how to enter it.

The Mystery of
Foxglove Lodge
by S. C. Toft

One afternoon in December, 1902, I left my practice early to purchase a Christmas present for my wife. My journey took me to a milliners shop not far from Baker Street, so I took the opportunity to pass on the season's greetings to my old friend, Mr. Sherlock Holmes. Of course, I couldn't do this without bringing a small gift for the famed detective.

"Ah, Watson, you have outdone yourself! And such a fine pipe as this deserves only the finest tobacco," he said, reaching into the familiar Persian slipper that he kept by the fireplace.

"Now tell me, dear fellow, what brings you to your former lodgings on such a cold, snowy afternoon? I see from the hat box at your side you have come via Fawcett's on Marylebone High Street – a present for your good lady wife no doubt, but pray tell, what is the true purpose for your visit? Perhaps you have a patient in need of my services?"

"Why, have you really become so cynical as to suggest that my visit could be anything other than a chance to share some festive cheer with my dear old friend?"

Holmes paused thoughtfully. "I dare say that my unique line of work me causes me to look for motives in even the most kindly of gestures. Please accept my most humble apologies. Now, let us enjoy a glass of port by the fireside, and I shall apprise you of my recent cases."

He stood at the sideboard, pouring the port from a crystal decanter, when he glanced up to look out the window. "Hullo, what do we have here? There is a very good chance that a man walking along Baker Street at a hurried pace, dressed without a hat or scarf on such a day as this, has urgent business with myself."

Moments later, as Holmes had predicted, the very same snow-dusted gentleman of around fifty years old was ushered into the warm sitting room by Mrs. Hudson.

"Gentlemen, my name is Dr. Barnabas Flint. I practice medicine in the market town of Essington, and this morning I witnessed something that has made me question my own sanity – or, if I haven't lost my mind, then I have witnessed something that throws the laws of science into doubt."

"Dr. Flint," Holmes interjected, with a gleam of excitement in his eyes. "I suggest that you join us in having a glass of this most excellent

265

port and enlighten us as to the sequence of events that have caused you such concern. Please state only the facts."

"Why, thank you, Mr. Holmes," said Flint, accepting the glass with a trembling hand. "As I stated, I attend to the medical needs of the people of Essington and have done so for the last twenty years. Like you, Dr. Watson, I served as an army surgeon in Afghanistan before commencing general practice. A week ago, one of my patients, an elderly spinster named Miss Harriet Aldington, passed away peacefully at the age of seventy-eight. Miss Aldington lived in a house on Church Road called Foxglove Lodge, and after her passing I have been given temporary custody of the keys to the property, until Charles, her nephew and only remaining relative, is able to travel down from Edinburgh after Christmas. I was happy to check on the property whilst it was uninhabited, and I began calling in each evening on the way home from my consulting rooms to see that everything was in order.

"This morning, however, while walking through the snowy market square on my way to work, I was stopped by Mary Baxter, landlady of The Saracen's Head, who told me that she had seen a light on at Foxglove Lodge at around midnight last night. I expressed scepticism, as I knew – or thought I knew – that the house was empty. None the less, I called by the late Miss Aldington's house and walked across the pristine snow, up to the front door. I couldn't see any lights inside but entered regardless, just to be certain that nothing was amiss. I walked cautiously into the tiled hallway of the property. How she kept such a pristine home at her age without a housekeeper was nothing short of miraculous. But I digress, and at my unfortunate tale's most critical point." Dr. Flint paused to take a long sip of his port.

"Once you have fortified yourself, please continue with your intriguing narrative," said Holmes, with his fingers pressed together and eyes narrowed as if in deep meditation.

"Mr. Holmes, I can scarcely believe what I am about to tell you, but I swear that it is all true. As I have said, I entered the hallway and called out, 'Hullo? Is there anybody there?' There came no answer, so I proceeded to enter the parlour to my left, and there slumped in the armchair was the body of a man of around thirty years with brown hair and beard. His eyes were wide open and his body was as cold as the snow that lay on the ground outside. There was no pulse and, out of professional habit, I checked my pocket-watch and declared him dead, to myself, at eight-forty-seven. There was no obvious cause of death.

"I couldn't fathom it – a dead stranger in Miss Aldington's parlour. It was completely inexplicable. After closing the eyelids of the unfortunate soul, I explored the rest of the house, but there was nobody else present, no one to explain the presence of the dead body at Foxglove Lodge. As such, I immediately walked to the small police station on King Street and told Sergeant Cribbins everything that I've just told you. We hurried back to the lodge, and the Sergeant's curiosity was obviously aroused. But it is at this point that my tale veers from the unusual to the extraordinary – or even, dare I say, the miraculous!

"When we arrived at the gate of Foxglove, I observed my own set of footprints leading to and from the front door, but there was also an extra set of footprints that had appeared in the snow, going not from the front door, but from the door at the side of the house to a smaller gate at the side of the property where there is a rough track, just wide enough for a carriage. These were certainly not there at the time of my previous visit to the house.

"'Let's see about this body then, Dr. Flint,' said Sergeant Cribbins cheerfully as we traced my earlier footprints up the path to the front door and entered the parlour via the hallway."

Dr. Flint paused, shook his head, and took another long sip of port before continuing his singular account. "Gentlemen, the corpse had gone – completely vanished, and there was no sign that it had ever been there.

"'It appears your cadaver has gone out to stretch his legs, eh Dr. Flint?' said Cribbins with a mocking tone. I looked around the room incredulously.

"'This can't be so!' I said, pacing to the side door, which I opened to see the footprints that led directly to the gate in the wall that runs along the track at the side of the property.

"'It's going to make an interesting report, this one. It'll give the boys at the station a laugh or two, that's for sure! A corpse that has been resurrected from the dead and gone for a walk! A touch of voodoo here in little old Essington."

"Cribbins then lowered his voice and said, 'In all seriousness, Dr. Flint, might I respectfully suggest that, if indeed there was a gentleman in this house, that he was perhaps in a particularly deep sleep, and he has subsequently woken up and left the property? I read in the papers the other week about a fellow who awakened in his coffin just before the undertakers laid him to rest!'

"'Impossible!' I cried. 'One thing I've seen more than my fair share of, Sergeant, is death. That man was as dead as a door nail – as cold as a block of ice! Yet it still makes no sense. You saw the footprints – the only prints that were in the snow were my own, and this new set leading off the property.'

"'Without a corpse or an intruder, there isn't much the police can do, I'm afraid. But let's check the rest of the property, just to make sure that aren't more surprises lurking!'

"The search of the house revealed nothing to shed any light on the mystery. Sergeant Cribbins said he would make some enquiries, but I couldn't help feeling that he believed that I was either lying, or that I had completely lost my mind. Please tell me, Mr. Holmes: Is there a rational explanation for what I have told you?"

Holmes took a deep breath and began. "It is certainly a compelling tale, with a number of unusual features. Tell me, was there any sign of a forced entry into the property?"

"Not that I could see."

"And you are quite certain that on your initial visit to the house that it was empty, with the exception of yourself and the deceased gentleman?"

"That is correct. I went into every room of the house after finding the body."

"Now the matter of footprints: You are positive that were only three sets of prints when you arrived back at Foxglove Lodge – your own to and from the front door, and the third set leaving the house from the side door?"

"I would swear to that on the Holy Bible."

Holmes jumped to his feet and said, "Then that settles it. I suggest we hastily drain our glasses and catch the next train to Essington. I believe it departs Paddington at ten-past-three – if we hurry we can make it. Watson, I assume you will be joining us."

"But Holmes – my wife is expecting me!"

"I have no doubt of that. We shall send her a telegram if necessary. Come, gentlemen – time is very much of the essence!"

Within an hour we had left the smoke and bustle of the city and were speeding through the snow-blanketed countryside towards the small town of Essington. Dr. Flint and I took this opportunity to share stories of our experiences in the Afghan campaign, whilst Holmes sat with his eyes closed, and the faintest glimmer of a smile on his face – a sign the detective was in his element, his spirit nourished by a new and puzzling case.

We arrived at Essington Station at half-past-four and wasted no time in making our way across the pretty town to Foxglove Lodge, home of the late Miss Harriet Aldington.

Holmes bristled with all the keenness of a hound on the scent of a fox. His eyes were suddenly alert and his mind, I imagined, was already ablaze, making critical observations and infinite calculations.

At the gates of the property, Holmes immediately dropped on to one knee, staring with concentration at the jumble of footprints that still remained in the snow leading to and from the front door. There was no snow falling, but there was a freshness in the air and the darkening sky was brooding with the intention of releasing another wintry flurry.

"It is quite clear," Holmes began, "even in this dusk-light, which prints are yours, and which belong to our friend, Sergeant Cribbins. There is no indication here of the presence of a third party on this path. Not since the snowfall this morning at any rate. Let us now examine the house. Dr. Flint, if you would be so kind."

He opened the front-door and gestured for Holmes and me to enter the hallway. Holmes went in first and moved quickly from room to room, examining seemingly invisible signs and clues with great intensity. Dr. Flint and I looked on in silent awe as the famous sleuth went about his work. Nothing seemed to escape his scrutiny. One cannot imagine what an onlooker would have made of this strange, lean man crawling on the floor and examining furniture with a magnifying glass, all the time fizzing with energy.

Suddenly Holmes leapt up from the rug he was examining and declared, "I've seen all that I need to see. I must now examine the footprints at the side of the house before they are lost."

We followed him as he walked slowly alongside the mysterious set of footprints. He stopped abruptly and turned to Flint. "Doctor, could you again describe the appearance of the corpse that briefly occupied the parlour of Foxglove Lodge?'"

"Of course. He was a gentleman of around thirty years, short brown hair, and a beard. I would guess he was approximately five-foot-nine inches in height."

"And his build?"

"Slim, I would say."

"Thank you. Beyond the gate there is the narrow track, and beyond that lies some woodland?"

"That is quite correct. Bishop's Wood, which leads down the river. Some fine fish of various species to be caught there too."

"Perhaps we'll have time for a spot of winter angling, eh Watson? I expect to solve the mystery of the walking corpse within a day. These footprints here tell us nearly everything, do they not? Combined with the two clues inside the house, we have the beginnings of an explanation. I can safely say, Dr. Flint, that you have neither lost your mind, nor do you need to abandon your scientific beliefs. Indeed, it is the very laws of physics that have illuminated this intriguing matter."

"But Holmes," I asked, "how can you possibly come to such a conclusion just from these footprints? I don't see anything that contradicts the account Dr. Flint has given us."

"Quite so. Doctor. You have given us a near-perfect narrative. But Watson, I'm disappointed that you don't see the answers that these footprints have provided."

I looked again at the prints – a gentleman's boot of average size – but beyond that I failed to deduce anything.

"I suggest we catch the next train back to London," said Holmes. "But not before we pay a brief visit to Sergeant Cribbins."

Darkness had now come to Essington, and as we walked through the market square towards the police station, gaslight illuminated the snow that had just begun to fall. The sound of laughter and revelry escaped from The Saracen's Head and The Royal Oak, Essington's two hostelries. One gentleman in particular, having clearly enjoyed a festive libation or two, was giving a rousing rendition of "God Rest Ye Merry Gentlemen" from the doorway of the latter. This man, it transpired, was none other than Sergeant Cribbins.

Dr. Flint called out, "Sergeant! Should you not be on duty?"

"Ah, Doctor, seen any more ghosts recently? Ha ha!"

"Sergeant, your manner is most unprofessional. Fortunately for both you and me, a real detective is now investigating the affair. May I introduce to you Mr. Sherlock Holmes and his colleague, Dr. Watson."

"You're having me on!" exclaimed Sergeant Cribbins.

"Alas, he is not," interrupted Holmes, "and I'm afraid I must urge you, Sergeant, to bring about a close to your festive celebrations for there is work to be done. Tomorrow morning at first light!"

"Well, I never! It's an honour to meet you, Mr. Holmes. Surely you aren't in Essington because of the doctor's disappearing corpse!" asked Cribbins with a chuckle.

"Indeed I am, and tomorrow morning you and your men will conduct a thorough search of Bishop's Wood. You can expect to find the body that Dr. Flint pronounced dead this morning in the parlour of Foxglove Lodge."

"What on earth is it doing in Bishop's Wood? Surely you can't be suggesting that the doctor was right, and this body got up and walked across the snow?"

"All will become clear in good time, Sergeant – just as long as you and your men do as I say, and search the woods thoroughly."

"Very well, Mr. Holmes, but first you must join me and the lads for a Christmas tipple. It would be an honour to share an ale with you."

"And I would be delighted to join you, Sergeant, but not until we have wrapped up this case. I shall be in touch tomorrow."

As we walked away from The Royal Oak, Holmes turned round and called out, "Remember, Sergeant: Search the woods thoroughly, and please – no more ale!"

On the train back to London, Holmes stretched out his legs and smiled with a feline satisfaction, "A productive little excursion, wouldn't you say?"

"Perhaps for you. I still fail to see how those footprints reveal anything other than the fact somebody wearing boots walked from the house to the gate. And I certainly don't see how a corpse can be in the parlour one minute and gone the next – not without anybody else's footprints arriving at the house to then take the body away – unless somebody walked up to the front door in the footprints that Dr. Flint had already made!"

"My dear Watson, why on earth somebody go to the trouble of doing that? And what a fine stroke of luck it would have been for this individual to have exactly the same shoes as the doctor. No, Watson, the matter of the footprints is really quite a simple one. The real mystery lies in exactly what happened before and after the events at Foxglove Lodge."

"Is too much to expect you to reveal what your next moves will be? I recall it was always your habit to keep me in the dark."

"That was often for your own sake. You are pathologically honest. Expecting you to lie or mislead individuals could put a case in jeopardy. You will recall my reasoning on this matter in the affair of Victor Savage's death. It's really to your credit that you have such integrity. But as it happens, I will gladly inform you of the next step in our investigation. Upon our return to Paddington, you will go home to your wife, partake in supper, and then retire to bed."

"Holmes!" I cried in frustration.

"And in the morning," he continued, "stop by Baker Street and see if there's any news to report."

The next day, it was with a sense of excitement that I took a carriage through the snow to Baker Street and, after exchanging pleasantries with Mrs. Hudson, hurried up the familiar staircase to Holmes's rooms.

To my astonishment, he was nowhere to be seen. Instead, a man of around sixty years old with a white moustache and spectacles was stooping over the fireplace, poking at the embers. He turned around towards me.

"Ah, Watson, I've been waiting for you!"

"Good Lord – is that you?"

"Yes, but to the criminals of London, I'm Jim Dudley, pedlar of household wares and, on occasion, goods of a less-than-legitimate nature."

Holmes opened the left side of his coat to reveal an assortment of watches, chains, and necklaces.

"Very convincing! If you ever decide to retire from detection, a career awaits on the stage."

"In order to effectively gather intelligence, one's adopted persona must be entirely incontrovertible, especially amongst the criminal fraternity who are naturally suspicious of strangers. Attention to the finest detail is crucial.

"Dare I enquire as to reason for your fine disguise?"

"I received a telegram from Sergeant Cribbins very early this morning requesting my presence in Essington as a matter of urgency. I obliged, taking the next available train from Paddington. As I predicted, the corpse had been found in Bishop's Wood. The body possessed some remarkable features that necessitates an excursion into London's underworld."

"So you were right!" I exclaimed. "But how on earth is the strange affair at Foxglove Lodge connected to the criminal fraternity of London?"

"I suggest you cast your mind back to the Christmas of 1887."

"The theft of the blue carbuncle? An extraordinary case."

"Indeed, and presented by yourself with such poetic flare."

"I fail to see the similarities between the two cases, other than the time of year, of course."

"All will become clear, but first I have important business to attend to as Mr. Jim Dudley, pedlar of dubious reputation."

"Do take care. It sounds like you're sailing in murky waters."

"Waters I have been navigating for many years. If my investigations proceed as planned, then I expect to be at The Saracen's Head in Essington at five o'clock this evening. I trust you will be there too."

"Of course. But be careful – you aren't as young as you once were."

"Ha!" exclaimed Holmes with a dismissive wave of his hand.

I had three patients to attend to before I was able to catch the train, but I found that I wasn't able to give them my usual degree of attention, consumed as I was by the mystery in which I had become so quickly entangled. I wondered if Holmes would have even told me about this fascinating case had I not been present, by pure chance, at the moment that Dr. Barnabas Flint entered 221b Baker Street. I also wondered how this curious puzzle could be explained, and how the sudden disappearance of a corpse in seemingly impossible circumstances could be associated with London's underworld and an old case involving a Christmas goose. It was these thoughts that still occupied my mind as I travelled on the train towards Essington.

The snow had stopped falling by the time I reached the old market town, and the temperature had dropped by a degree or two. What had previously crunched satisfyingly beneath my feet had turned to a treacherous sheet of ice. A scattering of stars had already begun to appear in the inky evening sky.

I was eager to meet up with Holmes, but the icy pavements slowed me down considerably. It was uncertain as to whether I should expect my old friend to still be assuming the disguise of Jim Dudley, or if he would have reverted back to his true identity. This question was quickly answered by the alarming sight of Sherlock Holmes, still wearing the white moustache and spectacles of Jim Dudley, wrestling with a red-haired man outside the entrance to The Saracen's Head.

I hesitated slightly before exclaiming, "Dudley!"

Holmes looked up, and at that very moment the red-headed man pulled a blade from his pocket and swiped at him. Holmes deftly dodged the blade, but in stepping back stumbled upon the ice. The other man took the opportunity to take flight, running with all the skill of a dancer along the icy road. He moved at such a speed that, instead of causing him to fall, each slip of his feet seemed to propel him further along. "Quickly, Watson!" called Holmes, who rose and then ran with the same astonishing dexterity as the red-headed man. I, however, stumbled a number of times, hampered by my old injury, as well as a lack of the grace that blessed the two men running ahead of me.

The red-headed man, pursued by Holmes, ran down Church Road, turning left onto the track alongside the mysterious Foxglove Lodge. From there he turned into Bishop's Wood. Here I caught up with Holmes as we pursued the young man down the wooded hill that was only partially illuminated by the moonlight showing through the branches of oak and ash. I ran with all my strength despite, at that moment, still being ignorant of exactly who we were chasing – or why. This query was partly answered by the sound of Holmes shouting, "Griffiths! There is no point in running!" The fugitive disregarded this suggestion and continued through the woods. The hill levelled out as it reached the frozen river referred to earlier by Dr. Flint. Here Griffiths turned right, and along a path that followed the bank.

Along this particular stretch, the river didn't meander, but instead ran with a straightness that made it appear more like a canal. Suddenly, beyond Griffiths, out of the darkness and into the moonlight, three figures emerged, running towards us. This sight was accompanied by the shrill blast of a police whistle. As the men came close, I identified the man with the whistle as none other than Sergeant Cribbins. He was accompanied by two burly looking constables.

The man I knew only as Griffiths stopped suddenly on the path and pulled out the blade with which he had earlier attempted to slash Holmes. "Come any closer and I'll slice yer!" Griffiths growled menacingly. We all paused, Holmes and me on one side of Griffiths, and Cribbins and his men on the other, both sets of pursuers about ten yards from the armed man. Griffiths waved the blade, frantically twisting round as if trying to face all of us at the same time. "I mean it!" he shouted.

What happened next took us completely by surprise. Instead of attempting to flee back up the wooded hill, or charge at us, Griffiths took a step to his side and lowered himself onto the frozen river. It was a good thirty yards wide, enough to have given him an advantage over us if he'd been able to get across to the meadow on the other side. We all hurried to the edge of the bank and watched him gingerly make his way across the ice, looking over his shoulder as he did so. Holmes turned to Cribbins and asked, "Where is the nearest bridge?"

"About a hundred yards that way," said Cribbins, gesturing over his shoulder in the direction from which they had come.

Before we had chance to recommence the chase, however, our attention was drawn back to Griffiths by the sound of cracking ice and his plaintive scream. "Please help me! I can't swim!" He had lost his previously sure footing and, as one of his feet broke through the ice just a few feet from shore, he fell, and his whole body crashed through into the morbidly cold river. He let out a great cry as he disappeared into the black water.

"Quickly, grab him before he perishes!" directed Holmes as the man resurfaced. "Cribbins," he continued, "hold my arm! I think that I'll be able to reach him!" Cribbins did exactly as he was instructed and, holding on to one of the constables, acted as an anchor for Holmes, who was leaning over the river, straining as he reached towards the thrashing Griffiths.

With some effort, Holmes grabbed Griffiths' hand and, with the help of Cribbins, hauled him up onto the bank. His body was steaming and shivering with cold. "Watson!" Holmes called to me with a tone of urgency.

"We must remove these cold, wet clothes," I instructed, "and get him by a warm fire with haste."

After peeling off Griffiths' sodden garments, Holmes covered him with his own overcoat, while Cribbins, taking no chances, handcuffed the man and passed the knife to one of the constables. "Right-o, gentlemen," began Cribbins. "The fires at the station will have died by now, so I suggest we temporarily take this fellow to The Royal Oak, where he can warm up by the fire in the lounge. We want to make sure he recovers enough to face justice." Cribbins then turned to Griffiths and said, "I can't say it'll be much of a merry Christmas for you though, me lad. But we may be able to spare a mince pie if you behave yourself!"

An hour later, after we had escorted Cribbins and his suitably restored prisoner to the cells at Essington Police Station, we returned to the open fire in the lounge of The Royal Oak. Also in attendance at this festive gathering was Dr. Barnabas Flint.

"A successful conclusion, I think you'll agree, gentlemen," said Holmes with a satisfied smile as he began to fill his pipe.

"So I gather" said Dr. Flint. "But what of the walking corpse? How on earth do you explain that? And how is Billy Griffiths mixed up in all this? I'm aware he has a reputation as something of a rogue, but never imagined he would be involved in this strange affair."

"The matter is really astonishingly simple, and ultimately a tale of criminality and greed. The initial solution presented itself when I was carrying out my examination of Foxglove Lodge. There were three clues that on their own may not have been significant, but together formed the beginnings of a hypothesis as to what had happened.

"Firstly, there was the wardrobe door in Miss Aldington's dressing room. The door of the wardrobe was slightly ajar. It was clear from what Dr. Flint had said, and the appearance of the rest of the house, that Miss Aldington was a fastidious and house-proud lady, and there was nothing out of place. Nothing except for the wardrobe door, indicating that someone had opened it. Did you think to look inside it, Doctor?"

Flint shook his head. "I did not. I simply moved from room to room, and it never occurred to me."

"Secondly," Holmes continued, "was the presence of a strand of red hair on the rug in the parlour. As Dr. Flint confirmed, the corpse had brown hair. Miss Aldington, one would surmise from her advanced years, had grey or white hair. Therefore, we can conclude the presence of a third party.

"Thirdly, and most significantly, were the footprints that went away from the side of the house. You will recall that I enquired as to the build of the corpse. Slim, you stated, Dr. Flint. A comparison between those prints and those at the front of the house revealed everything. The footprints leading to the track at the side of the house were an inch deeper than those made yourself, Dr. Flint – a man, if I may say so, of medium build. What could possibly explain footprints of such depth? They weren't made by a man of slim build. So perhaps a man of enormous size? Or, in fact, a man burdened by the weight of what he was carrying – a man carrying the dead weight of a corpse. It seemed reasonable to infer that the hurried movement of this corpse was as a result of your arrival, Dr. Flint, and as such, unplanned. Therefore it was highly probable that the body was somewhere in the woods – the nearest viable hiding place, as opposed to it having been transported by a pre-arranged carriage, for instance."

"Of course!" Flint exclaimed. "But what on earth were these two men doing in the house of Mrs. Aldigton?"

"Ah, this was explained by the discovery – or rediscovery – of the corpse by Sergeant Cribbins and his men this morning. The body possessed two extraordinary attributes. Firstly, I recognised the corpse to be none other than Arthur Smithson, notorious jewel thief, whom I have had the misfortune of encountering on a number of occasions. I was confident of his identity due to the distinctive mermaid that is tattooed on his arm, along with the initials *A.S.*. Secondly, his body had been disembowelled."

"So it was murder!" Flint exclaimed.

"Dr. Flint! The body was already dead when it was mutilated – it was you yourself who certified it. Now, the fact that the body had been disembowelled *post mortem* that led me to consider the possibility that there must have been something inside the stomach that was worth moving a corpse for, and for carrying out such an unpleasant procedure. Since the cadaver belonged to an infamous jewel thief, a hypothesis presented itself, and this formed my new line of enquiry. I reminded Watson earlier today of the case of the Blue Carbuncle, where a famous gem had been stolen and subsequently hidden inside a Christmas goose. There were grizzly echoes of that particular adventure, and I was quite certain that the disembowelment was not merely an act of violent deviancy, but was motivated by avarice."

"Good Lord!" exclaimed Flint. "But however did you come to learn of Griffiths' involvement in this dark tale?"

"This was where my character Jim Dudley came in to play," replied Holmes. "Arthur Smithson was like an aggressive weed that would appear across the south of England, but his roots were well and truly in the East End of London. I knew that if I were to uncover the secrets of this dark affair, I would need to visit those seedy alleyways and insalubrious hostelries. In my line of work, I have an intimate knowledge of London's criminal underworld. Thieves and fences are ultimately businessmen, and the prospect of a new money-making opportunity is usually too much for them to resist. Once you have their trust and there is the promise of a profit, they are unrelenting gossips, and it didn't take long for me to ascertain that Arthur Smithson was one of the men responsible for a recent burglary of precious stones, including diamonds, rubies, and emeralds from Cunningham's in Hatton Garden. My sources told me that his accomplice was a man whose name with which I was not acquainted – Billy Griffiths from Essington. And it was after a charitable glass of sherry in front of this very fire that Griffiths began to relax somewhat and talk freely. At the station, perhaps to ensure he avoided a murder charge, he begged forgiveness and made a full confession. Sergeant Cribbins, if you would be so kind."

Cribbins retrieved a folded piece of paper from his jacket pocket and handed it to Holmes, who began to read:

My name is William Griffiths of Essington. I admit I have not always made my living in an honest way. Since me missus gave birth to our son, I've struggled to provide for them, so I've been spending more time in the East End, working with The Monkey Parade Gang. More recently, I'd been doing jobs with Arthur Smithson, nicking from jewellers and the like, but never harming no one.

On the night of the 20th of December, me and Smithson broke into Cunningham's in Hatton Garden and stole a handful of their most valuable stones – diamonds, rubies, and emeralds. We knew what we was looking for. We then made straight for Paddington Station to get out of London. Smithson was well known to Scotland Yard and was panicking that he would be apprehended and searched, so he decided to swallow the gems, so nothing would be found, and we would be allowed on our way. From Paddington we caught the overnight train that stopped at Essington on its way to Glasgow.

The snow had begun to fall as Smithson picked the lock of the front door of Foxglove Lodge. I'm often in Essington visiting me Alice and our little son, so I knew that the property was empty after the passing of the old dear. It was an ideal place to lay low. Now that we was a safe distance from the London coppers, our plan was to wait until the stones had passed through Smithson's guts, clean them, then sell them once the eyes of Scotland Yard were not upon us.

Alas, our plan was scuppered when poor old Smithson, possibly as a result of all them stones he'd swallowed, fell suddenly ill and died in the night, leaving me with a very valuable corpse and a grim dilemma.

I thought of all the money at stake and made me decision. It was nearly morning when I prepared to cut open Smithson's belly and retrieve the precious contents. However, I happened to look out the window saw this gent walking up the path to the house. Before I'd even made an incision, I was forced to run upstairs and hide in the wardrobe in the dressing room.

As soon as I heard the gentleman leave the property I hastily left my hiding-place and ran downstairs. I suspected that the arrival of the local constabulary would be imminent, so I had no choice other than to haul Smithson onto me shoulders and escape. I know Essington like the back of me hand, so I made for the quiet track at the side of the house and the woods beyond. Once in safety of a hollow in the woods, I went to work with the knife . . . .

"It will have been at this moment that you returned to a now-empty Foxglove Lodge with the incredulous Sergeant Cribbins."

"Good Lord!" said Flint in astonishment. "What an extraordinary sequence of events!"

"But however did you come to be brawling outside the Saracen's Head?" I asked.

"It was suggested to me by my contacts in the East End that the two jewel thieves had planned to lie low in Griffiths' home town of Essington, so I hurried back and made further enquiries at The Saracen's Head. It was the obvious choice, as Sergeant Cribbin's presence yesterday at The Royal Oak would make that a highly unlikely choice of establishment for the criminal classes.

"After a couple of pints of ale, I had made enough new friends to arrange a meeting with Griffiths on the pretext of purchasing the gems. It was likely his intention to eventually return to London to sell the jewels there, but the temptation of a quick sale away from the capital proved too much to resist. However, my terms weren't to Griffiths' liking, Watson, and it was while he was demonstrating this that you arrived."

Sergeant Cribbins interrupted, "I'd been observing from the safety of The Royal Oak, and when I saw Griffiths run, I gathered a couple of the lads to head him off on the path further upstream."

"Well, Mr. Holmes," said a smiling Dr. Flint, "I'm deeply indebted to you. I fear that I might have lost my mind, had it not been for your hasty resolution of this mystery!"

"Surely the case isn't completely resolved," I interrupted. "What of the jewels themselves?"

Holmes reached into his pocket and pulled out a small black velvet bag. "You mean these?" he said with a smile as he emptied the sparkling contents on to the table. "I extracted them from Griffiths' pocket during

278

our confrontation. They'll make a welcome Christmas present for Cunningham the jeweller, I expect."

"Well, I'll be d----d!" said Cribbins in astonishment. "Just look how they twinkle in the firelight!"

Later, outside The Royal Oak, the stars were also twinkling as Holmes and I left the inhabitants of Essington to continue their yuletide merrymaking into the night.

The Strange Adventure of
Murder by Remote Control
by Leslie Charteris and Denis Green

Sherlock Holmes and The Saint
An Introduction by Ian Dickerson

Everyone has a story to tell about how they first met Sherlock Holmes. For me it was a Penguin paperback reprint my brother introduced me to in my pre-teen years. I read it, and went on to read all the original stories, but it didn't appeal to me in the way it appealed to others. This is probably because I discovered the adventures of The Saint long before I discovered Sherlock Holmes.

The Saint, for those readers who may need a little more education, was also known as Simon Templar and was a modern day Robin Hood who first appeared in 1928. Not unlike Holmes, he has appeared in books, films, TV shows, and comics. He was created by Leslie Charteris, a young man born in Singapore to a Chinese father and an English mother, who was just twenty years old when he wrote that first Saint adventure. He'd always wanted to be a writer – his first piece was published when he was just nine years of age – and he followed that Saint story, his third novel, with two further books, neither of which featured Simon Templar.

However, there's a notable similarity between the heroes of his early novels, and Charteris, recognising this, and being somewhat fed up of creating variations on the same theme, returned to writing adventures for The Saint. Short stories for a weekly magazine, *The Thriller*, and a change of publisher to the mainstream Hodder & Stoughton, helped him on his way to becoming a best-seller and something of a pop culture sensation in Great Britain.

But he was ambitious. Always fond of the USA, he started to spend more time over there, and it was the 1935 novel – and fifteenth Saint book – *The Saint in New York*, that made him a transatlantic success. He spent some time in Hollywood, writing for the movies and keeping an eye on The Saint films that were then in production at RKO studios. Whilst there, he struck up what would become a lifelong friendship with Denis Green, a British actor and writer, and his new wife, Mary.

Fast forward a couple of years . . . . Leslie was on the west coast of the States, still writing Saint stories to pay the bills, writing the occasional non-Saint piece for magazines, and getting increasingly frustrated with RKO who, he felt, weren't doing him, or his creation, justice. Denis Green, meanwhile, had established himself as a stage actor, and had embarked on a promising radio career both in front of and behind the microphone.

Charteris was also interested in radio. He had a belief that his creation could be adapted for every medium and was determined to try and prove it. In 1940, he commissioned a pilot programme to show how The Saint would work on radio, casting his friend Denis Green as Simon Templar. Unfortunately, it didn't sell, but just three years later, he tried again, commissioning a number of writers – including Green – to create or adapt Saint adventures for radio.

They also didn't sell, and after struggling to find a network or sponsor for The Saint on the radio, he handed the problem over to established radio show packager and producer, James L. Saphier. Charteris was able to solve one problem, however: At the behest of advertising agency Young & Rubicam, who represented the show's sponsors, Petri Wine, Denis Green had been sounded out about writing for *The New Adventures of Sherlock Holmes*, a weekly radio series that was then broadcasting on the Mutual Network.

Green confessed to his friend that, whilst he could write good radio dialogue, he simply hadn't a clue about plotting. He was, as his wife would later recall, a reluctant writer: "He didn't really like to write. He would wait until the last minute. He would put it off as long as possible by scrubbing the kitchen stove or wash the bathroom – anything before he sat down at the typewriter. I had a very clean house." Charteris offered a solution: They would go into partnership, with him creating the stories and Green writing the dialogue.

But there was another problem: *The New Adventures of Sherlock Holmes* aired on one of the radio networks that Leslie hoped might be interested in the adventures of The Saint, and it would not look good, he thought, for him to be involved with a rival production. Leslie adopted the pseudonym of *Bruce Taylor*, (as you will see at the end of the following script,) taking inspiration taking inspiration from the surname of the show's producer Glenhall Taylor and that of Rathbone's co-star, Nigel Bruce.

The Taylor/Green partnership was initiated with "The Strange Case of the Aluminum Crutch", which aired on July 24th, 1944, and would ultimately run until the following March, with *Bruce Taylor*'s final contribution to the Holmes Canon being "The Secret of Stonehenge", which aired on March 19th, 1945 – thirty-five episodes in all.

Bruce Taylor's short radio career came to an end in short because Charteris shifted his focus elsewhere. Thanks to Saphier, The Saint found a home on the NBC airwaves, and aside from the constant demand for literary Saint adventures, he was exploring the possibilities of launching a Saint magazine. He was replaced by noted writer and critic Anthony Boucher, who would establish a very successful writing partnership with Denis Green.

Fast forward quite a few more years – to 1988 to be precise: A young chap called Dickerson, a long standing member of *The Saint Club*, discovers a new TV series of The Saint is going into production. Suitably inspired, he writes to the then-secretary of the Club, suggesting that it was time the world was reminded of The Saint, and The Saint Club in particular. Unbeknownst to him, the secretary passes his letter on to Leslie Charteris himself. The teenaged Dickerson and the aging author struck up a friendship which involved, amongst other things, many fine lunches, followed by lazy chats over various libations. Some of those conversations featured the words "Sherlock" and "Holmes".

It was when Leslie died, in 1993, that I really got to know his widow, Audrey. We often spoke at length about many things, and from time to time discussed Leslie and the Holmes scripts, as well as her own career as an actress.

When she died in 2014, Leslie's family asked me to go through their flat in Dublin. Pretty much the first thing I found was a stack of radio scripts, many of which had been written by *Bruce Taylor* and Denis Green.

I was, needless to say, rather delighted. More so when his family gave me permission to get them into print. Back in the 1940's, no one foresaw an afterlife for shows such as this, and no recordings exist of this particular Sherlock Holmes adventure. So here you have the only documentation around of Charteris and Green's "The Strange Adventure of Murder by Remote Control" . . . .

Ian Dickerson

The Strange Adventure of Murder by Remote Control

Originally Broadcast on August 14th, 1944

CHARACTERS
- SHERLOCK HOLMES
- DR. JOHN H. WATSON
- MAID
- LORD BURFORD
- MLLE. CEJANE
- M. DUBOIS
- BARON LECHAISE
- BOB CAMPBELL (ANNOUNCER)

CAMPBELL (ANNOUNCER): Petri Wine brings you –

MUSIC: THEME (FADE ON CUE)

FORMAN: Basil Rathbone and Nigel Bruce in *The New Adventures of Sherlock Holmes.*

MUSIC: THEME – FULL FINISH

OPENING COMMERCIAL

CAMPBELL: The Petri family – the family that took time to bring you good wine – invites you to spend the next half-hour as Doctor Watson tells us about another exciting mystery solved by his old friend, Sherlock Holmes. I hope you enjoyed your dinner and are now in the mood for a good story. I *know* that you enjoyed your dinner if it was accompanied by a bottle of that good Petri Wine. Because that Petri Wine makes *everything* taste better – whether it's a hamburger sandwich or a six-course turkey dinner! You ought to just try a Petri California Burgundy with your dinner one of these fine evenings. That Petri Burgundy is a hearty red wine with a refreshing flavor that is wonderful with any kind of meat or meat dish. And if you ever have a spaghetti dinner – that Petri Burgundy is a definite "must". If, on one of these warm evenings, you're serving a *light* meal – like, say, a chicken salad . . . then you ought to tray a delicate, subtly flavored Petrie California Sauterne. Try that Sauterne chilled. Mmm mmm . . . There's a white wine that was just *made* for hot weather

283

meals. Believe me, *with food* nothing can take the place of that good Petri wine.

MUSIC: *SCOTCH POEM*

CAMPBELL: And now for our weekly visit with the good Doctor Watson, in the charming little ranch house overlooking the blue Pacific, where we will hear another one of those stories that Doctor Watson tells so well. Let's see what he has in store for us tonight. Good evening, Doctor.

WATSON: Ah, there you are, Mr. Campbell. I was beginning to think you'd forgotten your appointment.

CAMPBELL: And miss hearing you tell another new Sherlock Holmes adventure? (HE LAUGHS) No, sir. That's one doctor's appointment I'll always keep. And what story have you decided to tell us tonight, Doctor Watson?

WATSON: Well, tonight, as I promised you last week, I'm going to tell you about one of the strangest adventures that ever happened to Sherlock Holmes. D'you know, Mr. Campbell, that in this story, the great man became the laughing stock of Paris . . . and only quick thinking prevented him becoming publicly disgraced.

CAMPBELL: Are you kidding? Sherlock Holmes a public laughing stock? How on earth did that happen?

WATSON: Well, if you'll stop interrupting me, I'll tell you the story.

CAMPBELL: I'm sorry, Doctor. Go ahead.

WATSON: It was in the spring of 1904. Holmes had remained in France recuperating from the immense strain caused by his exertions that year in the celebrated Lyons train murders case. I was referring to my notes just before you came and I see that it was on the fourteenth of April that I received a telegram from Holmes telling that he was staying at the Hotel Crillon in Paris, and inviting me to spend a few days with him. I was a bit run-down myself, so I obtained a *locum* for my practice and was on the next cross-channel steamer. I found Holmes in excellent health and in one of his rare moods of gaiety. Shortly after my arrival, he informed me that we were going to a

284

party. (WITH A CHUCKLE) A party! Holmes – the recluse – the hermit – was positively gadding about. As we walked up the Champs-Élysées that night, I didn't hesitate to let him know how glad I was to see the change in him . . . .

MUSIC: GAY FRENCH THEME. (UP AND THEN OUT)

SOUND EFFECT: FOOTSTEPS ON PAVEMENT

WATSON: (LAUGHING) You know, Holmes, I still can't believe you're going to Lord Burford's party. What's come over you?

HOLMES: (DRYLY) I have my human moments, Watson. But without wishing to disillusion you, I'd better tell you that our visit tonight is not purely for pleasure – at least not on my part.

WATSON: I thought this was too good to be true. All right, tell me the worst. What is it this time? Are you expecting a dowager's diamonds to be stolen, or is it just a French murderer you're trailing?

HOLMES: (CHUCKLING) Nothing so dramatic, my dear fellow. No, my motive in accepting tonight's invitation is that Monsieur Dubois is going to be there. You've heard of him, of course?

WATSON: (THINKING) Dubois? Dubois? No . . . can't say I have.

HOLMES: Come, come, old fellow. A couple of months away from me and your brain returns to its normal state of atrophy.

WATSON: Well, really, Holmes. What a thing to say.

HOLMES: Andre Dubois is the head of the *Sûreté*. The greatest detective in France. I haven't seen him for years.

WATSON: Dubois! Of course. So he's going to be there?

HOLMES: A very interesting man, Watson. Also I'm curious to see what kind of parties a famous detective goes to. You never know, Watson, I might want to give a *soiree* at Baker Street one of these days.

WATSON: (LAUGHING) What an idea! 'Pon my soul, Holmes, this Parisian air has made you positively facetious!

285

HOLMES: Here we are. Number 275. Come on.

SOUND EFFECT: FOOTSTEPS MOUNTING STEPS. FOOTSTEPS STOP. PEAL OF DOORBELL JANGLING (OFF)

HOLMES: Is my tie straight?

WATSON: Is it ever? Here, let me fix it. (LAUGHING) I never thought I'd live to see the day you'd be going to a party in Paris dressed in evening clothes.

HOLMES: I must admit . . . .

SOUND EFFECT: DOOR OPENS. SOUNDS OF ORCHESTRA PLAYING IN BACKGROUND

MAID: (FRENCH) *Bon soir, messieurs.*

HOLMES: *Bon soir.*

WATSON: Evenin'

MAID: Lord Burford *vous osporo* . . . .

HOLMES: *Merci.*

SOUND EFFECT: DOOR CLOSES. MUSIC LOUDER

WATSON: What a crowd. Everyone in Paris must be here.

MAID: *Vous voulez laissor les chapeaux, messieurs?*

HOLMES: *A vec plaisir.* Watson, your hat.

WATSON: Hmm? Oh, my hat . . . Here.

MAID: *Merci, monsieur.*

WATSON: Thanks.

HOLMES: Come on. Let's go and find our host.

MAID: *Vous trouney* Lord Burford *sans le salon.*

<u>MUSIC: (UP LOUDER)</u>

(AD-LIB OF VOICES IN BACKGROUND)

WATSON: I say, Holmes, look at that ravishing creature over there with the crowd around her. Never seen a more beautiful woman in my life. I wonder who she is.

HOLMES: (DISINTERESTEDLY) I've no idea, but you can find out when we meet our host – and there he is, unless I'm much mistaken. Ah yes . . . Good evening, Lord Burford.

BURFORD: Ah, Mr. Sherlock Holmes. It's good to see you again.

HOLMES: May I introduce my friend and colleague, Dr. Watson.

(BURFORD AND WATSON AD LIB: *HOW D'YOU DO'S.*)

BURFORD: A glass of champagne?

HOLMES: I think not, thank you.

BURFORD: You, Doctor?

WATSON: Well, I'm never a man to say no. Thank you. A glass of bubbly'd be very nice.

BURFORD: (CALLING) Champagne *por monsieur* . . . .

HOLMES: I am very eager to meet M. Dubois tonight, Lord Burford. Has he arrived yet?

BURFORD: I don't think so – but he's coming. Here's your champagne, Doctor.

WATSON: Thanks very much.

BURFORD: By the way, Holmes, you'll be flattered to know Mlle. Cejane is very anxious to make your acquaintance.

HOLMES: Mlle. Cejane? I'm afraid I'm not familiar with her name.

BURFORD (LAUGHING) I wouldn't expect you to be familiar with it, my dear fellow. Mlle. Cejane is the famous – or some people say *infamous* – star of the Folies Bergere.

WATSON: (TREMENDOUSLY INTRIGUED) The Folies Bergere. I say, Holmes . . . .

BURFORD: She's standing over there with the group of men around her.

WATSON: By Jove, Holmes, it's the same woman! The one I spotted as we came in.

BURFORD: I see you have a Latin eye for beauty, Doctor Watson. She's particularly anxious to meet you, Holmes. Asked me to tell her as soon as you arrived. She wants to talk to you alone. All sounds very mysterious.

WATSON (CONCERNEDLY) Alone? She can't object to me being there. After all, I've –

HOLMES: Don't worry, old fellow. You'll meet her. Lord Burford, I shall be happy to meet the lady – though I can't for the life of me think what she wants.

BURFORD: Why don't you go out on the balcony there and I'll bring her to you. (FADING) I won't be a minute.

WATSON: I must say, Holmes, this is a strange business. Beautiful women wanting you alone. (LAUGHING) Good thing you've got me for a chaperone.

HOLMES: Really, Watson, your sense of humour gets a little cloying at times.

WATSON: (MUTTERING) That's better than having no sense of humour at all . . . .

HOLMES: What a wonderful view from this balcony. (INHALING) Ah, fill your lungs with that Parisian night air. Now, there's real champagne for you. And look at the Arc de Triumphe down there. Beautiful, beautiful . . . .

WATSON: You're waxing positively lyrical tonight, Holmes.

HOLMES: No doubt it's the influence of –

BURFORD: (FADING IN) Mademoiselle Cejane, May I have the pleasure of introducing Mr. Sherlock Holmes and Doctor Watson.

MLLE. CEJANE: *Enchanté.*

BURFORD: And now, Mademoiselle, I have kept my promise and I shall leave you. (FADING) I shall ask you for a dance later . . . .

MLLE. CEJANE: (YOUNGISH, WITH AN INFECTIOUS LAUGH AND A GREAT DEAL OF CHARM. FRENCH ACCENT) So you are the great Sherlock Holmes, eh? (SHE LAUGHS)

HOLMES: Sherlock Holmes is my name. The "great" is your own addition, Mademoiselle.

WATSON: (FERVENTLY) Mlle. Cejane, this is indeed a great pleasure. I haven't yet had the privilege of seeing you at the . . . ah . . . Folies Bergere, but I hope to remedy that omission before I return to England.

MLLE. CEJANE: I will arrange for you to have a box.

WATSON: I say, really? May I get you a glass of champagne, Mademoiselle?

MLLE. CEJANE: Do not bother, *cher* Doctor. Give me a sip of yours. We make it a loving cup. You do not mind, do you?

WATSON: (COMPLETELY ENSLAVED) Mind? I should say not. I can't tell you how –

289

HOLMES: (INTERRUPTING IMPATIENTLY) Mademoiselle, I understood from Lord Burford that you wished to see me in private. I am not exactly a lady's man, and I should be glad to learn the nature of your problem.

MLLE. CEJANE: (LAUGHING) I have no problem, Mr. Holmes. I wanted to meet you for two reasons. Firstly, I want to tell you that I think you are a fraud.

HOLMES: A fraud. How interesting. Pray continue.

MLLE. CEJANE: And secondly I want to make a wager with you for any sum you care to name that I can prove you are a fraud.

WATSON: (LAUGHING) Obviously you are joking, Mademoiselle.

MLLE. CEJANE: (SUDDENLY SERIOUS) I am not joking.

HOLMES: (KEENLY) I didn't think you were. Please continue. You interest me very much.

MLLE. CEJANE: In my modest way, am a student of criminology too. And I have studied your cases in the papers . . . very closely, and I say you have been very lucky because you have been dealing with fools. You are no cleverer than any other detective. You have only caught your criminals because they were stupid. Every time you cross swords with a clever man, you lose, For instance, my friend Professor Moriarty has consistently fooled you.

WATSON: Moriarty! Good Lord. D'you know that scoundrel?

MLLE. CEJANE: Very well. Many times we have laughed together over your feeble attempts to catch him, Mr. Holmes.

HOLMES: I only hope, for your own sakes, Mademoiselle that you continue to laugh. And now may I ask the nature of this wager you have just proposed?

MLLE. CEJANE: Tomorrow night I am giving a little supper party after the performance. I want you and your friend here Doctor . . . er . . . .

290

WATSON: (EAGERLY) Watson.

MLLE. CEJANE: Doctor Watson. I want you to attend the party, because I propose to kill a certain gentleman before your very eyes.

WATSON: Good Heavens! You're joking! The whole thing's a –

HOLMES: (INTERRUPTING) And the wager?

MLLE. CEJANE: Fifty-thousand francs – a hundred-thousand – any sum that you care to name that you cannot catch me. If you do, you will win the bet, and I shall say that you are a very great detective.

HOLMES: And if I fail?

MLLE. CEJANE: If you fail – and you will fail – I shall be many thousand francs richer, and you will be the laughing stock of Paris . . . and the world. What do you say, *mon cher degonfleu*?

HOLMES: It's an interesting offer, Mademoiselle. I shall think about it.

MLLE. CEJANE: If you have the courage to accept, I shall expect you at midnight tomorrow. 213 Place de l'Etoile. (FADING) *Au revoir, Messieurs* . . . .

HOLMES: *A bientot*, Mademoiselle.

WATSON: Good night, Mademoiselle Cejane. (AFTER A MOMENT) Holmes, what d'you make of it. Obviously an elaborate joke, don't you think?

HOLMES: I'm not so sure, Watson, The lady, for all her apparent flippancy, is obviously intelligent and shrewd. I shall have to think about it. In the meantime, let's go and find M. Dubois.

SOUND EFFECT: (MUSIC UP STRONGER) AD LIB VOICES IN BACKGROUND.

WATSON: Ravishingly beautiful woman. (LAUGHING) Did you notice the way she sipped out of my glass?

291

HOLMES: I did. Gross familiarity, my dear fellow. Besides being unsanitary.

WATSON: What d'you mean Holmes? There's nothing –

HOLMES: (INTERRUPTING) Ah, there's Dubois. (CALLING) M. Dubois, how are you?

DUBOIS: (FADING IN. ABOUT FIFTY. FRENCH ACCENT) Monsieur Holmes, I am glad to see you again. And this must be Dr. Watson.

WATSON: How d'you do, Monsieur Dubois.

DUBOIS: I trust you're having a pleasant stay in Paris. After your brilliant handling of the train murders in Lyons, you are certainly entitled to a peaceful holiday.

HOLMES: It's been peaceful enough – so much so that I'm starting to get a little restless.

DUBOIS: The war horse snorting for action, eh? (LAUGHING) I myself would welcome a little rest, but alas, unlike you, I have to handle every case that comes my way. That is the penalty of being a professional criminal investigator.

HOLMES: Monsieur Dubois, no doubt you are familiar with Mlle. Cejane?

DUBOIS: But certainly. Don't tell me you know her?

WATSON: We met her tonight. Fascinating woman.

HOLMES: What d'you know about her?

DUBOIS: Well, as Dr. Watson points out, she is very beautiful. One might say she is a woman of mystery. She has had four husbands, and all of them died rather mysteriously, leaving her large sums of money. At the moment she is contemplating a fifth marriage – to Baron Lechaise, the perfume manufacturer. Can't say I envy the gentleman.

HOLMES: You say her previous husbands died mysteriously?

292

DUBOIS: Yes. I'm speaking unofficially, of course. We've had our eyes on the charming lady for many years now.

HOLMES: Interesting. Very interesting. Watson, d'you remember the lady's address?

WATSON: Certainly. 213 Place de l'Etoile. You don't mean –

HOLMES: I mean, my dear fellow, that tomorrow we will join her midnight supper party. I accept Mademoiselle Cejane's challenge!

MUSIC: BRIDGE

SOUND EFFECT: DOOR OPENS

MLLE. CEJANE: (FADING IN) *Bonsoir*, Mr. Holmes. Doctor. I'm very happy that you accepted my invitation after all.

HOLMES: I found it irresistible, Mademoiselle.

SOUND EFFECT: DOOR CLOSES

WATSON: (FADING IN) Good evening.

MLLE. CEJANE: Will you place your hats and coats on the chair there? I let my maid go home. I shall serve supper myself. I think it will be more cosy that way, don't you?

WATSON: Oh, much. (LOWERING HIS VOICE) I can't tell you how much I enjoyed your performance tonight, Mademoiselle. (LAUGHING SELF-CONSCIOUSLY) A little . . . er . . . *daring*, if I may say so, but you were wonderful.

HOLMES: (OFF A LITTLE) Watson . . . did you attend the Folies Bergere tonight?

WATSON: Certainly I did. Why shouldn't I?

HOLMES: No reason at all, my dear fellow, except that you told me you had a special permit to study the paintings in the Louvre.

293

MLLE. CEJANE: Mr. Holmes, before we go into the other room, I should like to be quite clear about our wager. How much are you prepared to gamble?

HOLMES: I never gamble. I only bet on certainties.

MLLE. CEJANE: A hundred-thousand francs?

HOLMES: Very well.

WASOLN: That's a lot of money, Holmes.

MLLE. CEJANE: Your friend has a lot of confidence, Doctor, And so have I. Now, in the other room, awaiting us, is Baron Lechaise. Before tonight's supper is finished, he will be dead. If you are unable to prove I killed him, you will pay me a hundred-thousand francs, Mr. Holmes. Am I right?

HOLMES: Correct, Mademoiselle.

MLLE. CEJANE: Then shall we go in?

HOLMES: One moment, Mademoiselle. Does Baron Lechaise know he is in danger?

MLLE. CEJANE: Oh yes, though he doesn't really believe it.

HOLMES: Then I may speak freely in front of him?

MLLE. CEJANE: *Certainement.*

HOLMES: Very well. I am anxious to meet the gentleman.

MLLE. CEJANE: This way.

WATSON: This whole thing's absolutely fantastic.

SOUND EFFECT: DOOR OPEN

MLLE. CEJANE: Alex, *mon cher*, our party is complete. May I introduce Mr. Sherlock Holmes and Doctor Watson? Baron Lechaise.

(HOLMES, WATSON, and LECHAISE AD LIB: *HOW D'YOU DO'S*)

MLLE. CEJANE: And now I'll serve supper. (FADING) I'm famished, and I'm sure you are . . . .

HOLMES: Baron Lechaise., I understand that you know your fiancée. Mlle. Cejane, thinks there is to be an attempt on your life tonight?

LECHAISE: (ELDERLY, FRENCH ACCENT, CACKLING LAUGH) Of course I know. (LAUGHING) Eloise is a fanciful child, but we must humour her. If she thinks I'm going to die tonight . . . (CACKLING LOUDER) I'll just have to die, that's all. Eloise always gets her own way.

WATSON: Well, 'pon my soul –

MLLE. CEJANE: (OFF A LITTLE) Come on, gentlemen. Supper is ready. (COMING ON) You sit here, Mr. Holmes, on my right, and you on my left, Alex, so that Mr. Holmes can keep his eyes on you. And will you sit there, Doctor?

SOUND EFFECT: SCRAPING OF CHAIRS AS PEOPLE SEAT THEMSELVES

LECHAISE: Oysters. Delightful, Eloise. Delightful. Don't you think Mr. Holmes should examine them first to see if there's any powered glass in them? (HE CACKLES AGAIN)

WATSON: (NERVOUSLY) I say, Holmes, d'you really think there might be anything wrong with 'em?

MLLE. CEJANE: Don't worry, Doctor. Look – I am eating my oysters. And so is Mr. Holmes.

WATSON: I haven't got much of an appetite.

LECHAISE: Eat, drink, and be merry, for tomorrow . . . or rather tonight – we die! (HE CACKLES)

MLLE. CEJANE: How about some champagne? The perfect drink to wash down a dozen oysters. There's a bottle behind you in the ice bucket. Perhaps you'd open it, Mr. Holmes – so that you may be certain it hasn't been tampered with.

<u>MUSIC: BRIDGE</u>

LECHAISE: Eloise, my love, you have surpassed yourself. Never have I eaten a better dinner.

MLLE. CEJANE: Dinner is not finished. No meal is complete without coffee. Syrian coffee, brewed in this samovar. I shall pour it.

WATSON: Isn't it unusual to make coffee in a samovar, Mlle. Cejane?

MLLE. CEJANE: Yes, but then I'm an unusual woman, *cher* Doctor.

WATSON: You certainly are, madomiselle, and a very fascinating one too, if I may say so.

MLLE. CEJANE: My second husband – Prince Petroff – insisted on coffee made in the samovar. Will you pass this to the doctor, Mr. Holmes? And here's a cup for you. I hope you enjoy it.

HOLMES: I'm sure I shall, Mademoiselle.

MLLE. CEJANE: I think I should take a taste of it myself first (AFTER A MOMENT) *C'est bon.*

WATSON: (ADMIRINGLY) Perfect hostess. Perfect.

MLLE. CEJANE: Mr. Holmes, how do you feel about our wager now?

HOLMES: Keenly interested as to its outcome, Mademoiselle. The time is nearly up. Dinner is finished.

MLLE. CEJANE: Dinner finishes with the coffee.

WATSON: Why d'you look so serious, Holmes? Don't you realize yet that Mlle. Cejane is just playing an elaborate practical joke on you? Mmm, this coffee's absolutely delicious.

MLLE. CEJANE: Will you not taste it, Mr. Holmes?

LECHAISE: Yes, you'd better make sure it's not poisoned. (CACKLES)

HOLMES: (AFTER A MOMENT) Excellent. My congratulations, Mademoiselle.

LECHAISE: Eloise, my pigeon, mayn't I have a cup? It's quite safe – the great Sherlock Holmes has personally tasted it himself! (CACKLES)

MLLE. CEJANE: Here you are, Alex. May I suggest that M. Holmes pour it and hand it to you himself.

LECHAISE: Thank you, my love. Nothing like a cup of Eloise's Syrian coffee to finish off a good dinner.

HOLMES: Here you are, sir.

LECHAISE: Thank you.

SOUND EFFECT: THERE IS A MOMENT'S PAUSE, FOLLOWED BY A DESPERATE GASP OF AGONY. THEN THE CRASH OF GLASS AND SILVERWARE AS A BODY SLUMPS TO THE TABLE.

WATSON: Great Heavens! Holmes . . . Holmes . . . He's dead!

HOLMES: (SNIFFS) Yes. Poisoned!

MUSIC: (UP STRONG)

CAMPBELL: In just a few seconds, we'll continue with tonight's adventure, and I hope you've enjoyed the story so far. And say, I hope you've had the chance to try those wonderful after-dinner wines, Petri California Port and Petri California Muscatel. Everybody, of course, likes Port Wine, but just wait till you try a Petri Port and you'll learn just how delicious a Port can be. Rich and full flavored, hearty and full bodied, that deep red Petri Port is the kind of wine you want to linger over, so that you don't miss a single drop of its goodness. You'll love Petri Muscatel, too. It's a different wine, shining gold in color, and most unusual in flavor. Petri Muscatel is probably the most popular after-dinner wine with all the ladies. Try both wines – and serve them proudly – because the name *Petri* is the proudest name in the history of American wines.

297

MUSIC: STING

CAMPBELL: And now back to tonight's new Sherlock Holmes adventure. In Paris, Holmes has accepted a strange wager made to him by Mademoiselle Cejane, star of the Folies Bergere – a wager of one-hundred-thousand francs that she would murder a man under his very nose and that Holmes would be unable to prove it. Baron Lechaise has been poisoned with cyanide, and as we rejoin our story, Holmes and Watson are in their hotel room (FADING) discussing the strange mystery . . .

WATSON: Have you seen the papers this morning, Holmes?

HOLMES: Yes. Charming publicity, isn't it?

WATSON: Good Lord, Holmes . . . . (READING) *"Baron Lechaise murdered whilst being guarded by Sherlock Holmes"* – *"So This is England's Great Detective!"* – *"Mademoiselle Cejane Explains That She Warned Sherlock"* . . . .

HOLMES: (IRRITABLY) All right, all right. I've read them for myself.

WATSON: But what are you going to do, Holmes? This'll ruin you. You'll never be able to show your face in Baker Street again. You'll be the laughing stock of the world.

HOLMES: Don't worry, my dear fellow. I think I know how the murder was committed. The one thing I need is the proof.

WATSON: You know *how* it was done? We found the poison in the cup of coffee that Baron Lechaise drank. But you opened it. You poured the coffee – you tasted it yourself before you handed him the cup. How could it have been done?

HOLMES: I haven't time to explain now, Watson. Time is short and there is too much to be done. I wouldn't be able to convict Mlle. Cejane by ordinary methods, so I shall have to resort to extraordinary ones. Watson, I want you to see M. Dubois and tell him that if he will have dinner with me tonight here in our room, I promise to solve the death of Baron Lechaise for him. Then go to Mlle. Cejane and tell her that

298

if she will join me at the same time, I will give her my check for one-hundred-thousand francs.

WATSON: You mean you're going to –

HOLMES: I mean that I shall be host at tonight's party, and I think I can promise you at least as exciting a party as you attended last night!

MUSIC: BRIDGE

SOUND EFFECT: CLINK OF GLASSES, KNIVES, AND FORKS

MLLE. CEJANE: A very excellent dinner, Mr. Holmes. Allow me to congratulate you.

HOLMES: Thank you. And you, M. Dubois – I trust you enjoyed it.

DUBOIS: Splendid, but I am most anxious to hear your solution or the death of Baron Lechaise.

WATSON: So am I.

MLLE. CEJANE: (LAUGHING) So you have solved poor Alex's murder, Mr. Holmes. You are more clever than I thought you were. Don't tell me I'm not to get my hundred-thousand francs after all?

HOLMES: We shall see, Mademoiselle, we shall see.

SOUND: SCRAPING OF CHAIR BEING PUSHED BACK

HOLMES: And now, before I explain the murder to you, I wonder if you would be so kind, Mademoiselle, as to permit me to light my pipe? The soothing draught of tobacco is conducive to clear thinking.

MLLE. CEJANE: Please do, Mr. Holmes.

HOLMES: Thank you, Mademoiselle. Oh, by the way, as evidence of good faith let me present you with my check for one-hundred-thousand francs.

MLLE. CEJANE: *Merci.*

299

HOLMES: Suppose you don't take it just now. Let us give it to M. Dubois for the moment. He is the official representative of the police and can act as a sort-of referee.

MLLE. CEJANE: (LAUGHING) Really, Mr. Holmes, you're even more stupid than I thought you were. How can you possibly prove I murdered poor Alex? I was sitting beside you all the time.

HOLMES: You murdered him, Mademoiselle, by remote control.

DUBOIS: "Remote control"? Really, Holmes, I wish you'd be a little more explicit.

WATSON: So do I. I can't make heads or tails of the whole thing.

HOLMES: Very well. Let me reconstruct the crime. Baron Lechaise had made a will in Mademoiselle Cejane's favor, and she wanted him dead so that she could marry a younger man. That takes care of the motive. The execution was very ingenious. She told the Baron that she was going to play a trick on me to make me look foolish, and she asked his cooperation. She gave him a small capsule that he held in his hand during dinner last night. She had told him the capsule contained a harmless potion that would knock him out for a couple of hours. Actually, as we know the capsule contained cyanide and, believing he was helping you in a little joke, slipped the deadly potion into his coffee as I handed it to him.

MLLE. CEJANE: (LAUGHING) A clever theory, Mr. Sherlock Holmes. But what evidence, may I ask, do you have to substantiate it?

HOLMES: The only evidence I can possibly have will be your own signed confession. Mlle. Cejane. That is why I asked M. Dubois to be present.

DUBOIS: Mlle. Cejane, what have you got to say to this accusation?

MLLE. CEJANE: That it is ridiculous. It's typical of his methods. Here he has presented an entirely imaginary reconstruction of the crime, and he has not a single piece of evidence to prove it.

DUBOIS: I must say, Holmes, that ingenious though your theory is – it's just pure deduction.

WATSON: Yes. You can't prove that it wasn't suicide.

HOLMES: Mlle. Cejane, you refuse to sign a confession of guilt?

SOUND EFFECT: CHAIR BEING PUSHED BACK

MLLE. CEJANE (ANGRILY) This is ridiculous! I am not going to stay
here and –

HOLMES: Please sit down again, Mlle. Cejane. I have bad news for you.

MLLE. CEJANE: Bad news? What do you mean?

HOLMES: I foresaw that I would have difficulty in getting your
confession by legal methods, and so I have been compelled to go
outside the law myself. I realize, M. Dubois, that I may have to stand
trial for murder myself.

WATSON: Murder? Holmes, what are you . . . ?

MLLE. CEJANE: You're trying to frighten me and it will get you
nowhere.

HOLMES: We shall see. Mlle. Cejane, just new you complimented me on
the dinner. I regret to inform you that your own meal was not quite
as perfect as ours. You see, I poisoned *you*.

MLLE. CEJANE: (SHAKILY) I do not believe you.

HOLMES: I think you do believe me. You will recall that I left the room
just before the chicken was served, I took the liberty of injecting your
portion with a small, but extremely potent, substance that I shall not
name unless I have to. Suffice that it is lethal and at this very moment
is starting to work on you. However, if you change your mind and
decide to sign the confession, I shall be most happy to give you the
antidote.

MLLE. CEJANE: You're lying! I know you're lying! You can't frighten
me!

HOLMES: I'm not trying to. You're a practical woman and I'm treating you in a practical way. Sign the confession and I'll give you the antidote. If you don't, I'm very much afraid you'll die. Of course, you'll have the slight consolation of knowing that I may die too.

MLLE. CEJANE: If I were guilty – which I'm not – and I signed a confession, I'd die anyway under the guillotine. And this way at least you'd die with me.

HOLMES: I don't think you'd die under the guillotine, Mademoiselle. Beautiful women are seldom executed in France. I'm sure you would be judged on a "*crime passionale*".

MLLE. CEJANE: (HYSTERICALLY) You'll never get me to confess! Never! I'd rather die with poison . . . and take you with me!

HOLMES: We're progressing. You will notice, gentlemen, that Mademoiselle is admitting the possibility of a confession.

MLLE. CEJANE: It would be a pleasure to die if I could drag you down with me!

HOLMES: Now there you make a mistake, Mlle. Cejane. The death I have planned for you is far from pleasurable. I injected your chicken with a substance known as *radium salts*. It's really much subtler than cyanide.

MLLE. CEJANE: I don't care! I'm not afraid or pain!

HOLMES: But you are afraid of disfigurement, aren't you?

MLLE. CEJANE: Disfigurement?'

HOLMES: The qualities of radium salts are very unusual. It may take months or even years before you die, but the immediate results are far from pleasant. First of all, your complexion will change a sallow, scaly skin will replace that rose petal texture you cherish so carefully. Your hair will come out slowly at first. Everything will be slow at first. But it will be sure. Your hand – your beautiful hands –

MLLE. CEJANE: (SCREAMING) Stop it! Stop it!

HOLMES: (RELENTLESSLY) Your hand will wither and become gnarled. Your eyesight will fail. Your flesh will be eaten away like a leper's –

MLLE. CEJANE: (CRESCENDO) Quiet! Quiet! I'll sign the confession! Quickly give me the antidote!

HOLMES: Supposing you sign the confession first. Here it is. I have had the foresight to prepare it. All you need to do is to put your name to it. Watson, hand her that pen . . . .

SOUND EFFECT: SCRATCH OF PEN

MLLE. CEJANE: There . . . .

HOLMES: Thank you, Mademoiselle. Here, Dubois. A momento of a difficult case. A case solved without a scrap of evidence.

DUBOIS: Amazing, Holmes. Amazing.

WATSON: Yes, I must say –

MLLE. CEJANE: Stop talking, all of you, and give me the antidote!

HOLMES: The antidote? (HE PAUSES FOR A MOMENT AND THEN CHUCKLES) I'm afraid you're going to be rather angry, Mlle. Cejane. No antidote is needed, because I gave you no poison.

MLLE. CEJANE: No poison! Why you . . . .

HOLMES: Take per away, Dubois, there's a glint in her eyes I don't like. Goodbye, Mademoiselle, and my compliments to your friend Moriarty if you see him. By the way, you really owe me a hundred-thousand francs. I don't suppose you'll pay it, but if you do, make it payable to Madame Curie's Radium Research Fund, will you? She gave me such a beautiful idea.

MUSIC: (UP STRONG TO FINISH)

CAMPBELL: That was a most unusual story, Doctor.

WATSON: That's because Mlle. Celjane was a most unusual woman, Mr. Campbell.

CAMPBELL: A-ha! I see. You still have a warm spot in your heart for her.

WATSON: And why not? She was so beautiful, you could forgive her anything. Why, if she were to walk in here right now – you'd be speechless.

CAMPBELL: Oh, I don't know. I'd think of something to say.

WATSON: (LAUGHING) Yes, you probably would at that. You'd probably tell her all about the Petri family and Petri Wine. (CHUCKLES)

CAMPBELL: (LAUGHING) What a man. To hear you talk, you'd think I spent every waking minute thinking about Petri Wine.

WATSON: Well, don't you? (LAUGHING)

CAMPBELL: I admit I think about it a lot – but after all, it is a pretty terrific wine. And that's because the Petri family took *time* to bring you good wine. Don't forget – the Petri family has been making wine for a good many generations. They've owned the Petri business ever since it was founded – in the nineteenth century. And because they *have* kept the business in the family, everything they've ever learned about the art of turning plump, luscious grapes into clear, fragrant wine . . . they've been able to *hand down* in the family – from father to son, from father to son. So it's only natural that the Petri family are past masters when it comes to making delicious wine. Which means it's only logical that the next time you want a wine to serve before meals, with your dinner, or at *anytime*, you just can't miss with a *Petri* Wine . . . because Petri took time to bring you good wine!

MUSIC: *SCOTCH POEM*

CAMPBELL: Tonight's Sherlock Holmes adventure is written by Denis Green and Bruce Taylor and is based on an incident in the Sir Arthur Conan Doyle story, "The Adventure of the Empty House" *[sic]*. Mr. Rathbone appears through the courtesy of Metro-Goldwyn-Mayer, and Mr. Bruce through the courtesy of Universal Pictures, where they are now starring in the Sherlock Holmes series.

MUSIC: (THEME UP AND DOWN UNDER)

CAMPBELL: The Petri Wine Company of San Francisco, California invites you to tune in again next, week, same time, same station.

MUSIC: HIT JINGLE

SINGERS: *Oh, the Petri family took the time, to bring you such good wine, so when you eat and when you cook, Remember Petri Wine!*

CAMPBELL: Yes, Petri Wine made by the Petri Wine Company, San Francisco, California.

SINGERS: *Pet – Pet – Petri . . . Wine.*

CAMPBELL: This is Bob Campbell saying goodnight for the Petri family. *Sherlock Holmes* comes to you from the Don Lee studios in Hollywood. This is the Mutual Broadcasting Network!

The Case of
The Blue Parrot
by Roger Riccard

Chapter I

On a cool Saturday autumn morning in 1906, I was lounging in front of the fire at home, casually reading a newspaper, as I awaited my wife to join me for breakfast. My study of the goings-on in the metropolis of London was interrupted by a ring of the doorbell. The maid answered but wasn't allowed to announce our guest, as he pushed passed her straight to our parlor and called out in a French accent, "Are you *the* Dr. John Watson, associate of Mr. Sherlock Holmes?"

He was a rough-clad fellow in layman's garb that spoke more of the Continent than England. Wild, dark, unkempt hair protruded from under his beret and he bore a thin, curled moustache. He gestured wildly with one arm as he spoke, while leaning heavily on a *T*-handled cane with the other.

I stood and waved the maid away as I faced this rude intruder. "I am he. What can I do for you, sir?"

"You can tell me where Holmes is!" he bellowed. "I've been to Baker Street and that old landlady of his has no clue as to his whereabouts. I need his services, monsieur. It's a matter of life or death!"

He approached me as if he were going to wring the answer from my throat. I instinctively reached for the cane beside my chair to defend myself as I replied, "Holmes no longer lives in Baker Street. I'll thank you to stop bothering Mrs. Hudson, or you'll have to deal with me and the police."

Suddenly, another voice called out, "Stop right there or I'll shoot!"

This command was followed by the click of a cocking pistol and the man froze. He turned slowly with hands raised waist high and palms wide open as he dropped his walking stick. Behind him my wife had entered the room with my Webley revolver in her hand, held steady as a rock. The look on her face told the fellow she would brook no sudden action. After an uncomfortable silence that seemed to drag on interminably, he spoke again, this time with no accent at all.

"My dear Mrs. Watson, do be kind enough not to pull the trigger. I would much prefer a lump of sugar in my tea to a lump of lead in my chest so early on a Saturday morning."

I was taken aback. The voice now was unmistakably that of Sherlock Holmes himself. It was proven so when he pulled off the beret, long haired wig, the thin moustache, and straightened to his full height.

"Darling," I said calmly, "it appears our friend is up to his old tricks."

Facing the detective, I crossed my arms and said, "Really, Holmes, have we not outgrown this little game of yours?"

"I must keep up my hand at disguises, old chum," he replied as he tossed the beret, wig, and moustache into an empty chair, picked up the walking stick, and set it there as well. "You are my penultimate test. If I can pass muster with someone who shared my rooms for the better part of two decades and has seen many of my disguises, it is the threshold to perfection. I can rest assured that I may walk about freely without recognition."

"I would think Mycroft would be your ultimate test," I said, referring to his elder brother, whose observation skills Holmes had admitted, were even greater than his own.

"Exactly so, and one which I have never passed," he declared, with some chagrin. "Thus it falls to you, my dearest friend."

My wife, having set the pistol aside, broke in with a wry smile, "We were about to have breakfast. Would you care to join us and partake of some of that tea which you prefer to my gunshot?"

Holmes bowed and replied, "I would be delighted, madam."

We sat down to the breakfast table and were served with rashers and eggs. Holmes dug in with a relish which I usually attribute to his need to recharge after solving a case. Thus, I enquired about his latest activities.

"Nothing much, Watson. I was able to assist Hopkins in the capture of the Beddington jewelry heist robbers. You will probably read about it when you get to the rest of your morning paper."

"And what adventure brings you to seek out my husband's assistance on this fine autumn day, Mr. Holmes?" asked my wife as she took a sip of tea. "Nothing too dangerous, I hope?"

"Darling!" I exclaimed.

"Oh, really, John. How could you not know that is why he is here?" she said, with a look that made me feel obtuse.

Holmes folded his hands across his waist, "I've always admired your perceptivity, my dear." Turning to me, he said, "I do have an ulterior motive for my visit."

He pulled a letter from his pocket and handed it over, indicating that I should read it aloud. The attached envelope was postmarked Morocco and was oddly addressed to:

Erik Sigerson c/o Diogenes Club
Piccadilly, London, England

Dear Friend Sigerson,

> *I trust you remember your old friend, Ferrari. It has been a long time since you've been to Casablanca, yet I shall never forget the valuable assistance you gave to me and my family in our time of trouble. My son, Anton, is sixteen years old now! He was just a* bambino piccolo *when you were here. We have also been blessed with a daughter, Gabrielle, who is eleven.*
>
> *I realize I expect much, but I am a desperate man, my friend. I am being troubled by rogues who threaten me and my business. They operate in secrecy, so that I cannot even report anything useful to the police that would lead to their arrest. They demand protection money or say they will kill me and my family and simply take over the business themselves. They backed up their threats with samples of damage to my business, such as lighting a fire. I have since been paying it, but their methods of collection are so clever we cannot catch them in the act of picking it up.*
>
> *I am hoping that someone with the skills you exhibited all those years ago can help put an end to this evil. If you can come to our aid, please reply to the French Consulate where I do business regularly. I dare not have such mail come directly to my home.*
>
> *I pray you to look upon me with favor, friend Sigerson, in remembrance of our time together.*

Your ever grateful host,
Val Ferrari

I looked at my friend, "Obviously this relationship dates from your years immediately after Reichenbach. This Ferrari fellow only knew you by your alias. How did you come to know him?"

Holmes leaned back in his seat, teacup in one hand, saucer in the other, eyes gazing upward with the rising steam. "It was early in 1894," he recalled. "I was returning from my time in Tibet *en route* to Paris when

308

my ship stopped at Casablanca in Morocco. We were due to stay in port for two days and I chanced to stop into The Blue Parrot Café for a meal. I was taken ill before I even left the establishment and the owners, Valentino Ferrari and his wife, took me in. They made room for a cot in a spare room and called for a doctor. I was laid up for several days with a stomach ailment and missed my sailing. As it happened, several other patrons were similarly afflicted, though all the others presented symptoms after leaving the café.

"I was able to determine that the food had been deliberately poisoned by one of his competitors, which led to an arrest and the salvation of the café's reputation. It was a quite simple matter to an observant investigator. Ferrari makes far too much of my skills. But then, he is an emotional fellow."

I smiled at his modesty and asked, "Have you replied yet?"

"I've no intention of replying," he stated, to my surprise. Then he added, "Not in writing. Too many chances for interception. Also, while I may trust my French police sources in Paris, my travels through various European colonies has left me with the impression that corruption is too easily found when officials are far from home.

"Therefore, I shall instead reply in person. Which brings me to you, my dear fellow. If your bride and patients can spare you for perhaps two weeks, I should welcome your company."

We both turned to my wife, who was spreading butter onto a steaming hot crumpet. She stopped and looked at us strangely. "What? You thought I would say 'No'? As if that would deter you? I knew what I was getting into when I married you, John. I appreciate the fact that we make important decisions together. But I also know that Mr. Holmes does not take on trivial cases. This Ferrari family deserves his assistance, and if he needs you, I'll not stand in his way.

"However," she voiced, in a much more commanding tone as she pointed her butter knife at the detective, "I hold you responsible for him, Mr. Holmes. You bring my husband back to me safe and unharmed. Promise?"

Holmes held his hand to his heart and replied, "My word of honor, my dear lady."

"Then have a safe trip," she replied. Looking at me, she smiled and added "Don't forget your pistol."

I smiled at her across the table. Turning to Holmes I said, "I have one patient this afternoon that I must see to. I'll make arrangements with Dr. Burnside to cover the rest of my appointments."

Holmes slapped his palm on the table in agreement and replied, "Splendid! We shall leave on the ten o'clock Dover ferry tomorrow

309

morning for Calais. Then a train to Marseille to catch a steamer down to Morocco. I shall resurrect my Sigerson guise, but there is no need for you to be incognito. Although, if asked about *Sherlock Holmes*, I would prefer you to reply that you are not *that* Dr. Watson. Perhaps you could recall the burr of your Scottish roots and be *Dr. Watson of Edinburgh?*"

In my best recollection of my grandfather's voice I replied, "Aye, that I could do, Mr. Sigerson."

My wife looked at us like a couple of schoolboys about to pull a prank and just shook her head as she returned to her meal. Holmes gulped down his tea and rose from the table. "I've preparations to make. I shall see you in the morning." Turning to my wife he added, with a grin, "Thank you for your hospitality, madam," nodding toward my revolver on the end table where she had left it.

Chapter II

I arrived at the Charing Cross railway station precisely at 7:30 the following morning, carpet-bag in hand. I looked about, not sure exactly what appearance Holmes's took on when he was in his *Sigerson* persona.

"Ready to board, Watson?" came a voice from behind me. I turned and there was a tall man with short blond hair, moustache, and short beard. I recognized him at once from his voice, even with the Norwegian accent, but it took several seconds for me to penetrate the visual effect of his disguise.

"Sigerson, old friend!" I replied in my Scots burr as I stuck out my hand. *Sotto voce* I asked, "Was this your appearance when last in Casablanca?"

In a similar low voice he answered, "My facial hair back then was my own beard, grown out over the years of my travels. To appear more Scandinavian, I dyed my hair as you see and affected this accent. But come, it is time to board."

We made good time on the train to Dover, steaming through the countryside at a brisk pace. High clouds overhead had kept the temperature down, and I was glad I packed sufficient clothing for all kinds of weather. During the ride, I was able to learn more about Ferrari from Holmes.

"Valentino Ferrari is from Genoa," stated my companion. "Travels for his father's shipping business took him to Marseille where he met Rosette, the daughter of a French restaurateur. They fell in love, but neither of their families approved. Thus, they eloped and came to Casablanca, another coastal city, where both their cultures thrive. She knew the restaurant business and he knew how to obtain the best prices from shipping companies. That led them to open the café about twenty years ago."

The ferry crossing was a bit rough. Storms in the channel the previous night had left a choppy sea in their wake which slowed our progress. As a result, we had to rush to make our boarding on the next train to Marseille. We would then catch a steamship that would take us to Casablanca *en route* to its final destination in French Indo-China.

The next day aboard ship, we found ourselves among a contingent of French police officials, assigned to Casablanca as advisors to the Moroccan Police under the terms of the Algeciras Conference, signed earlier that year. One chap was a particularly chatty type who spoke English very well and seemed to want to practice on us. The single chevron on his sleeve indicated he was a recent recruit and a *Gardien de la Paix*. (Keeper of the Peace). He was about five-foot-six-inches with a sturdy build. Thick brown hair flowed back from his pleasant round face. My impression was that he wore a thin moustache to make himself appear older, for I doubted he had seen his twentieth birthday. He introduced himself as Louis Renault and asked if we had been to Casablanca before, as he hadn't and was anxious to learn about the place.

Holmes explained that he was an explorer who had passed through Casablanca many years before. He indicated that that he and I had met in Edinburgh some time ago when his ship stopped by, while bound to Greenland. He was taking me to Casablanca where he thought the dry climate might help a medical condition from which I was suffering.

We conversed for some time until the bell tolled for lunch. Throughout the remainder of that voyage, Renault always greeted us cheerily. It seemed that every time we saw him, he was chatting up other passengers, especially those whose destination was Casablanca.

I mentioned this to Holmes, "That Renault is a curious chap. I suppose it is rather smart of him to get to know citizens over whom he will have authority. The better he knows them, the better he can serve the community."

Holmes stroked his goatee and replied, "Remember the words of Sir Francis Bacon, Doctor. '*Knowledge is power*'. This fellow is adept at gaining an arsenal of knowledge which will undoubtedly assist him in his career. As it is, we shall need to be on our guard in any dealings with him."

At last we reached Casablanca. The weather was pleasant, being much closer to the equator than London, and I threw my overcoat over my carpet-bag as I carried it. Holmes made a suggestion which I thought prudent, remembering back to my army days. "Best to tie your sleeves through the handle. When last I was here pickpockets abounded."

311

Holmes observed how much the city had built up in the twelve years since he'd enjoyed the Ferrari's hospitality. Rather than take a chance on an unknown hotel, he requested the cab driver to take us to The Blue Parrot Café. "We'll drop in on Signor Ferrari and seek his advice on the safest hotel for our stay. He can also inform us of any new aspects of his situation."

The streets were bustling with traffic of horse drawn carts, pedestrians, and some few automobiles, such as our cab. I spotted the man-made perch with The Blue Parrot upon it, even before we could read the sign above the arched entryway. As Holmes paid off the cab driver I asked a rhetorical question: "I wonder if that is the same parrot which was here back when you were? This is hardly a natural habitat for such a creature. I imagine it would be expensive to replace."

Holmes walked up to the perch and stared briefly at the blue-and-gold bird and said, "You see . . . ." The bird cocked its head and gave a low gurgle. Holmes repeated the phrase, "You see . . . ." This time the creature bobbed its head up and down twice and replied, "You see, but do not observe – *Awk!*"

Holmes pulled a bit of biscuit he had secreted in a napkin in his pocket at breakfast and held it up for the bird to take. To me he said, "Blue Macaws can live up to fifty years or more in captivity," he replied. "This is Felice, Italian for '*happy*'. I distinctly remember her markings. The story of how she came to be in Casablanca is an interesting one, though not relevant to our case. If you are curious, I suggest you bring it up with Signor Ferrari."

"I should be happy to tell it again, my friend!" came a voice from the doorway. The man making that proclamation was about forty-five years old, of medium build with olive skin, dark hair, and full moustache. He was rather tall, just under six feet by my estimate. His build was average with a bit of a pot belly. He wore a white suit, *sans* coat, though he retained his blue-and-gold necktie which matched the parrot's colors perfectly. He marched right up to Holmes and threw his arms around my companion and gave him a kiss on each cheek.

"Signor Erik, I did not know you were coming!" In a lower voice he asked, "Are you here in response to my letter?"

In a similar low voice, Holmes replied, "Yes, I thought surprise might better fulfill our purpose. This is my friend, Dr. Watson. He has accompanied me on some of my explorations and thought a trip to your warm climes might be a nice change from the chill of his native Scotland."

Ferrari pumped my hand vigorously and said with enthusiasm, "Any compatriot of Erik is most welcome." Looking down, he saw we still had

312

our bags. "You have not checked into your hotel? Where were you going to stay?"

Holmes answered, "With the many changes to your city over the years, I thought it best to obtain your recommendation. Is there a safe place close by?"

Without a second thought our client piped up, "The Hotel Napolitano should be perfect for you and the Doctor. It is merely two streets down that way and around the corner to the right. But first you must come inside and refresh yourselves. I will send Anton to make your reservations."

We stepped into the cool atmosphere of the café. It took a moment for my eyes to adjust, after being out in the bright sunlight. When they did, I saw an expansive dining room with a bar and kitchen at one end, and a stage at the other. The stage held several seats with music stands to one side, which were unoccupied at the moment. The café itself wasn't crowded at this time of day, being a good hour before luncheon. Ferrari led us to the end of the room near the kitchen. He opened the kitchen door and called out, "Rosette, Anton, Gabrielle! Come see who is here!"

A tall woman of perhaps five-foot-eight led the way, wiping her hands on her apron. She was obviously his wife. Unlike her husband, she was stout and pale with light brown hair, and spoke with an accent more French than Italian. "What is it, Vito? We must get the food ready for the noon meal." Then she saw Holmes and cried out, "Monsieur Erik! *Mon Dieu!*" She strode over and subjected Holmes to another hug and more kisses. Holmes introduced me and she curtsied politely, then turned to the children who had followed her from the kitchen. "Gabrielle, Anton, this is Monsieur Erik Sigerson, who helped your papa when we almost lost the café years ago."

"And this is his friend, Dr. Watson." Ferrari added, gesturing to me.

Anton strode forward and held out his hand in greeting. He was large for sixteen. As tall as his father already, yet stout and pale like his mother. His English was perfect, and we later learned that he also spoke his fathers' Italian and his mothers' French fluently, as well as the local Arabic dialect. Gabrielle, with the universal shyness of all eleven-year-old girls, approached us slowly. She took more after her father with her olive skin, long dark hair, and brown eyes. One could see she would grow into a real beauty. She also curtsied and said "Hello." Holmes and I both bowed in our mostly gentlemanly manner, which brought a smile to her face as she retreated to her mothers' side.

Ferrari said to his son, "Anton, go over to the Napolitano. Speak to Signor Martino and tell him I would like him to arrange two adjoining rooms for Signor Sigerson and Dr. Watson."

"On my way, Papa. Gentlemen. If you will excuse me?" he bowed courteously to us and strode out the door to run his errand. His father waved us to seats at a table far from the rest of the light crowd as he requested his wife to bring food and wine. She and her daughter returned to the kitchen. We sat and Holmes asked, "Have there been any further developments in your situation, Valentino?"

The café owner looked about to ensure we weren't overheard, then replied, "There have been new demands, Signor Erik. I do not understand them, but I am compelled to comply."

"What makes these demands unusual?" asked Holmes.

"They are orders to expand my menus and change my entertainers. These extortionists say they want me to be more successful."

I spoke up and commented, "Perhaps they believe the more successful you are, the more money they can extort."

Ferrari shook his head in frustration, "My café has been built on my reputation for quality food and pleasant entertainment. We have been successful for years. There's no reason to change."

Holmes asked, "Does your menu still consist of Italian and French food?"

Ferrari nodded, "Yes. The tourists are comfortable with our cuisine. Yet, in their latest demand, these *criminali* want me to add traditional dishes of English and Spanish food – all because of the new status after the Algeciras Conference, [1] which is bringing in more foreigners than ever before."

Holmes nodded and continued his enquiry, "What changes in entertainment have they suggested? Any particular performer or group?"

Our host shook his head again, "No, no one in particular. They simply want me to change from our traditional Italian and French musicians to include Spanish and English acts as well. They are insisting that we become more *cosmopolita*, so as to attract all the variety of new tourists pouring into the city."

"Did they use that word – *cosmopolita*?"

Ferrari held his open palm to his chest, "No, Signor Erik. That is my own. All of their demands have been written in English."

"Interesting. Do you have the messages they sent?"

"*Sì*. I will get them for you." He left just as Rosette and Gabrielle brought two steaming plates of spaghetti with garlic bread and wine.

"I remember how you enjoyed my spaghetti when you were here before, Signor Erik," she said with an infectious smile. "*Bon appétit*, gentlemen. There is plenty if you want more."

I broke off some bread and began swirling the aromatic pasta around my fork. Holmes merely took a sip of wine and said "I recommend moderation, Doctor. It is a bit spicier than what you are used to at Rivano's in London. He tends to use milder ingredients in his gravy, due to the tastes of the English palate."

Following this caution, I reduced the size of the bite I was about to take. It was indeed spicier. Not so much as the Indian dishes I had been exposed to in my army days, but zesty all the same. I followed it with a sip of wine and was glad I had bicarbonate of soda in my medical bag.

Ferrari soon returned and gave Holmes a handful of typewritten sheets. My companion gazed intently at them, using his magnifying lens. As he did so, Anton returned and advised us that a bellman from the Napolitano was waiting outside with a cart to take our luggage to the hotel. Noting the papers, he asked his father something in Italian, to which Ferrari replied, "Do not be rude, my son. Signor Erik was of extreme help the last time someone tried to take over our business. I've asked for his assistance again. I trust him as a *fratello*. You will do anything he asks while he is here, so we may get to the bottom of this madness."

"As you say, Papa," he nodded. To us he bowed and added, "At your service, gentlemen."

"Thank you, Anton," replied Holmes. "Ferrari, I should like to take these with me to examine more closely."

"Anything you need."

"May we also take our food with us? I should not wish to insult Rosette, but I would like to settle into our rooms and get started on this problem quickly."

"Of course! Thank you, Erik!"

"Excellent! We shall return this afternoon."

Chapter III

We quickly settled into our rooms. Once unpacked, I knocked on the adjoining door and walked in at Holmes's invitation. I saw that he had set the various dishes used to transport our spaghetti on a small table, and he indicated I should go ahead and eat while it was still warm. He had spread the letters out on the bed in order by the dates Ferrari had written on them. Each was neatly typed, so there would be no handwriting to analyze. That in itself meant something to my friend.

"There are two primary reasons to type such messages, Watson: Either to disguise the person's handwriting, which implies that Ferrari may have been able to recognize it, or the writer has some deformity or handicap which makes handwriting difficult or impossible."

I nodded in agreement as I continued to eat and poured myself more wine from the bottle Ferrari had sent along. "I would think the former is

315

more likely. Although I suppose you can ask Ferrari if he knows any such handicapped person."

Holmes nodded and continued, "I also note that the requests seem to broaden as they move forward in time. This extortionist has become more confident by his successes and begins to suggest changes to the operations of the business. Also note the difference in the sums he demands. They do not remain the same, nor do they continually increase, as is common with this type of crime. He asks for smaller amounts of cash when he requires a change in the business that will require expenditures."

"What changes has he asked for?" I enquired.

"The first was to replace the coal burning stoves in the kitchen with gas ovens. That demand appeared in the third letter, after the first two were merely for cash. Then, the cash demands reduced for a time, apparently in response to the expense Ferrari incurred to put in the new ovens.

"The next improvement was to put the musicians on tiered levels instead of having them flat on the stage – apparently an effort to improve the sound quality of the entertainment."

I finished off my garlic bread and took a sip of the excellent Merlot before replying. "It appears Ferrari's extortionist has the man's success at heart. One could almost look upon it as having a paid consultant – albeit an enforced one."

"Which begs the question, Doctor: Who benefits from this arrangement?"

"Certainly the extortionist," I observed. "He's getting money through threats, and obviously the more successful Ferrari becomes, the greater this person can raise their demands."

"What have I said in the past about obvious facts?" countered my companion.

I searched my memory and recalled, "That there is nothing more deceiving."

"Precisely," answered Holmes. "We need to take a closer look at all the players in this game. There is more data to gather before we draw any definite conclusions. First we must determine the source of these letters."

He handed me his magnifying lens and the first letter. "Tell me what you see."

I read through the demand and it seemed straightforward enough. The money was to be paid in paper currency and placed in an envelope to be delivered by the boy, Anton. He was to walk along a specific street until confronted, and then turn the money over. There was the usual demand for no police or any tricks, or the boy would be the first to suffer. Since Holmes had handed me his lens, it seemed apparent that I was to study the document itself, rather than just read it. The paper was a clean, white, quarto-sized sheet. The typing was neatly done with no spelling errors. I looked at specific letters to see if there were any distinguishing characteristics. A few of them appeared smudgy, while the rest were clean and crisp. I commented upon these to Holmes, and he nodded approvingly.

"Anything else?" he queried.

I took another look and noticed the watermark, "This paper seems to have been manufactured in Italy. The name on the watermark appears to be Italian. Could he have an enemy from his home country who has come to Casablanca for some type of revenge? Or perhaps another Italian business rival?"

Holmes shook his head, "Not Italian, Watson. Latin, which could mean anywhere in Europe. But, there is a telling clue in the salutation. Look closely."

I leaned in as close as possible to the document with the lens and noticed that there appeared to be scrape marks above the letter *n* in *Signor Ferrari*. Almost as if someone attempted to peel away a layer of paper. I reported my finding to Holmes.

"Precisely. I believe the person who typed this letter was unfamiliar with the keyboard and didn't realize his error until it appeared on the page. He then used a pen knife or razor to attempt to scrape away the telltale mark."

"What mark?" I asked.

"I would contend that our extortionist was using a Spanish typewriter. While it has all the normal English letters, it also has a key for the letter *n* with a tilde above it for typing words like *señor*. He used the correct key later on for the rest of the *n*'s but he was afraid to let that one be noticed, and likely didn't have time to retype the letter. Another telling fact."

"What do you conclude from this?" I asked.

"We shall have to determine what businesses have Spanish typewriters. It will most likely be one where the person wasn't a regular employee, but was borrowing the typewriter surreptitiously and had limited time to use it. It may also mean that he is a Spaniard and typed that character out of habit."

I nodded and asked, "Just how do we go about that? With all the recent immigration since the Algeciras Conference, there must be dozens of new Spanish businesses, not to mention those that have been here for decades."

"I believe we shall start with the Spanish Consulate."

"There is a consular office here? I read that the Spanish Embassy is in Rabat."

317

"It is," affirmed Holmes. "However, with the population of Casablanca being the second largest in all Morocco, they have installed an office here as well.

"First, however, we shall return these dishes and silverware to The Blue Parrot and question Ferrari and his son further. I need to see just how this person or people were able to avoid capture."

Chapter IV

Not long after, we were back at The Blue Parrot. Holmes had chosen to return at a time when it was more likely that the lunch crowd had dwindled so that our client and his family wouldn't be too busy to speak with us.

We settled again near the kitchen, far from the few remaining patrons. Ferrari and his son sat with us and Holmes peppered them with questions. I could barely keep up my note-taking whenever the father spoke. Occasionally, he would slip into his native tongue and when he had to repeat himself in English, it allowed me to catch up. Anton, on the other hand, was very deliberate in his speech. He took his time with his answers, so that he might give all the detail he could remember.

"I walked down that street, as they demanded. It was dark at that time of night and the streetlamps in the area are far apart. I was just passing an alley when someone stepped out of the shadows and gave the code phrase."

"Can you describe him or her?" queried the detective.

Anton raised his eyebrows, "It never occurred to me that it might be a woman, although the voice was of a high pitch. I still believe it was a man. He was dressed all in black with a black fedora pulled low and a scarf covering up most of his face. He was a short fellow, less than five-and-a-half feet tall, I should think. He had a small pistol in his hand, so I wasn't inclined to argue. He demanded the envelope and I handed it over. He warned me not to follow and ran back down the alley, turning to the right when he got to the far end. As I am not athletic," he continued, looking down at his stout physique, "I did not pursue."

"Very likely a reason they chose you," said Holmes. "I should like to visit the scenes of all these drop-offs at your convenience."

"Certainly. I have a meeting with my tutor this evening, but I can be free up until seven o'clock."

"That will be a good start, thank you," replied my friend.

We spent next forty-five minutes going over the various scenarios where money was delivered. The places all varied, they were all at night, and they all provided a convenient escape route with multiple options in

318

case of pursuit. The person had no discernible accent, just the high-pitched voice. Other than being short, he was of average build and seemed well-coordinated as he ran. Anton had no knowledge of pistols. He could only tell us the weapon was a revolver.

As we still had some daylight left to us, Holmes requested that Anton and his father take us to the places where the money was taken. Ferrari informed his *maître d'* to take charge while he was gone. This man, whose name was Vito, was a short, balding fellow of average build with a handlebar moustache and a distinct Italian accent. He bowed and replied *"Assolutamente, signor,"* and returned to his duties.

Once outside, Holmes insisted that we visit our destinations in the order in which they occurred. Ferrari hailed a cab and gave directions to the driver. As we rode, Holmes asked our client, "How many employees do you have?"

Ferrari named them off on his fingers, "The family, of course. Then Vito, who has been with me for three years. I have two bartenders, Aramis and Gilberto. Aramis was here when you last visited. He is a cousin of Rosette. Gilberto came to us about a year ago, when old Carlos retired. He only works nights as he has a day job at the Spanish Consulate as a courier. We have two other cooks besides Rosette and Gabrielle. There are two waiters and three waitresses. Oh, yes, there are also three busboys and the cleaning staff, which is the three Manetti sisters."

Holmes nodded, while I was impressed at the size of the operation, and certain Holmes had caught the Spanish Consulate connection. The detective then asked, "Have you ever had any problems with any of them, or has anyone complained about their pay?"

Ferrari shook his head, "Never a complaint. I treat my employees very well."

I observed at that statement that Anton slightly shifted in his seat, bowed his head and pursed his lips briefly. They were all subtle movements and his father didn't notice, but I'm sure Holmes did, though he chose not to enquire at that time.

Ferrari went on, "Gilberto, the bartender, has twice asked me for an advance on his pay, in regards to some medical bills for his wife."

"Did you advance him the money?" asked Holmes.

"That favor is usually reserved only for my most long term and trusted employees, Signor Erik. However, I did take pity on him, for I have met his wife and she is a frail little thing. I insisted, however, on paying the doctor directly, just to be safe."

"A wise precaution," stated my friend.

We arrived at the first drop point, the alley where the thief took to his heels. It had been several weeks, so Holmes didn't expect to find any physical evidence. He primarily wanted to examine the scene as to why it was chosen. This would gain him some insight into the extortionists' mind.

He turned to Anton, "Where were you when you heard his voice?"

Anton took a stance on the pavement, "Right about here."

"And where was he standing?"

"From where you are, about two steps back and over next to the wall."

Holmes took up the indicated spot. "So he was here when he spoke to you. Did he have the gun pointed at you, or just in his hand?"

"He was holding it at his right hip, pointed at me."

Holmes nodded, "Walk through the motions of what happened."

"He called out my name and said, 'Come here!' Anton started walking toward Holmes and then stopped. "When I got to this point, he told me to stop and put the envelope on an old crate that was there against the wall. Then he made me take two steps backward. He picked up the envelope, peeked inside, and said, 'Very good. Now stand there until I'm out of sight. If you try to follow I will shoot.' He turned and ran down to that end of the alley and turned to the right."

Holmes examined the area where the perpetrator stood, noting a side door to the establishment next to the alley nearby. He then walked out to the street, looking up and down at the various businesses and streetlamp locations. Satisfied, he then led us down the alley to the far end and turned right to see what lay in that direction. It was another alley, a bit broader, where many of the businesses had their loading doors or rear entrances. A half-dozen possibilities presented themselves as to where the man had gone, or he could have even run on down that alley to another intersection. As long as he maintained a fair distance, there were a myriad of ways to elude capture. Again, a sound reason for insisting upon the bulky Anton as the carrier.

Holmes waved us back to the waiting cab to proceed to the next destination. As we walked he asked another question. "You say he looked into the envelope to ensure the money was there. Was the envelope sealed? Did he tear it open?"

The teenager replied, "It was not sealed, Mr. Sigerson. He merely lifted the flap and took a quick look. He did not take time to count it."

Holmes acknowledged this answer with a mere hum and we moved on to repeat the same routine at all the other destinations. Each one was chosen for its multiple escape routes. Some were foyers of hotels or shops, where Anton was called in off the street and the same person that made him go back outside while he slipped out one of many possible exits. One was a spot under a balcony where the culprit lowered a basket on a rope for the envelope. A little money slipped to the manager revealed that the room was supposed to be unoccupied, and no one recalled any person leaving through the lobby at the time in question. To be thorough, Holmes suggested a look at the roof, where evidence suggested someone had crossed over to a neighboring rooftop, though pinning down an exact time frame was impossible.

By this time, it was dusk and we returned to The Blue Parrot so that Anton could eat before going to his lesson. Ferrari insisted we join them for dinner. As we were eating – or rather, I was eating while Holmes smoked and drank coffee – I asked the young man what subjects he was being tutored in.

"I am studying Spanish, Doctor. I have a desire to increase my language skills to include all those spoken in our fair city."

Chapter V

Holmes eyebrows raised at that remark and he enquired, "A noble ambition, young man. Where do you study?"

"A friend of mine works at the Spanish Consulate. We meet at the city library and trade lessons. He teaches me Spanish and I teach him French."

"How convenient," replied Holmes. "What does this fellow do at the Consulate?"

Anton cocked his head and replied curiously, "He's just a clerk. He's a bit older than me, but not much. We met in the marketplace. We were at adjoining booths haggling over prices with merchants who chose not to understand what we were saying in order to frustrate us into paying their high prices. As we overheard what was going on, we came to each other's rescue by translating for one another."

"Most fortuitous," stated the detective. "I have some business with the Consulate. Perhaps I shall run into him. What is his name?"

The rotund teenager dabbed at his mouth with his napkin and replied. "Pablo. Pablo Ugarte. But he works in a little back office processing paperwork. I doubt that you would chance to see him."

Holmes raised his wineglass toward the youth, "Paperwork processing is exactly what I need. In my line of work, I often need permission from government officials to enter certain areas for exploration, especially when I'm working with archeologists. There is a British expedition scheduled for early next year. I thought I would visit the Spanish and French Consulates while I am here now, to see what papers will be necessary under this new ruling conglomerate of nations. What does this Ugarte look like?"

Anton stood to leave for his appointment and replied, "He is a short fellow, perhaps five-foot-three inches and maybe one-hundred-thirty pounds. He has black hair cut very short and is clean shaven. His face is very round with brown eyes that have a sort of sleepy look to them."

He then chortled. "He has a bit of a wheezy, nasal voice, but altogether he can be a charming fellow. Now, if you'll excuse me, I don't wish to be late. Shall I tell him you'll be coming by the Consulate?"

"Yes, that would be splendid," said Holmes. "It's always well to have an inside connection when doing business."

"But he's just a clerk, Monsieur Sigerson. He has little influence."

"Ah, you never know, Anton. Just as if you wish to know the intimate secrets of a household you ask the servants, so too, with most businesses, including government. You can often learn more from the staff members than the directors and officers. Have a good lesson."

The lad left us, as did his father to attend to his patrons now that the dinner hour was filling the café. I presumed Holmes would wish to go back to the hotel to smoke a few pipes over the information he had gathered today. I was thus surprised when he merely sat back and lit up a cigar as he shifted his chair for a better view of the small stage where musicians were about to begin the entertainment.

The leader of this little band announced from the stage that they were going to play a series of songs from a popular American Broadway musical, *Little Johnny Jones* [2]. He turned to his troupe and began a series of lively tunes comprised of ballads, ditties, and rousing cadences. For a group of a mere eight musicians, they performed extraordinarily well, even though the café was filled with the usual bustling noises of meals being served, tables being cleared, and multitudes of conversations taking place.

I thoroughly enjoyed them. Holmes, however, was busily scanning the room. At one point, he got up and walked a long circuitous route of the entire café, pausing on occasion to take a longer look at certain personages. He also closely observed the musicians from the side of the stage, applauding them as an admirer to allay suspicion of the fact that he was studying them.

He returned to the table and sparingly ate some bread and cheese while finishing off a second glass of wine. When the performers took a break, he suggested we make our *adieus* to Ferrari and return to the hotel. When we parted ways for our separate rooms, he informed me that he would be going back out for an hour or so and that he would see me in the morning at eight. I asked if he could use my assistance but he declined and replied, "Merely a little reconnoitering. I feel an urge to visit the library."

Chapter VI

The next morning I was at the hotel restaurant, enjoying a cup of coffee and debating whether to order breakfast, as I didn't know what Holmes's plans might be. He arrived at precisely eight o'clock and sat with me, motioning for a waiter.

"Order hearty, Doctor," he advised. "I don't know where our plans might take us. There is no guarantee as to when our next meal may be."

During our repast, my companion informed me of his nocturnal trip to the local library. "I went as myself, Watson, so as not to be recognized by young Anton. I found an excuse to research several volumes on shelves near the table where he and Ugarte were exchanging language phrases. I couldn't overhear everything said, but the gist of the conversation appeared to be what we were told. I managed to wait until they left and heard Ferrari's son tell Ugarte to expect a visit from me. The little Spaniard seemed puzzled but told him he would do what he could, though he hoped I wouldn't expect too much from a man in his position."

"So all seems legitimate," I commented. "What were you expecting?"

"Just examining all possibilities," he replied. "As you may have seen from Anton's description, Ugarte bears a striking resemblance to the person collecting the extortion money from Ferrari. Their behavior last night would appear to refute that notion, for now."

"For now?"

"You know I loathe to eliminate suspects too soon. But Ugarte has moved a little farther down the list."

Once fortified, we set out upon our day. We first visited the French Consulate on the Boulevard Rachidi, where Holmes sent a telegram off to his brother. While there, we happened to run into our fellow traveler, the *gardien*, Renault. He greeted us most enthusiastically and asked if he might speak to us in private.

The three of us stepped into a small anteroom, whereupon the policeman closed the door and bade us to sit down with him. Holmes, wary of the sly look upon the young man's face, spoke first. "How may we help you, Monsieur Renault?"

The fellow waved his hand as if brushing away a fly as he shook his head, "No, no, Monsieur, you misunderstand. It is I who wish to assist you, *Mr. Sherlock Holmes.*"

Holmes held the fellow's gaze, whereas I started, being not so practiced at concealing my emotions without advanced preparation. Renault turned to me and continued, "and Doctor John Watson, not of Edinburgh, but of London, by way Afghanistan in Her Majesty's service."

323

Holmes still refused to react, whereas I blurted out, "How . . . ?" until Holmes held up his hand to forestall any further outburst. "What is it you wish, sir?" the detective asked, without his Norwegian accent.

"Do not misunderstand me, gentlemen. I only wish to help you with whatever case has brought you to Casablanca. Of course, if my assistance proves worthy, I would be pleased of any commendation you might mention to my superiors. Imagine having the recommendation of the great Sherlock Holmes on my record!"

"Is that all?" asked Holmes, suspiciously.

Renault placed his right hand upon his heart, the white glove in sharp contrast to the deep blue uniform. "Upon my word of honor, Monsieur. I am merely a civil servant, anxious to do his duty and rise through the ranks to an appropriate station where I can administer justice proficiently.

"As to your unspoken question, Dr. Watson," he said, turning to me, "in my quest to master the English language, I've read many British books and magazines. One of which contained your story of 'The Empty House' and the revelation of your friend's *nom de guerre* of 'Sigerson'."

Returning to my companion he concluded, with a smile and a twinkle in his eyes, "As you might say, Mr. Holmes, the deduction was elementary."

Holmes mulled this over, finally nodded and replied, "You may possibly be of assistance to us, Renault. Being a newcomer to Casablanca, you are unknown, thus you could easily blend in with tourists. Have you any experience with undercover work?"

"Only what they taught us in our training. I should be happy to learn whatever you wish to teach me."

Holmes stood and stated, "I shall keep you apprised. I believe we may have need of your services soon to surreptitiously follow someone. The situation is currently delicate and I must wait for the next action of our culprit before putting a plan into place. I presume I may reach you here if needed?"

"*Oui,* Monsieur Holmes. What is the nature of your case?"

"An ongoing scheme of extortion. This is why I must wait for the next demand."

"How intriguing!" said the young man, rubbing his hands together, "I shall be ready, whenever you call."

Holmes held up a finger, "Not a word to anyone, Renault. If it becomes known that our victim has asked for outside assistance, the consequences could be disastrous. Also, when you receive word from me, you must come in civilian clothes. The presence of official police in the area will defeat our purpose."

"As you wish, Mr. Holmes. I am yours to command."

We left the Consulate and walked on toward the Spanish Consulate, which was just across a large park. As we did so, I questioned my friend on his bringing Renault into the case.

"At some point, Watson, we are likely to need official police to make an arrest. Better that we have someone of whom we have some knowledge."

"But are you sure you can trust this fellow?"

"No. We cannot yet classify him as friend or foe until he proves himself. But he knows who we are. It is better to play along with his proposal for now. We shall practice a saying I learned in the Orient. 'Keep your friends close and your enemies closer'."

Arriving at the Spanish Consulate, Holmes walked up to the reception desk and enquired in a rather halting fashion, "Pardon me, umm, *dónde esta Señor Ugarte, por favor?*"

The young man at the desk smiled and replied, "You may speak English. Señor Ugarte's office is down that way. Turn right and it will be the fourth door on the left."

"Thank you," replied Holmes, back to his Norwegian accent. As we walked I questioned him quietly. "I thought your Spanish was better than that?"

"It is. However, I have now established that I have little knowledge of it, and it may lead someone to believe they can speak it within our earshot without worrying about whether we can understand it."

I gave a little sniff of acknowledgement and we were soon at Ugarte's door. It stood wide open, revealing the little man at his desk with piles of papers before him. Holmes introduced us as Sigerson and Watson, friends of the Ferrari family, and the clerk bid us to sit down.

It was a small room, but it did have a window opposite the door which at least made the atmosphere slightly less oppressive. There were no paintings on the walls, merely a calendar behind his chair and rather worn file cabinets in one corner. The walls were a dingy cream color and in need of paint. The visitor chairs were small, wooden affairs with no cushions. His own chair was merely a slightly larger version of those where we were seated, but with arms to rest his elbows upon. Being short in stature, the edge of the desk was just below his breastbone. Working at that level caused his shoulders to hunch upward as he leaned over his paperwork.

Our visit seemed to be a welcome respite and he sat back somewhat in relief of what I, as a medical professional, was assured was an aching back. He spoke to us in that unusual voice which young Ferrari had described.

325

"Yes, gentlemen. Anton told me you would be calling. How may I help you?"

Holmes spoke up, "I have a group of archeologists in Great Britain that wish to explore the region of Lakhyayta to the south. With the implementation of the Algeciras Conference, I understand there are new protocols in place to gain permission for foreigners to conduct such expeditions. Is there some paperwork which I may obtain in order to start that process?"

Ugarte sighed, an odd sound coming from that nasal voice. Then replied, "There is much paperwork involved in such instances. There are also many fees as well as restrictions on what can be taken out of Morocco and what price will be exacted. But, as you are friends of Ferrari, I will collect nothing today. You may bring back a Geological Disruption Fee of one-thousand *peseta*'s [3] when you return the completed paperwork. When your expedition arrives, you will be assessed an additional fee per person."

I was outraged at this obvious attempt at bribery but held my tongue. Holmes replied that he would inform his expedition partners and asked if he could take the paperwork to be filled out. Ugarte went to a file cabinet and pulled several sheets out to hand to my companion. As Holmes looked the paperwork over, he gave special attention to one document that required approval from the French Consulate, He held it up and asked, "I will be visiting the French Consulate later. May I borrow your typewriter and fill this form out now?"

Ugarte hesitated, but the chance to get out of his chair and stretch for a bit was a welcome respite, so he offered his seat to Holmes and the detective slowly typed out the necessary information on the form. When complete he stood, shook the clerk's hand, and told him that we would be back when we had the approval and funds from our expedition sponsors.

"It's been a pleasure, Señor Sigerson. I hope to see you soon."

Chapter VII

I thought that would be the end of our visit to the Spanish Consulate, but as we made our way to the exit who should we run into but Ferrari's nighttime bartender, Gilberto, just returning from one of his courier runs. He seemed shorter, seeing him out from behind the bar, which I suppose is natural. One is usually looking up at the bartender when seated on a barstool. He was a wiry fellow in his mid-twenties with short curly hair and moustache. He spotted us immediately and cried out, "Dr. Watson! Señor Sigerson! What brings you here? Is everything all right at the Café?"

Holmes assured the fellow we were here on business and repeated the same story he had told Ugarte. Gilberto shook his head, "How much did he try to charge you?"

Holmes, acting naïve, voiced the amount, along with the fact that Ugarte didn't demand any payment today.

"*El bandito!*" declared the courier. "That fee is twice the normal amount and there is no 'per person' charge. The Moroccan government does require payment for artifacts taken out of country, but that goes through their officials, not ours."

"*Grácias,*" answered Holmes. "By the way, do you have access to a typewriter? I should like to type out a message to my expedition sponsors in London."

"*Si*, come with me. There is one in a common area for all to use."

He led us to a table outside the mailroom where a typewriter sat with reams of paper and a stack of envelopes. It was against a wall, but no one sat nearby who could see what was being typed. Holmes sat down and I engaged Gilberto in conversation so he couldn't observe what the detective was typing. When finished, Holmes thanked the gentleman.

"I can mail that through our mailroom, if you wish?" volunteered Gilberto.

Holmes waved the envelope, into which he had placed the paper and replied, "Thank you, Gilberto. However, I have some other documents that need to go with this back at my hotel. Your kindness is much appreciated."

"Any *compadre* of Ferrari is an *amigo* of mine," he replied, shaking our hands as he returned to his work in the mailroom.

Once back out on the street I turned to Holmes. "That was fortuitous. Now you have samples of two possible sources of the extortionist's demands."

"Yes, that saves me from the time my other plan would have required. Let us return to our hotel to compare these samples and see what we can conclude."

Meticulously Holmes compared the new typing samples with the original notes received by our client. He verified the watermark on the paper and examined each single letter and punctuation mark with his lens, attempting to find some unique characteristic that could be traced back to one typewriter or the other. He made several notes along the way. Finally, he set down his pencil and magnifying glass and leaned back in his chair. He had a contemplative look on his face, which told me something didn't set right with him. He got up and walked to the window, drawing his pipe and tobacco from his pocket. As he lit his old clay, he peered out into the street. I felt I had been patient long enough.

"Well, which one is it?"

"I have somewhat of a quandary, old friend. On the one hand, we have a loyal employee who has been forthcoming about his money troubles and been treated more than fairly by Ferrari. On the other, there is Ugarte, who has formed a symbiotic relationship with young Anton. Overriding all of that, what is the motive for either of these men to demand improvements to the café's operation?"

I nodded, "I see your point. But if I had to choose, I would say Ugarte's our man. He is dishonest and fits the general physical description Anton gave us. He could have disguised his voice, especially if it was muffled by a scarf. He keeps the money for himself, but does his friend a favor by ordering improvements to his father's business. If Gilberto is our man, he must have an accomplice who met with Anton, since many of those exchanges were at night when Gilberto was tending bar."

"I'm afraid our suspects haven't completely narrowed. While I'm certain now that it was Ugarte's typewriter that was used, it is easily accessible, since his office door has no lock. Any person with access to the Consulate could have slipped into the man's office and typed those notes."

"But, Ugarte also fits the description Anton gave us," I commented.

"To a certain extent, except for the voice," replied Holmes. "Ugarte's is very distinctive, and it is hard to believe that Anton wouldn't recognize his friend."

"So what do we do now?"

"I need a private discussion with Ferrari."

That evening, we returned to The Blue Parrot and met with our client. Holmes explained that we had narrowed our suspects, but that there could be accomplices involved. He didn't mention who his suspects were, for fear that Ferrari may inadvertently change his attitude toward them and make them suspicious. Holmes explained his plan to the restaurateur, emphasizing that no one else be told, not even a family member who might let it slip. Ferrari agreed and we set things in motion.

During dinner, Holmes announced that he had received news from Norway that his mother was gravely ill and he would be returning home. He didn't know when he might be able to come back to help his friend. Rosette was most sympathetic and I was sorry Holmes had to put her through such emotions for this lie that was necessary to our plan.

We checked out of the Napolitano the next day. Three days later, Ferrari received another demand.

Chapter VIII

The Vista Del Mar hotel was quite pleasant and offered an excellent view of the beaches west of Casablanca's main harbor. The sea air was invigorating and a pleasant change from that of the central city. We were lunching out on the patio when a familiar young man in a white wool suit arrived. He recognized us immediately and came over to our table.

"Mr. Holmes, Dr. Watson – a pleasure to see you gentlemen. I have the message you were expecting from Signor Ferrari." He handed over a sealed envelope which Holmes immediately tore open as he bid the fellow to sit down. He read through it quickly and commented, "Excellent! We now have an opportunity to spring our trap. Can you be available for some covert work tonight, Monsieur Renault?"

"I am at your service, sir. What do you need?"

"Just you in clothes which don't stand out on the streets after dark. Don't bring any other officers with you. If an arrest is to be made, you will be able to take full credit. However, I must advise you that there may be no arrest, depending on what we discover and the mood of the victim. In any case, I will advise your superiors of your valuable assistance."

"Thank you Mr. Holmes," replied the *gardien* with a smile. "Where and when do you need me?"

Holmes gave the fellow instructions and he agreed to meet us accordingly. After he left, I commented, "Are you sure you can trust him?"

"Absolutely not!" he replied to my surprise. "To quote the Bard, '*He has a lean and hungry look.*' However, we know he wasn't involved in this extortion scheme, since he is a new arrival. He is also an ambitious sort who will take any advantage he can. The fact that he knows who we are works in our favor. Thanks to your chronicling of our cases, I have gained a reputation of sorts as someone who may not to be crossed. He is young and smart enough to know not to make an enemy of me – at least, not this early in his career. If he can, instead, make an ally of me, it will be to his great advantage."

That evening, Anton Ferrari stepped out as before, instructions in hand and an envelope of cash in his pocket. Unbeknownst to him, he was being expertly followed by Holmes in a black Moroccan *tadjellabit* with the hood pulled up to hide his features, which were now his own rather than Sigerson's. Blending into the shadows, he was never detected by the young man, who lumbered his stout frame along the route he had been ordered to take.

Also in disguise, I stayed ahead of Anton, slipping into establishments where he might be confronted, until such time as he passed by. I then would leapfrog over the next such location by crossing the street and passing him by. Fortunately, his usual slow gait made this method feasible. Renault would cover the building I skipped, then he too would leapfrog over me and settle into one farther along the way.

We kept this pattern up for some time. After about three-quarters of a mile, I was in the lobby of a hotel with a dining room attached to its lobby. To my surprise, Anton walked in. I had seen no one signal him, yet he came in without hesitation and walked straight into the restaurant. I surreptitiously moved to a greater vantage point and took note of his actions. He had sat down and was soon joined by a young woman. She appeared to be in her late teens but was attempting to appear more mature with her hairstyle and makeup. She was dressed in a fine emerald-green evening gown with a cut which emphasized a full-figure. Her dark hair and tanned complexion suggested she was Italian, and were in sharp contrast to a beautiful white smile, pearl necklace, and pearl earrings. Overall, she was a very attractive young lady.

I slipped out to the street and signaled Holmes. As he came from an alley across the way, Renault also caught up, en route to his next surveillance post. I pointed out our young friend. The detective and *gardien* each took a clandestine look. Holmes indicated we retreat out to the street where we could speak freely without being overheard.

"This was the one option I feared most," declared the detective. "Apparently, the extortionist is Anton himself."

"Extraordinary!" I exclaimed. "You really had Anton among your suspects?"

"Everything the extortionist asked for benefits Anton as the son and heir," replied Holmes. "Had it just been for the money, the net casts wide. But the demands for business improvements smack of one who cares about the welfare of the family. Anton gets cash for himself to spend on his appetites, and the business prospers."

"Why wouldn't he just make these suggestions to his father directly?" I asked.

"He may have made some small suggestions in the past that were shunned by his father, coming from one so young with no experience. I've no doubt the young lady has also aroused his desires to succeed."

"Shall I arrest him?" asked Renault, eagerly.

Holmes looked at the young officer sternly. "Not all crime is black-and-white, Monsieur Renault. You will learn this as your career progresses. In this case, I doubt the father will actually press charges. I'm sure he will wish to settle the matter within the family. Putting the young man in prison for this will do more harm than good. May I suggest, among your reading material, you should add *Les Misérables* by Victor Hugo. It is an excellent example of how a policeman can be consumed by expecting perfection and strict interpretation of the law. You do not wish to become an *Inspector Javert*. You must learn when to temper legalism with forgiveness."

330

"So what do we do now?" I asked.

Holmes pulled back his hood and thought a moment. At last, he pulled the *tadjellabit* off over his head, revealing a black suit underneath. Even now, in European dress, he wasn't likely to be recognized by Anton, since he was clean shaven and his hair was its usual color.

He said to me, "Watson, go to the hotel and change back into your normal attire. Then proceed to The Blue Parrot and await me there. Say nothing to Ferrari until I arrive. Just report that I'm still following his son. I shall keep an eye on our young friend for the remainder of the evening."

Turning to our companion he declared, "Monsieur Renault, thank you for your assistance. You may take the rest of the evening off. I shall deliver a recommendation to your superiors before I leave Casablanca. Good luck with your career, young man."

He put out his hand and Renault shook it firmly, "Thank you for the opportunity, Mr. Holmes. Should you ever need my assistance again, I shall gladly be at your service."

I caught a cab to the Vista Del Mar and changed into my normal attire. As I rode back to The Blue Parrot, I wondered what I should say to Signor Ferrari. He would surely wonder why Holmes had sent me back. Walking through the door into the café and wending my way through the late evening crowd to the bar, I finally decided that I would merely report that the situation called for us to back off, for fear of being spotted, and that Holmes alone was continuing the surveillance.

In the meantime, Holmes was taking decisive action, which he later reported to me.

The detective observed Anton and the young woman as they ate. When the check came, Anton pulled the extortion payoff envelope from his inner breast pocket, took out some cash, and handed it to the waiter. That confirmed what had appeared obvious and, as they stood up, Holmes walked over to their table.

"Excuse me, miss. Mr. Ferrari and I have some business to discuss. I'm afraid he will not be available for the rest of the evening."

Anton glared at the detective, "Who are you, sir? How dare you interrupt us?"

Reverting to his Norwegian accent, Holmes replied, "You know me best as *Signor Sigerson*, and you know why we need to talk."

The young Ferrari was taken aback. Then he leaned closer to Holmes and said, "You are not Sigerson! Leave me alone!"

He started to brush past, but Holmes grabbed his upper arm and whispered in his ear in his normal voice, "I *am* occasionally Erik Sigerson, but at the moment I am Sherlock Holmes, a British detective. We must decide how to explain your extorting your father. I have sent the police away so that you and I can speak privately. If you insist, I can bring back the *gardien* who was very eager to arrest you."

Anton realized he was trapped and turned to his companion, "I am sorry, my dear. It appears my presence is needed elsewhere. I shall be in touch."

He kissed her hand. She curtsied and batted her eyes at him in a very coquettish fashion, which made Anton's interest in her quite obvious. Then she walked away, and Holmes bade Anton to sit back down. A waiter came by and Holmes ordered two coffees.

As they awaited their beverage, Anton asked, "Does my father know you are not who you appear to be?"

"Not yet," replied Holmes, "I shall reveal my true identity when I return to the café tonight. First, I have two questions for you: Does Ugarte know you used his typewriter to advance this scheme of yours? And was he ever involved, or did you just use his description as one being easy to remember?"

The youth folded his beefy hands across his ample belly and replied, "Ugarte allows me to borrow his typewriter from time to time, but he doesn't not know my true purpose, nor does he ever see the documents. He was not involved in this plan at all. I used his basic description because, as you said, it was easy to remember a real person. I also had him in mind as a contingency plan, should I ever need to use a second person to maintain this little fiction. But that is all."

Holmes nodded his acceptance of that statement and continued. "The last question is, what shall we tell your father about you? If you care to explain yourself, perhaps I can help."

Knowing he was caught with nothing to lose, Anton confided the reasons for his actions to Holmes. "My father is a decent employer and treats his workers well. However, over the past year, he has delegated more and more tasks to me. As a good son I felt obligated to obey, of course. But as time wore on, I came to realize he was taking advantage of our relationship. Yes, being a family member has its rewards in free room and board. He has also paid for my education and my basic needs. However, lately I have been doing the work that he used to pay others to do. I would prefer not to use the knowledge I've gained to go to work for one of his competitors. I have seen what they are doing, and if he does not keep up with the trends, his business will fall farther behind.

"Of course, he ignored my initial suggestions regarding change. That, and the fact that he has never even thought of paying me wages, resulted in this plan of mine. The money amounts were never excessive. I have access to the accounting ledgers and know what he can afford. At some point in the future, when he has absorbed the changes and realized their value, I will tell him all."

The coffee arrived and the young Ferrari took his up and drank. Holmes leaned back and looked him over. Myriad thoughts swirling through his mind as to options that lay before him.

Finally, he stated, "I cannot assist you in deceiving your father, Anton. However, I believe I have a plan."

He outlined his idea to Anton. The young man was skeptical, but saw that he had no choice. Within the hour they walked into The Blue Parrot.

Chapter IX

After I had answered Ferrari's questions about our mission, he left me at the bar to attend to his patrons. The café was crowded with people anxious to eat, drink, and be entertained. As it was getting well into the evening, I decided to order something while awaiting Holmes's arrival. I took a small table near the kitchen and was soon eating beef burgundy with scalloped onion potatoes, a small salad, and a glass of wine.

I was nearly finished when Holmes walked through the door with Anton in tow. I swallowed the last of my wine and walked over to join him. I arrived at the same time as Valentino Ferrari. Holmes held up his hand at the Italian's barrage of questions and suggested we go into the kitchen to bring Rosette into the conversation.

There was a table off to one side where the kitchen staff could take their meals in relative privacy and we all sat around it. Holmes then began his tale. "First of all, my friend, although I was traveling as *Sigerson* when last you saw me, my real name is Sherlock Holmes. I am a consulting detective from London."

"I have heard of Sherlock Holmes," recalled Ferrari, "but, I thought he died many years ago. Something about a waterfall."

"To quote the American author, Mark Twain, '*the rumors of my death have been greatly exaggerated*'. I escaped Professor Moriarty's trap, but to avoid his gang, I adopted the identity of *Sigerson* and traveled throughout the British Empire. After returning to London when it was safe, I asked Dr. Watson here to refrain from writing any more stories about me until just three years ago. It was then when the story finally came out about my escape and return to London.

"But enough of that. The man extorting you is in custody. The French police are ready to press charges."

Ferrari slapped his hand on the table and exclaimed, "*Bene! Bravo Signore!* Who was he? What was his motive for all these changes he demanded?"

"I'll get to that in a moment," answered my friend. "First, I have some questions for you. I am sure the French police would want to know these answers so as to determine the exact charges to impart."

"*Certamente!* What would you like to know?"

"May I see your accounting ledger?"

Ferrari shrugged his shoulders and raised his hands, palms up, "If you wish. *Un momento.*"

The café owner stepped into a back office. While he was gone, Anton instinctively reached for his mother's hand. She tilted her head at him curiously. Then, her countenance suddenly changed. Her mother's intuition made her realize that her son may be in trouble, though she couldn't understand how.

Ferrari returned, sat back down, and handed Holmes the ledger. Looking over my friend's shoulder, I could see that the entries were written in Italian, mostly in Ferrari's hand, though some exhibiting the more graceful writing of his wife. Fortunately, numbers are numbers throughout Europe, and I could see a distinct pattern over time. This appeared to be what Holmes was looking for.

"I see that your business has undergone significant increases in income over the last several months," said the detective.

"It is a good thing!" declared Ferrari. "Look at how my expenses have increased. I have had to buy a greater variety of food, pay for multiple entertainers, hire more staff who were multilingual – the list goes on!"

"Agreed," replied Holmes. "I would point out though, that your profit margins are greater than ever. Even after paying this fellow what is really a nominal amount, all things considered."

"*È un criminale!*" he cried. "He set a fire and threatened to do more!"

"As I understand it, the fire was in a metal barrel ten feet away from the building and in plain sight of the back windows, where it could easily be spotted. In fact, it was Anton who noticed the fire, was it not?"

"Yes. He was taking garbage out."

"Rather a menial task for someone who knows three languages and is learning a fourth," noted Holmes.

"He is young. He needs to learn all the aspects of the business if he is to take it over someday."

"Not so young as that," countered my companion. "Many young men his age are already working at their first jobs, saving money for their own home and marriage."

Ferrari answered in agitation, "Who would hire him without the knowledge I am giving him? What need has he of money, when I provide his room and board? Marriage and a home are years away. There will be time enough for that! What has any of this to do with the man you have in custody? Where do I go to file charges?"

During this diatribe, I noticed Anton's grip tighten on his mother's hand, to the point she had to place her other hand upon his to calm him. But it was too late.

The boy raised his considerable bulk out of his chair, shaking off his mother's grip and ignoring her plea, "*Non, ne pas!*"

He leaned forward across the table, knuckles grinding into the red-and-white checkered tablecloth. His father stared up in confusion at this reaction by his son and started to speak, "Anton! What – ?"

"Be quiet, Father! For once in your life you are going to sit there and listen to *me!*"

I could see by the look on Holmes's face that this wasn't the direction he had planned this conversation to take. His own muscles tensed as he shifted on his chair into a position where he could rise to prevent a physical attack. The lad's emotions were running high. His face was now red with barely controlled rage, and his eyes stared daggers at his father.

"*I* am the one in Mr. Holmes custody. It was *I* who set the fire! It was *I* who demanded money and then demanded the improvements that are making you richer by the day! You have never appreciated my ideas, nor my talents. I have two other establishments willing to hire me right now as an assistant business manager or purchasing agent."

Ferrari leaned back, startled by these revelations. Before he could respond, Anton went on. "I had planned on revealing all of this to you soon, so that you might realize what you had right under your own roof. But, Mr. Holmes managed to follow me tonight and accelerated my agenda. Now, to listen to you belittling me in front of mother and these men, I see that you are as blind as ever. You can't even acknowledge the profits I've made for you. Well, you can find yourself a new errand boy, old man. I'll not stay where I am not respected."

He turned to go as his mother grabbed his sleeve. He stopped momentarily and looked at her as he patted her hand. "I am sorry, *maman*. I will keep in touch." He walked on. His father stood and bellowed, "Anton, come back here at once!"

The boy kept walking, waving his hand above his head in a dismissive fashion and refusing to look back. Ferrari started after him, but Rosette stood and blocked his path.

"No, you will not confront him now! Not like this. You are both too angry and stubborn to speak to each other now. One of you will do something that cannot be forgiven. You will give him time and – if you are lucky – *maybe* he will come back to you,"

"He needs to learn respect! He cannot – "

"So do you!" she said, in a tone I would never have expected from her.

"Always *le tout Savior,*" she said, and then turned to us. "Thinks he knows everything, this one. His own son, he doesn't know. Nearly seventeen years under this roof and he does not understand him at all!"

She turned on her heel and stormed back to the kitchen, leaving him speechless and embarrassed. He sank back into his chair, his head falling forward into his hand with his eyes closed. After several seconds he leaned back and let his hand fall to the table.

"What is happening here? *Sono tutti pazzi?* First you tell me you are not Erik Sigerson, but Sherlock Holmes. My son disrespects me and walks out. My wife, my little Rosette, speaks to me as she never has before. What am I to think? What am I to do?"

Holmes responded, "I sympathize, Valentino. It must be disconcerting to have so much change come upon you so quickly. I am afraid my counsel in family matters is extremely limited, having never headed up one myself."

Then my friend, my companion, my comrade in arms, turned to me and dropped the question in my lap. "Watson," he said, affably, "you are much more experienced in the matters concerning marital bliss and the female mind. Perhaps you have an opinion in this situation?"

I started at this sudden request for my thoughts. Usually on a case, Holmes only seeks my medical advice, or tests out ideas on me to see what the common man might think. I cleared my throat, folded my hands upon the table, tilted my head to one side in thought, and willed my mind to race for the right thing to say.

At last I spoke, "Signor Ferrari, I can only speak to you from my experience in my culture. I do not know what the expectations are of an Italian, or should I say, a French-Italian, household. However, I have been married thrice, each time to very intelligent and formidable women. In my case, these were women whose opinions I respected and often sought out. I was still the head of the household, but my marriages were more a partnership than a patriarchy. I have found it much easier to work together on things than to try and take everything on myself. Why should I bear the total burdens of life when I have a helpmate as my wife? Perhaps this could be of use to you?"

Ferrari shook his head, "This is not how we do things in *Italia*, Doctor. My father, my father's father, all my ancestors, ruled their households. Their word was law, and no one was allowed to argue!"

"But you are not your father's son," chimed in Holmes.

The café owner bristled and turned red at this apparent attack on his birth-right, but Holmes held up his hand. "Hear me out, Ferrari. You, yourself, told me the story of how you defied your father in order to marry Rosette. The two of you came here to start a new life without his help or his blessing, nor that of her father, either. You *both* made that decision, for she was under no obligation to turn her back on her home just because you asked.

"Now your son, who may have his mother's looks, but certainly gained most of his spirit and stubbornness from you, has defied you. Just as you defied your own father for what you believed to be right, so he has followed in your footsteps."

This revelation took Ferrari aback. The tension went out of his countenance. He leaned forward, elbows on the table and rubbed his forehead and temples with both hands. Finally, he dropped one hand on the table and said, "So what do I do?"

Holmes leaned back and held his lapels in both hands, "For now, nothing. Your wife is right. You must let both your tempers cool. If he in fact is walking out, I'm certain I can find him and let you know where to reach him. But only when you are able to speak to him man to man, for he is no longer the errand boy you have created."

"Thank you, Signor Holmes. I must find Rosette. Please, go have something to eat in the café and I will find you later."

He walked back to the kitchen and we saw him and Rosette talking on the far side of the room as we made our way back out to the dining area. Rather than eat, however, Holmes suggested we try and track down Anton's whereabouts. Gilberto, the bartender, informed us that he saw Anton leave with a suitcase and his overcoat draped over his arm.

Holmes was able to track down the girl Anton had been with by talking to workers at the restaurant where they ate dinner. Over the next two days he was able to follow her to Anton and then him to his new domicile. We also found that he had started working for another establishment. Not a direct competitor of his father's, but a firm who would benefit from his purchasing connections and multi-lingual capabilities.

Three days after the confrontation, we were able to inform Ferrari and his wife where they could reach their son. We boarded our ship back to Calais and, exactly two weeks from Holmes's initial visit, we were back in Queen Anne Street, where I was greeted with open arms by my wife.

I had insisted upon Holmes coming home with me, as it was nearly dinner time. I had telegraphed ahead and the table was set for three. After a warm and affectionate welcome from my sweet lady, she turned and walked up to Holmes. She grabbed on to his coat lapels to pull him closer as she raised up on her toes to plant a kiss on his cheek.

"Thank you for keeping your promise, *Sherlock.*"

337

Straightening back up, Holmes brushed the spot on his cheek with his finger and replied, "It would never do for a British gentleman to not keep a promise to so gracious a lady, my dear. I just hope our friend Ferrari learns the lesson of a happy household from the example you and Watson have set."

POSTSCRIPT

Looking back over Watson's draft for this case, I realize he did not include the story of Felice, the actual blue parrot, in his manuscript. I shall attempt to reconcile that oversight here from his notes. – R.R.

As we sat enjoying our splendid meal, Signor Ferrari stopped by our table and asked if we needed anything else. I took the opportunity to enquire about the parrot at the door.

"Ah, *sí*, Dr. Watson. Felice came to us in 1892. According to her owner, Professor Abreu, she was just a year old at the time. He was a Brazilian archeologist and had rescued her when she apparently had fallen from her nest nearby one of his archaeological digs in the Amazon.

"She may have been attacked by another bird, because her wings were damaged and her ability to fly was limited to short bursts of only a few feet and no higher than six or seven feet into the air. She seemed quite content to remain with the professor. Thus, he took her on as a pet and named her *Feliz,* the Portuguese version of *Felice.*

"He came to Casablanca with an expedition to explore nearby ruins. This group was interested in comparing the ancient cultures of North Africa and South America to see if there were common roots. Apparently the distance between these continents is much less than that of England to Canada, so seafarers of ancient times may have made such voyages."

I nodded with interest. I had recently been reading the theory of the German scientist, Alfred Wegener, regarding continental drift. According to it, there was a possibility that these two continents were much closer in ancient times. That could help explain the scattering of cultures throughout the world.

Ferrari continued, "Professor Abreu brought his pet with him and he frequented our café on a regular basis, bringing *Felice* with him to entertain the children of our patrons with the simple phrases he had taught her. Eventually we became known as the café of the blue parrot.

"Of course, he always sat on the patio by the door, so that Felice would not make a mess on our floor. Before we put her perch out there, she would sit on the back of the chair next to him. He had a sort of leash to her leg which he tied off, in case she was frightened.

"There was one day, when he needed to use the water closet, that he left her there and had little Anton sit by to keep an eye on her. Now, Felice had a habit of picking up phrases. One never knows what triggers her brain to choose which ones. On this particular day, she must have overheard men at the next table. They left before the professor returned. But, when

339

he resumed his seat, she suddenly she started squawking, *'Steal the artifacts! Load the boat!'*

"Of course, that caused the professor great concern because they had uncovered many artifacts in their excavations. Anton was able to tell him a little bit about the men as to their general size and coloring. Thanks to this warning, they put on extra guards, including some secret ones, and captured these men in their attempt.

"Unfortunately, Professor Abreu, apparently, contracted something called *Valley Fever*, while in Brazil. In spite of our dry climate, his lung condition worsened while he was here. He succumbed to it after being with us for about three months. Because of the good times he had here with Felice and the children, he left the bird to us, along with a generous bequest. In his honor we changed the name of the café to what everyone was calling it. Thus, *The Blue Parrot,* got its name and Felice has been at the door ever since."

NOTES

Fun Fact: Sydney Greenstreet, who would play the grown up Anton Ferrari in the 1942 movie *Casablanca*, had his acting debut in a 1902 English stage production of Sherlock Holmes.

1. The Algeciras Conference of 1906 took place in Algeciras, Spain, and lasted from 16 January to 7 April. The purpose of the conference was to find a solution to the First Moroccan Crisis of 1905 between France and Germany, which arose as Germany responded to France's effort to establish a protectorate over the independent state of Morocco. Germany was not trying to stop French expansion. Its goal was to enhance its own international prestige, and it failed badly. The result was a much closer relationship between France and Britain, which strengthened the *Entente Cordiale*, since both London and Paris were increasingly suspicious and distrustful of Berlin. The Sultan of Morocco retained control of a police force in the six port cities, which was to be composed entirely of Moroccan Muslims (budgeted at an average salary of a mere one-thousand *pesetas* a year) but now to be instructed by French and Spanish officers, who would oversee the paymaster (the Amin), regulate discipline, and be able to be recalled and replaced by their governments.
2. George M. Cohan's first Broadway musical from 1904 about the American jockey, Tod Sloan, in England produced several popular songs such as, "Give My Regards to Broadway" and "Yankee Doodle Boy".
3. Approximately two-hundred dollars, or eight-hundred pounds, in 1906 currency.

The Adventure of the
Expelled Master
by Will Murray

I suppose at heart I'm like the old fox hound, one who has retired and is content to sit in the sun, but whom, upon scenting the familiar fox, rouses himself for one more enthralling chase.

I am content to tend to my bees by my modest villa in the South Downs, not far from the hamlet of Fulworth and very close to the great chalk cliffs overlooking the Channel. Life is pleasantly uneventful. Of my friend and biographer, Dr. John H. Watson, I had seen little during the summer months of the year of 1908.

It was noon of August 3ʳᵈ that Inspector Bardle of the Sussex Constabulary drove up to my residence in his small motorcar. I knew him to be a steady, plodding fellow, but the speed with which he approached was anything but unhurried. That fact that it was he and not Anderson the village constable was suggestive.

"A word with you, Mr. Holmes," he greeted, stepping out. "If you do not greatly mind."

"I don't mind at all," I replied cheerfully, for the day was hot, and I didn't intend to remain out of doors much longer.

"I come to you out of desperation, Mr. Holmes," he said. "I know that you're comfortable in your retirement, but you were so brilliant in solving the problem of the queer death of McPherson, I felt that I must consult with you."

"I was rather laggardly in seeing the obvious," I replied. "For by my own standards, I was slow off the mark."

"That may well be, sir, but when you landed, you landed square. No other brain alive could have done it."

"You have your good opinion whilst I harbor my own," I replied diffidently, for I had received so many generous portions of praise over my life that I had become quite allergic to hearing more.

"You are a wonder, and everyone knows it!" Bardle said effusively. "False modesty ill becomes you."

"Come inside," I invited. "My housekeeper will pour us some tea and you may tell your tale."

But Bardle was too anxious to unburden himself. During our short walk, he spoke rapidly, and a trifle breathlessly.

"There has been another queer death connected to The Gables," he said. "This time it is Murdoch, the mathematics teacher."

Ian Murdoch was well known to me. During the affair of the Lion's Mane, he had been the chief suspect in the death of Fitzroy McPherson. A strange man, given to fits of temper, he loomed large in my suspicions until the *recherché* truth eventually came out.

"How did Murdoch perish?" I asked.

"He was expelled!"

"You must make yourself clearer," I replied. "Scholars may be expelled, but masters are more properly let go."

We reached the door of my villa and there the policeman paused to collect his wits.

"You must excuse me, Mr. Holmes, but I have never encountered anything like it. I meant to say that Murdoch was expelled from his chimney and into the air, whereupon he fell to his death."

I knew that Ian Murdoch lived in a modest thatched cottage near The Gables. He preferred to live alone. He was that sort of fellow – solitary and given to moods.

As we entered, I invited, "Pray sit down and tell me more. Begin at the beginning, as you understand it."

Taking a seat, Inspector Bardle composed himself further. By this time, I confess that I was rather intrigued. It wasn't that mysteries no longer possessed their fascination, but rather that I had wearied of an unending round of needy persons, all requiring their troubles to be unknotted by my aging brain. Bees are less demanding.

"There was a witness, a young scholar named William Manners. He was walking by the cottage, and saw the entire miraculous spectacle unfold."

"Fortunate," I remarked. "If not convenient for your investigation."

As my housekeeper brewed a fresh pot of tea, Bardle poured out his story.

"According to the young man, his attention was captured by an impossible sight: A human figure flew out of the chimney top, and off into the woods, landing some small distance away from the home."

"How was the man dressed?"

Bardle looked briefly blank in his rather bovine way. "I don't understand how that pertains to the matter at hand."

"Kindly answer the question. It may be a trivial thing, but in trivialities there are sometimes concealed volumes of data."

"He wore a Norfolk jacket, tattersall shirt, black trousers, and Wellington boots. When the body was found, those very items were smeared with soot, much as they would from passing up a chimney flue."

"I see."

"The man had evidently landed on his head, for his neck was broken and his crown stove at the top."

"Did he wear a hat?"

"No hat was found near the body, which has been removed to Fulworth. If you care to see the remains, this can be arranged."

"All in due time. Tell me, Inspector, is the student who witnessed the fantastic show of good character?"

"Excellent character. He is the son of George Manners, Baron Tinsley."

"Was he a student of Murdoch's?"

"That he was."

"Did he recognize the man whilst flying through the air, or was he able to identify him after discovering the body?"

"Young Manners didn't discover the body. Mr. Holmes. He ran straightaway to The Gables and summoned Harold Stackhurst. It was he who discovered the body. Or should I say, Stackhurst was the first to identify the body, for another man discovered the body before that."

"And who is this fellow?"

"His name is Algernon Hubbard, of Fulworth. He was walking from the beach, where he had been fishing. By his own account, he heard the body land and investigated. Finding poor Murdoch lying dead, and recognizing him, he hurried to The Gables to report it. By that time, Stackhurst had telephoned the news to Fulworth. I hurried forthwith to take charge of the scene, and it was a terrible one to behold. I cannot for the life of me understand is how a man can be shot out of his own chimney like a cannonball!"

The tea poured, the inspector braced himself with a long sip, which he took without adding milk or sugar. Properly fortified, he looked to me and asked rather plaintively, "Mr. Holmes, What do you make of it?"

"It is remarkable, if factual."

"We have a witness, a body, and a bloody awful mystery to boot. All of these elements line up like links in a chair. I don't see a break in the chain."

"I assume you investigated the chimney from within the cottage?"

"Thoroughly. The hearth was cold, of course. There was nothing remarkable about it – not that my senses could perceive, I should add."

"I should like to speak with young Mr. Manners before I see the body," I told Bardle.

"I would be most grateful if you did so. I'm at an utter loss to explain any of it."

"Since Murdoch is deceased, there is no rush. Have another cup of tea. Then we will be on our way."

"Thank you. I don't know what more can be learned, but any light you can shed on this most disagreeable event must perforce be brighter than my meager efforts."

I had already drawn certain conclusions by that point in the conversation, but I wouldn't be a very entertaining narrator if I revealed them this early in my account. Watson was very clever in parceling out such tantalizing tidbits as to keep the reader on the edge of his seat, even if his cleverness was partly the result of his good-natured naivety, so I'll copy Watson in keeping my own counsel until I'm ready to reveal my deductions as they are proven too be correct, or otherwise.

After a short drive over the Downs, Inspector Bardle brought us to The Gables, which is a private coaching school of significant size and excellent reputation.

Entering, we went at once to Harold Stackhurst's office on the ground floor. He was headmaster, and had made it a rousing success. An athlete in his student days, he was the picture of vitality and respected by all.

Stackhurst greeted us warmly, I having known him since purchasing my little estate only half-a-mile distant.

"Holmes! My dear fellow! And I see you have brought with you Inspector Bardle. Or is it the other way around? It doesn't matter. I don't have to ask what brings you here. Alas, I know full well. The loss of Master Murdoch coming so after the death of McPherson is a terrible blow to The Gables. He was a credit to his field."

Stackhurst waved us to chairs and we were soon seated.

I got directly to the point. "I understand that you were the first to find the body. What was its condition?"

"It was stretched out in the dirt, the head half-twisted around so that I saw immediately that Murdoch's neck had been broken. His still features and hiking clothes were streaked with soot, giving credence to the wild tale of his demise."

"How did the body lie?"

"On its back, slightly turned. *Rigor mortis* had already set in."

"You rushed to the scene without delay?"

"I wasted no time."

"I thought not. Were there visible injuries to the face?"

"None that I saw. Its color was rather livid, which I suppose is normal enough."

I said, "I'm told that one of your scholars witnessed Murdoch's meteoric and improbable passing from this earth."

345

"Yes, William Manners. If I didn't know the young man so well, I would have thought him to be suffering from sun stroke. But the body confirmed the terrible tale."

"I would like to interview him. But first tell me, has there been any trouble around Murdoch in recent months?"

"No, not at all. His temper has been quite balanced of late. I suspect it's because he has begun seeing that young woman in Fulworth. It seems to have mellowed him a bit."

"Not Maude Bellamy?" I inquired.

"Well, yes. The two have once again warmed towards one another. As you might recall, his affections towards her were previously known, but he was gentleman enough to step aside when she showed a preference for McPherson."

"Has Miss Bellamy any other suitors?"

"Not that I'm aware of."

"Had marriage been discussed?"

"If it had, this hasn't been revealed to me. The rekindling of their friendship is a recent thing, given that Miss Bellamy has been grieving for McPherson all during the long winter months and into the spring."

"Understandable," said I. "Now, if you would produce Mr. Manners. I'm keen to speak with him."

"I shall be pleased to do so, Holmes. He's a very impressive young man."

Stackhurst left us briefly and Bardle, who had been silent throughout, offered, "I've spoken with the boy. He is forthright and honest, in spite of his wild tale. It's a story I wouldn't normally credit, but the evidence supports his account. Let us see what you make of it, Mr. Holmes."

"Something other than the fantastic, but I'm eager to hear his story in his own words."

William Manners was produced, and he proved to be a freckle-faced young fellow whose head was surmounted by crown of tow-colored hair that to my eye required more than a comb to keep it ruly.

"William, this is Mr. Sherlock Holmes," said Stackhurst. "Inspector Bardle, you have already met."

"I'm pleased to meet such an illustrious man, Mr. Holmes," said the freckled young man politely. "I have read much of your exploits. They are deeply impressive to me."

"They are the product of a strict regiment of observation, combined with a wide fund of knowledge which I apply liberally to the problems I encounter. But no more about me. I would like to hear your story in its entirety."

346

"Well, sir, I was walking the path not very far from Mr. Murdoch's cottage, when something caught my eye with a suddenness. I thought it was a bird taking flight, but it was nothing of the sort. Mr. Murdoch abruptly flew out of his chimney and into a copse of trees."

"Permit me to stop you here. You say that you saw him fly out of his chimney. But it was a commotion that drew your attention to this remarkable spectacle."

"Not precisely, sir. It wasn't a commotion such as one hears, but a commotion such as one notices from afar."

"You heard nothing, then?"

"Not initially."

"At what point did you see the figure of a man emerge from the chimney top?"

"I believe he had almost fully emerged. But it happened so fast, you see. In my memory, I caught sight of him as his boots were coming into view."

"Very good. You are certain on that point?"

"Quite certain, sir."

"And you would testify that the figure didn't merely sail over the chimney, but emerged from it?"

"I would, Mr. Holmes. I would swear a solemn oath on any Bible as to what I witnessed. Moreover, his clothes were black with soot."

"Now at the point where you first laid eyes on the fantastic flying figure," I pressed, "did you recognize him as Ian Murdoch?"

"I was certain it was he, for he wore Mr. Murdoch's hiking clothes, as well as his familiar cap."

"Ah. So he wore a cap, did he?"

"He did. A wool cap."

"Have you particulars to add?"

"It was an ivy cap, Mr. Holmes," the boy answered promptly. "Brown Donegal tweed, if I'm not mistaken, for such a cap Mr. Murdock habitually wore."

"Excellent! So you didn't see his hair?"

"Well, he flew past so swiftly, I'm not sure that I could have, had he been bare- headed."

"Did you glimpse his features?"

The young man shook his head firmly. "There was no time but to take in the glimpse of what appeared to be an impossibility."

"So I imagine," I said. "Now let us follow the trajectory of this errant figure. Did he fly straight up?"

"After his boots came clear of the chimney, he sailed off towards the elms. He was quickly gone from my sight."

"What sounds did you hear?"

"Only the crashing of the body through the treetop boughs."

"Of what duration would you judge?"

"Barely a minute, I suppose."

"Half-a-minute, would you say?"

"Closer to a full minute, sir. Although I didn't perceive him after he went into the treetops."

"And then?"

"And then there was silence."

"What did you do next?"

"I ran straight away to Mr. Stackhurst and told all that I had seen. I was ordered not to follow into the woods, so I didn't. Thus I was spared the sight of the body, which I'm told was terrible to behold."

"I'm sure that it would have done you no good to see what became of poor Murdoch, and possibly considerable mental harm. Tell me, did the man you saw flying from the chimney cry out at any point?"

"He did not. The only sound he made was that awful crashing through the treetops."

"I have one final question. You were a student of Murdoch's. Would you say the angle at which he exited the chimney was obtuse or acute?"

"I would say neither, sir. He seemed to fly in a kind of an arc."

"A high arc, or a shallow one?"

"It began high and very quickly turned shallow, at which point he disappeared from my view, becoming lost in the great old elm. It was a wonder to behold, but a terrible wonder, as you might imagine."

"Yes, I suppose that it was. I thank you for your thorough testimony. You are very observant and know how to get straight to the point."

"You may go now, William," said Stackhurst.

I objected, saying, "I would prefer that young William remain available, for I may have further questions."

"Oh, thank you, sir."

"William, wait outside, please," instructed Stackhurst.

After the young lad had departed, Bardle asked, "What is your opinion of his story?"

"It is plainly preposterous, and yet I believe his every word."

"How can that be, Mr. Holmes? It must be one or the other."

"It *should* be one or the other," I replied firmly. "But it is both in this case. Young Manners has told the truth as he witnessed it, but what he beheld is not what in fact transpired. I would like to pick through the woods and look for Murdoch's lost cap."

"Do you believe it to be significant?"

"I only wish to examine it. As for the significance, that remains to seen. I would like Mr. Manners to accompany us. There may be other points I wish I have illuminated."

"I should like to join you, as well," said Stackhurst.

"I was going to suggest that very thing," I told him, "for I have some questions for you too."

And off we went, leaving Bardle's automobile for the moment. The walk wasn't very long and took us through the rolling Downs, which was dotted with dense stands of trees, principally sturdy elms.

During this promenade, I was silent for a time as I considered all that I had heard. Certain points were clear to me now, but others remained obscure.

Addressing Stackhurst, I asked, "The man who found the body – tell me of him."

"I encountered Algernon Hubbard not long after Mr. Manners's alarm. As it happened, he was rushing to The Gables to bring word of his awful discovery."

"Describe him."

"A rangy sort of fellow, rather handsome in a rustic sort of way. A joiner, by trade, he is. He had just returned from the shore, where he was fishing."

"Now did he say that he'd been fishing, or was that an assumption on your part?"

"He was carrying a fishing pole and creel, and wore wading boots, so I drew a natural conclusion."

"Did he have much luck?"

"In the excitement, I didn't think to ask."

"Was his creel filled?"

"It was of wicker and the lid was shut firmly, so I cannot answer that question."

"Think back to the moment," I implored him. "Did he smell of fish?"

"Now that you mention it, he did not. I am certain on that point."

"Very good."

"As I recall," added Stackhurst, "he made a point of informing me that he was returning from the beach and discovered the body upon his return."

"And how did happen to find Murdoch's body? What drew him to it?"

"It was the dreadful sound the body made striking the ground. I believe he also mentioned the crashing noises that preceded the body landing, the very commotion William reports."

"He didn't see the body flying through the air, then?"

"No, he didn't remark on the outlandish feat. In fact, he expressed puzzlement over how Murdoch came to fall from such a height. He wondered aloud if the poor fellow had been climbing a tall tree and lost his grip."

"So he doesn't tell the quite same story as young Mr. Manners?"

"Only insofar as he missed the beginning of Manners's account."

We had penetrated into a thick stand of elms now, and were soon surrounded by the stately trunks on all sides. This was dominated by a hoary old elm of the weeping variety, its serrated leaves a cloud of still greenery. I began to look about.

Displaying a fine initiative, young Manners led us over to the path along the Downs from which he saw the acrobatic flight from the chimney. He described the arc of its flight and pointed to where the body had landed. I judged the distance to be over fifty yards.

I studied Ian Murdoch's cottage and saw from a distance that it was quite old, but in good repair. The stout walls were spotlessly white. The roof looked as if it had been thatched within the last few years, although I noticed that the eastern pitch was in need of repair. The chimney lacked some mortar, but it didn't lean appreciably. In fact, it was visibly in plumb, showing no totter.

Gauging the approximate trajectory from the chimney to the spot where the body was found, I commenced searching the ground. But my peregrinations brought no result, other than the scampering of agitated squirrels going about their woodsy business.

"I imagine Murdoch's cap was lost in the trees," I mused. "We must search high, rather than low."

We all four scanned the treetops for some time until young Manners's keen eye accomplished what our more mature orbs failed to discern.

"I spy it!" he cried out, pointing into the great weeping elm tree.

I looked up into the leafy crown, and there hung the cap.

"Do you think you could fetch it, William?" I asked.

"Count upon me, sir."

Agile as a monkey, William Manners clambered up the tree and snatched loose the cap, which had snagged on a branch. This he tossed down to us. Inspector Bardle caught it between two hands.

I took it from him and saw that it was an ivy cap. The pattern was grey herringbone. In the lining there was some straw, creating the impression that a squirrel might have already begun building a nest in its comfortable confines.

Turning it over in my hands, I saw that a pin had been stuck across the top. This I withdrew. It was quite long – clearly a woman's hat pin.

Noticing this, Bardle observed, "I would expect a woman to resort to such a device, but as you know it is quite blustery in these parts."

Harold Stackhurst chimed in. "Yes, keeping one's hat on his head is a challenge at times."

"No doubt," I commented. "Evidently a second pin transfixed this cap, but only the pinholes it left behind remain."

Addressing William Manners, I remarked, "Here is a lesson in observation for you. From the distance at which you beheld the flying form, you recognized Ian Murdoch's clothes, and your brain completed the picture, sketching in his brown tweed cap, as it were. But here you can plainly see that it is grey and of a different pattern. Never make assumptions, whether by observation or premature conclusion. Else they will lead you astray."

"I understand, sir. It is just that my memory insists that the cap was brown."

"Does it also insist upon a Donegal tweed pattern?"

Young William hesitated. "I fear that does, Mr. Holmes. But I now see that my recollection is in error."

"All the more reason to practice observing without prior prejudice. Now take me to the spot where the body was discovered."

Stackhurst lead the way, and we were soon surrounded by brambles that showed clear signs of having been broken and trampled recently.

In these brambles I found some bits of straw, suggesting that the squirrel had scavenged in this area for its nest. There were also a great many serrated elm leaves here and there, broken off no doubt when the flying form tore through the crown of the stupendous elm.

I spoke up. "Murdoch weighed approximately twelve stone, did he not?"

Stackhurst nodded. "I wouldn't disagree with that assessment."

I begin looking searching the branches above carefully. I observed only one broken limb, its exposed inner pulp still fresh to my eyes. This was midway up in the ancient elm, which stood about twelve yards from the spot where the body had been found.

"Are you game to climb another tree?" I asked William Manners.

"For you, Mr. Holmes, I would gladly climb the tallest tree in the land."

"Likely lad! Good for you. Now climb this elm and tell me what you see on that stoutest of branches at which I'm pointing."

Up the trunk went William Manners until he was balancing upon the heaviest bough. He searched his surroundings with eager eyes.

"I see marks."

"Describe them to me, please."

"They are rather like the sort of marks a body might make in scraping through the treetops."

"I didn't ask for an assessment. Your description will suffice, thank you."

"Of course, sir. There are scrapes and scuffs here, here, and here." He pointed with his forefinger.

"Are they fresh?"

"They appear to be so."

"Do you see anything else noteworthy?"

After craning his tow-head this way and that, William replied, "No, I do not."

"Can you see the roof of Master Murdoch's cottage from where you stand?"

"I can."

"Then you may come down."

As young William made his way back, I noticed that he disturbed bits of straw that fell to the base of the hoary elm.

Leaning over, I picked up a few meagre strands, examined them briefly, and then let them fall to the ground.

"I should like entry to Murdoch's cottage to continue my examination," I declared.

Inspector Bardle said, "It is locked up tight, Mr. Holmes, but I have the keys."

"More than one?"

"The front door is fitted with two locks."

"Unusual," I remarked.

"Murdoch lived alone. He may have feared for his safely."

"Yet he had no enemies?"

"None known to me," offered Stackhurst.

When we came to the door, I saw that in addition to the usual keyhole under the doorknob, there hung a padlock of the type that required a brass key.

Fumbling with his keys, Bardle let us in.

The policeman led us directly to the fireplace, and I saw at once that the iron fire basket had been set to one side. Stooping, I studied this, and perceived that it was quite new, not more than a year or so old. It was also quite clean, as might be expected of a fastidious owner. There would be no need for a hearth fire at this time of year, of course.

"Did you remove this fire basket?" I inquired of Bardle.

"Not at all, Mr. Holmes," he replied. "All is largely as I found it."

"Very good," said I, turning my attention to the fireplace hearth, which was of black granite.

It looked as if it had been recently swept, yet there was the traces here and there suggestive of matter that has been a dislodged from the flue.

Kneeling, I took up a fragment and saw that it was only a twist of straw, such as might have been used to seal such chinks as age had made in the brickwork. It was sooty to the touch, blackening my fingertips.

I took the liberty of appropriating a tablecloth and spreading it so that I might lie down upon the cloth without soiling my clothes. I cast my gaze upward.

The damper was open. Sunlight streamed down at such an angle that I could see the interior of the chimney clearly. It was sound and in good order – but I had expected that. The flue was black with soot, but not excessively so. I perceived indications that a chimney sweeper had been at work since winter last.

Extracting myself from the uncomfortable position, I stood up and again took stock of the hearth floor. I detected no mechanism that might have served as a catapult, but I didn't expect any such unlikely contrivance.

Young William Manners observed me closely. In his growing excitement, he blurted out, "What do you conjure, Mr. Holmes? Have you discovered any clues?"

"I'm currently eliminating possibilities," I told him with a smile. "You see, whilst clues are important, equally significant are the available facts that one may rule out. I have just ruled out the possibility of a catapult – but I never put any stock into that outlandish notion."

"I see. Does your thinking take any particular course?"

"There are certain things that are obvious. And here we have a case of something so obvious that it almost doesn't require comment."

"And what is that, sir, if I may be bold as to inquire?"

"English chimneys do not sneeze."

Mr. Manners's eager expression twisted up most remarkably and then his freckled face lit up with understanding.

"You don't hold that Mr. Murdoch was expelled from that this chimney?"

"I have already ruled out that farfetched possibility."

Bardle inserted, "But what about this young man's testimony? He appears to be above reproach."

"What William witnessed I believe was accurately described. Equally important to his account were things that weren't described or heard."

As I spoke, I scrutinized the granite floor of the hearth. There was something odd about it that had impinged upon my consciousness while I was lying with my back atop it.

"One moment," I said, stepping up to it. I placed my right foot upon its base. It seemed less substantial than it should. I gave that foot a hard stamp, and then another.

Dropping to the knees, I took out my jack knife and revealed the blade. This I inserted into a seam separating the portion covering the firebox floor from the part that intruded into the room. The blade slid in quite deeply. By pressure on the handle, I made a discovery that produced exclamations of astonishment from my companions.

The inner hearth slab opened upward, revealing a cavity beneath.

"I must have a lantern," I declared, laying aside my knife and lifting up the trap door until its top surface lay hard against the brick back of the firebox.

Stackhurst swiftly produced a lantern, which he lit with a Lucifer. This he handed to me and I dipped the warm illumination down into the cavity below.

The others leaned in and saw what I did from their own individual points of view.

"It is a tunnel!" declared young Manners.

"No doubt it's an old smuggler's tunnel," declared Bardle. "But what does that have to do with what happened to Murdoch?"

I spied a ladder leaning below and handed the lantern back to Stackhurst.

"One or more of you may follow me down with this, for I shall need strong illumination."

The ladder was a rough thing of joined wood, but it could be negotiated. I would have preferred to have been younger and more spry, but I made it to the bottom and in the earthen floor below.

Young Manners followed down with the lantern, and the others came after him.

I lifted the lantern high and could see that the tunnel ran straight south, in the direction of the beach. Here and there, the roof was shored up like old mine workings.

"Shall we see where it leads?" I asked.

No dissenting voice was heard, so we crept along the crumbling passage, our heads bowed low, soon enough arriving at a blank end and another leaning ladder.

"By my reckoning, I would judge that we are midway to the beach," said Stackhurst.

354

"I wouldn't disagree," said I, lifting the lantern so that I could see above my head.

There was a trap door, as I had expected there would be. I noticed also about my feet was a considerable quantity of straw. I knelt to examine this and saw that the stuff was comparatively fresh.

Handing the lantern to Manners, I went up the ladder and put my shoulder against the trap door. It lifted with some difficulty, but eventually I pushed it all the way up and over.

Climbing out into the bright sunshine, I found myself in a little dell that was sheltered by brush and bramble. The others quickly emerged to join me.

Walking about, I soon came to what appeared to be the remains of a campfire.

It consisted of several stout pieces of wood. Some were twigs of good size and others were planed square crosspieces. These have been largely burned away, and in the center was a calabash gourd that had been hollowed out, but was now a scorched ruin.

"Someone appears to have been cooking a rough meal," remarked Stackhurst.

Turning to young Manners, I asked, "What do you make of it, William?"

"I don't think that this is what is left of a meal, Mr. Holmes. I'd judge from the way the calabash has collapsed all forlorn that it was cooked after having been gutted of its meat."

"Bright lad! I quite concur. Does it look familiar to you?"

"No, it doesn't. If I'd seen it before, I should imagine it would have been whole."

"I suppose that you are correct," I replied.

Something had caught Harold Stackhurst's eye and he reached down to remove what proved to be a charred handle.

"What do you make of this?" he asked, holding the black thing up.

"I judge it to be an old hammer, but the head is missing."

We kicked the charred detritus apart with our feet, but nothing more interesting came to light.

There seem to be nothing else noteworthy to the little glen, so I suggested that it was time to return to the cottage and lock it up.

"I've seen all I need to see here. It's time to look at the body. Where is it being stored? By custom, Murdoch should be resting in his own bed, looked after by his family, but I didn't see it."

"Since he has no local kin, and there is an inquest, the remains were removed to Fulworth. The funeral parlor wasn't available, inasmuch as it is of modest proportions and presently showing old Mrs. Dunn. Other accommodations had to be made. Fortunately, Mr. Hubbard, who found the body, and has a fairish large workman's shed, and offered to store the remains out of the goodness of his heart."

"Extraordinary!" I remarked.

"Well, his brother is a cabinet maker by trade, and does a side trade in building coffins. So there is an element of the convenient involved. The brother does his work in Hubbard's shed alongside him."

"The element of convenience appears to be providential," I stated, "inasmuch as I'm as interested in Hubbard's account as I'm in Murdoch's body. Let us hasten there at once. Mr. Manners is excused from this duty. Stackhurst, it is up to you whether you care to accompany us."

A wry smile not very far from a grimace touched Harold Stackhurst's face. "I'm very taken by your methods, so I'll gird myself for the unpleasant ordeal."

After Bardle got the cottage locked up, and young Manners sent on his way, the automobile was reclaimed and we were motoring in the direction of Fulworth.

"Are you prepared to reveal any of your thoughts, Mr. Holmes?" asked the inspector.

"I believe I've traveled most of the way to my conclusion, but there are certain points that must be clarified. I prefer not to speak of them until they have been sorted out in my mind."

"As you see fit," the man said agreeably. "We are fortunate indeed to have your services."

We arrived in the seaside village of Fulworth in due course, and were soon knocking on the front door of Algernon Hubbard's substantial home.

It took some time before the owner showed his face and when he did, he broke out in a generous and very pleasant grin.

"Inspector Bardle! Jolly good to see you. And who have you brought with you? Come in, come in. Would you like some tea?"

"We are here to view the body," Bardle said morosely.

"Ah! You may follow me. It is of course where you left it. I have been working out back with my brother, who is building the casket. It has been an odd convenience for him, but he is making the best of an unhappy situation."

We all went around to the back of the house and into the shed, which was quite generous. The front was given over to a woodworking set-up. There a burly fellow was working on a casket. He didn't look up from his efforts. Indeed, he seemed to take no particular notice of us. My eyes immediately went to the cadaver, which lay on a bench, covered by a sheet in a far and dimly lit end. I hastened there.

356

Drawing back the sheet, I exposed Ian Murdoch's swarthy features. I will not describe them since they have nothing to do with my narrative. I'll only note that his head was askew, a result of fractured neck vertebrae and what appeared to be soot streaked his cold brow and cheeks, although not his nose, which I found curious.

I placed my right palm on top of his dark thatch of hair and felt gingerly, discovering that the topmost bones of his skull gave under pressure. My hand came away clean. There was no blood. But I didn't expect any.

"Could I have a lantern?" I asked.

"Certainly, sir," said Hubbard. There were several already burning, so he simply picked one up and brought it over.

"But I don't believe I have caught your name."

"Sherlock Holmes," I replied, "and I thank you for the lantern. Would you mind holding it up for me?"

"Of course, of course." The man showed no recognition of my name, which was a blessing since too often many fussed about, plying me with innumerable questions.

Under this light, I observed Murdoch's throat. It was dark with bruising. I took the head in both of my hands and moved it, which it did with scant resistance. The period of *rigor mortis* had passed and the muscles were now flaccid.

Turning down the sheet, I exposed the length of the corpse. Murdoch was dressed as they found him, in a Norfolk coat and Wellington boots. Coat and boots were quite blackened. His trousers, which were of brushed black cotton, showed no such smearing, of course.

"Follow me, please," I directed.

Algernon Hubbard kept the lantern close as we moved to the booted foot and I studied the leather soles. They were clean. I looked for traces of soot, but to no avail.

"Thank you, Mr. Hubbard. Now, may I ask you a few questions?"

"If you must."

Drawing away from the body, I faced the fellow.

"I would like to hear the story of how you came upon this man's corpse. From the beginning, if you would."

"It is very simple," said Hubbard. "I was hiking back from the beach, where I had been fishing."

"How many fish had you caught?"

Hubbard hesitated only slightly. "Whatever that does that have to do with for Murdoch's death?"

"It is probably nothing. But indulge me."

Hubbard laughed lightly. "And that is what I caught. Absolutely nothing!"

"Now what did you perceive that drew you to the body?"

"As I was walking along the path, I heard a crashing through the treetops, and when I looked up, I spied something moving from one side to another through the greenery, which I could only dimly perceive. Then I heard that terrible thud. I ran towards the sound. And when I broke through the brambles, I found poor Murdoch lying there, his neck broken. Alas, I could do nothing with him. He was already gone."

"And what did you think when you found the corpse?"

"I wondered if he had fallen out of a tree."

"A reasonable assumption under the circumstances. Except for one item."

"And what is that?"

"Bodies falling from trees tend to fall as gravity requires. Straight downwards. Yet you saw him crashing horizontally through the trees before he plummeted to ground."

"Exactly so. And I wasn't the only person to witness this odd spectacle. A young lad from The Gables happened to be passing by and saw the same thing."

"Yes, I have spoken to him. His story matches yours in that particular."

"So I am told."

"However, young Mr. Manners also witnessed the prologue, during which he insists that Murdoch's body flew out of the chimney and sailed broadly to its unhappy destination."

"I'm not so sure that I believe that," admitted Hubbard. "But I witnessed no such thing."

"It does beggar belief," I allowed.

Hubbard laughed rather loudly. "I would say that it is far *beyond* belief. But I cannot contradict the young man's account, except by the application of common sense."

"You are to be commended for your level-headedness in the face of the bizarre," said I. "No doubt you are a credit to Sussex."

Hubbard laughed pleasantly. "Would that my ancestors were present to hear your compliments!"

As we spoke, my eyes ranged the room. The industrious brother continued with his coffin making, and barely took notice of us. I thought that odd, but didn't remark upon it. Tradesmen sometimes are so absorbed in their work they don't easily stir from it for any reason.

I asked Hubbard, "Did you know Ian Murdoch?"

358

"I knew of him. I had seen him round from time to time, but he wasn't an acquaintance of mine."

"Therefore his passing is a small moment to you."

"It's very sad in its way. And also extremely perplexing. I still don't comprehend how it could have taken place."

"It's a difficult riddle to unravel, I will admit, but it isn't beyond our ken. Is that your cloth cap resting on the stool over yonder?"

Algernon Hubbard's head snapped around rather abruptly, and when his eyes fell upon the, his face took on a frozen expression.

"I believe that is my brother's cap," he said, keeping his voice low.

I asked politely, "Do you believe it, or do you know what to be true?"

"Of course it is David's cap. It is certainly not mine."

The brother straightened, for the first time spoke up.

"That is not my cap, gentleman."

"Then to whom does it belong?" I pressed.

Algernon Hubbard looked momentarily abashed. His thin smile returned and he said, "Why, of course! How foolish of me. It was Ian Murdoch's cap."

I walked over to the cap and picked it up.

"It was of good quality, and fashioned from brown Donegal tweed," I mused.

Showing it to Harold Stackhurst, I asked, "Do you recognize this cap as one Ian Murdoch wore?"

"Yes, it's his. I recognize it."

"I see," I mused. "Now this is very interesting. Inspector Bardle, did you not tell me that no cap was found near the body?"

"None was. The man was hatless."

"So how did Murdoch's cap come to be here?"

Hubbard said swiftly, "Why, it was in his pocket. I found it there. Then I laid it aside."

Bardle spoke up saying, thickly, "I went through the man's pockets before the removal of the body. There was no cap."

"I'm mistaken then. It was tucked into the waistband of his trousers."

"How peculiar," said I. "When Mr. Manners saw the flying form he believed it to be Ian Murdoch describing a parabola in the air, it was wearing a cap until it went into the trees. We did find a cap later on, snagged by a branch. But this one was of a grey herringbone weave. If this is Murdoch's brown tweed cap, how did it come to be here, and whose cap was discovered high in the treetop?"

At this point, I was studying Algernon Hubbard's pleasant features as they became loose and a trifle rubbery. His smile struggled for vitality.

"I cannot account for it," he said quickly. "I told you I found it in his waistband."

"Contrarily, you stated that you found it in his pocket. Now you recall otherwise. Would you like to change your statement again?"

Hubbard's open mouth sealed tightly, and his eyes became somewhat glassy.

From the other corner, the hitherto-silent brother spoke up. "You utter, abysmal fool! Why did you not throw that damned cap away?"

At that point, I said loudly, "Inspector Bardle, you may arrest Algernon Hubbard for the murder of Ian Murdoch. This case is resolved."

Bardle was slow to comprehend my words, clear as they were. Not so Algernon Hubbard. His response was immediate and violent. He broke for the door leading back towards the house.

Had I been younger, I would have pursued him. But it proved to be not necessary. Harold Stackhurst stepped up, blocking his way. Seizing him and in both of strong hands, he wrestled him to the ground while Bardle finally got his wits composed and applied the handcuffs.

At the far end where he was working on Ian Murdoch's coffin, the brother began sobbing raggedly.

Before very long, Hubbard and his brother David were taken straight away to the Fulworth jail, protesting their innocence with every step.

Once behind bars, Inspector Bardle, Harold Stackhurst, and I adjourned to the inspector's office where I unburdened myself of such theories as had coalesced in my mind.

"However did you puzzle it out, Mr. Holmes?" Bardle asked.

"I began with the obvious. As I told young William, chimneys do not sneeze. In any event, no explosive sound was heard prior to Ian Murdoch's apparent expulsion from his own chimney flue. Nor did the flying form cry out, as might be expected of a man hurtling to his doom. Therefore, it wasn't Murdoch who was seen by the witness. Working backwards from that premise, I reasoned my way to the following conclusions:

"I've always looked askance at coincidences, yet here I was confronted by a striking example of that nebulous phenomenon. At the precise moment that the chimney appeared to have coughed up Ian Murdoch, a young boy happened along to witness the unique event. This would ordinarily lead me to suspect the witness of conjuring up a false narrative, but for the evidence at hand – namely Murdoch's soot-smeared clothing, as well as a corroborating witness. I soon discarded collusion. William Manners had no guile about him.

"Then there were the mathematics of the matter. Chimneys cannot be made to launch men like cannonballs. If they could, the body should have shot straight up into the air and fallen back down onto the roof, or onto the immediate grounds of the property. It did not. Instead, it described a preposterous parabola, carrying it well into the elms, after which presumably Murdoch's neck was broken by contact with the ground."

Harold Stackhurst remarked, "Why, so it should, so it should."

"But it didn't. All of it was properly impossible. So I looked for another explanation. And found it in yet a third coincidence—the appearance of a second timely passerby, Mr. Hubbard, who heard the same commotion of a body passing through treetops, followed by the thud of said body landing." Here, I paused. "A thud that William Manners failed to hear."

"My word!" exclaimed Bardle. "This is a point I hadn't considered."

"What isn't said can often be as telling as what is freely offered. There was no thud of a body because no heavy body struck the ground. Let there be no doubt upon that point. It is obvious. Then there was the telling fact that Stackhurst found Murdoch to be in a state of *rigor mortis*, a condition taking between two and six hours to set in. It was incontrovertible proof that Ian Murdoch had died hours before his body was found, and significantly prior to his supposed ascent and fall."

"Another excellent point!" Bardle cried out.

"One that should have occurred to all," I pointed out gently. "But no matter. How then to account for the dead man being discovered by Algernon Hubbard? Again, the fellow's story didn't square with reality. Any more than his claim to have returned from fishing on an August day, when it would have been a very clumsy fisherman indeed who caught no fish at all, and who, I might add, was returning to Fulworth by the most roundabout route, over the Downs and not along the shore."

"If Hubbard hadn't been fishing, then what was he doing walking along the Downs with his fishing pole?" asked Stackhurst.

"He was casting for much more ingenious game. If the flying form was not, as I deduced, Ian Murdoch, then what could it be? Something light enough to be carried through the air by human action, swiftly enough to be glimpsed by a convenient witness, but so rapidly that certain crude details couldn't be detected."

"I have it!" Stackhurst burst out. "A straw man!"

"Precisely, the scorched remains of which we discovered at the woodland glen, along with the hollowed calabash that had served as the scarecrow's head.

"Burnt to destroy the incriminating evidence, no doubt," crowed Bardle with gleeful obviousness.

"Although a great deal of its straw stuffing had been liberally scattered throughout the woods over the course of the clumsy if ingenious

361

perpetration of the scheme," I added. "Putting myself in the shoes of the schemer, I conceived the following: He stood high in the great weeping elm, whose profusion of leaves concealed him from sight, and with both arms, snapped back with his rod, forcibly pulling the form from the chimney top, into which it had been stuffed, awaiting the chance arrival of a suitable, if credulous, witness.

"He landed it near his perch – which was marred by scuff marks made by the hard heels of his wading boots and reported by William Manners – during which straw was scattered about rather liberally. Recall also William's testimony that it took nearly a full minute for the form to crash through the treetop—suggesting to me something being *dragged* through a tangle of branches, which showed infinitely less damage than it would if a human missile weighing twelve stone had plummeted through. The many fallen leaves scattered about supported that theory. I noted also the fact that the body was discovered, not hung up in the crown as might be expected, nor crumped at its base, but twelve yards to the east. Rather far, I thought."

"But how did this form come to be in the chimney in the first place?" asked Bardle in what I thought was dull-witted wonder. "And how could he have cast his line so cleverly as to snag it at such a formidable distance?"

"That I could have reasoned without any clues, although they were readily apparent to my eyes. I saw that the eastern pitch of the cottage roof was in disorder. My imagination told me that it would be far easier to climb the roof and stuff the straw man into the flue, with the fish took already secured to its strongest point. Then, paying the line out as he returned to ground, he sought the perch from which he intended to withdraw his fanciful lure, as soon as a suitable witness passed by."

"It is a wonder that the scarecrow held together under such terrific strain," vouchsafed Stockhurst.

"It was well constructed," I pointed out. "Hubbard was a joiner, after all. His straw man was no makeshift contrivance, although it was largely twigs, light wooden crosspieces, screws, and twine. Presenting himself as the discoverer of the body, he hoped to remain above suspicion. And so he would have been, except for the absurdity of his scheme."

Inspector Bardle was by this time struggling to follow my account in his limited way.

"Mr. Holmes, I beg of you. Where was poor Ian Murdoch throughout all this fuss and bother?"

"Regrettably, he was deceased, his body secreted nearby, for it was to conceal and obscure the true circumstances of his murder that this preposterous spectacle was engineered. No doubt he was nearly naked, his clothes having been transferred to his duplicate. Once the scarecrow had landed softly in the wood, knowing that the young witness would almost certainly flee to The Gables to tell his tale, Hubbard hurriedly dressed the corpse in his proper clothes, which had already been smeared with soot to assist in the illusion calculated to hide the difficult fact that Murdoch's neck had been previously broken, and that there was an inconvenient hammer blow to the top of his head. These injuries needed to be accounted for and covered up. It didn't matter that his plan required more credulousness than reasonable. It was a scheme that he hatched and he had, I imagine, less than a day to carry it out. He counted on the incontrovertible need to bury Murdoch as swiftly as practical to aid in covering up his crimes!"

"I see it now!" Bardle shouted. "This was why Hubbard offered to store the body."

"He is a cold-blooded man," I allowed. "His great mistake was in not disposing of Murdoch's brown tweed cap after losing his own grey one."

"The matter of the two caps confuses me, Holmes," mused Stackhurst. "To whom did the grey herringbone cap belong?"

"Why, to Hubbard. It should be obvious. Young William correctly reported that the flying figure was wearing Murdoch's Donegal cap, which was affixed to the jury-rigged calabash-head by a long woman's hatpin so it wouldn't fly off. But it was snatched off once the scarecrow entered the treetops. As it happened, or so I imagine, Hubbard lost his own herringbone cap whilst up in the elm tree and, motivated by some quirk of personality, took Murdoch's cap as a replacement."

"But there was a hatpin in the gray cap found in the elms," Bardle stated. "How do you account for that?"

"Easily," said I. "Hubbard brought more than one hatpin with which to fix the brown cap in place. He found that only one was necessary, but he had carried the pins in his own cap, inasmuch as they were too long to go into his pocket safely. Thus, both caps were pierced. I noticed a second set of perforations in the grey cap, indicating a missing hatpin."

Stackhurst remarked, "Young William had wondered to me why Murdoch would be wearing his cap while exiting his cottage in such an unorthodox manner."

"He is a bright boy," I said readily. "The thought had occurred to me as well. A man rarely wears his cap indoors, which is another point arguing against the existence of a living chimney rocket. Still another was the liberal blackening of Murdoch's person. Hubbard went too far in his hasty attempts at verisimilitude. There was too much applied, especially to the face, where contact with the dirty flue bricks struck me as improbable, but

363

would also have resulted in scraping and abrading of the skin. Yet such injury was wholly absent. And it wasn't the dusty black of chimney soot, as it should have been had the body been shot up the flue. This substance was charcoal. Nor did I detect any upon Murdoch's black trousers, for no one had bothered applying any. The condition of the clothes told me as surely as a confession would that one of the Hubbard brothers had tampered with the body."

"It all fits rather nicely together, Holmes," said Stackhurst broadly. "But what are the circumstances of the murder itself? Where did the foul deed take place and what motived it? By his own account, Hubbard hardly knew Murdoch."

"Here, I can offer only conjecture. Beyond that, we must rely upon a confession in order that we may understand the details in full."

Bardle scoffed. "I wouldn't pitch a tent in wait of a confession. You heard Hubbard going on about his innocence."

"Perhaps. But his brother appears quite ready to crack open like an egg. In any event, I suspect that Ian Murdoch acquired an enemy in the course of rekindling an old flame." Noticing the befuddled expressions now facing me, I added, "I refer to Maude Bellamy, who had been engaged to the late Fitzroy McPherson, and in whom Ian Murdoch had a prior interest."

"Upon my word!" exclaimed Stackhurst. "Do you think Murdoch's feeling were reciprocated by Miss Bellamy?"

"We shall have to ask that of her," I responded candidly. "I can only say that, as before, a romantic rivalry ensued, with results that were tragic in the extreme. But I prefer that the guilty parties supply all concrete details, for my ideas are more properly surmise, not deductive in nature."

Inspector Bardle's bovine countenance took on a look of perplexity. "However did you come to conclude this from the available evidence? It is beyond me."

"From Ian Murdoch's choice of trousers. Although attired for a hike, he wore cotton trousers, not twill or canvas. This told me that he was bound for Fulworth. The hour suggested that he was paying court to a lady there."

"My word!" exclaimed Bardle rather tiresomely. "You *are* a wonder, sir!"

I misjudged the character of Algernon Hubbard. He, not his brother, broke down and confessed all.

I wasn't present for this confession. I only wish I had been. It was made two days following the arrest of the Hubbard brothers.

Bardle motored up to my villa that afternoon to reveal all that had been hitherto obscure.

"You were as right as rain, Mr. Holmes," he announced upon his arrival.

"Not in all particulars, surely," I countered.

"The whole sordid affair was over Maude Bellamy, as you surmised. It was a simple as all that."

"Surely not," I said, setting down my rake. "Come inside for a spot of tea and tell me all."

Over tea and biscuits, Bardle summarized the facts in the case.

"Poor Ian Murdoch had undertook to court Miss Bellamy, but Algernon Hubbard also had eyes for her. He took an immediate dislike to Murdoch, the two had words over the rivalry.

"I have it from Miss Bellamy that she fancied Murdoch over Hubbard, but was slow to make up her mind. Poor girl, she was enjoying the attention and thought nothing of taking her time in deciding between the two suitors.

"Although Murdoch was the one known for his temper in past years, and Hubbard a jolly sort, some perverse impulse took root in Hubbard's mind, and he began lying in wait for Murdoch on those evenings where he hiked over to see Miss Bellamy. Not wishing to draw unpleasant attention to himself, given his past reputation, Murdoch endeavored to avoid every snare and opportunity for conflict, for he could see that, despite Hubbard's greater size, if it came to a row, this would reflect badly upon him, given that he had mended his old temperamental ways."

"I can see that," I stated.

"Murdoch purchased an extra lock for his cabin door to safeguard himself whilst sleeping. He also knew that the cottage he had purchased with an eye toward a future marriage had the interesting feature of an old smuggling tunnel. He used this to good advantage in foiling Hubbard, who often lay in wait for him in the evening. By slipping down the tunnel after turning out his lights, he was able to emerge safely in the little sheltered glen, and make his way to Fulworth, while Mr. Hubbard wasted untold hours keeping an eye out for his emergence – for Hubbard was often able to pry from Miss Bellamy the advance dates of their assignations, as it were.

"It was a sound plan, but I suppose that it was doomed to failure eventually. Hubbard eventually discovered that somehow Murdoch had outwitted him. He became livid with rage.

"What happened the night of the murder was as much happenstance as it was premeditated. When Murdoch lifted the fireplace door trap, Hubbard was at his window watching, and saw him disappear below. He reasoned that there existed a tunnel and it must terminate in a stand of trees. So he raced into the woods in search of it.

"The sound of Murdoch throwing up the trap door drew him to the location. Furious, Hubbard fell upon Murdoch. Equally enraged, Murdoch fought back. Being the more powerful of the two, Hubbard managed to break Murdoch's neck. The man fell, but he was still breathing, and cried out for help most piteously, according to Hubbard. Unfortunately for Ian Murdoch, Algernon Hubbard recognized that he had gone too far. But there was no going back. Hubbard carried a hammer, and brought this down on the top of Murdoch's head, finishing him off most viciously.

"Here, Algernon Hubbard came to a full realization of what he had done. He immediately resolved cover it up. As he told me, he knew that he couldn't simply bury the body in the woods, for once Murdoch failed to appear at The Gables, a search would be undertaken, and any makeshift grave eventually discovered. He was uncertain as to who else knew of the tunnel – he couldn't hide him there. Nor dared he convey the deceased man to the cliffs and simply hurl the body over the precipice of Beachy Head in the hope that Murdoch's fall injuries would be ascribed to a fall. You will recall that the moon was full that night, and he feared that he would be seen doing the dastardly deed, and murder would be the obvious conclusion. A murder that would be easily proven by the prints of his wading boots and the drag-marks of the body." Bardle shook his head slowly. "No, that convenient artifice would not do.

"Rushing back to Fulworth, he enlisted his brother David in as mad a scheme as I have ever heard. They fashioned a wooden dummy and brought it to the stand of elms, where they dressed it as Murdoch, stuffing it with straw and rags and topping it off with a pale calabash for a head, which was supported by a truncated broomstick. Murdoch's brown tweed cap was affixed to the gourd by a hatpin to further disguise its artificiality."

"Ingenious in a crack-brained sort of way," I remarked.

"These lads thought quickly, I will give them that," admitted Bardle. "And Hubbard thought he was being clever when he feigned skepticism over young Manners's testimony. But all he was doing was stirring confusion into the stew, as it were."

"You have left out an important point, Bardle. At what point was the mad scheme hatched, and by whom?"

"Ah, so I have. Algernon Hubbard spent some time in the elms, pacing around the body, cogitating most fearfully. His future loomed very dark and dire in his mind. He knew he couldn't successfully hide the body, so his thoughts ran in the direction of concealing all signs of murder. Why his imagination fired so wildly, I couldn't tell from his explanations. I suspect that Hubbard isn't of the soundest mentality. No matter. He hatched his scheme and executed it as best he could. Counting on a

366

passerby to come by the next day for his plan to work, for broad daylight was necessary for the plot to pan out."

"The dummy was inserted into the chimney by dark of night, I take it?"

"Yes, it was. Both brothers were involved in that endeavor, which makes David Hubbard an accomplice after the fact to murder."

"Where was the body of Ian Murdoch while Hubbard climbed the old elm tree with his fishing rod to pluck out the scarecrow?"

"Down in the smuggler's tunnel, where no one would immediately discover it. It was a very convenient tunnel, as far as that was concerned."

"Convenience is a theme running throughout this entire affair," I pointed out. "From William Manners happening by, to the opportunity to store the body in Hubbard's own work shed so that few had the chance to examine it."

"Oh, Hubbard explained that he knew that many students passed by Murdoch's cottage hiking to and from the beach. At this time of year, it was only a matter of patience before a likely lad happened along."

"I see," I said. "Well, I imagine Algernon Hubbard's confession has tied up all the loose ends in the matter."

"All but one, Mr. Holmes. All but one."

"And what is that?" I asked, for I couldn't think of any dangling thread.

"With David Hubbard in jail, who will finish Ian Murdoch's casket? That is what I would like to know."

The Case of the
Suicidal Suffragist
by John Lawrence

How I wished Sherlock Holmes could have accompanied me to the Epsom Derby early in June of 1913, one of the social events of the season, made all the more appealing by the announcement that King George V and Queen Mary would be in attendance. Holmes had little interest in such pageantry, however, and was content to tend his bees in Sussex rather than attend a horse race, even one with so storied a history as the Epsom Derby.

The Derby has been run since the years of the American Revolution. This year, most eyes would be on Anmer, the King's admirable horse that would be ridden by the talented Herbert Jones, although considerable interest was focused on Craganour, the horse of Gower Ismay.

I had joined a number of friends from my club, not having any patients scheduled in my surgery for race day. Since the race would take me out of London, I called Holmes and arranged to travel from the track in Surrey to his retirement home for a leisurely weekend with my old friend. He happened to be back in England just then, having spent a great deal of the past year traveling in the United States under another name as part of a long-term investigation.

The trains down to Surrey were crowded with people in every state of dress from aristocratic finery to a more proletarian style. At Epsom, as many as five-hundred-thousand had arrived to witness the race from the viewing stands around the outer and inner perimeter of the track. After a good deal of pushing and stumbling, I found myself in an enviable position just before the "top of the stretch", where the horses would turn and make a straight dash to the finish line. The excellent location assured us the ability to see clearly the magnificent horses as they charged down the slight incline of the track at enormous speeds before having to climb on the last hundred yards, a demanding finale for any animal.

I enjoyed the camaraderie of my colleagues, several of whom flattered me with praise for my published exploits with Sherlock Holmes. They noted, with great accuracy I am afraid, that the Holmes tales had certainly brought me far greater notoriety (and money) than any activities of my medical office! However, I happily indulged their questions about Holmes, which invariably ended with murmurs of amazement at his extraordinary deductive skills.

To our right, at least a half-mile down the track at the finish line, the storied grandstand was festooned with banners and special flags marking the location of the King and Queen, whose presence was announced to great cheers. The crowd became quite animated and within a few moments, a shot proclaimed the beginning of the race. Even from our seats on the far side of the track, the sight of the massive animals, with their brightly clothed jockeys atop them, was thrilling. The horses were bunched together and threw up great cloud of dirt and dust as their hooves dug into the track. As they emerged from the cloud of debris, it was surprising that Anmer trailed badly, although there was plenty of time for his outstanding jockey to steer him around the other horses and into contention.

As the horses neared the top of the stretch, there occurred one of the most shocking events I have ever witnessed, and which soon became the most important story in the country. The horses rounded the turn and began the race down the stretch to the finish line. Several passed directly in front of me, and then there was a slight space between them and the next group of horses, which included Anmer, the King's entry.

Suddenly, a solitary figure ducked underneath the rail of the infield, against which hundreds of spectators were pressed to see the horses as they raced passed. From where I stood, it was clear that it was a woman who had either been pushed under the rail or who had purposefully ducked under it. The first group of horses passed by her and she made no effort to retreat to the security of the guard rail. Then as the second group of horses neared, she pulled a white scarf or banner from her coat and, to the horror of thousands of spectators, stepped directly in the path of the thundering horses.

The tragedy unfolded so quickly that it was difficult to recall the exact series of events. Fortunately, however, a moving picture camera filmed the scene, and so there can be no question about what transpired. In a moment, Anmer was upon the figure, raising its two front legs in a vain attempt to leap over the woman as if in a steeplechase. But the woman was far too tall for such a leap, and instead, a thousand pounds of horse traveling at perhaps thirty miles-an-hour collided with her. In a flash, the woman, Anmer, and the rider Jones were sprawled on the track like broken dolls as the remaining horses flew by on their way to the finish. The gasp of the crowd was like a muffled thunderclap! As thousands of stunned eyes watched, Anmer struggled to its feet and continued down the track, racing on pure instinct towards the finish line. Both the rider and the woman whose actions instigated the accident lay motionless on the track.

369

I was only a few rows from the track and reflexively, I climbed out of the stands and hastened to the rail from which the guards were staring at the carnage in the track.

"See here!" I cried, "I am a physician! Let me through!"

One of the guards came over to me.

"Are you really a physician?" he asked.

"Yes, of course," I replied. "Dr. John Watson! Let me through!"

The guard allowed me to climb under the rail and escorted me onto the track where a large crowd had already gathered about the two injured people. Far down towards the finish line, we could hear cheers for the winning horse, but we could also see a commotion in the grandstands. In a matter of seconds, I was knelling by the prostrate woman. She was perhaps thirty-five or forty, dressed almost all in black, apparently a well-to-do woman from the quality of her clothing. That the collision with the horse had inflicted grave damage was indisputable. She was unconscious and there were multiple lacerations about her head. Blood was running from her mouth and police were cradling her head. Amongst the other people congregated around her in mass confusion, a woman who was evidently a friend of the injured woman shrieked at the sight of the injuries.

"Bring a stretcher immediately!" I demanded. "This woman has been terribly injured."

I quickly ran over to Jones, who also had been hurt when Anmer rolled onto his leg.

"What happened?" the jockey asked, to no one in particular. "What happened?" he repeated. Then he asked, "Anmer. Is the horse all right?"

"Just relax," I advised. "Everything is just fine. I am a doctor. We'll get you to a hospital."

A medical team had appeared and I helped load the unconscious woman and jockey onto stretchers so they could be evacuated to a nearby hospital. The crowd was still in a tumult when I returned to my friends who pummelled me with questions about what I'd seen.

"A terrible accident," I reported. "I believe the rider has only minor injuries. He is trained to fall from a horse, of course."

"And the woman?" my friend Horace Basler asked.

I shook my head in response. "I suspect she has suffered a grievous injury, almost certainly a fractured skull and likely a brain haemorrhage," I responded. "It would be nothing short of a miracle if she survives."

"But what could she have been thinking?" asked Malcolm Polton, a fellow physician.

Again, I shook my head. "Who can possibly say?" I replied. "She may have had an objective, I suppose, or she may have been insane. Surely only someone who has lost all rationality would position themselves in front of a racing thoroughbred horse. In any event, there is little likelihood she will live to explain her motive."

The horrible incident cast a grim pall over the festivities as the stands emptied. As we through the crowd, a young man pushed his way through and accosted me.

"Say, you were down there on the track, weren't you?" he inquired. "Lyle Fitzgerald, *Daily Mirror*." He removed a small pad of paper from his pocket and a pencil from another, which he licked before continuing. "What did you see?" he asked "What can you tell the readers?"

I regarded the impudent reporter in a censorious manner. "I am a medical man," I replied. "I do not discuss cases with the press. This was a very great tragedy."

"Oh, come on!" he quickly responded. "Just doing my job. What did you see? Did she say anything? How did she look? It seemed awfully bad from where I was."

I pushed past the young man. "As I said," I reiterated, "I do not respond to press inquiries."

From behind me, I heard one of my friends reprimand the young journalist. "Don't you know that is Dr. John Watson, the associate of none other than Sherlock Holmes?" he said. I turned and saw it was the irrepressible Basler, and threw him a disapproving look.

"Dr. Watson!" the young reporter exclaimed in excitement. "That means Sherlock Holmes will be on the case, right?"

"Wrong," I responded. "Mr. Holmes is retired in Sussex, and I am finished with this interview!"

371

As planned, I returned to the train station and caught the next train to Sussex, where I was warmly welcomed by Sherlock Holmes. After a dinner at the nearby Tiger Inn, we returned to his charming home and I shared with him my account of the day's shocking events at the Epsom Derby.

Quite early the next morning, there was a knock on my bedroom door.

"Watson," Holmes called from the hallway outside my bedroom. "Are you now my publicity agent as well as my chronicler?"

"I have no idea what you are referencing," I responded.

"You really must see this morning's newspaper!" he answered.

"Would you mind explaining what you are reading?" I replied.

"Not at all, not at all," he said good naturedly. "Here is the headline in this morning's *Daily Mirror*. '*Sherlock Holmes to Investigate Epsom Derby Tragedy*'.

"*What?*" I exclaimed. "This is outrageous!"

"Oh, there is more," he added, reading, "'*Dr. John Watson, Mr. Holmes's close associate and biographer, attended the race and treated the injured rider and woman.*'"

I finished putting on my robe and opened the door. Holmes had the newspaper in his hand and was casually leaning against the wall.

"Holmes, I am mortified!" I declared, seizing the newspaper from his hands. "Surely you must know that I never suggested for a moment that you would in any become involved in this matter. Indeed, the only reason this reporter could identify me was because of the unwelcome remark of one of my friends."

"Watson, I didn't for a moment believe that you had volunteered me to become engaged," Holmes laughed. "I imagine this headline is about as involved in this misfortune as I am likely to become."

I quickly dressed and joined Holmes in the dining room, where a simple breakfast had been laid out by his housekeeper. As I buttered some bread and took a deep draught of strong coffee, I perused the front of *The Daily Mirror* for additional news of the previous day's calamity.

The unfortunate woman had been identified as Emily Davison, forty years old and a resident of London. She was an official of the Women's Social and Political Unit, the organization founded by the militant suffragette Emmeline Pankhurst to advocate for the vote for women. Like Mrs. Pankhurst, the injured woman was no stranger to militancy in pursuit of her political objectives. Indeed, she had been sent to prison multiple times for protests such as setting fire to postal boxes, climbing through the air ducts to reach the House of Commons, and hurling metal balls through windows. In 1909, she had been jailed for attempting to force her way into a room where David Lloyd George, the Chancellor of the Exchequer, was speaking. Soon thereafter, she was apprehended for chucking rocks at the Chancellor's automobile, each one wrapped in paper on which had been printed "*Rebellion against tyrants is obedience to God*".

"Quite a charming young lady," Holmes said disapprovingly. "How very American in her embrace of equal rights for all."

"Really Holmes!" I reproached. "The woman is lying near death!"

"And perhaps that was her intention," he replied. "We shall likely never know."

A knock on the door interrupted Holmes's comments, and his housekeeper entered the room. "Mr. Holmes, there's a wire here for you," she said, handing a yellow paper to my friend.

Holmes thanked her and quickly perused the telegram. "Well, Watson, I may have spoken too soon!" he said.

He handed the note to me and I read its contents.

Mr. Holmes:

I intrude on your retirement to seek your counsel, only because I have learned from The Daily Mirror *of your interest in investigating the tragic injury to our colleague, Miss Emily Davison. There are several unique questions regarding the incident that resulted in her injury that I would like to discuss with you. It is quite out of the question to raise such matters with the police. Please inform me as to your availability for a meeting in London in the next day or two.*

Very truly yours,
Emmeline Pankhurst

Holmes looked disapprovingly at me as he read of his "*interest*" in the Davison matter. "Well, what do you say, Watson?" he asked. "Should we journey to London and discuss the matter with Mrs. Pankhurst?"

"Holmes, I regret your becoming involved in this," I again apologized. "I assure you – "

He interrupted me with a wave of his hand. "The bees can manage on their own for a few days," he smiled. "Let's take up Mrs. Pankhurst on her offer. I would welcome the opportunity to meet the leader of the suffrage movement. Quite a different perspective, I suspect, from that illuminating discussion with your literary agent a year or so ago."

"I don't believe that Conan Doyle an ardent opponent of suffrage," I answered, "but he disapproves of the more radical wing of the movement."

I looked around in my briefcase and took out an envelope. "As it happens, I have brought along some recent clippings that I thought might be of interest to you, and here is a news article about Conan Doyle on this very subject."

"And what does the good doctor have to say?" Holmes inquired.

I pulled out a clipping from *The Times* of 29th April past and began to read.

> *Conan Doyle said it was necessary to differentiate between the honest constitutional suffragist, the female hooligans, and the even more contemptible class of people who supplied the latter with money to carry out their malicious monkey tricks.*

I shook my head in agreement. "Who could disagree with that proposition?" I asked. Continuing to read,

> *He believed that two years ago they might have had a chance of getting the vote, but now they would not get it in a generation.*

"Conan Doyle is quite critical of the more confrontational of the protestors," I remarked. "He speculates that their next foolhardy scheme for gaining public attention might be 'blowing up a blind man and his dog'."

Holmes snorted in response. "Or fomenting a tragic accident during a Derby," he added, "which ironically results only in the mangling of the demonstrator herself?" He reached for a briar pipe and filled it with tobacco. "Well, let us go meet Mrs. Pankhurst and perhaps she will supply us with some of the answers."

A few days later, a train to London and a cab deposited us at the home of Emmeline Pankhurst. The suffrage leader herself answered the door knock and ushered us into the tastefully decorated sitting room. Books were piled on the tables and even around the chairs, their titles focusing heavily on political and feminist matters. Mrs. Pankhurst was a dignified and still-attractive woman of sixty or so, I should say, dressed formally in a high-necked blouse and a black suit. Her graying hair was piled on her head, and her sober visage conferred a sense of calm and command.

"Thank you for coming, Mr. Holmes," she said. "And I think I can safely presume this is Dr. Watson," she added, nodding in my direction. She strode over to us and forthrightly extended her hand. Her handshake was firm and businesslike. She asked a young lady waiting by her side to bring some refreshments and gestured for us to be seated.

"I do not know whether you share your literary agent's disapproving view of the activities of the suffrage movement," she began. "I am aware of his . . . ambivalence towards our work."

"I assure you, Mrs. Pankhurst, that Sir Arthur's views on the matter of suffrage are of little interest to me and will have no bearing whatsoever on my role in this matter," Holmes responded. "I have always felt his energies were best left to ophthalmology, but he continues to promote the commercialization of my profession together with," and here, he gestured in my direction, "my 'Boswell', as Watson has been described. If I become engaged, you will have my full attention. I am interested in your suffrage movement only insofar as it is relevant to explaining the disturbing events at the Epsom Derby."

"It is not *my* suffrage movement, Mr. Holmes," Mrs. Pankhurst corrected. "It is a movement for all women, for all right-thinking people for that matter. In the Twentieth Century, it is intolerable to disenfranchise half the population, not to mention the half of the population that may well be better read, more compassionate and fair-minded, and equally hardworking as those who already enjoy the right to vote."

"Undoubtedly true," responded Holmes, his tone conveying a mild irrigation over being subjected to a speech. "I tend to avoid discussions of politics. Murder, blackmail, and thievery are more along the lines of my personal tastes."

Mrs. Pankhurst regarded him carefully, judging whether he was mocking her. She evidently decided to allow the comment to pass.

"I have been engaged in this struggle for many years," she continued, "having devoted my life to equal rights for women."

"Most commendable," I interjected.

"It is a matter of the highest principle for me and for the W.S.P.U.."

"Excuse me," I interrupted. "The W.S.P.U.?"

"The *Women's Social and Political Union*," she explained. "We believe in 'Deeds, not words'. In fact, that is our slogan."

"And I gather from the press that those deeds include arson," Holmes said, a topic that had caused ruptures in the Pankhurst organization recently.

"Battles for basic rights sometimes necessitate extraordinary measures," she replied.

"Including interference in a Derby, perhaps?" Holmes said.

"Yes, including interference in a Derby," she said. "I will not apologise for Miss Davison's action, although I will not claim to have known in advance of her intentions. But," she grew somber, "being run

375

down by the horse, being nearly killed – that certainly was never the intention, I am quite certain. Emily was quite practiced at what she was doing. I can only imagine the rider veered to collide with her, and I want you to look into that possibility."

Holmes shook his head. "I very much doubt that is the case," he replied. "A collision at that speed is bound to end tragically. No, a rider as experienced as Howard Jones would never have intentionally provoked a collision."

"Perhaps I did not make myself clear," Mrs. Pankhurst continued. "I believe that *is* what occurred, and I would like to engage you, and Dr. Watson, to provide the evidence so that we might take legal action against Jones and the King."

"The King?" I asked.

"It was his horse," Pankhurst replied. "We shall hold him responsible!"

Holmes stood up and picked up his hat. "Mrs. Pankhurst, I have no intention of beginning an inquiry burdened by a proscribed outcome, let alone one that implicates the Sovereign," he declared. "It is a cardinal mistake to draw a conclusion prematurely. Facts dictate the explanation, not the other way round. Watson?" he said, summoning me to my feet as well. "I am pleased to have met you, Mrs. Pankhurst," he concluded, moving towards the door.

"Do you mean that you will not take the case?" she archly asked.

"I will not take any case if there is any presumption about what I may investigate or conclude," he answered. "I would be interested in pursuing the matter on my own terms, with no restraints or preconditions."

Mrs. Pankhurst mulled over his comments for a moment and stood up herself. "Very well, Mr. Holmes," she responded. "Your way it will be. But I should not be surprised if there turned out to be more complex forces at work here than anyone suspects at the moment."

Holmes put his hat down and slumped again into the chair. "Oh, of that, I have no doubt. No doubt whatsoever."

The young girl appeared with coffee and tea and we poured ourselves steaming cups before settling back in the chairs.

"How may I help you?" the suffrage leader asked, suddenly more conciliatory. "I do wish to uncover what was behind poor Emily's rash action."

"It has been my experience that when a person acts in a way that is foreign to their nature, there is usually an explanation," said Holmes. "Of course, we don't know if that motive was honourable or not, and you must be prepared to discover aspects of Miss Davison's life that may reflect poorly or her, or on your organization, for that matter."

"I had not considered that possibility," Mrs. Pankhurst admitted. "However, I have little doubt that Emily's motivations were thoroughly honourable, however unfathomable in origin."

We quickly learned more about the activist's background. She was the rare woman to have attended Oxford, although she had not been granted a degree because of her gender. She had gravitated to the suffrage cause soon thereafter and had distinguished herself for her willingness to face arrest for engaging in confrontations with public officials and the police.

"She was sent to jail nine times," Mrs. Pankhurst declared with a sense of pride. "She was not afraid of the police or the courts. She viewed them all as part of a system designed to trample on the rights of women, and she was prepared to pay the price for her beliefs."

"Was she amongst those refusing to eat as part of their protest in jail?" I inquired.

"Most certainly. She was force fed while strong men held her in a chair. On forty-nine separate occasions! Forty-nine! I have been subjected to such abuse myself." She turned to face me. "I don't have to tell you, Doctor, that having a tube inserted into her nose and pushed into your stomach is anything but an enjoyable experience."

"Certainly not!" I agreed.

"Emily was not faint of heart, Mr. Holmes. Once at Strangeways Prison, she refused to leave her cell, and the matron flooded the cell with ice-cold water. Emily came close to drowning. And do you know what Emily did? She sued the prison and she won forty shillings! That is the price Emily was prepared to pay for equal rights. As are we all."

"Most admirable," murmured Holmes. "I am not persuaded it is the most efficacious means of achieving the ballot, but I cannot dispute the bravery required to endure such treatment. I also seem to recall Miss Davison spending several days in prison after horsewhipping a Baptist minister on the mistaken belief he was the Chancellor of the Exchequer."

"An unfortunate misidentification on her part," Mrs. Pankhurst admitted. "However, Mr. Holmes, I can assure you that politely asking Mr. Asquith has not proven especially efficacious," she said of the Prime Minister, with more than a hint of reproach in her voice. "I very much doubt that men, who have never lacked for political influence, can appreciate the humiliation and frustration felt by the women of Britain due to their legally inferior status. Please note, I said *legally* inferior."

"Not in my mind, I assure you," Holmes replied. "Not in my mind."

Mrs. Pankhurst narrowed her eyes as she stared at Holmes in an effort to assess whether he was being sincere. After a few moments, she turned to look at me.

377

"Unlike my friend, I have been married, and more than once," I quickly added. "I have only the very highest regard for the female sex, I assure you!"

"Marrying women does not signify a respect for them or their political rights, Dr. Watson," she reproached me.

"Let us put politics aside and focus on Miss Emily Davison," Holmes suggested. "What of her recent thinking might help explain her rash and tragic behavior at Epsom?"

"She had attended several meetings of the WSPU in recent weeks," Pankhurst began. "We have been engaged in discussions about the future of our movement."

"What about the future of your movement?" Holmes interrupted.

"Perhaps you are aware of the 'Cat and Mouse Act' that was passed just two months ago?" she responded. Both Holmes and I shook our heads. "Our refusal to eat whilst in prison has been rather bad publicity for Mr. Asquith," she continued, "and even more so the decision of the prison authorities to force feed us. The law allows for the release from prison of anyone engaged in a hunger strike – the term we use – if that person's health is threatened. But after the person has recovered, they are to be returned to prison to complete their sentence.

"Obviously, this new approach necessitates our thinking about innovative ways to protest other than hunger strikes. We have been meeting amongst ourselves and with some other protest groups to think about a new strategy."

"Which ones?" asked Holmes.

"Is that germane?"

"I will not know until you tell me," answered Holmes.

She mused about his request. "Well, frankly, Mr. Holmes, I do not know if I should be sharing such information with you."

Holmes stood up and reached for his hat. "There is no point in *my* playing cat and mouse, Mrs. Pankhurst," he reproached. "One cannot make bricks without straw, and I cannot analyse a problem without the facts. *All of* the facts. If you prefer to remain close-mouthed, that surely is your right. But I ask you to consider if the shoe were on the other foot, would your answer be satisfactory? I am, after all, working on your behalf."

Mrs. Pankhurst looked stonily at Holmes and me. "Very well, but I am relying on your discretion," she began. "Undoubtedly you are aware the Irish agitation has been gaining momentum."

"Yes, on both sides of the question unfortunately," replied Holmes. "The Home Rule bill seems to have stirred up both the Unionists who oppose a unified Catholic Ireland and the nationalists. The Irish

Republican Brotherhood is a group of dangerous extremists, in my view. But I fail to understand the connection between this group and your own, except for your mutual distrust and dislike of the government."

"We suffragists do not dislike the government, Mr. Holmes. We disapprove of its policies that treat millions of British women as second-class citizens," Mrs. Pankhurst responded with a hint of disapproval. "Still, I will not deny that disparate interests may find common cause against a mutual adversary."

"In this case, that *is* the government," I clarified.

"Yes. Miss Davison had been meeting with some of the I.R.B. nationalists during the past several weeks in an effort to explore how we might coordinate efforts towards our respective goals. However, the I.R.B. has shown little interest in working together, fearing suffragism distracts from the nationalist focus of their effort." She paused to ask Holmes, "Is that significant?"

"I cannot be sure," Holmes replied. "It is one more 'brick' for me to weigh."

Our investigation began with a rail trip back to Epsom and a drive to the Epsom Cottage Hospital to which Miss Davison had been transported after the tragedy had occurred. Mrs. Pankhurst hastily wrote a note to arrange for our visit and soon, we were knocking on the door of the hospital just after five o'clock in the afternoon. Four days had passed since the incident that resulted in her hospitalization.

"We are here in conjunction with the inquiry involving Miss Emily Davison," Holmes informed the clerk sitting at a desk at the admissions office. "We have been authorised to assist in the examination and treatment of Miss Davison, whom we understand is receiving care at this hospital."

The young man looked confused. "Are you with the police?" he responded. We replied in the negative. "Let me call the manager of the hospital," he suggested.

The clerk disappeared for several moments before returning with a sober middle-aged man who introduced himself as the manager of the facility, Sheffield Grimhold.

"Are you members of the family?" he inquired.

"I am Sherlock Holmes," my friend brusquely responded. "I imagine you are familiar with my name." Grimhold seemed a bit startled by Holmes's introduction, but nodded affirmatively. "And this is my colleague, Dr. Watson. We wish to see Miss Davison, as requested in this note from Mrs. Pankhurst. We understand your patient is in a very precarious state."

Grimhold looked at the note and then up at Holmes and shook his head. "Not any more she isn't, Mr. Holmes," he said. "She passed away just an hour ago from her injuries."

"Passed away?" I cried.

"The surgery could not help her," he responded. "We haven't even had the police here yet. I'm afraid they haven't given this case a very high priority."

"No police. Well, that is one piece of good news," Holmes said, drawing a quizzical look from the manager. "Would it be possible for us to examine her before the police arrive and further confuse the situation?"

"I certainly do not want any trouble," Grimhold replied. "It's just that there has been so much interest in what happened the other day at the racetrack."

"What kind of interest?" Holmes asked.

"The press," he replied. "And several Irish gentlemen called this morning as well."

"Really?" Holmes declared. "And did they have an opportunity to visit with Miss Davison?"

"Oh, no sir," he responded. "That would be strictly against the established procedures! They weren't admitted."

"Then it is all the more imperative that I view Miss Davison's remains immediately."

"I, well – all right, given as you're Sherlock Holmes and working for her friend," he responded, waving Mrs. Pankhurst's note.

He led us down to a room in which all the drapes had been drawn, which created a suitably somber atmosphere.

"Her end came quite peacefully," said Grimhold. "She never regained consciousness, and I very much doubt she was in any pain."

"Watson, would you mind?" Holmes said, turning on the room's electric lights and motioning to the bed where the body lay covered with a crisply starched white sheet. Folding back the covering, I again looked into the face of the woman I had seen for the first and only time lying on the dirt track at the Epsom Downs racetrack four days earlier. The blood had been cleaned from her face, and there were surgical scars on her scalp where some hair had been cut off. Her dark hair and wide mouth bespoke an air of elegance. She was very thin. A quick look confirmed that her neck had been broken by the force of the collision with the horse.

"Yes, dead perhaps an hour or so," I agreed, flexing her hand and wrist. "I would expect a massive hemorrhage of the brain, consistent with the collision and her fall to the track. It seems several vertebrae were severely damaged, which might have led to the failure of her respiratory system. A tragedy."

Grimhold nodded his head in agreement.

"Who else has been to see her?" Holmes asked.

"Her sister was here earlier in the day. Her brother Captain Davison as well, and several suffragists who had been at the Derby. Since they were family and close associates, we permitted them a brief visit."

"And they doubtless pinned this medal on her hospital gown?" asked Holmes, pointing to a badge affixed to the dead woman's bedclothes.

I looked at the printing on the badge. "'*Women's Social and Political Union*'," it read.

"I wonder if I might not look through her effects," Holmes said, looking about the room. "There could be a valuable piece of evidence that has been overlooked."

"I expected the police will want to see all that," Grimhold said, motioning to a table on which Miss Davison's clothing and other personal materials were neatly piled. "Please look quickly!"

Holmes's fingers pulled and pushed apart clothes, papers, and other materials. He opened her handbag and quickly looked at the contents. Every once in a while, he would utter a loud, "Hmm!" or click his tongue. Finally, he picked up a folded piece of paper and opened it. He read it quickly and returned it to the purse.

"And what is this?" Holmes asked, picking up a long scarf on which there was dirt from the racetrack as well as some printing. He held the scarf up with both hands. It was over six feet long and coloured with purple, green, and white stripes. On each end, in large block letters, were the words, "*Votes for Women*".

"That was brought in yesterday by Mr. Richard Burton, the clerk of the Epsom Derby track," Grimhold said. "It was found lying near Miss Davison on the track after the accident."

"Do we know that it was in her possession?" Holmes asked. "Might it have been placed there after the collision, to associate the accident more clearly with the suffrage cause?"

"I saw her pull that scarf from her coat just before the collision," I informed Holmes.

A knock on the door was followed by the entrance of an older man carrying a stethoscope and wearing a physicians' jacket. He looked about the room with a look of surprise on his face before waving his arms about. "What is the meaning of this?" he huskily whispered. "What are you doing in this patient's room? She cannot have visitors!"

"Visitors will do her no harm now," I said, bowing slightly in the direction of the corpse. I stepped forward, offering my hand. "I am Dr. John Watson of London, and this is my friend and colleague, Sherlock Holmes."

381

The physician was obviously uninterested in who we were. He moved quickly to the head of the bed and began to examine Miss Davison. After a moment, he stopped and looked at me with a pained look on his face. "I see, I see," he repeated. "I am not surprised."

"You are . . . ?" Holmes inquired.

"Mansell-Moullin," he replied, as though we should have recognized it.

"The author of *Surgery*!" I exclaimed. "A most outstanding text."

The surgeon slightly bowed in my direction. "I am the surgeon here. I operated on this woman four days ago." He placed the sheet back over her face. "A tragedy for racing and for the movement."

"You consider yourself a supporter of the suffrage movement?" Holmes inquired.

"What right-thinking person is not?" the surgeon responded. "I wish the government shared our point of view, in which case it would not have been necessary for Miss Davison to call attention to the cause by her sacrifice."

"I wonder," said Holmes, "how can you be sure that was her motive? I understand she didn't discuss her plans with her compatriots. Nor has an explanatory note been discovered. Perhaps something entirely different lies behind her action."

Dr. Mansell-Moullin shook his head. "I very much doubt that was the case," he responded. "I knew Emily through my wife, Edith, who is quite active as well. I have myself written a definitive report on the impacts of the barbarous practice of force-feeding the protestors."

"Why sacrifice her life by standing in front of a thousand-pound racehorse running thirty-five miles an hour?" Holmes responded.

"This is a woman who threw rocks in windows and endured force feedings in prison," the doctor answered.

"Yes, but those are far cries from effectively committing suicide before five-hundred-thousand people – not to mention risking the lives of riders and horses."

"Well, it certainly appears to have been suicidal to stand in front of that horse," the doctor said. "You know, she did once attempt suicide in prison."

"I was not aware of that incident," Holmes replied. He looked back at the bed. "Are there final arrangements?"

"Yes," the doctor replied. "Emily is going to be returned to London after the inquest is held. She is to be interred in Longhorsley, Northumberland following several days of ceremony attesting to her selfless sacrifice for the cause."

382

Holmes looked about the room one more time. "I think we have seen all there is to see here," he said. "Watson and I will remain for the inquest tomorrow. There are a number of matters which will require additional attention in the next several days to bring this matter to a conclusion."

"But surely the facts are not in dispute!" Grimhold said.

"Yes, Holmes," protested Dr. Mansell-Moullin. "Hundreds – perhaps thousands – of people saw Miss Davison duck under the rail and stand in front of Anmer. They saw the horrible collision. I fail to see how there is anything obscure about what occurred. It is a great tragedy, and senseless loss of life, but it is hardly a mystery."

Holmes looked at Grimhold and then at Mansell-Moullin. "Facts, you know, are curious things," he replied. "Some of the facts may well lead to the conclusions you have reached, gentlemen. But there are additional facts that suggest other explanations."

"Such as?" the doctor inquired.

"Such as the presence of a return ticket to London in her bag," Holmes said, holding up a piece of paper from the purse. "And this note from her sister expressing delight at their upcoming vacation together. Neither would suggest Miss Davison arrived in Epsom intending to take her own life. You see, I never draw conclusions until I have *all* the facts, and even then, I am rarely convinced that I have gathered every possible bit of evidence. On one point, however, I have no doubt whatsoever."

"And what point is that?" asked Dr. Mansell-Moullin.

"There is more here than meets the eye. I'm sure that in your surgery, you have often begun a case presuming a diagnosis only to discover something else, something even more sinister than you have anticipated, lurking hidden," Holmes suggested, and the doctor nodded. "We share that experience in common."

"What did you mean," I asked on the walk back to our hotel, "when you said something more 'sinister' was lurking in this case? Do you suspect Miss Davison was not the idealistic suffragist that has been portrayed?"

"Oh, I have no doubt her passion for the suffrage movement was sincere," he said. "But I don't think Miss Davison went to the Derby with the intention of committing suicide."

"How do you know that?" I asked.

"Because of that return ticket to London and the plans with her sister," he responded. "Those intending to commit suicide rarely make future travel plans. There are some other suggestive signs which lead me to question whether this case is as straightforward as it might appear to the undisciplined eye."

The inquest at the Epsom Police Court the following morning was a dry affair that offered little illumination about the circumstances surrounding the tragedy. Captain H. Jocelyn Davison, the dead woman's brother, offered a morose account of his sister's life, which he considered to have been utterly wasted by her irrational pursuit of a radical political objective. "Her achievements withered like Dead Sea fruit under the malignant influence of militancy," Captain Davison testified.

"I rather doubt he will be given a prominent speaking role at the memorial service," I whispered to Holmes, who grunted his agreement.

A police sergeant testified that no one had responded at the track when he had called out "Does anyone know this woman?" as Miss Davison lay crumpled on the track, although he had seen at least one woman hover briefly over the prostrate woman and then duck back into the infield area. A verdict of "Death by Misadventure" rather than "Suicide" was returned after the coroner described the fracture at the base of her skull, apparently caused by the collision with the racehorse. "It is exceedingly sad that an educated lady should sacrifice her life in so pointless a fashion," he concluded.

We departed the court building and returned to the station to await our train to London. "Wait here for me," Holmes requested as we stood on the platform. "I shall be right back." In five minutes, he had returned and we were soon aboard the train speeding back to Victoria Station. Holmes didn't show any interest in conversation during the journey but sat quietly with his eyes shut for most of the trip. I could tell he wasn't sleeping, but rather was deep in thought, and I knew better than to interrupt him during such periods of contemplation.

"I hope you don't mind that I've arranged a rendezvous at your home this evening," Holmes said as we alighted from the rail car. "If my invited guest chooses to join us, we might be able to make some quick progress on the remaining questions in this matter."

We had returned from a light dinner to my house and were settling into comfortable chairs for an after-dinner pipe when there was a knock on the door. Holmes looked at the mantel clock and nodded with satisfaction. "Eight o'clock precisely," he said. "I have no doubt many answers will be forthcoming very shortly."

"Mr. Holmes, is it?" the man said as I opened the front door, my hand instinctively resting on my service revolver in my coat pocket.

"I am Dr. Watson," I replied. "Mr. Holmes is in the sitting room."

A young man with red hair, at least six feet tall, strode across the sill and brushed past me, disappearing into the parlour. I was right on his heels in case his intentions were malevolent.

384

Holmes was standing by the fireplace, puffing on his briar. Looking up, he regarded our visitor for a moment before speaking.

"I presume I have the honour of addressing Mr. Liam McCorley," said Holmes.

The man looked surprised but responded, "Yes, I'm McCorley." He looked carefully at Holmes and then at me. In the better light of the room, I could see his eyes were red-rimmed, and it was evident the man had been distraught shortly before arriving. "What is it you want with me?"

"Please, be seated, Mr. McCorley," Holmes said in a welcoming tone. "Would you like something to drink? A pint, perhaps?"

The red-haired man waved off any suggestion of refreshments.

"I've read the news about Emily," he said. "What do you know of this business? How did you know of me or how to find me?" He looked around again. "Are you with the coppers, then?"

"Please sit down," Holmes repeated. "I'm not with the police and I have no interest in their becoming involved, although I cannot guarantee they will not intrude into the matter. I believe I can help ensure you aren't blamed for actions for which I strongly doubt you are responsible. But I will need your trust and your cooperation."

"I don't even know you!" he spat out. "Why should I trust an English aristocrat to care about me?"

"I assuredly am no aristocrat, and you have no particular reason to trust me save my reputation for integrity and discretion. At present, I have no reason to accuse you of wrongdoing. Unfortunately, I rather doubt the police will view the facts in the same light. I suggest we speak quickly and frankly."

McCorley eyed Holmes closely and collapsed in a chair. "Well, what do you know of Emily and me?" he asked.

"Not very much, to be truthful," Holmes said. "I do know you were acquainted, perhaps somewhat more than 'acquainted', to be perfectly truthful. I know you have a connection because of your mutual interest in suffragism, perhaps through your sister, Lucille, and that you disagreed over the levels of militancy required to achieve political reform. It is likely – no, probably more than likely – that you met Miss Davison at the Epsom Derby earlier this week, and I suspect you were as shocked as anyone by her rash action of ducking under the barricade and confronting the King's horse."

McCorley sat with his mouth slightly open for several moments after Holmes paused speaking.

"And do you know what I had for dinner last night?" he asked.

"Based on the arrangements of spots on your shirt," Holmes responded, "I would guess lamb stew, but that is really beside the point."

385

"Well, you're wrong about the lamb stew!" McCorley replied. "At least not last night. I didn't have any dinner, nor breakfast today. I cannot think of eating! I am distraught at the news of poor Emily, although I knew she was hurt grievously." He hesitated and covered his eyes with a large hand, rubbing them as though he could make the recent events disappear.

"Your note was in her purse advising that she meet you on the infield, at the top of the stretch run," Holmes began. "Contrary to your instructions, she had neglected to destroy it. It didn't require very much work on my part, given the other clues, to determine where you might be found and how I might get a message to you."

"And how's that?" he asked.

"I am aware of the growing connection between the British suffrage movement and some of the Irish nationalists," Holmes replied. "Of course, I don't know with which faction you are affiliated, but I felt a well-placed note to some of the London groups would find its way to you without much difficulty."

"Yes, it's true," McCorley admitted. "Emily and Lucille, my sister, had become friends in London, and when I arrived a few weeks ago, I met Mrs. Pankhurst and the others. I'm not one of the militants, Mr. Holmes. I am as much of a nationalist as anyone, and I make no apologies for that to you or to anyone else. But I take the word of my religion seriously, and I abhor violence in support of a free Ireland. Some of the suffragists thought me insufficiently committed and commenced to tutoring me to increase my level of militancy, much like they had when they formed the W.S.P.U. I spent quite a bit of time with them. I have to say it wasn't all politics and protesting and the like. I quite enjoyed their company – especially Emily's.

"Last week, she suggested we all meet at Epsom to see the races," he continued. "Lucille and Mary Richardson were coming along as well."

"And who is Mary Richardson?" Holmes interrupted.

"Oh, she's quite a disrupter," he said. "A few years ago, she saw the coppers beating up the demonstrators outside Parliament, and that was it for her. Mary said she was joining up – she called it a 'Holy Crusade' – and from then on, it was attacking police and smashing windows for the both of them. They both went to jail and got force fed. I'm sure you know that. Well, they looked on me as someone who needed a real lesson in militancy being the only way. I didn't have anything planned, and Epsom seemed like a nice diversion. I figured it would be one lecture after another, but I figured I could handle it."

"How would you describe their mood when you met them at Epsom?" I asked.

"Quite normal," he replied. "I'm not sure they ever got to the point of being jovial, if you know what I mean. Quite serious almost all the time.

But I certainly didn't think Emily was thinking of taking action down there with the crowds and the King present – not to mention all those police!"

"You all planned to return to London?"

"Absolutely," he confirmed.

"Yes, I thought as much," Holmes added, looking in my direction. He turned back to McCorley. "Please continue."

"Well, there's not much to tell, I suppose," he continued. "We met at the racetrack as planned at the inside viewing area, about a half-mile from the end of the race, I suppose."

"Did you know Miss Davison's plans?" Holmes asked. "Had she confided in you?"

McCorley looked down at his feel and remained silent. After several moments, he looked up with a plaintive look on his tortured face. "I knew she was up to something, but not her exact plan. I thought maybe they were planning to march down the track after the race, or some such thing. Oh, how I wish I'd told her not to do it!" he cried, his voice catching.

"It was the scarf." Holmes said. "The '*Votes for Women*' scarf she had concealed in her jacket."

"Yes, I saw it when she reached in for some money to pay for her admission," he said. "It was a sunny day and I could see no reason for a large scarf, so I asked her why she carried it all the way from London. She patted my hand like I was a schoolboy. 'Now, don't you mind that, Liam,' she says to me. 'But we're going to create some news here today.'"

"I couldn't imagine what she was talking about, but I gave it little thought because of all the people milling about."

"She didn't seem agitated or deeply concerned?" Holmes asked.

"No, not at first," McCorley said thoughtfully. "But I will say her mood changed after that other Irishman pushed past us."

Holmes sat upright. "What other Irishman?" he asked.

"Oh, Mr. Holmes, I'd rather not say, except he is a bad character well known to Scotland Yard. Not simply a supporter of a unified and free Ireland, but one of the army's deadliest."

"The Irish Republicans," Holmes clarified.

"Oh yes. They're a nasty lot, they are, happy to use the bomb and the bullet to secure their goals," McCorley continued. "I'm all for Ireland, but not at the expense of human life."

"Did Miss Davison speak with him?" Holmes asked.

"No," McCorley said thoughtfully. "But she seemed a changed person after that – edgier, more anxious – and I didn't blame her. I asked if she wanted to leave, but she said she preferred to stay, that there were too many people and it was too late to cross the racetrack to get to the exit."

"An interesting observation from someone who only minutes later did just that, despite several horses running towards her at full gallop," Holmes added. "What happened then?"

"Well it wasn't long before they announced the race would be beginning, so naturally everyone crowded to the rail so we would have a good view of the horses as they came round the track. Emily had positioned herself with an excellent view, but I did notice something peculiar. She suddenly seemed almost indifferent to the race, and instead, she kept looking down the track towards the finish line, down by where all the pennants and flags were flying.

"Down where the King and Queen were watching the race?" Holmes asked.

McCorley nodded. "Only a minute later, the first of the horses came by in a tremendous thundering of hooves," he continued, "but Anmer – that was the King's horse – wasn't in the first batch of horses, which seemed surprising. The crowd was cheering so loudly, and everyone was pressing against the rails to get the best view. But then, I could see the horse with the King's colors rounding the bend and seeming to pick up his speed. And that's when Emily ducked down under the barrier and stepped onto the track. I still cannot believe it!"

He covered his eyes again to block out the memory. "I thought she had lost her mind! The horses were coming so fast and there was so much noise. I admit, Mr. Holmes, I froze in fear, but it was fear for her, not for me. And in that instant, she pulled the scarf from her bag and planted her feet in the turf, directly in front of Anmer. She made no effort to move out of the way, not a step!"

McCorley stopped and closed his eyes as he recalled the scene. Holmes walked over to him and put a hand on the man's shoulder.

"Steady, McCorley, steady," he said. "Take a deep breath and continue."

"It makes no sense to me, Mr. Holmes," he sobbed. "Yes, I know they are saying she tried to commit suicide once before, but she seemed perfectly normal at the race – at least until she saw that big Irishman. She certainly didn't give the impression of someone about to sacrifice herself for 'The Cause', as they say."

"What did you do after the accident?" Holmes asked. "Did you go out to the track to check on Miss Davison?"

"I started to, but Mary – that's Miss Richardson – pushed me back. 'Don't you go out there!' she said to me. 'The coppers will grab you in an instant. They're looking for the likes of you. Get out of here as fast as you can. I can handle this.' It was against my better judgment, but she was insistent, and then she disappeared under the rail and onto the track so I

388

couldn't talk to her anymore. I figured she knew the situation better than me, and it didn't look like there was much I could do, so I disappeared into the crowd and then made my way back to London, where your note found me earlier today at the Emerald Island Pub."

Holmes stood up as he addressed McCorley. "Well, you have given me important information that I believe will help get to the bottom of all this," he said. "I appreciate your swift response to my request to come by. Meet me back here at ten o'clock this evening, and in the meantime, keep yourself well hidden. I suspect you are the target of very dangerous people."

After McCorley departed, Holmes went to the telephone and placed a call.

"Hello, this is Sherlock Holmes," he said into the receiver. "I need to speak with Mrs. Pankhurst, please." He waited a moment, and then added, "If you would please convey my request to her, I'm quite certain she will accede to my wish to speak with her." There was a short delay, and then apparently the suffrage leader was on the line.

After preliminary pleasantries and a quick updating of his activities, Holmes got to the point. "Forgive the hour, but I would like to meet with you immediately, if that would be convenient," he said. "Very good! And Mary Richardson. Yes, I would like her to be present as well. Why? Well, let's just say I think she will be able to provide some illumination to the issues. Nine o'clock? Very good, then," he concluded, hanging up the receiver.

"We have a nine o'clock appointment," he said to me. "By all means, let us assess where we are in this case."

"Some aspects of the matter seem quite clear," he declared. "Miss Davison was certainly a dedicated suffragist and not afraid to put herself at considerable risk to emphasize her political demands, as we have seen from her repeated arrests and self-starvation episodes in prison. I don't suppose, given her one known suicide attempt, that we can entirely rule out mental illness as a cause of her alarming decision at Epsom, which she must have known placed her life in peril."

"From a purely medical standpoint, I must agree," I responded. "She demonstrated what the new field of psychiatry calls 'self-destructive behaviour' on many occasions. Confronting a stampeding racehorse could well fall into such behaviour, in my opinion."

"Perhaps, but I'm not persuaded that was her intent," Holmes replied. "There are those several pieces of evidence that suggest she didn't intend to sacrifice herself at Epsom. And then there is the obvious question of why she would choose such a place to do away with herself, without apparently leaving any explanation for her action."

"There is the scarf with the '*Votes for Women*' message" I noted.

"Yes, but she could just as well have stepped in front of a streetcar or thrown herself off the Parliament clock tower," he said. "This was an especially dangerous and public act, one that I suspect was unplanned when she journeyed to Epsom."

"What do you suspect?" I asked. "Was the encounter with the other Irishman significant?"

"I don't think there is any doubt about that," he responded. "I suspect that we might well derive important information from Mary Richardson. Let us hasten to Mrs. Pankhurst's home where, I believe, the remaining facts of this case might be revealed."

We were soon ringing the bell once again at the home of Mrs. Pankhurst, who greeted us and ushered us into her parlor. Awaiting us was a woman of perhaps thirty or so with a hard glint in her eye and dark hair cut very much like that of a gentleman.

"This is Mary Richardson," said Mrs. Pankhurst, gesturing to her compatriot as we entered the room. "This is Mr. Sherlock Holmes and his associate, Dr. Watson – a medical doctor."

Miss Richardson's expression didn't change. "And what will you two gentlemen be wanting from me?" she asked in an indifferent tone.

"A pleasure," Holmes replied cheerily. We settled into chairs and Holmes turned towards Miss Richardson.

"Of course, you are under no obligation to speak with us," he said. "I have no doubt you will be given the opportunity of an interview with the police in the next few days."

"I certainly hope you don't think that is going to intimidate me!" she said in an exasperated tone. "They have interrogated me and worse for several years, and I have made clear I have no interest in cooperating with the likes of them no matter how they torture and abuse me."

"Yes, as I recall, your specific words were 'I shall be militant as long as I can stand or see. They cannot do more than kill me'," recited Holmes.

"I see you have made quite a study of me," she replied, her tone softening slightly. "Do you know what that policeman told me? He threatened to keep me till I was a skeleton and then throw me into an institution for mental wrecks!"

"No one is turning anyone into a skeleton here!" Mrs. Pankhurst interrupted.

"Believe it or not, Miss Richardson, I am personally quite sympathetic to your ultimate objective," said Holmes, "although I cannot condone your reliance on physical confrontation."

"Sometimes it is all that gets the attention of those who aren't sympathetic," she responded defiantly.

390

"Sometimes, but not always," Holmes countered. "For example, the other day at Epsom, I believe Miss Davison was concerned about something she learned just before the race began – something that caused her to change her own plans for the day and that, ultimately, cost her life. Something said to her by an Irishman she didn't expect to meet there."

Miss Richardson looked at Holmes intently, her jaw involuntarily working nervously.

"You see, it is clear to me that Miss Davison went to the race with the intention of creating an incident to draw attention to the suffrage cause, and undoubtedly, you were well aware of the plan. Otherwise, why would she have brought the 'Votes for Women' scarf with her?"

"Perhaps she wished to display it at the race," said Miss Richardson.

"I think there was something more planned," Holmes countered. "She kept the scarf hidden inside her jacket until she made her way onto the track. If she wanted to display it, the time had passed once the race began. Afterwards, there would little interest in the banner because all of the attention would be directed towards the winning horse and rider.

"Moreover, she discovered only once there that the King and Queen were in attendance. If she wanted to create an incident, surely the best time was before the race since, almost certainly, their Majesties would not linger long after its conclusion. She could have walked down the infield section to the area across from the seating area and unfurled her banner. The King could hardly have missed it."

"No, she couldn't," Miss Richardson countered. "The crowd was enormous, and you couldn't just walk through the infield like that. And besides, there was a great deal of security near the King. She probably couldn't have gotten close enough for him to have seen the printing on the banner."

"So she was effectively stuck where she was, perhaps a half-mile from the person who was doubtless the object of her demonstration," Holmes said. "How inconvenient. But that hardly explains her taking so drastic an action as stepping onto the track."

"Well, that goes to show how little you know!" Miss Richardson said disapprovingly. "As it so happens, we had been practicing exactly that little manoeuvre for a week, which was the reason she went onto the track."

"What 'manoeuvre' was that?'" I inquired.

"We spent several days at a stable, practicing how one might attach the banner to a horse as it sped by, so that when it crossed the finish line, it would be carrying the 'Votes for Women' banner," she explained. "It was Emily's idea, and she was getting quite good at it."

"And was she knocked down during these practice efforts?" Holmes pressed.

"Well, no, of course not," she replied, "she would stand to the side and stuff the banner into the saddle or the bridle."

"And she was successful in doing so?" Holmes asked.

"Yes, on several occasions, she was!" Miss Richardson answered.

"Well, then, that makes her action at Epsom even more difficult to explain," Holmes said. "It would have been one thing had she never attempted so foolhardy a stunt and was trampled in the process, but you are telling me she was practiced at it, and therefore, she knew where to stand and when to reach out to the horse as it sped by."

"And what significance to you ascribe to that observation?" asked Mrs. Pankhurst.

"The only one that is plausible," Holmes responded. "That her decision to stand in front of the King's stampeding horse was intentional!"

"Martyrdom!" commanded Miss Richardson. "She is a martyr to the cause of women's equality and suffrage."

"Perhaps," said Holmes. "What happened before she ducked under the guard rail?"

"A minute before the race started, Mr. McCorley tugged at her sleeve. He was holding a card in his hand. 'Look Emily, look what I have found slipped into my pocket!' he said with alarm. She took it to read and her entire expression changed. But then the race began and I forgot the incident until the horses came near.

"Emily had the card in her hand, and she was looking to her left, down the track to the finish line," she said.

"Towards the end of the track, and not towards the horses that were approaching from her right?" Holmes asked.

"Yes," Miss Richardson continued. "Just as the horses approached, she turned to see them. And then suddenly, she slipped under the rail and walked out into the middle of the racecourse. After the collision, I ran onto the track to comfort her," she continued.

"You undoubtedly encountered me there," I said, "as I ran onto the track to assist her."

Miss Richardson stared at me but said nothing.

"Come, Miss Richardson," said Holmes, standing and walking over to where she sat, his hand extended to her. "Let me have the card."

Miss Richardson stared at Holmes, as did Mrs. Pankhurst and myself. She said nothing, but her face hardened into a mask of defiance.

"I could simply call the police and have them charge you with withholding valuable information," he said, "although I have no desire to do so. I do not believe you were a part of a plot. Indeed, you might have

392

been as disturbed by what was written on the card as Miss Davison herself." He walked closer to the young woman with his hand still extended. He spoke, and his voice took on a sharper tone. "The card, Miss Richardson!" he commanded. "Or I will have no alternative but to detain you until Scotland Yard arrives. I remind you, we aren't dealing with the municipal police."

The young woman pursed her lips, then reached down and opened her handbag and removed a small card. She silently read the rough writing on it and then placed it in Holmes's hand.

Holmes looked at it with a serious mien and passed it to me:

> *The end of the race means the end of George. Freedom for Ireland!*

"Where did this come from?" Holmes demanded.

"Mr. McCorley said it must have been slipped into the pocket of his coat while we were passing through the throng. Emily was looking at it as the race began. She had it in her hand when she ducked under the rail."

"And you went onto the track to retrieve it immediately after the collision," Holmes declared.

"Yes. I didn't want that to be found on her," Miss Richardson confessed. "I was sure that whatever was to happen to the King at the end of the race would be blamed in part on the suffrage movement, perhaps by suggesting we were in collusion with the Irish Nationalists."

"You do share a common willingness to commit acts of violence," I interjected.

"To make our point, yes," she replied, "but we are not soldiers at war with the King. The I.R.B. or the I.R.A. might embrace regicide, but suffragists certainly do not! In fact, the I.R.B. doesn't even support the suffrage movement because they believe it detracts from their argument for Irish Home Rule."

"And what was McCorely's reaction to the tragedy?" Holmes asked.

"Oh, he left as swiftly as possible. I didn't even know until a day or two later how badly Emily had been injured, or that the King has been safely evacuated from the track, thank goodness."

Holmes sat on the arm of his chair, fingering the card in his hand.

"Yes, I think we have Miss Davison to thank for that," Holmes declared.

"Why do you say that?" Mrs. Pankhurst asked.

"I suspect that Miss Davison performed an act of extraordinary bravery – not simply for the suffrage movement, but for England as a whole."

393

He turned to the two women. "Please allow me to keep this note," he said to Miss Richardson. "If my inquiry has the outcome I expect it will, I am not going to mention that it ever found its way into your possession. I ask that you not discuss anything related to the incident with anyone but the police, should they find their way to you. I would tell them the story precisely as you have related it to me, but leave this paper out of it for now."

The two women nodded their heads in agreement, and Holmes and I returned to my rooms, where McCorley soon appeared looking anxious and furtive. He seemed grateful to find us.

"What have you learned?" he anxiously asked when we had closed the door.

"Among other things, I learned that you were not entirely straightforward with me," Holmes said reproachingly. McCorley silently looked at the floor. He withdrew the card from his pocket, and there was a gasp from McCorley.

"Where did you find *that*?" he asked as he rose from his chair, his eyes wide.

"Miss Davison had it in her hand when she was struck," Holmes said. "You have Miss Richardson to thank for retrieving it. Had it been found in Miss Davison's hand, she would surely have been connected to the Irish nationalism movement even more than the suffragists already are."

"But she wasn't I.R.B.," he protested, "and neither am I. They don't even like the suffragists! I don't know when that card came into my pocket. I assume while we were walking through the crowd."

"Yes, it undoubtedly was placed there by the Irishman you saw at the race. He surely intended that it would be found when you and Miss Richardson were questioned by the police – after the assassination of His Majesty King George!"

I stared thunderstruck at Holmes. McCorley looked at the detective seriously but without surprise.

"Mr. Holmes, you must believe, I knew nothing of any planned attack on the King," he insisted. "Nor did I have any sense of what Miss Davison would do before she ducked under the rail."

"But you showed her this card, which you had failed to mention to me."

"Yes, I found it in my pocket just as the race was commencing. She took it from my hand and asked what it meant. I saw the meaning immediately: The IRB was planning an attack on the King, presumably during the commotion after the race. I told Emily, 'My God, they mean to kill the King!' She got a horrified look on her face. I know the papers said she was smiling but it was no smile, it was a look of horror. I think she could see the danger to us all, to our movements, if such a despicable act were laid at our feet."

Holmes measured McCorley carefully. The young man seemed genuinely distraught at the thought of injury being done to King George.

"I believe Miss Davison made a split-second decision when she saw this note," Holmes said. "She had intended to attempt to place the '*Votes for Women*' scarf on Anmer's bridle, as she had practiced at the stable. But she realized that if the race were run as was planned, the King and Queen were likely to come down from the grandstand to congratulate the winning rider, and that there were assassins in the crowd waiting for just such an opportunity.

"She needed to create an incident, a much bigger incident than the symbolic one she had originally planned, to alert the King's security people from a half-mile away that there was imminent danger and they must escort him from the track instead of visiting with the winning horse. And so instead of stepping to the side as the horse went by, she stood where the horse could not help but collide with her. That catastrophic incident that was certain to alert the King's people, a half-mile away, that danger lurked at the Epsom Derby.

"I doubt she intended to sacrifice her life for the King's safety. I would imagine she thought she might be knocked away. She kept this card in her hand in case she couldn't alert those attending to her afterwards that there was a plot against the King."

"The she is a heroine!" McCorley cried.

"Not one we can afford to celebrate in public," Holmes said. "It would be extremely difficult to prove that she didn't know about the I.R.B. plan. It might even appear she was in league with the revolutionaries. But absent holding the card, her action probably wouldn't have prompted the evacuation of the King and the Queen from Epsom Downs."

McCorley was quiet. "I suppose I am to blame," he said. "I should have brought the card to the attention of the police. But I had no time or ability to do so. I didn't even find it in my pocket till after the race had started."

"The idea of slipping the card into your pocket was to point the finger of blame at you and your colleagues in the fight for Irish independence," Holmes explained. "By discrediting you, they undoubtedly believed they would build support for their own radical movement and at the expense of the suffragists whom they dismiss as busybodies.

"I suspect there is nothing good for you here in London, Mr. McCorley," Holmes said. "I suggest you return to Ireland until this matter calms down. If no attention is turned to the plot against the King, I think you'll be safe from the police. As to your safety from the I.R.B. – well, that, sir, is your concern and your concern alone."

McCorley stood with his hat in hand and stared at Holmes with a look of disbelief. "You're letting me go, then?" he asked with a look of relief on his face. "You're not turning me over to the police?"

"It would seem to me the most unwise thing I could do would be to sully the more reasonable wing of the Irish movement by linking all forms of nationalism to regicide," Holmes replied. "I trust you will continue to renounce the use of violence to achieve your ends. Otherwise, I will become your most tireless pursuer."

McCorley nodded several times and fled out of the room, but as Holmes feared, he didn't immediately depart from the city, and was far from safe. Two days later, there was a short report in the newspaper. "*Irish Nationalist Stabbed to Death Near London Docks*" the headline read. A small piece of cardboard was pinned to his chest on which had been written "*IRB*" in his own blood.

"A sordid group," Holmes said at breakfast as he read the account to me. "He could implicate the I.R.B. in the plot, so they had to get rid of him before he talked to the police. I'm not sympathetic with his goal of breaking apart our alliance with Ireland, but the way to fight that battle is surely through debate, not bullets, knives, and bombs. And, I believe, the same is true for Mrs. Pankhurst and her acolytes in the suffrage movement. Unfortunately, violence seems to have found McCorley despite his renunciation of direct action."

Holmes spent several days with Inspector Llewellyn at Scotland Yard, going through the information he had gathered on the I.R.B. plot against the King, although he was able to leave the connection to Miss Davison and the suffragists out of the story. Over the next several weeks, a number of arrests of I.R.A. and I.R.B. militants in London and Dublin were directly tied to the information Holmes had provided.

Miss Davison's body arrived in London to a spectacular welcome by over five-thousand women. Her coffin, inscribed with the slogan "*Fight on. God will give the victory*" was at the head of the procession that included hundreds of men supporting the right of suffrage for British women. Holmes and I did not attend the ceremony. Neither did Mrs. Pankhurst, who had been arrested that very morning under the Cat and Mouse Act.

The march proceeded from Victoria to Kings Cross, and then to St. George's Church in Bloomsbury for a service attended by members of the Church League for Women's Suffrage, and then along a parade route lined with fifty-thousand mourners, many wearing the distinctive colours of white, green, and purple of the suffrage movement. They were the same

396

colours that had been emblazoned on the scarf Miss Davison had carried inside her jacket, onto the Epsom Derby track and then, into history.

Emily Davison
11 October 1872 – 8 June 1913

The Welbeck Abbey
Shooting Party
by Thomas A. Turley

Chapter I – A Conference with the Elder Brother

On a mild but windy morning in November, eight months before the outbreak of the Great War, I found myself in Whitehall answering a summons to meet with Mycroft Holmes. It had been several years since I last encountered that remarkable civil servant. Nor had I seen his brother, my friend Sherlock Holmes, for several months. In those days (as I have written elsewhere), the detective was often absent in the United States, posing as an Irish-American agent known as "Altamont". The momentous results of his mission would be revealed in the case Sir Arthur has entitled "His Last Bow" – although it proved, of course, to be nothing of the kind.

I was relieved that our interview would take place in Mycroft's office, rather than inside the strange confines of the Diogenes Club. It was not often that I met alone with His Majesty's advisor, whom I found slightly intimidating even in his brother's presence. Fortunately, whatever nervousness I felt was groundless. The senior Holmes greeted me with his old-fashioned courtesy, removing a pile of documents from the chair before his desk and enquiring whether I preferred tea or sherry. Much like his brother, however, he evinced a degree of satisfaction when I declined both.

"Then let us proceed to business, Doctor, if you please." With a heavy sigh, Mycroft relapsed into his voluminous desk chair. I could not but notice that he looked much older than when I had seen him last. The iron-grey hair above his lofty brow was sparse. His Victorian side-whiskers had fallen victim to the modern age. While hardly slim, he was at least three stone lighter than when he served the Queen. Yet that in itself was no bad thing. Mycroft's colour was still excellent. His lethargy seemed no more pronounced than formerly. It occurred to me that Holmes's elder brother was five years older than myself, and my own countenance in the morning mirror was no longer an inspiring sight.

"In forty minutes, I must report to the Prime Minister on the Irish transport workers' strike," he grumbled, "so we are forced to make our plans in haste. I have an assignment for you and Sherlock, Dr. Watson: one that will bring you once more into the presence of European royalty."

"Holmes is back in England?" I had had no word from him to that effect.

"He docked last night in Liverpool and is on his way to London. I have arranged a room for him in the Diogenes Club. He will join you on Friday for the trip to Worksop, then return to Chicago when your mission is completed."

"Worksop?" I tried to recall the place and failed. It sounded less than euphonious as a destination for European royalty.

"In Nottinghamshire, Doctor!" Mycroft had no more patience than his cadet with slower-moving intellects. "It is the nearest town to Welbeck Abbey, the country house of the Duke of Portland, whom Franz Ferdinand intends to visit."

I knew Portland, at least by reputation. As a very young man, he had served in the élite Coldstream Guards, but a promising army career was cut short by his early succession to the dukedom. Since then, he had held several court positions, including Master of the Horse for both of Britain's recently departed Majesties. I remembered his leading Queen Victoria's Golden Jubilee Procession when I was married to poor Constance, in what seemed of late to be another lifetime.

"Is the Archduke acquainted with Portland?" The Austro-Hungarian heir-apparent and his morganatic wife were presently at Windsor, the guests of King George and Queen Mary. My own wife was following their visit with great interest.

"Yes, they met in Vienna years ago. The Portlands spend much time in Austria and have many friends there. The late Empress Elisabeth even sent the Duke a number of her Lipizzaner horses, in exchange for four of his Jersey cows. As you perhaps have heard, Franz Ferdinand is an obsessive hunter, and Welbeck Abbey is renowned for its shooting parties. You, along with my brother and the Archduke, will attend one there next week."

"But why?" Had I been summoned merely to fulfill a social obligation?

"Because I've no one else to send! Ireland, Doctor, is on the verge of civil war. My best men are in Dublin or Belfast. The others are shadowing those wretched Pankhursts, lest another suffragette do worse than throw herself under the King's horse. This country has gone to the Devil since that damnable Parliament Act two years ago! [1] The Austrian heir-apparent and his wife are safe enough in Windsor, but my agents (if I had any) cannot operate effectively on a private estate like Welbeck Abbey. No, it must be you and Sherlock. As guardians of a foreign potentate, you're all I've got."

"Is Franz Ferdinand in danger?"

"'The Great,' as I believe you habitually refer to them, are perpetually in danger. No doubt your experience of Herr Anton Meyer has convinced you of the Pan-Germans' lack of reverence for the House of Habsburg. The Archduke himself is widely hated, both within and without the borders of his realm. It is rumoured that on his accession, he will revise the *Ausgleich* with Hungary to improve the fortunes of the empire's Slavs. Besides antagonising the great Magyar nobles, that course quashes the ambitions of the Pan-Serb dynasty that has ruled in Belgrade since you and Sherlock failed to save King Alexander." [2] (Here I shifted restlessly in protest.) "Fortunately, Franz Ferdinand was able to restrain the Austrian military leaders who sought a reckoning with Serbia in the recent Balkan Wars."

"That surprises me. The newspapers often depicted him as a leading warmonger."

"Doctor, I have no time to correct the manifold imbecilities of the British press. Suffice it to say that the Heir-Apparent has a host of enemies. His marriage alone left him *persona non grata* with the Emperor. His wife was a lady-in-waiting, although of ancient lineage. The Duchess of Hohenberg, as she is now entitled, endures constant petty snubs at court, which naturally exacerbates Franz Ferdinand's ferocious temper. The Duchess has been treated far more respectfully at Windsor this past week than ever in Vienna."

Having been apprised of the lady's troubles by my fascinated, if sympathetic, wife, I only shook my head regretfully. "So if I understand you properly," I cautiously began, "Holmes and I – mere commoners – are to act as secret bodyguards for the heir-apparent to a European throne, attempting to look inconspicuous on a ducal estate teeming with aristocrats, all armed to the teeth with hunting weapons! How are we go about it? Do we join someone's retinue, or try to socialise on equal terms?"

Mycroft smiled with more compassion than I had expected. "I shall leave that to you and Sherlock. But guests invited to the shooting party – although admittedly august – are not exclusively nobility. Several Conservative ex-ministers from the House of Commons will attend, including Mr. Balfour." (I all but rolled my eyes – An ex-Premier, the nephew of a marquess, would bring down the tone of the occasion!) "There are likewise a good many soldiers, with whom you, as a veteran of Maiwand, ought to fit in well. If possible, I shall provide a guest list before your departure. Have you any other questions, Doctor?"

I had several, but I decided to pose the one that Priscilla, my wife, would have asked: "Does the invitation to Welbeck Abbey – which I presume you have secured – include my wife?"

400

"I fear not. To avoid any questions of precedence, ladies are excluded from the party unless they are related to the Duke or are already acquainted with the imperial couple. For the same reason, His Majesty did not invite the royal princesses to attend at Windsor. Moreover, the presence of your wife would be a needless complication, given the nature of your mission."

I looked forward to offering Priscilla *that* excuse! Nevertheless, my country called. It would be exciting, even at so late a date, to share another adventure with Mr. Sherlock Holmes. As ever, I acquiesced in what was asked of me, and Mycroft quickly outlined the logistics. Then I returned to Queen Anne Street to placate my wife.

"But I don't understand why *I* can't go," Priscilla wailed, "if other wives are invited to the shooting party. It's not as though *I* take precedence over the poor Duchess! It really is too bad of Mr. Holmes, John."

We were preparing for an evening out, so I was reluctantly donning evening dress, thankful again that a retired army surgeon was not required to keep a valet.

"My dear, it was not Mr. Holmes's decision." Suppressing a sigh and retrieving a dropped stud, I repeated Mycroft's explanation, which sounded unconvincing even to my ears. The simple truth was that Priscilla would be in the way, but I could hardly tell her so. I had not been permitted to reveal the nature of our mission.

"Well, I certainly hope this will be the last time," she said sulkily, passing me my cufflinks. "You promised before Belgrade there would be no more 'royal adventures'."

"I promised there would be no more *European journeys*," I corrected her. "Welbeck Abbey is in Nottinghamshire, three hours north of London. I'll be back within a week."

"I know that, John," my wife conceded. "It's just that I'd got used to your being at home since Mr. *Sherlock* Holmes left for America. And he always takes you into danger. Should you – should *either* of you, for that matter – still be having these adventures at your time of life?"

"We're not *quite* at death's door, you know," I muttered, fastening my collar. In truth, I had felt that fearful portal looming nearer since turning sixty-one. Like any aging man possessed of a still young and lovely wife, I saw the contrast between us more poignantly each time we passed a mirror. My expanding girth, grey hair, and tendency to gout – two of those attributes visible at this very moment – reminded me that the man I had been once I was no longer.

"She's very beautiful, I hear," a voice behind me murmured.

"Who's beautiful?"

"The Duchess. Of Portland, I mean, not the Archduke's wife. Sargent's painted her, as has Lázló."

"Quite so, my dear," I acknowledged, turning back to her with a manufactured smile. "The Duchess of Portland was undoubtedly the most beautiful woman I saw at the Devonshire House Ball. In 1897! She is at least a decade older than you are, and – I can honestly assure you – not half so beautiful even at the time."

My third wife *was* sufficiently beautiful that my exaggerated compliment was not an empty one. The high-waisted, flowing gown she wore matched her green eyes and suited her trim figure. Her chestnut hair (confined for the evening by a feathered headdress) was a glory when released. she dimpled sweetly as she reached over to adjust my tie, and the smile I gave her this time was sincere.

"We'll say no more about the trip to Welbeck," she decided, "but you must tell me all about it – the people, I mean, not the shooting – when you and Mr. Holmes return. And tonight, John: It's only a one-act play, so, please, no longing glances towards the lobby after fifteen minutes. You know how much I enjoy Mr. Shaw."

I did, but I also knew how much *I* enjoyed Mr. Shaw. Nevertheless, I managed to maintain an amiable demeanour for the remainder of the evening, consoling myself with the thought that – come Friday – the game would be afoot!

Chapter II – From London to Worksop

I arrived at King's Cross promptly on Friday afternoon, well ahead of the scheduled time of our departure. Stepping outside the first-class compartment Mycroft had reserved for us, I scanned the platform in search of Sherlock Holmes. It was eighteen minutes past three – with a mere seven minutes' grace remaining – when he at last appeared, moving through the milling crowd with the purposeful stride I well-remembered. I noted that he was wearing a most atypical tweed cap, matched by a suit that looked as though it had done service in the 'Nineties. Holmes had brought with him a surprisingly small amount of luggage, and when he turned to instruct the porter I re-entered the train and took my seat, not wishing to appear unduly anxious.

"Well, Holmes," I greeted my old companion as he joined me, "That's certainly not one of your more elaborate disguises. No Italian clerics or consumptive seamen in your repertoire today?"

"No," he replied with veiled amusement. "I abandoned my original disguise before leaving for the station. I did not wish to place *too* great a strain upon your powers of observation." We exchanged a laugh, and

Holmes tapped my knee with his briar pipe, a puckish gesture prompted by the lapse of time since our last meeting. "How are you, Watson?" he enquired, pulling out a bag of shag tobacco. "Eating too well of late, I see."

"Indeed," I ruefully admitted. "I only wish that I could say the same of you." The detective was as gaunt as he had been in Baker Street when using himself up too freely. "You look tired, Holmes. Was it the sea voyage? I recall from our last 'royal adventure' that you don't do well on ships."

"In part, I suppose," Holmes sighed. "I came over on *Olympic* – in the veritable lap of luxury – but it reminded me how close I was to embarking on *Titanic* last year for her maiden voyage. If not for a last-moment change of plans, I might be sitting on an iceberg instead of talking with you now."

"Indeed," I parroted once more. My friend's jocularity, I knew, masked his deep emotion at that awful tragedy. Several acquaintances had gone down on the ill-fated liner, among them Senator Gibson and his second wife, our former clients. After thirty years, however, it was evident to me that something more was wrong with Holmes. A sudden jolt, as our train began to leave the station, forestalled my enquiry.

"Sometimes, Watson," he remarked quietly, "I find myself doubting that the British Empire will survive the present century."

"Good heavens, old man!" I replied, quite shocked. "What on Earth has happened to leave you in any doubt of *that?*"

"Nothing I can coherently explain to you, or even to myself. Yet, my latest mission has convinced me that Great Britain lies in greater danger than at any time since Napoleon I ruled Europe. Another emperor (you have met the one I mean) now seeks the same hegemony. Before many years have passed, his country will be far better able to displace us than ever was 'The Little Corsican's'."

"This mission, Holmes," I prodded him, for he had previously said very little of his quest. "Of what does it consist? Why does it require these frequent journeys to America? What results have you accomplished during all these months?"

My friend stared out our compartment's window, where the environs of London had given way to countryside. It was a long while before he answered. Even then, his gaze remained fixed upon the passing scenery.

"It involves misleading our most likely enemy regarding our defensive capabilities. I cannot say more, old friend, even to you. However," he went on more brightly, "it has gone well of late. I have disarranged a number of my adversary's plans, and thus far he has not questioned the slightly flawed intelligence 'Altamont' has sold him. However, the crux of the affair cannot occur for quite some time. Until

403

then, I can take no risks that would expose me prematurely or upset the scheme I have in place. For that reason, Watson – " Here he turned back to me, and I could foretell the rest with dawning horror. " – I cannot accompany you to Welbeck Abbey."

"What?" I nearly shouted. "You're leaving me alone?"

"I must! This morning, Altamont met in secret with the German spy to whom he has been feeding information. There I learned my 'pigeon' has been invited to the Duke of Portland's shooting party. I have not altered Altamont's appearance from my own, save for adopting American attire and a hideous goatee. How can I take the risk of being recognised? Why, I might forget myself and lapse into a Yankee twang."

"Good heavens, Holmes! Your spy may have travelled with us on this train." Rather foolishly, I glanced out our compartment's doorway in alarm.

"No, no," my friend assured me. "Herr von Bork will accompany the rest of the German contingent tomorrow, the same day the Archduke is arriving."

"Von Bork?" I queried. "Who *is* the scoundrel?"

"Hardly a scoundrel, Watson. Merely a faithful – if not always scrupulous – servant of his sovereign, much like you or I. Von Bork is an amiable *bon vivant* who fills some minor position at the embassy. Since arriving here three years ago, he and his wife have become great favourites in society. *However*, beneath his charming surface, this young man has succeeded our late friends Oberstein and Meyer as the most dangerous of the Kaiser's agents. Should I be recognised at Welbeck Abbey, not only our two lives, but the safety of the British Empire would be forfeit."

"So I'm on my own to protect the 'widely hated' Heir-Apparent from your spy and every other assassin who attends the shoot. A fine plan you and Mycroft have conceived! What are *you* doing in the meantime? Having tea? Why are you even *here*, Holmes?"

"Don't blame Mycroft, my dear fellow. He had no inkling of my meeting with von Bork at the time he spoke to you. And it isn't quite as bad as that. I'll be within call, four miles away in Worksop. I can come to your aid if absolutely needed."

"Four miles? Why, thank – "

"And you *will* have other allies. Portland has been informed of your true function, and there are trustworthy people on the Heir-Apparent's staff. One soldier, in particular, you should get on with – a Colonel Brosch von Aarenau. He headed Franz Ferdinand's *Militärkanzlerei* – a kind of shadow chancellery in the Belvedere Palace – for five years before leaving to command a regiment of *Jägers*. His successor, young Count von Straten

Ponthoz, is an unknown quantity. Finally, there is Baron von Rumerkirch, the Archduke's chamberlain, who has served him long and faithfully."

"Anyone else?" Despite myself, the prospect of another independent mission was beginning to appeal to me.

Holmes smiled, taking from his jacket a thick portfolio. "As usual, Mycroft has prepared extensive notes on everyone whom you will meet. Study them carefully. Fortunately, neither the Austrians nor the Germans will arrive before tomorrow evening, which should give you ample time to speak privately with Portland. Ask him to find a reliable local lad to act as a messenger between us. You remember my procedure in the Dartmoor case so long ago. Make any other preparations the two of you deem fit. But *do not* say anything to Portland to give away von Bork."

"But why? Why not arrest the fellow and be done with it?"

"It would never do, Watson. In the first place, he has done nothing – nothing we can yet reveal, at least – to justify arrest. Although his presence at the shooting party makes me uncomfortable, we are in much the same position as we were with Adolf Meyer in Geneva, back in '98." [3]

"Well, you know how *that* turned out!" I put in caustically.

"Of course I do, but here the stakes are even higher. In the last analysis, the life of Franz Ferdinand is secondary to my greater mission. Habsburg heir-apparents – as we have seen – can always be replaced. Whatever may happen to the Archduke, it cannot be allowed to compromise the delicate plans I have arranged. It is in Sussex, and not at Welbeck Abbey, that I must entrap von Bork."

I could only accept this decision. It was then that my friend told me of his audience, eleven years earlier, with the Emperor Franz Josef, an event I have recounted elsewhere. To judge by that chilling conversation, the Heir-Apparent faced more dangers in Vienna than beyond the borders of his realm. Next, Holmes described the rest of the German contingent that would attend the shoot.

"Von Bork's 'handler' – to employ one of Mycroft's terms – is the embassy's chief secretary, Baron von Herling. A huge man, slow of speech, but my no means slow of wit. Watch him closely, for he is known to be disloyal to the present ambassador, Prince Lichnowsky, who has done his best to ease tensions between London and Berlin. Whether the Baron's ultimate allegiance is to his Kaiser or the Pan-Germanists remains uncertain."

"Are they not one and the same?" I suggested. "Your brother apprised us long ago of William's boast that he would seize the Habsburgs' German-speaking provinces."

"Ah, but that was before the present system of alliances came fully into force. Now Germany finds herself caught between France – her bitter enemy – and the Russian bear. Given Italy's unreliability, Austria-Hungary is the Kaiser's only trustworthy ally. He has therefore taken pains to cultivate her heir-apparent. Four years ago, William invited the Archduke and his consort to Berlin. There he made quite a show of treating Duchess Sophie with full royal honours, and the two men have become fast friends. Recently, the Kaiser even visited Franz Ferdinand at Konopischt to view his rose gardens."

"The Archduke grows roses?" I asked incredulously. "That belies almost everything I've heard about his personality!"

"Do not rely solely on court gossip from Vienna. Mycroft informs me that Franz Ferdinand, despite his reputation for ferocity, is a man of considerable intelligence. Nor is his wife the ambitious climber her enemies portray. They both made an excellent impression upon the King and Queen at Windsor. As I have often told you, we must not cloud our observations with pre-judgements."

"Quite so, Holmes." I meekly admitted.

"There is one other person of whom you need to be aware," my friend concluded, "and that is Prince von Fürstenberg. Frankly, Watson, I don't know what to make of him. He is extremely wealthy, with vast estates in both Germany and Austria, and serves as a trusted messenger between Vienna and Berlin. Yet he appears to be a foolish, foppish fellow in himself. More oddly still, his friendship with the Kaiser is reputed to be of such a nature that the Kaiserin objects to it."

"Surely not!" For all my dislike of our old enemy, I was astonished to hear such an imputation made against the man.

"So I have been told. Mycroft – who, as you know, has an eye at every European keyhole – reports that William's previous 'best friend', Prince Eulenburg, was disgraced some years ago in an unseemly scandal, as was earlier the great munitions manufacturer, Herr Krupp. The latter gentleman is rumoured to have killed himself after the Kaiser was unable to hush the matter up."

"Now we have descended into gossip!" I grumbled, turning to my window. Outside, twilight was fading as we left Nottingham behind. "If you don't mind, Holmes, I would rather discuss my mission than these German peccadilloes."

"Very well," conceded the detective. However, he was silent for some moments, as though reluctant to broach the next item on his list. "Watson," he continued finally, "the Austrians may ask you about a certain Herr Wolfe, who was invited to Welbeck Abbey but declined to come. Franz Ferdinand had desired to thank Wolfe for an assignment he recently conducted for Vienna in the Balkans."

"Herr Wolfe? I've never heard of him. Do you know the fellow?"

406

"Quite well. 'Nero Wolfe' is a rather fanciful alias used by my son, Scott."

"Scott?" I marvelled. "Surely the boy was very young for such a mission!"

"He was not yet twenty-one in May, when it began," replied the proud father. "As you know, Mycroft has been grooming Scott for intelligence work ever since his days at Harrow. You may recall that Austria-Hungary and Russia nearly came to blows during the spring, after the Serb and Montenegrin armies invaded Albania, that new country whose creation blocked Serbia from the Adriatic – one of the London Conference's more unwise decisions, in my view."

"I remember all too well," I said. For several weeks, it had appeared the Balkan conflict would plunge all Europe into war. With the Great Powers divided into two armed camps, Austria's and Russia's respective allies were obliged by treaty to support them.

"The Austrian heir-apparent was determined to have peace, despite the clamouring of his generals to crush the Serbs. In order to defuse the crisis, Franz Ferdinand secretly approached Sir Edward Grey [4] to despatch a British envoy to negotiate the Montenegrins' withdrawal from Scutari, the Albanian port they had just taken after a long siege."

"I remember that as well. The Turkish garrison and their Albanian allies held out for months against the Montenegrins. Scutari's fortress surrendered only after its commander was murdered by his traitorous successor."

"Yes, Watson," Holmes replied a bit impatiently, "To return to my story, Scott – as the stepson of Count Vukčić – was the obvious choice to serve as envoy. He and Vukčić, escorted by agents of the Austrian *Evidenzbureau*, met with King Nicholas in Scutari and urged him to surrender its fortress to the international naval force outside the harbour. The old king reluctantly acceded to his councillor's assurances. The Montenegrin troops withdrew, and a broader European conflict was successfully averted."

"What a diplomatic triumph for your son!"

"Not so," my friend responded glumly. "You see, Scott and his stepfather, relying upon Austrian promises, pledged to King Nicholas that he would regain Scutari in the peace settlement. As you recall from the treaty signed in Bucharest, this did not occur. 'Nero Wolfe' feels that he unwittingly affronted his adoptive family's honour. Mycroft may soon discover that his promising new agent's first assignment will also be his last." [5]

"Was the Archduke guilty of bad faith?"

"I daresay not. The Emperor himself cannot predict the machinations of his foreign office, nor had the Austrians the final word in Bucharest. Even so, I shall be interested to learn what Franz Ferdinand may have to say about the matter."

By now, our train was rolling into Worksop. It was a town of moderate size, notable chiefly for mining and malting, and famous in Elizabethan times for growing liquorice. The station at which we arrived was architecturally reminiscent of that age, although on this night it was being decorated to delight another royal visitor. Few other Worksopians were then in evidence, so Holmes and I had no difficulty in securing transportation to the business district. Because we were not yet expected at the Abbey, Mycroft had suggested spending the night in the town's newest hotel and making our own way to Welbeck in the morning. Inevitably, his brother had a different plan. Holmes gave an address on Bridge Street to our driver, who soon halted before a decrepit structure named the Old Ship Inn. It appeared to pre-date, if not Queen Elizabeth herself, at least most of her successors.

"I say, Holmes," I called dubiously as he began taking down his luggage, "Do you intend for us to share the tap-room with Captain Billy Bones?"

"Not 'arf, Guv'nor," my friend replied, his accent unexpectedly dropping into lower-class vernacular. Quickly, he gestured for me to leave the cab. After requesting its owner to remain, I joined him in the doorway beneath the juttied upper floor.

"I shall be residing here for the duration," the detective muttered. "While its appearance may be unprepossessing and its comforts minimal, this hostelry possesses a unique feature that will be highly advantageous to our mission. Please address any communications you may send to Bobby Jenkinson, a retired groom or trainer. I have not yet decided which."

"Will I see you at Welbeck in this guise?" I wondered, recalling that Portland kept a renowned stable and had won the Derby for two years running in the 'Eighties.

"Not – as the saying goes – if I see you first!" Holmes smiled. "Seriously, I shall not venture onto the estate without improving this disguise. At present, it is too like my actual appearance. Now," my friend concluded, "you had best proceed as scheduled to the new French Horn Hotel. Our cabbie appears to be becoming restive. Good luck, Watson! I shall await your first report with interest."

With that, he nodded cordially, and we went our separate ways. Although I spent the remainder of the evening quietly researching

408

Mycroft's notes, inwardly I was simmering with anticipation of the morrow, feeling younger than I had in years.

Chapter III – Three Days Among "The Great"

I arose early on Saturday, happy to see that the clear autumn weather still prevailed. After an excellent breakfast in the French Horn's dining room, I hired a dogcart for the drive to Welbeck Abbey. So pleasant was the morning that I alighted as we entered the estate's magnificent park, instructing the driver to take my luggage to the house while I walked the remainder of the way alone. Soon I arrived in a green dell populated by enormous oaks, reminding me that Welbeck's grounds lay within the original boundaries of Sherwood Forest. One ancient specimen – a veritable Methuselah of trees – undoubtedly pre-dated Robin Hood and might have been producing acorns at the Conquest. Sadly, it was all but dead, for the trunk had long ago been pierced by an archway wide enough to accommodate a coach-and-four. I later learned from Portland that this was the famous Greendale Oak, mutilated in the eighteenth century by a predecessor out to win a wager. Here was one noble ancestor I should not have cared to claim.

The house, I had read some years ago in *Country Life*, was "*a sombre pile, massive and ugly in many styles*". It had indeed been founded as an abbey, but in the century after the Dissolutions had been substantially rebuilt by a younger son of Bess of Hardwick. Later, it had fallen to the Bentinck family, whose founder accompanied "Dutch William" to England in 1688 and thereby gained a dukedom. The present Duke of Portland was the sixth to hold the title. Despite its chequered history, the Abbey was assuredly, as John Evelyn once described it, "*a noble but melancholy seate*". Its west front, which I came to at the end of a long drive, boasted battled parapets and a great square tower, while the gabled east front rose high above broad terraced lawns that faced a narrow lake. On my left, I could see two imposing Jacobean erections, one of which (I remembered from the article) housed the stables and a riding school. The other had been remodeled by the fifth duke for a picture gallery, but that aged, eccentric nobleman became preoccupied with constructing tunnels between the Abbey's several buildings and vast, underground rooms. All was left a shambles when the old man died, and I wondered what the present duke had made of it when he inherited Welbeck from his cousin at only twenty-one.

For the moment, however, I was more concerned with announcing my arrival to anyone who might take note of it. Fortunately, my unpaid driver was still waiting, and the household servants were at that moment carrying my bags to whatever fate awaited them. I was kindly advised by Portland's butler that as I had not (as he delicately put it) brought my valet with me, a footman would be sent to assist with my unpacking and, when I had refreshed myself, convey me to the Duke. His Grace would await me in the Titchfield Library.

Properly refreshed, I was admitted to the library, where I found a grey-mustached, slightly portly gentleman rather like myself, although better tailored. He strode across the ornately shelved and decorated chamber with his hand outstretched.

"I am pleased to welcome you to Welbeck Abbey, Dr. Watson," Portland graciously assured me. "Mr. Holmes – I refer, of course, to Mr. *Mycroft* Holmes – has told me a good deal about you. And having briefly been a soldier in my youth, I am honoured to meet a veteran of Maiwand and recipient of the Afghan Medal."

"I fear, Your Grace, that I did little to deserve it," I admitted ruefully, "aside from being shot. Rather less than Bobbie, our regimental dog, who also got the medal." [6]

"Yes, I recall Her Majesty's broad smile when she presented it," my host chuckled. "A gallant little fellow. But to return to present day, *your* Mr. Holmes will not be joining us, I understand?"

"No, but he is at hand and can be called if needed." I paused, uncertain how much information the detective would wish me to reveal. "For now, he is residing at an obscure inn in Worksop."

"That was at my suggestion. The Old Ship has . . . peculiar advantages that may be of some use." Portland, who seemed somewhat preoccupied, did not enlighten me as to those advantages. "*Well*, Doctor, I am afraid I shall see little of you before the shooting starts, except at dinner." At his courteous gesture, we left the library and progressed down a long corridor leading to the driveway I had entered. "Our imperial guests arrive tonight from London, and for the next few days Winnie and I shall be showing them the other great houses in the neighbourhood. Our own Bolsover, of course, and Chatsworth. Have you seen Chatsworth?"

"Holmes and I were there on an occasion in the old duke's day." I did not describe for him my last encounter with the Germans: A night in 1901, during the secret alliance negotiations held at Chatsworth, when the two of us had nearly lost our lives. [7]

"Quite a character, old Hartington," laughed the Duke. "I still miss him. His nephew and I shall take Their Highnesses to view the house of Bess of Hardwick, our common ancestor." Here we passed through Welbeck's imposing portal out onto the drive, where a beautiful Lorraine-Dietrich limousine awaited Portland's pleasure. I had heard that His Grace – unusually for a devotee of the track – was also an enthusiastic motorist.

"I am off to Worksop, Dr. Watson, where Gibson, my head gardener, is decorating the station for the Archduke's visit. We're planning an avenue of palms and shrubs, with great pots of chrysanthemums. You may not know that his Imperial and Royal Highness is a flower fancier."

"I do, actually, and find the fact surprising."

"You will find Franz Ferdinand a surprise in many ways. His public personality, which results largely from the way his wife is treated in Vienna, is very different from the face he shows to those he trusts. The latter is the true measure of the man. Those who know His Highness well (and Winnie and I feel fortunate to count ourselves among them) believe him to be the only man who can transform his uncle's ramshackle realm into a modern state. If Austria-Hungary's nationalities problem can be solved peacefully *within* the empire, it will go a long way towards preventing another European war.

"Forgive me," Portland added, nodding to his chauffeur to open the car door. "I did not intend to lecture. Tomorrow, some good fellows will arrive with whom you will have much in common. Do you know Lord Lovat, Doctor, of South African fame? And my old friend Harry Stonor – a crack shot, Harry. I believe he has a message from a former client to impart." He paused and glanced at me enquiringly. "Anything else before I go?"

"Talking of messages," I suddenly remembered, "Holmes requested that Your Grace recruit a lad from the estate to carry my reports and any instructions he may wish to send. Would that be possible?"

"Of course," the Duke replied a little doubtfully, "if Mr. Holmes believes it would be useful. I'll instruct my head gamekeeper to find a likely boy. We shall be meeting this afternoon to plan the shoot." He raised his stick to me in parting. "Farewell, Dr. Watson, until dinner. I am very glad to have you with us."

I stood bemused as the white limousine moved slowly down the drive. Although Portland could hardly have been friendlier, something in his manner puzzled me. It was as if certain facts had been withheld from me, and I had no understanding why. With an inward sigh, I turned back to the house, wondering – as I seemed so far to be the only guest – whether I should appear for luncheon or have a tray brought to my room. For all my admiration of "The Great", it had been years since I spent time in a great house, and seldom ever without Holmes. On my own, would I be ignored by the luminaries – ("Who is that man? Why is he here?") – who had expected to meet the great detective? Would Franz Ferdinand be as disdainful of a proxy as the young archduchess I had once encountered in Trieste? If so, successfully accomplishing my mission would be difficult indeed. Then I recalled my old friend's precept: "Theorising without data,

411

Watson, is a futile exercise." Comforted somewhat by his words, I regressed to my quarters to await the coming meal.

Happily, my first three days at Welbeck did much to alleviate these foolish qualms. By Monday evening, I felt sufficiently well-grounded to write a full report to Holmes. I did not detail the Abbey's manifold delights, for they would have been of little interest to my friend. I said nothing of its splendid drawing rooms. Nor did I describe the maze of tunnels the fifth duke had constructed, or the subterranean ballroom his successor had converted to a portrait gallery. Portland's stables, with thoroughbreds in a hundred stalls, went unrecorded. Of his art collection, which was worthy of a royal palace, I wrote only of Sargent's portraits of the ducal couple: Her Grace lounging languidly against a mantel, His Grace returning from a walk with his two collies. Recalling the detective's tale of Reginald Musgrave, I did mention one item in the curios: The goblet from which Charles I took his last communion on the morning that he died. But Holmes learned nothing of our splendid dinners, presided over by a lady who seemed (despite my assurance to Priscilla) as beautiful as she had been in 1897. For me, these three days were a private taste of "life among The Great". I regretted only that my wife could not be there to share it with me.

> *Welbeck Abbey, 24ᵗʰ Nov.*
> *My dear Holmes (or Jenkinson):*
>
> *As you instructed, I asked Portland (who has been very amiable) to find a local boy to carry messages. This afternoon, he sent one by the name of Willy White, who is twelve years old and seems intelligent. His father is an under-gardener, and the family live in Worksop, which will be convenient. Willy promises that if I complete this missive before dinner, it will be delivered by tonight. How this feat will be accomplished I have no idea.*
>
> *A happy feature of these house-parties, as you know, is that guests are generally left to their own devices until dinner. I have therefore been able to mingle with my fellow* hoi polloi *while dukes and archdukes go their way. Two new acquaintances are rather more than* hoi polloi: *Lord Lovat, besides being chief of Clan Fraser, raised a regiment of scouts to fight the Boers and won the D.S.O. Harry Stonor ("a crack shot", according to our host) is a Groom-in-Waiting and – despite the disparity in spelling – a cousin of our early client*

412

Helen Stoner. "Helen," he kindly let me know, "has passed a very happy life, thanks to you and Mr. Holmes." Both Stonor and Lovat will be good men to have in our corner if a crisis comes.

The Opposition politicians are well represented, particularly the Cecils. All recall our many services to "Lord Bellinger", whose nephew Mr. Balfour was gracious enough to praise my careful handling of a certain ticklish case. [8] *The only politician who snubbed me was that "most superior person" Lord Curzon, the ex-Viceroy, to whom I was unwise enough to mention my own time in India.*

The Germans are a more intriguing study. My relations with them, understandably, are distant, for they are well aware of our association. Baron von Herling regards me with hauteur and suspicion. I generally avoid the Prince of Fürstenberg, whose gushing, mincing personality contrasts oddly with his burly, mustachioed physique. Von Bork – as you warned me – is a hard person to dislike. Even Portland admits "He is a good fellow, for a German": Amusing at the dinner table, expert at both chess and billiards, a tireless companion on a ramble, and (ominously!) a first-class shot. His young and pretty wife, one of the few untitled ladies invited to the Abbey (which would not please Priscilla!), is popular as well. As one bejeweled dowager whispered to me last night at dinner, "It is strange to remember that those nice von Borks aren't English!"

The Austrian delegation arrived on Saturday evening, but only today was I able to speak to one of them. The imperial couple have been touring with the Portlands, so I have seen them only from afar at my end of the dinner table. Franz Ferdinand is a man of fifty, somewhat heavy-set and almost as flamboyantly mustached as the Kaiser. His wife is a tall and striking lady in her forties. She exhibits grace and dignity that make a mockery of her supposed ambition. Both seem delighted with everything they see, and from what I have observed the Archduke's fearful reputation must surely be exaggerated.

This afternoon, I had the opportunity to discuss him with the man you had suggested that I cultivate: Colonel Brosch von Aarenau. Brosch had been exempted from the latest motor tour, so I invited him to join me in a walk. The Colonel is not far past forty, young for that rank in Franz Josef's superannuated army. Even in mufti, he bears himself like a born soldier. It was evident that despite having left the Militärkanzlerei, he still holds his former chief in high regard.

Brosch told me of the Archduke's early life: How he contracted tuberculosis and was given up for dead, the Emperor openly more satisfied with his other nephew, Otto, as the heir. "Otto, who later died of syphilis!" the Colonel cried indignantly. "Add to this insult the Hofburg's treatment of the Heir-Apparent's wife. The Choteks are among the oldest families in Bohemia, but Prince Montenuovo (who merely reflects the wishes of His Apostolic Majesty) affects to find no difference between a high-born countess and a milkmaid! Is it a wonder, Herr Doktor, that Franz Ferdinand's anger sometimes overwhelms him? Truly, the Duchess's influence has done nothing but good. Those who knew His Highness before their marriage say he has become a different man."

"Even so," I noted, "so volatile a master must have been difficult to serve."

"Fortunately," the Colonel laughed, "I began on the right footing. When I arrived for my interview, I found the Heir-Apparent sitting on the floor, playing with his children. All three were quite small in those days. As I stood stiffly at attention, the younger son, Prince Ernst, toddled up and offered me a toy. His father (you may be sure) was watching closely to see how I would react. After a moment of panic, I knelt down, accepted the gift, and thanked the little fellow. The Archduke smiled and rose to welcome me, and I knew that I had passed the test."

I had hesitated before including this remembrance, knowing my friend's dislike of what he would regard as mawkish sentiment. Of more import to Sherlock Holmes would be Franz Ferdinand's political opinions. Here, too, my companion had provided valuable insight during our ramble, particularly regarding the Heir-Apparent's plans to reorganise the empire. To return to my letter:

In his youth, the Archduke visited the United States, where he discovered the federal model as a possible solution to Austria's nationalities problem. Four years ago, Brosch accompanied Their Highnesses on a state visit to Bucharest. There, Franz Ferdinand met a Roumanian named Popovici,

414

the author of a book entitled The United States of Greater Austria. *It proposed dividing the Dual Monarchy into no fewer than fifteen federated states, based as far as possible on ethnic lines. The Heir-Apparent, says the Colonel, now prefers this plan to his old idea of "Trialism", which would only benefit the Slavs.*

I enquired whether the Hungarians would not be likely to oppose the plan, recalling that they looked to the last Habsburg heir-apparent as a champion of the Magyar cause. Brosch assured me that upon that subject, Franz Ferdinand has nothing in common with his cousin Rudolf. Indeed, he has talked of reconquering Hungary by the sword if needed. Noting my look of consternation, the Colonel added, "I feel sure that this was but hyperbole. The Archduke is often harsh and hasty in his judgements. At times he can even be unjust, but once he realises his mistake, he does not hesitate to put things right."

By then, we had reached our destination, a row of greystone almshouses that Portland's duchess had encouraged him to build with his winnings from the track. It was not a site of scenic interest, but we guests had been requested to avoid the woods and fields before tomorrow's shoot. Brosch and I paused for a brief rest, while the Duke's collie (who had accompanied us for exercise in her master's absence) strained at her leash to be away. The Colonel turned to me with a thoughtful countenance.

"You asked me, Herr Doktor, whether I found my master difficult to serve. It was not always easy. He will not abide direct contradiction, but his saving grace is that – unlike every other Habsburg – he wants to know the truth. When one has learned how to be frank with him in an acceptable manner, one can accomplish almost anything. The Archduke's education was broad, not deep, but he possesses an incredible quickness of perception. Even in areas where he has only the most basic knowledge, he instinctively makes the right decision. And when one at last has won his confidence, his trust endures. I was called from my regiment to join His Highness on this journey simply because he wanted my opinion of you Englanders!"

I replied lightly that I hoped we had not disappointed. While he reassured me on that point, Brosch expressed discomfort with those now in his master's retinue. He fears especially that young Count von Straten Ponthoz may be a spy for "Conrad and the military clique". Culling my memory of the notes we had received, I realised that he was referring to General Conrad von Hötzendorf, the army's Chief of Staff. It appears that Conrad was once the Archduke's protégé, but they have fallen out. Franz Ferdinand was rightly furious when Conrad allowed the traitorous Colonel Redl to shoot himself before he could be questioned. Later, during the Balkan Wars, he lost patience with the Chief of Staff's demands for war with Serbia, even if it meant fighting Russia, too. Twice he has dismissed Conrad from his post, but the Emperor promptly reinstated him. It was, Brosch grumbled, only the latest instance of their failure to agree. My companion shook his head and, handing me our charge's leash, walked on at an agitated pace. The collie and I were hard-pressed to keep up. When we returned to the lawn of Welbeck Abbey, the Colonel halted, offering me an apologetic smile. Then he told me gravely:

"I truly believe, Herr Doktor, that Franz Ferdinand is Austria's last hope. The reign of His Apostolic Majesty has been a long decline since 1848. His one idea, the Ausgleich, simply permits the Magyars to ride rough-shod over everybody else. Now, the Serbs, the Roumanians – even our Italian and our German 'allies' – flock like vultures, conspiring with their compatriots inside our borders while they wait for us to die. Do you know the saying in Vienna: 'The situation is hopeless, but not serious'? We muddle onward with our well-known Schlamperei. [9] But the Heir-Apparent sees things clearly, and he has his plans in place. I pray nightly that he will be spared until the sad old man in Schönbrunn Palace joins his wife and son at last."

In pursuit of our mission, I asked Brosch whether he considered the Archduke to be in danger. "No man in the empire," he replied, "has more enemies, and it now appears they are beginning to combine against him. Several months ago, the Emperor appointed Franz Ferdinand Inspector-General. It may have been a poisoned gift! Next summer's maneuvers – which the Archduke's new duties require him to attend – will be held in Bosnia. Already, the Bosnian Serb newspapers in Sarajevo are calling for his murder. Yet, General Potiorek, the provincial governor, implores His Highness to make a ceremonial visit to the city – on June 28,

416

the day of Kosovo, when the Serbian Empire fell five-hundred years ago. It would be madness! And it is no coincidence, perhaps, that the two old rivals, Conrad and Potiorek, are now as thick as thieves.

Although for security's sake I did not comment on the fact to Holmes, the Colonel's revelations showed that Mycroft's knowledge of the dangers that beset Franz Ferdinand was as accurate as ever. Alas, the suspicion that a plot was being hatched in Sarajevo did not ensure the Archduke's safety for the next few days. I therefore sought my friend's advice regarding how I should proceed, urging him to write a quick reply.

One final conversation on that Monday – and a far more pleasant one – occurred too late to find a place in my report. Having finished the epistle and given it to Willy, with instructions to deliver it to "Mr. Bobby Jenkinson", I had almost two hours remaining before dinner. On impulse, I decided to revisit the underground ballroom which housed the portrait gallery. Leaving the main building, I passed through a long, curving corridor whose walls were covered with framed prints. At a distance, I spied two ladies walking towards me. One I identified as the Duchess of Hohenberg, the other as a younger lady I had heard mentioned as her niece. To my surprise, Her Highness appeared to recognise me as the two drew near. With a quiet word to her companion, she stepped across the hallway, smiling warmly.

"Herr Doktor Watson! I am indeed happy to make your acquaintance. How is your 'friend and colleague', Herr Sherlock Holmes?'"

I bowed deeply. "Quite well, Your Highness, thank you. He regrets very much that he was unable to join us at Welbeck Abbey. I had no idea you even realised I was here."

"*Jawohl,*" she laughed. "My husband, too, is well aware of it, although consulting detectives are less likely than our police detectives to fall within his ken. He hopes to meet you when the shooting starts. But I recognised your name at once! Did you know that as a girl, I read aloud your *Study in Scarlet* to my sisters? During the years I served Archduchess Isabella, I always found a way to smuggle in the latest issue of *The Strand*. Even now, I read your tales of Mr. Holmes's adventures to my children."

"Mr. Holmes and I are honoured, ma'am. May I ask which story is your favourite?"

"Why, 'A Scandal in Bohemia', of course! Its title references my homeland, and I enjoyed seeing a woman get the better of a man. Little did I imagine, Herr Doktor, when I sat reading that story for the first time, that one day I would marry the King of Bohemia myself!" [10] The Duchess sighed a little wistfully, "There were so many things I did not imagine in *those* days, I fear.

"But now," she added, nodding to her niece to join us, "I must introduce you to this pretty lady. Elisabeth, my dear, here is Dr. John H. Watson, the friend and biographer of Sherlock Holmes. Herr Doktor, my niece, the Countess de Baillet-Latour."

I bowed, if it were possible, more deeply than before. The Countess was well short of thirty and quite lovely. Her face reflected the same intelligence and kindliness as did her aunt's, and her smile was charming. When I enquired whether she was enjoying her visit, she replied, "Much more so than when we came last year, and I got appendicitis!" Both ladies chortled merrily, and I felt vexed by my inanity. To my relief, the Duchess noticed Baron von Rumerkirch, the Archduke's chamberlain, signalling urgently to her some distance down the corridor.

"Heavens, I must go, Elisabeth! The Portlands promised to show your uncle and me their Lipizzaners before dinner! Herr Doktor, would you mind escorting my niece back to the main house? *Danke,* and my apologies." She hurried away while I was still attempting to say something gallant. The Countess smiled indulgently when I turned back to her.

"Her Highness is a very gracious lady," I opined, in an effort to restore my standing.

"Dear Aunt Sophie is the noblest, kindest woman in the world," her niece responded stoutly. "She is my closest friend. It is tragic how little she and the Heir are really known and understood. So much of what is written of them is untrue! Even your English papers speculate that Uncle Franzi will renounce his oath and declare his wife empress when he takes the throne."

"Is there no prospect of that happening? She is certainly worthy of the title."

"But he swore an oath to God!" the Countess cried. "To Catholics as devout as they and I, breaking such an oath condemns one's soul to Hell. As a Protestant, Herr Doktor, you do not understand, but I assure you that my aunt's presumed ambition to be empress is a myth. For her, it will suffice to end the years of slights and insults, and be honoured simply as the emperor's consort. The title in itself means nothing to her."

I thought it best to change the subject. "Your own title, Countess," I said artfully, "intrigues me. Surely it is not Austrian in origin."

"Indeed not, Herr Doktor. My husband is a count of Belgium."

By this time, we had returned to Welbeck Abbey's entrance hall. I prepared, with some regret, to say farewell to my companion, for it was nearly time to change for dinner. Unhappily, we were accosted at that moment by the Prince of Fürstenberg, who occupied us for a quarter-hour with chatter even more inane than mine. We were finally rescued by none other than von Bork, who happened by and smoothly invited the Prince to join him in a game of billiards. From the ironic wink he gave us when the two departed, it was obvious he had performed such services before. Once again, I was left with an unwonted, and unwanted, liking for my friend and country's adversary.

I made my way back to my room. It was on the ground floor of the oldest portion of the Abbey, which I understood was seldom used. No other guest was anywhere in sight. While I failed to understand the reason for my isolation, the chamber itself was comfortable enough, so I did not request another. That night, as I lay abed, it occurred to me that I had learned more of the Archduke and his consort than most of their own subjects were privileged to know. Moreover, what I knew engendered a protective instinct I had not felt towards our other royal "clients" – not even Emperor Frederick. For whereas that monarch was already doomed, Franz Ferdinand represented (as Colonel Brosch expressed it) the last remaining hope for Austria. Having failed disastrously in our earlier mission for the House of Habsburg, it seemed that this time Holmes and I had a positive duty to succeed. Not, assuredly, for the sake of "the sad old man in Schönbrunn Palace" – to him we owed very little. Our duty was rather to the far-seeing Heir-Apparent, whose accession might preserve the future of an empire and – even more importantly – the peace of Europe.

Chapter IV – The Shooting Party [11]

When I awoke the next morning, a letter lay upon my bedside table. I was baffled as to how it had arrived there, for I am not an abnormally sound sleeper, and the long-fallen door into my room had shrieked unbearably each time I opened it. Upon inspecting them, I saw that my two ground-floor windows were secure.

Though the letter's method of delivery remained unknown, its authorship was not in question. I identified the folded sheet (there was no envelope) as a type used by country inns and third-rate London hostelries. It was with no surprise, therefore, that I recognised the hand of Sherlock Holmes. Dated only "*Monday night*", the text read as follows:

My dear Watson:

> *Your report, although admirably thorough, was extremely long in coming. I had not expected to wait three days to hear from you. While I recognise that you lacked an early opportunity to observe the imperial couple and their*

419

minions, information on Portland's other guests would have been more useful to me yesterday. With the shooting due to start tomorrow, it becomes difficult if not impossible to ensure the safety of His Highness.

Nevertheless, I urge you and Portland to do everything that can be done as soon as possible. Surround Franz Ferdinand with the guards you have identified (Lovat, Stonor, and Colonel Brosch von Aarenau), whose reliability we shall have to trust. Keep every German – particularly von Bork – as far away from him as feasible. Verify that all those enlisted as beaters and loaders are well known to the Duke. Whatever protection this plan provides may be illusory, for I do not expect anyone attending the shoot to attempt the Archduke's life directly. The likely threat will come from a sharpshooter armed with a long-range rifle, like the one Adolf Meyer intended to use against the Empress Elisabeth. (Our Teutonic foes are not noted for imagination!) Let me remind you that Brosch commands a regiment of sharpshooters, as did Lovat in South Africa. They must not be overlooked. Finally, in making your arrangements with the Duke, remember not to implicate the Germans or von Bork specifically – although Portland, unlike most members of the aristocracy, may be sharp enough to put two and two together.

I was annoyed by the detective's imputation against Brosch, who could not be an assassin unless he was also a monster of deceit. Otherwise, Holmes's plan seemed well-conceived. It was too late, however, to implement the precautions he desired at once. On arriving for breakfast, I learned that Portland had departed, making it impossible to revise his preparations for the morning's shoot. I did manage to have a private word with Stonor and Lovat while we helped ourselves from the sideboard. Both readily agreed to serve as bodyguards. His Lordship, without prompting, identified the Germans as the major threat. Neither they nor the Austrians appeared downstairs until we left the house.

Shortly before half-past nine, a cavalcade of automobiles and shooting brakes [12] drew up outside the Abbey, as the Duke, his head gamekeeper, and the Archduke with his chamberlain returned from a reconnaissance. We guests piled into the other conveyances, and the party set off for the shooting-ground. I shared a brake with my two compatriots and those twin pillars of British country life, dogs and horses. Naturally, the dogs enjoyed our excursion more than anyone, keenly anticipating the day that was to come.

Not all my readers may be familiar with the shooting parties held at noble houses. They are less common now than formerly, if only due to the expense involved. Under the supervision of a tribe of gamekeepers, the birds (pheasant, grouse, woodcock, and duck) are bred, hatched, and reared on the estate. On the day of a shoot, the gentlemen attending (or "guns", as they are called) take a designated place beside their "loader" with a pair of shotguns. The man reloads one weapon while the other is in use. Meanwhile, an army of "beaters" (all men from the estate) walk through the adjacent woods and undergrowth, making sufficient noise to rout the birds. They fly over, and the "guns" attempt to bring them down, taking care not to poach into the territory of their neighbours. Dogs are employed to retrieve the fallen game, while ladies who accompany the party stand or sit nearby. At such a shoot as Welbeck Abbey's, hundreds or thousands of pheasants – plus the odd, luckless hare or rabbit – could be slaughtered during each day's sport. To fire at deer, or other beasts too big to be humanely killed by buckshot, was of course bad form. To use the term "humanely" may seem strange, but I heard Portland state his prefer-ence that guests miss altogether rather than merely wound a bird.

Regrettably, I was too often in compliance with the first alternative. Though I count myself a fair shot with my service revolver, the recoil (or "kick", as my American friends called it) from a shotgun soon becomes painful to my damaged shoulder. To my chagrin, my prowess declined steadily as the day wore on, even when I adjusted to the borrowed guns. That is not to say we were not treated to remarkable displays of marksmanship. I do not recall that Mr. Balfour killed a single pheasant, but most of the party shot quite well. Stonor, Lovat, and von Bork were miraculous. As for Franz Ferdinand, his reputation as a rifleman was legendary. He had shot all types of game, from tigers in India to chamois in the Alps. Konopischt, his castle in Bohemia, held among its trophies his three-thousandth stag. Some found this bloodlust a disturbing feature of the Heir-Apparent's personality. Yet, as the event we were attending proved, it was shared by royalty and aristocrats in Britain and across the Continent.

On that morning, either the Archduke's eye was out or Nottinghamshire pheasants flew higher than those to which he was accustomed. Even we "guns" down the line noted His Highness's repressed fury as the birds eluded him. It was the only time at Welbeck I saw him out of temper. Added to his trials was the Prince of Fürstenberg, who prattled on incessantly from the adjacent station. How that gentleman expected to converse above the din I could not fathom. Fortunately, his obnoxiousness offered me an opportunity. During luncheon (served under a marquee behind the shooting-ground), I spoke to Portland. The Duke was obviously worried by his august guest's frustration. We agreed to rearrange the stations, exiling the Prince to join his fellow Germans down the line. Brosch replaced him beside the Heir-Apparent, with Stonor and Lovat both nearby. By grouping all the "crack shots" except von Bork together, this change was highly unfair to the other shooters. The rest of us hardly saw a pheasant for the balance of the day. Even so, the main object was achieved. Relieved of Fürstenberg, Franz Ferdinand shot much better in the afternoon and regained his good humour, quite unaware of the motive behind his improved luck.

That evening after dinner, I was approached by Herr von Bork. We had managed to avoid the bridge tables (a dislike of cards being one point we had in common), and he invited me to try my hand at billiards. Although I had not played often since my games with Thurston, I readily agreed. The German was clearly my superior, but my old skill revived enough to offer a degree of competition. When von Bork paused to chalk his cue, I took the opportunity to thank him for rescuing the Countess de Baillet-Latour and me from the talkative Fürstenberg the day before.

"*Bitte sehr!*" he replied amiably. "Poor old Fürstenberg! The Prince can be a trial, I must admit. He was quite heartbroken to be removed today from the Imperial and Royal Presence. Am I wrong in thinking, Herr Doktor, that you played a part in that decision? I saw you speaking to His Grace at luncheon."

"The Duke did ask for my opinion," I misleadingly agreed.

"So many famous 'guns' around the Archduke in the afternoon! He was assuredly very well protected. I was surprised not to be invited to serve as a bodyguard myself."

"In fact," von Bork added as I bent to the awkward shot he left for me, "it almost seemed we Germans were being isolated from Franz Ferdinand. If His Grace's wish was to protect his guest, why were we singled out? Austria-Hungary is Germany's good ally. He is her heir-apparent."

"I am sure the Duke intended no affront," I answered, feigning concentration, "save, possibly, to Fürstenberg. It was evident that the Prince was treading on the Archduke's nerves." Contrary to my expectations, I sank the ball before me and moved around the table for another shot. My opponent politely stepped aside.

"Do I sense behind these odd precautions," he demanded quietly, "some unknown, guiding hand? Von Herling and I were extremely disappointed that Herr Holmes did not attend the shoot at Welbeck Abbey. Yet, I cannot help but wonder if he is *somewhere* in the neighborhood."

422

"Anything is possible," I admitted lightly. My last ball shuddered in the pocket but just failed to drop, leaving von Bork well situated to close out the game. With a smile of resignation, I invited the spy to take his turn.

"Well played, Herr Doktor," he acknowledged afterwards, "but the game is mine. As will be, I think, the one to come."

"This one, perhaps," I replied evenly, replacing my cue in the rack beside the table. "We shall see about the one to come. Good night, Herr von Bork. I wish you pleasant dreams." We exchanged well-mannered bows, and I retired to my room to write my next report to Sherlock Holmes.

It was well past midnight when that report was finished. Weariness soon overcame my resolve to sleep "with one eye open" in case I should be visited again. On awakening, I was not surprised to find a second note. This one was considerably terser:

> Watson,
>
> A word in haste, for I must keep a watch tonight. This evening, there appeared at the Old Ship a man I recognised, an Irish vagabond who calls himself O'Roarke. He is an embittered ex-Fenian, not much younger than ourselves. Besides several more unsavoury activities, he acts as a messenger in London between the agent known as "Altamont" and Herr von Bork. Michael O'Roarke was responsible for some bloody work in Ireland, and I have no doubt that if our spy intends to employ a non-German to assassinate Franz Ferdinand, he has at hand a man well-suited to the task. I have it on good authority from a source you know that O'Roarke is an expert marksman with a long-range rifle.
>
> Redouble your precautions, therefore, and let me hear from you as soon as possible.
>
> S.H.

As always, the detective made no reference to his own proceedings, so in this regard his message left me none the wiser. It was again impracticable to comply in full with his instructions. On enquiring for young Willy, I learned he had been sent to join the beaters, one of Portland's regulars having fallen out. This decision had been taken by the head gamekeeper without his master's knowledge.

In consequence, I spent a very nervous day. Before leaving for the shooting-ground, I apprised the Duke of the altered situation. He advised his butler and head gamekeeper to beware of any unknown persons posing as servants, gamekeepers, or the like. We both recognised, however, that an assassin could easily remain anonymous in the retinue of a treacherous visitor. It was the first time in living memory, Portland dourly remarked, that a squire of Welbeck Abbey had reason to distrust his guests.

Thanks to our rearrangement of the stations, the morning shoot went well. Portland had quietly entreated Stonor and Lovat to leave a few birds for others down the line, and Colonel Brosch seemed to restrain himself voluntarily. Only the Archduke blazed away as he had done the day before, and more effectually. Having (at his host's suggestion) changed to a heavier-bore shotgun, he proved himself a truly deadly shot. I, meanwhile, spent more time scanning the wood for riflemen than the sky for pheasants, much to the disgust of my poor loader. My contribution to Welbeck's bag that day was small indeed.

When we returned to the marquee for luncheon, I made my way among the beaters, searching each homely English face for a disguised O'Roarke or Holmes. It was a wasted exercise, for I had never seen the Irishman, and none of the older beaters was tall enough to be my friend. On finding Willy White, I asked him to deliver my report to Jenkinson at once. Unfortunately, the boy's duties did not permit him to comply. Willy promised to leave the moment the head gamekeeper released him, assuring me that he could reach the Old Ship Inn within an hour. I remarked that it had taken me a longer time to walk from Worksop, and in response was cheekily reminded of my age.

Our afternoon was enlivened by an upsetting incident which might well have been more serious. It occurred during the last drive. Just as the flushed birds were appearing overhead, an aged gentleman emerged from the trees and began walking down the line in front of us. He was carrying a placard on which was inscribed the Biblical injunction: *"Thou shalt not kill."* Oblivious to every outraged shout of warning, he proceeded on his way serenely, bringing our slaughter of the innocents to a ragged halt. I heard the Heir-Apparent's startled enquiry, first to Colonel Brosch in German and then in English to the Duke. Otherwise, we shooters stood dumbfounded, while the lady observers (including both the Duchess of Hohenberg and the Countess de Baillet-Latour) exhibited bewildered sympathy for the old fool. He was taken firmly in hand by two loaders and delivered to Portland, whom he began to address in an indignant bellow. I wandered near enough to hear the end of the diatribe, which involved "universal kinship" and the rights of animals. Franz Ferdinand snorted in derision, while our host ignored the charge that he was "a disgrace to your good lady", a noted champion of birds and beasts. The intruder – a Mr. Cardew, I learned later – was escorted off the premises without further ado. However, his object was accomplished, for His Grace declared the day's shooting at an end.

I walked back to the house with Brosch and Lovat, close behind the imperial and ducal party. Poor Portland was apologising to the Archduke at some length.

"I am really very sorry, Your Imperial and Royal Highness. That fellow Cardew is a well-known crank. I ought to have suspected that he might appear. He did the same thing at Nettleby last month, just before that unfortunate incident in which Lord H------- shot a beater."

Franz Ferdinand had retained his equanimity throughout the disturbance. "It is of no importance, my dear Portland," he assured the Duke in heavily accented English. "We have such lunatics in Austria as well. I have not decided whether they should be shot for insolence or given a medal for their courage, rather like your British suffragettes." His wife gently chided him for this opinion, and Colonel Brosch shot me an amused glance.

I had noticed both him and Lovat eyeing the nearby trees intently during Cardew's interruption. Obviously, their soldierly instincts were aroused. I had also feared that the diversion might conceal a greater threat, but soon realised that an elderly eccentric would be a most unlikely ally for a paid assassin. If von Bork and his Irishman were indeed the danger, why, I wondered, were they so slow to show their hand?

That night, the Portlands held an informal ball in their vast underground portrait gallery. A hired band played the usual waltzes, plus a bit of ragtime, as the subjects of Van Dyck or Reynolds gazed nostalgically upon the dancers from their odd pink walls. Besides dancing (badly) with my hostess and the Countess de Baillet-Latour, I was able to converse briefly with the Archduke. He was a different man that evening than on the shooting-ground: Affable, easy-going, and even courtly to the ladies. When His Highness led out the night's last waltz with Duchess Sophie, their mutual affection and delight in the occasion were apparent to us all.

Von Bork avoided me, both at the ball and during the late-night supper afterwards. At one point, I saw him in close consultation with young Count von Straten Ponthoz and the Prince of Fürstenberg, whose demeanour was more serious and sensible than usual. I later observed the senior German present, Baron von Herling, speaking almost angrily to Portland. Upon returning to my room, I could not divine what these discussions boded. I knew only that the last day of shooting would provide a final opportunity to the assassin. My only course, it seemed, was to remain vigilant and await help from Sherlock Holmes.

Chapter V – An Encounter in the Dark

His help, when it came, came as a rude awakening. Two hours before dawn, a well-remembered voice disturbed my sleeping consciousness, speaking in the same calm tones it once had used in Baker Street.

"My abject apologies, Watson, for intruding at this ungodly hour. I would take it as a great favour if you would rise and dress. I am in need of your professional services."

I sat up groggily and switched on the electric lamp beside my bed. Holmes, still attired as Bobby Jenkinson, reclined in the overstuffed armchair across the room. My friend looked utterly exhausted. His Norfolk jacket's sleeve was torn, and there was a deep cut upon his left forearm, which he had made an ineffectual attempt to bandage with a handkerchief. Pushing back the bedclothes, I got to my feet and went to the nearby wardrobe to retrieve my doctor's bag.

"My dear fellow! What on Earth has happened to you? And *how*," I added in sudden realisation, "have you managed to enter this room three times without my hearing you?"

The detective smirked as I bent to examine his wounded extremity. "As ever, friend Watson, you see but you do not observe. Take a look behind this chair." The chair (I did observe) sat before an alcove adjacent to the elaborate Jacobean mantel surrounding the hearth. In the near-darkness, I saw nothing out of the ordinary in that corner of the room.

"The chair can wait," I told Holmes firmly. "Take off your coat. That arm needs my immediate attention." Setting the ewer and washbasin on the table next to him, I carefully washed, disinfected, and bandaged the gash, removing only enough of the caked blood to permit stitching. My friend endured these painful ministrations stoically, although before the stitching he did request a pause to light his pipe. When I had finished, he murmured "Thank you," and with a nod directed me again to search behind the chair.

There I saw an open panel in the alcove's wainscoting. An electric torch lay beside it on the oaken floor. Picking up the torch, I shone it down into the darkness, revealing an old but sound wooden stairway leading to an earthen passage six or seven feet below.

"A tunnel?" I enquired incredulously. "I was aware that the fifth duke had dug like a mole beneath the Abbey's grounds, but no one mentioned this part of the house."

"This tunnel was a much earlier duke's project," Holmes informed me. "During the Civil War, the future Duke of Newcastle employed it to escape to Hamburg after Marston Moor. Portland's mad old cousin extended it to join his own tunnel to the riding school. Where do you suppose the other end emerges, Watson?"

I recalled Portland's reticence and Willy's unexpected speed. "The Old Ship Inn!" I cried, adding, less triumphantly, "and, as usual, I'm the last to know. I suppose the Duke told Mycroft of it when they made their arrangements for our mission."

"Exactly so," my friend confirmed, having come to stand beside me, "which made the Old Ship a perfect base of operations. The tunnel saves twenty minutes on the walk from Worksop, and until an hour ago I had believed it was secure."

"What happened?" I gestured to him to take his seat while I began to dress. The detective collapsed into his chair, and I saw for the first time the mien of shock upon his face. For a long moment, he only sat and smoked. Then he answered quietly, "The fact is, Watson, that I have killed a man."

"Good Lord, Holmes! I presume it was O'Roarke. Did he recognise you?"

"Indeed," Holmes replied, gazing at me curiously. "I must say, old friend, that you seem less appalled than I'd expected. I forget sometimes that you were once a soldier."

"Well, I shall certainly require an explanation. I know nothing of your activities over these past days."

"In that case, we had best descend, for we have a body to dispose of. I fear," Holmes added wincingly, slipping his injured arm into its sleeve, "that you must do the digging. As it happens, the Old Ship's landlord keeps shovels in the tunnel." I wondered, though I did not ask, how many other bodies had been buried there.

During our three-mile trek in ill-lit gloom, my friend recounted the events that had led to O'Roarke's death. Holmes had first augmented his "Jenkinson" apparel with a wig and beard of greying russet. He had gone to Welbeck Abbey's stables, bearing a testimonial from Portland, in the guise of a retired horse trainer. There he met the Duke's own trainer and the grooms and jockeys who would later serve as beaters for the shoot. As my friend remarked, our long-ago visit to King's Pyland had stood him in good stead.

"Normally," he laughed, "there is no one more close-mouthed with a stranger than a Nottinghamshire countryman. 'Horsey' men, however, share a fraternity that transcends provincial ties. While you were hobnobbing with 'The Great', I was touring the estate on horseback,

427

memorising the locations of the 'drives' for each day's shoot. By the end of our last ride on Monday, I was fully informed of the geography.

"The next morning, having delivered my reply to your report, I emerged from the tunnel near the riding school. It was too late to have an impact on the first day's shoot, for I could not reveal my presence to the beaters. Instead, I examined the terrain reserved for the succeeding days, marking the most favourable lines of sight for an assassin. On my way back that afternoon, I passed the first day's shooting-ground and was pleased to note from a nearby hillside that you had effected the precautions suggested in my letter. At dusk, I returned via the tunnel to the Old Ship Inn. There my satisfaction with the day's events abruptly ended."

"O'Roarke arrived," I hazarded, employing my *"blinding talent for the obvious"*.

"Soundly deduced, Watson! He was imbibing in the Old Ship's tap-room when I went down for supper. Having met O'Roarke four times during my negotiations with von Bork, I knew that any scruples he possessed had died in the cause of Irish independence. If he should recognise Bobby Jenkinson as Altamont, one of us would not depart the Old Ship Inn alive.

"Fortunately, whisky is the man's Achilles Heel. He was already well into his cups, trying to elicit news about the shoot from the grooms and jockeys I had ridden with that morning. Hoping to remain unremarked, I took a corner bench. O'Roarke's interrogation was not going well. His hatred of the landed class was on display, and Portland's loyal tenants had little fellow-feeling for an Irishman. I heard one snap, 'The Duke's the best landlord in England, you bloody Mick!' as they abruptly moved away. Unluckily, two of the grooms noticed me. They cried out 'Well met, Mr. Jenkinson!' and stopped to have a word. O'Roarke eyed me suspiciously when he staggered from the room. After escaping my inconvenient friends, I ascertained from the landlord that my foe had gone to bed. Then, having had no word from you, I wrote and left at the Abbey the note that you found yesterday."

I explained the reasons for Willy's delayed delivery of my report, a delay that would have fatal consequences. The next morning, O'Roarke had followed the same procedure as had Holmes the day before. He walked to Welbeck along the same road I had used on my arrival, trailed surreptitiously by Bobby Jenkinson. Either von Bork's instructions or his own enquiries had given the Irishman a clear idea of the terrain. He entered the estate through a break in a stone wall and made directly for the third day's shooting-ground.

"There," continued Holmes, "he chose the precise location from which to shoot the Archduke that I had myself earmarked the day before.

What I did *not* know, Watson, was that O'Roarke had seen me shadowing him and penetrated my disguise. Late that evening, he also saw young Willy leave my room after delivering your message. He followed the boy into the Old Ship's basement and discovered the tunnel. What still amazes me is that he did not proceed immediately to Welbeck Abbey and inform his German master of my identity as Altamont."

It was possible, of course, that O'Roarke had tried to do exactly that. As I started to report the previous night's ball, we came upon the Irishman's dead body. He was a wicked-looking fellow, shot cleanly through the forehead but still glaring fiercely above his short, grey beard. A bloody knife and broken lantern lay beside him in the dirt. The corpse had not yet entered *rigor mortis*, so I closed the eyes, straightened the limbs, and performed other decencies. Then I began to dig while the detective went on talking. Even in the presence of his victim, his voice retained its usual urbanity.

"I had intended to arrive at the Abbey as Bobby Jenkinson, well before O'Roarke. However, upon entering the tunnel I saw the gleam of his light ahead of me. It was only then that I realised the horrid risk of my exposure. I extinguished my torch, praying that O'Roarke hadn't seen it, and moved quickly and quietly towards him through the dark. Fortunately, the tunnel's course was relatively straight, and I knew it well enough by now to avoid impediments and follow the faint glow ahead of me. Like yourself, my Irish foe was slightly lame, so I gained rapidly upon him. By the time he noticed my approach and turned, it was too late to raise his rifle, which in any case he had not loaded. Moreover, I was already covering him with my revolver. With few other options left, O'Roarke set his lantern down and met me with an evil grin.

"'How do, Mister Altamont?' he greeted me. 'Ye *look* like an Irishman in that fine beard, but I never believed ye *were* one, even one from the far side of the Atlantic. Nor did ye *sound* like one when we drank two nights ago, talkin' to the laddies from the fine, great manor. "Bobby Jenkinson", is it? Or would yer name be *Holmes*, a'tall?'

"When I heard *that*, I must admit that inwardly I panicked, Watson. For a moment, I feared for Willie's safety, but he knew only Bobby Jenkinson. Had O'Roarke somehow found your letters in my room? The real question, of course, was whether von Bork now knew his trusted contact Altamont was an imposter. If that revelation had not occurred already, it simply could not be allowed. The contest between us was no longer 'Michael O'Roarke or Sherlock Holmes'. It had become 'Germany or England'.

"Apparently, the old Fenian saw this conclusion in my face, for with a roar he drew a knife and rushed at me, kicking aside his lantern in the

429

process. With better luck than aim, I shot him dead, but not until he got in a last thrust with the knife. I trust, gentle*man* of the jury, that you'll agree I shot in self-defence and for my country."

I could not answer Holmes immediately, for I was climbing from the grave to catch my breath. "O'Roarke could not have seen von Bork last night," I gasped. "It was long past one before the Portlands' post-ball supper ended. Had they met afterwards, he could not have been returning to the Abbey at the time that you encountered him. Now, please help me get the poor devil below ground."

"I was under the impression that he was there already," the detective quipped (quite unsuitably, I thought). Together, we buried the dead Irishman, and I extracted a promise that Holmes would inform Mycroft of the shooting and have O'Roarke removed and buried decently. Thankfully, considering my friend's wound and my own weariness, our remaining journey was a short one. Dawn was just breaking when we emerged from the basement tunnel in the Old Ship Inn.

Chapter VI – The Last Day's Shoot

In contemplating our next action, Holmes and I could not agree as to how we should proceed. He insisted upon joining me at Welbeck Abbey, whereas I believed that with O'Roarke's demise the threat to Franz Ferdinand had largely been removed.

"No, Watson, you do not know von Bork. The loss of his assassin will certainly be a blow, but he is an adaptable fellow. With another day of shooting yet to come, the Archduke's safety is by no means assured. Our spy's improvisations will be unpredictable, so I had best be on the scene."

"But what if you are recognised?"

"I shall take measures to avoid that possibility." His assurance led us to a discussion of disguises. Bobby Jenkinson, my friend decided, had outlived his usefulness. He was well-known to the beaters and would inevitably attract attention. Holmes rejected the idea of masquerading as my overdue valet, for in our modern age it would require him to appear clean-shaven. Instead, he opted to colour the wig and beard of Jenkinson with lampblack, also shortening the latter. Having brought a grey cloth cap and suit of clothes appropriate for loaders, he elected to fulfill that role for me. I saw numerous objections to this plan, two being the state of his left arm and the fact that the party's other loaders would know him for a stranger. Holmes thought these deficiencies offset by the likelihood that our aristocratic German foes would take less notice of a "peasant". As he reminded me, our time and options were both limited.

430

So it was back into the tunnel for another trek. We returned to my room in Welbeck Abbey still in time for breakfast. Having refreshed my toilette, I left my friend to cool his heels and made an appearance at the table. Luckily, the Duke came down soon afterwards without his imperial guests. Colonel Brosch was there as well, and I was able to persuade both him and Portland to accompany me to an urgent consultation. Holmes had vetoed my request to invite Harry Stonor and Lord Lovat. "Too many allies," he warned me, "are as useless as too few."

On entering my lonely chamber, the Duke shook Holmes gravely by the hand. "I am very glad to see you, sir, but I fear I must report a setback. Last night, Baron von Herder came to me and insisted, quite indignantly, that the German shooters be placed closer to Franz Ferdinand today. He felt they were being intentionally excluded – which," Portland added with an uncertain glance at me, "seemed indeed to be the Doctor's plan. I assumed that Monday's change of shooting stations had come at your direction."

"Quite so, Your Grace. I had reason to suspect a threat that did in fact materialise. Happily, that threat has been averted, but I am not convinced that it will be the last."

"And this threat comes from our faithful allies?" Brosch demanded. I had spent the journey to my part of the Abbey apprising him of our mission and Holmes's involvement in the case. Although the Colonel recalled Duchess Sophie's fondness for my stories, he had been amazed to learn that the detective was not a fictional creation.

My friend confirmed that a member of the German party was undeniably involved. "Then I must add my part to the tale," growled Brosch. "This morning, von Straten Ponthoz asked me to relinquish my stand beside His Imperial and Royal Highness to Herr von Bork, with Prince von Fürstenberg to be nearby. I had supposed that the Archduke sanctioned this request, although why he should subject himself again to Fürstenberg I could not fathom. As I have no official standing, I did not feel able to refuse." Portland gloomily agreed that he as host was in a similar position.

"Then we must take counter-measures to ensure His Highness's continuing protection," Holmes declared. "Who among the British shooters is closest to Franz Ferdinand?"

"Simon – er, that is, Lord Lovat," the Duke replied. "His station is on the other side of Fürstenberg's."

"Then Watson and I must take his place. I am to be the Doctor's loader," he added, holding up his inky wig and beard in explanation.

"His Lordship is the better shot," I noted, with no false modesty.

"True, but you and I are 'in the know' and must be placed to take prompt action."

However, both Portland and I urged that Lovat was not a man to be discarded, so the detective grudgingly agreed that he might be informed and placed nearby. His Grace thereupon suggested that Brosch and I return with him to breakfast, lest our prolonged absence be remarked. "I shall have Hudson, my head-keeper, Mr. Holmes, tell his loaders to take no notice of the new man serving Dr. Watson." I thought privately that Victor, my long-suffering loader of the past two days, would only be relieved!

When we came to the shooting-ground an hour later, the air had turned considerably colder, with the sky a clear, unclouded blue. It was ideal weather to pass a pleasant day among high-flying pheasants, eager dogs, and good companions. Sadly, for Holmes and me there would be little relaxation.

I began by having a quiet word with Lovat, who understood the requirement for the change immediately and moved without protest to my other side. Prince von Fürstenberg spoke to me cordially, clearly delighted by his return to imperial proximity. As for Franz Ferdinand, he grew a bit impatient with the renewed flux but settled into his murderous routine once the shooting started. Von Bork, now my near neighbour, greeted me with an ironic bow. To my relief, he appeared not to notice my new loader before turning his attention to the birds. Holmes went about his business with quiet inefficiency. So far as I knew, my friend had never participated in a shooting party, but naturally he was familiar with all types of firearms. Nevertheless, his wounded arm impeded him, and our mutual disabilities made my rate of fire even slower than before. The genial spy did not neglect to chaff me at the end of the first drive.

"*Gott im Himmel*, Herr Doktor! I did not believe it possible to shoot worse than you did yesterday, but you have surpassed yourself! Did the first loader His Grace assigned to you give up in disgust?" Von Bork grinned at the first loader's successor, who had taken up a cringing crouch in order to mitigate his height. Fortunately, a deferentially touched cap sufficed to end the German's interest.

Over the succeeding drives, it was our adversary's prowess that started to decline. He became ever more distracted, as if uneasily awaiting a delayed event he had expected to occur. When it had not occurred by the time we broke for luncheon, I saw von Bork in agitated consultation with von Herder on their way to the marquee. Abruptly, the spy collared a young beater, handed him what looked like half-a-crown, and sent him flying to the Abbey. "From now on, Watson," muttered Sherlock Holmes, "we must increase our vigilance to the nth degree."

When the shooting party reconvened, I was not the only one with a new loader. "I know that fellow, Holmes," I whispered when I saw the man now handling the German's guns. It was von Bork's valet, who had appeared and spoken briefly to his master on the evening of our billiards game. Moreover, it had been clear on that occasion that the valet had the size and bearing of a soldier. Now he loaded and passed the weapons flawlessly, and von Bork's rate of fire and accuracy began even to exceed the Archduke's. It became almost a contest between the two of them. Before the afternoon's first drive was over, Portland, Brosch, and several of the other shooters (myself among them) had abandoned their own efforts just to watch.

"Well shot, my dear von Bork!" Franz Ferdinand cried jovially as we moved to our next stations. The German, by now looking a bit ashen-faced, merely bowed agreeably in reply. For myself, I could not help but be a little sickened when I saw the enormity of the slaughter our party had inflicted. So profusely lay the dead or dying pheasants that the dogs ran themselves ragged trying to retrieve them. Welbeck Abbey's was the last such shoot that I attended. My reasons had nothing to do with the dire event that was shortly to unfold.

At the time, the lust for destruction proved contagious. No longer willing simply to acclaim their champions, every German, Austrian, and Briton kept up an infernal fusillade that soon would echo across the battlefields of Europe. So overwhelming was the din that I actually forgot our mission and the danger threatening its august object. One man, thank God, did not.

In a momentary lull, I heard a gasp behind me. The Duchess of Hohenberg had risen from her chair, pointing in alarm in the direction of her husband. Following her lead, I saw von Bork's loader casually aiming a waist-high shotgun directly at Franz Ferdinand, who was intent upon his shooting perhaps twenty feet away. Von Bork also seemed to be oblivious. Then the Archduke brought down an unusually high-flying bird. Portland and von Bork paused to express their admiration. The spy's henchman began to raise his gun. I glanced despairingly at Holmes, realising we could never move in time to stop him.

"*Ausweichen!* I *must* congratulate His Imperial and Royal Highness!" It was the Prince of Fürstenberg, pushing aside his own loader and blundering towards von Bork's. Sherlock Holmes leapt after him, shoving the aristocrat into the valet at the moment that he fired. I could hear the Prince's startled cry and my friend's groan at the insult to his wounded arm. The lethal pellets, scattered between Portland and Franz Ferdinand, miraculously hit neither one. Instantly, all shooting ceased, and there was a cacophony of outraged enquiries, shamefaced explanations, and profound apologies. Meanwhile, the day's last flight of pheasants passed safely overhead, unmolested by a single shot.

Earlier than usual that night, the surviving members of the Welbeck Abbey shooting party sat down to a well-earned dinner of roast game. I use the term "surviving" because several members of the party had decided, somewhat abruptly, to take an early train to London. Oddly, all of them shared German nationality: Baron von Herder, the von Borks, and the Prince of Fürstenberg. The poor prince was almost weeping with humiliation as he bade his hosts farewell, having been refused an audience to apologize in person to the Habsburg heir-apparent.

As for the spy, he had gamely withstood Portland's solicitous concern ("My *dear* fellow, you're not going?") as Duchess Winnie attempted to console his devastated wife. It was not as if the popular von Borks had suffered a disgrace. Their unlucky valet had stoutly pled his innocence when seized by Lovat, Brosch, and Harry Stonor – ("He ran right into me, *meine Herren!*") – and Franz Ferdinand had graciously conceded that his near-assassination had been accidental. In fact, he presented his own gold watch to the Abbey's head gamekeeper, in order to commemorate "three days of the most marvellous shooting I have ever enjoyed."

Even so, before departing Herr von Bork found time to have a word with me. "My heartiest congratulations, Herr Doktor! It seems that, after all, you have won the second round of our billiards match. But the match is not over, *mein Freund* – and you may pass that message on to *Meister* Holmes – whenever he puts in his appearance. Until that time, farewell!" With a respectful heel-click of Teutonic salutation, the German spy was gone.

With his arm in a sling, but otherwise in his usual persona, Holmes emerged from my room soon after dinner. I had earlier seen that he was sent a plate of pheasant. While the Portlands entertained their other guests, we were privately admitted to Franz Ferdinand's apartments, where we found the Archduke and his wife, the Countess de Baillet-Latour, and Colonel Brosch von Aarenau. Duchess Sophie crossed the room to take my friend's hands in her own, smiling at us beatifically.

"Dear Herr Holmes, how can we ever thank you and the Herr Doktor? I *knew* that 'the great detective and his Boswell' would not let us down!" The young countess added her own tribute by kissing us both softly on the cheek, which I considered more than ample compensation for my efforts. Franz Ferdinand regarded this display with tolerance, albeit a bit quizzically. He appeared ready to offer us his hand, but the detective forestalled the gesture with a brief and formal bow. Rebuffed, the Archduke also took refuge in formality. Fortunately, he instinctively chose the right approach.

"Even before today's incident, Herr Holmes, I had wished to meet you. I understand you are acquainted with the mysterious Herr Wolfe, who recently refused a decoration I had offered him. Please tell him how much I regret that certain promises made during his mission to Scutari could not be fulfilled. I shall attempt to make amends to King Nicholas when I am emperor. I shall make any amends to Herr Wolfe he wishes to propose."

My friend seemed taken aback by this unexpected condescension. "I thank Your Imperial and Royal Highness," he replied, "and I shall certainly pass on your remarks to my – to Herr Wolfe when I return to London."

"*Danke. Und vielen Dank, meine Herren*, for the service you provided me today. Brosch has explained that there was more to this afternoon's comedy than met the eye. It seems the loyalty of our young friend von Straten Ponthoz is in question."

"If Colonel Brosch has issued such a warning, it is not for me to contradict it. If I may add a warning of my own, I would advise Your Highness that it may be well to turn a jaundiced eye upon your empire's German allies."

The Archduke laughed and, rather belatedly, invited us to take a chair. "I was not born yesterday, Herr Holmes, and I have lived my life in the snake pit of my uncle's court. I have long known that Count von Straten Ponthoz is a spy for Conrad – but two may play at that game. As for these Pan-German fellows, be assured that I took your conclusions regarding the death of my dear aunt – when at last they reached me! – far more to heart than did His Majesty. Was that not true, Brosch? When next the German Kaiser visits me (as will happen in the spring), I shall speak to him of today's mischief. I am confident that Wilhelm will put a stop to any further machinations."

My friend, I could see, was not convinced. "If I may raise one more point . . . ?" he began carefully.

"*Natürlich.*"

"The trip to Sarajevo, which Dr. Watson informs me is to take place next summer. Watson and I have personal knowledge of the regime in Belgrade, and of those who are fomenting a Pan-Serb insurgency in Bosnia and Herzegovina. Again, I would urge Your Highness to be extremely cautious. Indeed, I would advise strongly against making such a trip at all."

Franz Ferdinand sighed, exchanging a troubled look with Colonel Brosch. "I assure you, Herr Holmes – as I have assured my loyal Brosch – that I have no wish to go to Sarajevo. It is another nest of vipers, and Bosnia in mid-summer is as hot as Hell itself! But it will be my duty as

435

Inspector-General to observe our summer maneuvers in the province, and I rather think my uncle will insist. No doubt I shall be safe enough. When His Apostolic Majesty visited the town three years ago, every street he travelled on was lined with soldiers."

When the detective still looked dubious, the Archduke added, almost kindly: "Pray do not worry yourselves unduly, gentlemen. I have known for some time now that it is possible I shall be murdered." Franz Ferdinand regarded us serenely with the clear blue eyes he would one day turn on his assassin. He turned to smile at Duchess Sophie as she touched his hand. "Each of us, you know, can die at any time. For a man in my position, there can be no help for it. I can only trust in God."

"In that case, Your Imperial and Royal Highness," murmured Sherlock Holmes, "I can but echo the prayer offered in your empire's anthem: May '*Gott erhalte Franz den Kaiser.*'"

My friend bowed, far more respectfully than he had done on entering the room. The two of us departed Welbeck Abbey, leaving the doomed couple to their fate.

Later, on our own train back to London, I told Holmes of my conversation with von Bork, including his warning that the contest between us had not ended.

"He is quite right, you know, Watson," replied the detective. "Today's was purely a defensive victory. We were able to thwart our adversary's plan, save the Heir-Apparent, and protect my Altamont identity. But the real contest is yet to come. Nor have its stakes in any way diminished. No less than the peace of Europe and the survival of the British Empire still hang in the balance."

So matters stood until the evening of August 2, 1914, when Holmes completed his mission and brought the German spy to heel. By then, the Archduke and his consort had died in Sarajevo, victims of Pan-Serb assassins and inadequate security, just as Colonel Brosch had feared. The Powers of Europe, trapped by their alliances, rushed as heedlessly as lemmings into the abyss. In the end, our best efforts had but postponed the catastrophe and preserved our country from immediate destruction. Yet that in itself is a good deal. It may be, as Sir Edward Grey once prophesied, that the lamps of Europe will never burn as brightly as on the fateful night he spoke those words. So long as the British Empire still endures, they cannot be extinguished altogether.

Archduke Franz Ferdinand seven months before Sarajevo. At the time, he and his wife Sophie were visiting their friends the Duke and Duchess of Portland, at the Portlands' estate in Nottinghamshire. The Archduke is at right, beside the Duchess of Portland. Sophie is beside the Duke of Portland to the left.

Welbeck Abbey, "a noble but melancholy seate".

NOTES

1. The 1911 Parliament Act, the imminence of civil war in Ireland, the suffragette movement, and other domestic crises facing Britain on the eve of World War I are treated in George Dangerfield's classic *The Strange Death of Liberal England, 1910-1914* (New York: Capricorn Books, 1961 [1935]) Dangerfield stresses the helplessness of Prime Minister Asquith's traditional Liberal methodology to solve them.

2. Holmes and Watson's failed mission to Belgrade in 1903 is recounted in "A Scandal in Serbia," found in *The MX Book of New Sherlock Holmes Stories, Part VI: 2017 Annual*, edited by David Marcum [London: MX Publishing, 2017], pp. 545-572). The tale is also included in the forthcoming book *Sherlock Holmes and the Crowned Heads of Europe*, now in pre-publication with MX Publishing. It was during the mission to Belgrade that Holmes met for the last time with Irene Adler, and Watson learned that the two of them had had a child together (Scott Adler Holmes), who is mentioned later in this story.

3. Here, and several times later in the story, Holmes and Watson refer to their 1898 mission to Geneva, where they sought to prevent Empress Elisabeth of Austria's assassination engineered by the Pan-German spy Adolf Meyer. Holmes later reported on this mission on the deaths of Elisabeth and Crown Prince Rudolf, at Mayerling, to Emperor Franz Josef. The new Habsburg heir-apparent, Franz Ferdinand, eventually learned of then as well. See "The Adventure of the Inconvenient Heir-Apparent", the second story in *Sherlock Holmes and the Crowned Heads of Europe*.

4. British Foreign Secretary from 1905 to 1916. On August 3, 1914, the night before Great Britain declared war on Germany, Grey saw from his office window the lamps of Whitehall being lit. "*The lamps,*" he said, "*are going out all over Europe. We shall not see them lit again in our lifetime.*"

5. As recounted in "A Scandal in Serbia", Count Vukčić was Irene Adler's last husband and thus the stepfather of Holmes and Adler's son Scott, who (according to W.S. Baring-Gould, and tacitly accepted by Rex Stout) grew up to become the detective Nero Wolfe. Wolfe referred to his 1913 mission on behalf of Austria, as well as subsequent adventures in World War I and post-war Yugoslavia, in Rex Stout's *Over My Dead Body* (New York: Bantam Books, 1994 [1940], pp. 10-11, 18-23, and 117-121. Wolfe repaid the Austrians' treachery by fighting for Montenegro in the war.

6. Bobbie, a mongrel from Reading and regimental pet, stood with the 66th Berkshires' "Last Eleven" in their heroic last stand against the Afghans. Although injured, he was able to rejoin Dr. Watson and other wounded members of the regiment. On returning to England, Bobbie and other survivors of the 66th received the Afghan War medal personally from Queen Victoria.
https://www.britishbattles.com/ second-afghan-war/battle-of-maiwand/.

7. One phase of the abortive Anglo-German alliance negotiations was held at Chatsworth, the Duke of Devonshire's estate, in January 1901. Devonshire's wife was German by birth, and both he and the Colonial Secretary, Joseph Chamberlain, favored an alliance with Berlin. The Chatsworth talks were interrupted by the death of Queen Victoria, and the alliance negotiations (which the Prime Minister opposed) ended soon afterwards. Exactly how Holmes and Watson nearly came to lose their lives remains an untold tale. However, they had met the Devonshires years before the two had married, as recounted in "A Game of Skittles" from *The MX Book of New Sherlock Holmes Stories, Part XIX: 2020 Annual (1882-1890)* (London: MX Publishing, 2020), pp. 221-246.

8.	In his earlier stories, when Watson was disguising the identities of eminent statesmen, "Lord Bellinger" was his alias for Robert Gascoyne-Cecil, 3rd Marquess of Salisbury (1830-1903), who formed three governments between 1885 and 1902. His nephew, Arthur Balfour, succeeded him as Prime Minister and served from 1902 to 1905. The case Watson refers to is "The Adventure of the Second Stain", which took place in 1896 and not (as Baring-Gould asserts) in 1886.

9.	A peculiarly Austrian term for laziness, *muddleheadedness*, and inefficiency – thus, fully appropriate to describe Franz Josef's empire.

10.	Sadly, here the Duchess was anticipating her husband's eventual accession. As noted in "A Scandal in Serbia" (found in *The MX Book of New Sherlock Holmes Stories, Part VI: 2017 Annual*, edited by David Marcum [London: MX Publishing, 2017], pp. 545-572), the crown of Bohemia had passed to the Austrian emperor several centuries before. Watson used the title as an alias for the real king (Milan I of Serbia) involved in the case he had originally recorded as "A Scandal in Bohemia".

11.	Coincidentally, Dr. Watson's chapter title duplicates the title of Isabel Colegate's 1980 novel. It, and the 1985 film starring James Mason, perfectly capture the social and diplomatic anxieties that beset the British aristocracy on the eve of World War I. Ms. Colegate's novel may have been based on a real incident, for one of her characters appears in Watson's account of the Welbeck Abbey shooting party.

12.	At this time, a type of horse-drawn wagon used to transport shooting parties, along with their dogs, guns, ammunition, and dead game. Later, the term was applied to automobiles suited for the purpose.

Case No. 358

The Final Case of
Inspector Tobias Gregson,
Scotland Yard
Transcribed by John H. Watson, M.D.

by Marcia Wilson
Translations by Stella Danelius

In my mind, Tobias Gregson is still in his prime – a large, powerful man with the cold blue eye and wheaten hair of his Northern race, impatient with weakness and in possession of the iciest nerves I have ever seen. Beneath his fighter's build lurked a brain sharp and coy, like the watch-cogs that cut the hand foolish enough to probe its innards.

Upon retirement, he was freed from the discretion of his duties. We spent many garrulous hours discussing London, crime, and people. He had no patience for writing but was a rarified storyteller, and our collaborations for print amused him to no end. He would laugh at me now but I prefer to think of him this way and not as the weary pensioner content to sit in his sunny rocking-chair. He died satisfied and I shall die content that I had some part in the wrapping up of his final affairs.

It was a crisp day when I came home to find the expected letter crowning the evening post. Though my heart sank, I read the contents to my wife.

"I must go to the Lestrades. They will care for Gregson until he needs more than they can give. He has asked to see Holmes and me one last time."

"As well as you ought," was her response. "And our son [1] will breathe all the easier without you telling him how to diagnose the patients for a bit. Will you be taking Mr. Gregson's Final Story?"

"The best for last."

"Wonderful! I can't think of a better way to spend Hallowe'en than with old comrades before the fire and a ghost story."

"Mayn't I remind you that Holmes will be present?"

"No ghosts need apply!" we chimed together.

My trip required a stopover in the Sussex Downs where I collected my old friend Sherlock Holmes. It was his preference to ride as a passenger and drive only when he must. From there we headed to our destination, the boreal slope of Plymouth where, despite all expectations, Friend Lestrade had abandoned London and retired.

As lively as ever despite his rustication with a cane and leg-brace, Geoffrey Lestrade met us at the gate and hosted our informal affair under a matriarchal apple in a sweet autumn wind. Clever grandchildren had carved a forest of Hallowe'en grins and grimaces from root-crops, and these bobbed and twisted from the branches like the wealth of a head-hunting tribe as dry leaves skirled about us.

Gregson sat beneath these in his throne of a splint chair by the brazier. He had declined swiftly that year, whey-faced and withered of flesh, but remained sharp-eyed and sharp-tongued. Few kings could hold their courts with so much wit, and it was with a knowing smile that he watched Sherlock Holmes walk slowly up the winding path to the party.

My friend Holmes was the youngest of our quartet. His black hair had become as silver as Lestrade's and arthritis bowed his fingers from the violin. The marks of the cocaine-needle were long replaced with honeystings and there was a peace to his *mien* that his hives and the Downs had brought to his soul. He brought us jars of thick ling honey and pulled on a pipe laced with groundsel for his lungs as he bemoaned the lack of cleverness in country crimes. When Lestrade smirkingly asked if he, too, had been robbed by the honey-thieves currently running through the south, his mournful, "No," sent us into peals of laughter. Who indeed, would be foolish enough to poke Sherlock Holmes, even when he was within his self-proclaimed senectitude? In this way we spent the day, which departed with the swiftness of the season.

Lestrade lit the punkies at dusk. The brazier popped with nuts and we hushed to watch a silver curtain of frost settle upon the fields of stubble. We were the only souls out. Everyone else was away to the villages, trying their hap in little *soirees* dedicated to fortune-telling and marital prophecy. The wild ponies of the moor were long gone, sheltering within the warmer hollows. Against the occasional owl-hoot, the jack o' lanterns cast a glow more comical than sinister, and I said so.

"Why should a season be sinister?" Holmes challenged. In the firelight, his grey eyes sparked in amusement salted with annoyance. "We think nothing of upholding Christmas for charity and soft emotions, but there is nothing more English than a ghost story for Christmas."

Thus began an inspired discussion. Holmes was a proud Anglo-Saxon with a drop of artistic – some might say mad – French blood.

442

Gregson was a staunch Norman with a rational Greek (" – *and stoic*, thank you very much!") grandmother. Lestrade was a Channel-Briton of lineage that did not make particular distinction between the living and the dead. I was a babe north of Hadrian's Wall. We all kept the custom of saving the "shivery tales" for winter. And winter, so far as we agreed, began after Hallowe'en.

"Twaddle!" Holmes finished. "Ghosts take the centre of the stage with all else thrown aside! I have never encountered the horror within the so-called 'supernatural' – what man does is terror enough, and we needn't turn the key players of our little dramas into wailing banshees to remember it!"

"Hah!" Gregson laughed, for he had found his opening. "Then help us start a new custom! Watson had the right idea with *The Hound of the Baskervilles*. Make people believe they're getting a ghost story, and trick them into a much worse tale of cold, hard truth!" He coughed energetically, and leveled his pipe-stem at my breast-bone.

I pulled the newly-printed book from my pocket.

"Good man. Holmes, Ratty – I finally surrendered to this Incurable Romantic's push to publish." That said, Gregson reached down and pulled out a box heavy with items and spread them about the table between the cider-mugs and nuts:

> A wax linen sandwich wrap;
> A battered coin of a cat sailing in a cradle;
> A cloth spyglass unfurled with its two lenses; and finally,
> A relic of the Great War: A German *Dräger* Rebreather,
> incongruous as it was attached to a Royal Navy diving
> mask!

With baffled expressions Lestrade and Holmes stared at the items, and then at each other, before looking to us in a silent plea for answers.

Gregson grinned smugly.

"We've been at this hammer-and-tongs since spring and here it is, my last case, and the reason for my honourable retirement. Watson was good enough to write for me, as we can agree words are his genius and not mine . . . "

Lestrade gasped and Holmes nearly dropped his pipe into the charcoal.

" . . . But as I haven't the lungs nor the patience, we shall simply ask to be treated to Mr. Holmes's fine speaking voice . . . ?"

Holmes flushed at the praise and lifted his cider. "I should be honoured. If someone would kindly bring a few of those turnips closer for

443

light . . . ?" As we complied, he opened the book and coughed. *"Dearest Holmes. Together Gregson and I put his cases in order and he saved the best for the last. Out of respect for this collection we have the title for this story . . . ."*

Case No. 358

This story begins not long after the Great War. Deluded by the blandishments of late spring, every captain on the Whale Road from Denmark to England was surprised at a polar squall that lapped against all shores held by the North Sea. Each man pressed his craft for the nearest port, and one that survived this horror, a small passenger steamer, made hasty landing on Boothy Island.

Asleep in their berths since Esbjerg, the passengers woke at the dawn rattle of ice. They listened as the crew apologised for a docking less southerly than promised, but what to do against a leaking hull? Wasn't it better than hitting an old naval mine? They nodded and accepted billets to room at any Boothy establishments during address, free of charge, courtesy of the *North-Royal Line.* What choice did they have? The crew assisted them to *terra firma,* all the faster to wash their hands of lubbers.

Boothy Island, the captain explained, was sure to welcome them. Kindly remember the name came from the old corrupted word for *Puffin,* and the natives called themselves "Pufflings". The weather was now clear for seeing the famous Cappadocian Chapel, gem of the North Sea! Photographs were allowed!

An elderly passenger curiously eyed that famous gem. It was a black blot cut atop a spike of Old Red Sandstone overlooking Boothy's original Harbour (now a filled-in salt marsh). The path to Divinity was a rickety spiral cut into the stone like the Dragon Lines of old. From here it gave the impression that Puffling ancestors hung desperately to the earth with one hand as they chiseled out a trail with the other. He shrugged and tightened a new Homberg about his head before stepping gingerly amongst the hailstones that salted the dock. His bags had been carried down by a young sailor and thoughtfully abandoned in favour of a stunning young lady with a parasol. He sighed and broke down his walking-stick into sections that fit in his huge pockets, manfully becoming his own porter.

Happier people spent money, and the Pufflings were selflessly showing the visitors all the ways in which this was possible: The tiny open-air market with its *provençal* charm, the women's knitting for sale, a handful of guides promising the most charming scenes for *en*

444

plein air viewing, drink pressed from the rare fruits, homes crafted thriftily from retired fishing-boats, flipped upside down.

Sweet and pleasant though these offerings were, the centre of new commerce was The New Harbour Inn, also the largest structure in the Isle. Her brick arms were open for storm-orphans and the smell of roast beef beckoned. To her the lubbers fled like ants, save those more interested in the alehouses.

The old man chose nothing. Amongst the colour and brass he was alone, a slow-moving giant beneath a sea of squared-off shoulders under an Inverness. Two travelling-satchels depended from his gigantic hands, ballasting his weight on the rough terrain.

He paused at a lump of deeply inscribed sandstone in the middle of the community's cross-roads. It wasn't a rude stone from the Celtic savage, nor the graceful ruin of Norman invaders, but given adjustment for the erratic spelling of its day, it read:

> *This stone*
> *marks*
> *where fell*
> *Sir George the Deaf,*
> *May-Day, 1534.*
>
> *Shipwrecked*
> *Optatus' Day 1501*
> *and submitted*
> *to the Will of*
> *Our Divine Lord*
> *in building*
> *this Chapel*
> *in honour of his youth*
> *in Cappadocia.*
>
> *By hand and chisel he carved This tribute to God*
> *for the souls of Butheyd*
>
> *May it stand as long*
> *as Our Charter with England*

"Mr. Reynolds?"

The traveller looked down – and down – at a small black boy oblivious to the melting slush in his willow *blokken*. A single brace held up the short pants under his open sailor's smock. A matching sailor's cap

445

struggled to hold down a thicket of black curls. Despite the frisky air, the child was proudly displaying an all-too familiar grief: A tiny flag at his breast proclaiming his relationship to a fallen soldier.

The boy looked up and down as well. He had the demeanor of a curious feline, lacking only a twitching tail and whiskers. The elder almost smiled at the fineness of his observation, for there was a large disc of metal pinned to and holding up his brace: A hammered-out cat sailing in a cradle.

"And who might you be?" The question was answered with a question.

"Cat's-Cradle." Said with pride. "We were told to expect ye' on one'a'tha' ships if ya came at all, sir. 'A big man inna Homburg stopping by the Spur.' You don't look much like a ghost fighter."

"I'm not at all surprised to hear that . . . but nor d'you sound much an Englishman."

"'Cause I ain't but half."

"Oh? And the other half of you would be – ?"

"A sailor!" The tiny chest puffed with pride.

The gentlemen kept his composure only from a lifetime of hard practice.

"Come on, Mr. Reynolds. Have a sup against the dank." The hope for his own shone in lively black eyes.

Cats do not own curiosity. The old man condescended to his.

"Lead on, MacDuff – or Cat's-Cradle."

In the storm's wake, the sun struggled to regain its lost territory. Here and there weak patches of light blinked through blue clouds, and fog snaked off the earth from the melting hail. They made for a lean grey tavern crushed between two wind-washed warehouses that had, sadly, given up the battle of its paint versus the elements generations ago. The grim-lipped cleanliness of the fresh-painted walls of the tavern appealed, and the sign, The Wheel, was simple and straightforward: A green solar cross on a white back. This was the natives' roost.

A window flew open and a plump green-sleeved arm threw crusts to birds.

Cat's-Cradle howled, "I wanted that, Tante Maisie! An' here's Mr. Reynolds!"

"Goed!" snapped a Dutch accent. "Bring him in! And this not fit, Cat!"

"Yes it is!" Cat whispered and the newcomer took heed. Maisie brooked no argument.

446

Indoors was hot from exhausted bodies before a sea-coal fire over which cooked a black iron pot of brown bean soup, fragrant with clove and juniper berries. Tarry watermen drank with their land-twins: Thick bipeds of square beards and farmer's hats surrounded by baskets of pease and tiny strawberries. The *viginti* huddled over mugs and puffed at pipes or shaved their plugs. In the wake of the war there were overlaps between the old delineations of society: One salt was as black as the little guide, but the snorter was a meaty farmwoman with trousers under her skirts.

All blinked as this new comrade uprooted his Homberg, releasing a square red face under a startled white shock of hair that could have been a flag of truce for the interloping.

He chose a table and gave coin for Cat's-Cradle to drop his bags beneath. The child skipped a circle, his weight rattling the tables. The old man settled and lifted his hand for a drink but found his porter had returned to the land of business acumen.

"Errands?"

"I might need a clever lad." The gentleman opened the floor for bargaining. "Who be your father?"

"Don't have one." Cat's-Cradle started to puff up again, but a glitter of eye-frost stopped him. "Tante says cats don't have masters."

That wise woman was stamping downstairs, her wide green skirts polishing the wooden rails. She was plump as Providence, and white mossy hair popped from the sides of a headache-tight cap of peacock-green paisley. She wore no jewellry save a string of green-and-brown beads upon her left wrist, yet she was a Queen.

And she had taken in his measure before he'd done the same. There was a feeling she found him wanting. This didn't stop her from pouring a steaming mug of tea for his cold hands.

"I haven't paid."

"We all gets a good drink in bad weather, Mr. . . . . Reynolds?" She spoke slowly, not challenging her guest but neither endorsing a clean bed. Like the boy, she had an outlandish way of talking that sounded like she'd spent time around the Queen's Pipe Dutch in London.

"I've been called worse. That's twice I wasn't allowed time to give my own name."

"I did!" Cat's-Cradle protested.

"For all of three seconds, lad. You are hasty."

"Forgive us, please. We're glad to see you." To Cat's-Cradle: "You're right. I didn't believe he'd come. It was good you waited."

"How long have you been waiting?"

"How long you been a ghost-fighter?" interrupted a young fisher with a twisted leg. There was a nasty glint behind his large blue eyes.

447

"Armour!" Maisie scolded.

For answer, Reynolds pointed at his head. "How many whites?"

"Huh." Armour was impressed at his wit if nothing else. "We need a *professional*, Mr. Reynolds, not a charlatan or Cunny-man."

The newcomer squared up his broad shoulders and straightened up. Tall and powerful his thick neck bent down. "Then perhaps you should tell me what it all means, sir." His voice had gone from bland to authoritative. "I've not said yes or no, but I'll choose one once I've got your story." He lifted his large right hand to stall the just-rising Armour. *"I said I would listen."*

Armour dropped down. "W-well we don't need a faking psychic."

"Good to know! What *do* you need?"

"Well, I don't know! But we don't need an oaf who pretends to see past the Veil!"

"You needn't shout! Whsht!" The farmwife blew through her teeth, at the same time a man who had wrinkles upon his wrinkles spat "Shush!"

"I'll say what I please, Una!"

"Ingen vet att uppskatta lugn och ro nu för tiden." [2] a salt-pickled old Swede muttered. He was well-wrapped within a black knitted top, button-listed to the side in the Baltic Sea style, and looked like the more pagan version of Father Nicholas – the kind of jolly old elf that would hit you with a stick. The guest later learned he was a monoglot, incapable of any speech but his own, though he understood others. His glare at Mr. Reynolds was conspiratory against this room of impatient youth.

"Stop, all of you!" A pink man in shabby black and a dog's collar choked on his sudden tears.

"It's all right," Maisie murmured. She rested one hand on his shoulders. "This is our Sexton, Jamie Peake. He took Father Joel's murder hard." She straightened up, much as the old fighter had, and put her fists into her hips. "And we thought you'd be younger . . . if you came at all. We never got word back."

"And yet I'm here. Is this the place for talk?"

"We've no one to talk t'." One of the bloodshot smokers spoke from the back. There was a rumble of resigned agreement. The farmwife shrugged.

Reynolds took a deep breath for patience. "Father Joel was murdered?"

"Yes. We told the Church he was quarantined with cholera, but soon we'll have to tell them he's dead. That's why we paid you to come sight unseen."

"You never answered," Armour sneered.

"Ghosts and murder? If this were a court of law, what would you say to someone who asked how you knew the murderer was a ghost?"

"Because we buried the killer ourselves."

Mr. Reynolds took a drink for patience. He took three. "What say the authorities?"

"Our Constable's out with his ague."

Mr. Reynolds slowly pulled out the segments of his walking-stick and put them together with a great show of deliberation. He let the silence stretch out quite a bit, and when he judged there was enough shuffling and nervous eye-casting, continued the interrogation. "And the other churches?"

"What, the Methodists on Pig Island?" The sniff was the strongest energy in the room since the Sexton's outburst.

"Methodists exorcise, young Miss. *'For Christ cast out the unclean spirits into the swine, and the word of the Book is to be met as the whole of the Law. My ground is the Bible. Yea, I am a Bible Bigot. I follow it in all things, great and small.'* That was John Wesley himself."

This Wesleyan intelligence was met with surprise and a sudden respect. The temperature of the room thawed from cautious to tender hope.

"Hmm." Mr. Reynolds studied his drink. "Everyone talks their own way, but bits and pieces make for good puzzles, not good reports." The frosty eyes glittered at all. "You may all tell me your side of it, or one of you may do all the telling. It is all the same to me."

What tumbled out next from multiple throats was confusing, but Maisie overrode them all. "We wrote it down!" She exclaimed. "Cat, go fetch it – top left drawer. I held it waiting for your response . . . ."

"Quite all right," Mr. Reynolds grunted. "I imagine the lines have been tangled a time or two as they clean up."

"Streuth," the farmwife swore. "We're *still* plucking shards of those evil Mark 6's out o' the nets and the pools where the liddle 'uns play."

Cat returned with a sealed letter. Mr. Reynolds carefully set it open alongside a small notebook – the sort one might see with a policeman – and a mechanical pencil. The interrogation had begun.

On Collop Monday [*"That was the 3rd, wannit, Maisie?"*] of this year, *The Good Orchard* docked asking for a passenger's burial. Mr. Rickard Lamb had fallen overboard and died from exposure before he could be rescued.

449

From the start there were troubles. Grave-soil was scanty for the Pufflings, and a coffin wanted more space than their customary canvas shroud. But . . . it was the dead man's wish to be buried in wood, and money was offered. With great effort, the coffin was squeezed into a narrow notch in the tiny church plot. They had no aid from the only mourner, Jacob Sears, the *Orchard's* carpenter and coffin maker. He was, it turned out, the ship-mate who rescued poor Mr. Lamb, but not in time to spare his life. He was a dour sot who chewed his cud through Father Joel's sermon. The Pufflings remembered this well, for his gansey had triple rib-stitches underneath his arms and across his chest, a mark of skill associated with (dare we say) a *better* class of seaman than an unshaven soak who couldn't put his weed down long enough to pay respects to his fellow man.

That night a white shape was seen flitting about the graveyard. This was tossed off as moonbeams and the usual thrill of a ship in port. Then Sears vanished after a public drinking-round in all four taverns. *The Orchard* hastily sailed lighter than ever. A troubled pall dampened the Island.

Sixten [*Here the old Swede lifted a wrinkled hand.*] found Sears two Fridays later, bobbing in the glassworts of Old Harbour. The head and hands were gone, natural to anyone who died in water, but everyone remembered that gansey. They buried him at sea with a canvas coffin and a stone anchor at his feet. But how did Sears drown in the marsh?

The nightly hauntings in the graveyard continued. Lamb was unhappy with his burial, said gossips. If Father Joel hoped to still their tongues, there was no chance after the news hit the telegraph station: Lamb was "Pincher" Lamb, a convicted garrotter and London gang assassin escaping the law! He had not accidentally fallen overboard, but drowned to escape capture!

This failed escape smacked of suicide, and *everyone* knew a suicide must never be buried within sight of the sea, else the fish would be too insulted to go into the nets. The Pufflings leapt to a hard inventory of their catches and found them wanting against the past years. Either way you had it, the isle was torn with complaints of consequence. Father Joel was caught in the middle, and ever the peacemaker, withdrew to contemplate as he made the Chapel's repairs.

[*"What repairs?"*]

The Chapel Window's yearly duty. Each of the four quarters of glass needed removal, cleaning, and returning to the frame. Only the priest could touch this precious glass, and only one-quarter could be replaced at a time. It took days.

When children came into The Wheel babbling of a white shape *in the Chapel*, the Father left his supper and soothed their fears by promising to stay there all night, working on the window. His subordinate, Peake, came the next morning with his breakfast to find him dead on the Chapel transept, throat pinched in half and no foot-prints in the dust! With the island's constable in the grip of malaria, the people had few options.

[*"And we dug him up! We thought if we moved him out of sight of the sea . . . there's a cleft in the heart of the double hills . . . we put suicides there . . . ." But Mr. Peake could not speak past this point.*

"The grave was empty," Alain muttered reluctantly. "I know. I drew the lot."]

With nothing to lose, the Pufflings applied for whatever aid they could find, and that included Nevis Reynolds, Spiritual Investigator, and the self-proclaimed inspiration for Carnacki the Ghost Finder –

– The very gentleman before them, who was actually Scotland Yard Inspector Tobias Gregson, on special assignment, and who had kindly accepted their application fee of £25.

Gregson leaned back in his chair and sipped a hot toddy.

"Cat's-Cradle, mind your deliveries." Maisie pointed with a jerk of her chin to a strawberry crate. "You're wasting money. *Stap snel.* There'll be pie after your bath. You'll eat *my* food with clean fingers."

Gregson wasn't ready to allow others control. "Do you have a question of me, Mr. Peake?"

The poor sacristan blinked. "You are a fighter. You didn't get that ox-neck writing letters."

The guest flexed his knuckles, setting off a series of loud pops like pine trees in a freeze. "Other than restless ghosts, would anyone want to kill Father Joel? This carpenter sounds just as murdered – but I heard no whisper of this outside the isle, and I read no words about it in the papers."

"We lied to the papers."

Gregson's mouth fell open. No one could appreciate this, but Maisie's answer was the first and last time he had ever been so surprised by honest candor.

"This is most serious. *How* did you keep this secret?"

"Oh, dear." The Sexton swallowed hard. "Outsiders won't talk to us much. They stick to the Hotel run by those Mainlanders. So far we've put up word that the Chapel is closed for repair and Father Joel is inside it with quarantine. But we're running out of time."

Fresh tears welled in his eyes and his head bowed. He was crying again. *"If Lamb is not walking, where is he?"*

Behind the sacristan, one, another, and a third, reached down and touched their fingertips to the iron nail-heads poking from their bench. Gregson pretended blindness. He was more impressed with the fact that the unity was a sailor, a ropewalker, and the farmwife. This was serious enough to stretch across the boundaries of land and sea, race and sex.

"You saw Father Joel last?"

"We were at supper. The children ran in and their faces were white as whey." (Cat's-Cradle turned purple and Gregson correctly guessed the identity of one child.) "I could barely understand them. He sent them home and told me to eat, not to wait up. He'd . . . go back to the window and keep an eye out as he worked . . . It was beginning to rain, so he wrapped up a sandwich in his pocket and smiled and said . . . he'd tell me about it all at breakfast. But he didn't come in for breakfast. I went up and . . . and he was . . . his neck was . . . ."

The Sexton bowed his head again and no one mocked the little drops that slid from his face to the table.

"The Chapel is old and precious and this will bring the Mainlanders," Masie mourned. *"They'll ask questions*! The Church barely survives as is."

"And what do you wish of me?"

"Investigate the Chapel," grumbled a one-handed porter. "We see a white shape, but when we go in there's nothing."

"Have you not gone to the Chapel and spent the night? None of you?"

"If we did we'd be noticed."

And you are afraid, the old man thought. The shame hovered in the room.

"What if Lamb's body is found?"

"The sea can have it! Murderers and suicides have no business in sweet earth. He was both. Burn him with fire and give the ashes to the sea!"

"The Pastor's things. What did he have?"

A box was produced from the back and he poked and prodded its contents with his crayon. There was a small calendar, box of holy water and wafer, chalk, match-box, and a bit of wax. The poor man had been buried with his beloved cross, stole, and prayer-book.

He was silent a long time.

"Is something wrong?" Alain asked rudely.

452

"Where is his sandwich?"

"His sandwich? Be a bit stale by now!"

Gregson didn't answer. He was smiling.

Gregson was given the Wheel's best room, a narrow chamber boasting an outside exit. He put up his luggage and keyed open the seaward door to the scent of fresh melting ice and an odd mix of stable and motor-oil. Blessing the solitude, he produced a silver smoking-tin from his pocket.

He paused to look about. The vantage gave him an excellent view of the circle-shaped city over the roof-tops, and the now-friendly sea. His little balcony was a good eight feet straight up of a venerable old stable and mews. Half of both were tailored to motor-cars and one well-used Model H Triumph. He chuckled that it was parked adjacent to the stall of a piebald hay-burner, and noted the tiny forge in the back for the repairs of the motor-cycle – and possibly for the horse.

A rattling caught his reddened ears, and the piccolo-splinter of glass. With his precious cigarette aloft in one hand, Gregson leaned over the narrow rail to the darkened pool of shade beneath his roost. Cat's-Cradle, the young imp, was perched with his knees to his chest in the cold and taking a ball-peen hammer to a box of brightly washed Codd Bottles. The boy neatly opened the throat of his next victim, and plucked up the small glass marble hiding inside. The glass slivers were hastily removed from the frozen earth – more for the comfort of the horse, Gregson suspected, than to clean up after one's crime.

Child and elder met their squints in the middle. As suspected, the first round went to impertinence. "Got a fag?"

"For the likes of you?"

"I can pay." The urchin held up a handful of glass marbles.

"Or I might offer you the end. You're not a very good businessman if you offer money before a deal opens."

"I respect my elders." The boy tucked the hammer in a loop somewhere in his trousers and swung up as able as any ship's mate to land neatly on the plank boards. As a proper man of business he did not directly ask for a part of the smoke, but leaned with his forearms on the rail to grin at the petrol bike below.

"What do you think?" Gregson asked.

For a moment the mask slipped. A much-older and sadder being was behind the little face to the world. "We heard something in the Chapel. I wanted to stay but the others run off." He bit his lip. "We didn't think you'd come. Heard you didn't work for less than a hundred pounds. Pretty soon, word'll get off the island."

453

"That scares you?"

"They . . . took us in. Didn't care we were Conchies [3]. Everybody else did. But they didn't." He nodded to the machine, hastily changing the subject. "Front fork spring's knackered. Trusty's ain't bad otherwise."

"Is that so?"

"I know! Boch-Simms' high tension Magneto! Did second at the Isle of Man race. Took a Matchless to beat it! This the same model in '07 what did 1,279 miles in less'n a week! Ixion 'imself looked it over! Worth fifty pounds broke!"

"Don't care for horses?"

"Harder to fix."

The old fellow smirked at the sauce of youth, so unquenchable. "If you like to go places, you can take me to the Constable."

Cat's-Cradle's cap nearly fell off. "Why-for?"

"To tell him I'm here."

Overwhelmed, Cat gave Gregson the blessing of tobacco in silence, and when the end was offered, took it with only a dazed nod.

Gregson was led down a shell path until it ended at a tiny station behind which were the living quarters – a room just big enough for a wall-bed and stove. The books and clothes were boxed under the bed. The host was Country Constable Baum, still set within the grip of malarial fever. He trembled and shook under his heavy blanket and squinted at his guest's business card, well covered in penciled notations. When he finally read it through he blanched, tried to salute, and made a disaster of serving stove-top tea. Gregson was given the only chair and the constable sat on his bed. Cat's-Cradle had the floor by the stove and a box holding a mother cat and her kittens.

"Maisie will take 'em. Rescued from a drowner, if you can believe it, while the whole island's run over with rats!" Baum muttered as he huddled in his woolly shelter. "That's usually our worst crime over here. Stupidity."

"And there's only you to watch the whole island?"

Baum shrugged awkwardly at the other's astonishment. "The island's a big'un, yes, but population's gone down. Most the men are gone. It's amazing how much mischief goes away with young men."

Baum's point was acknowledged with a grin.

"What about Father Joel?" Cat blurted.

"Lad, if you can keep silent until we get back to the Tavern, I'll give you a shilling."

The boy clapped both hands over his mouth and kept them there until a paw tugged them back down for play.

"Don't mind him." Baum sighed. "He's a cat – never occurs to him *not* to tell the truth. But he's right. Joel's neck is stove in. I was trying to find answers when I 'us struck, and the whole island wants this kept quiet. I thought about sending a ciphered wire, but this is the first day you've seen me standing."

"Never mind all that. It looks like there's a bit of a ghostly mystery."

"Beggars my mind, and I'm helpless as a babe until the fit passes." He reached under the bed and with wobbling arms, pulled out a leather sack with three holes. "I found this in the empty coffin. I'm thinking you might recognise it."

Gregson looked hard, and nodded. His face was dark with rage. "No one can help? Can you decree the church off-limits?"

"No one's going *near* a defiled church! Anyway, Boothy's too thin of manpower."

"Is it that bad? I saw some beefy arms back at the inn."

"And that's most of what we've got. Yes, it is that bad. That and some, sir. We've lost half our menfolk to the War, either by prison as Conchies, or by joining up and falling, or getting murdered by those German mines. A sub destroyed our best fishing ships in one night, and it was the women and children who had to pull the bodies from the sea on the following tide. What you see of us . . . it what's left. Just a sprain can hold up a whole family's livelihood. They don't dare risk getting hurt. Just one day of not working means someone's child goes hungry."

"I am surprised there isn't a drunken mob."

"Sir George's Charter is clear. The acre's allocated to Pufflings for the length of Crown Rule, *as long as no weapons enter the chapel.*"

"Good Lord!"

"That's not the oddest bit. Most of the Chapel's protectors don't even belong to it – they're holding it fast for their loved ones."

"The War's done!"

"And C.O.s still in prison! Kith and kin keep faith for them but they ferry o'er to Pig Island's Methodists or the Rowantrees when there's time to pray. We've only a matter of time before some visiting drunkards walk in with knives or guns or even a billy-club and that will be the end of the charter. The Chapel will be up for whoever has the money. The Mainlanders want it – they've offered! That's the end of our heart and soul when they gets it!" A shiver sent Baum backwards. "Bring in the police, and everyone here will lie on a stack of Bibles and deny what they just told you. They'll risk their souls over the Ninth Commandment if it means saving the Chapel . . . The War was hard on them, sir. Too hard. Most of the Boothies are Conchies. Soldiers would come in just to abuse them, scare the children . . . the War's not over for them. They're terrified investigators will come in with weapons in pursuit of justice and ruin four-hundred years of peace – and that's if the Mainlanders don't smell blood and interfere. They want the whole island for themselves, not just the land for their fancy brick inn."

"And you've been struggling with this alone? You need a hospital. Malaria isn't a joke."

"When this is over."

The two sat and thought.

"I have a plan," Gregson said at last. "But I need your help."

"You have it, sir. But . . . er . . . what can a ghost-fighter do?"

"Fight."

Cat's-Cradle was silent, but his eyes were loud.

Gregson held his own silence until he was back in The Wheel.

"Pack me some food and a dark lantern. I'll be staying in the Chapel. No knives. No forks. Nothing sharp. I'll not risk losing you the Charter."

Maisie stammered. "But we still owe you – "

"This is a special case."

Armour tried to sneer "What are you going to do against a murderin' ghost?"

"Preach St. Augustine."

"What if you lose?"

"Have the constable send a wire to my brethren. I gave him my address. Put my remains in storage – Untouched! – for them to dispense." He stared at all of them. "Win or lose, I promise you this will be the end. I'll make certain of it." With a final point he produced a pungent cigarette and lit it within his hands. "Now if someone would be kind enough to escort me to the Chapel?"

In the end there were three someones: Armour, Sixten, and John Burner, eldest netmaker. Sixten had the last mutter: *"Jag skulle hellre fiska upp en till kropp ur träsket/marsken än att gå igenom detta igen."* [4]

To which Mr. Gregson astounded him by grinning and answering, *"Tack."* [5]

Cat's-Cradle grumbled to stay behind, but Maisie's hand was firm upon his shoulder. Woman and child watched the old man go with Armour and two dock-hands.

"What'd he mean, Tante? Preach St. Augustine?"

"Preach the Gospel at all times, and when necessary, use words."

Armour limped the way with an iron key swinging from his hand. Gregson was glad for the daylight. It was required for the spiraling path up the grass-blotched mound of sandstone. In keeping with local custom, the wildling plants among the burials were left free. Here and there sank long notches where the interred slowly became red earth. Father Joel's notch was already a loamy swell decorated with starflowers, for his beloved parishioners had tenderly replaced the sod after cutting it off the soil.

Gregson paused at "The Pincher's Grave". The Pufflings smiled uncertainly as he knelt to examine the weather-damaged coffin, still rudely ripped from the ground and exposed to the elements. He poked inside the planks and pocketed a torn scrap of cloth and a stray bit of curved metal with no explanation.

The Cappadocian Chapel was smaller than it appeared from the waterside. It was about the size and shape of a sardine ship. Her one window faced north to Old Harbour, where the long-dead Sir George once marvelled at hulks and caravels.

"Don't mind the birds." Armour unlocked the door. "They fly in when the glass is off. There's bats too. Maybe mice."

"Is there any way in and out besides this door?

"Eh, no."

"*This* is the whole chapel? A single room?"

"Oh, no! Sir George cut a second chamber beneath the Chapel. You get in by the door behint' t'altar. We'd keep those who'd died in the winter there, and move 'em out in the spring. All that ended back in the Sailor King's day! Now we keep stores for emergencies there, but Father Joel's the only one who knows – knew – where its key was kept."

"So there's nothing there?"

"Well, how would there be? We can't find the key, and the door's locked tight."

Gregson grunted. "I shall see you in the morning, gentlemen."

The door closed.

"Here," Armour whispered. "We paid him to take care of this. Let's make sure he does."

"Eh?" said John.

"We lock him in. He could just step out, have a nap under the stars and come back before dawn saying it's all taken care of. He'll fix it or he won't, but either way we won't be out any more money. I've got young ones to feed same as you. I can't lose any more."

457

So wrapped were they in their underhanded guilt they never noticed the little catlike shape creeping up to rest beneath the Chapel's window.

The old man heard the gong of the lock behind him and shrugged, more interested in his new quarters.

It was a lovely house of worship, shaped from the soft red living sandstone like the upside-down keel of a boat. Faded saints inside stick-thin bodies were painted along the bowed walls and the slope made them lean over the pews like worried old grannies upon their young charges. The only man-made light was provided by screw-mounted lamps, placed directly into the painted hands of the Saints – a clever touch. The lamps stood dark and cold, for they had burned themselves out, oil and wick, without Father Joel to mind the flames.

The round window was now the only illumination, and the chapel's equal in beauty. The old man fancied himself too hard-bit to follow Catholic fripperies, but the window truly was amazing. The Stella Maris stood in the heart of a zaffre sea, one hand cradling a spindle for repairing nets as the other cast out to rescue the souls of the drowning along with the fish. Her Persian Blue robes were trimmed with the golden stars that floated from her mantle past the curling white clouds to the firmament above. Father Joel had replaced the glass in its locking frame, but not the inner casings, so she beamed in four quarters around a cross-shaped gap of missing iron. The gap blew a fresh salt breeze and the cry of gulls. It was a splendid view of the marsh and a good bit of the New Harbour.

The Dead-Vault's door was found, a thriftily fashioned lapstrake plank from some long-dead ship, deep-set in the wall to the side of the tiny altar. It was painted and carved to look like a lean Peter with his hands folded in prayer. In accordance to the old symbols, his large eyes were only half-closed, standing guard between the rooms for the living and the dead, and the keys of his profession hung through his fingers as part of his rosary. Like the saint, the door was not properly shut. It was old and warped. A finger of space existed behind its frame.

The old fighter touched this edge and felt a deep chill. He bent and peered, and it swayed on wooden hinges. Black was the space where no light reached.

The plate of the keyhole was freshly scratched.

For some time he stood before this door, thinking and listening. It would have been a simple thing to pluck up his lantern and go inside, but he finally turned away. In doing this he accidentally encountered a final message: A natural bulge of stone in the wall had been coaxed by chisel and paint into Paul, that small, ferocious Jewish mystic who fought for Christ with all the arrogance of a man who does not know how to fear death. The bas-relief glittered with stern power, the Benjamite's left hand lifted to show a sincere lack of fear. It gestured to the darkness Peter guarded, conciliatory and accountable. The living visitor considered this, for Paul's zealotry for truth had always appealed to his nature. Half-wondering, the old man leaned over and touched the stone gently with pale hands swollen with age and weather. The moment passed. He turned away.

He ate with the Saints for company, using the light-beams from the smiling Mary. The breezes lifted and turned like the sighing breath of the chapel itself, gathering the dust in one spot, then another in graceful feather-trails that dissolved all foot-marks upon the floor.

At sunset a prickle of fine gold slipped across the stone, shaped by the cross-shaped gap in the glass. The guest thought this a fine example of speaking with sunlight, and watched as a burning lava track ran hot against one tight plane, then another.

By six o'clock it was quite dark and the once-blue seaglass had absorbed a plum-like tinge as deep as dried blood. Many long hours passed before the moon emerged. After half-an-hour he saw the first gentle slide of dusty moonlight. It hallowed the ancient glass by inches, casting fey new shadows in icy white upon the tiny world.

Then, as the silver-light cross touched its foremost tip against the pulpit, a *scrape* sent the vermin a-fly. The church held its breath. No sounds barred the old man from hearing the low gasps coming closer and closer with each slap of skin upon stone.

The driftwood door parted. Peter was turning away. And behind that holy figure was no divine illumination but infernal dark.

Fingers emerged, bone poorly wrapped in white flesh. They curled spiders over the edge of the Saint's Door, and a bald head followed. So small were those eyes, so black the wells of socket that it was as though a field-turnip had been carved into a Hallowe'en lantern but left unlit.

That smooth white bulb bobbed side to side, sniffing the air as the spiders twitched. Then, the gross head tipped up as the long beaky nose sniffed the living flesh. A blood-red gleed burned from the bottom of the skull's wells, and the sclera wrapped around those red eyes were yellow as plague. They saw the lump against the corner, and its purpose froze in place.

"Aye," grunted its foe. "You like it when they run, don't you? I've never run, Pincher."

459

He was barely on his feet in time. The apparition sprang and clutched its ragged claws into the space that just held the old man's throat.

Up close only the most superstitious brain would fail to recognize this foe: The Pincher was a full albino, valued as a killer to his ghastly employers because he could ply his vile trade in the dark. He lived and murdered in darkness, and now he had finally gone mad in it. He was a devil in rage. How long they battled, the old man could not say. He was wrestling a skeleton with wild, clacking teeth and banshee squeals. There was no equal standing with this monster and its hands – grotesquely oversized and strong, clicked and pinched like crab-claws whenever it thought his throat was in reach.

Finally, in between the gasps and grunts – a clue: Those terrible yellow-red lamps blinkered out like the shutter of the old lantern. The madman could not bear the brightness of direct moonlight coming through the Silver Cross!

The old fighter saw the blink and the waver. He took his advantage with cold nerve and allowed the fiend to strike at him, again and again, each time painfully giving way a bit more to his left side, slowly turning them by bruising combat into a circle, until his aching body judged no better moment and lunged back, no longer blocking the Silver Cross of light from the other's red eyes.

A single cry, like a newborn mewing its protest, and the lunatic fell to his knees with its claws over its face. It wriggled its head wildly from side to side, and, in its haste struck its own head upon the stone floor and stopped, rattling like a pinned spider and just as dead.

The old man sank down. Something in him was broken, he knew. Finally, he could reach inside his coat and pull out a tiny police-whistle. He wasn't certain he had enough air in his lungs to sound it, but as his eyes gave up the struggle to stay open he heard pounding feet running down the spiral path to the town. Cat's-Cradle, as he had gambled, had stayed close to watch.

You can always trust a cat to be a cat, he thought.

As the investigation revealed, the Pincher hastily boarded the *Orchard* when the Law was too close to his trail. Sears, a member of that gang's secret fraternity, was assigned to engineer his escape. The coffin had been large enough to hide himself, a supply of hardtack, and a confiscated Dräger diving rebreather. His death was duly faked, and his unpleasant appearance was enough to discourage an inspection by the curious. Few outside the law knew the Pincher was an albino, and the captain was just glad to be rid of a Jonah.

Inside the rebreather were traces of imitation Oxylite, otherwise known as sodium superoxide. Normally it expelled oxygen when contacted with the CO_2 in the user's breath, but cobbled British chemistry did not quite mix with German equipment. He may have already been mad when the coffin lid closed over his head, but the inadequate air supply did not help his fading grip on sanity. He was a complete maniac by nightfall, but sane enough to remember that Sears was the only one to know his secret. Sears must have been garroted after the exhumation and tossed into the Marsh. Pincher would have been smarter if he'd weighed the body with his heavy rebreather, but again, his mind was not above question.

A cloth spyglass was found in his cache, proving he was using the Chapel as a lookout. Every night he posted himself at the window with the spyglass, looking for some signal along the mysterious language of his criminal Brotherhood that would assure him escape was at hand. But as time wore on without a friendly ship, his self-control slipped further away. Poor Father Joel had been killed because the Pincher couldn't bear the thought of being kept from his vigil a single night. His sandwich was gobbled and the wrapper absently taken with it, which gave his pursuer the first proof he was dealing with flesh and blood.

As for "Mr. Reynolds", he was treated for grievous injuries and a mainland policeman aided his departure. He left as mysteriously as he arrived, although twenty-five pounds were soon mailed to The Wheel (*"Refunded: I was paid to fight a ghost and this was not a ghost."*).

By that time a few might have suspected that *Reynolds* was an imposter, but who would complain about the helping hand of the famous Tobias Gregson, Scotland Yard?

The punkies had burnt low by the time Holmes lowered the book, and the smouldering flames gave them a brooding illusion of contemplation. Gregson was leaned back in his chair with his warm drink and peace upon his tired face.

In contrast sat Lestrade, one finger tapping a restless pattern upon the table. Beside him Holmes quietly set the book down in trade for his long-awaited tobacco. In silence we sat, and Holmes smoked.

"That boy." Lestrade was the first to break the silence. "You put a lot of him into the tale."

Gregson only chuckled.

"I did wonder," Holmes interrupted whatever Lestrade had been about to say, "of your retirement. It was ahead of my projected schedule."

"Ah, that." The old Yarder drew his blanket closer to his chest. "A man out of his wits will hurt more than a sane man ever will. He broke me

461

good and I didn't heal proper. Asymptomatic, they said. Once I was over the pneumonia I was done."

"That is an . . . *amazing* final case, Tobias." Lestrade's voice had dropped. "But I always wondered what would happen if you went up against something bigger than yourself." Only I could see how his hands had stilled about his drink. Lestrade's own retirement had been humdrum and dull – insultingly so to a man who fought so passionately for British Justice and the law and there had been some rumour that it had not been a matter of choice. Had Sir Henry Baskerville not known about and remembered his aid over the business with the Hound, he might have stayed in London with its unhappy memories. Luckily, the baronet *had* remembered his worth, and offered him the rebuilt Merripit House where he could look after his now-blind wife and her own weakened lungs in peace.

I often hear policemen wistfully speaking of "a great case" without which they could not be truly retired with honours. Even though I knew Lestrade had many admirable cases to his name, it was clear he had never achieved "a great case" before his departure.

Gregson coughed again, breaking the congestion in his lungs. This was his daily battle now, and each day was worse.

Lestrade plucked up the little coin where we could now see the back had been riveted into a sort of crude brooch to hold up a child's braces. "He was mightily attached to this token. I am surprised he gave it to you."

"I believe our good friend has left threads for us to follow." Holmes mused around a smoke ring. "Are you not up to your old tricks again, Gregson? Telling part of the story but letting the rest lurk in the shadows?"

Gregson's chortle was pinched from lack of proper air. "Old habits die hard, don't they?" He waggled a chiding finger at a bewildered Lestrade. "You can't tell me you never walked into that man's sitting room with only half your story on your lips with the other half going down your throat with a swallow, Geoffrey. I did it. We all did it, and he'd see those swallowed bits anyway."

"You will *never* let me live down that murder in Herefordshire."

"I should hope not. But as it is late I should make myself for bed. Unlike the rest of you fine fellows, I must be ready for the doctor upon seven o'clock, and it is deep *nachmitternacht*."

"I'll see you off to bed proper." Lestrade ignored Gregson's protests, claiming that his wife would hear him and spill his brains with her frying-pan before she knew his identity. The two old men made their way to the house. In the misty light of the punkies Holmes was smiling ear-to-ear, and that was unfailingly indicative of a story hiding within his sharp mind.

"What do you think, Holmes?"

"That Lestrade best not tell anyone he has so many healthy *Apis mellifera*. The honey-rustlers know their prime value on the market as well as the impossibility of diluting the comb with boiled maize cobs." He leaned backwards in his country chair and made a show of examining the stars over our heads.

"Holmes! What did you see? I have been with Gregson since we started collaborating with this last case, and I was certain I saw nothing more than what he told me!"

"And that is what you were supposed to do, old friend! Gregson needed your help and you did a splendid job. I cannot imagine how anyone else could have done better."

I tried to think around the glow of his praise, for this story had turned from familiar to queer. I examined my brain for insights as Holmes continued to smoke and star-gaze, his expression as thoughtful as it was pensive.

"Ah." I sat upright, shocked. "Gregson began his adventure past the point of its natural beginning . . . why was he in Esbjerg? Why would a policeman be abroad?"

"Why, indeed?"

"You have realised this riddle. Will you share it with me?"

"It would require discretion."

"Lestrade? Gregson hid something in this story for Lestrade to find?"

"Gregson is a widower and penniless, his savings empty, and his disease a mockery of his pension. Lestrade has taken in his old comrade in arms and refused to accept any payment for his room and board, for he can afford it – modestly – and the Brotherhood of policemen is strong.

"Did you think for even a moment Gregson would meekly accept Lestrade's generosity? After decades of rivalry amongst their profession?" Holmes shook his head at my naivety. "Watson, Watson! When has Gregson *ever* peacefully surrendered the field to Lestrade?"

"But Lestrade wouldn't hear of reparation. He wanted to help Gregson because it was the proper thing to do!"

"And of the two, Gregson has achieved something Lestrade has not: A terrible crime recognised and solved with sharp thought and frozen nerve. What each policeman dreams of having – a *Great Case*." Holmes knocked his ashes into the cranium of a burnt-out turnip.

"Though I begin to see what you are saying, I am still lost."

"Take your time, old fellow, just remember that it will take Lestrade about ten minutes to return."

463

"Was it the boy, Cat's-Cradle?"

"One of the prettier little puzzles of the Great War was the disappearance of The Dutch Agates." Holmes had found a wisp of straw to steal a light from a still-burning lantern and he spent a moment in puffing his small combustible into full throttle. "Do you remember them, Watson? My expertise was consulted but before long I chose to bow out of the matter."

"I remember nothing of the first half of the War, Holmes. I was in the trenches with my men."

"Ah, then I shall illuminate. Agates are not normally of note among jewelers, but the Dutch Agates were mined from a seam of rare fossilised coral, and instead of the usual red amber colour, the seam was a remarkable translucent blue. Queen Wilhelmina had sent them to her favoured jeweller Aren de Oude, or, Aaron the Old, to make a fine piece for a minor relative's wedding.

"Said relative, whom discretion forbids me to name, was dallying both sides concerning her rule. Salic Law will decree the House of Orange-Nassau-Dietz extinct upon her passing, even though the Succession Laws of the Dutch ignore this ruling. The Queen's finances were severely curtailed by then, and it didn't take long for the Agates to look attractive for a low worm of the court seeking leverage.

"German Loyalists soon burgled the office of De Oude. He and his wife were murdered, but the crime was cheated for the stones were missing – along with the toddler son Aren De Jung and his loyal Nanny, Jacinthe Macy.

"I had followed all interesting crimes that came my way in the fickle lines of the news, and the last thread had been a search for the missing Heir in Denmark, for De Oude had nephews in the trade under an Esbjerg address. The close Fraternity of gem-cutters was a good enough reason to seek the child there, but the war muddied all plans. There had been one week in which the ships would have sailed without too much harassment from the English Blockades or the German boats . . . but that week was plagued with heavy storms and the lack of news led the world to conclude that the child, his Nanny, and the priceless coral agates were lost beneath the waves along with several other ships."

"That is a terrible story, Holmes."

"Many stories are exactly that."

"And yet I believe you have not finished."

"*The story* has not finished, Watson. Tut-tut! Be precise.

464

"Not many people know the Arens were Black Dutch, their family originating from slaves freed almost two centuries past. Even fewer know that De Jung was born in Kinderdijk. Have you never been there, Watson? You would enjoy it, with your writer's pen and overly romantic eye for detail. It has picturesque scenery with its windmills and floral-clad canals."

"Perhaps someday, Holmes," I said in exasperation. "But I surely cannot plan for such a trip if I am sitting here waiting for you to end my impatience."

Holmes's eyes twinkled in mischief. "Ah, but it is such an interesting story! Do you know how the town got the name of Kinderdijk? It means 'Children-Dike' after the St. Elizabeth Flood in 1421. All living souls perished, or so everyone thought, but a small cradle was seen bobbing in a peculiar pattern about the flood-waves. Whenever that frail craft seemed about to tip over, it righted itself just in time.

"At long last it floated within reach of a rescuer, who found an infant sound asleep and the reason for its life in the form of a small cat. The cat would jump from side to side, correcting the tipping of the vessel. Thus did the people name the town, and made its seal a cat sailing in a cradle."

Holmes stood to straighten his back with a grimace. "When you do go there, Watson, make certain you pay the local cats proper respect. They are considered something of a good-luck charm, and I wouldn't like to be the man caught mistreating one."

"But this is incredible! How would such a case fall to Gregson?"

"Resources were thin for the Crown after the War, Watson. As well you know." Holmes sighed. "They would not have asked him to join in the hunt had someone else been available. I daresay someone remembered his success with foreigners with the subtle hint that he would be retiring soon, allowing a more deserving young man to inherit his post in a labour-troubled market."

"You haven't explained how this child and his Nanny wound up on that tiny island."

"Evidence leads me to a plausible conjecture. Just as Gregson and the worthy Sir George – blew off course from a storm. All this time the governments had been tracing the wrong ships in the wrong place." Holmes didn't shrug but he expelled a cheerful plume of smoke high into the branches of the apple tree. "I adduce from the sudden sounds in the kitchen that Lestrade is coming back out after he examines his foot for broken toes. Really, he needs to do something about that pig-iron doorstop."

I was trying not to laugh at this absurd situation. "This is worse than a Dickens novel! Holmes, aren't you going to tell Lestrade about this?"

"Are you?"

"I cannot!" I blustered. "It is so clear now that you have explained it. But . . . what if Lestrade does not see this hidden mystery?"

"Gregson is smug and that is enough. Lestrade is already suspicious. The seeds have fallen, I daresay, upon fruitful soil. Lestrade never could let go of a dandling question. He will seek and find the young heir and his formidable guardian. Should I be senile enough to believe in a crystal ball, my friend, I daresay they will continue to live their quiet, unassuming lives, away from the hatred and jealousies outside the Isle. They will give him the Corals and he will come up with a plausible explanation for their existence – possibly another shipwreck's leavings on the windward side."

Holmes returned to his chair. "Hallowe'en has passed, Watson. It is the time to honour Hallowmass, where the Saints take notice of all selfless acts, even a Protestant such as Gregson. A fortuitous sense of timing, would you not agree?"

NOTES

1. This story is dated a few years before Watson's death, and we know he was increasingly protective of his privacy. This may be why he doesn't identify his "son" (stepson) or wife by name. We take his reticence as further evidence of his work in Intelligence for His Majesty.
2. "Nobody knows to appreciate calm and peace nowadays." (Old style ca 1900-1950). *Swedish translation by Stella Danelius.*
3. *Conchie*: Conscientious Objector
4. "I'd rather fish another corpse out of the Marsh than go through this again." *Translation by Stella Danelius*
5. "Thank you."

About the Contributors

The following contributors appear in this volume:
The MX Book of New Sherlock Holmes Stories
Part XXVII – 2021 Annual (1898-1927)

Brian Belanger is a publisher, editor, illustrator, author, and graphic designer. In 2015, he co-founded Belanger Books along with his brother, author Derrick Belanger. He designs the covers for every Belanger Books release, and his illustrations have appeared in the MacDougall Twins with Sherlock Holmes series, as well as *Dragonella, Scones and Bones on Baker Street*, and *Sherlock Holmes: A Three-Pipe Problem*. Brian has published a number of Sherlock Holmes anthologies, as well as new editions of August Derleth's classic Solar Pons mysteries. Since 2016, Brian has written and designed letters for the *Dear Holmes* series, and illustrated a comic book for indie band The Moonlight Initiative. In 2019, Brian received his investiture in the PSI as "Sir Ronald Duveen". Find him online at *www.belangerbooks.com, www.zhahadun.wixsite.com/221b*, and *www.redbubble.com/people/zhahadun*

Leslie Charteris was born in Singapore on May 12th, 1907. With his mother and brother, he moved to England in 1919 and attended Rossall School in Lancashire before moving on to Cambridge University to study law. His studies there came to a halt when a publisher accepted his first novel. His third one, entitled *Meet the Tiger*, was written when he was twenty years old and published in September 1928. It introduced the world to Simon Templar, *aka* The Saint. He continued to write about The Saint until 1983 when the last book, *Salvage for The Saint*, was published. The books, which have been translated into over thirty languages, number nearly a hundred and have sold over forty-million copies around the world. They've inspired, to date, fifteen feature films, three television series, ten radio series, and a comic strip that was written by Charteris and syndicated around the world for over a decade. He enjoyed travelling, but settled for long periods in Hollywood, Florida, and finally in Surrey, England. He was awarded the Cartier Diamond Dagger by the *Crime Writers' Association* in 1992, in recognition of a lifetime of achievement. He died the following year.

Craig Stephen Copland confesses that he discovered Sherlock Holmes when, sometime in the muddled early 1960's, he pinched his older brother's copy of the immortal stories and was forever afterward thoroughly hooked. He is very grateful to his high school English teachers in Toronto who inculcated in him a love of literature and writing, and even inspired him to be an English major at the University of Toronto. There he was blessed to sit at the feet of both Northrup Frye and Marshall McLuhan, and other great literary professors, who led him to believe that he was called to be a high school English teacher. It was his good fortune to come to his pecuniary senses, abandon that goal, and pursue a varied professional career that took him to over one-hundred countries and endless adventures. He considers himself to have been and to continue to be one of the luckiest men on God's good earth. A few years back he took a step in the direction of Sherlockian studies and joined the *Sherlock Holmes Society of Canada* – also known as *The Toronto Bootmakers*. In May of 2014, this esteemed group of scholars announced a contest for the writing of a new Sherlock Holmes mystery. Although he had never tried his hand at fiction before, Craig entered and was pleasantly surprised to be selected as one of the winners. Having enjoyed the experience, he decided to write more of the same, and is now on a

471

mission to write a new Sherlock Holmes mystery that is related to and inspired by each of the sixty stories in the original Canon. He currently lives and writes in Toronto and Dubai, and looks forward to finally settling down when he turns ninety.

John William Davis is a retired US Army counterintelligence officer, civil servant, and linguist. He was commissioned from Washington University in St. Louis as an artillery officer in the 101st Air Assault Division. Thereafter, he went into counterintelligence and served some thirty-seven years. A linguist, Mr. Davis learned foreign languages in each country he served. After the Cold War and its bitter aftermath, he wrote *Rainy Street Stories, Reflections on Secret Wars, Terrorism, and Espionage.* He wanted to write about not only true events themselves, but also the moral and ethical aspects of the secret world. With the publication of *Around the Corner*, Davis expanded his reflections on conflicted human nature to our present day traumas of fear, and causes for hope. A dedicated Sherlockian, he's contributed to telling the story of the Great Detective in retirement.

Ian Dickerson was just nine years old when he discovered The Saint. Shortly after that, he discovered Sherlock Holmes. The Saint won, for a while anyway. He struck up a friendship with The Saint's creator, Leslie Charteris, and his family. With their permission, he spent six weeks studying the Leslie Charteris collection at Boston University and went on to write, direct, and produce documentaries on the making of *The Saint* and *Return of The Saint,* which have been released on DVD. He oversaw the recent reprints of almost fifty of the original Saint books in both the US and UK, and was a co-producer on the 2017 TV movie of *The Saint.* When he discovered that Charteris had written Sherlock Holmes stories as well – well, there was the excuse he needed to revisit The Canon. He's consequently written and edited three books on Holmes' radio adventures. For the sake of what little sanity he has, Ian has also written about a wide range of subjects, none of which come with a halo, including talking mashed potatoes, Lord Grade, and satellite links. Ian lives in Hampshire with his wife and two children. And an awful lot of books by Leslie Charteris. Not quite so many by Conan Doyle, though.

Sir Arthur Conan Doyle (1859-1930) *Holmes Chronicler Emeritus.* If not for him, this anthology would not exist. Author, physician, patriot, sportsman, spiritualist, husband and father, and advocate for the oppressed. He is remembered and honored for the purposes of this collection by being the man who introduced Sherlock Holmes to the world. Through fifty-six Holmes short stories, four novels, and additional Apocryphal entries, Doyle revolutionized mystery stories and also greatly influenced and improved police forensic methods and techniques for the betterment of all. *Steel True Blade Straight.*

Steve Emecz's main field is technology, in which he has been working for about twenty years. Steve is a regular trade show speaker on the subject of eCommerce, and his tech career has taken him to more than fifty countries – so he's no stranger to planes and airports. He wrote two novels (one a bestseller) in the 1990's, and a screenplay in 2001. Shortly after, he set up MX Publishing, specialising in NLP books. In 2008, MX published its first Sherlock Holmes book, and MX has gone on to become the largest specialist Holmes publisher in the world. MX is a social enterprise and supports three main causes. The first is Happy Life, a children's rescue project in Nairobi, Kenya, where he and his wife, Sharon, spend every Christmas at the rescue centre in Kasarani. In 2014, they wrote a short book about the project, *The Happy Life Story.* The second is the Stepping Stones School, of which Steve is a patron. Stepping Stones is located at Undershaw, Sir Arthur Conan Doyle's former home. Steve has been a mentor for the World Food Programme for the last several years, supporting their innovation bootcamps and giving 1-2-1 mentoring to several projects.

Mark A. Gagen BSI is co-founder of Wessex Press, sponsor of the popular *From Gillette to Brett* conferences, and publisher of *The Sherlock Holmes Reference Library* and many other fine Sherlockian titles. A life-long Holmes enthusiast, he is a member of *The Baker Street Irregulars* and *The Illustrious Clients of Indianapolis*. A graphic artist by profession, his work is often seen on the covers of *The Baker Street Journal* and various BSI books.

Tim Gambrell lives in Exeter, Devon, with his wife, two young sons, three cats, and now only four chickens. He has previously contributed stories to *The MX Book of New Sherlock Holmes Stories*, and also to *Sherlock Holmes and Dr Watson: The Early Adventures* and *Sherlock Holmes and The Occult Detectives*, also from Belanger Books. Outside of the world of Holmes, Tim has written extensively for Doctor Who spin-off ranges. His books include two linked novels from Candy Jar Books: *Lethbridge-Stewart: The Laughing Gnome – Lucy Wilson & The Bledoe Cadets*, and *The Lucy Wilson Mysteries: The Brigadier and The Bledoe Cadets* (both 2019), and *Lethbridge-Stewart: Bloodlines – An Ordinary Man* (Candy Jar, 2020, written with Andy Frankham-Allen). He's also written a novella, *The Way of The Bry'hunee* (2019) for the Erimem range from Thebes Publishing. Tim's short fiction includes stories in *Lethbridge-Stewart: The HAVOC Files 3* (Candy Jar, 2017, revised edition 2020), *Bernice Summerfield: True Stories* (Big Finish, 2017) and *Relics . . . An Anthology* (Red Ted Books, 2018), plus a number of charity anthologies.

Denis Green was born in London, England in April 1905. He grew up mostly in London's Savoy Theatre where his father, Richard Green, was a principal in many Gilbert and Sullivan productions, A Flying Officer with RAF until 1924, he then spent four years managing a tea estate in North India before making his stage debut in *Hamlet* with Leslie Howard in 1928. He made his first visit to America in 1931 and established a respectable stage career before appearing in films – including minor roles in the first two Rathbone and Bruce Holmes films – and developing a career in front of and behind the microphone during the golden age of radio. Green and Leslie Charteris met in 1938 and struck up a lifelong friendship. Always busy, be it on stage, radio, film or television, Green passed away at the age of fifty in New York.

John Atkinson Grimshaw (1836-1893) was born in Leeds, England. His amazing paintings, usually featuring twilight or night scenes illuminated by gas-lamps or moonlight, are easily recognizable, and are often used on the covers of books about The Great Detective to set the mood, as shadowy figures move in the distance through misty mysterious settings and over rain-slicked streets.

Arthur Hall was born in Aston, Birmingham, UK, in 1944. He discovered his interest in writing during his schooldays, along with a love of fictional adventure and suspense. His first novel, *Sole Contact*, was an espionage story about an ultra-secret government department known as "Sector Three", and was followed, to date, by three sequels. Other works include five Sherlock Holmes novels, *The Demon of the Dusk*, *The One Hundred Percent Society*, *The Secret Assassin*, *The Phantom Killer*, and *In Pursuit of the Dead*, as well as a collection of short stories, and a modern detective novel. He lives in the West Midlands, United Kingdom.

Stephen Herczeg is an IT Geek, writer, actor, and film-maker based in Canberra Australia. He has been writing for over twenty years and has completed a couple of dodgy novels, sixteen feature-length screenplays, and numerous short stories and scripts. Stephen was very successful in 2017's International Horror Hotel screenplay competition, with his scripts *TITAN* winning the Sci-Fi category and *Dark are the Woods* placing second in the horror category. His three-volume short story collection, *The Curious Cases of Sherlock Holmes*, will be published in 2021. His work has featured in *Sproutlings – A Compendium of Little Fictions* from Hunter Anthologies, the *Hells Bells* Christmas horror anthology published by the Australasian Horror Writers Association, and the *Below the Stairs*, *Trickster's Treats*, *Shades of Santa*, *Behind the Mask*, and *Beyond the Infinite* anthologies from OzHorror.Con, *The Body Horror Book*, *Anemone Enemy*, and *Petrified Punks* from Oscillate Wildly Press, and *Sherlock Holmes In the Realms of H.G. Wells* and *Sherlock Holmes: Adventures Beyond the Canon* from Belanger Books.

Jeremy Branton Holstein first discovered Sherlock Holmes at age five when he became convinced that the Hound of the Baskervilles lived in his bedroom closet. A life-long enthusiast of radio dramas, Jeremy is currently the lead dramatist and director for the Post Meridian Radio Players adaptations of Sherlock Holmes, where he has adapted *The Hound of the Baskervilles*, *The Sign of Four*, and "Jack the Harlot Killer" (retitled "The Whitechapel Murders") from William S. Baring-Gould's *Sherlock Holmes of Baker Street* for the company. Jeremy has also written Sherlock Holmes scripts for Jim French's *Imagination Theatre*. He lives with his wife and daughter in the Boston, MA area.

Roger Johnson BSI, ASH is a retired librarian, now working as a volunteer assistant at the Essex Police Museum. In his spare time, he is commissioning editor of *The Sherlock Holmes Journal*, an occasional lecturer, and a frequent contributor to *The Writings about the Writings*. His sole work of Holmesian pastiche was published in 1997 in Mike Ashley's anthology *The Mammoth Book of New Sherlock Holmes Adventures*, and he has the greatest respect for the many authors who have contributed new tales to the present mighty trilogy. Like his wife, Jean Upton, he is a member of both *The Baker Street Irregulars* and *The Adventuresses of Sherlock Holmes*.

John Lawrence served for thirty-eight years as a staff member in the U.S. House of Representatives, the last eight as Chief of Staff to Speaker Nancy Pelosi (2005-2013). He has been a Visiting Professor at the University of California's Washington Center since 2013. He is the author of *The Class of '74: Congress After Watergate and the Roots of Partisanship* (2018), and has a Ph.D. in history from the University of California (Berkeley).

Peter Lovesey is the author of the Peter Diamond mysteries, well known for their use of surprise, strong characters and hard-to-crack puzzles. He was awarded the Cartier Diamond Dagger in 2000, the *Grand Prix de Litterature Policiere*, the Anthony, the Ellery Queen Readers' Award, and is Grand Master of the Swedish Academy of Detection. He has been a full-time author since 1975, and was formerly in further education. Earlier series include the Sergeant Cribb mysteries seen on TV and the Bertie, Prince of Wales novels. Peter and his wife Jax, have a son, Phil, also a teacher and mystery writer, and a daughter Kathy, who was a Vice-President of J.P.Morgan-Chase, and now lives with her family in Greenwich, Ct. Peter currently lives in Chichester, England. His website at *www.peterlovesey.com* gives fuller details of his life and books. "Try him. You'll love him," wrote the doyen of the mystery world, Otto Penzler, in *The New York Sun*.

David Marcum plays *The Game* with deadly seriousness. He first discovered Sherlock Holmes in 1975 at the age of ten, and since that time, he has collected, read, and chronologicized literally thousands of traditional Holmes pastiches in the form of novels, short stories, radio and television episodes, movies and scripts, comics, fan-fiction, and unpublished manuscripts. He is the author of nearly eighty Sherlockian pastiches, some published in anthologies and magazines such as *The Strand*, and others collected in his own books, *The Papers of Sherlock Holmes, Sherlock Holmes and A Quantity of Debt*, and *Sherlock Holmes – Tangled Skeins*. He has almost sixty books, including several dozen traditional Sherlockian anthologies, such as the ongoing series *The MX Book of New Sherlock Holmes Stories*, which he created in 2015. This collection is now up to 27 volumes, with more in preparation. He was responsible for bringing back August Derleth's Solar Pons for a new generation, first with his collection of authorized Pons stories, *The Papers of Solar Pons*, and then by editing the reissued authorized versions of the original Pons books, and then volumes of new Pons adventures. He has done the same for the adventures of Dr. Thorndyke, and has plans for similar projects in the future. He has contributed numerous essays to various publications, and is a member of a number of Sherlockian groups and Scions. His irregular Sherlockian blog, *A Seventeen Step Program*, addresses various topics related to his favorite book friends (as his son used to call them when he was small), and can be found at *http://17stepprogram.blogspot.com/* He is a licensed Civil Engineer, living in Tennessee with his wife and son. Since the age of nineteen, he has worn a deerstalker as his regular-and-only hat. In 2013, he and his deerstalker were finally able make his first trip-of-a-lifetime Holmes Pilgrimage to England, with return Pilgrimages in 2015 and 2016, where you may have spotted him. If you ever run into him and his deerstalker out and about, feel free to say hello!

Will Murray has been writing about popular culture since 1973, principally on the subjects of comic books, pulp magazine heroes, and film. As a fiction writer, he's the author of over 70 novels featuring characters as diverse as Nick Fury and Remo Williams. With the late Steve Ditko, he created the Unbeatable Squirrel Girl for Marvel Comics. Murray has written numerous short stories, many on Lovecraftian themes. Currently, he writes The Wild Adventures of Doc Savage for Altus Press. His acclaimed Doc Savage novel, *Skull Island*, pits the pioneer superhero against the legendary King Kong. This was followed by *King Kong vs. Tarzan* and two Doc Savage novels guest-starring The Shadow. *Tarzan, Conqueror of Mars*, a crossover with John Carter of Mars, was just published. *www.adventuresinbronze.com* is his website.

Sidney Paget (1860-1908), a few of whose illustrations are used within this anthology, was born in London, and like his two older brothers, became a famed illustrator and painter. He completed over three-hundred-and-fifty drawings for the Sherlock Holmes stories that were first published in *The Strand* magazine, defining Holmes's image forever after in the public mind.

Tracy J. Revels, a Sherlockian from the age of eleven, is a professor of history at Wofford College in Spartanburg, South Carolina. She is a member of *The Survivors of the Gloria Scott* and *The Studious Scarlets Society*, and is a past recipient of the Beacon Society Award. Almost every semester, she teaches a class that covers The Canon, either to college students or to senior citizens. She is also the author of three supernatural Sherlockian pastiches with MX (*Shadowfall*, *Shadowblood*, and *Shadowwraith*), and a regular contributor to her scion's newsletter. She also has some notoriety as an author of very silly skits: For proof, see "The Adventure of the Adversarial Adventuress" and "Occupy Baker Street" on YouTube. When not studying Sherlock, she can be found researching the history of her native state, and has written books on Florida in the Civil War and on the development of Florida's tourism industry.

Roger Riccard of Los Angeles, California, U.S.A., is a descendant of the Roses of Kilravock in Highland Scotland. He is the author of two previous Sherlock Holmes novels, *The Case of the Poisoned Lilly* and *The Case of the Twain Papers*, a series of short stories in two volumes, *Sherlock Holmes: Adventures for the Twelve Days of Christmas* and *Further Adventures for the Twelve Days of Christmas*, and the ongoing series *A Sherlock Holmes Alphabet of Cases,* all of which are published by Baker Street Studios. He has another novel and a non-fiction Holmes reference work in various stages of completion. He became a Sherlock Holmes enthusiast as a teenager (many, many years ago), and, like all fans of The Great Detective, yearned for more stories after reading The Canon over and over. It was the Granada Television performances of Jeremy Brett and Edward Hardwicke, and the encouragement of his wife, Rosilyn, that at last inspired him to write his own Holmes adventures, using the Granada actor portrayals as his guide. He has been called "The best pastiche writer since Val Andrews" by the *Sherlockian E-Times.*

Jacqueline Silver is the Headteacher of Stepping Stones School. She has developed her career from her early days as an accomplished Drama teacher and has a strong background in school leadership. She has always had a passion for creating nurturing and positive school environments for mixed ability children. Her recent career history has seen her spearhead pastoral care provision at a number of schools where she has also been resolute in her vision for safeguarding, particularly of the most vulnerable children in our society. Since her appointment as Headteacher of Stepping Stones School, she can realise her prime personal focus for improving the employability of young people with learning needs. Quality of life, independence, and positive engagement with society are linchpins of Jacqueline's vision for the future. Stepping Stones will flourish under her leadership.

Joseph W. Svec III is retired from Oceanography, Satellite Test Engineering, and college teaching. He has lived on a forty-foot cruising sailboat, on a ranch in the Sierra Nevada Foothills, in a country rose-garden cottage, and currently lives in the shadow of a castle with his childhood sweetheart and several long coated German shepherds. He enjoys writing, gardening, creating dioramas, world travel, and enjoying time with his sweetheart.

Stephen Toft is a homelessness worker and writer who lives in Lancaster, UK with his wife and their children. He has published three collections of poetry, and has recently began writing crime stories.

Thomas A. (Tom) Turley has been "hooked on Holmes" since finishing *The Hound of the Baskervilles* at about the age of twelve. However, his interest in Sherlockian pastiches didn't take off until he wrote one. *Sherlock Holmes and the Adventure of the Tainted Canister* (2014) is available as an e-book and an audiobook from MX Publishing. It also appeared in *The Art of Sherlock Holmes – USA Edition 1*. In 2017, two of Tom's stories, "A Scandal in Serbia" and "A Ghost from Christmas Past" were published in Parts VI and VII of this anthology. "Ghost" was also included in *The Art of Sherlock Holmes – West Palm Beach Edition.* Meanwhile, Tom is finishing a collection of historical pastiches entitled *Sherlock Holmes and the Crowned Heads of Europe*, to be published in 2021 The first story, "Sherlock Holmes and the Case of the Dying Emperor" (2018) is available from MX Publishing as a separate e-book. Set in the brief reign of Emperor Frederick III (1888), it inaugurates Sherlock Holmes's espionage campaign against the German Empire, which ended only in August 1914 with "His Last Bow". When completed, *Sherlock Holmes and the Crowned Heads of Europe* will also include "A Scandal in Serbia" and two additional historical tales. Although he has a Ph.D. in British history, Tom spent most of his professional career as an archivist with the State of Alabama. He and his wife Paula (an aspiring science fiction novelist) live in Montgomery, Alabama. Interested readers may contact Tom through MX Publishing or his Goodreads author's page.

Marcia Wilson is a freelance researcher and illustrator who likes to work in a style compatible for the color blind and visually impaired. She is Canon-centric, and her first MX offering, *You Buy Bones*, uses the point-of-view of Scotland Yard to show the unique talents of Dr. Watson. This continued with the publication of *Test of the Professionals: The Adventure of the Flying Blue Pidgeon* and *The Peaceful Night Poisonings*. She can be contacted at: *gravelgirty.deviantart.com*

The following contributors appear in the companion volumes:

The MX Book of New Sherlock Holmes Stories
Part XXV – 2021 Annual (1881-1887)
Part XXVI – 2021 Annual (1888-1897)

Ian Ableson is an ecologist by training and a writer by choice. When not reading or writing, he can reliably be found scowling at a clipboard while ankle-deep in a marsh somewhere in Michigan. His love for the stories of Arthur Conan Doyle started when his grandfather gave him a copy of *The Original Illustrated Sherlock Holmes* when he was in high school, and he's proud to have been able to contribute to the continuation of the tales of Sherlock Holmes and Dr. Watson.

Hugh Ashton was born in the U.K., and moved to Japan in 1988, where he remained until 2016, living with his wife Yoshiko in the historic city of Kamakura, a little to the south of Yokohama. He and Yoshiko have now moved to Lichfield, a small cathedral city in the Midlands of the U.K., the birthplace of Samuel Johnson, and one-time home of Erasmus Darwin. In the past, he has worked in the technology and financial services industries, which have provided him with material for some of his books set in the 21st century. He currently works as a writer: Novelist, freelance editor, and copywriter, (his work for large Japanese corporations has appeared in international business journals), and journalist, as well as producing industry reports on various aspects of the financial services industry. However, his lifelong interest in Sherlock Holmes has developed into an acclaimed series of adventures featuring the world's most famous detective, written in the style of the originals. In addition to these, he has also published historical and alternate historical novels, short stories, and thrillers. Together with artist Andy Boerger, he has produced the *Sherlock Ferret* series of stories for children, featuring the world's cutest detective.

Chris Chan is a writer, educator, and historian. He works as a researcher and "International Goodwill Ambassador" for Agatha Christie Ltd. His true crime articles, reviews, and short fiction have appeared (or will soon appear) in *The Strand, The Wisconsin Magazine of History, Mystery Weekly, Gilbert!, Nerd HQ*, Akashic Books' *Mondays are Murder* web series, *The Baker Street Journal*, and *Sherlock Holmes Mystery Magazine*. His latest book is *Sherlock and Irene: The Secret Truth Behind "A Scandal in Bohemia"*.

Martin Daley was born in Carlisle, Cumbria in 1964. He cites Doyle's Holmes and Watson as his favourite literary characters, who continue to inspire his own detective writing. His fiction and non-fiction books include a Holmes pastiche set predominantly in his home city in 1903. In the adventure, he introduced his own detective, Inspector Cornelius Armstrong,

477

who has subsequently had some of his own cases published by MX Publishing. For more information visit *www.martindaley.co.uk*

Harry DeMaio is a *nom de plume* of Harry B. DeMaio, successful author of several books on Information Security and Business Networks, as well as the fourteen-volume *Casebooks of Octavius Bear*. He is also a published author for Belanger Books and the MX Sherlock Holmes series edited by David Marcum. A retired business executive, former consultant, information security specialist, private pilot, disk jockey, and graduate school adjunct professor, he whiles away his time traveling and writing preposterous books, articles and stories. He has appeared on many radio and TV shows and is an accomplished, frequent public speaker. Former New York City natives, he and his extremely patient and helpful wife, Virginia, live in Cincinnati (and several other parallel universes.) They have two sons, living in Scottsdale, Arizona and Cortlandt Manor, New York, both of whom are quite successful and quite normal, thus putting the lie to the theory that insanity is hereditary. His books are available on Amazon, Barnes and Noble, directly from MX Publishing and at other fine bookstores. His e-mail is *hdemaio@zoomtown.com* You can also find him on Facebook. His website is *www.octaviusbearslair.com*

Matthew J. Elliott is the author of *Big Trouble in Mother Russia* (2016), the official sequel to the cult movie *Big Trouble in Little China, Lost in Time and Space: An Unofficial Guide to the Uncharted Journeys of Doctor Who* (2014), *Sherlock Holmes on the Air* (2012), *Sherlock Holmes in Pursuit* (2013), *The Immortals: An Unauthorized Guide to* Sherlock *and* Elementary (2013), and *The Throne Eternal* (2014). His articles, fiction, and reviews have appeared in the magazines *Scarlet Street, Total DVD, SHERLOCK,* and *Sherlock Holmes Mystery Magazine,* and the collections *The Game's Afoot, Curious Incidents 2, Gaslight Grimoire, The Mammoth Book of Best British Crime 8,* and *The MX Book of New Sherlock Holmes Stories – Part III: 1896-1929.* He has scripted over 260 radio plays, including episodes of *Doctor Who, The Further Adventures of Sherlock Holmes, The Twilight Zone, The New Adventures of Mickey Spillane's Mike Hammer, Fangoria's Dreadtime Stories,* and award-winning adaptations of *The Hound of the Baskervilles* and *The War of the Worlds.* He is the only radio dramatist to adapt all sixty original stories from The Canon for the series *The Classic Adventures of Sherlock Holmes.* Matthew is a writer and performer on *RiffTrax.com,* the online comedy experience from the creators of cult sci-fi TV series *Mystery Science Theater 3000 (MST3K* to the initiated). He's also written a few comic books.

Stephen Gaspar is a writer of historical detective fiction. He has written two Sherlock Holmes books: *The Canadian Adventures of Sherlock Holmes* and *Cold-Hearted Murder.* Some of his detectives are a Roman Tribune, a medieval monk, and a Templar knight. He was born and lives in Windsor, Ontario, Canada.

James Gelter is a director and playwright living in Brattleboro, VT. His produced written works for the stage include adaptations of *Frankenstein* and *A Christmas Carol,* several children's plays for the New England Youth Theatre, as well as seven outdoor plays co-written with his wife, Jessica, in their *Forest of Mystery* series. In 2018, he founded The Baker Street Readers, a group of performers that present dramatic readings of Arthur Conan Doyle's original Canon of Sherlock Holmes stories, featuring Gelter as Holmes, his longtime collaborator Tony Grobe as Dr. Watson, and a rotating list of guests. When the COVID-19 pandemic stopped their live performances, Gelter transformed the show into The Baker Street Readers Podcast. Some episodes are available for free on Apple Podcasts and Stitcher, with many more available to patrons at *patreon.com/bakerstreetreaders.*

Dick Gillman is an English writer and acrylic artist living in Brittany, France with his wife Alex, Truffle, their Black Labrador, and Jean-Claude, their Breton cat. During his retirement from teaching, he has written over twenty Sherlock Holmes short stories which are published as both e-books and paperbacks. His initial contribution to the superb MX Sherlock Holmes collection, published in October 2015, was entitled "The Man on Westminster Bridge" and had the privilege of being chosen as the anchor story in *The MX Book of New Sherlock Holmes Stories – Part II (1890-1895)*.

Hal Glatzer is the author of the Katy Green historical mystery series, set in musical milieux just before World War II. He has written and produced audio/radio plays, scripted and produced the Charlie Chan mystery *The House Without a Key* on stage, and adapted "The Adventure of the Devil's Foot" into a stage and video play called *Sherlock Holmes & The Volcano Horror*, set on the Island of Hawaii, where he has lived for twenty-five of the past fifty years. See more at: *www.halglatzer.com*

In real life, **Anthony Gurney** lectures in Computer Science at a university in Scotland where he lives with his wife and children. The first books that he bought for himself were a two volume hardback collection of the Holmes Short Stories and the Long Stories for 10p each at a church jumble sale. It was the start of a lifelong affair.

Arthur Hall *also has a story in Part XXVI*

Keith Hann is a Canadian Ph.D. student, slaving away in the realm of military and diplomatic history. To dodge dissertation deadlines, he enjoys pulp fiction, trash cinema, and crafting the occasional Holmes piece, one of which has appeared in *Ellery Queen's Mystery Magazine*.

Paul Hiscock is an author of crime, fantasy, and science fiction tales. His short stories have appeared in several anthologies and include a seventeenth century whodunnit, a science fiction western, and a steampunk Sherlock Holmes story. Paul lives with his family in Kent, England, and spends his days chasing a toddler with more energy than the Duracell Bunny. He mainly does his writing in coffee shops with members of the local NaNoWriMo group, or in the middle of the night when his family has gone to sleep. Consequently, his stories tend to be fuelled by large amounts of black coffee. You can find out more about his writing at *www.detectivesanddragons.uk.*

Mike Hogan writes mostly historical novels and short stories, many set in Victorian London and featuring Sherlock Holmes and Doctor Watson. He read the Conan Doyle stories at school with great enjoyment, but hadn't thought much about Sherlock Holmes until, having missed the Granada/Jeremy Brett TV series when it was originally shown in the eighties, he came across a box set of videos in a street market and was hooked on Holmes again. He started writing Sherlock Holmes pastiches several years ago, having great fun re-imagining situations for the Conan Doyle characters to act in. The relationship between Holmes and Watson fascinates him as one of the great literary friendships. (He's also a huge admirer of Patrick O'Brian's Aubrey-Maturin novels). Like Captain Aubrey and Doctor Maturin, Holmes and Watson are an odd couple, differing in almost every facet of their characters, but sharing a common sense of decency and a common humanity. Living with Sherlock Holmes can't have been easy, and Mike enjoys adding a stronger vein of "pawky humour" into the Conan Doyle mix, even letting Watson have the second-to-last word on occasions. His books include *Sherlock Holmes and the Scottish Question,*

The Gory Season – Sherlock Holmes, Jack the Ripper and the Thames Torso Murders, and the *Sherlock Holmes & Young Winston 1887 Trilogy* (*The Deadwood Stage, The Jubilee Plot,* and *The Giant Moles*), He has also written the following short story collections: *Sherlock Holmes: Murder at the Savoy and Other Stories, Sherlock Holmes: The Skull of Kohada Koheiji and Other Stories,* and *Sherlock Holmes: Murder on the Brighton Line and Other Stories,* among others. *www.mikehoganbooks.com*

In the year 1998 **Craig Janacek** took his degree of Doctor of Medicine at Vanderbilt University, and proceeded to Stanford to go through the training prescribed for pediatricians in practice. Having completed his studies there, he was duly attached to the University of California, San Francisco as Associate Professor. The author of over seventy medical monographs upon a variety of obscure lesions, his travel-worn and battered tin dispatch-box is crammed with papers, nearly all of which are records of his fictional works. To date, these have been published solely in electronic format, including two non-Holmes novels (*The Oxford Deception* and *The Anger of Achilles Peterson*), the trio of holiday adventures collected as *The Midwinter Mysteries of Sherlock Holmes,* the Holmes story collections *The First of Criminals, The Assassination of Sherlock Holmes, The Treasury of Sherlock Holmes, Light in the Darkness, The Gathering Gloom, The Travels of Sherlock Holmes,* and the Watsonian novels *The Isle of Devils* and *The Gate of Gold.* Craig Janacek is a *nom de plume.*

Kelvin I. Jones is the author of six books about Sherlock Holmes and the definitive biography of Conan Doyle as a spiritualist, *Conan Doyle and The Spirits.* A member of *The Sherlock Holmes Society of London,* he has published numerous short occult and ghost stories in British anthologies over the last thirty years. His work has appeared on BBC Radio, and in 1984 he won the Mason Hall Literary Award for his poem cycle about the survivors of Hiroshima and Nagasaki, recently reprinted as "Omega". (Oakmagic Publications) A one-time teacher of creative writing at the University of East Anglia, he is also the author of four crime novels featuring his ex-met sleuth John Bottrell, who first appeared in *Stone Dead.* He has over fifty titles on Kindle, and is also the author of several novellas and short story collections featuring a Norwich based detective, DCI Ketch, an intrepid sleuth who investigates East Anglian murder cases. He also published a series of short stories about an Edwardian psychic detective, Dr. John Carter (*Carter's Occult Casebook*). Ramsey Campbell, the British horror writer, and Francis King, the renowned novelist, have both compared his supernatural stories to those of M. R. James. He has also published children's fiction, namely *Odin's Eye,* and, in collaboration with his wife Debbie, *The Dark Entry.* Since 1995, he has been the proprietor of Oakmagic Publications, publishers of British folklore and of his fiction titles. He lives in Norfolk. (See www.oakmagicpublications.co.uk)

Naching T. Kassa is a wife, mother, and writer. She's created short stories, novellas, poems, and co-created three children. She lives in Eastern Washington State with her husband, Dan Kassa. Naching is a member of the *Horror Writers Association,* Head of Publishing and Interviewer for *HorrorAddicts.net,* and an assistant and staff writer for Still Water Bay at Crystal Lake Publishing. She has been a Sherlockian since the age of ten and is a member of *The Sound of the Baskervilles.* You can find her work on Amazon. *https://www.amazon.com/Naching-T-Kassa/e/B005ZGHTI0*

Susan Knight's newest novel from MX publishing, *Mrs. Hudson Goes to Ireland,* is a follow-up to her well-received collection of stories, *Mrs. Hudson Investigates* of 2019. She is the author of two other non-Sherlockian story collections, as well as three novels, a book of non-fiction, and several plays, and has won several prizes for her writing. She lives in Dublin where she teaches Creative Writing. Her next Mrs. Hudson novel is already a gleam in her eye.

David Marcum *also has stories in Parts XXV and XXVI*

Kevin Patrick McCann has published eight collections of poems for adults, one for children (*Diary of a Shapeshifter*, Beul Aithris), a book of ghost stories (*It's Gone Dark*, The Otherside Books), *Teach Yourself Self-Publishing* (Hodder) co-written with the playwright Tom Green, and *Ov* (Beul Aithris Publications) a fantasy novel for children.

Adrian Middleton is a Staffordshire-born independent publisher. The son of a real-world detective, he is a former civil servant and policy adviser who now writes and edits science fiction, fantasy, and a popular series of steampunked Sherlock Holmes stories.

James Moffett is a Masters graduate in Professional Writing, with a specialisation in novel and non-fiction writing. He also has an extensive background in media studies. James began developing a passion for writing when contributing to his University's student magazine. His interest in the literary character of Sherlock Holmes was deep-rooted in his youth. He released his first publication of eight interconnected short stories titled *The Trials of Sherlock Holmes* in 2017, along with a contribution to *The MX Book of New Sherlock Holmes Stories - Part VII: Eliminate The Impossible: 1880-1891*, with a short story entitled "The Blank Photograph".

Mark Mower is a crime writer and historian whose passion for tales about Sherlock Holmes and Dr. Watson began at the age of twelve, when he watched an early black-and-white film featuring the unrivalled screen pairing of Basil Rathbone and Nigel Bruce. Hastily seeking out the original stories of Sir Arthur Conan Doyle, and continually searching for further film and television adaptations, his has been a lifelong obsession. Now a member of the Crime Writers' Association, The Sherlock Holmes Society of London, and The Solar Pons Society of London, he has written numerous crime books. Mark has contributed to over 20 Holmes anthologies, including 13 parts of *The MX Book of New Sherlock Holmes Stories*, *The Book of Extraordinary New Sherlock Holmes Stories* (Mango Publishing) and *Sherlock Holmes – Before Baker Street* (Belanger Books). His own books include *A Farewell to Baker Street*, *Sherlock Holmes: The Baker Street Case-Files*, and *Sherlock Holmes: The Baker Street Legacy*, and *Sherlock Holmes: The Baker Street Epilogue* (all with MX Publishing).

Jane Rubino is the author of *A Jersey Shore* mystery series, featuring a Jane Austen-loving amateur sleuth and a Sherlock Holmes-quoting detective, *Knight Errant*, *Lady Vernon and Her Daughter*, (a novel-length adaptation of Jane Austen's novella *Lady Susan*, co-authored with her daughter Caitlen Rubino-Bradway, *What Would Austen Do?*, also co-authored with her daughter, a short story in the anthology *Jane Austen Made Me Do It*, *The Rucastles' Pawn*, *The Copper Beeches from Violet Turner's POV*, and, of course, there's the Sherlockian novel in the drawer – who doesn't have one? Jane lives on a barrier island at the New Jersey shore.

Geri Schear is a novelist and short story writer. Her work has been published in literary journals in the U.S. and Ireland. Her first novel, *A Biased Judgement: The Diaries of Sherlock Holmes 1897* was released to critical acclaim in 2014. The sequel, *Sherlock*

Holmes and the Other Woman was published in 2015, and *Return to Reichenbach* in 2016. She lives in Kells, Ireland.

Frank Schildiner is a martial arts instructor at Amorosi's Mixed Martial Arts in New Jersey. He is the writer of the novels, *The Quest of Frankenstein, The Triumph of Frankenstein, Napoleon's Vampire Hunters, The Devil Plague of Naples, The Klaus Protocol*, and *Irma Vep and The Great Brain of Mars*. Frank is a regular contributor to the fictional series *Tales of the Shadowmen* and has been published in *From Bayou to Abyss: Examining John Constantine, Hellblazer, The Joy of Joe, The New Adventures of Thunder Jim Wade, Secret Agent X* Volumes 3, 4, 5, and 6, *The Lone Ranger and Tonto: Frontier Justice*, and *The Avenger: The Justice Files*. He resides in New Jersey with his wife Gail, who is his top supporter, and two cats who are indifferent on the subject.

Brenda Seabrooke's stories have been published in a number of reviews, journals, and anthologies. She has received grants from the National Endowment for the Arts and Emerson College's Robbie Macauley Award. She is the author of twenty-three books for young readers including *Scones and Bones on Baker Street: Sherlock's (maybe!) Dog and the Dirt Dilemma*, and *The Rascal in the Castle: Sherlock's (possible!) Dog and the Queen's Revenge*. Brenda states: "*It was fun to write from Dr. Watson's point of view and not have to worry about fleas, smelly pits, ralphing, or scratching at inopportune times.*"

Matthew Simmonds hails from Bedford, in the South East of England, and has been a confirmed devotee of Sir Arthur Conan Doyle's most famous creation since first watching Jeremy Brett's incomparable portrayal of the world's first consulting detective, on a Tuesday evening in April, 1984, while curled up on the sofa with his father. He has written numerous short stories, and his first novel, *Sherlock Holmes: The Adventure of The Pigtail Twist*, was published in 2018. A sequel is nearly complete, which he hopes to publish in the near future. Matthew currently co-owns Harrison & Simmonds, the fifth-generation family business, a renowned County tobacconist, pipe, and gift shop on Bedford High Street.

Denis O. Smith's first published story of Sherlock Holmes and Doctor Watson, "The Adventure of The Purple Hand", appeared in 1982. Since then, numerous other such accounts have been published in magazines and anthologies both in the U.K. and the U.S. In the 1990's, four volumes of his stories were published under the general title of *The Chronicles of Sherlock Holmes*, and, more recently his stories have been collected as *The Lost Chronicles of Sherlock Holmes* (2014), *The Lost Chronicles of Sherlock Holmes Volume II* (2016), *The Further Chronicles of Sherlock Holmes* (201). He also wrote a Holmes novel, *The Riddle of Foxwood Grange* (2017). Born in Yorkshire, in the north of England, Denis Smith has lived and worked in various parts of the country, including London, and has now been resident in Norfolk for many years. His interests range widely, but apart from his dedication to the career of Sherlock Holmes, he has a passion for historical mysteries of all kinds, the railways of Britain and the history of London

Robert V. Stapleton was born and brought up in Leeds, Yorkshire, England, and studied at Durham University. After working in various parts of the country as an Anglican parish priest, he is now retired and lives with his wife in North Yorkshire. As a member of his local writing group, he now has time to develop his other life as a writer of adventure stories. He has recently had a number of short stories published, and he is hoping to have a couple of completed novels published at some time in the future.

Kevin P. Thornton is a seven-time Arthur Ellis Award Nominee. He is a former director of the local Heritage Society and Library, and he has been a soldier in Africa, a contractor for the Canadian Military in Afghanistan, a newspaper and magazine columnist, a Director of both the *Crime Writers of Canada* and the *Writers' Guild of Alberta*, a founding member of *Northword Literary Magazine*, and is either a current or former member of *The Mystery Writers of America, The Crime Writers Association, The Calgary Crime Writers, The International Thriller Writers, The International Association of Crime Writers, The Keys* – a Catholic Writers group founded by Monsignor Knox and G.K. Chesterton – as well as, somewhat inexplicably, *The Mesdames of Mayhem* and *Sisters in Crime*. If you ask, he will join. Born in Kenya, Kevin has lived or worked in South Africa, Dubai, England, Afghanistan, New Zealand, Ontario, and now Northern Alberta. He lives on his wits and his wit, and is doing better than expected. He is not one to willingly split infinitives, and while never pedantic, is on occasion known to be ever so slightly punctilious.

DJ Tyrer is the person behind Atlantean Publishing, was placed second in the Writing Magazine "Local Reporter" competition, and has been widely published in anthologies and magazines around the world, such as *Disturbance* (Laurel Highlands), *Mysteries of Suspense* (Zimbell House), *History and Mystery, Oh My!* (Mystery & Horror LLC), and *Love 'Em, Shoot 'Em* (Wolfsinger), and issues of *Awesome Tales*, and in addition, has a novella available in paperback and on the Kindle, *The Yellow House* (Dunhams Manor) and a comic horror e-novelette, *A Trip to the Middle of the World*, available from Alban Lake through Infinite Realms Bookstore.
His website is: *https://djtyrer.blogspot.co.uk/*
The Atlantean Publishing website is at *https://atlanteanpublishing.wordpress.com/*

Peter Coe Verbica grew up on a commercial cattle ranch in Northern California, where he learned the value of a strong work ethic. He works for the Wealth Management Group of a global investment bank, and is an Adjunct Professor in the Economics Department at SJSU. He is the author of numerous books, including *Left at the Gate and Other Poems, Hard-Won Cowboy Wisdom (Not Necessarily in Order of Importance), A Key to the Grove and Other Poems*, and two volumes of *The Missing Tales of Sherlock Holmes* (as Compiled by Peter Coe Verbica, JD). Mr. Verbica obtained a JD from Santa Clara University School of Law, an MS from Massachusetts Institute of Technology, and a BA in English from Santa Clara University. He is the co-inventor on a number of patents, has served as a Managing Member of three venture capital firms, and the CFO of one of the portfolio companies. He is an unabashed advocate of cowboy culture and enjoys creative writing, hiking, and tennis. He is married with four daughters. For more information, or to contact the author, please go to *www.hardwoncowboywisdom.com*

Margaret Walsh was born Auckland, New Zealand and now lives in Melbourne, Australia. She is the author of *Sherlock Holmes and the Molly-Boy Murders, Sherlock Holmes and the Case of the Perplexed Politician*, and *Sherlock Holmes and the Case of the London Dock Deaths*, all published by MX Publishing. Margaret has been a devotee of Sherlock Holmes since childhood and has had several Holmesian related essays printed in anthologies, and is a member of the online society *Doyle's Rotary Coffin*. She has an ongoing love affair with the city of London. When she's not working or planning trips to London. Margaret can be found frequenting the many and varied bookshops of Melbourne.

I.A. Watson, great-grand-nephew of Dr. John H. Watson, has been intrigued by the notorious "black sheep" of the family since childhood, and was fascinated to inherit from his grandmother a number of unedited manuscripts removed circa 1956 from a rather larger collection reposing at Lloyds Bank Ltd (which acquired Cox & Co Bank in 1923). Upon discovering the published corpus of accounts regarding the detective Sherlock Holmes from which a censorious upbringing had shielded him, he felt obliged to allow an interested public access to these additional memoranda, and is gradually undertaking the task of transcribing them for admirers of Mr. Holmes and Dr. Watson's works. In the meantime, I.A. Watson continues to pen other books, the latest of which is *The Incunabulum of Sherlock Holmes*. A full list of his seventy or so published works are available at: *http://www.chillwater.org.uk/writing/iawatsonhome.htm*

Matthew White is an up-and-coming author from Richmond, Virginia in the USA. He has been a passionate devotee of Sherlock Holmes since childhood. He can be reached at *matthewwhite.writer@gmail.com*

Marcia Wilson *also has stories in Parts XXV and XXVI*

The MX Book of New Sherlock Holmes Stories
Edited by David Marcum
(MX Publishing, 2015-   )

"This is the finest volume of Sherlockian fiction I have ever read, and I have read, literally, thousands." – Philip K. Jones

"Beyond Impressive . . . This is a splendid venture for a great cause!
– Roger Johnson, Editor, *The Sherlock Holmes Journal,*
The Sherlock Holmes Society of London

In Preparation
Part XXVIII – More Christmas Adventures

. . . and more to come!

The MX Book of New Sherlock Holmes Stories
Edited by David Marcum
(MX Publishing, 2015-)

Part VI: *The traditional pastiche is alive and well . . . .*

Part VII: *Sherlockians eager for faithful-to-the-canon plots and characters will be delighted.*

Part VIII: *The imagination of the contributors in coming up with variations on the volume's theme is matched by their ingenious resolutions.*

Part IX: *The 18 stories . . . will satisfy fans of Conan Doyle's originals. Sherlockians will rejoice that more volumes are on the way.*

Part X: *. . . new Sherlock Holmes adventures of consistently high quality.*

Part XI: *. . . an essential volume for Sherlock Holmes fans.*

Part XII: *. . . continues to amaze with the number of high-quality pastiches.*

Part XIII: *. . . Amazingly, Marcum has found 22 superb pastiches . . . This is more catnip for fans of stories faithful to Conan Doyle's original*

Part XIV: *. . . this standout anthology of 21 short stories written in the spirit of Conan Doyle's originals.*

Part XV: *Stories pitting Sherlock Holmes against seemingly supernatural phenomena highlight Marcum's 15th anthology of superior short pastiches.*

Part XVI: *Marcum has once again done fans of Conan Doyle's originals a service.*

Part XVII: *This is yet another impressive array of new but traditional Holmes stories.*

Part XVIII: *Sherlockians will again be grateful to Marcum and MX for high-quality new Holmes tales.*

Part XIX: *Inventive plots and intriguing explorations of aspects of Dr. Watson's life and beliefs lift the 24 pastiches in Marcum's impressive 19th Sherlock Holmes anthology*

Part XX: *Marcum's reserve of high-quality new Holmes exploits seems endless.*

Part XXI: *This is another must-have for Sherlockians.*

Part XXII: *Marcum's superlative 22nd Sherlock Holmes pastiche anthology features 21 short stories that successfully emulate the spirit of Conan Doyle's originals while expanding on the canon's tantalizing references to mysteries Dr. Watson never got around to chronicling.*

Part XXIII: *Marcum's well of talented authors able to mimic the feel of The Canon seems bottomless.*

Part XXIV: *Marcum's expertise at selecting high-quality pastiches remains impressive.*

The MX Book of New Sherlock Holmes Stories
Edited by David Marcum
(MX Publishing, 2015-   )

MX Publishing

MX Publishing is the world's largest specialist Sherlock Holmes publisher, with several hundred titles and over a hundred authors creating the latest in Sherlock Holmes fiction and non-fiction.

From traditional short stories and novels to travel guides and quiz books, MX Publishing caters to all Holmes fans.

The collection includes leading titles such as *Benedict Cumberbatch In Transition* and *The Norwood Author*, which won the 2011 *Tony Howlett Award* (Sherlock Holmes Book of the Year).

MX Publishing also has one of the largest communities of Holmes fans on *Facebook*, with regular contributions from dozens of authors.

www.mxpublishing.co.uk (UK) and *www.mxpublishing.com* (USA)

Printed in the USA
CPSIA information can be obtained
at www.ICGtesting.com
CBHW031118140124
3393CB00011B/334/J

9 781787 057838